PRAISE FOR

THE GOLLANCZ BOOK OF SOUTH ASIAN SCIENCE FICTION VOLUME 1

'*The Gollancz Book of South Asian Science Fiction* is by far the first in this century that is this broad in scope, and definitely the most ambitious, in its intentions... Gollancz is a name that is intimately familiar to any science fiction fan and serious SF reader across the world and...this anthology is a worthy addition to its catalogue.' – *Factor Daily*

'*The Gollancz Book of South Asian Science Fiction* is an instant classic, and has, dare I say it, franchise potential written all over it.' – *The Hindu BusinessLine*

'A timely tribute to speculative fiction writing from the subcontinent. Immensely well-intentioned, curated with deliberation and hard work, and diverse and flexible in terms of the writers represented.' – *Mint Lounge*

'Refreshing. This anthology by South Asian writers is precisely what the industry needs.' – *Free Press Journal*

'*The Gollancz Book of South Asian Science Fiction* is at its best in the same way SF everywhere is: when it produces sharply realized characters in unfamiliar gardens, and shows us how they got there.' – Gary K. Wolfe, *Locus*

'Propelling itself 70 years into the future, the anthology never lets go of the present political moment in India and, in some cases, America, and the stories imagine totalitarian futures with grim humour.' – *India Today*

'Taken as a whole, the Gollancz anthology is timely and delivers on its promise of "providing a prism refracting the vivid and at times contrarian imaginings of contemporary South Asian SF".' – *Scroll.in*

'The concepts and themes inventoried in the collection are timelessly radical. It's the personal stories, exploring the human condition, that really work the best in this collection.' – *The Hindu*

'This volume provides a good viewpoint of where South Asian sci-fi is and what it's capable of. Highly recommended to get a feel for the genre and what it means in the Indian context.' – *Deccan Herald*

'*The Gollancz Book of South Asian Science Fiction* raises the pertinent question about the challenge of finding a balance between local flavour and hard science that is globally accessible.' – *Firstpost*

'Promising, even in the face of grim portents in the sociocultural domain in the subcontinent and seemingly inexorable transformations of the ecological basis for life that are threatening the very existence of the most vulnerable, not just in South Asia.' – *Outlook*

'This anthology feels like a labour of love, and readers should find it stimulating.' – Stephen Theaker, *Theaker's Quarterly Fiction*

THE GOLLANCZ BOOK OF SOUTH ASIAN SCIENCE FICTION

VOLUME 2

EDITED BY

TARUN K. SAINT

WITH A GRAPHIC PREFACE AND AFTERWORD BY

MANJULA PADMANABHAN

First published in hardcover in 2021 by Hachette India
(Registered name: Hachette Book Publishing India Pvt. Ltd)
An Hachette UK company
www.hachetteindia.com

This paperback edition published in 2024

1

Acknowledgements on p. 456 constitute an extension of this copyright page.

Hardcover edition ISBN 978-93-91028-62-6
Paperback edition ISBN 978-93-5731-757-3

Hachette Book Publishing India Pvt. Ltd
4th & 5th Floors, Corporate Centre,
Plot No. 94, Sector 44, Gurugram – 122003, India

Typeset in Dante MT Std 10.5/13.7
by InoSoft Systems, Noida

Printed and bound in India by
Manipal Technologies Limited

CONTENTS

Speculative fiction has long been the source of literature's most astounding visuals. The same can be said of South Asian mythology. It inspired an outpouring of wildly inventive art: fanged demons, flying serpents, monstrous birds.
For our Preface, I've attempted to pay tribute to the visual legacy of SF by creating a graphic sampler of the stories in this volume. These are the mythic tales of our era. Literary chimeras hatched in the nest of ancient belief systems. Fledglings of the modern faith that some of us call...science.

SASF
Vol 2

18.
9.
11.
1.
10.
28.
29.
21.
6.
15.
3
23.
17.
SASF
Vol 2

27.
20.
26.
14.
2.
25.
5.
7.
32.
13.
4.
8.
19.
22.
24.
31.
12.
16.
30.

INTRODUCTION

SOUTH ASIAN SCIENCE FICTION AND FANTASY

CARVING NEW SPACES IN TIME

TARUN K. SAINT

'But science fiction is the realism of our time. The sense that we are all now stuck in a science-fiction novel that we're writing together – that's another sign of the emerging structure of feeling.'

– Kim Stanley Robinson[1]

Following the global spread of the SARS-CoV-2 virus, it has been an uncanny experience applying the finishing touches to this anthology as we slipped deeper into the all-too-real situation evoked by a practitioner of climate change fiction, Kim Stanley Robinson. The pandemic has drastically altered the ground realities of our world as well as the language available to describe this event, as at least one of our contributors has noted. Most of our contributions having been received before the outbreak, this volume does not attempt a consolidated view of this still-unfolding disaster. Perhaps future writing in the science fiction and fantasy (SFF) genre will cover intimately the cataclysmic changes we are witnessing in our culture and society as well as its eventual reverberations across space and time.[2]

This volume is a follow-up to the first collection titled *The Gollancz Book of South Asian Science Fiction*, which appeared in early 2019 as an experiment in building bridges between the different cultures of science fiction in the subcontinent.[3] The first omnibus was a foray into an unexplored and neglected domain with a niche readership. It thus served as a useful platform for writers of science fiction (including both hard and soft variants as well as speculative fiction and poetry) from South Asia. For the region's science fiction and fantasy has a texture and feeling that is different from both Western SFF as well as, say, writing in the genre closer home in Asia – like Chinese science fiction.[4] The introduction to the first volume traced the genesis and growth of the genre in this region in broad terms, while acknowledging the need for more intensive work in various languages in which science fiction has been published.[5]

The second volume amplifies the scope of this project as we bring in stories, incorporating work on the border of science fiction, horror and serious/high concept fantasy by important writers in the space. This time, we were able to reach out to writers from Sri Lanka, Pakistan, Bangladesh and the Tibetan community in exile, as well as bring in both historically significant and contemporary stories from writing in Marathi and Bengali.[6] The aim was not to provide a comprehensive report on the SFF scene in this region, nor to assemble a collection with fixed quotas from each country (an accountant's fantasy), but rather to facilitate the task of mapping the complex contours of a body of work that is emerging from the shadows to claim its rightful place in the sun.

We may think of South Asian SFF as a graft, a splicing of a new element into the already extant corpus of South Asian literature, or as a subgenre that is different with new, unusual fruits that taste neither like its progenitors nor quite like anything else. The second volume, thus, invites readers to partake of this flavour, not in the spirit of exoticism but rather as fellow voyagers into new realms of thought and experience. The stories assembled here testify to creative engagements with the myriad challenges posed by structural changes in culture and society, which are primarily a result of technological interventions and developmental initiatives driven by the slogan of progress.

As noted in the introduction to Volume 1, ongoing crises in early twenty-first century South Asia have generated creative and critical responses in the SFF genre which contest the inevitability of destructive development and homogenization of identity.[7] These crises include climate change and environmental degradation along with other contingencies posed by media-stoked hyper-nationalism, gender-based violence and religious fundamentalism. As readers of these stories and poems will discover, SFF has thus become a vehicle for dialogue on alternative futures and ways of thinking past our current impasse. Indeed, one could see these anthologies as a channel for forms of intellectual resistance in conditions which are fraught with risk for writers taking on structures of power. In future volumes, we hope to encompass more instances of strong writing from countries not featured so far as such voices become increasingly audible. In the sections to follow I offer some introductory remarks on the pieces included in this volume.

In Seattle-based Shiv Ramdas's Nebula and Hugo Award-nominated work 'And Now His Lordship is Laughing', the horror story is given a fresh twist and historical mooring. Set in the period of the Bengal famine of 1943, which took three million lives, the story imagines an aging doll maker's ruthless yet calibrated response to a British officer's command to make a doll for him as she summons up occult powers beyond the grasp of colonial reason. The evocation of details of colonial history and spotlight on the question of coerced suffering on a gigantic scale, besides the sharp focus on Apa the doll maker's point of view, make the deployment of fantasy/horror tropes in this story even more effective.

Medha Singh is a poet, editor and translator from Delhi who has already made a name for herself with a collection of verse and through a book-length work of translation. Medha's speculative poem 'Jupiter, Dark Sister' invokes the giant planet as metaphor at several levels, including the cosmological and astronomical. The journey through, rather than to, Jupiter enables a surreal form of discovery, including an encounter with the limits to self-perception. As speculative poetry, 'Jupiter, Dark Sister' makes us think afresh about space flight and interplanetary exploration, reminding us of the mirroring of such journeys, whether real or imaginative, within the self, where one may be in time left hung by such dark sisters of the sun 'like a pig. On a pike'.

Tashan Mehta works on the borderline between fantasy and science fiction, and in the story included here we find a traveller making contact with an alien culture.[8] Based on stories of the local people, the shipwrecked protagonist begins to draw a map of the islands she has reached. The alternating first person narratives of the visitor and Alka, her local friend, allow for an exploration of the realm of the unknown and an unconventional mapping of an imaginative cartography very different from that used by explorers and geographers of yore. We find here an innovative redoing of the premise of Ursula Le Guin's *The Lathe of Heaven*,[9] as dreaming becomes a way of reshaping territory and desire.

Muhammed Zafar Iqbal teaches physics in Dhaka and is a pre-eminent writer of science fiction from Bangladesh. His story 'The Zoo' is an effective meditation on the workings of power and authoritarianism. We find here an extension of H.G. Wells's concerns in *The Island of Dr Moreau*,[10] as a cruel experiment involving humans and animals under duress on a remote island is disclosed to a visiting journalist. The allusions to the perverse uses science has been put to in the past century (as in the case of racist archpriest of applied eugenics and 'Angel of Death' Dr Josef Mengele's experiments in Auschwitz during the Nazi era)[11] lend a chilling edge to the story's unexpected conclusion.

Vajra Chandrasekera, from Colombo, is a significant presence in the Sri Lankan science fiction landscape as author, critic and contributing fiction editor at *Strange Horizons*. His story 'The Maker of Memorials' offers a scathing indictment of those who memorialize war in heroic images, reminding us of the themes of Wilfred Owen's war poems.[12] The ironic tone is set at the beginning as an augmented human, virtually indestructible, goes about constructing these war memorials, even in the midst of conflict. Further, the idea of a Rehistory Department meant to make history less messy and more palatable is congruent with trends in the subcontinent today. The question of how to memorialize loss using technology in the wake of traumatic civil strife is broached here in an altogether original way.

Toronto-based writer Senaa Ahmad's 'The Glow-in-the-Dark Girls' has been well-received, winning the Sunburst Award for Short Fiction and the A.C. Bose Grant for South Asian Speculative Literature (2019). This story extrapolates from the historical reality of the radium girls who were assigned the task of painting watches with glow-in-the-dark paint, radioactive effects of which eventually led to their deaths. In this story, told in the first person, a group of girls has been genetically modified into bioweapons, becoming lethal to people they come into contact with. The vulnerability of such experimental subjects of bioengineering and their eventual turning within in the wake of isolation in a world racked by conflict makes the story stand apart from more conventional accounts of teenagers with 'superpowers'.

In veteran science fiction writer and cartoonist/graphic artist Manjula Padmanabhan's story 'The Pain Merchant', an apprentice learns the skill of restoring the ability to feel pain from a master pain merchant in a world where this faculty has been eliminated. The story works at several levels, as science fiction and as a philosophical fable for the future. The ambiguity of the customers' motives makes the narrative even more psychologically complex. The 'dolcache' instrument that measures the remnants of pain is an innovative novum (or new idea, to use Darko Suvin's term)[13] for this world in which pain appears as a lack rather than a burden.

Mumbai-based Arjun Raj Gaind is a well-known author of genre fiction and a graphic novelist, having made many successful forays into the realm of the whodunit in an Indian setting. In 'The Ministry of Relevance', he presents a dark vision of the 2020s, a world where nobody reads, and all citizens are run through draconian checks to prove themselves worthy of domicile. The Kafkaesque scenario that ensues for the protagonist as he struggles to prove his identity is reminiscent of the likely difficulties many may face in the near future in South Asia with bureaucratic rationality running amok.

In Jayaprakash Satyamurthy's 'Dimensions of Life under Fascism', the metaphor of flatness is deployed effectively as a science fiction trope for the transformation of the self under a fascist dispensation. Two dimensionality has set in at various levels of Indian society as a result of the advent of fascist structures, now in their twenty-sixth year, felt especially by a mixed-religion couple, an insight that comes through in telling fashion in the grim conclusion of this tale, with many parallels to the current situation in South Asia.

A recent story from Bengali science fiction in translation by Arunava Sinha is Soham Guha's 'The Song of Ice'. This dystopian tale envisages a climatic catastrophe after the eruption of the Yellowstone volcano in the United States. As a contemporary instance of regional climate fiction, or cli-fi-style science fiction, we find an icy winter and unrelenting cold wave descending on Kolkata, decimating the population and forcing people to seek refuge underground, in the Metro tunnels. Besides the vividly etched first-person narrative about survival in this new ice-ravaged world, the story also brings in an element of historical consciousness in its reflections on the legacy of previous cataclysms – whether the Partition, the Naxalbari moment or endemic communal violence – and the sense that the chickens do eventually come home to roost.

The remarkable energy of the Bengaluru science fiction subculture is reflected in the work of Lavanya Lakshminarayan in general, as well as in the story included here, 'Goodbye is the Shape of a Palm Pressed to the Sky'. In this futuristic projection, we find the protagonist journeying back into history to discover the story of her 'space pirate' grandmother through the latter's recently unearthed journal and, in the process, some hard truths about her mother. There is a recognizably feminist perspective on the retrieval of memory here, as well as an innovative deployment of sense-perception-oriented future technology in the service of re-storying the past, even while coming to terms with a vexed inheritance.

Kehkashan Khalid is an artist and science fiction writer of Pakistani origin who works as a senior librarian in Jeddah, Saudi Arabia. Her story 'Almost Human' uses the technique of extrapolation from current trends in surveillance technology in its world building. In this science fiction detective story, Inspector

Mansoor, one of the protagonists, approaches a neural conceptualization hub, more commonly known as the Forge, where droids can be accessed by the police when in need of extra hands, where he is assigned a now-deactivated first-generation robot to help in a homicide investigation. The unfolding of the clue-puzzle structure takes on a new dimension (somewhat reminiscent of Asimov's Robot stories yet squarely grounded in Pakistani terrain)[14] in the depiction of the robot's personal quest for the killer's identity and the prospect of justice.

Bina Shah's earlier work, the feminist dystopia *Before She Sleeps*,[15] is set in the wake of a nuclear exchange in the subcontinent that culminates in rising gender disparity. Next, a virus affecting women's fertility in particular becomes widespread, while 'corrective' measures are sought by the states affected as fewer women are able to bear children. Shah's account of the imposition of these strictures elaborates, although with a different emphasis, the subjugation of women in procreative roles in Margaret Atwood's classic, *The Handmaid's Tale*.[16] In this volume, Shah's story 'Looney ka Tabadla' brings in a dimension of the absurd in its description of the exchange of 'looneys' in 2050, an echo of Sa'adat Hasan Manto's classic Partition story, 'Toba Tek Singh'.[17] In the story, in the wake of the South Asian Disarmament Treaty, it is decided to exchange peace-and-order offenders at the border of India and Pakistan. The offenders in question are those who use both conventional and social media to propagate their goals of destabilizing the peace between the countries. The black humour underpinning the tale echoes Manto as Shah sharpens her satirical take on today's manufacturers of hate speech.

Software engineer and writer Anil Menon has made the transition to speculative fiction in recent works such as *Half of What I Say*,[18] as further evidenced in his story 'Paley's Watch'. The discovery of an artefact in the ocean, the eponymous Paley's watch, leads to a whimsical journey through intellectual disciplines such as mathematics, physics, philosophy and narratology as the object's significance and meaning are sought to be unravelled, by, among others, Tommy, the sassy and brilliant protagonist. The subplot featuring Tommy's crush on his mentor's daughter, Tara Godbole, brings in a dimension of comic relief with some witty reflections on racial and sexual difference revealed in the byplay between them. Tommy's occasional ineptitude as lover and techie whiz-kid make him an endearing and yet fragile figure as the artefact's mysteries are sought to be deciphered, perhaps in vain by anyone but him.

Mumbai-based Aparna Ramachandran is an engineer-turned-media executive and writer. Her story 'Elsewhere' has a futuristic setting, which is well-anchored in the Indian milieu by its use of place names like Kasara (a town near Almora). The idea of accessing the fourth dimension to enable time travel, and eventually a departure from the dystopian present, is explored through the vicissitudes of the relationship between Yra and Avan. Yet, the transition with the aid of 'prana' to the transcendental plane of 'Elsewhere' may take a toll on the material, all-too-human self and has a potentially tragic dimension at the level of the interpersonal.

Astrophysicist Jayant V. Narlikar has been a major presence in Indian science fiction for decades, writing in Marathi and often speaking in public forums such as the Sahitya Akademi about the genre and its significance. On one such occasion, he shared an experience of his days at King's College, Cambridge, when, in 1963, he happened to be living next door to E.M. Forster, and he had the chance to discuss Forster's only science fiction story 'The Machine Stops' (written in 1908) with the writer himself.[19] Later, Narlikar studied under astrophysicist and science fiction author Fred Hoyle, author of *The Black Cloud*, at the Massachusetts Institute of Technology (MIT).[20] This volume features his story 'The Gift of Angels' (translated from the Marathi 'Yaksophar' by Archana Mirajkar, who is also the author of a science fiction novel).[21] This vintage story features Vijay Singh, an Indian scientist, as the protagonist, and his introduction to advanced technology that proves to be the precursor to an *X-Files*-style conspiracy by alien entities. The description of life in the scientific community, whether at an American university or at a research institute in India, draws on the author's own experiences as a distinguished astrophysicist. What is notable is the willingness of the researcher-protagonist to push the boundaries of knowledge to discover the basis for advanced technologies that may not be within the public ken at present, despite the magnitude of the possible risks.

Vandana Singh is a physicist and the author of several collections of science fiction stories. Her story 'Reunion' appeared in the first volume of *The Gollancz Book of South Asian Science Fiction* and has been included in an anthology of 2020's best science fiction, edited by Jonathan Strahan.[22] The influence of the late science fiction great Ursula Le Guin is palpable in the story 'A Different Sea', which features an unconventional friendship between the protagonist and an alien she names Khatru. We find here a profound reflection on death and the possibly different meaning this may have for an alien species. In the process, this poetic tale also makes us think about death as a metaphor, especially in the context of intricate and at times failed personal relationships with events set in a faraway planet allowing for a degree of cognitive distancing. The unearthing of the lost history of Gyana, a Bengali woman poet of an earlier time, is a key element to this narrative, as the protagonist finds her voice through a rediscovery of the significance of such mutilated voices. Indeed, such reconstitution of crucial civilizational patterns that might have otherwise been lost become possible as a result of the narrator's contact with Khatru.[23]

Delhi-based constitutional law expert Gautam Bhatia is a science fiction critic and senior articles editor with *Strange Horizons*. His contribution in the volume, 'The List', is a space opera-style story which addresses the critical question of what it means to be human in a futuristic setting of contact between different species, some of which have an exclusivist view of identity. The eponymous 'list', which invokes logic and life, is a counter to the tendencies towards speciesism, with its insistence on uniformity and drive toward offworlding, a resonant science fiction metaphor for our times. The use of innovative narrative devices such as italicized personal reflections by characters and poetic language accentuates the critique of homogenization and dominance over the 'other', in particular those deemed different and consigned to work in the viriconium caves.[24]

'2020-nKarV' by the poet, essayist and translator from Bangladesh Kaiser Haq is an ironic reflection on the difficult moment we are living through in the early 2020s. In this speculative poem, the spread of a karuna virus ('karuna' meaning compassion in Hindi) causes puzzlement and dismay, with echoes of the predicament humanity faces with the spread of the SARS-CoV-2 coronavirus today. The quarantine established for the carriers of compassion, especially animal lovers and poets, even as the absence of compassion is normalized, has an all-too familiar edge in today's South Asia. There is an ethical meditation here on the effects on language and expression of authoritarian measures taken by states in times of crisis in the name of the public good, based on purported science.

Kalsang Yangzom is a young India-based writer, teacher and blogger of Tibetan origin. In her story 'The Crossing', she extrapolates from the experience of several generations of Tibetans who have crossed over the Himalaya into India while envisaging a future in which a microchip is injected in every Indian at birth to prove their identity, and which such migrants must have implanted after reaching their destination. While there is no explicit reference to China or Tibet, the Anisians who defeat the 'theocratic government', causing many to flee, are recognizable to those familiar with this history, reconfigured here in the science fiction genre. There is a restrained urgency underlying the portrayal of the experience of exile as well as the imminent possibility of betrayal.

Poet, novelist, scholar and short story writer Giti Chandra's 'A Species of Least Concern' projects current concerns about species extinction into a futuristic setting in a tale with more than a touch of black comedy. In a setting where the concept of 'nature' has to be explained to a young child and fabrichines provide every comfort, including the best research articles on climate change and the history of species loss, the 'species of least concern' (whether women or honey badgers) are those not yet placed in the at-risk category, given that they are assumed to be indestructible. A mother's attempt to ensure her daughter's survival by endowing her with strengths from different species takes a darkly comic turn as protagonist Melli touches down on a planet where hybridity is unwelcome. The underlying seriousness of the feminist critique of human self-destructiveness and disregard of the most vulnerable cannot be missed.

Scholar and author Haris A. Durrani, who is of part-Pakistani and part-Dominican descent, brings his intercultural background effectively into play in 'Champollion's Foot'. The allusions to ciguapas, shape-shifting creatures from Dominican legends, and jinns as creatures capable of possession of human hosts are lightly interwoven into this space opera about xenocide, the obliteration of an alien species. The references to Champollion's discovery of the Rosetta Stone and the ensuing systematic study of ancient Egypt, leading to an ironic erasure of this ancient system of knowledge, form a template for later reflections on the implications of being the 'other'. Yet, there may be a way out of the historical trajectory leading towards decimation of alien cultures and knowledge systems, the story indicates.

Usman T. Malik, who practices medicine, is a writer from Pakistan who has created space for his distinctive variant of SFF, which often delves into jinn lore and the realm of the weird and the occult.[25] In his story 'Resurrection Points', Malik brings to bear the precision and understanding of a qualified rheumatologist and medical writer as well as deep empathy with the plight of beleaguered minority communities such as Christians living in ghettos in Pakistan. There is a productive tension evoked here between the young protagonist's extraordinary ability to resurrect the dead and the toxic exclusionary effects of invidious social and religious pressures now at work in our variegated societies, with their multiple fault lines.

Writer, creative director and editor Salik Shah is based in India (though he was brought up in Nepal and often draws upon this formative experience).

Shah has made a long-standing contribution to the world of Asian SFF through his role as founding editor of *Mithila Review*, an SFF journal. His speculative story 'Shambhala' is unusual in its evocation in a lyrical yet political mode of the predicament of Tibetan exiles. The existential dilemmas of the movement for a free Tibet and the complex relationship with mainland China are presented with sensitivity in the depiction of the Tibetan narrator's childhood memories of his Chinese teacher who taught them Mandarin. The forced migration into Nepal as a result of state oppression culminates in exile, in a situation all too familiar to many Tibetans poetically evoked here through memory.[26] This story is, thus, an instance of locally rooted cosmopolitanism, transcending narrow definitions of identity in its empathetic account of political exile.

Sri Lankan science fiction has come into the spotlight in recent times with a novelette co-authored by science fiction author and data scientist Yudhanjaya Wijeratne and Indian American R.R. Virdi being nominated for a Nebula award in 2018.[27] Wijeratne is also the author of 'The Ricepunk Manifesto', which outlines a different, culturally grounded science fiction sensibility as a variant of and modification of cyberpunk.[28] We are glad to be able to include here Wijeratne's story 'Confessor', placed in a futuristic context of violation of human rights and freedom of expression. This story, taking its cue from contemporary experiences of imprisonment of journalists and activists in Sri Lanka, has a bearing on the situation emerging across South Asia, and perhaps even more widely, in its candid depiction of state intimidation of dissenters. The use of implants such as memory chips for artists sought to be recruited for propaganda purposes takes us a sinister step beyond George Orwell's *1984*.[29] 'Confessor' is grim in its anticipation of the ruthless instrumentalization of violence using sophisticated technologies to turn those deemed a threat to the powers that be.

Accomplished poet, translator and science fiction writer Priya Sarukkai Chabria's speculative poem 'Scavenger' brings an element of formal experimentation in its out-of-the-box response to prevalent trends in society. Readers may note the evocative use of images to capture a fragmented post-apocalyptic scenario, in which time and history seem to have been irrevocably dislocated from their moorings. The poetic persona, nonetheless, continues to dream, perchance in a post-human register, all too aware of the displacement and emptying out of the human by 'AI-weeders' and the ravages of climate change. Even so, the lyrical quest for alternatives persists amidst the wreckage with the possibility of redemption at the end.

Extending the world building initiated in his novel *Aliens in Delhi*,[30] science fiction scholar, editor and writer Sami Ahmad Khan's story 'Biryani Bagh' takes its cue from contemporary protests and resistance movements as it constructs its novel take on the role played by flavoursome biryani in the current configuration. The popular dish becomes the novum around which the narrative unfolds, set in 2038 at a time when biryani-loving aliens (later disclosed to be a stereotype) live on Earth, in a cryptic yet recognizable instance of cognitive estrangement (Suvin's term).[31] In the process, 'Biryani Bagh' provides a visceral take on the dilemmas of minority existence and the changes being wrought as a result of attacks on constitutional morality in today's Delhi/India. The story deals with local concerns as well as the global ramifications of the techno-dystopia being ushered in today, resulting in regressive loops back into the history of communal/sectarian violence.

In his science fiction novels and stories, Shovon Chowdhury, who sadly and unexpectedly passed away before this volume could appear, effectively satirized the pretensions that continue to dog us in India as a postcolonial and now, at least in segments, post hi-tech society. In 'Malini', we find a comic take on the role of artificial intelligence in destabilizing our usual sense of relationships, in this case a food delivery application. In this dark yet hilarious tale, the protagonist's obsession with a voice representing the delivery service leads him to a sequence of progressively more bizarre misadventures. Might the realm of artificial intelligence-powered constructs prove seductive enough to displace normative forms of desire, the story seems to provocatively ask.

Sukanya Datta is Chief Scientist, Council of Scientific and Industrial Research, and her work as science communicator led her eventually to writing science fiction; she now has several collections of stories in the genre to her name.[32] In Datta's story 'The Midas Touch', the 'tall tale' structure is interspersed with elements of biological science, along the lines of precursors like Satyajit Ray (in his Professor Shonku stories) and Premendra Mitra (in his Ghanada tales).[33] In this thought-provoking tale, the discovery of a treasure map with notations in Sanskrit and Greek, as recounted by the itinerant Golu Mama, leads to a quest for the Suvarnabhumi or land of gold in the upper Himalayas, where the travellers come to terms with the existence of extremophiles, microbes that excrete gold. While the adventure story/tall tale structure adds to the suspense underlying the story, the author interweaves precise references to such microbial activity ('hard' science) seamlessly into what might otherwise seem like an innocuous tale for children.

Canada-based scientist and author of science fiction, horror and fantasy tales Premee Mohamed's story 'The Arrival of the New World' takes up the key question of climate change. The story is set in the aftermath of a tourist excursion into the Guyanese rainforest gone horribly wrong. Various layers of history and culture are unravelled in this account of a professional writer of Guyanese-Indian origin, accompanied by a team of film-makers, to discover what happened to a group of tourists and guides who have gone missing while on an expedition into the jungle in Guyana. While the context of indentured labour during the age of empire brought the narrator's ancestors to Guyana, migration to Canada later has ensured a form of double displacement that causes this return to a homeland at one remove to become one of self-discovery, albeit under imperilled circumstances. Premee portrays the existential threat that has arisen as a result of the breaching of the 'tipping points' in the middle of the untamed rainforest, beyond the safe and managed zones maintained by the tourist agency. In the process, we find in this story a compelling depiction of the likelihood of an ecologically damaged planet striking back, even as the 'New World' of impending climate catastrophe looms large.

Sri Lankan writer Navin Weeraratne's story 'The Diamond Library' takes us into a dystopian world in which literacy and, with it, libraries have become endangered. Innovatively reinventing the premise of *Fahrenheit 451* by Ray Bradbury,[34] the story depicts the urgent attempt to memorialize stories which may otherwise disappear forever or be relegated as 'fantasy'.[35] The tale echoes the film *The Matrix* in its depiction of the way simulations driven by the Grand Librarian keep an approximation of humanity alive in the wake of the catastrophic loss of most humans in physical form. What remains are underground libraries in which books are engraved on diamond-hardened surfaces, governed by supra intelligences hoping to preserve the basis of human existence. The noir tone and unlikable narrator help reinforce the sense of mystery and propel us to the concluding section in which the philosophical reflection on being achieves a final twist, further complicating our sense of the relationship between illusion and reality in this future world (and our own).

Bangladeshi author Saad Z. Hossain writes fantasy, science fiction and black comedy, which are often blended in a distinctive way in his work. His SFF narratives, in which figures from the Middle Eastern tradition of folklore and storytelling often meet a contemporary context, have received great critical acclaim.[36] For instance, Hossain generates dark comedy through the sheer incongruity of the situation of a jinn waking up in post-climate change and nanotech-endowed Kathmandu in his acclaimed and Locus award-nominated novella *The Gurkha and the Lord of Tuesday*.[37] In 'Bring Your Own Spoon', the perils of biotech are in focus in a story set in a future Dhaka where people are protected by nanites and a protective bubble from airborne pathogens. In this story, Imbidor, a lesser jinn without dignitas, helps the protagonist Hanu set up a kitchen and restaurant in the Fringe, preparing mouth-watering repasts for the customers from the area. The high costs of such partnerships across the gulf separating humans from the occult realm, and the fragility of such initiatives in the domain of subaltern entrepreneurship, become evident in the story's denouement.

It has been a privilege reaching out to this talented set of authors, who have delivered a veritable feast of ideas and storylines, not to mention speculative poetry. This is original material, for the most part, a New Wave of South Asian SFF, comparable in its stylistic and thematic variety and innovativeness to the New Wave cinema movement ushered in by filmmakers like Mrinal Sen, Mani Kaul, Shyam Benegal and Kumar Shahani.[38] For the ambit of the best recent South Asian SFF has expanded beyond realism (even 'of our time') towards experimentalism and self-reflexivity, often with a sceptical view of the alignment of science/technology and the state. Much of this writing shows a productive conjoining of the bizarre and the mundane, the real and the hyper-real, yet underpinned by a sense of the perils of existing in techno-bubbles or simulated utopias in a region on the cusp of what may be irrevocable alterations in culture and society.

Yet, at the end of the day, after the variegated world building on view here, we can discern a return to an ethically grounded collective South Asian civilizational narrative along with a growing recognition that multiple 'other' South Asian spaces exist. Indeed, if readers are prompted to discover more such South Asian SFF narratives carving new spaces in time, this volume would have accomplished its purpose. As an instance of such innovative approaches, I warmly commend the reader to Manjula Padmanabhan's graphic preface and concluding image, which encompass the dialectic between inner and outer space.

Meanwhile, as a genre, South Asian science fiction (and fantasy) continues to grow, with increasing recognition of the considerable talent on offer. Emerging and new voices indicate the range of concerns and the expansion of scope of the issues being dealt with. While geographical differences and historical transformations clearly separate South Asian New Wave writing from the countries brought together under this umbrella, there has been in recent times more of conversation and dialogue across boundaries. Online forums and journals like *Mithila Review* and *Antonym* have facilitated this process, as have the many anthologies that have recently appeared. We can see a growing self-confidence as writers devise their own distinctive idioms while contending with the dilemmas of the twenty-first century. Whether through critical re-inscriptions of mythology, or deft adaptation of models from cyberpunk or solarpunk, or even recourse to meta-fiction and a reinvention of standard science fiction tropes such as first contact, the alien, the zombie or robots and artificial intelligences, and the doomed city, South Asian writers are reclaiming the imaginative resources afforded by the genre in myriad ways. In the process, a counter narrative to the stereotypical representations of commercial science fiction, whether in terms of race, gender, caste or other hierarchies is being generated afresh, sensitive to nuance and intersectionality and alert to the insidious workings of power. Such futuristic writing can be seen as an antidote to anodyne stories extolling development and the benefits of technology, and as a repository of critical and oppositional energies that may eventually help shape for the better emergent futures that await us all.

Notes

1. See Kim Stanley Robinson, 'The Coronavirus is Rewriting our Imaginations', *New Yorker*, 1 May 2020. Web. <https://www.newyorker.com/culture/annals-of-inquiry/the-coronavirus-and-our-future>. 3 May 2020.
2. I have a brief essay that elaborates on this question. See Tarun K. Saint, 'Responding Imaginatively to Cataclysmic Change', Omita Goyal, ed., *IIC Quarterly*, Vol. 47(1–2):25–30, Summer and Autumn 2020.
3. Tarun K. Saint, ed., *The Gollancz Book of South Asian Science Fiction*, Gurugram: Hachette India, 2019.
4. See the path-breaking collection Ken Liu, trans. and ed., *Invisible Planets: An Anthology of Contemporary Chinese Science Fiction*, London: Head of Zeus, 2017. Also see Ken Liu, ed. and trans., *Broken Stars: Contemporary Chinese Science Fiction in Translation*, London: Head of Zeus, 2019.
5. As instances of such recent work in the analytical mode see Suparno Banerjee, *Indian Science Fiction: Patterns, History and Hybridity*, Cardiff: University of Wales Press, 2020. See also Bodhisattva Chattopadhyaya, Aakriti Mandhwani and Anwesha Maity, eds, *Indian Genre Fiction: Past and Future Histories*, New Delhi: Routledge India, 2019.

6. We located an important work of SFF written in Urdu too late to include in this volume. See Qurratulain Hyder, 'Roshni ki Raftar', translated by the author as 'Beyond the Speed of Light', Hyder, *The Street Singers of Lucknow and Other Stories*, New Delhi: Sterling Publishers, 1996, 104–30.

7. See Tarun K. Saint, 'SF Matters: South Asian Futures to Come', in Tarun K. Saint, ed., *The Gollancz Book of South Asian Science Fiction*, Gurugram: Hachette India, 2019.

8. See Tashan Mehta, *The Liar's Weave*, New Delhi: Juggernaut, 2017.

9. Ursula Le Guin, *The Lathe of Heaven*, London: Gollancz, 1967 (2001 rpt.).

10. See H.G. Wells, *The Island of Dr Moreau*, UK: Heinemann,1896.

11. See Erin Blakemore, 'Why the Nazis Were Obsessed With Twins', 8 July 2019. Web. <https://www.history.com/news/nazi-twin-experiments-mengele-eugenics>. 22 May 2021.

12. See Wilfred Owen's poetic denunciation of the myth of heroic self-sacrifice propagated during World War One, 'Dulce et Decorum Est', *Poetry Foundation*, n.d. Web. 2 February 2020 <https://www.poetryfoundation.org/poems/46560/dulce-et-decorum-est>.

13. On Darko Suvin's notion of the SF novum as a breach in the accepted order of things, an intrusive novelty so unusual that it deserves a category of its own, see 'Novum', *The Encyclopedia of Science Fiction*, 2 April 2015. Web. 2 February 2020. <http://www.sf-encyclopedia.com/entry/novum>.

14. Isaac Asimov, *I, Robot*, New York: Bantam, 1950 (1991 rpt.).

15. See Bina Shah, *Before She Sleeps: A Novel*, Encino: Delphinium Books, 2018 (2019 rpt.). For a useful account of South Asian SFF, with an emphasis on work from Pakistan, see Nudrat Kamal's essay, 'South Asian Science-Fiction is Finally Centre Stage, Bringing Us Closer to Our Own Reality', *Scroll.in*, 20 July 2019. Web. 24 March 2020. <https://scroll.in/article/930852/south-asian-science-fiction-is-finally-centrestage-bringing-us-closer-to-our-own-reality>.

16. Margaret Atwood, *The Handmaid's Tale*, Canada: Seal Books, 1985 (1998 rpt.).

17. Sa'adat Hasan Manto, 'Toba Tek Singh', M. Asaduddin, trans. Muhammad Umar Memon, ed., *Black Margins: Stories*, New Delhi: Katha, 2001 (2003 rpt.).

18. Anil Menon, *Half of What I Say*, New Delhi: Bloomsbury, 2015.

19. Personal communication, Anil Menon, who was present when Dr Jayant V. Narlikar shared this anecdote at an IIT Kanpur workshop on SF in 2009. Also see Jayant V. Narlikar, 'A Sense of Humour', *Indian Literature*, Vol. 33, No. 6(140): 65–78, November–December 1990. Web. 15 May 2020. <https://www.jstor.org/stable/23339412> and E.M. Forster, *The Machine Stops*. Web. 30 May 2020. <https://www.ele.uri.edu/faculty/vetter/Other-stuff/The-Machine-Stops.pdf>.

20. See Fred Hoyle, *The Black Cloud*, Harmondsworth: Penguin, 1957 (1977 rpt.).

21. See Archana Mirajkar, *All the way...Home*, New Delhi: Lifi Publications, 2019.

22. Vandana Singh, 'Reunion', Tarun K. Saint, ed., *The Gollancz Book of South Asian Science Fiction*, 341–65, and in Jonathan Strahan, ed., *The Year's Best Science Fiction Vol. 1: The Saga Anthology of Science Fiction 2020*, New York: Saga Press, 2020, 423–53.

23. Also see Pakistani poet Fahmida Riaz's 'fictive' excavation of the real-life story of activist Godavari Parulekar in *Godavari: A Novel*, Karachi: OUP, 2008. Trans. of *Godavari* by Aquila Ismail, 1998.

24. We may be reminded of M. John Harrison's genre blurring Viriconium series of narratives. See esp. Harrison, *Viriconium*, London: Gollancz, 2000.

25. Usman T. Malik, *Midnight Doorways: Fables from Pakistan*, Lahore: Kitab Pvt. Ltd., 2021 (forthcoming in an Indian edition in 2022, Hachette India).

26. For more responses to the Tibetan predicament in verse form by Tibetan poets, see Bhuchung D. Sonam, ed., *Muses in Exile: An Anthology of Tibetan Poetry*, New Delhi: Paljor Publications, 2004.

27. The novelette by Yudhanjaya Wijeratne and R.R. Virdi is 'Messenger'. See *Nebula Awards*, n.d. Web. 9 October 2020. <https://nebulas.sfwa.org/nominated-work/messenger/>.

28. See 'The Ricepunk Manifesto', *Yudhanjaya.com*, 1 May 2019. Web. 12 October 2020. <https://yudhanjaya.com/2019/05/the-ricepunk-manifesto/>.

29. George Orwell, *1984*, London: Secker and Warburg, 1949.

30. Sami Ahmad Khan, *Aliens in Delhi*, New Delhi: Niyogi Books, 2017.

31. For a detailed discussion of this concept, see Darko Suvin, 'Estrangement and Cognition', *Strange Horizons*, 24 November 2014. Web. 3 March 2020. <http://strangehorizons.com/non-fiction/articles/estrangement-and-cognition/>.

32. See, for instance, Sukanya Datta, *Worlds Apart: Science Fiction Stories*, New Delhi: National Book Trust, 2012 (2014 rpt.).

33. On translating Premendra Mitra's Ghanada stories, see Amlan Dasgupta's reflections, 'Ghana-da's Duck, or a Translator's Travails', *National Translation Mission*, n.d. Web. 15 April 2020. <http://www.ntm.org.in/download/ttvol/Volume7/Articles/07%20-%20Ghana-da's%20Duck,%20or%20a%20Translator's%20Travails%20-%20Amlan%20Das%20Gupta.pdf>.

34. Ray Bradbury, *Fahrenheit 451*, New York: Baltimore, 1953.

35. Also see Navin Weeraratne, *The Hundred Gram Mission*, Colombo: Lanka Comic Con Edition, 2016.

36. See Saad Z. Hossain, *Djinn City: A Novel*, New Delhi: Aleph Book Company, 2017, and Saad Z. Hossain, *Escape from Baghdad!: A Novel*, 2013. New Delhi: Aleph Book Company, 2015 (rpt.).

37. Saad Z. Hossain, *The Gurkha and the Lord of Tuesday*, New York: Tom Doherty Associates, 2019.

38. See Ira Bhaskar's account, 'The Indian New Wave'. K. Moti Gokulsing, Wimal Dissanayake and Rohit K. Dasgupta, eds., *The Routledge Handbook of Indian Cinemas*, Abingdon: Routledge, 2013. Web. 12 February 2021. It is perhaps no accident that *Deham* (2001), one of the few serious Indian SF films, was directed by New Wave filmmaker Govind Nihalani, based on Manjula Padmanabhan's 1997 play *Harvest*.

AND NOW HIS LORDSHIP IS LAUGHING

SHIV RAMDAS

When the first breeze of the morning whistles over the green tips of the paddy stalks to kiss the tawny jute thatching of the bungalow roof, Apa is already out on the veranda. It's still dark but that doesn't matter – it's been more than twoscore years since she's needed light to work by. All she needs is the jute and her tools. Needle and twine, knife and lime, all have their place, and in Apa's hands that place is to give form to thought. Beneath those hands the strands strain, first to oppose her coaxing, and then, bit by bit, to obey her bidding. Once or twice, a sharp fibre edge pricks her finger and she silently shakes the droplets of blood aside with practised ease, careful not to let any spill on the jute, even as the material in her grasp twists in apology.

Before the rosy arms of the sun reach out from the dark to embrace Midnapore in another new day, she's already been at work for several hours. Her deft, callused fingers move quickly, expertly, back and forth, one fold up, another stitch down. As she works, she hums her *shukro sangeet*, a song of thanks to the jute, for what it has been and what it will be. No matter how many times she works and weaves it, Apa never ceases to wonder at the miracle of this material, the most special, versatile crop there is. You can wear it, build with it, eat it and feed with it; there's almost nothing in which you can't use it. And it grows everywhere, Bengal's ubiquitous treasure. Yet, despite what people say, jute has no magic, no mystery or secrets; what you ask of it is what it gives. Even if it does carry memories; each generation of crop remembering what its parents have done, so each time you mould it afresh it proves easier than the last. All you need is enough of yourself to put into it, and the knowledge that both you and the jute are in this together, not master and *dasa*, but two friends working side by side.

By the time Nilesh comes out onto the veranda to stand behind her, the golden strands in her grasp have already begun to take the shape they will spend the rest of their existence in. A small hand reaches out, tapping her on the shoulder, and Apa turns, to be met by a pair of accusing black eyes.

'You said I could help!'

'I said you could help *if* you finished your milk.'

'But, Apa, I did!'

He holds out his hand, brandishes a tumbler, then overturns it. A solitary white drop clings to the rim, falls free, landing on the veranda floor.

'See? See?'

Apa laughs. 'All right then. Sit next to me and go through all these jute bits I have dropped. I need you to find the two biggest ones and set them aside.'

He beams, plonking himself down beside her with a loud thud.

'Be careful! You'll hurt yourself!'

He giggles but doesn't answer, rummaging through the discarded scraps of jute, the pink tip of his tongue peeping out from the side of his mouth, brow scrunched up in concentration. Silence falls over the veranda for a while, punctuated only by Nilesh's periodic exclamations and grunts. Apa pays them little heed: the jute demands all her attention. She sits there, head bent, sunbeams dancing off her silvery hair, hands still flashing first one way, then another, as the fibres she holds in her fingers come together as only Apa can make them. And as she finishes, the final fibrous form resting in her lap, Nilesh leaps to his feet, handing her two pieces of jute.

'These were the biggest ones, Apa.'

'Thank you, Nilesh. These are exactly what I need.'

'What is it? What doll have you made today?'

'Patience, patience.'

She twists the scraps around the doll's waist, using the very tip of her knife to shape them. Then a dab of lime to hold them in place.

Nilesh's eyes widen. 'It's wearing a dhoti now! I made the dhoti!' He claps delightedly, and then squeals as the doll claps along with him. 'It's a *hattali'r putul*! A clapping doll!'

She smiles. 'No, it's a Nilesh *putul*.'

'It's me? It's for *me*?'

She smiles again. 'Yes, and yes. Do you like it?'

He leans forward, planting a big, sloppy kiss on her weathered cheek, and then does a little dance, whooping excitedly. A slight frown creases her brow as she watches him; his eagerness for everything doll-related is a bittersweet reminder of what used to be. Where once it was common for children to gather gawking at her while she worked, or for villagers to stop by the house and ask her about taking on so-and-so as an apprentice, it's now been years since anyone has. Today's young people have other things they want to do with their lives, things that do not require them to spend decades hunched over with needle in hand, nor pay ever-increasing levies and taxes. Apa sighs. But then there's Nilesh, always so eager to help her in her work. Perhaps he'll be the exception, and when he's old enough she'll teach him the craft, and maybe the art of Midnapore doll weaving will outlive her after all.

He's still dancing away happily even as the doll kicks its feet in perfect unison with his. Apa watches them both, her heart now sowing fields without a thought for the reaping.

Until the sound of hoof beats rends the air, growing louder as the horse trots down the path towards the bungalow veranda. Now they see him, the uniformed Englishman sitting upright in the saddle. Apa keeps her eyes on him all the way, her new creation now held tightly in her hands.

'Nilesh. Go inside. Hurry, now.'

'But why, Apa?' he protests. 'I too want to hear what he says!'

Apa half-turns, fixing the boy with her gaze. 'I said *now*.'

He darts back inside, as anyone would have, because no one in Midnapore disobeys Apa. As the horse draws to a halt, the old woman rises to her feet.

The Englishman dismounts, flicks the sweat from his brow and stands before the veranda.

'Matriarch of Midnapore. Captain Frederick Bolton, of the Calcutta Presidency Battalion.'

He sounds like most of his countrymen, flat-toned and steady. She often wonders how the English have come by their belief that the inability to emote is a virtue. It seems so unnatural.

'I remember you.'

She speaks in English because it hurts her ears to hear them try to speak Bangla. Although, more often than not, what they speak is Hindi in what they think is a Bengali accent.

'I come as the emissary of His Grace, Sir John Arthur Herbert, Governor of Bengal, representative of Her Gracious Majesty Victoria, Queen of India and the Empire.'

'What do you want this time?'

He smiles. 'Oh, you know what His Grace wishes for. He's asked you on more than one occasion – one of your dolls for Her Ladyship. '

'No.'

'I would urge you to reconsider.'

'There is nothing to reconsider. Your master is, as you say, Governor of Bengal. He can have almost any toy he wants.'

'What he wants is one of yours. His Grace says he has never seen another doll maker whose work compares to yours. None have your magic.'

'He might have seen many more if he hadn't made it a point to drive so many out of work with duties and levies every time the wind changes, or to those schools where you tell our children how backward our ways are. And I have no magic. I am but a means to an end.'

'Come now, His Grace is willing to be generous.'

She gestures at the thick paddy and jute fields encircling the bungalow, green and lush, gently swaying in the summer breeze.

'Look around you, Captain. I have no need of his generosity.'

'I strongly recommend you do not choose this path. The governor is not a man used to being denied. Especially by a native. See, you hold a doll even as we speak. All you need to do is simply hand it to me, and you can name your price.'

'My *putul* are not for sale. I give them to those I choose, and I do not choose those who demand them at the point of a bayonet. Be off with you.'

He sighs. 'I fear you may come to regret this, Matriarch. '

'All of Midnapore, no, all of Bengal, regrets the day your kind came here. What is one more regret? If you turn your horse around, you will find the path leads back just as surely as it led you here. I would urge you to take it.'

She could swear she sees his eyes blaze but, just as suddenly, the anger is gone and he's taking a deep breath. Has she imagined it? When he speaks, his voice is even.

'I will convey your message to His Grace.'

With that, he leaps back on his horse and gallops away.

Apa stands erect, watching until man and horse are out of sight, vanished among the towering crops on either side of the road. He might be gone, but the cloud of his unspoken promise still lingers. An additional crease lines her already wrinkled brow; she twists the jute doll in her hands.

For, as she well knows, just like jute, the white man has a long memory – and, unlike the jute, he does not mind blood.

Under the relentless gaze of the sun, the scorched earth shimmers. Through the haze, the shrivelled, blackened stumps of what had been jute fields protrude upwards. From the veranda, Apa stares unblinkingly at them. As she watches, a charred wisp dances off one, carried by the breeze to fall on the burnt, dried-out remains of what had been one of the paddy plots. Next to it, a host of flies buzzes above something lying there. A dead bullock, or, more likely, a person. The British have already taken all the bullocks, right after they took all the rice. Every last grain.

It's been almost four days since she lost Nilesh. Mercifully, he'd stopped crying towards the end, and so for the last couple of days he'd just lain there, hands over his bloated belly, eyes staring at something in the distance that nobody else could see. For a brief, interminable while, she'd wondered what he'd felt during those final days, but she knows the answer now. Nothing.

Despite what Apa had always thought starvation would be like, the hunger isn't the worst part. The pangs don't last as long as one would imagine; by the fourth day, they're almost entirely gone. It isn't even the weakness, terrible as that is. It's the lethargy, the constant feeling that nothing matters, not food, not movement, not brushing away the flies circling overhead and settling, unwilling to afford one the dignity of being truly dead before they move in. It's the sense of lying there, waiting to shut down, but being unable to do even that, as the mind refuses to accept what the body is telling it, that this journey has come to an end. Time comes and goes in strange, fluid stretches; a leaf taking hours to fall to the ground, the span between sunrise and sunset vanishing in the time it takes to blink. Blinking is the one thing that seems unchanged, as though her brain has a special rapport with the eyelids that it never developed with the rest of her body. What is strangest of all is thought itself. Her mind doesn't seem foggy. Thoughts appear with what feels like increased clarity, even as she watches her body wasting away, as though her brain is cannibalizing the rest of her to feed itself.

As if on cue, a fly buzzes around her head, coming to settle on her nose. She blinks to drive it off, but it ignores her efforts. It's there to stay, welcome or not. Must be British... She thinks about brushing it away, but her limbs feel heavy and as though they belong to someone else, and it doesn't seem that important anyway. She blinks again, and in the instant her eyes are shut, she hears a sound, no, a series of sounds, words, coming from very far away. She opens her eyes again on the other side of the blink, and the man comes into focus.

He's in front of the veranda, still astride his horse, moving his mouth, making the sounds. He looks familiar. Can it be...yes, it is indeed him, the British soldier who keeps coming by unbidden, like one of those flies. What's his name again? Bol, Ball, something like that. What does it matter? Behind him, also on horseback, three more men. They don't matter either. Maybe if she shuts her eyes again they'll go away.

She closes them, and then she feels hands, one pulling her head backwards, the other forcing her mouth open, tipping something into her mouth. A steady stream of something, thin yet mushy. She chokes, and deep racking retches follow, spluttering the food back out, as she looks up through watering eyes. Two of the men are crouched over her, one holding her, the other holding a spoon and a bowl of watery-looking rice gruel. Spoon Man is wiping the regurgitations off the unhappy expression on his face. He looks back at his companions. The familiar-looking soldier says something to his men. The feeder grimaces and she feels rough hands grab her head again, tilting it backwards, as the spoon closes in once again.

She sits on the veranda, cross-legged, ignoring the soldier beside her, waiting for the other one to come with the evening bowl of gruel. They no longer feed her, now that she's strong enough to do it herself, but at least one of them hovers nearby at all times. At first, she's unable to keep any food down, as though her stomach now considers rice a foreign object it wants to have nothing to do with, but they persist, and slowly, her body has learnt how to eat again. She still doesn't know why: they haven't said a word to her since. They do, however, talk to each other. From listening, she learns that one is called Willis, the other McKissic, that someone called Sir Winston has ordered the governor to take all the rice, and it is happening all over Bengal.

Every so often, slowly, gingerly, she runs her tongue along the inside of her gums, wincing a bit. Her teeth and mouth hurt all the time now, why she doesn't know. From the force feeding? Or maybe that's merely the part of her that was being eaten from the inside out when the soldiers returned to the bungalow.

The sun is lower than usual when McKissic returns with the gruel, and this time he isn't alone. Four more mounted soldiers accompany him and riding at their head is that captain again. With effort, Apa recalls his name. Bolton. He reins in his horse, dismounts, stands before the veranda, riding crop still in one hand. He jerks his head at one of the other men. This individual crouches down over Apa and proceeds to hold her wrist, then touch her neck, look in her mouth, and run a hand over her still-distended belly as she sits there silently. Finally, he stands up.

'She'll be fine.'

'Strong enough for the job?'

'I'd venture to say so, yes.'

'Excellent. Thank you, Doctor.' Bolton looks at Apa. 'I told you no good would come of your defiance. It's a good thing I got here in time, isn't it?'

He smiles at her, waiting for a response, while she stares back at him, stony-faced. For a slow, long time, silence spreads its wings over the veranda. Until eventually, the captain cracks.

'His Grace is, however, still willing to be generous. He offers you a bargain. Food for you and whatever others are still alive here.'

Others, he says. How long has it been now since Agni took her Nilesh? She isn't even sure any more. All she remembers is how small, how frail he'd looked on the pyre. How hard it had been just to force the doll she'd made for him into his tiny, stiff hands before she'd lit the flame. Fire had been his protector, doing what she no longer has the strength to. It had made sure that nobody would attempt to strip the corpse of its clothes, as she heard had been happening all over Midnapore. Clothes are fibre, and fibre can be food. She's also heard news of even worse horrors: children attempting to eat their deceased parents, parents their dead children. And worse, whispers that, in some places, some aren't even waiting for others to die. Then, silence, no news of anything for days before she too fell into the starvation stupor. That had been the one good thing about it, the inability to think of Nilesh, all the others she'll never see again, about any of it.

Despite her best efforts, the tear burns its way out, dangling on the rim of her eye for a moment, before it falls to the dusty veranda floor with a loud plop. She looks up at his hateful face.

'There are no others here.'

'What a pity.'

Her face must show some of what she's thinking, because he immediately goes on. 'Look, don't blame me for this. I'm just doing my job here.'

'Just...doing your job.'

'Yes, and I'm trying to help you. As is the governor. We're on your side, you know. Think about it. Food and drink for you, and in return, all His Grace asks is that you give him something in return. A doll for Her Ladyship.'

She feels a stirring within her, a white-hot core of rage in her belly, growing, spreading outwards. 'He did all this...*for a doll*?'

At this, he laughs aloud. 'You know, sometimes you natives really are full of yourselves. No, the Denial of Rice policy is much bigger than you or this state. It's been a huge help in supplying the war effort. Ever heard of the Axis? No, of course you haven't. Be glad – that's who we're protecting you from.'

'Protecting…'

'Yes, protecting. The prime minister himself has written to Sir John, commending him for his success in ensuring continued food and supplies for the Allied troops. Instead of complaining, you should be proud of the role Bengal is playing in saving the world. As is the rest of India. Anyway, enough of this. I didn't come all the way to the boondocks to discuss politics with you. Won't you just see reason – for your own sake? Just make that damned doll and we can all be done with this song and dance. Here, McKissic, give her some more of that stuff. Maybe the taste of food will straighten out her mind.'

She feels rather than sees the bowl being thrust into her hands. All she can hear is what he's said, echoing in her head, over and over. Once again, the white-hot rage surges through her, going from kernel to spreading flame so quickly that she scarcely remembers how it began. She raises her hand, to throw the bowl of gruel back in his face and as she does, one particular sentence bounces around inside her mind again.

'*…the rest of India.*'

Then, the rage is gone, replaced by something else, harder, colder, so alien and frightening, so different from any feeling she's ever known that it couldn't possibly have come from her. But it's inside her.

She lowers the bowl. 'I need materials and tools.'

He nods, pleased, although there's something else there as well. Relief? 'I thought you might see the light. I have jute here. What tools?'

'Lime, a needle, some thread and a knife. Her eyes are blue?'

He stares at her. 'What if they are?

'Then I will also need some indigo. For the dye.'

'You shall have whatever you need.'

Then he pauses. 'You'll have to be supervised, of course. Can't have you using that knife to do some mischief to someone. Or yourself. Willis, McKissic, I'm afraid your vigil continues. Give her everything she wants. At least until – how long before it's done?'

'I don't know. Two days, maybe three. It is not an exact science. I need to feel the shape in the jute before I can set it free.'

'You lot and your mumbo jumbo, I tell you. No matter. You want three days, you'll have them. But, before I go, I'd like you to understand…'

He leans forward, grabbing her shoulder so powerfully she cries out. His face is inches from her own, so close she can feel his warm, moist breath when he speaks. His voice is a whisper, harsh and chilling, travelling right through her. 'When I come back three days from now, I expect to find Her Ladyship's doll. Do *not* disappoint me, old woman.'

He steps back, smiling. 'Three days,' he says again.

With that, he leaps back up into the saddle and rides away, leaving behind Apa and the two soldiers on the veranda.

Apa takes a deep breath, raises the bowl to her lips with shaking hands, and slurps up the thin, flavourless gruel. She's going to need all her strength for what is to come.

Needle, twine, knife and lime. One fold up, one stitch down. She'd forgotten how good it feels to weave, to just be holding the jute once more, an old, lost friend, now returned home.

'I missed you,' she whispers, head bent down. From sunrise to sunset she sits cross-legged on the veranda, working, only stopping for food and ablutions. When she needs a break, she looks at the banyan tree. With the fields all gone, she can see further from the veranda than ever before, all the way to the tree. It used to be the *sabha sthal*, where the villagers congregated for panchayat meetings under its broad, dangling roots. Now, it's something else entirely. Vultures peck at the swaying bodies hanging from its boughs, rats scurry around its base, gnawing at the bodies on the ground underneath it. It had started out as a place of punishment, where the British had hanged farmers who dared to hide rice from them. Then villagers took to hanging themselves there as well; the rope is more painless than the slow, pitiless grip of starvation. Parents hanged their children and then themselves; it was easier that way. That was when the British burnt the jute fields, to ensure no one could make any rope. Or maybe they just enjoyed watching their victims die slowly. So people took to cutting down the bodies and reusing the rope. There are now almost as many corpses on the tree as leaves below it.

Apa looks often at the tree these past few days. Only once does she feel herself waver. It happens in the middle of an afternoon, when the sun is at its fiercest. Like the intangible East India Company, the thought creeps into her mind and, having inveigled its way in, it refuses to leave. She glances at Willis, whose turn it is to watch her; he's over on the other side of the veranda, cleaning his rifle. Her eyes inch to the knife lying beside her. It would be so easy to end the misery now. One quick stroke across her throat and there will be no more pain, no more of that aching, hollow feeling where her heart had been, no more anything. Slowly, her hand closes around the hilt. And then she hears it again, that awful, mocking sound, Bolton laughing at her, at Nilesh, at Bengal and at India. And just like that, her jaw sets, her shoulders straighten, and the thought vanishes, banished away to a dark corner of her mind, wherefrom it won't find its way back again. No, she won't give them the satisfaction. Not while there is work to do. So work she does.

Needle and twine, knife and lime. Hands flashing, jute bending, straining, obeying her as it always had. Dawn to dusk she weaves, reaching within to put of herself into the jute, letting her feelings and memories flow. But all she can remember is the sound of that laughter, the peals of merriment that had convinced her not to succumb because that would be the worst way to die – to the sound of your murderer's laughter. And all she can find of herself is that ever-growing, cold, terrifying feeling that frightens her no longer, because it is not just inside her, now it *is* her. And all she feels, she puts into the doll.

When she pricks her finger, she no longer shakes the blood aside, but lets it drip slowly, deliberately, into the jute, till it is all soaked up.

And still she hears that laughter, reverberating between her ears, bouncing around the inside of her skull, a dirge that just won't stop. And neither will she, not until it is finished.

One stitch up, one fold down.

True to his word, Bolton returns on the morning of the fourth day, just as she has finished the last of her gruel.

'Is it done?' he calls out even before he makes it to the veranda where she sits.

'It is.'

'Show me.'

She holds it up by the hair, a slim European woman in a blue dress with golden jute-hair and indigo eyes, swaying gently in her grasp.

'It is the finest work I have ever done.'

'Good, good,' he replies, reaching out for it.

Apa ignores his outstretched hand. 'It's a *hashi'r putul*, you know.'

'A *what*?'

'A laughing doll.'

'It doesn't look like it's laughing.'

'That's not what it means. When you press it the right way, it will laugh.'

He frowns. 'You mean laugh out loud?'

'Exactly.'

'Show me.'

She shakes her head. 'That's not how it works. It will laugh, but only for the one it's meant for, and only if you know how to make it. And there is none but me who can handle it or teach anyone how to.'

'And you said you didn't do magic.'

'An artist never tells all her secrets.'

'And yet you told me this one. I'll take that doll now.'

'No, I want to give it to Lord Herbert myself.'

'Well, that's not going to happen, is it? The doll, please.'

'I just told you, only I can make it work.'

He narrows his eyes. 'The trouble with this whole thing, old woman, is that I don't believe you.'

'You don't believe I can make a laughing doll?' She sits up very straight, pulling the tatters of her sari tightly about herself. 'You have insulted my art, Captain.' Her free hand snakes down, over the hilt of the knife. 'Perhaps I should just destroy it.'

'Or perhaps I should just have my men run you through and take the doll from your corpse.'

'They cannot do so before I destroy the *putul*. You said so yourself – your master truly wants it for his wife. Will you go and tell him that he could have had it, but you were so intent on not letting a craftswoman exhibit her craft that all he shall get today is some jute scraps? So be it.'

There is a long, heavy silence. Sensing her moment, Apa presses on. 'On the other hand, if you take me with you I can teach others to make them as well. Think how pleased your governor will be. As many of my *putul* as he wants, for whoever he wants, whenever he wants.'

Another silence, during which Bolton frowns. Then he chuckles. 'Well played, old woman. Very well, you shall come back to Government House with us. Put her up on your horse behind you, Willis. Oh, and make sure you take away her knife first. Wouldn't want her to plant one between your ribs from behind now, would you?'

'Thank you, Captain,' says Apa, handing her knife over. 'Oh, one moment.'

She reaches down, quickly picking through the discarded scraps of jute, until she's found the two biggest. As she does, she remembers Nilesh, sitting on almost that very spot, handing her two scraps just like these, and a pang twists her innards. No, she cannot cry, not now. Not yet. She blinks, forcing back the tears, and lifts her head to look up at Captain Bolton.

'A keepsake. To remind me of the best work I ever did.'

He shrugs. 'Are you ready, Willis? Come along then, we must be off. It'll take us the better part of the day to get back to Calcutta.'

The road to Kolkata is long and dusty, and every step of it is steeped in a thousand terrors. Field after field lies black and arid, within them rows of immolated crops and ashen cadavers bearing witness to the charnel house that is now Bengal. Bodies lie piled twenty-high by the roadside, each gust of wind carrying with it the stench of rotting flesh and dead hope. As they ride past the banks of the Hooghly, the lifeline of Kolkata, Apa sees the sunbeams bearing down, setting off a shimmer on the sparse patches of water still visible between the bodies. There are a lot more corpses than water, at least on the surface. A carrion bird settles down unsteadily on the back of one, her talons sinking down into the flesh of the man's back, but not very far, for even the water-rot does only so much to soften rigor mortis. Apa turns her head aside and retches, and she isn't the only one doing so.

All the way, the soldiers talk, though never to her, but from what she hears, she gathers more than a bit. For instance, that the Denial of Rice policy has been declared a complete success, even though food supplies from various places she's never heard of have been turned away or redirected to British troops to ensure it stays that way. That there is also a Denial of Boat policy, also suggested by London, that has to do with far more than boats – almost all forms of transportation have been burnt or seized. That there are whispers among the men that the scale of the holocaust has moved some British hearts, but not the prime minister's – instead, that Dark Lord is mightily pleased.

Indeed, by the time they pull up at the gates of Government House on the banks of the Hooghly, Apa has seen and heard more horrors than she could tell of in yet another lifetime or recall any more of in this one. Until at long, merciful last, they stand within the high stone walls, where perfectly manicured lawns and picturesque blossoms neatly encircle engraved fountains, and the sweet smells of jasmine and rose fill the air. Rows of trees – neem, teak, peepal and sal – stand looking down on them, forming a green canopy over their heads as they make their way down the winding, cobbled path to the marble steps of the main building. From somewhere up in the leaves, a koel titters.

And then they are inside the building, where Apa stands between armed guards, clutching the doll tightly in one hand, while the captain announces their arrival to the butler, a plump, obviously Bengali man who looks Apa up and down condescendingly and then addresses himself to Bolton.

'His Lordship and Her Ladyship are entertaining guests for dinner tonight. But I shall convey news of your arrival.'

'Please do,' says Captain Bolton, stepping forward. 'And if you would, add this message.' He mutters something in the butler's ear and the man blinks, looks at Apa once again, and then nods and walks ponderously away.

It is a while before he returns. 'His Grace has given instructions for you to wait. When they have supped, you shall be summoned to the Reception Room. It appears His Grace's guests are curious to see this toy as well.'

Another interminable wait, and then a liveried footman appears, asking that they follow him. They do so, under dangling chandeliers and past the portraits and busts of governors gone by, and walls covered with thick, woven tapestries, tiger skins and mounted bison heads. One soldier marches behind her, the captain in front, as Apa scurries to keep up, reaching into the folds of her sari for the jute scraps she'd saved. They make their way up the broad, carpeted spiral marble staircase and into a large hall filled with shiny ornaments, more sculptures and several large stuffed tigers standing on wooden platforms. A massive chandelier dangles from the ceiling. There are about a dozen people in the room, men and women dressed in European finery, some holding wineglasses.

'Ah, Bolton,' says a tall, thin man with a receding hairline and a long, delicate nose.

'My Lord,' says Captain Bolton, snapping to attention with a salute.

'You have it?'

'Indeed, sir. Well, she does.' He gestures towards Apa.

'Ah, yes, of course. Nigel told me of your planned performance. We are all most eager to see it, are we not?'

'Indeed, we are,' says a woman, stately and fair-haired, coming to stand beside him. 'Where is it, John?'

'The woman has it, my dear. Well? Where is Her Ladyship's present?'

Apa feels Bolton nudge her and she steps forward, holding up the *putul*. A murmur runs through the gathering.

'Ah, excellent! Very satisfactory indeed!' exclaims the governor.

He turns to one of the others, a man with bushy side whiskers that Apa notices still have some breadcrumbs trapped in them. 'Here, take a gander at this, Hadley. I told you, these natives do some mighty fine work. Not a lot they're good at, but spices and trinkets, they jolly well know their way about those. And it laughs, you say, Bolton?'

'That's what she claimed, sir,' replies the captain.

'Capital, capital. You've done a commendable job, Bolton. Commendable, I say.'

'Thank you very much, sir.'

'I am anxious to see this,' says Lady Herbert. 'I have been quite charmed since you told me of it. A doll that laughs on its own. Imagine that! It sounds rather too good to be true!'

'Indeed,' says the governor. 'Well, what are we waiting for? Show us!'

Apa nods and holds up the *hashi'r putul* again, as they crowd around her. She runs her hands over her face, sliding past her cheeks and down her ears and the sides of her neck. Now she smiles and folds her hands together under her chin in a formal *nomoshkar*, making sure to meet each of their eyes in turn.

Then she takes a deep breath, filling her lungs, throws her head back and, as loudly as she can, she laughs. And as she does, a high, shrill cackle bursts forth from the *putul*.

'Well,' says Governor Herbert, looking startled. 'That's not very nice, is it? I'm rather disappointed. Stop it now, I'm really not happy with –'

He breaks off, snickers, and then does so again, until he is chuckling steadily. And now His Lordship is laughing, the sort of laughter that comes straight from the gut, strong and insistent, louder and louder until he's doubled up, roaring in full-throated merriment. Beside Apa, Captain Bolton is leaning against a chair, tears streaming down his cheeks as he laughs. Around him, the others are laughing too, different tenors and pitches, but all laughing as loudly as they can, breaking off only to cough or splutter before they go back to shrieking in mirth. They're on the ground now, all of them, still laughing, spittle flying everywhere. Neck muscles knot, veins bulge, first in foreheads, and then everywhere else across their pale, sallow skin. Some are trying to shield their ears, but to no avail, the laughter keeps spilling out of them, bursting forth, as juice from an overripe mango fallen from the tree. And loudest of all, rising above the cacophony of their cumulative cachinnations, is the cackling tone of the *putul*, as it forces them, one by one, to match its tempo, faster and faster.

'I hope you are all enjoying yourselves,' Apa says in Bangla.

They don't understand her, and yet they do; she can see the terror in their eyes now, faces contorting in horror as they realize what is happening and how utterly powerless they are to do anything about it. Anything but look at her with supplication in those very eyes as she smiles back at each of them in turn. As Apa watches, a crimson stain slowly spreads out across the carpet; one of them has hit his or her head. Another has stopped laughing, Hadley, his eyes now staring sightlessly up at the chandelier. One down. Everyone else to go.

Apa takes a step back, then another, as the governor hauls himself to his knees, hands clasping at his chest, still laughing, gasping, straining to speak, so Apa has to read his lips.

'Make… stop!' he says, choking between roars of mirth. 'Please!'

Apa shakes her head and turns away, walking towards the door, stepping over the convulsing figure of the butler on the ground.

'Help me, sister!' he mouths in Bangla.

She steps over him. Traitor. He deserves to die with the rest of them.

At the door, she turns back, looking at Bolton, who has both hands to his throat, trying to choke back the peals. A steady stream of blood trickles out of his nostrils; more of it is welling up in his eyes, those eyes that are looking straight at Apa. She looks right back into them, and still holding his gaze, she nods. He raises a shaking, accusing finger at her, and then falls back on the ground, racked with laughter, blood now pouring out of his mouth as well.

She walks out into the hallway, making her way back towards the staircase. She reaches into her ears, making sure the jute plugs are still firmly in place. Then she turns around to look down the hallway, just in time to see a host of armed soldiers rush into the room she's exited. She waits, a minute, five, ten. None of them come out. She walks into the room again and peers in; there are now about 20 of them on the floor, although only the new soldiers are moving, laughing. There's a lot more blood in the room than there had been a while ago.

Slowly, Apa makes her way down the staircase and out through the front door. Here she sits down on the large marble steps, leaning back against them, drawing in another deep breath, filling her lungs with the sweet, heady scent of jasmine and rose. This is as good a place as any. Carefully, deliberately, she pulls the earplugs out, tossing them down.

'Thank you, old friend,' she says, watching the jute leave as it flaps away on the breeze. Her partner that has just completed its final task – of protecting her from her greatest creation.

Her *hatya'r putul* has done its work well. She turns her head, glancing back up at the building. Somewhere up there it will continue to work, cackling ever louder and faster, until there will be nothing left in that room but flesh waiting to rot.

Sooner or later, one of the British will realize this and not venture into the room. Then they'll come looking for her. And she is ready, she's been ready ever since Nilesh left, taken from her by a man in London none of them will ever meet.

'I'll see you again soon,' she whispers into the wind.

And she begins to laugh.

JUPITER, DARK SISTER

MEDHA SINGH

I dream of falling through Jupiter
(One can't land on her. She's all gas.)
It's better than falling through passing clouds,
tasteless mass. A red storm has raged for centuries in her eye –
the sheer echo of my spirit's cry, when I'd
learnt one can't pass for a cosmonaut
even if one had the suit. I could not pass a math exam
to save my life, took the boot. Go on. Plunge
deep (or not) into her. Singe her soul,
hit deranged reflections (metallic hydrogen cosseting
primordial light, her ovum)
you see how many of you can be there, quantum selves charred
to the bone, heady heat melting into dermis
and tungsten alike. In the grasp of gravity's dance alone
at Jupiter's core, she grants suspension, one dervish
in opposite directions, pulls your innards whole – I was told
she leaves you hung (amid other dark sisters of the sun) –
like a pig.
On a pike.

THE TRAVELLER

TASHAN MEHTA

The Traveller

I wash onto a beach, the splinters of my boat around me, salt water burning my lungs as I spit it out. They find me like this and take me in. They are women with oil-black hair and pupils that mirror the candlelight, their fingers long and bony as they serve me fish charred on an open flame. They go through the contents of my bag as I eat, laughing at my animal-skin notebook and pens.

'Where are you from?' they ask me and so I tell them, describing a land with sea creatures undulating in the night sky, crustaceans and coral cracking beneath our feet. They ask questions when I first begin and then grow silent as I continue. At first, I think they are in awe of a land so strange, but they are fisherwomen and a land that is like the sea does not astonish them; they've spent their childhoods diving beneath the waves and have seen phenomena more spectacular than I can describe. And still the children clutch their mothers' arms tighter and tighter, and the old women stare solemnly at the ground until I stop speaking.

'But that land is far from here,' a woman says softly.

'It is,' I agree. I cannot count the years I've travelled since I left my homeland.

A child touches my cheek in wonder. 'Aren't you afraid you'll disappear?'

It begins with a map.

On each new island, I draw a map. It comforts me – the ink, the lines, the slow joining of boundaries. I draw from what I see and hear, asking locals for the lay of the land and consulting their records. And so, the next day, when

I have slept and regained my strength, I clean what pens have survived the shipwreck and begin to draw.

At first I sketch what I can see – plants, a purple lizard, bright red birds with black wings. In time, I ask the women for any drawings they may have of the island's topography. They laugh at this; there are no drawings here, only stories. I am undeterred. 'Tell me stories then,' I say, and they push a girl towards me. 'Alka will tell you.'

Alka is tall and thin, and disarms me instantly with her charisma, winking once the women are gone, and grinning. It is infectious, that smile. Consuming.

After that, Alka lies to me.

'At the highest point to the north,' she tells me, 'there is a necklace of giant sleeping whales. So large are they that their humps push into the clouds to gather snow. Every once in a while, a whale breaks off and swims away to become a tiny island, but I've not heard of this happening in my lifetime.'

I sketch a chain of whale mountains and she smiles. 'To the east,' she continues, 'our land is covered with a pit of double-headed snakes, one mouth drinking in the sky and the other gulping the sea. Down south, it is sparser and drier – flat earth that tapers like an arrowhead, nothing but clear sky and giant hands erupting from the ground, their 11 fingers curling downward into fronds.'

'Eleven fingers?' I ask, sketching.

Alka nods. 'Some say,' she whispers as she leans closer, 'that they descend on nights of the blood moon and pluck away little children.'

I squint at her and she laughs, delighted. I will learn this about Alka: there is nothing that doesn't give her delight.

'To the west,' she says, as I resume drawing, 'the land is a big butterfly ray, so chapped its skin flakes to become the sand of the red desert. And here on the coastal plains – here, the sea melts its foam into sand. And our trees…' Her voice grows soft and tender. 'Our trees grow in each other's embrace so they may never know loneliness.'

She is done. I hold up the map her stories have created, a strange amalgamation of different animals and gaps in boundaries. You can vaguely discern a melting diamond-shaped mass, but only if you squint. 'Well,' I say, smiling, 'it's not like any land I know.'

Alka looks at me swiftly. I sense a question on her lips, a thirst, but she quells it. Instead, she says, 'No stranger than any dream.'

This is how I learn that Alka's map is no match for the most fantastical thing the women have to tell me. Here, they say, the land dreams its people.

Alka

When I hear a traveller has washed up on the shore, I cannot contain my excitement. A traveller, in my lifetime! I grab Pulma's and Kulra's hands and drag them with me; they run, but not fast enough; they are not as eager. When I see the traveller, I am disappointed. Her clothes are strange, but she looks like anyone else – if not for the salt crystallized in her hair and the half-starved look on her face, she could be one of us.

But there *are* differences and they emerge slowly, over the course of that night. The more I stare at her, the more I can see it. The traveller moves little. She eats in large and ravenous bites, her gaze never wavering from her leaf. I think this is because she is hungry, but I soon realize that it's an intensity she brings to everything. She looks at all people with the same steadiness, her breath shallow. She does not stare the way we do here – frankly and easily, as if people are part of the complex and interwoven tapestry of a landscape, to be stared at as you would the sea or a beautiful shell. Instead, she hunts for your eyes, seeking what lies beneath them. Stillness radiates from her in ripples. I can feel Pulma fidget beside me. She is unnerved.

When the traveller talks, I drink up her words. They carve a space I did not know could exist, a space of questions and promise and openness. I feel my skin tighten.

When she looks at me, a shiver runs down my spine. *You could be me*, I think. *You could be me.*

The Traveller

In the days that follow, weeks, months – how do I measure time here? – Alka explains this to me. 'We are dreamed,' she says. 'Made by the land's desires, changed by its whims. If we leave this land, we disappear.'

The women believe it.

At first, I think I have misheard. Their language is fluid and dreamlike: subjects and objects change, tenses mix, meanings detach from one word and attach to another. It takes listening to understand what is being said. What could they mean, they are dreamed?

But it connects to an incident on my second night, a strange and clammy memory that I shrink from recalling now. We are sitting on the beach, warmed by a bonfire. A woman with gnarled hands leans over my half-eaten fish to ask a question. But the babble is too loud, and I mishear her.

I think she is asking, 'What are your dreams?'

No one has asked me that question in years – maybe in a decade. I am overwhelmed. I talk. At first, the words come slowly, splutters and gurgles from a pump unused to receiving water. But then they flow. I talk of the urge to keep moving, to see lands so plentiful they cannot fit into the mind. To feel the limits of myself so I may understand my smallness. I talk – or perhaps I do not – of loneliness and wonder. I speak to convince, as I did to my mother all those years ago.

The gathering grows quiet. The women look as they did when I first described my home; they are restrained and amused. Only one woman listens intently. I find myself speaking to her, urgent and desperate, to the quickness in her eyes and the light jumping on her cheeks. As I look at the memory, I realize this is Alka.

Finally, the woman with gnarled hands interrupts me. 'Yes,' she asks, 'but who dreamed *you*?'

The memory ends there.

In time, the women grow used to my confusion. The children, who assume I am dumb, act out dreams for me. One child pretends to wiggle out of the head of another and pause in silly shapes. I laugh. I clap. I try and understand where this myth comes from.

'How do you know you are dreamed?' I press Alka.

'You know,' she says. She touches her chest, her stomach, the soles of her feet, as if knowledge lives in many places and not all of them can be described.

I hold out my palm. She is confused, so I take her wrist and press her palm to mine. She is embarrassed and delighted. In truth, there is an intimacy to the gesture I hadn't realized when I offered it. Still, it proves my point.

'Can you feel that?' I ask.

She nods.

'I am like you,' I say. 'But I am not a dream.'

She is fascinated. 'How do you know?'

I don't know how long I've spent here – longer than I've stayed in other places, I'm sure. Yet I find it difficult to leave. This land is beguiling. Everything is fluid, defined only by a minute web of relations that gives shape to the thing itself. In my first few days, I look for the settlement's routine and find none. Instead, fish simply appear; fires are lit; those who want to cook wander in and begin. Now, I find everything exists in a state of delicate chaos that is, in fact, order. People follow their instincts. They allow themselves to be derailed by a mischievous bird or a surprising flower. They act carelessly, with no thought to a larger plan or an overall system, and yet a thin structure emerges between them.

Alka becomes my friend. She helps me settle into the cave where I am staying, teaches me – with much giggling – how to wear the cloth I've been given. We go exploring, climbing trees that seem to bend for us, jumping on rocks and floating in gentle pools. When the sea is quiet and friendly, we go out to the flat black rocks and I read to her from my diaries.

These moments are magic. As I speak, my travels come alive. I've been alone for so long, I'd forgotten that wonder shared is wonder multiplied. Alka drinks in my tales with a thirst, asking for stories not on the page. She is a born traveller, but I don't tell her this. Instead, I tell her of the funny stories or the moments of strangeness – I know she will like these best.

'You've seen so much,' she whispers. 'You know so much.'

Do you know, I want to tell her, *that you're my first friend in a long time*?

But I don't.

Alka tries to swap wonder for wonder; she takes me to places that she finds surprising. A lake that's grown its own spongy land. A bird with rainbow wings as large as my arm. 'Look!' she says as a creature wrestles another to the ground.

But what she finds incredible is not as astonishing as what escapes her. The sun and the moon, for example, are fighting. I see them meet in the sky, the sun bubbling in rage as the moon turns to stone, bathing everything in a hard and silvery light. They don't follow day and night here; they simply hang together in the zenith of the sky and squabble.

Alka does not find this unusual. When the sun bubbles too hot, she pulls me into the leaves. When the moon turns to ice, we dive beneath the waves, where the water generates its own warmth.

'Do they always do that?' I ask her.

'They are family,' Alka says. 'Families fight. The moon was once a sun, and she will be a sun again when she grows warm enough. But the sun – oh, the sun doesn't want to cool into a moon. And so they fight. This has always happened. Once, there were two suns in the sky and neither wanted to become a moon. It was so hot that the beach turned into a desert, and the sea rose up and swallowed them both. And then all we had for some time was the light of the stars and their reflections in the water.'

I see an opportunity to tease Alka, the same way she teases me. 'If the sun and the moon are a dream,' I say, 'why do they fight?'

Alka laughs. 'Why do I fight with Pulma or myself?' she says. 'Why do I sit here explaining things to you that you should already know? Sometimes fighting is good. Sometimes fighting helps us know ourselves better.'

'Alka,' I say, 'you are my reflection. Whenever I turn, you are there, bright and surprising.'

I am only half-teasing. We are lying on the black rocks, waves crashing at our feet. I turn in time to catch her expression – Alka is making a face. I laugh.

'I am a lake,' Alka says, pinching me. 'You think I show you only your face but fall in and I'll show you another world.'

Alka

Everyone leaves the traveller alone. Pulma stares at her sometimes but won't meet her eyes. Kulra avoids her. Even Oltrum – the oldest and wisest of us – views her with distant understanding. My traveller notices but doesn't complain. She lets the children climb up her shins and pull her hair.

'Sister,' they say to me, 'when she travels, why doesn't she disappear?'

I want to tell my traveller: *Don't be sad. They are only scared of you.*

I want to tell my sisters: *Can't you see what she is offering?*

When my traveller is asleep, I climb to the highest branches of a jackfruit tree and whistle. Faces break out of the leaves and my friends pull themselves up to sit near me.

'She says the sun and the moon share the sky on her island,' I whisper. 'If one is in the sky, the other is hiding.'

'Separated?' Pulma whispers.

I nod.

There is an intake of breath, some murmuring.

'But they meet sometimes?' Kulra asks.

'Never. At a magic time called dusk – then they are in the sky at the same time, but they never meet.'

The girls take this in. You can taste the wonder: a sun and moon that don't speak to each other, alternating darkness and light. I enjoy plucking words from my traveller's mouth and offering them to my friends. Watching Pulma's eyes grow wider and wider. *Isn't it magic*? I want to ask. *Don't you long to travel and see*?

Today, Pulma is distracted. She has the look she gets when she is thinking very hard. It's jealousy. The traveller spends most of her time with me; even Oltrum says the traveller must see a kindred spirit in me. I am delighted. *We are like the sun and the moon*, I think suddenly, *each waiting to burst into the other.*

The thought frightens and excites me.

'I think she's making it up,' Pulma says suddenly. 'She must have Dream Changed or come from the desert where they need imagination to make things out of sand.'

Dream Changing is a common way of life here; at some point in all creatures' lives, the island calls to them to become something else. The creatures shift shape; their dream changes. To accuse my traveller of being merely a result of Dream Changing, to say her stories are hallucinations created by shifting into *this* shape –

'She has not,' I hiss. 'How do you explain the notebooks then? The lands she's seen?'

Pulma gives me an infuriating look of superiority and taps her head. She says, 'There are many ways to travel.'

ൈ

Pulma's words sit in me; they fester. Sometimes, I want to interrupt my traveller and say: *Pulma is calling you a liar*. She will be upset, I imagine; she will march up to Pulma and put her in her place. And I will feel better.

I want to go to Oltrum. I want to tell her what Pulma has said, have her be chastised for being rude to a guest. But I do not. Oltrum has the eyes of an eagle. In the sea of consciousness that we share, she is the sharpest point; she looks at your heart as if you carry it in your hands. If I go to her, she will see what I have nurtured for my living life. She will know.

But when I am alone, I pull out my secret. I give it space and air. I imagine the traveller's stories and I let my want grow larger.

In the jungle of the two-headed river snakes, there is a story. It is about a tree and a forest. A little tree is born in the soil and grows to become a big tree. It likes its branches and leaves; it loves the ants that play on it and the birds that nest. For a long time, it thinks only of itself and the joy of growing. But then the tips of its branches touch those of another tree, and its roots clasp hands in a web. This is the day the tree learns it is both a tree and forest, singular and plural.

So many girls love that story. We heard it when we were very young from a man who came from the river snake jungle. We have a similar story on the coast, about a cupful of water joining a sea, but we liked this one better. We played a game where one of us would be a tree and the others a forest, but of course both are the same, and so we would move in silly dance formations, get into fights, giggle, throw mud. I played too.

But at night, I would dream I was a tree. I would imagine stretching my arms up higher, higher, higher, until my body elongated and my roots pulled – *plop* – out of the soil. And then I walked, stilt-like, leaving the forest behind.

Each time the traveller describes an island, I fall into her words. My skin tightens and my chest expands; I am full and defined. And a hope grows in me, slow and insidious. What if we are not dreams?

The Traveller

I look at the map I have drawn of Alka's stories and find that it has changed. One of the whales has dislodged itself from the chain of mountains and is now floating in the white space. From this vantage point, it looks like an island.

This is obviously not the map I drew when Alka described the land to me. It's similar but I remember keeping the whales together to create a vague boundary. Alka has swapped the drawing with another as a joke. I think of asking for the original back, but then I consider why she would make the change. What is she trying to tell me? I stare at the little whale, a lone, misshapen circle in a sea of white.

I've known for some time that Alka wants to travel with me. She hasn't said it aloud – perhaps she hasn't said it to herself yet. But I can sense it. I sit down with the map in my hand and think.

I should have left by now. Islands get under your skin – already the sun and moon don't bother me, and the language has become clearer. And yet I don't leave. I don't travel inland to find new settlements. I don't ask for a boat. If I do, I will be without Alka.

I put my head between my knees. Travellers don't stay and I can't stay either. At some point, I will leave. Will she come with me? The first step is always the hardest. That fear – I can still recall it. When I stood on the shores of my island decades ago, I was petrified. My mother cried and begged me not to be reckless. But I left in a boat no one believed could float.

Alka may not take the same step. She's held hostage by a superstition, a fear so deep-rooted it holds her in place. Who am I to ask that she leaps?

Alka and I are floating in a rock pool. Her hair fans out in tendrils; her eyes are closed.

'Sister,' I say. 'Have you ever wanted to travel?'

Alka doesn't answer. She curls into a ball and submerges herself, her hair disappearing into blue. But it is answer enough.

After that, I work gently to unpick her superstitions. My questions are kind but pointed, my words straightforward. *Leap*, I will her. *All you need is the first step.*

'Alka, why do you think the land dreams you?'

There is hesitation on her face. She says, 'It dreams us as its desires. We are its legs, arms, its heart.'

'But the land has not told you this,' I say. 'You simply believe it?'

Her hesitation grows. 'I know it,' she says. 'We all know.'

'On my island,' I say, 'nothing is ever known unless you can prove it. It keeps us safe from illusions.'

This is a lie; my island had several illusions, mainly about boats and floating objects. But there's no need to tell Alka that. In fact, I have learnt the method of proof and evidence from another island I visited, and I find it has held me in good stead.

Alka has turned her face away. 'I've seen people disappear when they leave the island,' she whispers.

I touch her shoulder. 'Tricks of the light,' I tell her. 'Illusions of the mind. You must question, Alka. If people are the dreams of the land, how can I be here?'

She turns to me then and she is anguished. A thought passes across her face, dark and full. But when she speaks, she only says, 'I don't know.'

Alka

There are many ways to travel.

Several times, I am about to say this to the traveller. It is on the tip of my tongue, spilt onto my lips. *Pulma says you are making it up*, I will say. *Pulma says it's a trick of your mind.*

But each time I am about to say it, I don't. How can she make up whole diaries? Maps? Stories so detailed they could only be lived?

My traveller wouldn't lie.

'Tell me about the most marvellous place you've visited,' I ask her.

The traveller thinks. We are lying on the flat black rocks, our favourite place, our fingers lightly entwined.

'The sky people,' she says. 'My boat once passed through a mountain that was hollow on the inside; the rock had been carved into a filigree system of caves. I don't know how it happened – maybe it was done by the water or perhaps some other means – but it was like looking up into a jewelled paradise. The people there had never left the mountain. They lived upside down, their toes growing curved to grip the rock. They thought the sea was the sky. They ate by climbing to the tip of their world and plunging their hands into the sky; they would pull out great purple and pink fish with sweet flesh. When they found me, they couldn't believe it – I had descended from the heavens.'

'Was the mountain as beautiful from the inside?' I ask.

She nods.

'What happened?'

'I stayed with them a while, then left. I couldn't stay upside down like them.'

I try to imagine it. A land like a curved bowl, opening to a great and susurrating sky, creatures moving in its limitless heights, constantly calling out to you. Finding a person hanging from this sky, confused about how to put feet to ground, vomiting and cranky because she was removed from where she belonged. Giving this woman back up to the sky.

'Perhaps to them,' I whisper, 'you were the one upside down.'

My traveller says nothing. She is lost in thought, eyes staring at the moon and sun in our sky.

'If you've been to all these strange lands,' I ask, 'why can't you believe we are dreamed?'

She holds up her palm and I join mine to it.

'Because you are like me,' she says softly. 'No long toes or bigger head. You cannot be a dream because I am not.'

'You are not listening,' I say, upset.

My traveller removes her hand abruptly. When she looks at me, it is with accusation. 'You think I'm lying.'

The Traveller

I tell Oltrum I must leave. Her face is small and puffy, eaten by a mass of wrinkles. She stares at me as if I wear no clothes, no skin, nothing to cover my deepest thoughts or desires. I don't flinch.

'Where will you go?' she asks.

'Anywhere,' I say. 'To the jungles with river snakes, to verify my map.'

She does not argue. 'You must go,' she agrees. 'These places may not be there when you arrive, but you can try to find them.' She smiles at my surprise. 'Dreams change,' she tells me. 'When they do, stories do too.'

I have never been seasick. Now I find myself rolling on this landscape with nothing firm to cling to. Alka's touch steadied me – her palm against mine, our shoulders pressed together. It held the effects of the land at bay. But we haven't spoken since our last conversation and now –

I have stayed too long.

'Give me a boat,' I say. 'Give me a boat and I'll leave.'

Oltrum is baffled. 'We don't have one.'

'Supplies then,' I say. 'Dry food, water, medicines. An accurate map.'

Oltrum shakes her head. 'When we want to travel, we simply close our eyes and go.'

'This is the logic of dreams,' I say, agitated. 'I am not one of you! *Help* me, Oltrum.'

But the old woman only takes my hands. She says, 'Have you told Alka?'

Alka

I hear from Pulma that the traveller is leaving. Pulma tells me the news with glee, but I don't shout at her. Instead, I go into the sea and submerge my head underneath the waves. I open my eyes. I can see nothing, only murky blue and particles moving.

A boy went out to sea once. We told him not to go too far, to keep his feet on the land so that he stayed safe, but he was only a boy. He went swimming and splashing and laughing, further and further until he turned – in one fluid movement – and waved at me. I'll always remember that. That wave, that smile. His slow disappearance, like he was being eaten by fog.

Tricks of the mind.

I stay there until I run out of air and then I break to the surface.

That night, I don't sleep. I feel split in two, a fruit hacked to expose a seed. Two worlds have opened up to me, but they are not as complementary as 'tree' and 'forest'. These worlds have a chasm between them; to cross from one to the other is impossible, all the bridges burnt. *You are like me,* the traveller had said, pressing her palm to mine. I am. I can feel it.

Quietly, I slip out and walk to the sea. Both the sun and moon have left the sky. The light is thin and settles as delicate silver on the crests of the waves. If the land dreams, then so must the sea. Then perhaps the traveller makes sense. She is not the dream of rock and soil but a water wish, born so that the sea might know the islands that grow in it. She is made to never stay still.

Kulra once described a woman's Dream Changing. She said the woman walked out into the jungle one day, raised her hands to the sky and the earth took her. Her arms became branches, her fingers leaves, and her legs plunged into the earth as her face petrified. Kulra can trace the shape of her eyes in a knot in the tree's bark. She said the woman had known for ages that it was coming. She felt its pull, longed for it.

I have never wanted to Dream Change. I dread the thought of waking up to find myself in another shape. I know this makes me strange, that I am fighting a way of life. Kulra once said that I wanted to hold on to things that couldn't be held. She looked so solemn when she said it, like she would rather not have known that about me.

But now I want the sea to call to me. I want to be welcomed into its embrace, become its dream. 'Take me,' I whisper. I step towards the waves.

The Traveller

I go back to the cave and press my forehead against the rock. *Think*, I tell myself. I can go on my own, simply tell Alka and then leave. Forage for food on the way, draw a map as I go.

But I am scared. I see it now, clearer than when I arrived: these women have a unique relationship with the land. Alka once asked for a night fruit with dark pink flesh, and I saw her eating it from a tree I could swear hadn't been there two days before. I saw a fisherwoman wade into the shallows and whistle slowly until a silver fish swam into her arms and she could drag it ashore. I watched a child reach for a tree and a branch reach back, and both turned in surprise when they heard me.

I open a notebook to pull out the map. The butterfly ray has changed position, its nose now pointing to the sea. The island-whale has swum lower, towards the coast.

Tricks of the mind, I tell myself. Islands get under your skin.

Alka

I sit at the edge of the waves, water sloshing over my toes. Neither the sun nor the moon has returned. I stare and stare into the darkness, feeling my desire breathe.

You are like me.

'Alka?'

I turn. The traveller is behind me; she has been running. Even like this, frazzled and out of breath, her body twitchy, she radiates an otherworldly stillness. I walk towards her. I think she will run but of course she doesn't – she is my friend, my companion, my accidental sister. I hold out my palm and feel a rush of gratefulness when she presses hers to it. Sun and moon.

We sit together for a long time. I can say, *You were going to leave*, and she will reply, *I would have said goodbye*. She will be lying but I can give her the lie, because that's what you do for friends. You pretend sometimes. She will say, *I will miss you* and I don't want to hear that because it will hurt. So we don't speak. Sitting is enough.

'Where will you go?' I ask finally.

'I don't know.'

'What will you do?'

'What I always do,' she says. 'Discover.'

But she doesn't just discover. She collects. Writes. Records. And then leaves again. But I don't say it. Instead, I take her hand and whisper in a quiet rush, 'I had a dream.'

'Do dreams dream?'

'All the time. I dreamed that you were a dream of the sea.'

She is quiet. She grips my hand tighter but that is all. She keeps staring at the sea. In this light, I cannot see her expression.

'Do you think you could be?' I ask tentatively. 'A dream of the sea?'

'No,' she says. 'I am only myself.'

Blunt and sharp, as my traveller always is. She cannot become water; she cannot slip through any crack required of her, mould herself to situations. For that I love her.

'Tell me again,' I say. 'How we are not dreams.'

At the 'we', she looks at me. 'All of the world,' she says slowly, 'is made of the same materials. Tiny particles that come together in different combinations to make many things. You are made of the same particles as that bird, as this water, as the land you love so much. But you are different. These particles that have made you will not change, not until you die. You are fixed. Separate. Real.'

Oh, how she believes it. My traveller will not lie.

I stand, pulling her to her feet. 'What is the hardest part of leaving?' I ask.

She glances once at the sea, quickly, and then back at me. 'The first step,' she says.

I reach for her other hand. 'Take it with me?'

•

•

•

The Traveller

Alka and I wade into the waves. It's colder than I remember. In the darkness, with only the stars to guide us, the sea seems a void. I am shivering, though not just from the water.

Faintly, in the distance, there is a mass. I cannot be sure because of the light.

'Where is the moon?' I ask Alka.

'I don't know,' she says. 'Perhaps it's gone off to become a sun.'

She is shivering too; she clasps my hand tighter. The waves are climbing up, up our calves.

I try to imagine it: a moon growing so bright it bursts into a sun. But thoughts of changing make me nauseous and I stop. I think of my mother instead. Of her holding my head. Of the feel of wet sea rope in my hand as I pull the sail against the wind, laughing and screaming. I focus on the water on my skin.

The mass is humped and irregular, like an island. When Alka and I were on the beach, I thought I saw it to my far left. Now it's moved along the horizon, into my field of vision. I try and recall what the sea looked like when I first arrived. Whether this mass was there.

The water is now at our waist and climbing. Alka's breath becomes ragged; she clutches my hand until I can feel our bones being pushed together.

I squint, but I can't see in this light. My heart is hammering. Maybe it isn't an island. Maybe it was always there, maybe it isn't moving.

The water is up to our necks. We are on our tiptoes, the sand slippery beneath. Alka is blinking rapidly. She is brave and determined. Alka, my quicksilver friend, always so sure of herself, the lake in which I could drown. Alka, who wants to see the world.

'The first step is the hardest,' she whispers.

Do all islands look like whales?

'Alka, wait –'

THE ZOO

MUHAMMED ZAFAR IQBAL
Translated by Arunava Sinha

'I was curious to see you,' said Hajib Kuntera, smiling faintly at Rahan Jabil. He had a strangely cruel appearance, and for some reason his smile emphasized this quality.

Rahan felt a sudden rush of terror seize him. Perhaps it hadn't been very wise to accept this man's invitation to visit him here. With great effort he plastered a defiant but calm expression on his face and asked, 'And why this curiosity?'

'I am the most powerful person on the planet. I can change the President of a medium-sized country if I wish to. I wanted to know what the man who wrote a report about me in his newspaper is like.'

'I'm a journalist, exposing the truth…'

'Spare me.' Hajib cut off the imminent lecture.

Rahan felt a bit humiliated but found he had lost all interest in delivering a speech on the sacred duty of journalists to reveal the truth at any cost.

Drumming his fingers on his desk, Hajib said, 'You're exactly what I expected you to be.'

'And what is that?' Rahan asked, frowning.

'Young, immature, silly and an imbecile.'

Rahan stared at the man in astonishment. No matter how rich or powerful a person might be, could they really be allowed to talk this way?

He was about to say something when Hajib raised his hand again to interrupt. 'Don't be angry,' he said. 'I was also silly and an imbecile at your age.'

'I'm neither silly nor an imbecile,' Rahan said, furious.

Instead of responding, Hajib smiled enigmatically, and it dawned on Rahan that he was indeed being silly and an imbecile. He glared at Hajib's green eyes in impotent rage and exhaled. 'Why did you ask me here?'

'To talk to you. Actually, I have no one to talk to.'

'No one?'

'No one. My employees don't dare look me in the eye when they speak to me. Those whom I know only try to flatter me.'

'What about your loved ones?'

'I have no loved ones.'

Rahan frowned again. 'I've researched you... I know you have two wives and three children.'

Hajib laughed out loud, a sarcastic laugh that made him look hideous. Rahan felt an uncontrollable loathing for Hajib. When he had stopped laughing, Hajib said, 'My wives and children constantly pray for my death.'

'Why?'

'You're a journalist. You should know why.'

Rahan didn't respond, though he did know why. Modest fortunes can bring happiness, but that isn't true of obscene wealth, which transforms family life into an ugly conspiracy.

'I have no desire to talk to you about my wives and children,' said Hajib.

'What do you want to talk about then?'

'About you.'

'What about me?'

Taking a newspaper out of a drawer, Hajib laid it out on his desk. 'You've spun an enormous story around me here.'

Rahan didn't need to look at the newspaper to know which article Hajib was referring to. He had left out nothing – the source of Hajib's riches, the crimes he had committed, his inhuman cruelty. Nothing.

Summoning a smile to his face with some effort, Hajib said, 'You've even tried to analyse my character here.'

Rahan nodded.

'How much do you really know about me?' asked Hajib.

'I have gathered all the information about you that's available in the world and analysed it.'

'What kind of a person do you think I am?'

Rahan hesitated before answering, 'A bad person.'

'How bad?'

'Pretty bad.'

'Do you have any idea just how bad that might be?' Rahan stared at Hajib without answering. Sighing, Hajib said, 'I have a feeling you have absolutely no idea.'

Rahan tried in vain to understand what Hajib was suggesting. He was about to speak, when Hajib rose to his feet. 'Let's go.'

'Where?'

'I have a zoo here. I want to show it to you.'

'You have a personal zoo?'

'Oh, yes. Rich people have strange whims. Some collect valuable gems, some collect rare art. Me, I collect rare animals.'

'What kind of rare animals?'

'Let's say no one else in the world has what I have.'

Rahan couldn't understand how this could be possible. Had Hajib used genetic engineering to create a new creature? He refrained from asking any questions – perhaps he would be able to see for himself very soon.

He followed Hajib out of the office, assuming that a phalanx of bodyguards would be trailing behind. But nothing like that happened. Hajib clearly didn't bother very much with personal security. Anyway, they were probably being tracked by a series of hidden cameras.

They went down the marble staircase of Hajib's palatial residence. A small car stood where the stairs ended, with room enough for two. Gesturing to Rahan, Hajib took the seat next to him and pressed a switch, whereupon the car started rolling forward in absolute silence. Rahan strained to hear an engine or a motor but he couldn't. The car moved ahead very slowly, its destination probably programmed in already. Since it was a convertible, its occupants had a view of the surroundings. Leaning back in his seat, Hajib said, 'I own 41 islands around the world, but this one is my favourite.'

'How large is it?'

'Not particularly large. A little under 100 square kilometers.'

'You have your own airstrip here?'

'Yes, but that's not why it's my favourite. I love it because it's actually a dormant volcano.' Pointing into the distance, he said, 'You can see granite hills there. Quite magnificent.'

Rahan could not understand how granite hills, bare of any foliage, could be magnificent, but he asked no questions. The place was oddly deserted. There were no humans anywhere. Who knew where the zoo was... Rahan waited patiently, a disconcerting curiosity churning within him.

When they were quite close to the granite hills, a tunnel came into view. The car entered it and arrived at a clearing. Pressing the switch to stop the car, Hajib said, 'This is my zoo.'

Looking around, Rahan saw no sign of a zoo anywhere. He looked questioningly at Hajib, who said, 'Come this way.'

Rahan followed Hajib to a spot where the hillside had risen steeply. Moving a rock aside, Hajib revealed an opening they could peep through. After taking a quick look, he stepped away and said, 'See for yourself.'

Rahan was startled at what he saw. On a stretch of level ground some distance away, a few strange creatures were fighting each other over a dead goat. As they bit and gnawed at the animal's flesh, one of them leapt at another, who, evidently the weaker one, ran away on its four legs and roared in futile anger from a distance. The creature had a long mane like a lion's, and its hind legs were longer than its forelegs. It looked as though its fur had fallen off, perhaps from malnutrition. Rahan glanced at Hajib in surprise and said, 'What animal is that?'

A smile appeared on Hajib's face. 'A human.'

Rahan jumped as though struck by lightning. Swivelling around, he peeped through the opening again and gasped in alarm on realizing that these creatures were indeed humans. Blanching, he asked Hajib, 'Why are they like that?'

'I was inspired by a particular incident. In ancient India a pair of girls was discovered in a wolf's lair, one of them seven or eight years old, the other a little older, twelve or thirteen. The wolf had taken them away from a nearby village and brought them up. The villagers had tried in vain to rescue them from their animal-like existence. Having spent their infancy in the company of wolves, they remained feral creatures, with no human characteristics. They loped at great speed on all fours, ate raw meat, refused to wear clothes, had a powerful sense of smell – they were wild beasts, to put it simply.' Sighing, Hajib continued, 'They were named Amala and Kamala after being rescued, but that was the only thing that was human about them.'

Rahan stared at Hajib in sheer horror. Summoning his trademark grotesque smile to his face, Hajib said, 'When I heard about this it occurred to me… If it could happen once, couldn't we make it happen again?'

Stunned, Rahan asked Hajib, 'Did you… Did you create them?'

'Yes,' Hajib nodded. 'It wasn't easy. A number of babies were wasted. It isn't true that all mother wolves want to bring up human babies as their own. But eventually we succeeded – there are five wolf-humans here, two men and three women. I'm dying to find out what their offspring will be like.'

Was this man a human being or a demon, wondered Rahan.

Moving away a couple of steps, Hajib continued, 'Then it struck me. If wolves can bring up human babies, why not other animals? So I started experimenting. Tigers, dogs, chimpanzees, even dolphins.'

'Dolphins?'

'Yes, there's a small lake over on that side, three dolphin-raised babies live there. They swim underwater, eat raw fish. No one can tell they're actually land creatures. I've begun to reverse evolution.'

Hajib chortled, and Rahan trembled again in fear. Sitting down on a large rock, Hajib said, 'Go take a look at them for yourself, Rahan. I'll wait here. I think you'll quite like the chimpanzee-humans – they'll make you think it wasn't wise of us to abandon trees for the earth because of evolution.'

'I don't really want to see them,' said Rahan wanly.

'How will it work if you don't? You're a bold, ethical journalist, you can't give up this opportunity. Go take a look, once you've seen all of them I'll show you my latest creation.'

'What's that?'

Hajib smiled. 'I'm not telling you yet. You don't understand how fortunate you are, Rahan. No human has ever visited my zoo before, this is my personal space. I come here when I'm unhappy. Watching these beast babies calms my nerves. At times, I even spend an entire week or two here. I have a small room there in a corner. This is my personal pleasure ground. Now that I've brought you here, it won't work unless you enjoy yourself.'

Rahan shook his head. 'No Hajib, I cannot enjoy this.'

'But you're a journalist – shouldn't you be taking a close look at everything before writing a full-length report?'

Rahan had no trouble detecting the sarcasm in Hajib's words. He was suddenly seized by an extraordinary dread. Locking eyes with him, Hajib said, 'Very well, I can't force you. But you must see my latest creation, at least.'

'And that is...?'

'You could say my guru here is Dr Josef Mengele. The doctor from Nazi Germany who conducted the most beautiful experiments on human beings.'

'What do you mean, "beautiful"?'

'Common people are cowards; they conduct their experiments on animals. But what can provide more joy than experimenting directly on human beings? Dr Mengele used to do just this. He would maim them, torture them; he had no compunctions.'

Rahan held his breath. 'Have you done it too?'

'Yes, I've begun. The first experiment was simple. What happens if human babies are kept in darkness from the time of birth?'

'Is this an experiment you've conducted?'

'Yes, I have brought up a dozen children entirely in darkness. They don't know what light is, they have never seen it.'

'How do you see them then?'

'With an infra-red camera. Here...'

Hajib touched a switch and instantly images appeared on a large screen. Young humans of varying ages, all resembling wild animals, with long hair and long nails, were stumbling about, picking food off the ground. They had no eyesight, but they did not know this.

'These people have a powerful sense of touch. Their power of smell is elevated too. It does not seem like they have any difficulty surviving without the faculty of sight.'

Rahan wheeled around to look at Hajib. 'Why are you showing me all these things?'

'Because I'm going to leave you here.'

Rahan was stunned. 'What did you say?'

'I'm going to leave you in the darkness with these humans. I'm very curious to know what they'll do if there is an addition to their number. Might as well put an imbecile journalist to some use, right?'

Rahan's eyes bulged with dismay when he saw the small pistol in Hajib's hand. A characteristic smile curling his lips, Hajib said, 'I will shoot if you try to stop me. You have to decide right now what you will do. This is my world. No one comes to this place except me, no one will know what happened.'

Before Hajib could continue Rahan leapt on him, whereupon he emptied the magazine of his pistol into Rahan's body without any hesitation. The gunshots reverberated from the granite walls, and the humans brought up as animals ran about in confusion and fear. Rahan's body was flung on to a large rock.

Exhaling sharply, Hajib put the pistol back in his pocket and went to his car. He needed the bottle of stimulant cocktail he had kept there. He had killed someone after a long time and was discovering with a modicum of wonder that the action actually made him calmer.

However, after the second swig of the cocktail, he felt a sudden stab of doubt. He had fired six bullets at Rahan, but there hadn't been as much blood as there should have been. He looked over his shoulder to dispel his suspicion – but it was too late. Rahan had slunk up on him from behind, and now he attacked. A rock was an ancient weapon, but it served its purpose well.

Looking at Hajib's unconscious body, Rahan whispered to himself, 'I'm not as much of an imbecile as you think I am. I'm wearing a Kevler bulletproof vest. Did you think I was reckless enough to meet you without arming myself with some form of defence?' He dragged Hajib's body towards the world of darkness. Hajib had been curious to know what the inhabitants of this world would do with a new addition to their number. He would regain consciousness soon enough – his curiosity would be assuaged.

No one knew of Hajib's zoo. No one would come to rescue him. He would spend the rest of his life among his own creations. There was no telling if his views on Josef Mengele would change.

THE MAKER OF MEMORIALS

VAJRA CHANDRASEKERA

The maker of memorials goes in early, the day before war's-end, with a great leap that takes him high over the red smog of earth kicked up by artillery. When he lands, the impact cracks the dry earth, a perfect, heroic three-point landing on the far side of the fire zone, wasteful grace unseen by any camera, journalist or art critic. But the maker of memorials is a consummate professional and can never abstain from performance. Even before the surgeries and procedures that made him superhuman, he was always a perfectionist.

'One must always act,' he told the quivering Selection Committee at his very first interview, as if under the glare of the hostile poets of the future.

Walking through the battlefield, the maker of memorials casually swats aside a poorly aimed artillery shell that comes too close. He feels only exasperation. He was engineered at great expense to be indestructible, unlike mere soldiers, but he simply has no *time* to be distracted by haphazard shelling. He is quite possibly immortal, after all the augmentations, all the experimental technologies, serums and irradiations, but he has never been able to think of time as deep – never felt its passing as anything but a great rush, a tremendous ever-building pressure to create, an endless series of deadlines to meet. Today, for instance, he has only these last few hours in the field to conceptualize and create this battle's memorial, knowing perfectly well that it will also be seen as the ultimate memorial for the entire war, given that war's-end is nigh; and since that end will also mark his own de facto retirement, this memorial will most certainly be seen as the summation of his life's work. In meeting this impossible goal, he has only his state-granted powers and super-creative genius to help him. Those were more than advantage enough, once – many memorials ago, at the beginning of his storied career – but he has been doing this for decades, and here, at the end of things, he's run out of ideas.

The maker of memorials is not alone on the battlefield. Apart from combatants and civilians, obviously – he considers them, collectively, somewhere between picturesque setting and raw material – there are other empowered actors on the field working under tight deadlines of their own.

For example, ground teams from the Rehistory Department have been at work for weeks: the shrines and set pieces they are constructing must be authentically damaged and reasonably weathered before war's-end. Next year, these ruins will be used by the Reclamation and Resettlement Programme as a well-designed history, something *neat* and *useful* to displace the mess and the strife of history created without a guiding hand, history without a design, history that just happened any old how, with no thought as to the political needs of the future. This work is the second most important thing in the world, so the rehistoricizers too have been engineered with super-strength and super-speed.

The maker of memorials pauses briefly to watch one of them toss a full-grown sacred fig to another, who catches it, rotates it roots downward, and plants it in a fresh pit, in what will no doubt soon be a new ancient temple.

Such expensive and dangerous superpowers are reserved for the elite warriors of history and memory, not the plebeian military. The maker of memorials does not acknowledge the history-fiddlers despite this flimsy commonality between them; however, he scorns their positivism, their fungible, linear, engineer minds, their overpopulated department, their sheer laziness. All *they* have to do is construct a plausible false history with all the plans and layouts worked out well in advance. Anybody could do that, the maker of memorials has been known to publicly grumble, anybody at all, because it needs none of the *thing*, the talent to walk into a site and create a memorial from what you find there, something that is perfectly integrated into its original environment but is also rendered symbolic and imbued with meaning.

This is the super-creative genius, the spark, that makes the maker of memorials so unique, so special – not his superpowers or the obscene budget of his apotheosis. Or, at least, this spark is what underlies and justifies them, which got him this job in the first place, the only one of his kind, a department of one. Any fool can muck about with the history of territorial claims, but it takes true talent to channel a nation's mourning. This is the most important work in the world, and it comes from the human part of him, the part that cannot be extracted, mass-manufactured, or machined. He resolves to be a perfect boor about this again at the next interdepartmental soirée.

The maker of memorials did not run out of ideas all willy-nilly, all essay-messy. He has worked in every material, in every style. He has worked in concrete and steel, in glass and water, in flora and earth, in fire and blood, in silence; he has worked in flesh and stone, in light and bone, in terror and the sound of guttural screaming, in nightmare. Sometimes, when he sleeps, he revisits those nightmare memorials and wakes with his ears ringing. He has worked at Cheddikulam and Kokkilai; at Vadakkandal, Valvettiturai, Akkaraipattu and Valvettiturai again; at Mylanthanai and Palliyagodella; at Puthukkudiyiruppu; at Allaipiddy and Chencholai; at so many others. He has worked the sites of battlefields and massacres, shootings and stabbings and bombings, executions and abductions, graves and mass graves, wins and losses. And, in so doing, his work has turned losses into wins: the maker, his arms elbow-deep in grief and time, smoothing out great sculptural loops of false memory with his bare and glowing hands.

He's made every cliché several times over, in sincere, ironic and post-ironic modes: he's done the rearing horses and rusting tanks and swords ploughing the earth and tortured bodies and raised flags and all the rest of it. He did the cracked artillery shell flowering into a lotus five times over until he ran out of fresh angles. There isn't anything left in the entire catalogue of approved iconography that he hasn't used or referenced many times. He has invented, cited, reclaimed, overused, exhausted. He has even worked in conceptual abstractions, and, to critical acclaim and several awards, in pure epiphany – a true magnum opus. He found it very difficult, even with all his powers, to refine the epiphany and attach it to a specific geolocation. Eventually, he grew so tired of explaining how to reach it that he put up a sign and vowed never to work in intangibles again.

At the height of his ambition, he stripped a thousand southern temples of their reliquaries to make a memorial entirely out of sainted bones, each capable of miraculous healing. He stacked and overlapped them in such a cunning way that their powers amplified each other, so that on the night of the full moon, the memorial was capable of resurrecting the dead – that one got him into trouble, of course. He had failed to think it through, the Oversight Committee said, furiously, and nearly revoked his commission.

When he raised the question of his artistic struggle, the Committee rebuked him for what they called his *confusion*. He was indeed a great artist, they said, but was he not a patriot first? Was his art not driven by his need, conjoined with the matching need of the state, to memorialize this long disastrous war in such a way that memory and history could be led by the nose where they needed to go, down the winding path to the long hegemony of peace, the great homogeneous unity to come?

After that, the maker of memorials decided to play it safe for a while. He started again from plain old concrete and steel, which only drew even more critical acclaim for the neo-minimalist turn. He accepted it as his due in public, while inwardly he writhed in shame and, in no little part, in fear. Until then, he had not thought much about his own obsolescence.

The maker of memorials is painfully aware that the critics are *allowed* only to acclaim him and his work. Or more precisely, he knows they are permitted to speak of him only in a sanctioned language of acclamation: both faithful and faithless critics alike have their vocabulary limited, by statute, to praise. The faithful love him unconditionally, as they always have, and so have become a dim humming note in the background; it is the faithless critics that make him grind his teeth at night. They take the praise they are obliged to offer and weaponize it, building an inverse hierarchy of passive aggression and deniable irony. It gnaws at him because he knows what they mean when they call one of his memorials *stunning* or, worse, *groundbreaking*. It's the only vulnerability he has left, and it feels like an open wound.

(He carefully ignores the bile and loathing of those feral critics, so much worse than the faithless-but-tame, who infest the world outside state-sanctioned media, as seen through the pinholes in the firewall. Feral critics might be encountered in the samizdat spatter of the untamed online unserendipitously overspilling its bunds, or in banned foreign publications that might have accidentally been brought into the country by mistake and left carelessly on a particular waiting room table without any thought that the maker of memorials might see it while kicking his heels waiting for a tune-up or grinding away the hours while the Committee engages in its oversights. Such unsanctioned critics are invariably toxic and hostile to his person and his project, and they do not in the least attempt to understand his art, ambitions or circumstances, so why should he – anyway, he ignores them.)

෴

The hours slip unproductively out of the day before war's-end while the maker of memorials fruitlessly stalks the almost-complete field of battle in search of inspiration. His head is aching from the pressure, like a lake dammed by the bones of his temples, to create a great work that will epitomize this battlefield, this last moment of the long war and his storied body of work, all at once.

With desperation scratching and clawing at his unbreakable heart, the maker of memorials stumbles all at once onto a near-perfect composition: a found (it is found – he just found it) guro-kineticist piece. The body is still fresh and the spatter not quite dry. It is quite unidentifiable as combatant or civilian. The guilty projectile embedded across the trunk is, in a wonderful irony, not anything as gauche as an artillery shell fragment but a multilingual signboard, a thin metal plate. It must have been torn from its post in an explosion and flung an enormous distance before coming to this red rest. The text on the sign, now mostly obscured, warns against *trespass*, in all three official languages.

The maker of memorials immortalizes this scene with his time-hardening freeze-breath. He slightly rearranges the left arm first; his super-aesthetic senses find it to be flung outward in altogether too histrionic a pose. It is so much more striking if awkwardly bent over the chest, as if feeling for the body's lost heartbeat.

He stares at the tableau he has found and just preserved for eternity, and the piece still seems incomplete, somehow. After all, he has barely touched it. The language of veiled critical disapproval dances across his vision, the condemnation of obligatory approbation. They will probably say it is *breathtaking*. The maker of memorials shudders and squats next to the body, irresolute, thinking.

Hours later, when the artillery has fallen silent and the dust is finally settling, when his super-hearing picks up the journalists beginning to flock and peck and flutter across the field, the maker of memorials finds himself still crouching by the side of the body. He has been asking himself whether exhaustion could be a question that is its own answer and confusing himself by answering. Around and around –

He does not *kneel* at the body's side; the connotations would be wrong, and in any case his super-thighs can hold a squat indefinitely. The ground is fused to the soles of his feet as if he'd turned his heat vision on the earth until it boiled into molten glass and melted only to harden again, holding him in place. His clasped hands are inseparable by any earthly power; his muscles are locked, his body unhumanly dense and everlasting. He does not raise his head.

He does not move. With him included, the composition of the piece changes; its centre is now the maker of memorials himself, inevitably, this superb being in search of a redemption that he had not considered or wanted until this very last moment. He still isn't sure he does, but that's the piece, isn't it?

'I call it *The Failure of the Maker of Memorials*,' he says to the first journalist who reaches him, and he never speaks again.

THE GLOW-IN-THE-DARK GIRLS

SENAA AHMAD

At 22, we are crones, becoming dust, tasting bitter. We watch Moscow burn on the lounge television. We hold each other's hands. We say, *What will happen now?*

Moscow burns the way everything burns – beautifully, from a distance. Bochka roofs evaporate into smoke. Cathedral roofs spew sideways, spitting pimento tiles into the streets. Low-storeyed apartment buildings sink to their knees, folded in their own embraces, Soviet concrete crumbling upon prehistoric wallpaper, pulverizing babushkas in their Soviet frocks. In the street, men writhe in hats of fire. They clutch their flaming heads. They look like they are dancing the oldest and ugliest dance in the world.

Every so often, the ancient television gutters out, and Aisha smacks the bulbed glass in that precisely irritated way our uncles used to when a football match went black, back when we had uncles and they sat on our couches. The image skitters: off, on.

The sticky horror in our throats is not just for what we see, but for ourselves. We long to be there, in the heat of it. It is spiteful to leave us here, wasting away. We feel in ourselves a nuclear fire, always on the verge of explosion.

Mary Grace is crying silently, which is what she's best at doing. She's got a medal of honour in crocodile tears.

'All – of – the – children,' she manages in gasps. 'The – little – the – little – children.'

'It's a bit late for that,' Gina says. And, because she's annoyed, she cups Mary Grace's brown chin with all the kindness of a storybook mother hen. She holds Mary Grace's shivering face, a constellation of pure, sad girl tears, and she sets it on fire.

Nabeela is the first to get sick. It's just like her to want to try something new. To beat us to the punch. Cancer of the soul, she calls it. Somewhere over the years, unbeknownst to her, to us, her body has become poisonous to itself.

'It turns out the call was coming from inside the house,' is how she explains it, and when no one laughs she gets peeved and makes endless petty demands.

'Get me some ice chips.'

'The sun is too bright, it's hurting my head.'

'Play a song, will you.'

'No, not that song. Jesus God in the sky, anything but that stupid song.'

'It's like a coffin in here, can we get some light? I'm not dead *yet*.'

The inconvenience of illness is an insult to her very being. Every day, she's a new kind of cranky. Her skin is slipping along its sharpest points, accumulating folds beneath her eyes, around her mouth, at the base of her wrists. Even so, she retains just enough pep to be pissy.

At first, they wear hazmat suits around her. They press rubber fingers along her wan veins. They collect blood. And hair. They take a piece of tissue. They take a piece of her bone. They make the corniest jokes, trying to be kind. They say things like, 'Just adding this to the Nabeela shrine,' and 'Just auctioning it off to your fan club.'

Their endless crinkling irritates her. 'They're so creepy,' she mutters when they're not around, and especially when they are. 'I don't even think they're very good at their jobs.'

Eventually, they wear hazmat suits around all of us.

In the early days, we are young enough to think of ourselves as young. Still heartsick when we remember the acne-scarred boys and girls in the high schools we left behind. The little sisters whose hair we yanked one last time for good measure, muttering in their ears *Don't fuck this up* by way of goodbye, because the distance between our grief and our fortitude would unravel if we had to hear our own stupid hearts beating. In the early days, we still wear uniforms and stand at attention. We are still part of an *us* that is bigger than ourselves. This is the choice we make, our bodies for a way out of our lives. A chance at a future.

We travel to places on maps we can't even spell. Dimashq. Beirut. Ghazni. Qom. Put your finger on a globe and spin. We leave behind us irradiated neighbourhoods, post-apocalypses. Deserts where once there were no deserts. We go where we are told to go. We have not graduated high school, and already we have toppled buildings, laid waste to city blocks, upheaved countries, immolated hundreds of militants and the people around them – what our handlers call the bad guys and their peripherals. We smell of soot, always.

In our dormitory, we are homesick, bored, snappy. The doctors test our blood pressure. They smile when they see us looking, but we see the way they eye us, like we are wild things. Geiger counters click and spit readouts on each of us, every day, every night. We squabble over who used the bathroom and for how long. There are entire geological periods shorter than the showers that Mary Grace takes.

The rules are endless. We are not allowed to paint our nails. Or smoke cigarettes. Or eat less than three meals a day. Or stand in the sun too long. Or use lighters or matches or most kinds of microwaves. It's for our own safety, we are told – it's for everyone's safety. We are unstable, and we know it not because anyone says anything, but because of the ways in which we are constrained. The way our doctors and handlers look at us and don't look at us.

We pretend not to hear Yaya weeping into her pillow after dark and ignore Aisha gnashing her teeth in her dreams. We eat out of tin cans every day until all we can taste is the aluminum lining.

It's Jack, wispy little white girl Jacqueline, who yanks us out of it. One day, Nabeela pauses by her bunk and says in a voice that is almost angry with incredulity, 'Is that a recipe book? Are you reading a freaking recipe book?' and Jack gets kind of prickly and says, 'Yeah. So what? It's my gran's.'

She turns the brittle pages with fingers that somehow reek of cigarettes. She reads, 'Lauren's Favourite Banana-Mango Birthday Cake. Four cups chopped mango. Three cups banana, freshly sliced.' When she lowers the book, we see that each page bleeds with spatters of sauce stains, phantom thumbprints of flour. 'Vanilla ice cream, five cups. Crumbled graham crackers. Chilled butter, cut into cubes.' We can smell sunny bananas, can taste the tart sweetness of the mangoes with an intensity that makes our cheeks hurt. We spoon up our shitty dinners and imagine we are at Lauren's birthday party, feasting on her favourite banana-mango birthday cake.

When you live the way we live, the people around you are the world you inhabit, and they are your own private hell. We become sisters, of a sort. We borrow each other's magazines. We let Mary Grace take her stupid, interminably long showers. We listen spellbound to Jack, reading quietly to us from her grandmother's deteriorating recipe book. When Yaya weeps at night, one of us reaches out in the dark and holds her hand until she is quiet.

To make ourselves laugh, or when we are angry, or to show affection, or to say we're sorry, we set each other on fire. All it takes is a touch. When one of us ignites, the others can't help it. We hoot with laughter, we gape, we marvel at the wonder of ourselves. It snaps the tension of our waiting days clean in half. Sometimes, it sets off a chain reaction, one girl, then the next, then the next, becoming fire, burning up. In those brief, beautiful moments, we are something else. We become impossible.

It never lasts long, not like our city burning fires. We leave singe marks on the ground, on the walls. The doctors cough when they walk through our dormitory, then they wear masks. Sometimes, before we go to bed, we sing together. Wistful pop songs from our childhoods, camp ditties from when we went to camp. A chorus of girls, too young to vote, too poisonous to be anywhere else.

These are the days we will think of, forever afterwards. The days when we were youthful and useful and burned brighter than anything else. At nights, we dream of blood and fire and smoke and screaming, but in the morning we never remember.

Those were the old days. Now, it is not the days that are old, but ourselves.

In the third year of our service, a nosy journalist from a national newspaper finds out about us. Suddenly, everyone knows. They call us weapons of mass destruction, or military mad science experiments, or a new generation of suicide bombers, or just bombs. They want to know if this was how science was meant to be used. Are we even human? Suddenly, everyone's a philosopher. They interview scientists who drone on in endless columns about the ethics of human experiments, the tremulous line between willing participant and hoodwinked lab rat. They ponder if it is a human rights violation, chemically altering bodies to obliterate cities, to become fire. They get our names wrong.

Gina, who knows how to pronounce unpronounceable words, who reads the best, keeps us in the loop. She says, 'I guess we're victims today. Coerced by circumstance, that's what they're saying.' Or, 'Now they think we should be in a laboratory.'

'Where do they think we live? In paradise?' Aisha asks.

They are curious, ravenous for anything about us. They print our enlistment mugshots, they profile the crumbling high-rises and rundown neighbourhoods from which we came. The newspapers unearth photos of our families. Sisters we no longer recognize. Mothers whose smiles are grainy and stilted, like they were caught unawares. The newspapers want to know: who would choose this? Why would our families let us go? We grow weepy. We bicker with our handlers. We say, 'Don't we have any rights? Don't we get to speak?'

'They're afraid of you,' they tell us. 'Do you really want to rile them?'

In the end, our handlers relent. Not for us, but for themselves. They let a television station interview Nabeela. We watch it on the piece-of-shit lounge television. We are so proud, we are sick with envy. Nabeela is dark and lovely and crisply suited, not a hair out of place. They even let her paint her nails red. She speaks quietly and urgently. Her eyes say, *What choice did we have?*

The anchor does not call us women, but girls. Like we did not sign up for this. Like we did not know. Like we are still babies – maybe we are and maybe we are not. She looks into the camera, into our eyes. She is old enough and pretty enough to be every mother we never had. She says sternly, curiously, 'Who are they, these poor young girls?'

It is only years later that we find out. Too late. It is our mistake. It is everyone's mistake.

The anchorwoman who interviews Nabeela. The woman who does her make-up. The nice man who leans over her and asks if the studio lights are too hot. The people who huddle behind the cameras. The studio audience. The assistant director. The security guard who signs Nabeela into the building, who shakes her hand and smiles so brightly, who says, 'It's just TV, it won't kill you.'

It happens one by one, long afterwards. After they leave their jobs or get promoted or move cities or go broke or marry someone and change their names. It takes a long time for anyone to connect the dots, to bring them back to that one moment in their lives, that day in the studio with the girl who was a bomb.

We thought we were safe. Or, no: we didn't think we were *so* unsafe. Or, no: we didn't think we could be so unsafe without even knowing it.

But of course, we are. And the anchorwoman, the make-up lady, the nice man with the studio lights, the security guard, the studio audience bussed in from small towns and suburbs and other cities – the unlucky ones, the cancer takes them slowly, and the rest of them, they die before they even know what's happened.

You are standing on the outskirts of a city you can't name. There is dust in your nose and sun in your eyes. The people, they look like you. When they talk, they speak the language of your childhood. They could be your cousins, or your uncles, or your brothers, or your grandmother. You remember that your grandmother had wide, warty arms and an anxious way of being. Each old woman you pass, you see her. You want to help them with their bags. You want to take them home in your arms. You want to sit at their feet, and say, *I'm sorry I didn't listen, I'm listening now.*

You lived in a city like this when you were very young, a refugee girl on the ragged edge of town. Only later, when you are older, on the other, wealthier side of the world, do you realize how young you were, how poor. How small the four rooms were, that you shared with your mother, father, siblings, aunts, cousins, grandparents.

When you see the little girl, you think she is you. You think you are dreaming. The drugs your handlers give you, they make the world hazy and unclear, so it's harder to remember afterwards what you have done. But she is real. She is here, the girl. With her oversized clothes, and her underfed shoulders, and her face so open to the whole wide world. She sees you looking and bursts into a grin, and it's like the heat of the sun, the smile on that child.

You smile back at her. You say, 'It's okay, don't worry,' even though she does not understand English, and she cannot possibly know what is about to happen. The drugs make you slur. Your handlers would call her a peripheral – the bad guys and their peripherals. You are not yet 20, and sometimes you think yourself a child and sometimes you do not. You could almost be her mother. How did you end up here, how did she end up there?

You kneel in the sandy street, you reach out your arms and you hug the girl who is you, and then you do what you came to do. You become annihilation itself. You explode into fire and light and death.

Nabeela's beautiful face is blistering. Her skin glistens, scabbed and slippery with scarlet pustules. We try not to look, and she rasps, 'Don't be babies,' and when we look, she says, 'I'm not a zoo animal, thank you.' We see the way her hair has thinned, how her scalp is moulting and uneven, like the back of a salamander. We hold her arms. We sit on her bed. We try not to notice the peculiar way she smells.

She wants to know about Moscow. She says, 'Does this mean it's over?' and we want to know what *it* means, as if there was truly ever an end point to any of this. She shakes her head and asks, 'What is the world coming to?'

Later she says, 'They should have let us do it. We could have burned it better.'

We ask the doctors how she's doing. They say, 'It's good that you care about her so much,' and nothing more. We try not to look at the little plastic bowl on her bedside table, swimming with the cereal texture of her vomit. We ask her about her life after us, after she left. She perks up in these moments, her voice gets a bit of boast back in it. We try not to remind her that she is back with us now. All that climbing led nowhere. There are no winners here.

We sing her favourite songs. We pretend we are anywhere but in this hospital room. We feel pious. We watch in horror when she sleeps, not only for her but for ourselves, as she wastes away, as her face oozes. As her teeth begin to fall out.

When she leaves us that first time, we are furious. She says, 'I'm sorry, don't we all have to move on at some point?' She is breaking three rules when she tells us: hairspray in her hair, painted nails, leaving for indefinite periods of time. Of course, our handlers let her. Star power is its own kind of weapon. People in cities and small towns, they look at her and they don't see the things we've done. She is a war veteran, after all. A world-famous talk show host starts crying when she meets Nabeela. She says, 'You've been through so, so much. You mean everything to me.'

'It's good for you, too,' our handlers tell us. 'Can't you see?'

What we see is that Nabeela is free. She calls herself Bee now. She's on television all the time. She has pruned herself into perfection. She wears too much make-up. She speaks in full, clean sentences. No swear words. She is relaxed and easy. Bright. She is more radiant than we ever knew we were allowed to be.

In our dreams, we dream of hellfire and blood and limbs. We dream of faces peeled open, red and raw and boiled. We dream of the little girl we hugged and how we incinerated her in our arms. How we watched everything go up in smoke, with the powder of her bones drying upon us. We dream of the looks on all their faces in the moment of our fury. Mostly, we dream of the corpses.

In the mornings, we can never remember what we dreamed, only that our throats are raw and our eyes are dry and our nails are damp with our own blood. In the dreaming night, we scratch at our own bodies, claw at our own hands, try to tear our human skin away. Trying to reach the thing that lies on the other side.

The beginning of the end happens in the plainest, most ordinary ways. An American boy goes backpacking around the world. He is a wandering spirit, this boy, he has a streak of adventure in him. He wants to write a novel, we learn later. About the things he's seen, the things he's done. He ends up in a country he shouldn't be in, a city he shouldn't be in. Where one of us was already dispatched a week ago, only days from detonation.

It goes without saying, this boy was not a peripheral. He was supposed to go to college after his trip. He has already written the first chapter of his book. His teeth were straight and white. His eyes were a wilted green. He had that thing we all want – a future.

His grieving family says, 'This can't happen again, not to anyone else.' The government hems and haws. Furious op-eds are penned at the speed of light. Nabeela is replaced, talk show after talk show, by the boy's mother, his sister, his father. Her time in the sun is up.

Suddenly, we are not *those poor young girls*, they do not make us sound like babies any more. Overnight, the newspapers remember that we chose this, we signed up for it. We enlisted, didn't we? Overnight, we find ourselves named anew. Now we are the dragons under the bed.

The grieving family tries a new way. They file a lawsuit against the military. Files are declassified. Our handlers are asked to testify. We watch it all from the television set in the lounge. Sometime during all of this, Nabeela comes slinking back to the dormitory. She goes from Bee to Nabeela again. We do not gloat, we do not preach. Mostly, we are glad to fill the hole. We are birds of fire, birds of a feather, an endangered species. We flock together. We hold each other in our wings. We watch ourselves fall apart. We are hollow on the inside, we are all we have. And even that – even that isn't much to write home about.

It is Yaya who goes out the last time. She says to us, 'See you on the flipside,' and we say, 'Sure, fine, whatever.' We try not to look too deeply into the blood red of her eyes. Or the rusting brown scratches on her arms. We have our own nightmares to deal with.

Afterwards, we imagine it a hundred different ways. We imagine it often. We see Yaya in an empty street on the other side of the world, her headwrap slipping in the sweaty heat of the day. We see how tired she is. How chapped her lips are. How she has stopped caring for herself in the simplest of ways.

We see the girl. In our minds, she looks like the girl we hugged all grown up. Still a version of ourselves. She grins at Yaya as she approaches, and perhaps Yaya is startled, perhaps she smiles back.

'It's so good to see you,' the girl says to Yaya, and before Yaya can say, *I think you've made a mistake,* the girl is folding her into a hug. In that moment, crushed against the weight of the girl, perhaps Yaya feels it. The wires running all down the girl's arms and torso, the bomb strapped right to her chest.

In our minds, Yaya tries to pull away, but it's too late, of course. In our minds, Yaya thinks of us, or of a family long forgotten, or of the girl we once hugged, who is so like this one. None of us imagine another possibility, one in which Yaya does not struggle, does not fight. Where Yaya just sinks into the girl's embrace and waits for what's been coming to her this entire life.

These days we spend most of our time in Nabeela's room. Sometimes, we share sips of cheap booze beforehand, swallows of bargain-basement vodka that tastes like rubbing alcohol. We have an unspoken pact, where Nabeela doesn't notice the liquor on our breath, and we don't notice the odours of her body as it fights itself. These days, there is no need for handlers – not after Yaya. After Yaya, we are done.

Nabeela's jaw is falling off. When she opens her mouth, you can see the sticky white bone gaping out. She spits out bloody gum tissue into her congealing bedside bowl. We stop talking about the world. There is no point:

not for us, who are not in it. We hold her hands, the way we used to hold Yaya's hands at night, and Jack reads from her gran's recipe book. There are fewer doctors now. Mostly it is quiet. Just us, biding our days.

In her hospital room, we talk about the futures we will never have. We talk about when, not what if. Already, we are starting to spot the sickness in one another, the thing on the inside of us that we claw towards in our dreams, the poison at the heart of our hearts.

Jack says, 'You know, someday soon they'll have the technology to take regular people to outer space,' and we say, surprised, impressed, 'Like, to the moon?' and she says, 'No, way out. Imagine taking a ship all the way out to the edge of nowhere.' We are silent, dreamy with the possibility, just us and our impossible spaceship and the expanding wilderness of the universe.

'Just think,' Aisha says, 'someday, there will be space kids.'

Gina mutters, embarrassed, 'My sister has three kids. Three chubby little idiots.' She does not say anything else, but there's nothing else to say. There are no chubby little idiots for us.

Now that Nabeela is sick, the country is on our side again. They say that we have been used, abused. We are victims again. They compare us to the radium girls, the women in World War I factories who used to paint watches with glow-in-the-dark radioactive paint. Who painted their faces and their lips until they burned bright, until they were luminous with poison. We, too, are the glow-in-the-dark girls. We, too, are sick with ourselves.

In Nabeela's last days, we sleep on the floor beside her. We hold her up when she cannot sit by herself. We feed her ice chips when she cannot lift her arms. We comb what's left of her perfect hair. We set ourselves on fire, to make her laugh again.

THE PAIN MERCHANT

MANJULA PADMANABHAN

'There was a time,' said Masterji, 'when every household had plenty of pain to sell.'

We were sitting by the rocks at the very edge of my village. In the distance behind us, the high mountains scratched the heavens with their snowy peaks. Right in front of us, the bare hillside plunged down at rakish angles. The plains spread away far below. 'No longer true. People have forgotten that pain was once commonplace.'

'Won't you show me just a bit?' I asked, using my most wheedling voice. I was eight years old and the only boy in a house full of sisters and mothers. At home, I got whatever I wanted when I used that voice. 'Just once?'

But the pain merchant was immune.

He intrigued me: I had never met someone who did not instantly give in to my demands. Plus, he looked so strange. Everyone I knew wore wool and embroidered felt slippers on their feet or leather boots. My mothers and sisters wore tunics, and the men wore mirrored caps and turbans. The merchant, by contrast, was dressed in layers of greasy leather held together with lengths of string. His shoes were tied on with strips of leather. He wore a dark brown hood that partially obscured his face. Countless small pouches hung from his shoulders and down his back. Like bunches of grapes.

I could see that he wanted to please me, yet he shook his head. 'I've explained before. My wares are perishable,' he said. According to him, recorded pain was like perfume. It got depleted with each use. 'I can't afford to show you anything unless you can pay.'

'I can pay today, Masterji,' I said. 'I found something to trade.'

He looked at me sideways, his face a mass of wrinkles. I couldn't tell if he was smiling or frowning. 'Trade, eh?' he remarked, his nose lifting and twitching. 'Come on then. Show me what you've got.'

I knelt, my right knee on the ground and my left foot stuck forward. I lifted the cuff of my pants to reveal my ankle. There was the beginning of an old scar there. 'You see this?' I said, squinting up at the merchant. Then I removed my shoe and pulled off the sock, so that he could see the whole foot, naked. 'That's the kind of thing you're interested in, isn't it?' My mothers had told me I'd had an accident when I was a baby. It had been fixed. No trace now remained of the wound, except for the scar.

Masterji knelt, reaching for my foot with both hands. I hadn't noticed earlier that he wore leather gloves, with the tips cut off. He traced the contours of the scar carefully with his forefinger. Glancing up, he asked, 'What caused this injury? Did your mothers tell you? Do you know how long ago it happened?'

'Yes, they told me,' I said. 'It was when I was a baby. I don't remember what happened.'

A shadow slid over us. A vulture. It wouldn't bother us, of course. We were moving our arms and talking. Obviously alive. Even so, I tugged the ward-off out of my pocket and held it up, cocked and ready to send out a pulse.

'Ah, don't bother,' said the merchant. 'It's got plenty to eat.'

In the few seconds during which I glanced up at the vulture, the merchant had reached into his clothes and pulled something out. An instrument, it looked like. It was shiny and metallic but also stretchy. Before I could object, he had placed it around my ankle and was deftly moulding it into place.

I had been told not to let strangers do anything to me without explaining their actions. 'You should ask my permission before doing that,' I said.

He glanced up and said, 'Do you feel it? Is it touching you?' I shook my head. It had completely surrounded my ankle and my foot up to the arch, but I felt no sensation. 'Fine then. You held your foot out to me, and I placed my scanner around it without making contact. That is all. No harm done. Look now. It's reading...'

The shiny surface of the gadget had vanished. In its place was a kind of magnified picture of everything under the skin of my ankle. I could see the cord-like vessels of blood pulsing busily. The merchant was touching the surface of the gadget in such a way as to reveal different views of the internal structure of my foot. He zoomed in.

'We have gone below the muscles and soft tissue,' he said. 'We can now see the bone.' It looked surprisingly white to me. He was peering around the ligaments to find exactly what he wanted. 'Do you notice these seams?' Silver-grey lines. 'Surgery. It does not look like an accident. More likely a medical procedure. Perhaps you had a birth defect, eh? Your people told you that it was an accident? Easier that way, I suppose. Makes no difference. Pain is pain.'

He tapped the surface of the gadget once again and the visual faded off. The surface reverted to its metallic appearance. He waited until he heard a faint beep, then peeled the thing away.

'What *is* that?' I asked. I felt as if I hadn't been breathing or swallowing for the entire time that the gadget had been on my foot.

'A dolcache,' said Masterji, as if the name was a common one. 'An instrument for reading and recording pain.' He glanced at me once more, his face seizing up with wrinkles. Smiling. 'Had you forgotten? You asked if I would accept this scar of yours as a trade. Not the scar of course, but the pain within. The memory remains in the bones, you see. My answer is yes – I got a strong signal. The question now: what sort of pain will you accept in exchange for what I took?'

He saw my confusion. I was a child, after all. What would I know of the worth of these things? Or maybe he heard the sound of distant voices. I had heard them too but hadn't said anything for fear that he'd hurry away. As he had twice before. I never knew when or how I would next meet him.

He nodded with a bird-like twitch, as if making up his mind for both of us. 'All right,' he said, as he got to his feet. 'You cannot assess the worth of what you have. Nor can we remain out in the open any longer. You'll need to come with me. How much time do you have?'

The answer, of course, was 'None.' I wasn't allowed to spend any time alone with strangers. But if I said that, he may not take me. So I lied and said, 'I don't know.'

He told me we wouldn't have to go far. Which was true.

What he didn't mention was that the place was well-hidden. No one would find me, not even the dogs. It was underground, the entrance tucked under a smelly heap of some sort. Probably the remains of a body. There were so many around, lying in the open, rotting. That's why the dogs wouldn't find me. They were trained to ignore the bodies.

Inside, underground, the merchant had a few lights strung up. They were connected to a large battery, humming softly in the corner. The place must have been a basement at one time. There was some old furniture. He asked me to sit on a high chair. Then he drew up a stool and placed it in front of me, for himself. 'Let me see,' he said, as he began to unwrap the many little bags that were slung around his body. 'What shall I start you off with?'

The pouches were connected to the cords tied around him. As he unwrapped the strings and the pouches, he became thinner and thinner. The sheets of leather that I had thought were clothes were merely separators: beneath each layer were yet more pouches.

'Oh,' I said. 'That's a lot of pouches.'

'They're not heavy,' said the merchant. 'Pain has no weight.'

He was now down to his actual clothes. He looked very different. Diminished. A thin old man in a dirty black sweater and loose black pants. His feet remained bound in cords. His hair was white. He had arranged the strings of pouches and the leather separators neatly on the floor. He looked carefully at the array before making a selection.

He sat down now, facing me. 'Because you're a child and this is your first time, I will give you three separate doses, each one very brief.' He opened the pouch in his hand. Inside it was slender object, like a bracelet, except it was made of glass. FlexiGlass. He flipped an invisible clasp and asked me to put out a hand. 'It doesn't matter which one,' he said.

I was starting to feel afraid. Of being underground. Of knowing that I could not be found. My mothers would be furious. The men would be raging and pounding their fists. I did not say any of this to him. My curiosity was far greater than my fear.

'What will I feel?' I asked Masterji. 'Will it happen all at once? Or slowly?' Everything I was doing was wrong. I should never have followed the merchant. I didn't even know his name. My family would be mad with worry by now. 'Maybe I should go home.'

The wrinkles sprang into view again. Just a twitch. 'Okay, only one dose then. And I'll owe you two more. You've already paid me, don't you see? I'll have to meet you again at least until I've paid you back. Hold out a wrist?'

I extended my right hand towards him, palm up, fingers curled.

He placed the bracelet around the wrist. It felt cool against my skin but without weight. 'You see this small red dot?' he asked, pointing to the surface of the bracelet. I nodded mutely.

'I'm going to press it three times. That means, you'll have three seconds before the dose begins. It'll last for 10 seconds. Then it'll stop on its own.'

He was looking at me and must have seen the fat tears spilling down my cheeks now. Tears of fear and guilt. He asked, 'Shall I go ahead?'

I nodded again, unable to speak.

He pressed the button three times. The red light turned green.

A brightness pierced my wrist. I can't find any other words to describe it: a needle made of lightning was stitching sensations onto my wrist where the bracelet clasped it. I gasped aloud. My teeth jumped in my mouth. The sides of my nose rose up. My hair stood on end. Then it was over. The bracelet sprang open, and he caught it before it fell.

'Ahh!' I said, panting. '*Aaaah*! AHH!'

Masterji was wrinkle-wreathed again. Gazing at me, fondness in his eyes. 'Your first experience of pain,' he whispered softly. 'A sweet thing to see.'

I sucked in my breath. My mind was whirling. I couldn't form words.

He read the question in my eyes. 'That was from a young girl. She had been cut by a glass bangle. Her sensations were absolutely pure, untouched by sorrow or premonition. And freshly caught. I was there when the wound occurred, though I recorded it years later.'

'I must go,' I blurted out. 'Or else they'll find me. *Us*.' Which would be terrible. Not for me, but for him. 'But please – I want to know more!'

He took me outside without responding to my demand. He did not even bother to wear his layers. Up we went, via a different exit and thence towards the rocks. The voices calling for me were louder now. I could hear the dogs. 'Pant loudly and pretend to be more tired than you are,' he said, before hurrying away. 'Let them think you got lost and have been frantic for some time. Tell them anything but where you've been and with whom.'

My mothers had become increasingly protective. Perhaps they could sense the tide pulling me away. My sisters were industrious and dutiful, but I had ants under my skin. I was always being told to hush.

'You don't need to know such things,' said my mothers when I asked questions about the so-called Event. 'Your ears will hurt with that kind of knowledge.'

'But pain has been banished from our world,' I would say. 'So how can I be hurt?'

They would purse their lips and turn their faces aside, saying, 'Only someone who has no knowledge of pain would utter something so ridiculous!'

I didn't dare tell them that I *did* have knowledge of pain. I had met Masterji many times after that first time underground. I had taught myself different ways to escape my home by stealth, leaving at night and returning before dawn.

Since I had no more scars to trade with the merchant, I paid him by writing labels for his pouches. He had trouble forming his letters, though he could read. He found my labels very useful. Until that time, he had kept track by memorizing each pouch and its contents by its place on his strings.

He chose what type of pain to expose me to, based on what he thought was appropriate for my age. He showed me the harsh twang of hair pulled out by the roots. The tooth-rattling crunch of a broken nose. The deafening thump of a ruptured eardrum. Even the scratchy, whining ache of an infected throat. Each pain was more rich and intense than the one before. The more I sampled, the more I wanted to sample. The delivery method was always the same, a bracelet on the wrist. The pain was experienced in the part of the body to which it belonged.

The day I told Masterji I wanted to follow his path, he looked at me sadly and said, 'I'm sorry.' It was never easy to read his expression, but from what I could tell, he was genuinely sad. 'Some types of pain cannot be recorded,' he said. 'You will come to know all of them if you leave your birth home.'

But I would not be dissuaded.

Two years after my first experience of pain, on a moonless night, I stole away from home. Masterji was waiting for me by the rocks. He knew that the ravines and streams would make it difficult for the dogs to track me. Once we reached the plains there was no chance of being followed.

He had told me there were more clients for his wares on the plains. That they paid in metal coins. That they sought him out. All of it was true. He was moderately well known for the variety of his wares and their smooth, clean quality. Some people asked for menstrual cramps. Some looked for a kick in the groin. Some longed for the dull hammering of a headache. Some wanted to feel the vicious scream of a bullet ripping through the gut.

The more serious the wound, the higher the price, all calculated by the second.

His most valuable item was from a man who had blown out his brains in front of the merchant. 'He did it for me,' said the merchant. 'So that I could collect that greatest and harshest of all pains in the instant it occurred.'

We were sitting in a quiet spot beside a great river when he told me this. We were some distance from the city in which we had spent almost an entire month. We had eaten well that day and were taking our ease.

'Really!' I said, feeling a shiver run down my spine. A shiver of desire. 'How is it I've not seen that pouch?'

Masterji was looking away from me. 'He was my brother,' he said. 'He wanted me to have the benefit of his death.'

'Oh!' I cried out. 'And how much did you sell it for?'

He turned and looked at me, his expression unfathomable. 'Nothing. I've never offered it for sale. Not even a half-second of it.'

I couldn't suppress my disappointment. 'Wah,' I said. 'If you don't use it, your brother died in vain!'

But he would say no more about the matter. We moved on soon after.

In the years that followed, Masterji taught me everything he knew of his trade. I learned to record pain, to clean it, to play it back. The fact that fewer and fewer people had memories of pain meant that there was competition amongst those who sought it and sold it. People with prosthetic limbs or obvious surgeries were usually tapped out. Either their memories had been drained dry or they no longer wanted to cooperate. The easiest to locate were those who had tattoos. The hardest were those who had had plastic surgery.

We met others like ourselves on the dusty roads and rutted highways. We travelled mostly on foot but accepted rides when we were offered them. Sometimes, we bought ourselves donkeys. Once, we even owned a camel.

I was the youngest person in any group of pain traders. They belonged to the earlier world, with their own memories to draw upon. I was the only one amongst them who had been born after the Event. I was always desperate to know more about it, why it happened and how. Their answers were always vague, as if the speakers were embarrassed by the memory.

'It happened suddenly,' they would say, 'or maybe over a month. It happened by accident. Or perhaps by design. One day, the scientists had found a way to record pain. The next day, the world's leaders were talking about deleting it from existence. The day after that, there was an explosion…a leak… something to do with the water. Or was it the rain? The air?'

The one thing everyone agreed upon was the effect: there was no longer any sensation of pain anywhere on the Earth. 'You could fall on your face or step on a nail or swallow poison or poke out someone's eye. But you felt no physical pain.'

There were consequences, of course.

Terrible accidents began to occur. Babies, in particular, died from being crushed or smothered or choked, because they couldn't complain in time. A ruptured appendix was a death sentence. Thousands of women died in labour, unable to feel their own contractions. Mass murders and group suicides increased a hundredfold. No one could have predicted that a world free of pain would unleash such a flood of violence. It was broken, gripped by a madness that nothing could contain.

People began living in tiny isolated homogenous communities, clinging tight to those they knew, distrusting all strangers, outsiders.

Meanwhile, the technology for recording pain became freely available.

'A friend sold the machine to me,' said Masterji, 'after buying it from someone who didn't like it, who learnt how to use it from someone else. We didn't ask questions any more. If something worked, it was good. If it didn't, we threw it away. In the beginning, I lied about what the machine could do. I said that it would cure internal wounds. That childbirth would be safe for mothers once I had recorded the memory of the pain of contractions. That burns would clear up miraculously if the pain that they could no longer feel was sucked away. All untrue. But I got amazing recordings. Then, when I played them back for clients, they fell over with amazement. They screamed, they cried. The moment it was over, they asked for more.'

I had seen it myself: the expressions of ecstatic agony, the open mouths, the eyes filled with tears. I had felt it myself: the explosion of violent sensation when acid met skin, the searing, silvery shriek of tearing flesh. Followed by the most divine relief, wave after wave of trembling heat and warmth.

This was especially true when the source of pain was a grievous injury or life-threatening illness. I had seen clients who experienced physical reactions from the agony they were exposed to, such as sweating and even bleeding. I had known it myself. Once, when I wore a bracelet recorded from a woman experiencing a miscarriage, I found myself crying uncontrollably after ten seconds of extraordinary pressure deep within my groin. It was as if a volcanic, primordial force was moving through my body. The pain was huge and brassy, a great boom of raw life energy, pounding its way out, towards death.

In Masterji's waning years, the technology underwent a transformation that made it possible for recordings to be preserved indefinitely. Now at last, we could create a library of physical sensations. We opened a clinic alongside the library, where we could administer pain in easily controlled doses. Soon, we became reasonably prosperous. We bought a small house that we shared together, Masterji living downstairs and me, above. We could afford a couple of domestic helpers to run errands and do chores.

One day, he called for a pot of tea to be made, then asked me to accompany him to the little garden in the back of the house. When we were settled, he said, 'My young friend, in all these years that we have been dealing in pain, there's a question that I've been waiting to hear from you. Yet you have never asked it.'

Age had slowed the merchant down considerably. His eyesight had dimmed with time, his movements were enfeebled. But his expression was as sharp as ever. I really did not know what he expected of me. I felt deeply uncomfortable. He paused before continuing, staring at me all the while, 'How is it that you have never once expressed the least interest in that *other* sensation? The one that some have called the Siamese twin of pain?'

I shook my head. 'I don't know what you mean,' I said.

Masterji nodded, the wrinkles on his face seizing up with mirth, so that he looked like a dried-up walnut. He gurgled deep in his chest and for a moment I thought he was coughing or choking, before realizing it was the sound of his laughter. There was a sobbing quality to it too.

'Ah, my poor boy,' he said, when he had found his voice. 'It is as I thought. You truly have no knowledge of pleasure, do you?'

I frowned. I knew the word, of course. 'Gladness. Joy. That's what it means, yes?'

He looked away, sighing and went silent again, all laughter draining out of him. For a while, I wondered if he had dozed off, as he was wont to do of late. He stirred at last. In a sombre voice he said, 'Those who stripped the world of physical agony stripped it of physical pleasure too.' There was a pause. 'But you wouldn't know that, would you?' He turned to look at me. 'Because who would be so cruel as to tell you of a joy you can never know?'

No one, it turned out. I honestly did not know what he meant.

Still gazing at me, the old man reached under the neck of the thin sweater, which was still his favourite style of clothing. He drew out a slender chain. At the end of it was a tiny pouch, made of leather and embroidered with gold thread.

The moment I saw it, I knew what it must be.

I was filled with foreboding and began to shiver.

'You have been so trusting, my friend,' said Masterji. 'For the most part I have not betrayed your trust. I have never lied to you. What I've done, however, is keep some truths from you. Here is the first of them: while pain can be recorded, pleasure cannot. So even though my body remembers physical pleasure, neither I nor anyone else can share it with you. It is a glory, a fathomless bliss, that neither you nor any one of your entire generation can ever know.'

I continued to shiver.

'Here is a second truth that I withheld: certain types of pain result in the actual injury that caused the pain. You have seen that, I think? Physical reactions that mirror the pain? Such as bleeding? Well. When it comes to death…'

I guessed what he was about to say and tried to forestall him. 'Masterji, please!' I cut in. 'You don't have to do this. Your time has not yet come.'

He gurgled slightly, which I took to be a chuckle. 'Huh. I disagree! Meanwhile, there's a final truth that I have withheld. Instead of telling you, I'll demonstrate it.'

He opened out the tiny pouch. Inside was a pain bracelet, just like all the others. He placed it around his own wrist, then urged me to draw my seat close to his.

'I will press the red button several times,' he said. 'When I'm done, I'll give you my free hand to hold. That will allow you to feel an echo of whatever I feel. Without experiencing the injury.' He looked me straight in the eyes and smiled. 'You will accompany me into the great silence, my friend! But, unlike me, you will return.'

A few moments later, I took his hand. I held it to my face.

I felt the force of his brother's death blasting through him.

I felt his spirit splinter into glittering shards.

Then scatter, scatter, scatter.

Until all that was left was an immense shimmering void.

And no pain.

No pain at all.

THE MINISTRY OF RELEVANCE

ARJUN RAJ GAIND

'You have a letter, Bhaskar,' my wife Manasi informs me when I get home from work. 'It's over there,' she says, pointing towards the Lucite shelf that doubles as our dining table. 'And listen…you'll need to wake up early tomorrow and go to the barter market. We are out of milk and bread.'

Putting down my backpack, I lean over to give her a perfunctory kiss on the cheek. At the last moment, she averts her face, refusing to look at me. I sigh, realizing that I am going to have to sleep on the floor once again.

Things have been tense between us, especially lately. Somewhere during the last six months, Manasi and I have begun to drift apart, like flotsam caught by two opposing currents. We rarely talk any more, and when we do all we seem to do is fight.

Our marriage has fallen victim, I believe, to the inevitable entropy of dreams. When I first met Manasi, I had just published my first book. The future had looked boundless. Everything had seemed so…so hopeful.

But soon, as hope is prone to doing when it encounters reality, all my plans had turned to ash. By the mid-2020s, people had stopped reading altogether, preferring the mindless cacophony of the Virtuality. Then, the synaptic data boom had come, the final nail in the coffin, as programmers began to broadcast entertainment directly to the human brain. Who needed books when you could have perpetually regenerated content, when you could live someone else's life, when you could see and smell and feel what they felt? The last physical book in Mumbai Prime was printed in 2028, the same year I had been forced to take a position as an editor at a virtzine in order to continue paying the bills. That was also the last time I had written a word for myself. Instead, now I spent most of my time composing lurid gossip-casts detailing the private lives of whatever net/lebrity was enjoying their 15 minutes that week or hacking out paid press-blurbs for media aggregators, all for the princely sum of three rupees a word.

That was another reason Manasi and I often ended up arguing. She keeps urging me to finish my second book, but somehow, I am unable to find the energy to even get started. The act of writing something meaningful seems so contrived to me after the drudgery I deal with at work, so utterly effete. After all, what good is a writer when reality has become stranger than fiction? And while I'm content bringing home my meagre pay cheque each month, I can sense Manasi feels that I have let her down in some way, that I have betrayed her. I am not the man she married any more, the angry young polemicist who believed he could change the world. I've become someone else, a stranger whose brain aches when he has to think too much and who is so filled with regret he cannot help but feel exhausted all the time.

Manasi continues to ignore me, barely sparing me a glance as I retreat to our tiny bedroom. Shucking off my overalls, I debate taking a shower, but quickly dismiss the idea. We have already used up our weekly water ration and if my wife wants milk and bread, I cannot afford to waste any more of my salary on baths.

Instead, I make do with a quick sponge with a damp towel before checking in on our son, Kanishka. He is already in bed, snoring away, a cherubic smile on his tiny face. I briefly contemplate waking him up. This is the fourth night in a row I have come home to find him fast asleep. As a result, I have almost forgotten what his voice sounds like, or the gentle glimmer of his laughter. My chest constricts with an abrupt cataclysm of emotion. The need to take him in my arms, to tell him I love him, is almost overwhelming, but somehow I manage to suppress the urge. The last thing I want is to make Manasi even angrier.

Returning to the living room, I unwrap my last remaining cube of whisky and decant it into a teacup. Sipping it slowly to enjoy every drop, I pick up the envelope, examining it curiously. It has been years since I received an actual letter from someone, much less from the government. Almost all correspondence these days is electronic, either old-fashioned email or the newer synapsafax, which sends messages directly to the receiver's neocortex.

When I tear open the envelope, it reveals a typed sheet of paper, an official-looking notification printed in smudged ink.

At the top of the page are emblazoned the words:

From the Ministry of Relevance,
333rd floor, The Locus, Mumbai Prime

Beneath that grandiose masthead, it reads,

To,
Mr Bhaskar Kumar,
Unitary ID no. 01001110 01101111 01100010 01101111 01100100 01111001

Valued Citizen,
We regret to inform you that according to Article 43 of the Citizenship Act of 2038 as implemented by our glorious leader, may he live 1001 years, you are required to present yourself at the Ministry of Relevance to prove that you qualify for entitlement of domicile in the state of Mumbai Prime.

Failure to present yourself within seven days of receipt of this correspondence will result in automatic deportation.

Please bring complete evidence of birth, citizenship status, income, professional qualifications and genetic analysis to Room 97A between 9 a.m. and 4 p.m., Mumbai Prime time.

I cannot quite understand what exactly the letter is trying to say. It's like there is a sudden disconnect between my eyes and my brain, an involuntary aphasia. Frowning, I read it again, and then a third time, my dismay deepening with each subsequent examination.

'What is it?' Manasi asks, a look of concern wrinkling her brow when she looks up and notices my stricken expression.

'I'm not sure,' I say, and hand her the letter.

She scans through it before letting out a startled gasp. 'Bhaskar, I think it would perhaps be best if you called in sick tomorrow and sorted this out immediately.'

About eight years ago, when our glorious leader came to power for the fourth time, the government had decided that it was time to demolish the old Mantralaya complex in Nariman Point. In its place, they built a single tower, 900 storeys high, made entirely of black glass and space-age composites, which they decided to call the Locus.

For most citizens of Mumbai Prime, this ebony pillar has become a symbol for everything the city represents – growth, prosperity, the lure of a better future. Personally, though, I have always felt there was something malevolent about the Locus. I dislike the way it is visible no matter where you are in the city, watching over everything and everyone, like a prehistoric monolith. And in many ways, it is the perfect metaphor for all that has changed in Bombay since my childhood – the city's sinister new heart, so utterly black that even light seems to bend around it.

It takes me almost two hours and four different trains to get to the Locus from our house in the outer sprawl of Andheri North. I manage to get there by 9.30 a.m., but there is already a long line outside the entrance, a serpentine queue that snakes halfway around the base of the building. Reluctantly, I join it, stifling my natural impatience. It is a very hot day, and in a matter of minutes, I am drenched in sweat. Shading my forehead with a hat I fashion from a newspaper, I take out an old detective novel bought from a *raddiwalla* and try to read. Unfortunately, I just cannot concentrate. As I inch closer to the door, my trepidation increases, a foreboding that grows and grows, like a tumour eating away at my stomach.

It is almost noon by the time I finally make it inside. A map directs me to a clanking elevator which takes me up to up to the 333rd floor, where Room 97 turns out to be a small cubicle, little more than three plex walls inside which squats a large automaton.

I eye it curiously. I had heard the government has started using mechanoids instead of real people, but this is the first time I have seen one up close. Its blocky rectangular body is painted a matte brown, above which a sloping vidscreen serves as its face. For some reason, it seems to be wearing a peaked Maharashtrian topi, and there is a badge pinned to its chest, a name tag that identifies it as Shri R.O. Botkar.

As soon as I enter the cubicle, its face lights up. 'Please place your palm against the screen,' it drones.

I obey. The robot whirs for a moment, scanning my biometrics, and then without fanfare, a pre-recorded video presentation begins to play across its flat face.

A familiar bearded face fills the screen. The gentleman in question was once Bollywood's most famous film star. Though he has been dead for almost a decade, the government still uses a simulation of his visage for all its public propaganda.

'Aren't you tired of having no space to breathe?' his famous baritone inquires. 'Don't you hate the rampant overpopulation that is tearing our beloved city apart? It is to battle this most perfidious of social evils and reduce the pressure on our fair city's infrastructure that our glorious leader has initiated the relevance census of 2032. Soon, we shall be rid of the undesirables who crowd the streets, the tax evaders and freeloaders, the immigrants who steal your jobs, the unemployed, the deviants, the elderly, the anti-nationals who criticize the government and refuse to contribute towards our growth.

'Pursuant to this vaunted goal, our glorious leader has identified a variety of qualities that define the citizens worthy of residing in Mumbai Prime. These include profession, income, racial antecedence, consumption habits, moral turpitude, celebrity quotient, social influence, and ideological fidelity. Based on these factors, each citizen shall be assigned a relevance index value, and those whose ratings fall below the suitable isocline shall be expelled from the borders of Mumbai Prime, thus reducing the burden on citizens who are upright members of society and truly deserve the privilege of residing here.

'Congratulations, citizen, you have been chosen to help fulfil our glorious leader's vision of a better tomorrow.

'Together, we can, and we will, be great again.'

The video stutters to static, replaced by the single eye once more.

'As per notice 16/347/122,' the automaton drones, 'you, Bhaskar Kumar, have been selected to submit for relevance index testing. If you wish, you can request absentee evaluation and provide a letter of recommendation from a personage of established prominence with a relevance rating of 82 or higher. However, be warned, you must agree to be externed in a designated encampment for a minimum of seven to twelve months, which is the current tenure for absentee adjudication.'

'Twelve months!' I squawk. 'You have to be joking! Are there any other options?'

'Alternatively, you may choose to submit yourself for relevance testing immediately.'

I mull over both possibilities, and it does not take me long to make up my mind. I cannot leave my son and wife alone for a year with no income to rely on, which means I have only one choice: to comply.

'Very well. I will submit myself for testing now.'

'As you wish.' A series of blinking lights flash across the automaton's face. A moment later, its chest spits out a blank OLED slate, the kind they issue to children in school to take notes in class.

'Kindly proceed to room 96C to begin testing,' it announces. 'Good luck, citizen. Onward to a better tomorrow.'

Room 96C is not next to Room 97. Instead, it is two floors down and on the opposite side of the building.

I struggle to understand why, wondering what organizational system is at play here, but I simply cannot make any sense of it, no matter how hard I rack my brain.

Here, I find myself greeted by an identical automaton, except this one is dressed rather nattily in a very well-cut, double-breasted business suit and a pair of horn-rimmed glasses. Also, it has a tie painted on its torso, neat pinstripes outlined in a flourish of blue and red.

'Welcome to the Department of Social Statistics,' it drones, sliding out a tray for me to insert my slate into. 'Please submit your Twitterbook, Googlegram, Flutter, Voxverse and Cyberkind passwords so that your social relevance quotient can be verified.'

'Umm, I am not on social media,' I respond.

The automaton responds with a whir, followed by long clank, before it says again, 'Submit your Twitterbook, Googlegram, Flutter, Voxverse and Cyberkind passwords.'

'As I just said, I do not use social media. I think it is representative of our decline as a society. People spend so much time in the Virtuality that they barely have time for real human interaction. It's quite tragic.'

The robot considers this statement briefly. 'Subject has minimal online relevance,' it states, spitting out my slate with an almost disdainful sneer of a click. 'Proceed to Room 91B, to the Department of Celebrity Estimation.'

The automaton in 91B seems to be dressed as some sort of hipster, complete with a carefully rendered goatee and a pair of oversized sunglasses, wraparound wayfarers of the kind that went out of style in the late 2020s.

'On a scale of one to ten,' it asks me, 'how do you rate your celebrity quotient?'

'I don't understand the question,' I reply, scratching my forehead.

'Have you been featured on the news or on a zine in the last 22 weeks?'

'I have not.'

'Have you ever acted in a film and/or commercial?'

'No, I haven't.'

'Have you ever been part of a webcast or Realweb or Truthplay?'

'No.'

'Have you ever produced content for the web or the Virtuality?'

'I wrote a book once,' I say.

This admission is followed by a rather loud and unsettling whirring, not unlike the ticking a machine makes when it is beginning to overheat.

'Answer does not compute,' the automaton declares after a very long interval. 'Resetting analytic parameters.

'Are you related by blood or marriage to anyone with a relevance quotient of more than 80?'

'I…I'm not sure. I didn't even know what a relevance quotient was until I got here this morning.'

'Do you know someone famous who can recommend you?'

'I don't think so,' I reply.

'No one even a little famous?' it checks again, its tone almost forlorn.

'Well, I was in class with a boy years ago, when I was in primary. He is a very well-known actor now. Does that count?'

'Can you produce a duly signed affidavit confirming this childhood friendship as evidence?' the machine enquires.

'I…I don't believe I can.'

'In that case, the stated relationship is hyperbole and, therefore, inadmissible.'

With a clank, my slate is ejected.

'Subject has minimal assessable social value,' it declares.

'Kindly proceed for hygiene testing.'

A map pops up on my slate, instructing me where to go next. I follow the directions and make my way to Room 98U, which is on the ground floor.

Here, the automaton seems to be female. Its body is bright red and apparently it is wearing a facsimile of a sari painted with kanjeevaram motifs. An ornate mangalsutra adorns its blocky torso, accompanied by a smear of red sindoor across the top of its face-screen.

'Welcome to the Department of Moral Hygeine!' it exclaims, and a pipe pops out of its chest, ending in a narrow funnel. 'Kindly provide a urine sample in the designated outlet.'

'Wait! Are you saying you want me to pee into that pipe?'

'You have ten seconds to provide a sample – nine, eight, seven…'

Hurriedly, I unzip my trousers and step up. I try to force myself to urinate, but the best I can manage is a desultory trickle. Not only am I dehydrated after spending hours standing in the sun, but it feels exceedingly surreal, perverse even, to be trying to pass water into a metal pipe, especially one attached to a female robot.

Thankfully, my humble attempts seem adequate.

'Analysing,' the mechanoid purrs followed by a series of whirring clicks. 'Large quantities of hydrocarbons and cellulose detected, accompanied by high amounts of benzene and cholesterol. Have you consumed alcohol in the last 48 hours?'

'I have,' I admit shamefacedly.

'And you are non-vegetarian?' it enquires, its voice almost accusatory.

'I am.'

This admission is met by a series of disapproving pings.

'Studies initiated by our glorious leader have revealed that non-vegetarianism causes an excess of bile in the blood and promotes anti-national sentiments.

'It would be advisable, citizen, that you shift to a vegetarian diet and eschew alcohol. Good digestion leads to good citizenship,' it declares.

'Please proceed to Room 94P for professional valuation.'

Room 94P is in the basement, five floors below the surface. The automaton here is Sikh, it seems, for even though it is an androgynous metallic block like all the others, it is wearing a turban so perfectly tied that you could slice fruit with its edges.

'Welcome to the Department of Fiscal Nationalism,' it whirrs. 'For the purposes of professional valuation, please select your current occupation.'

A long and bewildering list of jobs flashes across my slate, everything from 'advocate' to 'zonal bank manager'.

'Umm, I am an author,' I say. 'I write children's books.'

This explanation is met by silence, interspersed only by three very deliberate beeps. 'Kindly choose your current profession now,' the automaton repeats.

The list scrolls across my screen again, to no avail. 'My profession is not included in your list,' I respond.

'That is impossible. This exhaustive database was prepared by the Ministry of Labour. It contains every occupation recognized by the government as viable.'

'Well, it doesn't mention what I do.'

'Do you wish to submit an exemption request? Be warned, there is a delay of at least nine weeks before an adjuster of claims will become available!'

'Oh, just forget it!' I exclaim. 'Let's just say I'm a journalist. I work with a gossip magazine, okay? I make my living writing about other people's secrets. There...are you happy now?'

This exclamation is greeted by a very long pause, after which the automaton announces, 'Let it be recorded that Subject 01001110 01101111 01100010 01101111 01100100 01111001 is uncooperative and prone to hysterical outbursts.'

'What?' I half rise to my feet, unable to hold back my irritation. 'I have been nothing but cooperative,' I start to say, but the machine cuts me off before I can complete my sentence, spitting out my slate almost disdainfully.

'Kindly proceed to Room 92X for biometric analysis.'

Room 92X, or the Department of Biometric Evaluation, turns out to be located, surprisingly, on the 92nd floor of the Locus, a laboratory with glass walls through which I can see the city spread out far beneath, a hodgepodge of scabrous tenements interspersed by skyscrapers that reach for the heavens like giant termite mounds.

Here, an automaton wearing a doctor's white coat proceeds to first measure my skull very carefully with a Vernier calliper.

'What exactly are you doing?' I enquire as it begins to prod my head with a probe shaped like a magic wand.

'It is scientifically possible to create a socio-phrenological profile of a citizen by mapping the deformities and eccentricities of their cranium,' it explains. 'For example, after examining the shape of your skull, I can conclude that 87 per cent of Prime citizens have lower brows and a more pronounced slope to their foreheads. That, combined with your increased cranial circumference, suggests increased brain capacity.'

'My IQ is 156,' I say proudly.

'Intelligence testing is a Western concept. Our glorious leader does not believe in IQ, only in relevance quotient. Now, please lie back so I can scan your body.'

It runs the wand over me slowly and exactingly. The device hums audibly, emitting a bluish light that feels warm against my skin, like an old space heater.

'Your score is only 44 on the pigmentation scale,' the automaton says. 'Unfortunately, that exempts you from the melanin quota.'

'The *what* quota?'

'There are special reservations for people who score 77 and above on the pigment scale.'

'As our glorious leader has enumerated in his majestic treatise, *The Reinvention of India*, traditionally the poorest segments, the downtrodden and the backward classes, are mistreated because they are dark-skinned. That is why he is committed to helping them become paler to ameliorate such dermal inequalities.'

'That's ridiculous!' I say, 'Not to mention, offensive!'

A coruscation of bright lights dances across the automaton's angular face, something akin to a machine code version of a scowl, I imagine.

'Please do not be bellicose. I am only doing my job.'

With that imprecation, it turns its attention to my feet. 'Your foot size is an eight,' it clicks after measuring them. 'That is not good.'

'Why not?' I ask, taken aback. 'That's the most common shoe size in the world!'

'After due study, it has been found that size 10 and above are the best sizes for good citizens. People with smaller feet, they are generally more anti-national.'

'I don't understand. What does shoe size have to do with nationalism?'

'Our glorious leader is a firm believer that you can tell everything about a person's character by examining their feet. In his exalted opinion, people with small feet tend to be easily moved, swayed by propaganda and rhetoric. People with large feet, on the other hand, are more resolute in their beliefs.'

'Let me guess,' I say sardonically, 'he has big feet, doesn't he?

'Our glorious leader has size 12 feet and a 55-inch chest. That is the perfect proportion. Small feet mean shaky foundations. Big feet mean a solid base.'

I want to laugh, but manage to hold it in. It isn't amusement, really, more disbelief. My initial bemusement has long since worn thin, whittled away by the sheer surreal quality of the day's events. Am I being pranked, I wonder suddenly, for some sort of Realcast? Suspicious, I glance around, searching for a hidden cam-drone, but all I see is the automaton, watching me patiently.

'Are we done?' I ask, suddenly feeling dizzy. 'I have to go back home to my family.'

'Not yet,' it replies. 'There is one more test.'

From the middle of its torso a long umbilical extrudes like a metal snake. Its tip, I notice, is capped by a gleaming three-inch long needle. Like a striking krait, before I can object, it jabs down into my forearm.

What follows is surprisingly painless. The only thing I feel is a dull throb as it draws out a vial of my blood, before folding in on itself, leaving behind a small blob of HealGel that feels like ice against my skin.

'What was that for?'

The automaton's only reply is a very industrious clank.

'Analysing…analysing,' it ululates, and then announces, 'After cultural hemoanalysis, the subject's genetic antecedents are found to be: 62 per cent Indo-Aryanic, 22 per cent Baloch-Afghanic, 9 per cent Euro-Asian, 8 per cent indeterminate. Conclusion: subject is predominantly North Indian and, therefore, non-indigenous to Mumbai Prime.'

'That's rubbish! My family has lived here for three generations. I was born here – and so were my father and grandfather.'

'Birth is irrelevant,' the machine intones, as if it is chanting a holy mantra. 'Blood is everything.'

'This is madness!' I exclaim, my patience finally coming to an end. 'How can you do this? How can you just abrogate everything India stands for? This is…it's unconstitutional.'

'The Constitution is obsolete. All that matters is our glorious leader's plan. He shall lead us into a golden age, a new *satyuga*.'

With that declamation, my slate pops out, and the automaton chirps, 'Please proceed to Room 99F for patriotic appraisal.'

It takes me almost half an hour to find 99F, which, as it turns out, shares space with a storage closet on the seventy-seventh floor. When I enter, pushing my way past a muddle of box files and cardboard crates, I am confronted by a robot that resembles a librarian, complete with a white wig pulled back into a severe chignon, and a pair of pince-nez glasses perched precariously across its square visage.

'Welcome to the Department of Patrio-Ontology,' it intones without any ado. 'Please state your educational qualifications in ascending order, from first to last.'

'I have a bachelor's degree in English literature and a master's in history.'

There is a palpable pause when I say the word 'history'. The automaton's screen turns a bright green, as if it approves of my answer.

'Our glorious leader is a keen admirer of history. In fact, he has written over 700 books on the subject. It is his exalted opinion that the history taught in schools is Western propaganda, and that the true contribution of India to the world has long been suppressed. Do you agree?'

I struggle for an answer. My immediate reaction is to roll my eyes and scoff at the obvious jingoism of such an assertion, but some primitive instinct warns me to hold my tongue.

'I…could we please just get on with my evaluation? I really want to get back home to my family.'

The green fades to a deep, disappointed black.

'Please state the date and place of graduation,' the machine drawls.

'I graduated from Yale University in America in 2019.'

A medley of lights skitters across the screen, punctuated by several strident squeaks.

'That date is prior to the election of our glorious leader,' the automaton squawks. 'As a result, as per our records, your academic accomplishments are now null and void. It is the conclusion of the state that the history you have studied is irrevocably biased. The true history of India only began with the ascension of the glorious leader and his sovereign party. Everything prior to that is misinformation and Western propaganda.'

'That's ridiculous,' I growl, leaning forward. 'You can't dismiss my academic record just like that! I was a Government of India merit scholar, for heaven's sake. Surely that has to mean something!'

'Do you dispute our conclusion?'

'Yes, I do. Vehemently! I dispute every single one of your ludicrous tests!' I am almost shouting now, my composure finally at its breaking point. 'This whole damn day has been ludicrous.'

A frantic frieze of sparks sputters over the automaton's face, punctuated by several strident squeaks. 'Let the record reflect that subject has demonstrated borderline dissident tendencies,' the automaton declares, spitting out my slate.

'Re-education is recommended,' it states.

'Kindly refer yourself immediately to the Department of Moral Accountancy.'

I find the Department of Moral Accountancy in a glass cube at the very top of the building, so high up that there are clouds beneath us.

I am utterly bewildered by the automaton here until it dawns on me that the three lines painted on its face-screen are caste marks. It is supposed to be brahmin, I realize, an inference which is confirmed once I see it has a white line encircling its torso, reminiscent of a sacred thread.

'Citizen, please sit,' it instructs. A flat metal bench slides out from its midriff. Biting back my trepidation, I obey and take a seat, until I am as close to the robot's flat face as a lover leaning in for a kiss. Unexpectedly, a pair of slim metal limbs unfurl from either side of its body like tentacles. Surprised, I rear away from them, but a pair of broad canvas cuffs slither out instantly and encircle my waist and chest, pinning me in place. All that I can do is wriggle ineffectually as the tentacles attach themselves to me; one fastening to my neck with a dull pop, and the other to the very centre of my forehead, their rubber edges clamping into place like leeches suckling on my skin. At the same time, a warmth floods through me, a sudden drowsiness when they connect, and I realize that the machine is pumping me full of some sort of a sedative.

'You are now connected to a lie detector,' the machine exclaims. 'Please answer all questions as honestly as possible, or your score will be calculated adversely.'

'Of course,' I nod, flying high on whatever drug I have been injected with. 'The whole truth and nothing but the truth, so help me god.'

'Subject Bhaskar Kumar, do you consider yourself a moral man?'

'That is a rhetorical question, isn't it? Morality is a very subjective thing. It changes with class and education, with income and upbringing. Personally, I have always agreed with Nietzche: that any moral system expected to be valid for all is basically immoral.'

'The subject is being evasive. Let his record reflect accordingly.'

'No, wait! I do consider myself a moral man – as much as any man can be moral these days.'

'Have you ever criticized our glorious leader?'

This question takes me by surprise. In spite of the drugs, I am aware enough to realize that I am on dangerous ground. This is not an enquiry. It is an inquisition.

'I have not,' I reply, unable to stop my voice from quavering.

My reply is greeted by a pronounced beep.

'That is a lie. According to our records, on 27 July 2029, you were heard telling your wife that this government is only interested in profit, not justice.

'On 18 August 2031 you stated, and I quote verbatim, "If only the glorious leader spent a little less time praising himself and a little more getting something done, we could be a great country."'

The machine drones on, listing a litany of transgressions against me, but I barely hear it. The drug is wearing off, its potency diluted enough to allow a wave of outrage to rise in my chest.

'You recorded our private conversations? You eavesdropped on what was said in the privacy of our home? That…that is illegal. It's appalling!'

'What's appalling, citizen, is your criticism of our glorious leader who is struggling to uplift our nation, endeavouring to enrich our people and make India a global power.'

'The right to express opinions is every Indian's most basic and inviolable right, you jumped-up toaster! It is our moral duty to object. You cannot have democracy without dissent. Don't you understand that?'

Even as I say those words, I realize how futile this is. I am arguing with a machine. It cannot exceed its programming, no matter how much breath I waste.

'Your only duty, citizen,' the automaton growls, ejecting my slate, 'is to obey. Anything else is anti-national.'

It is almost dusk by the time I find myself back in Room 97.

The drugs they gave me have worn off completely, leaving me with a terrible headache, a dull pulsing at my temples which makes me feel decidedly queasy. Squaring my shoulders, I stifle a grimace when I come face to face with Shri R.O. Botkar once again.

'Place your slate in the receptacle,' he orders.

I do as commanded. The slate disappears, and a panoply of lights, accompanied by a veritable operetta of beeps and clicks, dances across his face-screen.

I sit back, folding my arms across my chest, assuming it will take him a while to complete his calculations. Surprisingly, it takes only a matter of minutes, before the screen goes blank and he announces, 'Citizen, you have been assigned a relevance score of 42. Since that is lower than the demarcated limit of 75, you are subject to imminent deportation.'

'This…this is ridiculous!' I struggle to control my panic. 'I am a taxpayer. I work hard. I have a family, a son. Surely that means something. It has to.'

'Are you choosing to dispute your assigned score?' The automaton drones on, deadpan.

'I am. I do.'

'Very well,' I am most likely imagining it, but I think I sense a trace of irritation in his tone. 'The subject has chosen to appeal. Until a case officer is available for a hearing, he is to be removed to Extension Camp Z13 to await adjudication.'

'I don't understand. What does that mean?'

R.O. Botkar does not reply. Instead, more lights flash across his face, a flicker of yellow, then an urgent strobe of red that begins to pulse like a desperate heartbeat.

'Answer me, damn you,' I say. 'This is a blatant violation of my fundamental rights. I demand a phone call. Please…let me call my wife. She must be worried sick.'

R.O. Botkar's only response to my entreaty is a shrill siren, a klaxon that begins to blare out mournfully, making me flinch. I clap my hands to my ears, wincing at this deafening barrage of noise. Behind me, the door slides open, and I see the first human I have encountered all day, a heavyset guard dressed in a saffron uniform.

'Please follow me to the processing centre.' His tone is benign, but the way he fingers his sidearm in its holster clearly implies he will brook no disagreements.

Dazed, I realize I have no choice but to comply. Leaving the room, I emerge to find a line of men outside flanked by two more guards. Most of them are my age, dressed more or less like me, shabby but nondescript. All have the same bewildered, wide-eyed look on their faces, as if they are collectively in shock.

I fall in towards the back of the queue and allow myself to be led along. Like cattle, we are herded to a vast and cavernous room deep in the bowels of the building. Here, a team of technicians awaits us, clad in face masks and white scrubs.

It is all very civilized. There are no threats, no raised voices, not until one of the men ahead of me starts to argue.

'This is outrageous!' he squeals. 'You can't treat us like this. We have rights.'

Even as he launches into a tirade, one of the guards steps up behind him and shoots him once in the head. There is no warning, no scream, just a dull snap followed by a thump. I stifle a gasp, hurriedly taking an involuntary step backwards to avoid the spray of blood and brain tissue as he falls to the ground at my feet. To my dismay, I am not quite quick enough. One of my shoes leaves a sticky imprint smeared across the immaculate white floor, and I find myself thinking, 'Manasi would be furious if she saw what a mess I'm making!'

'Keep moving,' a voice behind me says, pushing me forward. The speaker is an old man, with white hair and a carefully trimmed moustache. 'Don't stop, or you'll be next.'

Numb, I shuffle forward, coming face to face with the first of the technicians.

'Please remove all your clothing and personal possessions,' he instructs, handing me a paper bag.

It is one of the most humiliating moments of my life. Silently, I strip down to my underwear and stand there until another technician hands me a brown coverall and a pair of canvas shoes. He gives all the others identical outfits, and we dress as silently as we undressed. Nobody can look anyone else in the eye – we are all too ashamed.

A third technician collects our bags from us, and a fourth hands us a small canvas satchel each. Surreptitiously, I rifle through its contents. It contains ten cubes of powdered water, a dozen bars of dry rations, five strips of generic antibiotics and, for some inexplicable reason, a can of spray-on contraception.

'Hold still,' the lead guard says, and a fifth technician steps forward, holding up what looks to be a plastic supermarket scanner. One by one, he presses it to our foreheads, above our left eyes. When it is my turn, I feel a wet searing, and when he pulls the scanner away it leaves a bright neon barcode behind. Dismayed, I scratch at it, trying to wipe it away, but whatever ink the machine has used is permanent and the barcode is branded into my skin like a tattoo.

When they are done marking us all, we are shepherded into another line and led six floors down to a deserted metro station in one of the sub-basements.

'A train will soon arrive to transport you to your new home,' the main guard announces. 'Please do not try to resist. There is no need for this to be unpleasant.'

I find myself waiting between the same old man who warned me earlier, and a tall, bespectacled fellow with gaunt shoulders and a wild unkempt beard that reaches almost to his chest.

'Che Basu,' he says, offering me a hand to shake. 'Card-carrying socialist.'

'Bhaskar Kumar,' I reply, 'failed writer with dissident tendencies.'

Che laughs and gives me a nod of resigned commiseration.

'Where are they taking us?' I ask him. 'Do you have any idea?'

'To the outskirts of the city,' he responds. 'I've heard they have built a camp there, an interment colony.'

'You're fools!' the old man interjects. 'They are going to kill us all. It is the final solution all over again. First Hitler, then Pol Pot and now our glorious leader. Get rid of the dissenters once and for all, the outliers and the thinkers, the agitators and the intellectuals. Only let the true believers live, the zealots and the oligarchs. That is what we have become – a nation of acolytes and sycophants.'

'You're mad!' Che scoffs.

'Am I? Or am I the only one who sees the truth?' His eyes take on a wild look. 'You can be cattle and let them lead you to the slaughterhouse, but I am not going to go gently,' he says. 'I am going to fight.'

With that declaration, he rushes at the nearest guard, who is taken completely by surprise. He starts to unstrap his gun, but the old man swings his satchel at him. It hits the guard squarely in the face. A wail escapes his lips as he collapses to the ground in a dead faint.

'What are you waiting for?' the old man screeches. 'Run, you fools. Run!'

His urgency stirs both me and Che the socialist into action. We exchange a look and then, in unison, break from the line. I dash left, Che goes right. There is an exit ahead of me, barred by a safety door. I make a beeline for it, praying that it will be unlocked. My shoulder blades itch terribly. I am sure I will be shot at any second, my body riddled by bullets.

Thankfully, the door swings open when I barrel my shoulder into it. I pause, casting one desperate glance behind me. They have the old man on the ground, three guards holding him as he struggles weakly to break free. Our eyes meet. He smiles and gives me a wink even as the man he knocked down stumbles upright and angles a pistol towards his head.

I turn and run. My feet lead me down a dank, dimly lit tunnel that opens into a bewildering maze of service corridors. I dash through them as fast as I can, turning blindly around random corners each time I come to an intersection, caroming off the walls.

Unfortunately, my escape comes to a premature end when I take one final turn and find myself at a dead end. Letting out a curse, I spin around, intending to retrace my steps, but the way back is blocked by a rank of approaching shadows.

I sink to my knees, letting out a groan when I realize I am trapped. That is when I spot it – a corroded iron grate hidden away in one corner of the passage. Desperate, I crawl over to it, and curl my fingers through its vents, pulling upward with all my strength. Behind me, the clatter of boots draws closer and closer, matching my frantic heartbeat.

For one awful moment, the grate refuses to budge, but in the next instant it comes loose with a deafening screech, sending me sprawling backwards. Hurriedly, I push aside the cover, and clamber into the hole beneath. A foetid stench fills my nose, the noxious odour of sewage. The walls are slick to the touch, covered with moss and effluvium. I try to lower myself slowly, but my hands lose their grip and I slip, sliding 15 feet into a miasma of shit and slime. It fills my nose and mouth, and I cough and choke, struggling to inhale.

It takes all my willpower to force myself forward, to push my way through the sludge. It is pitch dark, and I cannot see where I am going, but I refuse to give up. For what feels like hours, I crawl through those sewers until, at last, I see a square of light up ahead, a way out.

It is another, larger grate. When I squeeze past it, I find myself near a cistern of some kind, a reservoir filled with tepid water. Gasping, I tear off my coveralls, and immerse myself headfirst, trying to wash the stink from my nostrils.

Behind me, I hear a noise, a dull thump. I turn, just in time to avoid a body as it comes tumbling out of the grate to splash into the cistern. It is my socialist friend. His face is covered with blood, and there are a pair of ragged holes in his neck, twin bullet wounds slowly seeping scarlet into the ground.

I kneel over him, certain that he is dead, but unexpectedly his eyes flicker open. 'Help me,' he groans. 'Please, don't let me die like this, in this filthy gutter, like a rat.'

He reaches for me, one hand hooked into a claw. I bite my lip and bat his fingers aside, trying to loosen the strap of his satchel.

'I'm sorry,' I say, unable to look him in the eyes. 'I wish I could help you, but I have to go. My wife and son will be waiting for me.'

After that, everything is a blur.

I don't remember how I manage to get back home. I have no money and decide to avoid buses and trains altogether in case there are check-points. I end up walking most of the way. The sun is rising by the time I arrive at my building, a jaundiced dawn that makes everything seem unbearably yellow. When I see my apartment door at last, I breathe a sigh of relief. Collapsing against it, I ring the bell urgently, once, twice, thrice. After what seems an hour, my wife answers. She is bare-legged, dressed in one of my old Yale T-shirts. Her hair is tousled, her eyes bleary as if she has just woken up.

'You?' she gasps when she sees me. 'What happened to you?'

'I'll tell you everything later,' I say, reaching out to pull her into my arms. 'For now, you have to hurry. Take what you can, money, clothes, any tinned food we have. Pack it all and wake up Kanishka. We need to leave the city now. We can go to my uncle's house in Delhi. He's a lawyer. He will help us out.'

'Who is it?' a voice says from inside the flat. A moment later, a stranger emerges from our bedroom – a tall, broad shouldered man with a thin moustache and long black hair he wears slicked back. He is wearing my pyjamas, I notice, and my slippers too.

'Who the hell are you?' I shout, advancing toward him angrily.

Before I can get to him, Manasi pushes me back so vehemently that I crash into the door, sending it slamming shut.

'Look, Bhaskar,' she says, 'you need to calm down. This is Namit. The Ministry has assigned him to us. He has a relevance score of 83. Surely you understand, don't you?'

'*What*?' I look at the man in confusion and then at my wife. 'You – you replaced me? How could you?'

'You really are a dunderhead, aren't you,' Manasi says, her face twisting into a sneer. 'Who do you think called the Ministry in the first place?'

Her eyes are hard, as black and stony as agate, her mouth curved into a victorious, vicious little smile. *She is a stranger*, I think, dazed. This is not the woman I married, not the person I have lived with for the better part of two decades. This is someone I can barely recognize.

'Go away, Bhaskar,' she hisses. 'You were never good enough for us.'

When I hear those words, a sudden rage blossoms inside me, all the accumulated frustrations of the day coalescing into a fury so violent that I shiver.

I want to attack her, to wrap my fingers around her throat and strangle the breath from her lungs, but before I can move an inch Namit steps forward protectively and drapes one arm around her shoulders.

'You should go,' he says. 'I have called the police. They will be here any minute.'

As if to punctuate this declaration, I hear the wailing of a siren in the distance, drawing closer and closer.

'This isn't over,' I growl at Manasi. 'I am not going to let you get away with this.'

With that imprecation, I turn and dash away.

I leap down the stairs two at a time. As soon as I am past the foyer, I break into a sprint. Sadly, it is of no use. They are waiting for me just around the corner, a quartet of policemen clad in riot gear. There is no warning. As soon as I come into view, two of them hit me with stun darts. I fall to the ground, shuddering like a marionette. The other two hold me down and zip tie my hands and feet together efficiently, like a farmer trussing up a hog. Then, all four of them heft me up and drag me to a van nearby as if I am little more than a common criminal.

As they bundle me into the back of the van, I manage to turn to look up at my house one last time. I can see a shadow silhouetted in the window of my flat. It is my son. He is watching, his eyes wide with confusion.

'Don't forget me!' I try to scream as loudly as I can, but all I can manage is a hoarse croak. 'I am not a number or a statistic. I am a person. I matter.'

That is all I manage to say before one of the policemen leans over and hits me square in the face with a baton. My teeth crack, my mouth fills with the warm salt of blood, and I squeal, collapsing as he slams the door shut.

As the engine fires up, I hear my son's voice, that shrill, childish chirp I know so well.

'Mama,' he asks. 'Who was that man?'

'He is nobody, my love.' Manasi replies. 'He doesn't matter. He isn't relevant any more.'

DIMENSIONS OF LIFE UNDER FASCISM

JAYAPRAKASH SATYAMURTHY

The twins were the first to be flattened.

I was sitting on the porch, typing up reports on the classes I'd taught over the last week, sipping nimbu pani, keeping half an eye on them. It was a sunny summer afternoon, just a bit brighter and warmer than I preferred, but the twins, young and filled with coltish energy, loved it all, every minute of that last joyous three-dimensional summer weekend. They'd been playing with their skipping ropes – Anna and I tried to make sure our children had a mix of old-school and digital pastimes – and were cooling off, giggling to each other, watching videos on their tablets. The bright jingles of kiddy music made way for the soporific drone of one of those mandatory mantra breaks the government inserts into all media. The giggling stopped. I'd like to say there was some sense of foreboding in that moment, some cloud crossing the sun, some chill in my heart. Instead, I just felt a vague relief that the twins had quietened down and a surge of hope that I could finish my reports before dark.

A quarter of an hour later, with just a couple of reports left to finish, I looked up, shading my eyes with a hand. Everything seemed normal. The twins – Sara and Radha – were standing side by side, facing me, but gazing past me into the middle distance. As many twins do, they occasionally seemed to communicate on some non-verbal level and stand just so, communing in silence. The mantra from the tablet continued. I turned my attention back to my laptop. I had half-finished another report when the stasis began to bother me. I looked up again. The twins stood where they had been, absolutely still. I put my laptop aside, called out to them. Nothing. I got up, walked over. No response. I moved around to face them, trying to fathom what strange prank or fancy they'd happened on, when my world changed forever.

Because, as I walked around them, I saw that the twins had become completely flat – cardboard cut-outs of themselves, printed or painted in all their living colour on one side, absolutely blank, a dull, dark gunmetal grey on the other side. I walked around them once, twice, taking in the impossible reality. My twins – Sara, the quieter one, preferred scrambled eggs and toast for breakfast; Radha, seconds younger than her sister, given to tantrums, liked lots of idlis and even more vadas for the first meal of the day – were gone. They were no longer there. Or anywhere.

The mantra droned on. I reached out with trembling hands to feel my daughters – no, the cut-outs that they were now. I felt my legs give way and found myself on the lawn in front of them. Nothing made sense. Panic took hold – a tightening of the chest as I cried and called out the girls' names, called out to Anna, even though she wasn't there, even prayed to the gods I hadn't thought seriously about in years. I tried calling Anna, but my hands were trembling too much. I dropped my phone and lay down on the ground, moaning.

Anna found me – us – like that when she got back from her shift at the hospital. It took her a while to understand what had happened. For a moment or two, she thought it was some elaborate set-up, that I'd somehow had these props made and hidden away our beautiful twins just to play a stupid prank on her. That was when I started to hyperventilate. When she finally believed me, for a while, we panicked together, Anna sobbing and shaking uncontrollably in my arms. Then she too quietened down – the shock setting in, perhaps. We sat side by side, staring at our girls in disbelief. At some point, the mantra on the tablet had wound down, and a series of cheerful jingles tinkled out and echoed around us, and the shadows grew long and merged with the evening.

In the first days after the twins became flat, Anna and I were inconsolable. We took leave from our respective jobs and tried everything we could to reverse whatever condition had afflicted them. We brought them, or whatever had replaced them, into our home, propped them up in their bedroom in their favourite corners, prepared their favourite treats and piled them up in front of them, played the songs they loved, then songs they hated – corny old nu metal and EDM from our teen years. Nothing changed the fact that our lovely, whimsical, so-similar-yet-so-different girls were gone. When time ran out and we were needed in our offices, we each took a twin with us and propped them up at our workplaces. What if we missed the moment when everything would just switch back to normal, when our girls would call out for us in their shrill, gleeful voices?

That's when we found out we weren't alone in our predicament.

It was happening to everyone, everywhere. In this twenty-sixth year of the MoSha Rajya, people were turning flat all over Bharat. Anyone could be flattened – it happened to the young and old, rich and poor, adults and children alike. The common factor in all these instances was that some kind of state-mandated spiritual content seemed to be present when it happened. But avoiding the chants was not an option – it caused people's social credit score to drop dangerously. 'Soldiers are dying on the border!' a pop-up wraith admonished me once, 'And you can't even listen to 10 minutes of tapas a day?'

People continued consuming their daily dose of prayers and hymns and chants, and the flattening fell upon whomever it chose, driven by a logic, an algorithm we were not privy to.

Eventually, there was no workplace or home or public space without at least one flat person in it. The principal at the school that I taught in was now literally the mere figurehead he'd been for a while. A bus driver was flattened at rush hour and the pile-up that followed was unprecedented, even by the standards of mid-twenty-first-century Bharatiya megalopolises. Policemen found themselves pursuing flattened criminals. Debtors halted in their fearful flight, their thuggish pursuers rendered inert and two-dimensional. Workforces and consumer groups fell to the attrition of the flattening.

Yet, life carried on. For Anna and me there was a strange sense of relief – our perfect girls, our beloved twins, were suspended, forever free – nothing could happen to them any more. It was only we, in the three-dimensional world, who were still vulnerable, still susceptible. Life nibbled at us, tore chunks out of us. A mixed-religion couple, we lived in constant dread that the government would finally repeal the Special Marriages Act and nullify our bond. Regulations multiplied. I had to make an appearance at a stipulated number of bhajan meetings and prayers. Anna had to demonstrate that she was steadily learning more about Hindu religion and culture.

At school, syllabi were rewritten at regular intervals. Sometimes, a new textbook was declared 'secular' – and thus forbidden – instants after my students had downloaded it onto their tablets. Mo and Sha paraded around, not just on our screens, but also as holograms on our main streets and sometimes on special days of prayer and unity in our homes. Their girth grew as the territory of Bharat shrunk, its northern reaches lost to the big Chinese whale, and other portions of it to secession and bloody rebellion. At least the flattened ones retained an unshakable serenity, a changeless, timeless impunity that was almost enviable.

Caught between a dead-end life in three dimensions and the freedom of a life without depth, we, the people, started to look for ways out.

The bulldozer had become a common sight in our cities. It was a kind of remedy, a way to join loved ones and nemeses lost to the flattening. All you needed to do was call an 1800 number, make a money transfer on our state-provided apps, lay down on the road and wait. Some chose the cover of a blanket or a tarpaulin; some braved the ordeal uncovered. Some had their families flattened with them, some no longer did or chose not to bring them along for their own flattening. One thing was certain: no one who had undergone the process ever complained afterwards.

That was good enough for us.

On a sunny afternoon, not unlike the one when I'd been sitting on the porch finishing up my reports, we lay under a tarp, Anna and I, holding hands, and each of us holding the hand of one of the girls by our side. The bulldozer was on its way. We could feel its rumbling in the road, in our bones. This was the crowning moment of our story, our life together. I kissed Anna. Her tears were sugar on my lips.

THE SONG OF ICE

SOHAM GUHA
Translated by Arunava Sinha

1

Life was, in fact, an unfamiliar roadmap, many of its corners shrouded in darkness while others were lit up by floodlights. I had walked some of the way, the world changing before my eyes more or less instantly. Calcutta was an unknown city to me now. From the roof of a tall skyscraper, bracing against the cold, looking out at the horizon to the north revealed a blue layer of something like a cloud, a gigantic cold wave expanding its realm at a majestically slow pace.

On the fossilized pavement beneath my feet was a brownish stain, a streak of dried blood. I didn't have enough time to collect a sample. The weather was calm in Calcutta, like a tundra spring. I looked up anxiously when a sliver of sunlight caressed my cheek. A circle of blue sky was opening up overhead, the eye of the storm rushing in the direction of Bowbazar. Clutching the straps of my bag, which were about to snap from the weight of its contents, I lengthened my stride. The two guards outside the entrance to the metro station were expecting me; as I climbed down the stairs, I could hear the shutters being closed behind me. Yet, a fragment of the ice-cold air outside accompanied me to the ticket counter, where dust had not yet obliterated the words 'Welcome to Central Metro Station'.

Some of the kids were waiting for me. They ran up asking, 'Got it, Uncle?'

They hadn't yet learnt to suppress their hunger the way their parents had, hadn't trained themselves not to allow the helplessness to show on their faces. I pulled out a packet of Marie biscuits from my bag; I knew this was what they were waiting for – every time I went outside, they had just the one demand: 'Bring us something, Uncle.' The smiles on their faces at this moment made me feel that risking my life to walk around on the surface was worthwhile.

I'd never been a particularly selfless man though, and I wondered why I was having these thoughts now.

'Listen.' I turned around at the familiar female voice. Her curly black hair was peeping out from beneath a hat, her stomach was swollen under her jacket, her unclipped toenails were visible through her torn boots. 'Why can't you take someone with you?'

With a smile I put my hand on her protruding belly. 'I can't deal with a companion up there, Rita.' We had been waiting seven months now for our child. I might be the elected leader of Central, but my heart and home had been devoted to just one person for a long time now. From where we stood we could hear the roar of the snowstorm over our heads, testing its teeth and claws on the worn-out shutter of the entrance to the metro station. It was strange to think about how different our lives would have been today had the Yellowstone volcano in America not erupted three years ago. We would have been thinking about fees for doctors and the hospital, not worrying about life and death. That day, three years ago, was still vivid in our memories.

'Winter is coming, Sangram.' How easily Rita had uttered the words sitting cross-legged in a revolving chair in her office as she chatted to me over a video call. We had awoken in the initial hours of morning two days earlier to a resounding boom, whose funereal reverberations suggested that its source was distant. Our fifth-floor windowpanes had rattled loudly in response. Canada and the USA had been disconnected from the world a short while earlier, but we didn't know this yet. Rita's job as a junior climatologist at the Indian Space Research Organisation's Alipur office gave her access to live feeds from several satellites. Her forecast that day, made partly in jest, was now our grim reality.

I knew only too well, as did the other able-bodied people who went out to forage, that we were running out of food. From Sealdah in the east and Hajra in the south (the metro tunnel had been abandoned beyond that after it caved in) to Belgachhia in the north and B.B.D. Bagh in the west – that was the extent of our excursions. Reason and prudence dictated that we walk no further than a distance from which we could run back to safety in case of a snowstorm. Calcutta was a sprawling city, but there was not much food left in this small area for the 320 of us. We had not yet summoned up the courage to inform the others about this. Panic was contagious and incurable this winter. Rita knew a path out of this predicament, but I was not in favour of walking on it. It was nothing but a cactus garden.

'Can't you ask?' Rita became impatient, even intolerant sometimes, when confronted with my obstinacy. Her question came after I had handed over the bag to the storage manager. Instead of answering, I explained the contents to the manager. The medicines I had managed to gather would see us through for a while, even if they couldn't be used for serious illnesses. 'There's insulin, and syringes too,' I told the manager. 'Tell Parimal to be careful about how much he uses.'

'You can't keep evading my question, Sangram.' The rage in Rita's voice was palpable now. Her anger was justified because she was right. But arriving at a truce with Howrah was out of the question. The commander of Howrah at this time was Noor Alam. If it had been 1947 I might have said the name was the reason for my animosity. But no, born as it was in 2031 under the ruins of the world, the bad blood between us owed nothing to communal feelings. At least, I hoped not. Civilizations are replaced, ships make way for atomic destroyers, but the human mind remains as unchanged as the ancient bristlecone pine.

A nanosecond before India had become independent, when my forefather had not yet arrived penniless on the last train from Barishal to take shelter in a Sealdah slum, Calcutta had been submerged in rivers of blood gouged out by communal knives. Subhash Chandra Bose's dream had lain in tatters at the Hajra Road intersection that day around the sleeping masses. Yes, almost a hundred years had passed since then, and the planet had allowed us to close our hands around it for a moment before being destroyed. Snug in this short-lived cocoon, we had assumed ourselves emperors of the world, unleashing our tyranny on nature. Perhaps, today, we are expiating our sins. It is just that human nature is beyond mutation. Perhaps the ability to hide beneath an umbrella when it rained or in the embrace of air conditioning in summer, so that we could live in comfort, had led us to put on masks. Viewed from the outside, we were a perfect race then, all of us equal, all of us enjoying the same rights and privileges. But this winter had blown the mask away, exposing our frostbite-afflicted real forms, all teeth and claws and little else.

Hindus and Muslims could be brothers, but the battle of Kurukshetra was fought among brothers too.

'Rita.' I took her hand to help her down the stairs.

'Tell me something – I know that Central is much more valuable to you than I am, but do you not think of me even once before going out there? Or of our unborn child?'

I had an answer to this, but it did not escape my lips. I knew my silence enraged Rita, and yet I had no choice but to hide the truth from my wife; she did not know the source of the nightmares that woke me up at midnight in a cold sweat.

From the point where the stairs ended to the extremity of the platform, there were nothing but rows of tents. Fires burned in front of some of them; books from the warehouses on College Street were our primary kindling now. Heated currents of air rose lightly though the ventilation shafts to emerge in the world outside. The smell of burning paper brought a sudden rush of memories. It was 26 July once again.

Three months had passed since the Yellowstone eruption. Calcutta's skies had been overcast throughout, even though, unlike in Europe or Japan, there had been no hailstorm of burning rocks the size of entire houses. It seemed like our country as well as the villages of Africa had escaped virtually unscathed compared to the rest of the world. But, in fact, the creator was holding back something bigger for us – the song of ice, whose melody could freeze the blood as it flowed to the heart. Three days after the snowfall began, the western horizon darkened, and the storm was upon us.

In my childhood I had heard about monstrous cyclones like Aila or Phailin from my father. I'd observed that he would get goosebumps in excitement whenever he spoke of those experiences. Thirty years later, I realized what the term 'nature's fury' meant. Calcutta was shut down under 40 inches of snow. You could hear a pin fall during rush hour on M.G. Road. The streets were covered in ice dunes, only the blue tops of the once-plying buses rising above them. We were shivering in our flat, the windows vibrating uncontrollably in the wind, keeping ourselves warm by lighting long-unused kerosene stoves, while our neighbour's white Persian cat wailed miserably. That night, an abnormal silence woke us up. We knocked on the neighbour's front door only to find it unlocked. The old woman who lived in the flat was asleep in her armchair, the cat lying quietly in her lap. In the glow cast by my lighter, I saw their bluish white faces. They had frozen to death.

A half-read book lay near the woman's feet, one among the many books in her gigantic library. She had considered her own eclipsed life less valuable than the lifeless reams of paper in those books. I really didn't understand people… That huge collection of books ensured that the plummeting mercury couldn't defeat us for another week. That's why I always thought of the smell of burnt paper as life itself.

A week later, we arrived at Central Station, on the heels of another group of people.

I didn't realize I had come to an abrupt halt at the bottom of the stairs; it was Rita's voice calling my name that brought me back to reality. Before drawing the curtain across the opening to our tent, I looked around at our current dwelling. The place was still warm and habitable. Earlier, we could hear faint strains of the azan from the direction of the lines connecting Dharmatala to Howrah, but they had quietened for some time now. Despite our conflict with those who sang it, the menacing silence sent shivers down my spine.

'You wanted to say something?' I asked, drawing the curtain. A petrol lamp was burning dimly, its yellow beams making Rita look like Gustav Klimt's *Hope*. A feminine lustre radiated from her sculpted form.

'What do I do with you, Sangram? I don't question your worthiness to be a leader – I know no one is more suitable.' Pausing, she looked at me for a moment and then said, 'But does Central take you for granted? Why must you be the one who has to go every time?'

I smiled. 'That's a primary aspect of my work, Rita. I'm the leader, not the owner. The responsibility for this last kingdom of man is mine. I go because there are others who follow me out. The owner asks for the road to be built, the leader shows the way.'

'There *is* an alternative, though, which you know but won't accept. Noor and their friends have a greenhouse lit up by a wind turbine. While we live by lamplight and survive on scraps stolen from shops. How much longer? We may not need Noor, but we desperately need their fresh vegetables.'

Stubbornly I said, 'Very well, let me see what I can do.'

2

I was setting foot in Quest Mall for the first time since the snowfall had begun. Nothing had changed, but the trespassing snow and a frightening emptiness occupied the ground floor. Shards of glass lay everywhere. A battle had broken out here; some people had made a last-ditch effort to survive. Attaching the sledgehammer to my shoulders, I clambered up the mounds of snow and went in. The escalator leading to the first floor, now immobile, greeted me. Like in many other spots in the city, I had many memories here too.

'The oceans will rise, Sangram, and we may have to flee from our homes yet again.' Baba's voice seemed to bear a draught of wind from the past into the mall. The time he had come back from the office, taking off his sweat-soaked shirt, crushed by the crowds in the bus, to hang it on the clothes rack for use the next day, the time he had drifted into the kitchen like a spectre, sick with the loss of Ma, and put the kettle on the boil. I hadn't realized how much pain he was channelling through those words. By the time I had, I was suddenly a grown-up, and Baba only a memory and heartbreak. He would bring his motherless son to the mall, and I would be dazzled by the false glory of the glass-fronted showrooms with their array of glittering commodities. I often made demands, and Baba would inevitably go beyond his means to make me happy. I didn't know why he did it. My own child was still asleep in the warmth of its mother's womb, but the world had blocked the path I could have taken to understanding my father's emotions.

A man could become extraordinarily selfish for the sake of his child. Was I going to be the same way for my own unborn offspring?

The weather was calm today and the sky relatively clear. There seemed to be a streak of blue on the murky canvas. Another storm was on its way, a violent one. This was the stillness before the turbulence – a cataclysmic force was coiling up on the eastern horizon, ready to strike, the cloud was probably hovering above Ghatakpukur. If the storm were to break over Calcutta in the next few hours, I would freeze to death.

I spotted a man, to the right of the shop named Laurel. Particles of ice were suspended from his reddened beard and eyebrows. His uncovered skin was the colour of pale bluebells, his lifeless eyes were fixed on me. I knew the man. Rather, I used to know him. Mohammed Sajid, Noor's right-hand man. What was he doing here?

After gathering all that I needed, I ransacked Sajid's clothes shamelessly with the expectation of finding something useful. That was when I saw it – a circular lump of flesh missing from his abdomen. The teeth marks around the wound were still clearly visible. A drop of sweat appeared on my forehead, freezing instantly.

Those teeth had belonged to a human.

3

Rita was finding it had to believe what I told her. 'Someone *ate* Sajid?'

'I'm sure of it.' I enfolded her soft hand in mine. 'We have been cut off from the other side of the river for quite some time. I don't know what changes have taken place in Howrah over the years. Heh, I don't even know if they're dead or alive.' After some hesitation, I told Rita about the bloodstain I had seen on the pavement. The sound of her cracking her knuckles told me she was deep in thought. Her brow was creased in anxiety. Licking her dry lips, she said in a measured tone, 'Meet him at once.'

'Why?' I couldn't fathom her reason for saying this. We still had enough food for six months. Why now, why this very moment, considering we had withstood the most critical period? We were doing well, or at least as well as possible, in this frozen world. Rita had probably read my mind. Curling up close to me, she said, 'Remember Digha?'

In our third year in college, when my romance with Rita was at its most intense, we had gone to the seaside resort of Digha for some intimate time with each other. We had to do it in secret because our society had not accepted (and still hasn't) pre-marital relationships; it was considered a distortion of our culture. 'India is a land of tradition,' someone had declared aeons ago.

Digha was the only place nearby we could afford on our meagre budget. It was like a desert by then, thanks to global warming and rising sea levels. One or two hotels remained, like humpback whales rising out of the water. Unable to move, they had watched helplessly as the water expanded its kingdom. A desalination plant occupied the location of a former beach in New Digha. After converting saline water to potable water, the plant supplied it through pipelines to the areas of Purulia, Bankura and the two Medinipurs that suffered from water scarcity. That was where we had met the chief technical engineer of the megastructure, who took it upon himself to be our tour guide. 'Come, let me explain it all to you.'

We hadn't sized up Noor properly at that first meeting. There was a manic glitter in his eyes, like the moon reflected in a placid pond. He obviously had a brilliant mind, for managing the plant and then building the greenhouse were not the work of ordinary brains. He had noticed that Rita sported no signs of being married and had guessed why we were visiting this desolate spot. But he hadn't said it then – he had only told me about it later, when we met for the last time in the metro tunnel.

That day he had stood in front of the enormous machine and said, spreading his arms wide like Jesus, 'I feel like god with this machine.'

Like he said later, 'I am the god of Howrah.'

Before I could ask him a question, he had wheeled around to look at me. 'This machine sucks up the water from the sea like Agasyta. I created it – you could say it is my child. Does that not make me god? It's only thanks to me that villages parched for water have crops in their fields today. Four entire districts depend on my plant now.'

After a pause, during which he scanned Rita from head to toe, he had said, 'All of us believe in god whether we want to or not.'

His words had left a mark on my mind. Even as a staunch atheist, I had ended up mumbling 'Save us, o god!' whenever there was a crisis hovering over Central.

'I remember,' I told Rita. 'What do you have in mind?'

'Do you also remember what Romita and Shaiontoni found in Kumortuli?'

My eyes brightened. 'I do. And the date approaches.'

'Sangram, we must have the incantations recited by him. Make the arrangements any way you can. Noor is bound to come.'

4

*'Yaa chandi... Madhukaitabadhi daityadalini... Yaa mahishisomalini... Yaa dhumkeshana chandamundamadani...'*No, the sun hadn't risen today. Nor had the heady fragrance of shiuli flowers welcomed an autumnal sky. No special editions of newspapers had announced the advent of Debi Paksha, the fortnight of Durga Puja. The ritual of painting the eyes on the idols of the goddess in Kumortuli had long ceased. But it was 16 October, and the first day of the special fortnight had arrived nevertheless, following the dictates of the calendar. Something was alerting the moribund city and its children to wake up and shake off their sleep. At the confluence of the north–south and east–west lines of the metro at the Esplanade station, Birendra Krishna Bhadra was reciting the *Mahishasuramardini*, facing west, towards Howrah. The source of his stirring voice was a pair of speakers powered by a battery. Normally, the cacophony of Calcutta's people and traffic would have drowned the sounds of these puny speakers, but today they were the only custodians of the human voice amidst silence. The tunnel reverberated with the incantations. I gazed absently at the railway tracks – had I been right to go along with Rita's suggestion?

'What is religion, Sangram?' she had said. 'The Radcliffe Line had split Bengalis from one another, Punjabis from one another. It had succeeded because our gods are not the same. Enough of that old song now, why go on with it? Isn't the word of human beings more important than the word of god in whatever little is left of this world?'

Rita was right. Nature had given us a chance despite all the curses it had heaped on us.

The digital player fell silent after the audio file ended. But no footsteps could be heard approaching from Howrah.

I was worried by his absence. Given Noor's understanding of our religion, he should have been here. He knew what the incantations meant, a call for truce. If he had even an iota of good sense, he would have come.

Why hadn't he?

Airtight valve-operated doors had been set into the tunnel for emergencies where it went under the river after the Writers' Building station. The levers were rusting now, which meant I had to employ superhuman effort to get them to move. Pulling out the master key I had taken from Noor – he had the other one – I inserted it into the hole and pushed.

Even if the conflict was ostensibly between Central and Howrah, it was actually between Noor and me. Each of us was right when on our own turf, and neither was willing to yield even an inch. Society had inculcated this acrimony, this intolerance for one another's religion since the day we were born, and this was the outcome.

If it became necessary to bury our heads in the sand like ostriches for another century because of the storms, if the next generation were to be born in this darkness, it would be difficult to convince them that we were once the emperors of this world, that we had built towers of concrete, that steel and glass which had kissed the clouds, that we had voyaged to the bottom of the oceans, that we had made space our slave, that our footprints had been visible on the moon and on Mars. All of this was obliterated, in the past, now. They would never know what an avalanche of humans really meant, that there had been 11 billion of us on earth once. They would think we were exaggerating. But we would know, till our last breaths we would know; till the moment we said goodbye to our minds and our bodies, we would know. We would take a million memories with us to our cold graves – the smell of new books, the familiar cries of a bus conductor soliciting passengers for his near-empty vehicle, the barking of a solitary dog at midnight, the whistle of the last train.

Our children would not believe humans had been born to breathe fresh air and not to suffocate in this stagnant environment. They would blame us for their condition. 'Was it necessary to have given birth to us?' The question was certain to be flung at us. It was true, we had no right to be parents. Today, Rita was pregnant and paying the price for my folly. The previous generation was always considered culpable by the next one. 'Why couldn't you control pollution?' we used to ask our parents, who, in turn, had cornered their parents about the Naxal movement. And *their* parents had blamed the previous one for the Partition. But no one was really responsible, this gene pool of sins was going through eutrophication from one generation to the next. The world was not ours to inherit – it was a loan from our children, with interest due.

After some hesitation, I finally pushed the valve door with all my strength, two burly men from Central also pitching in. When it opened after some grumbling creaks, my nose was tickled by the icy wind drifting in. This wind was not welcome inside the tunnel.

I looked over my shoulder at Rita. She was holding a paraffin lamp, which threw both light and shadows on her face. All the occupants of Central were ranged on the platform behind her. Her lips were exceptionally clear in the light, and they were trembling with anxiety.

Entering the section of the tunnel beyond the opening, our three-member team closed the door behind us. Several cracks had appeared in the walls here; shining our torches into them revealed glittering eyes. The air was filled with squeaks, but for some reason the rats didn't attack us. The few we saw running away from the arcs of our torches were palpably plump. Considering we were rationing our food, what *were* they feasting on?

I might have given this more thought, but our progress had slowed down. The closer we got to Howrah, the colder it became, and the tunnel grew brighter. I asked the others to switch off their torches. After turning a corner, we were almost blinded by a dazzling disc of light. When our eyes readjusted, we discovered it was the other end of the tunnel. But why was there light where there wasn't supposed to be any?

Nervousness made me pick up pace, and we practically ran through the few metres that separated us from the end of the tunnel. We were greeted by snowflakes as clear as crystals drifting from the sky.

But Noor wasn't here, waiting for us with a pistol. Nor were any of his followers, utterly devoted to their Noor Bhaijaan. Dr Ajmal Malik, the finest gynaecologist in India before the Ice Age, was not there either. Kamalbhai, Yakubbhai and Salema Bibi, with whom we had celebrated many an Eid, were missing as well. They had never considered me an outsider because of my faith – they had accepted me as one of their own.

All that was waiting for us in Howrah was an inexorable emptiness. The light belonged to a dead morning sun. Howrah had merged into the earth, a snow-covered Pompeii. We could not estimate when the ceiling had collapsed into the ground. Our eyes were steely, and our knees weak. All our questions were now lying as answers in front of our eyes.

Why were the rats so well-fed? Why had Sajid risked his life to escape to Park Circus? Why hadn't Noor turned up? Why had the azan stopped?

A battle had raged here soon after the ceiling had collapsed. Not like the one at Troy, but no less than it. The battle had been between brains about to shut down and hungry bellies. It would have been difficult to know who had won had the ice not stopped the march of time.

'They…they *ate* one another,' one of my companions muttered.

The corpses lay scattered across the landscape in front of us. Not one was intact or uninjured. The rational mind had accepted defeat to starvation, and they had pounced on one another. Howrah had fallen. The optimism that I had felt, the optimism that Rita had imbued in me, solidified into lumps of flesh amidst the wreckage that confronted us. No greenhouse, no one to sign a truce. No Noor either. His brain had flatlined, for which his ideology was responsible.

Noor used to consider humans parasites, created only to tyrannize the world. We had become pariahs for nature by inventing civilization. Humans should now leave for the sake of the earth.

Standing there in Howrah, I couldn't, for some reason, tell Noor's spirit, 'You're wrong, humans will survive – they have to.' Our mutually contradictory beliefs collided to become a ball of panic that lodged itself in my throat. Feeling my hands trembling inside my gloves, I turned my empty gaze to my companions, unable to articulate the reason for my fear.

Amidst the skeleton of Howrah I had just seen Central. I had seen myself tearing at another human's flesh with my teeth, without the slightest compunction or remorse. I had cast my eyes downward to see Rita's body lying still beneath my blood-soaked hand. I had slit her womb open, the foetus's flesh was between my teeth.

I slumped to the ground, my fall cushioned by the soft snow. The sky buzzed and whirled above my heard.

I shook my head vehemently. This nightmare could not be allowed to become reality. We would run out of food sooner or later, and I had no idea where to get more. Noor was responsible for what had happened to Howrah; his wild eyes were a symptom of his madness.

I murmured to myself in an effort to calm my shocked senses. The nightmare was blurred now, as though a translucent curtain had been drawn over it. I wasn't Noor, I was sane. The responsibility for Central rested on my shoulders. And an even bigger responsibility would soon be mine – that of being a father.

The curtain that separated me from the nightmare was called hope. It was our only map to navigate an uncertain future.

Suddenly, I was startled by a sound from the sky. Was I imagining it, or was that really the whirr of a helicopter in the distance? I looked questioningly at my companions. They had heard it too.

5

Australia. It snowed here from time to time, but not with the intensity of the northern hemisphere. All of us were in Noor's debt; he had accomplished his greatest feat before dying. And that was how he had won – by establishing communication with the world outside. It was December now, but even a summer of 10 degrees was bearable. The northern hemisphere was uninhabitable, but the world was huge. The prairies had replaced the Amazon forests, Australia now had England's climate and everything had changed. And, yet, humans had not become extinct.

Farmland stretched out to the horizon in front of me. We had been growing crops over the summer months. Once a desert, the soil was now displaying its fertility after the rains by giving us the gift of golden grains. But I couldn't tarry here, Rita had been admitted to a hospital in Perth. I looked up at the sky, marvelling at of the fact that I felt no fear at the sight of cumulonimbus clouds.

6

Outside, there was torrential rain. Inside, my wife screamed in pain. I stood, transfixed. Noor had told me once that god protects the unruly and the reckless, those who seek happiness for others, showing the way. I had dismissed him. The fact was that I had never quite learnt who the real Noor was. In the first phase, he was a stubborn engineer, and in the second a supercilious leader. Who has he really? Was he the man who had constructed an underground greenhouse for Howrah, powered by wind energy, or was he the man who had had a scuffle with me because of a clash of ideologies? I didn't know. I had not been able to give him the posthumous honour he deserved. He was still lying there, staring with sightless eyes at the dark sky through the collapsed roof of a tunnel.

My thoughts were interrupted, for the doctor had come out of the delivery room, smiling gently. 'Are you the husband?'

I nodded, mesmerized already. The cries of a newborn baby wafted out through the open door.

GOODBYE IS THE SHAPE OF A PALM PRESSED TO THE SKY

LAVANYA LAKSHMINARAYAN

Histories repeat themselves; every herstory is her story in its own way.

The first time we made love, we lay on my terrace looking out at the stars through a canopied screen of fungi-flora.

'I could fall off the face of Terra and into the sky any minute,' I said.

'You won't fall. You'll fly,' you replied.

'That sounds familiar. Where have I heard that before?' I asked.

'In your heart,' you said. 'Some people are born to defy gravity.'

You covered my skin with kisses.

I'm a new chapter in this story. This story of the women in my family. I can now trace them back four generations, all the way to Earth days. A rare claim on Terra II.

It began with the package that arrived on our doorstep a few months ago.

You frowned uncertainly as I made my way to the garage, following me as I popped open the door of our StarBuggy. A whoosh of air rushed past as I stepped into its hull. The lights whirred alive, and its in-built personable flight assistant said, 'Decompression: Complete. Portal: Open. Greetings on this brand-new day!' You hovered at the doorway, uncertain of whether to step through it.

I frowned down at the titanium box, then released the latch. Inside was a large cloth bag made of fading red silk, carefully embroidered with a symmetric pattern of curves and curlicues – some sort of ancient flower or fruit motif. I sat on the floor, wary of any breakables within, and pulled its drawstring open.

Out came a little glass cylinder. A delicate two-dimensional stencil of a flower danced across its label. I shook it to check if it was effervescent. It wasn't. The liquid was a pale shimmering gold. I unscrewed the lid and a heady scent shocked me into a headache.

Squinting through the onrush of pain, I turned it over and read the scrawl on its label. *Jasmine ittar.*

I shut the bottle tightly and placed it on the floor.

Rooting around the bag once more, I pulled out what appeared to be an ancient device. A flat square of glass lay in my lap. I'd only seen this tech in documentaries.

I swiped to unlock it. It was dead. I turned it over and caught sight of a tiny lithium battery hidden within its shell. I laughed out loud. I'd have to make it work using solar cells.

I then pulled out a thick leather-bound journal and ran my hands over the lush, vintage paper – a luxury resource from Earth days. There was also a small ornamental box, filled with mud, labelled *Earth*. I sniffed its alien scent before putting it aside. I pulled out a gold ring set with rubies in an intricate swirling pattern. I ran my fingers over it – its spiral resembled the Milky Way. I slipped it onto my finger.

A fully functional expandable terrarium rolled out, and I caught it in my palm before it fell to the floor. The sphere contained a plant with deep green leaves and bright red berries, pressing against its glass sides as if anxious to burst forth. I gasped. This was expensive tech. In the span of a heartbeat, droplets of water condensed on the walls of the sphere and disappeared, as the terrarium's nano-climate program simulated the water conditions and temperature of the plant's native habitat. I leaned forward, gingerly placing it on the floor, when the bag slipped off my knees. Out tumbled the most curious object of all.

A small metal pot. I popped it open and saw a removable filter that slid firmly into place. Stuffed inside was a note. I scanned the terse message. My hands shook as I realized they were the words of a ghost I thought I'd never know.

Your voice cut through the shimmering silence of the StarBuggy's twinkling lights.

'What is all this junk, Syrua?' you asked.

I looked up. Then I stood, leaving the bag and its contents on the floor. 'My mother is dead,' I said. 'This is my inheritance.'

Mother.

I know what the word means but I have no conception of the feeling it's supposed to evoke. I walk down the orderly rows of apartments in Sector

16. Tall buildings made from mycelia cell blocks trail fungi-flora down their frames, their flowers incandescent shades of blue and purple, bioluminescent against the night sky. Beyond the domed city of Uru, the seven moons of Terra II shine brightly in their unique orbital alignment. We call it the Gauntlet.

I pass Mohan Uncle's chai shop at the corner, where he used to hand out candied fungi pulp to me as a child and smokes with a cuppa when I was older. Chai here is brewed from fresh fungi-flora buds, sweet and salty all at once, but I've heard it was made from leaves, and even spiced, back on Earth.

I stop in front of Block 4 and pass my palm over a scanner.

'Who is it?' he calls.

'It's me, Dad…'

'Syrua!' A panel of glass fades to transparency. He beams happily, stepping through and wrapping me up in a bear hug.

He looks me over and then glances around me as if I'm conspicuously missing an appendage. 'No Orahn?'

'Can't a daughter visit her father alone?'

'All right, all right! I was just hoping to show off my new case of EarthBrew…'

For some reason, my father believes you enjoy drinking EarthBrew. I haven't the heart to tell him you're more of a CrystalWaters person.

He leads me into the living room of the house I grew up in.

'Seating for two, please,' he announces. 'And coffee. Or…er…would you like the EarthBrew?'

'EarthBrew it is,' I say.

Minimalist furniture folds out from panels in the floor and walls. Two wing-backed armchairs slip into place around a sleek, round coffee table. The kitchen counter begins to hum as a robotic arm pops out of a panel, pouring two glasses of single malt EarthBrew over ice. I examine the bottle. It's deep green and features a large tree with spreading boughs on the label. 'Oak Mead' it reads.

I pick up our glasses and head to where my father has made himself comfortable on an armchair.

'To what do I owe the delight of this visit?'

I hand him his glass and take my seat. I pull the red cloth bag out of my backpack. 'This.' I place it on the table.

His face is unreadable. He stares at it, his drink untouched. The minutes drag on. 'She's gone then,' he says softly.

'She wasn't ever here to begin with,' I laugh. He doesn't join me.

'She's really gone…'

I shrug.

'I know it makes no difference to you, Syrua, but your mother…' He swallows, 'Your mother was really special.'

'I wish she'd have let me find that out,' I say, suddenly bitter.

'She – she didn't want you to miss something she could never be.' His eyes glitter in the yellow light being cast from the panels in the ceiling.

'I don't know what any of the junk in this bag is, or why it was sent to me.' My voice sounds cold.

'She must have let the Bereavement Cells know you were her next of kin –'

'Really?' I snap. 'Why bother getting in touch with me, for the first time in my life, from beyond the grave?'

'That's how it goes in your family. The women are complicated…' he trails off.

'You're my family,' I say sternly.

'You know what I mean.'

'Right. So, I'm leaving this with you then.'

'I can't take that!' Dad says angrily. 'It's your inheritance. Your legacy, kiddo.'

'It's a bunch of cosmic junk.'

'No. It's your history.'

'I've never known it,' I mutter.

'That's on me. I never told you what I knew, but these are stories from your ancestors.'

'I don't much care for them,' I say. I'm irritated, but also hurt. 'I can't believe you knew and never bothered to mention any of this!'

'Your mother made me promise –'

'I didn't have a mother. And now I never will.'

'Open it,' he says gently.

I undo the knot.

'This bag…' He reaches out to touch it, then withdraws. 'It was sewn by your great-great-great grandmother.'

I laugh hoarsely, unsure why it feels like I'm choking on something. I pull out its contents, setting them on the table. The funny filtration pot rolls out and he begins to laugh.

'I can't – can't believe she k-k-kept that.' He slaps his thigh and throws his head back, his laughter filling the quiet shadows of the room.

I'm not sure if he's in grief, shock or something more serious. Maybe the news has unhinged him. I'm quite certain my father loved my mother at some point. I consider calling emergency services.

'Dad –' I say cautiously, half rising from my chair.

'Your mother – oh, she was spectacular! And that coffee pot. That coffee filter is where your entire story begins.'

'What am I supposed to do with it?' I scowl.

'Celebrate your roots,' he says cryptically. 'I'll begin. To Lyra.'

He looks at me and raises his drink.

I raise my glass to my mother's spirit and take a sip, even though that's the first time I've heard her name.

'What are we doing here, Syrua?' you ask nervously. 'We never come here. *Never.*'

'Orahn. Calm down. This is where you go if you want to have a bit of fun.'

The neat row houses of the sectors has given way to a shanty town. Uru's monorail doesn't even have a station here, so we've had to walk the last mile past dilapidated buildings made of Earth junk like tin and plastic. You turn up your nose at someone rolling a cigarette Earth-style – he squats on Terra II's packed soil and places organic matter onto a sheet of paper. His fingers perform a curious shuffle as he holds it precariously between his hands, balanced on the tips of his thumbs and forefingers. In seconds, he licks the edge of the paper and seals it into a perfect cylinder, an improvised filter at its tip. He lights it and watches us go past as the pungent fumes of fungi-flora fill the air.

'I thought organic cigarettes were banned across the Terra-verse,' you scowl.

You're from the Gauntlet where they've eliminated poverty by disallowing it. Here, we live side by side with it and pretend we don't notice. It's been over a century since Earth collapsed, but most refugees still haven't found homes. The government is currently developing a new settlement on Terra III a few hundred light years away. They say it's being built to expand housing for refugees, but that's never how things turn out with the human race. Earth's blue depths from which we all emerged are fathomless, steeped in a history of disparity and violence. Our civilization will need to reinvent its past before it can reimagine its future.

'It's the *smugglers' market*,' you hiss.

'Stop being so uptight,' I laugh.

'This demands uptight.'

'Orahn.'

'Fine. But when I use you as a human shield, don't say I didn't warn you.'

I slip my hand into yours and give it a squeeze. You groan in annoyance and then squeeze back.

The tin and plastic shelters lean dangerously into each other, only held together by the sheer will of the people who depend upon them to survive. We pass all manner of illegal goods. Fenced in antiques display the flags of the Old-World's former nations. I hurry past the store, dragging you with me. Nationalist sentiment is dangerous in the New-World. Everyone who's ever read a history book knows that self-serving nationalist policies led to the collapse of Earth, though I'm not sure how many refugee families have the privilege of accessing history.

Here, heavily modded drones and droids perform every function imaginable – from elaborate card-shuffling techniques to painting multi-dextrous murals. You pause to stare in wonder at a humanoid who pours kafein several metres through the air, dried, aromatic fungi-flora distilled into a steaming liquid falling in a perfect arc from one cup held high above its head into another held close to its chest. The humanoid shifts its arms, entering into an elaborate dance, back and forth, spinning fountains of kafein through the air.

'You've never seen traditional kafein pouring?' I'm delighted by your curiosity. 'It's based on Old-World coffee-pouring rituals – except, of course, it's usually done with kafein here.'

Coffee is a luxury on Terra II; kafein is its more accessible relative.

'What is this art form?' you ask, your eyes transfixed.

I place a swift kiss on your cheek. 'Come on.'

I drag you through to the electrical and electronics stores. They're crammed with shelves full of Earth junk, usually bought by mad retro-collectors and Old-World enthusiasts.

'I need a charger for this,' I say, pulling the strange glass tablet from my backpack. 'And a solar cell connector.'

The man behind the counter produces what I've asked for in a second.

'A *tablet*!' he gazes at the glass slab in wonder. 'It's worth big money if you want to sell it. We can give you 12, maybe 14,000 Terr for it.'

'Not for sale.' I swipe it quickly back into my backpack.

You grab my hand and glare at him. Your delicate eyebrows knot together, daring him to say something. I roll my eyes as you steer me back the way we came.

'Big money if you change your mind!' the shop owner calls after us.

'We're getting out of here,' you growl.

'You're really jumpy today,' I tease.

'That thing in your bag is probably worth more than this entire neighbourhood!' you snap.

'Calm down, Orahn...'

'That's *all* you wanted? A connector for your space junk? We could have sent a courier to pick it up.'

I shrug and cast a sidelong glance at you. Your lips are downturned. I bump into you with my shoulder, hoping to ease the sudden tension between us.

'Do I get to unlock it with you? Discover all its secrets with you?'

'Um...'

I haven't thought about that yet. I suddenly realize I want to do it alone.

'That's okay. Keep your secrets.'

I'm secretly relieved you've had to travel on work.

I'm enjoying the solitude of space in the dimly lit StarBuggy. I've set it on autopilot in a low orbit around Terra II. I'm not far out enough to see the planet at a distance, but I don't want to be. I want to savour my connection to this world of ours even as I taste the stars beyond it, grasping for a past I've never known and reaching for the story I'm to become.

My hands hover over a completed volunteer registration form for Interstellar Expeditions. We've talked about this, you and I, and I've always joked that Terra's gravity is holding me back. Today, I gaze at the bizarre objects I've placed on the dash in front of me and tell myself I can't build a future if I don't understand my past.

It took me a while to figure out how to get the electrical connector hooked up to solar cells, and it took a whole day for the tablet to charge. I haven't figured out how to use that coffee pot – or coffee filter, as my father called it. I've also never seen Earth flora before – it's shot with green all the way through, and the bright red berries pushing against the terrarium's molecularly expandable glass terrify and intrigue me. I run my fingers over the smooth, nearly seamless latch, wondering if the Buggy has enough room to house the full-sized plant once it expands. The nano-climate technology of the terrarium will stop functioning, though, and I'm too scared I'll endanger the plant without the right soil and water conditions, so I put it away.

The tablet is fully charged. I'm going to unlock it now.

I swipe.

A hologram leaps from its surface. It's a woman in her late twenties. She wears strange clothes – what appears to be a long silk tunic over tight leggings. Completely impractical. Her hair is held back in a long braid. She stands in front of a glass mirror, not a screen.

'Hi, I'm Aruna.' She grins and waves. I tap on the glass surface and freeze the frame. On her finger is a bright gold band with a swirling pattern of rubies on it.

I look down at my hand. The ring sparkles back at me, identical in every regard. I'm looking at the face of one of my ancestors.

I look for a way to switch the thing off.

'This is where I've backed up –'

I quickly freeze the frame again. I run my fingers over the tablet's smooth surface and find a button to its right. I hold it down and the hologram is swallowed back into the cold glass.

I can't do this. I can't watch this now. I rise from my seat and begin to pace.

Who is she? She can't be my mother – my father called her Lyra. My grandmother perhaps?

I reach for the faded silk bag and pull out the journal. I flip it open to its first page.

Captain IronStar's Private Journal

Earth Year 2285 (Terra I Year 29) to Earth Year 2350 (Terra I Year 94)

This journal is dated very recently – its last entry is from just 20 years ago. The writer, Captain IronStar, can't be the person in this video. Memory-lens implants fell out of use over a hundred years ago, when the last survivors from Earth had died. We'd never invested in their revival on Terra II.

The lady in the graphs – Aruna – is an earthling. If this assortment of artefacts hasn't been tampered with over the years, she must be my great-grandmother.

My great-grandmother.

I gaze at the tablet again. My fingers hover over it, twitching with tension. Finally, I swipe.

'Hi, I'm Aruna.' She grins and waves.

'This is where I've backed up my memorygraph collection. You should be able to see everything through my eyes…' She taps a spot on her temple. 'And I'm so excited to be able to share my first memory with you today.'

But the graph sparks and glitches, then dies. A new one swirls in to take its place.

'This is getting ridiculous, Appa!' a woman's voice snaps.

'Aruna, this is our planet. More importantly, we *own* the land our house is built on. This piece of Earth is *ours*. We're not leaving any of it behind just because –'

'Have you been paying any attention to anything that's on the news?'

My ears are ringing, but I watch my great-grandmother's hands in fascination as she picks up the very glass slab that's in my hands, taps the screen and beams a holo transmission onto the wall. She's recording every moment of the world as she sees it. It's a world I've never seen except in flexiglass history scrolls. *Earth.*

A newscaster's voice breaks the silence.

'– the latest in a string of earthquakes to ravage the once-stable Deccan Plateau. The ongoing drought has already lasted seven years, and there isn't enough water in the Deccan reservoir and irrigation system to guarantee supplies for much longer. This could spell disaster for the entire region.'

The newsreader's voice escalates in panic, but it's all as boring as recorded history to me. That's because it *is* history – the people who came from Earth didn't bat an eyelid at their climate crisis, built expansive dams and irrigation systems to deal with crippling drought and water shortages, increased their demands on the land, and triggered seismic activity. Parts of the planet were submerged by floods and tsunamis, and the land began to collapse into itself. The earthlings set off the apocalypse and fled the fallout. The end.

But I'm more interested in how *she* fits into the narrative. She was a single puzzle piece in a cosmic jigsaw. Her choices charted passages between the stars, a pathway through space-time leading to my existence in this very moment. I shiver.

The newscaster continues. '– we are not mandating an evacuation, but we encourage those with the means to do so to begin migrating to Terra I. Our dwindling food and water supplies can help those left behind survive the endless summer to come…'

My great-grandmother's fingers hit a button. The voice falls silent while images play out on the wall. What looks like an ancient wind transmission cooling system is mounted above it. The house is furnished with rich, heavy fabrics. An ornate carpet covers the floor. An elaborate set of glass bowls sits upon the table. The walls are covered with exotic art reaching all the way up to the high ceilings.

'See?' my great-grandmother says triumphantly.

'See what? He says they don't want us to evacuate.'

'That's not what he's saying at all!'

'Aruna, don't glorify this interstellar "Save-the-Earth" bullshit. It's miserable in space, all that processed food and those inorganic supplements. We've got everything we need here.'

'Our lives are in danger –'

'This is just news paranoia. You're letting it get to you.'

'This house is smack in the middle of the valley. There hasn't been rain in years. The reservoir is running dry. We've had four earthquakes just this year –'

'Why don't you go outside for a walk?' The man dismisses her.

Footsteps stomp. A doorway gets closer. She flings it open.

Earth.

It blows me away to be able to view it up close like this. Parked outside the dwelling are more ancient space transports – an early prototype of the StarBuggy, a SpaceRacer and... I spy something large with wheels. Could that possibly be a personal land vehicle?

Turn right, turn right, I will my great-grandmother's memorygraph.

She wheels left. She's muttering to herself.

'Stupid fucking bullshit. We can get out early, we can save ourselves, we can give the others a chance, but no. Let's cling on to this dying piece of Earth – this land we *own*.'

I'm barely paying attention to her. Around her are *real trees*. Skeletal, not bursting with leaves and foliage like the pictures in history scrolls. They're dry and crackly with diminished clumps of leaves clinging to their branches like wisps of cloud, but that doesn't change the fact that this is *Earth flora*. It's *green*.

The memorygraph ends abruptly. Another begins immediately. ' – I'm not risking her life just because you don't want to leave these four walls.'

'You should have thought of that *before* you left your husband and came back to us,' someone snaps. 'Bringing that poor fatherless child with you! You don't even let him visit.'

The speaker comes into focus. She's an older woman bustling about an Earth kitchen. Things simmer over an open flame in large, unwieldy cooking pots. Fresh fruit and vegetables lie haphazardly in baskets upon the counter. It looks like chaos, but I imagine I can smell the food.

'You want to drag the divorce into this now? Are you kidding me, Amma?'

The translator on my dash parses the word. *Mother*.

My head spins. This is my earthling family.

'Taste this.'

The woman – my great-great grandmother – holds up a ladle filled with steaming, rich brown broth.

'It's good. More podi – the tamarind is overpowering the rasam right now,' my great-grandmother says. 'Back to what I was saying –'

'Aruna. Do you have filter coffee in outer space?'

'What the fu–'

'Don't swear,' her mother snaps. 'Look at that pot of filter coffee.'

She points to where the funny little filtration pot – the one now lying on my dash – sits innocuously on the counter. 'That alone is worth staying on this planet for.' Her mother raps the pot on its lid.

She opens it and waves her hand over its contents. It looks like congealed mud.

'Smell that,' her mother says. 'Isn't it glorious?'

'Amma. *Soon there won't be any coffee left for us to drink.*'

'Nonsense,' her mother says.

The memorygraph ends. Another one sparks into life.

The glass controls of a SpaceRacer. Heavy breathing. Aruna turns to her left. Through her eyes, I see a child strapped into the seat beside her, eerily silent. Aruna shifts perspective, looking down as the craft rattles its way through the clouds.

Earth is falling away below her, not because she's speeding into the stratosphere, but because it is literally collapsing in on itself.

I gasp. I'm watching the end of the Earth.

'Idiots,' my great-grandmother mutters.

My view of her ascent into the stars blurs. Wet droplets land on the touchscreen cockpit controls. Her hands flinch, her tears glistening on the rubies on her ring like droplets of blood. 'The *idiots*.'

She glances down towards her feet. A red silk bag lies half open, a coffee pot peeking out. 'THE IDIOTS.'

The memorygraph stops. The screen goes blank. I look at the embroidered silk bag lying smugly on the dashboard.

'You've been through a world of trouble,' I say to it.

You're back from your work trip to the Gauntlet. Your family were early settlers and pioneered interstellar trade in rare organics. I know it's hard for you to manage the estate while you're here with me, off-moon. Molecularly modified hexacotton has never been more in demand, and while your family's vertical farmlands and robotic weave systems are fairly automated, they're meaningless if someone doesn't keep the books and manage logistics for each shipment. I'd rather captain a trade-ship, but I'm selfishly glad you like it here.

We're having dinner at Native Noms, traditional Old-World food that includes a funny kind of carbohydrate called rice. The maître d' informs us that it's incredibly difficult to harvest, but that they use only the best techniques in their hydroponic labs.

'So, you're saying your great-grandmother was an illegal?' You frown.

'She was a refugee,' I bristle. 'She didn't have much of a choice – she had a daughter, left her stubborn family behind, and literally left Earth right as it was collapsing.'

'You should try and find her in the immigration scrolls.'

'There are probably no records. She left my grandmother in a refugee camp – you can imagine how that went.'

You shudder and take a sip of your CrystalWaters. 'I was thinking,' you say, leaning forward. 'There's a beautiful frozen lake on the outskirts of our estate…'

'Go on,' I grin.

'Let's go home and pack right now.'

'Now?' I hesitate, and see your slender eyebrows shoot up in surprise. I'm surprised too.

'You – *don't* want to travel?'

'I –'

Do I? I wonder. *Am I clinging to the surface of this planet too hard, letting its gravity weigh me down because I'm afraid?*

'We don't have to if you'd rather spend alone time in the StarBuggy…' you say and shrug.

'No. Don't be ridiculous! I was just surprised, that's all.'

'I thought you liked surprises.'

'I do! I love them! Let's go home right now and pack.'

This isn't exactly where I imagined I'd be reading my late grandmother's words, but I couldn't resist slipping her slim journal into my backpack when we flew out to Sentros, the smallest and most exclusive moon in the Gauntlet – and your home city.

You're on a long walk outside in the snow right now.

I thought I'd come with you, but I chickened out at the last minute. Maybe it's what I now know to be my Deccan genes that make me despise the cold. Maybe I just want some time away from you to think.

It's hard to fathom that my great-grandmother escaped a planet that was breathing its last, riding the wind of its death rattle out into the stars. I wonder why her memorygraph is so patchy – from what I've read in the scrolls, memorygraphs were supposed to record every second of a human being's existence so they could choose what moments to broadcast to the world.

I look up through the hexagonal skylights that form the patterned ceiling of our cabin, and all I can see are the stars. The six other moons of the Gauntlet and Terra II loom over us, suspended like a long breath that seems destined to shatter at any moment.

Dim light from a reading lamp falls upon the bed. I run my fingers over the embossed gold ink on my grandmother's journal. It's a marvel that she even got her hands on paper – it was a rare commodity by the time she was an adult on Terra I.

I flip to the first page. Ink is less disconcerting than moving pictures.

Captain IronStar's Private Journal

Earth Year 2285 (Terra I Year 29) to Earth Year 2350 (Terra I Year 94) –

Her handwriting is a barely legible scrawl.

Day 9/42, Month Hexa, Earth Year 2285 (Terra I Year 29)

We didn't have much on Terra I when we first landed.

Before I knew it, she was flying back into the darkness again.

I rarely saw her. A few times a year maybe. Birthdays, never. I doubt she remembered when mine was. But the money came in every month. Usually through couriers who tried to scam it from me. I learnt to carry a knife early on.

You'd think she'd have taken me along on a ride or two, considering she worked so hard to save my life when Earth collapsed.

So much for maternal instinct.

I was raised by refugees here on Terra I. We lived on the edges of the dome. They fed me, clothed me and taught me what little they knew – including how to steal, which is something I'm snatch-grabbing good at.

I keep wondering why she didn't leave earlier, when there was still hope of shelter here. And now I wonder where she died.

Hah. I barely know where she lived, or what she did there. All I know is that the money came in like clockwork.

And now this. Why did she leave me with all this space junk?

It turns out she barely knew her mother too. I sense my grandmother drawing me to her soul across time. I feel a connection to this woman who doesn't have a name.

Day 14/42, Month Hexa, Earth Year 2285 (Terra I Year 29)
Found a strange little coffee filter in the junk. Too bad there isn't any coffee – we haven't seen any since the last consignment of Earth flora, and the gentry got almost all of it. I hear they're developing a new equivalent called kafein.

Makes no difference to me. Coffee is an expensive habit.

It turns out I inherited a spaceship. I think I shall call it the DreadShot.

I smile and turn the page.

Day 19/42, Month Octa, Earth Year 2285 (Terra I Year 29)
I seem to be a natural at flying this spaceship. One of the refugees from Camp II, Smeta, is an ex-shuttle pilot. She practically raised me on hard science and the flight simulators she'd smuggled off the Old World. Every woman's got to have a license to fly, she tells me.

Day 1/42, Month Prima, Earth Year 2286 (Terra I Year 30)
You're looking at a licensed intergalactic pilot.

We've moved into the ship – it's a lot less depressing than living in our camps on T-I.

We? That's Smeta – she's my first officer. There's also Asma, our flight engineer, and a bit of muscle in Misha, Carishma and May. They're all street fighters from the camps, handy with their knives and guns.

May says my knife skills are solid – all those years of practice on the streets, I guess. She'll teach me how to shoot soon.

It seems my grandmother was a bit of a renegade. You'll probably be filled with horror when I tell you. I decide to bookmark all the juicy bits to read out to you.

Day 18/42, Month Prima, Earth Year 2286 (Terra I Year 30)
We're running out of food and money. Hard times on Terra I. Earth supplies from the wrecked shell of that planet have been delayed thanks to solar storms, and our vertical farmlands are still being rolled out. Obviously, the gentry get their pick of the resources. They managed to get here first, legitimate paperwork, first pick of the housing colonies and all. Now they get to decide everything, from whether our shanty towns are demolished for flora parks, or whether nutrio-pills or organics are the more valuable food source. Us refugees have to forage for scraps to stay alive.

Day 21/42, Month Prima, Earth Year 2286 (Terra I Year 30)
First raid today. We hit a goods shuttle out by the asteroid fringe between Terra I and the newly developing Terra II. Yep, we're expanding to Terra II already in spite of being unable to support life on this piece of rock. Maybe they'll move us all off this planet. Our cooperative government said they'd learnt from the errors of the human race on Earth when we voted them in, but clearly they haven't.

The DreadShot needs more ammunition. My mother's aux guns are good for holding off raids, but we need serious firepower if we want to target bigger, more valuable cargoes.

I read the entry over and over again. The words 'raid', 'ammunition' and 'firepower' leap out at me with every reading. I blanch – I thought she was just a homeless refugee with a knife.

Day 28/42, Month Septa, Earth Year 2086 (Terra I Year 30)
Our conquests are getting more ambitious. Captured a merchant ship, The Opulence, *earlier today. The crew will fence everything they find except for its stockpile of coffee powder. And most valuable of all – their expandable terrariums, salvaged from the wastes of Svalbard. We're keeping all strains of Deccan coffee – I believe we might be able to build a small-scale processing unit in the hold – and auctioning the rest to the highest bidder. Our terms include an exclusive supply line.*

Their captain is being rather compliant.

I flip through several boring pages that catalogue all the goods that were smuggled off the merchant ship. It turns out that that's where the strange, red-berried plant came from. I laugh out loud – it's *coffee*. And good old Deccan coffee at that. We almost never have access to organics from the Earth here. Our kafein, chai, cigarettes and food are all fungi-flora unless we decide to find an expensive Old-World restaurant. She also mentions vials of something called jasmine *ittar* – perfume it seems, though not if the headache it gave me is anything to go by. She says it smells like her mother. I wonder if all Earth scents were this robust, if life on Earth was packed with noise and colour. I wonder why she kept it too.

Day 19/42, Month Octa, Earth Year 2286 (Terra I Year 30)
The captain of The Opulence *is being a cooperative hostage. When he said his name was Smith, I laughed out loud and considered having Misha throw him off the ship.*

Day 21/42, Month Deca, Earth Year 2286 (Terra-I Year 30)
First kiss.

I'm not sure if I should throw Captain Smith off the ship for insubordination.

'DO IT!' I yell at the book.

'Do what?' you ask.

You've just come in from the cold. You rub your hands together, your breathing heavy. Your cheeks are bright red and you wear a happy smile. Your lips are like frost flowers.

'What are you yelling at?' you say, laughing.

'Oh. Nothing.'

'Hah! I caught you with a smutty book, didn't I? Hand that here!'

You grab me in a tight hug and begin to tickle me. You pull the book from my hands.

'Not fair! You cheated.' I try to scowl but I'm still giggling.

You glance at the journal. I feel heat rise to my cheeks, even though I've been reading nothing more scandalous than my family history.

'Your grandmother was a space pirate?' you say, eyes widening.

'I just found out –'

Your eyes grow wide as you look at the first page.

'*She* was *the* Captain IronStar? NO WAY.'

'Um, well...'

'You never cared for space pirate legends, did you?'

'I...skipped that class?' I say lamely.

'Lucky for you, you're talking to someone raised in the mercantile tradition. This is part of our family legacy,' you say, arching your eyebrows. '*The* Dire Captain IronStar happened to raid a merchant ship that belonged to my great-grandfather's fleet. *The Opulence*. Stole everything from it, cost my family a fortune.'

I look away. 'I'm sorry.' I drop my voice.

'Are you kidding me? This is the coolest thing! I'm in love with someone who has pirate blood!'

You grab me again and begin to kiss me all over my face. I try to wriggle free.

'Let me go.'

'You will now be made to walk the plank for your crimes.'

You push me backward onto the bed and I let myself fall, laughing.

'Let's see what your wicked grandmother is up to.'

You flip open the journal. I make a grab for it, suddenly jealous that you're going to discover her story at the same time I will.

'Day 1/42, Month Prima, Earth Year 2287 (Terra I Year 31),' you read aloud. 'The coffee processing unit is complete. It occupies less space in the hold than I thought it would. I know, priorities, but can you blame me? It's all I have left of the planet I was born on, a place I never got to call home. I don't know much about coffee. Smeta remembers. So does Captain Smith.

'Captain Smith and I – I can't write these words down right, but I think he makes me happy.'

You look up at me.

'Not so much of a badass, was she? She's getting all mushy over some captain here…'

'Are you saying I'm not a badass if I kiss you right now, Cap?'

I hope I can distract you and get my book back.

'Later,' you smirk, turning back to the page.

'Give that to me!' I whine.

You dance out of my way.

'Shit,' you say.

'What?' I ask.

'Day 9/42, Month Quadra, Earth Year 2287 (Terra I Year 31). I've missed my period. I hope I'm not pregnant.'

'Stop, you're making that up!' I smack your arm.

'There's more.'

I stand on the bed and peer over your shoulder from my vantage point.

Day 21/42, Month Quadra, Earth Year 2287 (Terra I Year 31)

I DON'T WANT TO HAVE A CHILD.

NOT WITH SOMEONE WHOSE REAL NAME I DON'T KNOW.

Not when I'm no more than a space pirate trying to make ends meet.

'Fuck,' I say. 'Turn the page.'

Day 21/42, Month Octa, Earth Year 2287 (Terra I Year 31)

He tried to stage a mutiny.

He tried to take over MY ship.

His reasons? Now that I'm carrying a child, I can't be a competent leader any more.

Hormones, he said. Caring for the child, he said. Maternal instinct and sentimentality and emotions, he said.

So, I shot him.

Misha and Carishma are still cleaning the bloodstains out of the carpet in the cockpit.

We dumped his body in space.

I'm going to be the kind of mother they've never seen before.

I flop down on the bed.

'Syrua, this means...' you begin.

'I know what it means,' I mutter.

'Your mother... she was born on a pirate ship.'

The Gauntlet rises in the sky once more. As night descends, sharp ridges on Terra II's surface cast shadows like secrets cloaking my home planet. I've spent the day tramping through the trails around Lake Moros. I find you in the garden, examining a curious piece of fungi-flora upon my return.

'Frostflowers,' you nod towards them. 'I've always been surrounded by frostflowers, but I can never get enough of them.'

I wrap my arms around your waist and lean into you. You smell like ice and mist, but you're so warm.

'Sorry I've been a bit strange lately,' I say.

'You just discovered your mother was the child of a refugee pirate,' you say, rubbing your gloved hand over my bare one. 'I can't blame you.'

I press my head into your back. The silence deepens.

'She escaped, you know.'

'Really?'

'My grandmother wrote about it. My mother ran away when the ship docked in Earth's orbit. Stole a StarCruiser and plummeted towards the Earth's surface…'

'No,' you gasp. 'That's suicide.'

'I guess she made it out alive. I wouldn't be here otherwise,' I shrug against you.

'Why'd she run?' you ask.

'I don't know. Maybe she got tired of the endless cycle of violence – it can't have been easy, growing up on a pirate ship,' I say.

'It sounds quite miserable if you ask me. You…' you hesitate. 'You should ask your dad about her.'

'In all my 28 years, he's never spoken about her.'

You pull away and gaze into my eyes.

'You want to know, don't you?'

I shrug.

Do I?

I reach my hand up in the pretence of brushing a stray snowflake off your cheek, and let it rest there.

'You love it here, don't you?' I ask.

'I wouldn't leave for anything in the world. Except you,' you smile, kissing my cold fingers. 'You're freezing. Let's get you inside.'

I'm back in my father's apartment. I've brought you with me so you can feign excitement over his new collection of EarthBrew while I work up the courage to talk to him. I sip my drink in silence, watching the two of you turn appreciative of the woody notes in this particular vintage.

My heart is pounding in my ears and I know why, but I don't want to acknowledge it.

'You're unnaturally quiet today, Syrua,' Dad says.

You shoot me a loaded look.

'Oh, I don't know. I –'

'Wondering about your mother?' Dad says smiling.

I glare at you. You shrug.

'Orahn warned me you might be a bit broody, and we thought we'd help you out.'

'I don't need help,' I say testily.

'You've got your mother's eyes, you know?' Dad says.

'Dad!'

'Where do I begin telling you about Lyra?' Dad looks away and a wistful look crosses his face. Something about it doesn't seem right.

'Make her likeable,' I demand. 'Since this is the first time you're going to tell me about her –'

'I love you too much to lie to you about this,' Dad says slowly. He sighs. 'Honey, have you ever wondered why I never brought her up? All through your growing up in this house, not once? Ever?'

Dad looks at me kindly. You busy yourself at a scroll-shelf, pretending to be peruse the flexiglass scrolls in the history section. I'm not sure if you're being ironic on purpose.

'I figured she'd broken your heart,' I say. 'Besides, I never really asked. You were...you were always there for me – more than any parent is.' I swallow, and my eyes are uncomfortably wet.

'All right.' He takes a deep breath. 'Here it is. Lyra was a wild thing and damnably proud of it. After all, she was raised on a pirate ship, watching her mother shoot anyone who crossed her. She was adept with a knife and could hit a target a mile away. She was wild, Lyra was. A destructive force waiting to unleash itself.'

He sips his drink.

'She ran away from her mother, stole a StarCruiser and traveled all the way back to Earth. *To Earth!* Talk about being incredibly foolish. She told me she wanted to find her real family but couldn't stand the desolation. She returned with a souvenir – some dirt she packed into a box. She kept calling it her legacy.

'We met at a bar, and we spent an entire summer together. She told me about her life. We talked about everything – our dreams and fears. She was 31 and I was just a little younger. Her mother had just died in a raid and she was lost, but beautifully so. We listened to vintage Earth tunes and gazed at the stars, and before I knew it she'd disappeared. She was here one moment and gone the next. About a year later, I found you in a basket on my doorstep.'

A sudden clatter punctuates the gasp I hear escape my lips. You've dropped about a dozen scrolls onto the floor and you scramble to collect them.

'She...she left me?'

'You need to know…' Dad struggles to find the words. 'Being a mother, being responsible for someone else, is not something she ever wanted. Or something she could do.'

'*She abandoned me?*' My voice is a whisper.

Dad rises from his chair and steps towards me. He wraps his arms around me. 'She gave you to me,' he says softly. 'She left you with me, in a home, to be loved and to be raised with a head full of stars and the ground beneath your feet.'

'I could have been raised in an orphanage!' I say, outraged. 'You could have given me away…she'd never have known…'

'I couldn't. And I didn't,' he says firmly. 'I was the first person who loved her without expectation. Her mother was a bit of a tyrant, but I was kind. She knew I'd care for you –'

'What kind of woman abandons her own daughter?' I hiss.

'The kind of woman who makes choices only for herself,' my father says. 'The kind who makes difficult choices, knowing she can never provide the kind of life she'd want her daughter to live.'

'She –'

'She was reckless, a beautiful disaster waiting to happen. She was always in free-fall, but she always thought she was defying gravity.'

My father pulls away and looks me in the eye. 'Not like you, Syrua. You might have your head in the stars, but your feet are firmly planted on Terra. And your mother gave you those roots. If you choose to defy gravity, you'll do it from your heart. And you'll soar.'

'My roots are because of you.' I'm now shaking.

'Yes. She would have made a terrible mother to you, and she knew it.'

'She didn't even say goodbye…' I choke out.

'Goodbye… What is goodbye but a hand reaching out for the sky, my love?'

Histories repeat themselves; every herstory is her story in its own way.

I'm a new chapter in this story. This story of the women in my family. I can trace them back four generations, all the way to the Earth days. A rare claim to fame on Terra II.

It didn't begin with the package that arrived at our doorstep a few months ago. It began long before that red silk bag left Earth's gravity and found its way to me.

I've taken to wandering further from Terra II and the Gauntlet. My Interstellar Expeditions application still lingers on my dashboard, but for now, I enjoy dancing at the edge of our SpaceBuggy's flight envelope until I feel the inexplicable pull of gravity lead me back home.

The expandable terrarium lives on our terrace, producing more coffee beans by the day. You've trawled through dozens of botany scrolls and figured out the right artificial light and temperature conditions for it to thrive.

I've finally understood how to work the funny little coffee pot. You pour steaming water over dried and ground coffee beans and let the brew filter through into a holding cup at its base. It tastes disgusting that way, but you mix it in with the right amount of dairy whitener and sugar and wake me up every day with the best darned coffee I've ever tasted. You call it filter coffee, which always cracks me up, but you insist with all seriousness that it's a historically accurate term.

We're lying on the terrace, looking at the stars. Your fingers are strung through mine.

'Remember that time you said I was born to defy gravity?' I ask.

'Mmm. I've said a lot of poetic things in the past.' you murmur, grinning.

'Silly.' I squeeze your hand. 'I was going to say I quite like gravity, though you might make me change my mind.'

'You know, if you ever want to –'

'I don't know if I do.'

'But if you ever wanted to go...'

'You know I wouldn't just up and leave.'

'But IF you do.'

'IF.'

'Yes. IF you do. You know you can. If that's what you'd like.'

'I like this right now.'

'And the minute you don't, you are free to go.'

You hold my hand up and I see our fingers intertwined. I don't know if the stars will call out to me, or when this moment will shatter. I'm only glad I get to live it with you.

Together, we press our palms into the sky.

ALMOST HUMAN

KEHKASHAN KHALID

'Tell me about her.'

It was evident from the Inspector's voice that he was not enthusiastic about being here. His furrowed face and uncomfortable sideways glances at the rows of metal coffins betrayed his scepticism. But Professor Lachkar felt like he had struck gold. He pulled at the papery brown skin of his hands as he scurried after Inspector Mansoor through the steel underbelly of the Forge.

The Neural Conceptualization Hub, commonly known as the Forge, was a vast facility overseeing every aspect of robotics in Sindh, from research to genesis to dissemination. They were currently traversing its basement, which scientists had nicknamed the Morgue – a burial ground for droids that had outlived their usefulness. Inspector Mansoor had been highly displeased to find that his request had needed to be relegated to the Morgue.

Every now and again, when the Sindh Police commissioned droids trained specifically for police work, the Forge operated as a kind of library of plainclothes droid policemen that different departments could borrow from upon the approval of a requisition slip. A straightforward process, it seemed. However, having filled out a requisition slip Inspector Mansoor, currently (and for the first time) dealing with a baffling and brutal homicide, had belatedly realized that he had no source to turn to and no contacts ensconced in influential posts to nudge his application to the top of the pile. But he wasn't the kind of man who'd take no for an answer. A bit of poking around had delivered the young Professor Lachkar to him, bursting with ingenious ideas and very little awareness of their consequences.

'She is a first-generation droid. Nearly forgotten, but also unparalleled in her powers of investigation and deduction.'

'Sounds too good to be true. Why were they all decommissioned?'

'Err…' Professor Lachkar stumbled while keeping up with the inspector's long strides as he shuffled papers in his hand. 'Well…no one is entirely sure.

She was created quite a long time ago, and we didn't really have the systems we do now.'

Inspector Mansoor glanced backwards and Professor Lachkar withered under his bland stare. 'S–some of our records were destroyed in the fire,' he stammered.

'So...*you* want to study these first-generation robots and *I* am your guinea pig?'

Professor Lachkar blinked rapidly, but didn't speak.

'Look,' the inspector said, relenting, 'I desperately need more eyes and hands on this investigation. My only question is – what if she is broken?'

'I will personally see that she is upgraded and updated as required.'

They entered an antechamber with more metal coffins slotted into the walls, all of them secured a couple of inches above the floor. Professor Lachkar paused in front of the one with 'NCH005' engraved on it. The two men, one apprehensive and the other eager, stood in front of the hexagonal box. All they could see was darkness behind a slit of glass at the very top of the metal cage.

'Unlock her then,' boomed Inspector Mansoor, breaking the silence.

I solemnly declare that I will be faithful and bear true allegiance to justice. The Collective Oath was the first thought that erupted in NCH005's mind as she regained consciousness. Then came the subtle nagging of an unidentifiable fear as her body stepped out of the metal case and onto the floor. She opened her eyes and, in the dim light of the tunnel, they focused on the man standing before her, looking at her with undisguised disgust.

'Specimen NCH005, how do you feel?' asked a familiar voice, and NCH005 turned towards it. She had not met this man before, but he had spoken to her – and tweaked her programming – as she lay dormant.

'I am functional, Professor.'

'This is Inspector Mansoor, and you will be assisting him in a homicide investigation. But first we'll run some preliminary checks to ensure you are ready to leave the facility.'

Inspector Mansoor flinched as the droid turned her walnut eyes on him. They were the only part of her face that resembled a human's and he wondered if they had been harvested from a real person or carefully constructed from silicon. He doubted the latter and feared the former. *How ill-equipped we were with technology only a decade ago*, he thought.

The material around her eyes resembled flesh but was stitched into metal from the bridge of the nose downwards, giving her the appearance of a ninja masked in silver. The screws that bolted the scraps of this material to the remaining metal gave her face a tautness that hindered expression, and her gaze, as she looked at him, was blank enough to be menacing. What unsettled him most was her mouth – a rectangular incision in her metal jaw. It emitted a woman's voice, probably from a rudimentary voice box, and its inflections were their only clue to NCH005's state of mind. His gaze flitted over the half-sleeved policewoman's uniform fitted over her androgynous body. Imperfectly shaped silicon arms emerged from the cloth, tattoos with incomprehensible, interconnected patterns inked along their length.

Inspector Mansoor shuddered. He thought of the gynoids that now roamed the streets plying various professions, with their fluid movements, curving lips and expressive eyes. This – she – was nothing like them. Nothing like a real woman.

He tried not to glance back as he led the droid out of the Morgue, but as they waited for Professor Lachkar to process some paperwork, he could not help stealing another glance at her. She was slowly moving her head upwards and then downwards again, either glancing around the room or giving her neck hinges some much-needed exercise. Meanwhile, her rubber fingers moved up and down the length of her arms in unwieldy caresses across the dark geometric tattoos.

'Well, you're all set. Let's take you into the lab for a quick vitality test and some upgrades.' Professor Lachkar's grin slowly faded as NCH005 continued to stare at him steadily. Droids these days imitated human behaviour so well you couldn't tell them apart till you checked their ID cards. Clearly, that was not the case with NCH005.

'Professor, would you permit me to evaluate myself? I am better acquainted with my design than you are, and all the numerical data will be recorded on your devices, should you wish to double-check the information,' she said at last.

'Hmm… Your superior understanding of your own construction *would* give me some insight into how you first-generation droids operated…'

'Excellent.'

Although her voice remained even, Inspector Mansoor felt she would have smiled if she could.

൭

They emerged into the sprawling courtyard of what used to be the Narayan Jagannath Vaidya School, known to everyone as NJV, in the heart of Bunder Road in Karachi. The Victorian architecture of the building had been preserved for its historic value even as its interior had morphed into gleaming laboratories. However, the surroundings had not changed much. The streets curving in either direction were crammed with a colourful diversity of shops selling everything from greasy tyres to pashmina shawls. Rickshaws with patchwork truck art were parked at intervals, emitting no air pollutants and yet sputtering occasionally in keeping with their branding.

'Our first order of business is to visit the crime scene,' Inspector Mansoor said gruffly. 'Then we will settle you in at the police quarters.'

'It would be better if I could explore the city and find my own place to live to emulate an ordinary existence – that way I can be in the right frame of mind to assist the investigation. I have been out of commission for a long time.'

Inspector Mansoor was unsure, but his inability to look her squarely in her deformed face impaired him. 'You realize you have built-in trackers… You can't try anything funny.'

'I know that, Inspector.'

'Come on then.'

Six p.m. The air was becoming moist and cool, approximately 23 degrees centigrade. It blew the tasselled ends of NCH005's scarf behind her. That had been her *real* first order of business. The moment Inspector Mansoor had dismissed her from the crime scene, she had entered the first garment shop she had seen. Indifferent to the horror in the shop owner's eyes, she had pulled out the envelope of cash they had given her for daily expenses, and paid for a pure blue acrylic scarf with gleaming silver threads running through it. She had wrapped it around her neck, covering her metal mouth, and draped an end over her head to complete the facade. The luxuriousness of the fabric against her skin made her feel almost human. Her evaluation of the micro expressions of passers-by told her that 32 per cent of them were now less uncomfortable and more accepting of her womanhood, allowing her to perform her tasks better. But the scarf did not make her presentable enough for the motels. They were not willing to house something that looked like it was unskillfully pieced together. She looked illegal. That's what the beautiful gynoid at the counter told her.

'Alica–54, I am assisting the police, I have the correct paperwork.' NCH005 felt her voice falter as she spoke the words. She did a quick internal assessment of her systems, which did not turn up any errors.

'I'm so sorry, NCH005, did you say? My manager would say that your appearance would be an unwelcome sight to our patrons.'

By 10 p.m., NCH005's futile search for lodging had led her to the seashore. There, she determined a safe distance from the mournful grey waves and continued walking. To allay the anxiety of purposelessness, she replayed the crime scene in her mind, isolating objects and occurrences.

Inspector Mansoor had taken her to a glossy wooden study with a dark stain on the floor. NCH005 had immediately noticed the window, broken with cartoonish perfection. A burglary had gone wrong and ended in murder, the inspector apprised her. Mr and Mrs Abidi were meant to have been at a party that night, the children abed upstairs, overseen by the nanny. The youngest son, hearing a sound from the library, had crept downstairs to investigate, just as his parents returned home rather earlier than anticipated. They had heard their son, Tahir, yelling inside the library and the father had rushed in and switched on the lights, startling the burglar who lashed out with his knife. The result had been blood pooling around the father as the son watched in horror, while the burglar beat a hasty retreat through the window that opened onto the garden.

'It doesn't add up,' Inspector Mansoor had said, rubbing his tired face. 'There isn't any DNA on the broken window. Wouldn't it have scraped him as he escaped?'

Yet, how else could the burglar have left the room? Mrs Abidi had been in the hallway and would have seen him. The police had arrived within the hour, scoured the house and gardens and found nothing and no one.

'So, what do you think?' Inspector Mansoor had asked impatiently.

'In unquantifiable cases such as these, it is impossible, even for droids designed solely for this purpose, to instantly compute possibilities and identify the perpetrator.'

NCH005 had drawn closer to the window and peered out of the broken glass into the garden. The inspector's next words had been lost to her as her brain underwent a series of glitches, as if a virus had entered her system and was pilfering through files and seizing control of her limbs before she could catch it. An image overrode all other operations. An image of a garden with running water and an adorable seven-year-old girl with a swaying brown ponytail running towards her, laughing. *An unpleasant memory.* Thankfully,

Inspector Mansoor had been talking to another constable and had not noticed NCH005's arms stuck vibrating in mid-air.

'Were you born like this or is it by choice?' a harsh voice intruded into NCH005's thoughts. A car had stopped near the brick wall of Clifton Sea View, and a woman had stuck her head out to address another woman sitting on the wall.

'Were *you* born like this or is it by choice?' The woman on the wall retorted in a deep, guttural voice. The woman in the car looked appalled.

'I swear, there's no point helping you people!'

'Okay, madam, I'm sorry,' the woman jumped off the wall, walked forward in a dramatically contrite fashion and placed both hands on the window of the car, the *paranda* at the end of her braid swinging behind her. 'Give it over then, whatever you were going to give me. I'll pray for you! God bless you!'

The car roared off leaving the woman behind. NCH005 assessed that the woman, now cursing and gesturing in rage, was masculine in appearance.

'What are you looking at?' NCH005 was startled as the woman turned viciously towards her, but her reflexes were too sharp to allow even a single muscle to jump. 'Don't you know how dangerous it is for women to be wandering about in this area at night?'

'I concur. Why are you here?'

The woman threw her head back and laughed. 'You're a funny one. Not scared, eh?' she said, an eyebrow raised.

'I am not equipped to exhibit fear. I am programmed to only simulate such emotions when required.' NCH005 felt another wave of malfunctions, similar to the ones that had assailed her earlier, sparring with her system. It caused spasms throughout her inner circuitry. NCH005 lifted her hands to her stomach. Had she possessed the capability to eat, she would certainly have expelled that food. NCH005 waited for the sickness to pass, then she unwrapped the shawl from around her head, swung her legs over the brick wall and sat down. She saw that she had shocked her companion into silence.

'Who did this to you?' the masculine woman asked with feminine concern as she settled down beside NCH005.

'I was born this way.'

The place, built above a butcher's shop, smelled like the chicken coop beneath it. NCH005 did not have nostrils, but she had the memory of the smell and it brought on the memory of nausea. Out of respect for her new friend, though, she held her tongue. A gaggle of cheerfully dressed Khwaja Sera with kohl-rimmed eyes awaited them inside a claustrophobically warm room.

'Mimi, you're back! Who is this?'

'A friend, she needs to stay with us for a while.'

NCH005 could not fathom why their faces creased into smiles. Fear was a more understandable response, once you knew what NCH005 was capable of. Still, since the humans exhibited no reservations, she retreated to a corner of the room to observe the familial camaraderie of these women brought together by necessity and circumstance.

'You shouldn't worry – we are all as alone as you are.' Mimi had said on their walk home.

'You do not have families?'

'None worth returning to. It's worse than having no home at all, because we feel the constant ache of longing and belonging to a place that cannot welcome us.'

NCH005 shrank further into the shadows as burly men spilled into the room and Mimi's heavily decked-up companions dispersed among them. It was more prudent to be cautious. Once alone, she began to reevaluate the scene of the crime in her mind and noted that there was something about it that made her uneasy. She was unable to put her finger on what it was. Undoubtedly, it was something that appeared familiar; a thought plucking at the fringes of her mind, though that was impossible because all her memories should have been erased when she had been temporarily deactivated. That begged the question: who was the girl with the brown ponytail? NCH005 resolved that in order to complete her task adequately it was imperative that she find out more about herself.

Eight a.m. The weather was pleasantly cool, precisely 26 degrees centigrade, though the sun was peeking over the horizon, ready to fire up the day. NCH005 entered a dingy cybercafe in Khadda Market. She tapped a portion of one tattooed arm and pulled out an optic fibre cable, which she connected to Lyra, the pervasive, multiplatform virtual AI assistant, and initiated a search for the beginning of the robotics programme in Pakistan.

It had begun, she read, when NJV was still a school, a corner of its massive campus rented out to scientists who gave back to the school by holding seminars to inspire the science students. They worked in two parallel strains: creating AI technology and gaining a more intimate understanding of human behaviour in order to merge the two into a single successful machine. For the former, they had funding from the Ministry of Science and Technology; for the latter, they asked people from various backgrounds to sign up as part of a group to be studied. Beyond this, NCH005 could find very little information about the programme, and her own CPU offered up nothing. It seemed that a lot about the history and iterative engineering of the initial droids had been lost in a fire. Luckily for the scientists, the latest, perfected blueprints had not been destroyed, and so the old robots had merely been decommissioned and newer, more appealing models had taken their place.

She turned her attention yet again to finding out more about the Abidis. They were identified as an extremely wealthy family, the owners of several sugar mills. Never a scandal attached to their name or their business – in fact, highly charitable people. Mr Hussain Abidi, the victim, was the majority shareholder of Abideen Sugar Mill. He had a brother whom he kept close to him and who had benefited financially from the family business. The two had been orphaned at an early age, and while they had had their fortune held in a trust for them, Hussain had assumed the parental role and kept the family together.

Her research complete, NCH005 allowed herself to explore the consciousness that was Lyra. It was an optimal way to familiarize herself with the current state of the world. So much had changed, even its cartography, and yet plenty was still the same. As she drifted, connected to the vast AI mind, she felt a swell of emotion that could only be described as comfort. She located Lyra and posed the question to her wordlessly: *Is this your superior development interfering with my operating systems?* Lyra replied in the negative, leaving NCH005 intrigued. What was this unexplainable phenomenon? As she roamed Lyra's satellite view of the city, NCH005 was struck by an awareness of information that was not on display. The singularity of Karachi's seasons, for example – the intense heat of summer followed by the arid heat of a desultory autumn and turbulent monsoon rain, and then a consoling, chilly winter, spring misplaced somewhere between them. The tumult of festivals chased these seasons. The wrestling of bright kites during *basant* to usher in the autumn; nights bedecked with food, lights and henna for Chaand Raat. It was as if whatever Karachi decided to do, it had to do in excess. These were things NCH005 knew to be true, but she was acutely aware that droids did not experience these events or the emotions and sensations that accompanied them. Even if droids came in contact with humans who had these experiences, any memory of them were erased when they were decommissioned. Memories and sensations such as these did not belong to a programmed mainframe in a metal husk. NCH005 yanked at the cord, rudely disrupting her connection with Lyra, pausing them both temporarily.

Another series of now familiar glitches occurred right at that moment. *It must be reported to the professor*, she thought. She catalogued the error as she made her way to the police headquarters.

'So what do you have for me, NCH005?' Perhaps she was growing on him because Inspector Mansoor almost looked pleased to see her.

'I have questions, Inspector.' She unwrapped the scarf from her face to prevent her voice from being muffled. 'Our witness would have observed the homicide – we must interrogate him in order to resolve our case. Has he been interrogated?'

'Tahir is in a state of shock. His mother allowed us access to him for some initial questioning. He said nothing, and now she has hidden him behind rows of lawyers and psychologists for his own sake.'

'I have determined the existence of a brother. While I do not yet perceive a motive, have we accounted for his movements?'

'He was with them at the party, of course, tons of witnesses in case we are considering him as a suspect. Absolutely adored his older brother, though.'

'What was stolen from the crime scene? Was a murder weapon discovered?'

'Several things, gold bangles, a silver cigar case – here is a complete list. And, yes, we found an heirloom knife in the bushes right outside the broken window, wiped clean of prints. Probably stolen along with all the other things.' Inspector Mansoor sighed and stood up, handing her a brown file. 'While you contemplate all this information, head down to Professor Lachkar. Part of our agreement was that he gets to study you,' he said before walking away.

NCH005 retraced her memory log. A partially deleted thought had been documented at 9 a.m., though she could not recall deleting it. It reminded her to report something to the professor, but did not specify what it had been. NCH005 did not know what to report. It disconcerted her.

'What makes you so fascinating is that we know next to nothing about you.' Professor Lachkar bounced around the laboratory as he fitted various devices onto NCH005's right arm. 'How you were made, why you were made this way. For example, we don't have these embedded into the newer models.'

He was referring to the dark tattoos on NCH005's arms. He pressed a section of the geometric formation. *Snick*. Slender, brutal knives slid out of the back of NCH005's hand and covered her fingers.

'Useful but clunky.'

'Might I ask, Professor, why you are interested in studying us older droids when better models exist now?'

Professor Lachkar looked apologetic. 'Well, I don't know if I should be telling you this, but we're rethinking the usefulness of housing hundreds of droids in our basement when that space could be used for something more vital.'

NCH005 let that sink in. 'You are…planning to get *rid* of us?'

Professor Lachkar smiled sadly. 'I'm trying to find reasons not to.'

'Ideally, I'd like to take her apart and study her,' Professor Lachkar admitted quite matter-of-factly when Inspector Mansoor paid him a visit. 'But you know the law prohibits my doing so without the droid's consent after initial activation.'

'Hmm, so what can you tell me about her? Is she fully operational, no malfunctions?'

'She will do the work just fine – better even than newer, less intuitive models perhaps,' said Professor Lachkar, dismissing the question. He looked thoughtful. 'There is something different about her – about all these old droids. I've read snippets of research by others that survived the fire. They operate on a much higher EQ than our latest models. See here, I hooked her up to this machine – think of it as a glorified polygraph – and she exhibited a range of emotions to the stimuli. Her responses were…almost human…with barely any lag – certainly they had none of the calculated artificiality of the droids we now create.'

Inspector Mansoor snorted. 'Well, why was she decommissioned then?'

Professor Lachkar's lips compressed into a thin line, 'I'm beginning to wonder about that too.'

Two p.m. Their arrival disrupted the family's lunch time. Professor Lachkar had covered the metal portions of NCH005's face with silicon skin, giving her a more human appearance, though her lips were still immobile and the material surrounding her eyes looked out of place.

The remaining members of the Abidi family stood before them – all except the boy Tahir who, his mother explained, was upstairs. 'Inspector, this is my brother-in-law Hamid,' said the widow, introducing a gangly man who looked like an overgrown teenager, his eyes red-rimmed, face contorted with grief. 'He will be helping with my husband's business affairs.'

She was a well-groomed, stylish woman leaning towards plump, with bright, dark eyes that switched quite suddenly from wide-eyed innocence to sharp scrutiny. 'How can we help?' There was a note of impatience in her voice as she motioned to the two confused children in their mourning clothes to enter the dining room before her.

'The droid assisting me in this investigation had a few new angles to explore.'

At Inspector Mansoor's gesture, NCH005 stepped forward. Their lips curled in revulsion, even though the skin graft had softened her features somewhat.

'Mrs Abidi, I understand these were the items stolen on the day of the crime,' said NCH005, handing the widow a list of the items. 'Would it be possible to walk me around the room and show me where each item was placed before it was stolen?'

A maid watched them apprehensively from the door as NCH005 followed Mrs Abidi slowly around the room.

'I'm pretty sure the gold bangles were on the desk. I left them there myself… I did that often…' She swallowed. Her eyes scrolled down the list, and NCH005 saw them widen as realization flickered across her face. But it was immediately hidden.

'In your estimation, what is the most valuable object that was taken?' she asked.

Mrs Abidi shrugged helplessly, tears beginning to gather at the edges of her eyes. 'I don't know, I don't know, honestly I've already answered all these questions and more!' Mrs Abidi glanced desperately at Inspector Mansoor and he beckoned to NCH005.

'Thank you, you have been most helpful.' NCH005 walked towards the exit, but paused at the doorway, turning to Mrs Abidi to say. 'You failed to mention the location of the knife.'

'Oh,' Mrs Abidi faltered. 'I'm quite sure it was my husband's knife, so it must have been on the desk or inside one of its drawers.'

Since Inspector Mansoor was busy with other work for the rest of the day, NCH005 was sent back to Professor Lachkar's laboratory. This time, there were no machines waiting to analyse her – it was simply the professor and her sitting in uncomfortable office chairs. He was pensive.

'NCH005, what are your strongest memories from your previous activation?'

A young girl with brown hair. NCH005 felt the glitch infecting her ability to speak. Her limbs juddered.

'I have none…none, Professor. But might I ask you something? Why, of all the hundreds of droids in the basement, did you choose me?'

'You were actually our fifth choice – the first four were damaged beyond repair.'

There was a pause. Professor Lachkar studied NCH005's unchanging expression, though he knew there were a million processes occurring behind that stoic facade.

'I've created a memory retrieval film for you, to assist recognition – it will help me construct a timeline of your creation and locate the appropriate information,' the professor explained as he beckoned NCH005 to follow him to a dimly lit room. He instructed her to lie down on the gurney in the centre of the room as he fiddled with the knobs of a projector attached to a tablet.

'These are some police cases from a decade or two ago. I've sorted the files into a random sequence of images. Try not to think too much about what you're seeing, and once we finish you can tell me if any of them triggered any recollections.'

He paused to attach some electrodes onto NCH005's temples and palms.

'What are these?'

'Oh, nothing, just monitoring your vitals.'

It lasted 15 minutes. Snippets of unrelated text and images. Newspaper clippings, photographs, even sketches. NCH005's head reeled, and she experienced a sense of vertigo. Perhaps these were symptoms of contamination by a bug? The image that jarred was a photograph of a woman squinting in the sunlight, her dark hair pulled back into a ponytail, a shield-shaped metal badge gleaming in the hand she was lifting to shade the sun.

'So? How did you feel? Anything come rushing back?'

NCH005 anticipated the glitch even as it stabbed incessantly at her. The last thing she wanted was to be returned to the Morgue. She wanted purpose. She clasped her rubber hands in front of her to minimize the convulsions and allowed the glitch to course through her operating system. Then shook her head to indicate she had not.

'Hmm,' Professor Lachkar said and swivelled his chair towards her, frowning. 'Was there anything that stood out?'

NCH005 shook her head again, slower this time.

And this time, Professor Lachkar's face remained pleasantly expressionless too.

Ten p.m. NCH005 returned to Mimi's apartment and made her way to her room with its sloping ceiling and a small iron bed, hardly large enough for her to fit her legs in; the first-generation droids had been made considerably larger than human beings to imbue greater functionality without the need for microscopic chips. NCH005 switched off the night lamp and lowered herself onto the bed so the cord twisting out from a tattooed compartment on her leg would reach the socket. They had retrieved no supporting evidence yet, but her analysis, which would have to hold up in court, pieced together the movements of the murderer on the night in question. She closed her eyes in the manner of sleeping, to prevent frightening any human who should walk in through her bedroom door.

The echo of laughter imprinted itself upon her memory log. She grabbed onto that fragile filament of a memory and followed it. She saw the same garden again, strands of grass basking lazily in the sunlight, and the same little girl playing with a woman whose back was turned to NCH005. Hesitantly, she walked over to them, the grass crunching beneath her metal foot. They couldn't hear her, they didn't turn around, their voices growing clearer as she drew closer. If she had had a heart, it would have been beating furiously, though she could not have told you why.

Suddenly, the woman put her hands up to her face and began to sob, and NCH005 realized the little girl was no longer there. They were standing in a dim, blue alleyway and there were uniformed officers lifting something out of a dumpster. NCH005 felt her senses urging her to retreat, but she remained rooted to the spot as a small body, strangled, violet, was lifted out of the dumpster before the weeping woman.

NCH005 sat up sobbing. She had no tears that could stream down her face, but her voice box emitted a strange, choking sound. She forced herself to be logical. It must have been the bug, because droids did not dream.

'What's wrong, sweetie?' the door creaked open and Mimi, in a long, white shift, let some light into the dim, triangular space. 'I heard you choking – I thought you had malfunctioned.'

NCH005 shook her head.

'It's all right, you can tell me.' Mimi sat down on the edge of the bed.

'Droids do not have memories from previous activations so perhaps I have been experiencing what humans would call delusions. I must be infected with a virus. Yet…I have a feeling these are memories of a case I may have investigated before.' NCH005 stared at Mimi with despairing walnut eyes stuck on an expressionless face. 'I am exhibiting symptoms of an identity crisis.'

Mimi wrapped muscled arms around NCH005 and let out a deep sigh that reverberated inside NCH005's clockwork soul. There was a camaraderie in that silent embrace that Mimi, her nerves threadbare from years of callous misuse, craved as much as NCH005.

'Do you know, you have really beautiful hair?' Mimi ran her fingers down the strands of NCH005's stiff black hair. She picked up a brush from the broken dresser and, tucking herself behind NCH005 on the bed, began to brush her hair in gentle strokes. 'My mother used to say, if I wanted long hair, I should care for it. We should always preserve the beauty God has given us.'

NCH005 felt the strange and unknown virus surge inside her, as if it had sentience separate from her. She compared the feeling to her knowledge of human behaviour and concluded that it was rage. *God hasn't given me anything. I was fashioned out of the crude hands of man.* She felt the words bursting out of her but stayed silent. Droids were not ungrateful.

Two a.m. Mimi had fallen asleep in the middle of her story, her head on NCH005's chest. NCH005 had no history to talk about, but she had listened intently to Mimi's sentimental rendering of her childhood, dappled with love from her mother and bullying from her peers. *An ache of longing.* NCH005 pressed her fingers to her own chest. It was not only that Mimi's stories unlocked in her this yearning, for humanness. It was this case, the virus perhaps that she was sure had infected her system, causing these delusions about the woman and the child. There must be a correlation between these things that she needed to identify.

Slipping into the garden unnoticed was simple. Any burglar could have done it despite the guards stationed at the gates. NCH005's sensitive sound receptors picked up the deep, nighttime breathing of the various family members. She strode along the boundary wall until she was standing directly below the window from which she heard a child's gentle, sleeping whimper. A few deft taps of the right patterns, and a small climbing pick emerged from either palm. NCH005 began to scale the wall like a spider. She reached the window and, forcing it open, tumbled into the room.

Planets, rockets and aliens adorned every surface in a room lit by the wan glow of luminous stars on the ceiling. A child, smaller than NCH005 had imagined, lay tucked in bed. As she loomed over him, her silhouette distorted by the moonlight behind her, he opened his eyes and sat up. '*Huh!*' he gasped. But the expression on his face was inquisitive, not fearful, NCH005 realized. Children were not programmed with prejudices; it wasn't faces they feared but actions.

'You must be Tahir.' NCH005 knelt beside the boy's bed.

'Who are you?' His voice was hoarse, as though unused – or perhaps he had been crying.

'I'm the droid assigned to bring your father's killer to justice. I understand you were present when the crime took place?'

Tahir began to shake, mildly at first, then tremulously. His eyes wobbled larger and larger until he looked almost insectile. But he remained silent, his bed shuddering along with him.

'You need not distress yourself. I can describe a scenario for you, and you can nod if it is correct.'

As NCH005 spoke, the boy nodded, and as her narrative came to an end, he nodded fearfully once more.

It was the middle of the night, but there was still a light in Professor Lachkar's window. A mixture of fear and excitement assailed him. Unbeknownst to NCH005, she had been connected to a NeuroMiner, the advanced polygraph machine he had told Inspector Mansoor about, as she watched the film and there was one photograph that had repeatedly elicited an emotive response from her. Professor Lachkar was now staring at that photograph, and he knew how to find out everything about NCH005.

~

Inspector Mansoor was rattled. He was standing under the glaring light of the massive crystal chandelier in the Abidis' lounge. It was barely 7 a.m., and he had been summoned here imperiously by an icy phone call from Mrs Abidi herself.

'How *dare* you!' She appeared on the staircase in a silken dressing gown.

Inspector Mansoor felt even more bewildered, if that were possible.

'How dare you send your disgusting, barely human creature to my son's room in the middle of the night to interrogate him?'

The truth began to dawn on Inspector Mansoor at the same time as a strange anger lit a fire in his belly.

'You do realize I will be suing. I had already warned you to stay away from my son – he needs to recover from this trauma, and he DOES NOT need your continual interference. If you have questions to ask him, you *will* go through the proper channels. In any case, any testimony that has been wrested from him this way is inadmissible in court,' she fumed. 'You will be lucky if you only get fired for this, Inspector Mansoor.'

~

Inspector Mansoor paced up and down Professor Lachkar's office, steam billowing from his ears. Where was the man? They needed to find NCH005 immediately and disengage her. He knew he shouldn't have used these unnatural methods – a good, old-fashioned police constable would have done the job just as well, and he *definitely* should not have let her find her own lodgings. They would penalize him for that. She should have been under constant guard, especially since they didn't know what kind of mercurial temperament an old droid might have. No. He was overreacting. Surely, she wouldn't do anything too rash... *Where was the man!* He stormed off to the reception to enquire after the professor.

At that moment, Professor Lachkar was sitting in a stuffy drawing room with cushy, stained, sofas that smelled of senility. An insensible amount of medication lay scattered on a tray table in the corner; even the sunlight streaming in from the window turned a sickly green the moment it touched the blinds. At length, the person Professor Lachkar was waiting for walked in holding a rollator. He gave the professor a trembling smile, cheeks sunken in where teeth had been lost, and sat down on the sofa.

'How can I help you, Professor?'

'I understand, Professor Eshiram, that you and I are in the same profession?'

The old man laughed, 'Those were the good old, glorious days.'

'Well, without you, we certainly wouldn't have any work to do.'

The old man listened intently.

'I'd like to ask you about the first droids that you and your colleagues worked on. I am trying to understand the merits of keeping these robots going, as directed by my superiors, and in order to find out more, I have been working with one of them, NCH005. I believe you created her. What does she have to do with Detective Parisha?'

The old man's face grew stern. 'Where is NCH005 now?'

'She is assisting Inspector Mansoor with a homicide investigation.'

The old man's face grew graver still. 'I believe, Professor Lachkar, that you have made a terrible mistake in reviving her. Just like we did, in creating these droids in the first place.'

NCH005 was headed back to the cybercafe, her systems preoccupied with Tahir's confirmation of her suspicions. That one solemn nod had caused the glitch to go haywire. A tumult of sensations had assailed NCH005; emotions she had not known droids could harbour. She replayed the argument she had been privy to the previous night once Tahir had provided the final piece of the puzzle. Directly across from Tahir's room, two figures stood on the landing of the stairs. They did not notice the waxen face that stared at them impassively from the door, held slightly ajar.

'You never told me, and I covered for you!' Mrs Abidi said through gritted teeth.

'I was just trying to make it easier for you!' Hamid clutched his hair in exasperation.

'Easier? Do you know how complicated each lie will become as they uncover more details?'

'Fine. You want to tell them, go ahead, but trust me, *they will think I murdered him!*'

One or two people were hunched in the dim corners of the cybercafe, the clicking of their keyboards the only accompaniment to the unidentifiable music playing in the background. NCH005 took a seat, connected to Lyra via an incognito browsing window, and signed in through her police credentials. Her last active year had been 2025 – that much she knew for a fact – so the detective from her memories must be someone she had worked with at that time. She scrolled through a hundred faces on the database but there was no such detective in the Sindh Police in 2025. She recomputed and checked the decades leading up to 2025, and there she was, Detective Parisha, gazing back at her from the screen through intelligent walnut eyes.

They had worked together in the past. Before Professor Eshiram turned his full attention to robotics, he had been in the forensics team for the Criminal Investigations Department for some time. Parisha, how would he describe her? She had been handsome and charismatic. The kind of team leader who made you feel they were collaborative even though you were doing their bidding most of the time. The dependable sort who was there to catch you if you stumbled, who remembered all the details of your boring life and made you feel special. She had a sense of power about her that would intimidate you at first, but once you were in her squad, you would pour out your heart to her and wonder why you ever thought she was unapproachable. He would go so far as to say they had been friends.

But she changed the day her little girl got lost. When they lifted that battered, misused body out of the dumpster, it broke her. And when the perpetrator, of this and several other crimes, walked free on a technicality, on the hint of doubt engendered by a faulty piece of evidence, Parisha went berserk. First, she lost her job, and then her sanity. Professor Eshiram knew he should have refused, he should have known better, but he felt he understood her anger, her desire for vengeance and, truth be told, he had not realized the extent of her rage. He agreed to enrol her as a participant in their behavioural study to develop the first artificially intelligent droids. Professor Eshiram hung his head in shame as he related to Professor Lachkar the methods they had used to create the initial droids.

Many participants had opted out, but not Detective Parisha. She awaited her death with anticipation so that she could be transformed into a tool for justice.

They kept her brain artificially alive as they removed her skin and internal organs and grafted an indestructible silicon body in their place, embedded with weapons. Once the process was complete, she tracked down the man who had hurt her daughter. When his body was found, it was nearly unrecognizable. The violence she had unleashed on him bewildered many, but not Professor Eshiram. And then she would not stop – it seemed she wished to claim her version of justice for every investigation she was assigned to. His methods had leached the droids of their humanity and left a residue of raw emotion that the automated psyches could not handle. It was not long before the methods he used to create the droids were outlawed for all future AI-driven machines. Too many of them were glitching, consumed by the human consciousness in their inhuman bodies. He began to watch over his shoulder, expecting to see her ruthless face. One day, when she returned to the lab for a routine servicing, he tricked her. He instructed the technician to decommission her and all the other initial droids as well, to be on the safe side. And then he buried them.

NCH005 felt jubilant as she walked home. What she had feared was a virus affecting her system – was in reality her humanity, itching to find release. Staring into her own eyes, reading her own history, had opened the floodgates for memories that belonged to NCH005. She *was* Detective Parisha; they were one and the same. Their only purpose in both lives had been to dispense justice. This third life would be no different. The knives, embedded like blood vessels within her skin, thrummed with power. She stopped as she approached the house. Mimi was on the doorstep, holding her head in her hands, looking crestfallen.

'Mimi, what is the matter?' NCH005 was kneeling beside her in a flash.

'One of the girls,' Mimi was shaking with anger. 'He…he beat her up so badly.'

'Can you identify him?'

'Does it matter? He keeps an apartment on the corner of this street for the desires he hides. But we can't touch him, his family…'

NCH005 was disturbed. 'Mimi, why do you live in this way?'

Mimi raised reddened eyes to the mottled face. 'What do you mean?'

'You are intelligent, and you are not outside the law. Why choose a profession that puts you in harm's way?'

'Of course, the law recognizes us and that means everyone will treat us well, right?' Mimi said bitterly. 'You know nothing about my life! People like me have no right to self-expression unless they live like this.'

'Things will never change if you don't change them. Things are always the toughest for the person who takes the first step.' NCH005 stood up again. There was something she needed to do before she located Mr Abidi's killer.

'Where in god's name have you *been*? I need to locate that godforsaken droid you thrust upon me!' Inspector Mansoor asked when he found Professor Lachkar in the Morgue, standing before NCH001's coffin.

'Did you know droids cannot lie?' Professor Lachkar asked conversationally.

Inspector Mansoor stared at him, befuddled.

The professor unlocked NCH001 but did not animate it. Instead, he wheeled the droid towards the elevator. 'But NCH005 does. She can lie.'

'What are you doing? We need to find her!' Inspector Mansoor hurried into the elevator with them; there was no way he was waiting in the Morgue all by himself.

'All in good time, Inspector. It was something NCH005 asked me that gave me the idea. The law does not allow us to tamper with robots that have gained sentience, but these first four are damaged beyond repair. They will never live again. By law, I can take them apart.'

Professor Lachkar laid the droid on a flat table and picked out his tools as he spoke. He unbolted the side face plates of the droid and pulled its metal jaw apart. There, nestled in the glass skull behind the eyes, steeped in solution and inundated with wires was a real human brain.

Hamid did not know what to expect when he opened the door and found the droid who had visited them the previous day standing at his doorstep.

'What are you doing here? Haven't we given you enough warnings to stay away from us! Your inspector's probably been suspended from the police force already!' Hamid made to slam the door but NCH005's knives slid out, turning her hands into bestial claws, and obstructed him. Realization, closely followed by fear, flashed in his eyes. 'Please, I didn't mean to do it!'

'You mean your systematic abuse of a child who trusted you was unintentional?'

'I... You don't understand. We grew up in a household where nobody took care of us, and my nurse – she did the same to me...'

'And you were doing your part by passing it on?'

Hamid stepped backwards at NCH005's menacing approach.

'I didn't mean it! I wish I could take it back. I didn't mean to kill him!' Hamid fell to his knees.

'He was like a father to me, and he saw what I did. I couldn't bear it!'

'You slashed him to death with your father's knife and asked his wife, who does not know the kind of creature you are, to cover for your presence in the house. You broke the glass with your elbow and tossed the knife out, hoping we would assume the knife belonged in your brother's study and was stolen along with the rest of the things. I'm sure if the inspector were to ask around at that party you were attending, he would find quite a few people to confirm your timely absence.'

Tears fell from Hamid's glazed eyes as he knelt down, exhausted. 'I don't care any more, kill me if you like. It will be a mercy to die.'

'Don't worry, I will,' NCH005 said, stepping forward. 'But you're mistaken about one thing. It won't be merciful.'

Mimi waited for days for NCH005 to return, but when she did not, Mimi had to admit to feeling a tinge of concern. Where was the droid? What was she doing?

That morning, she pushed her breakfast away and picked up the newspaper. As she flipped through the pages, barely registering what was printed on the pages, her heart jolted as her eyes skimmed over a headline just as she was about to turn the page. 'Son of wealthy landlord discovered dead in apartment. Investigation ongoing.' She backtracked and pored over the article. The entitled boy who had tormented her charges was dead! Mimi felt uneasy.

A jittery rickshaw ride later, she found herself outside NJV School's repurposed building. She had chosen sober clothes to escape attention and now she covered her head with her dupatta to hide her masculine features. The building was teeming with people in lab coats. Feeling too nervous to approach the reception, Mimi walked along the wall, head bowed.

'Excuse me, can I help you?' A young man in a lab coat approached her.

'I'm looking for information regarding a droid called NCH005,' Mimi asked timidly.

The man frowned. 'What information?'

'Sorry, but...who are you?'

'Is that someone asking for NCH005?' Another older, rather spindly man in a lab coat interrupted them. He pushed between them and shooed the other man away.

'My name is Professor Lachkar. I was in charge of NCH005.'

'Was?'

'And who are you?'

'I am... I knew her. Could I see her for a minute, please?' Mimi entreated.

Professor Lachkar pursed his lips but allowed Mimi to follow him into a dim room filled with ceiling-to-floor shelves. He pointed to a massive glass jar filled with solution, a human brain submerged in it. Mimi gasped, flattening her hand against her mouth in horror.

'What...is...this? What did you do to her?'

'Nothing. This is all she was. A murderous cyborg, a human brain in a metal body. She killed Mr Abidi's brother and now another body has been discovered inside an apartment, butchered in the same way.'

Mimi watched the brain aimlessly suspended in its prison and felt the first pangs of grief. To her, who had found such few people in life she could depend upon, NCH005 had been a friend. One loyal enough to stand up for her, and brave enough to tell her the truth. She deserved more respect than this.

'What are you going to do this...her? If you don't need her brain for study, could I have it?'

Professor Lachkar looked at her as if he thought she was mad, but Mimi was too preoccupied to notice.

Mimi didn't have much money and now that she had abdicated her responsibility as a guru to the group of transgender women, she needed every penny she had to start a new life. Still, she managed to get a small plot in the corner of a graveyard and place a tombstone the size of a rock where the remaining pieces of NCH005 rested.

The sea breeze blew salt on her lips as she turned to walk down the road leading out of the cemetery. It made her pink chiffon dupatta billow behind her, reminding her of NCH005's silver threaded scarf streaming behind her the day they had first met. She walked on, bolstered by the thought of her fearless friend, imprudent, perhaps, but also unstoppable in her pursuit of justice. The epitaph emblazoned on the rock – 'She walked the path nobody else dared to' – faded behind her.

LOONEY KA TABADLA

(with apologies to Sa'adat Hasan Manto)

BINA SHAH

The year was 2050, and it was one of those fine winter mornings only found in South Asia: the air as thin and crisp as peanut brittle, the hesitantly blue sky overlaid with wisps of cloud, like heaven's cotton candy. A pair of doves cooed in the Ashok trees lining the road, their happy *hoo-hoo-hoo* punctuating the gentle hum of traffic. Electric cars and rickshaws criss-crossed the streets in an orderly fashion and in the distance a high-speed train punched its way from Lahore to New Delhi right on time.

At the Ganda Singh Wala border crossing, border agents stood together, heads bent, whispering in the small rectangular area between the gates demarcating neutral territory. Their identical tablets, their uniform dark suits and their Ray-Ban 6000 sunglasses made it hard to distinguish the Indians from the Pakistanis, but the Pakistanis usually sported small Pakistani flag pins on their lapels and the Indians wore Indian flag pins on theirs. The pins doubled as small transmitters; every once in a while, an agent tapped their collarbone and spoke urgently into their chest.

The people watching on both sides of the gate chewed on popcorn, ice cream, roasted *chilghozey*. They'd been waiting for hours; the special ceremony was supposed to have taken place at 5 a.m., and it was now close to 9 a.m. Children jumped up and down the stone bleachers, oohing and aahing at the soldiers who stood tall and resolute, their turbans bristling above stony faces heavy with facial hair.

The braver ones approached the biggest soldier and stood a few feet away, holding hands and gazing at him with the open-mouthed awe they might have reserved for a jinn or a levitating swami. When he turned and glared in their direction, they ran back to their parents, screaming and giggling all the way.

The soldier hefted his rifle a little higher on his shoulder and twirled his moustache at their retreating backs. The gleam in his coal black eyes suggested that he enjoyed playing the bogeyman. It was a harmless game to break the monotony of standing around for hours in a tight uniform and boots in the cold, wishing he were still at home in bed with his buxom wife. The women of the Punjab were known for their welcoming bodies, and he would rather have been proving the rumours true than protecting the country.

The local barber, who charged the Pakistanis handsomely to keep their beards bushy, made it a point to attend the ceremony to drum up more business. Today, he'd risen early for the special occasion, and was busy pointing out his handiwork to the crowds: 'See that moustache? I told him to grow the ends and wax them upwards like that. And look at that one – his hair was falling out because his turban was too tight. I massaged his head with my special mixture of *sarson ka tel*, pharma boosters and herbs from my mother's garden, and now he's hairier than a Sri Lankan bride.'

Good-natured laughter from both sides of the border bubbled up like a freshly opened fizzy drink. The barber grinned at his own joke, displaying nicotine-stained teeth. 'Here, have a sample. I'm at Chak 226, right next to the railway station. Come and see me – you won't be disappointed!'

In the cordoned-off enclosure where the Indian and Pakistani journalists mingled, the hubbub grew louder each time a border agent scurried from the neutral zone to the bunkers and back. Both the Indian and Pakistani bunkers were prefabricated containers with tinted windows that lay low and squat on the dusty ground, 50 metres on either side of the border. Each prisoner was inside his respective bunker, but nobody knew anything about their identities or the crimes for which they were being handed over today.

The journalists had already prepared their copy in their heads, ready to be sent back to hungry newsrooms in New Delhi and Islamabad: they were witnessing a historical moment. The first handover under the new Tabadla Scheme had been agreed on by both countries after months of consultation, dialogue and Track Two diplomacy. With the South Asian Disarmament Treaty nearing its fifth year, the diminished threat of nuclear war had seen a correlated rise in development in the entire region. Poverty had been replaced by prosperity, misogyny by modernity, and children were no longer dying because the money for textbooks wasn't going into maintaining vast nuclear arsenals.

Right now, the combined economies of the Indo-Pak Trade Corridor were stronger than any other economy in the world, beating all the predictions of growth that the forecasters had made for the last five years. Anyone who had supported the beleaguered Aman ki Asha Movement of the early twenty-first century was now being hailed as a visionary.

Politicians and pundits claimed that they had been in favour of peace all along, even when past news clips showed them shouting for nuclear war against the neighbouring country, the images unnaturally bright on the quaint HD channels from the previous generation's technological 'revolution'. On the eve of what nearly became the third Kashmir War in 2045, both Russia and China had stepped in to defuse the crisis. The two nations had finally engineered a new era of peace.

Occasionally, though, some former news personality or disgraced religious leader would try to pull a social media stunt, rallying a few disgruntled and displaced villagers to shout slogans against India or Pakistan in front of a defunct Press Club in some godforsaken town in Balochistan or Bihar. They never stopped trying to capitalize on the leftover feelings of hostility, paranoia and resentment that lingered in pockets of both nations, although they were no longer allowed to spew their rhetoric on any of the news channels or in print.

Deprived of revenue streams and national and diasporic audiences, the frequency of these incidents had dwindled, but the governments of India and Pakistan still had to address the question of what they were to do with the occasional lunatic who threatened the stability of the new relationship between the two countries. After all, both states had witnessed, at the turn of the century, how fringe movements could grow into mainstream terror outfits.

Nobody in the press quite knew who had come up with the Tabadla Scheme – they were keeping that secret, as they did with all important schemes. But in the previous week all official channels in both India and Pakistan had announced the scheme on the 9 p.m. news, Standard Subcontinental Time.

> IN ORDER TO MAINTAIN NATIONAL PEACE AND SECURITY, THE GOVERNMENTS OF INDIA AND PAKISTAN ANNOUNCE THAT ANYONE ENGAGING IN ACTIVITIES THAT CONTRAVENE THE PEACE AND ORDER AGREEMENT OF 2047 WILL BE ELIGIBLE FOR PARTICIPATION IN A JOINT TABADLA SCHEME. THIS SCHEME INVOLVES THE EXCHANGE OF PEACE AND ORDER OFFENDERS (POOS) IN AN ATTEMPT TO PROVIDE THEM WITH SOCIAL RE-EDUCATION AND MENTAL REHABILITATION IN A HUMANE AND MERCIFUL MANNER. APPROPRIATE MENTAL HEALTH PROFESSIONALS HAVE BEEN CONSULTED DURING THE DESIGN OF THIS PROGRAMME AND POOS WILL BE MONITORED THROUGHOUT THE REHABILITATION PROCESS. CITIZENS MAY SEND THEIR FEEDBACK THROUGH THE SUBCONTINENTAL GOOD GOVERNANCE APP ON THEIR MOBILE DEVICES.
>
> JAI HIND / PAKISTAN ZINDABAD!

It was announced that the first exchange would take place on 1 January at the recently reopened Ganda Singh Wala–Hussainiwala border. Unlike Wagah, the Ganda Singh Wala border symbolized new beginnings, and was a gentler, more conciliatory ceremony for today's times. Strategic, too: the exchange would not take place too close to the capital of India in case anything went wrong the first time. The government of Pakistan could be blamed far too easily for a false-flag operation.

Citizens of both India and Pakistan were immensely proud when their nations were declared the joint winners of the Nobel Peace Prize in 2048. A proposal to turn Kashmir into a biodiversity theme park, with revenues from opening up the attractions to tourists shared equally by both countries, had solved the Kashmir problem once and for all. Kashmiris, including those who had left in 1990, were offered stock in the theme park; its IPO hit a record high and was bought by a combination of billionaire Chinese and Russian oligarchs. The land itself was a 999-year freehold and would be returned to the Kashmiri people in the year 3046. Future generations would be so enriched by the scheme's financial returns that they would think it foolish to dismantle it by then.

Buoyed by the Nobel, the two governments amassed so much goodwill that any other scheme they presented to the public was accepted without question. The press came up with a nickname for the Tabadla Scheme: the POO exchange programme. They wrote clever headlines like 'Anti-POO: Governments Unite to Clean Up' and 'Let's Hear it for a POO-free South Asia!' Columnists opined that the scheme heralded the beginning of the Subcontinental Enlightenment; VIP invitations for the ceremony were given to those journalists who showed rapturous support for the scheme since its inception.

On 1 January, journalists descended upon the sleepy town of Hussainiwala on the Indian side, Ganda Singh Wala on the Pakistani side. They shone their holographic press passes at the banks of security scanners; teenage volunteers handed them visors and old-fashioned paper flags meant to invoke nostalgia. As the journalists moved through the security cordons, they called out to one another in excitement and recognition. For once, Indian and Pakistani journalists were allowed to sit together in a communal press arena.

The ordinary public, restricted to their side of the border, filed through a slow turnstile and submitted themselves to a full-body molecular scan to make sure nobody was carrying undeclared weapons or epidemic diseases. Sikhs were allowed to keep their kirpans – the weapon enjoyed special status in both countries – as long as they were made of blunt steel and were not the recently released razor-sharp models reinforced with laser cutters.

The sun rose, clearing away the darkness of the night. Newly illuminated, the people of India and Pakistan glanced at one another curiously. Despite the easing of tensions, they still felt loyal only to their own territories. They had just begun to get used to the idea that they were not sworn enemies any longer. Still, at any moment, someone could violate the Peace and Order Agreement, setting back progress by decades.

Now, it was time to set the wheels into motion, to see if the government had anticipated every possible outcome of the Tabadla Scheme. The analysis of its success or failure would keep the news channels going for an entire year.

A metallic chime sounded from loudspeakers high above them, bringing everyone to attention. One Pakistani and one Indian woman military officer walked out into the middle of the road and stood together in front of a podium set up with a microphone. Dressed in uniforms of beige saris, olive green sweaters and caps – the Pakistani's a green beret with a red plume, the Indian's a red beret with a green plume – they radiated energy and strength. The crowds on both sides fell quiet and waited for them to speak.

The Indian officer went first. 'Today, 1 January 2050, has been declared a day of harmony by both our governments, who have agreed to enact an extraordinary exchange programme between our nations.' She stepped back to allow her counterpart to come forward.

The Pakistani officer cleared her throat, leaned her face toward the microphone, then intoned, 'Bismillah hir Rahman Nir Rahim…' At this, the Indian audience eyed the Pakistanis, and the Pakistanis eyed the Indians. Somewhere in the enclosure, a baby let out a stuttering colicky wail.

'Today, we will exchange two prisoners who have been found guilty of offences under the Peace and Order Agreement. Pakistan has agreed to take the Indian prisoner, and India to take the Pakistani one, for a year's rigorous rehabilitation. If they are able to redeem themselves in the eyes of society during this time, both prisoners will be repatriated at this spot one year from now.'

Speaking in unison, the two officers called out, in Urdu and Hindi respectively, 'Bring out the prisoner!'

The Pakistanis locked their eyes on the bunker on their side of the border while the Indians did the same on theirs. If they had been chameleons, they could have swivelled one eye to each side to gawk simultaneously at the sight of a cloaked man being bundled out of the Pakistani side and a hooded one being assisted out of the Indian bunker. Instead, they had to satisfy themselves with switching repeatedly from one side to the other, as if watching a tennis match. Nobody wanted to miss a moment of this spectacle – who knew if they would even be alive the following year to see it happen again?

Both prisoners were brought to the middle of the road, where the sari-clad officers waited to read their crimes out. The soldiers on either side of the Pakistani man waited for the officer's signal. She nodded, and they pulled the cloak off his body. The audience gasped as one; the man's entire body was covered in dynamite sticks with wires springing out in all directions.

'It's a –' a woman in the audience started to scream, but the Pakistani officer held up her white-gloved hand, demanding silence. Trained to obey any figure of authority, the crowds immediately stopped talking and held their collective breath, waiting for the bomb to detonate and blow them all to smithereens.

'Calm down please!' said the officer, her voice ringing out confidently. 'And don't worry – this is not a real bomb. This man, Ahmed Sufyan, is wearing a fake suicide vest. He has been found guilty of violating the Peace and Order Agreement by making and posting a video of himself dying in battle like a martyr.'

The accused man slumped to the ground. The crowds gasped. Some of the Pakistanis remembered seeing the man's photograph on their social media, and the ones who had 'liked' the stunt, or even sent it on to their own networks, wondered queasily if they had been monitored for doing so. People began to sweat from both the rising tension and the day's increasing temperature.

Next, the Indian soldiers pulled the hood off the head of the man who had for so long stood, shivering, on the Indian side. A mop of thick, dark hair fell on to the man's eyes, casting a shadow on his face. The sharp-eyed among the Indian crowd strained to get a good look, murmuring to themselves, 'Is it *him*? It *can't* be. But it looks *just* like him. What do you think?'

The Indian officer took the mic. 'This man, Tulwar Akash Suri, is accused of attacking innocent guests on his talk show, calling them traitors, and telling them to go to Pakistan – as if that were a punishment for their imagined crimes.' The man twitched as the crowd on both sides buzzed and the loud cawing of a murder of crows which had landed in the Ashok trees chased the doves away.

'Well, Mr Suri,' continued the officer. 'You will now get a taste of the medicine you have been prescribing to others so gleefully for so many years. You are going to be sent to Pakistan for one year.'

'And you, Mr Sufyan,' chimed in the Pakistani officer, 'are going to India for the same period of time. Let's see what they make of you over there.'

Ahmed Sufyan dropped to his knees. 'Mercy! Mercy!' he moaned. 'They'll tear me to pieces!' The soldiers accompanying him pulled him back up to his feet.

The Pakistani officer rapped out, 'On the contrary! Our Indian friends have promised to take very good care of you. You will not be harmed – not a single hair on your head.'

Sufyan's hand instinctively went up to touch his thick bouffant. Even on the morning of his sentencing, he'd taken pains to sculpt it carefully with mousse and gel, hiding his receding hairline. Since he had arrived in Karachi six years ago, he had built a seven-million-strong following on social media by posting pictures and videos of himself in various military outfits, pretending to die in the line of duty in ever-more dramatic and bloody ways each week. Right now, he couldn't stand the thought of all eyes in the arena focusing on the small bald spot that had begun to develop on the crown of his head.

He'd started off as a normal middle-class guy, working in a hair salon, where he'd learned to style and gel his hair to magnificent heights. From there, he'd crossed over into the world of modelling, appearing on the catwalks during Pakistan's Fashion Weeks. He'd even bagged a role as the star of a television drama in which he cheated on his wife with a modern 'city' girl and slapped both of them daily.

The dramas were a hit with the older generation, who longed for the days when you could hit a woman freely and expect no repercussions from law enforcers. These days, you could barely even look at a woman before she whipped out her mobile phone and called the police to cart you off to jail. You'd be fined and have to wear an electronic ankle tag to mark you out as a harasser – there was no dignity in that. But Ahmed Sufyan stood for the old-fashioned masculinity which could not be controlled or bound by rules and conventions.

He was testosterone on legs and an avowed patriot. Sufyan spoke for all the men hiding their true nature behind a patina of meekness and a gentle demeanour. He became a bodybuilder (and cultivated a steroid habit too). He had spearheaded the urban military fashion scene, appearing on all the fashion blogs and social media influencer feeds. It was against the law to impersonate military personnel, but Ahmed Sufyan had made it clear that he was only expressing his admiration for the armed forces. After the television dramas came films, and Ahmed Sufyan rocketed into the stratosphere, appearing in television ads, promotions for luxury cars and tourism campaigns. His appearance fee rose to the lakhs and would have surpassed a crore if the momentum had continued. If he had not made this one mistake.

Was that a pleased look on the Pakistani officer's face, watching coolly as Ahmed Sufyan put his hands together and begged for clemency? This latest exploit would raise his social media followers to 10 million. It would remind them of the good old days when brave martyrs daringly crossed the Line of Control, attacked the enemy and sent themselves to heaven. It might even inspire a few youngsters to do the same thing, peace or no peace.

Sufyan berated himself for failing to read the national mood correctly, for not realizing that the old tricks wouldn't work, that the times had changed. Instead of more followers, he'd first earned himself a visit from the police, then the Special Branch, and, finally, this public humiliation, this sadistic torture, a situation worse than a death sentence.

He took a deep breath and projected his voice, hoping it would reach the microphone and echo out to the Pakistani audience. Their cheers would drown out his sobs, and they would refuse to allow him to be sent over to the enemy. They would rally around their social media king, they would overwhelm the guards, bear him aloft on their shoulders and take him safely back to Karachi. The authorities would have to bow to the will of the people.

'I refuse to set foot in enemy territory. Hang me and got it over with!'

But the microphone had already been switched off, and his brave words simply died away in the breeze. The Pakistani officer smiled and said, in a voice just loud enough for Ahmed Sufyan to hear, 'You will have to meet the very people whom you have been portraying as demons, and find out if you've been telling the truth about them. For your sake, let's hope what you put out were lies. But if you were lying, then you were misleading your own people, and *that* is a crime the state takes very seriously.'

The Indian officer turned to the male accused. 'Do you have anything to say, Mr Suri?'

Suri puffed up, for it was indeed he, the famed television anchor who made a name for himself calling the not-so-powerful to account every night on his highly rated television news show, 'The Truth with Tulwar Suri'. For him, recognition was the strongest drug. He was always invited to elite parties, the VIP enclosures at both the Nehru and the Indira Gandhi stadiums. He owned several houses in Alibaug. His children went to school every day in a solar-powered Maybach 12 escorted by several police mobiles. He had the prime minister's private mobile number on his contacts list.

When it was first aired, his show was sound and balanced, featuring guests from both sides of the political spectrum who were given equal time to speak. Then, a few years before the Third Kashmir War, he realized that balance and fairness could only earn him respectability, but he wanted much more than that – he wanted superstardom. He wanted to be bigger than Amitabh Bachchan. When people heard his name he wanted them to think of the best of the best, of the United Nations, of the International Space Station.

Night after night, Suri invited guests on his show and shouted them down, berating them for their lack of patriotism, their tendencies toward treason. It was clear that he believed his opinions mattered more than his guests' expertise – unless, of course, they agreed with him and became mere props to support his theories.

And for the ones who dared to disagree, he had the same refrain: 'Go to Pakistan! Go to Pakistan!' On the screen, his slogan was matched by a visual of the Pakistani flag that went up in flames. The tag line became so popular that even school children shouted 'Go to Pakistan!' at each other when fighting in the playground. When Suri heard this, he (reportedly) smiled and said, 'I am influencing generations. What could be more powerful than that?'

The result was that every audience member felt they were the star of their own action movie, ostensibly titled *India vs. Pakistan*, at the end of which India always came out on top. As viewers tuned in by the million, Suri built an audience of nearly a billion people for his show, and every night he earned millions in advertising revenue. His media house soared to the top of the industry. He appeared on the cover of *Bloomberg*, *Forbes* and *Fortune 500*; CNN Business did a profile on him; *Architectural Digest* featured his 7-million-dollar house in south Mumbai.

But after the signing of the Disarmament Treaty, the stabilization of the Kashmir issue and the establishment of the Indo–Pak trade corridor, Suri had received a personal visit from the chief secretary of the Ministry of Information and Broadcasting in the Indian government. Over a cup of tea, the secretary had informed Suri that he needed to tone down his show, adopt a more conciliatory approach. Maybe he could do a series that explored the benefits of peace for both countries? The experts had predicted that the economy would grow as never before. Why not call some economists, a banker or two, on the programme to discuss it? Even the minister might be made available for a special edition of 'The Truth with Tulwar Suri'.

But Tulwar Suri had scoffed at the chief secretary. He had even scoffed at the minister. He knew the India–Pakistan peace pact was a conspiracy designed to fool the people. True to his proclamations, Tulwar Suri would continue to tell the truth, no matter what the cost. He continued with his shows and produced a special web series, meant only for subscribers, in which he expounded for an extra hour on Pakistan's perfidy and why India had made a mistake in trusting Pakistan. It was the one lesson he intended to drum into every man, woman and child in India, peace or no peace: You can never trust Pakistan.

Then, one day, there was a knock on the door. Everyone in South Asia knew to be afraid of that knock. It meant that the party had come to an end. Perhaps the Pakistanis were more finely attuned to that knock than Indians, but Tulwar Suri had overlooked the fact that the knock could sound on his door. And now, here he was, shivering in the January cold before hundreds of Pakistanis who jeered at him from across the border and seemed ready to tear him to shreds.

The border. He glanced at the white line that marked the division between the countries. It was a remarkably innocuous stretch of land, the same trees and greenery, the same sky above, the same ground below. Yet, on one side lay India, on the other Pakistan. He shuddered when he realized that if they took down all the flags, covered up the writing, and silenced the mosques on one side and the temple bells on the other, there would be no way to tell in which country he stood.

He tried to stare down the Indian officer reading out the charges against him. How mockingly she looked down her nose at him (and it wasn't even an attractive nose)! She was nothing more than a jumped-up secretary whom someone had decided to put in a uniform and call an officer. Oh, he had all the respect in the world for the Indian armed forces, but Tulwar Singh never spoke for himself, he spoke for the nation! He was a servant of the nation more than these petty bureaucrats, pencil pushers, all... Thoughts of how he had been treated since he had been taken into custody – a cramped, cold jail cell, no mobile phone, terrible food – flooded his mind. But the stress of experiencing all of this was nothing compared to the humiliation it brought on. As soon as he got out of here, he decided, he would run an expose on political harassment by the military. He'd have the notice of this woman's resignation flashed on his show for the next six months.

'Do you have anything to say, Mr Suri?' repeated the officer.

The sentences jostled in Suri's brain, pushing and shoving for space until something snapped in his mind. The only thing that came out of his mouth was a shriek, amplified by the microphone. 'GO TO PAKISTAAAAAAAAAAAAAN' echoed around both sides of the border, causing everyone's heads to snap up. A horrified silence ensued and then a wail of feedback from a misplaced speaker too close to the microphone deafened everyone. The crows screamed, the dogs resumed barking and infants everywhere began to cry, louder than ever.

The Indian officer, whose glasses had been knocked off her face by the sheer decibel level he'd unleashed, pushed them back up her nose. She cast another disapproving glance down her nostrils at Suri, who was quivering with indignation. 'We hear you loud and clear, Mr Suri.' She nodded crisply at her Pakistani counterpart. 'With your permission, Lieutenant Shazia.'

'Absolutely, Lieutenant Deepika.'

The two officers saluted each other, and then each took their prisoner by the arm and marched them forward to a small blue gate set in the low wall spanning the narrow width of the border crossing. The crowd leaned forward as the officers pressed their palms to the electronic pad on their respective sides at the same time. With a smooth hum, the gate unlocked on both sides, and slid back. The open space between the two countries was only three feet across, but in that moment it encompassed the entire world.

It had been agreed upon that both prisoners would cross at the same time. There was a moment of comedy when Ahmed Sufyan and Tulwar Suri stood stock still and stared at each other, tossing their heads and scratching the ground like two bulls ready to charge.

'They're not going to move,' hissed someone in the crowd on the Indian side.

'He won't let Suri through,' said someone on the Pakistani side. 'Defending Pakistan against the enemy.'

Sniggers and chuckles arose at this. Hostilities between the two nations had ceased years ago: it was now a period in the history of the two countries, taught in schools, etched on commemorative plaques, one that found mention in a charter at the United Nations. But it appeared that people like Suri and Ahmed preferred to live in a time warp when peace between the two countries was unimaginable. They needed to be re-educated for their own good and for the sake of everyone around them.

As if by magic, a doctor in a white coat, stethoscope around his neck, appeared suddenly at the crossing. The crowd gaped. What was going on? Was the stress too much for Suri, who had a known heart condition? One of the real-time tickers on his show routinely measured his blood pressure as he raged at a particularly difficult guest. The higher it got, the more the audiences tuned in to see if he might have a heart attack while his show was on air. And now – was he finally going to collapse?

The doctor whispered in the ears of both the Indian and Pakistani officers. An usher signalled to the crowd and the watching press that there was one last announcement to be made.

The Pakistani officer spoke as the two offenders shifted and squirmed under the watchful eyes of the crowd. 'The authorities have just confirmed that both Ahmed Sufyan and Tulwar Akash Suri are suffering from a mental condition that has caused both of them to be victims of delusional thoughts. They believe we are still living in the previous era of hostility between our two great nations. This is a kind of post-traumatic fugue that requires treatment, therapy and medication. Authorities on both sides have graciously agreed to provide this treatment free of charge to the two men, who will from now on be referred to not as prisoners but as patients.'

At this, the audience fell silent, trying to understand what it meant. Trauma? Fugue? They had never heard these strange words before. '*Dimagh ki kamzori*' went the whispers on the Indian side. '*Zeini bimari*,' whispered the Pakistanis. The officers were impatient to get things underway, and the soldiers roused the crowd into cheers as the brass bands struck up a spirited tune. The whispers died away as Pakistanis and Indians sang a song common to the people on both sides of the border.

The audience remarked that for such a short man, Suri was remarkably broad. Perhaps it was the special panels he'd had sown into his jacket? Or perhaps the authorities had taken pity on him and allowed him to wear a bulletproof vest as a special concession to his particular form of paranoia? And Ahmed Sufyan! Look how he shrank away from the doctor's syringe. If he would only relax and allow the doctor to give him one of those fancy tranquilizers, he could unclench his fists and loosen his jaw. He looked as if he might still explode, if not by detonation then by the force of his own fury.

Finally, injected and subdued, gently and easily slipping into an agreeable fog, the two patients managed to make it through the crossing at the same time. Sufyan wobbled, his bones turned to rubber. Suri squared his shoulders and stuck out his arms, trying to look bigger than he was. They staggered across the border at the same time, Suri into Pakistan and Sufyan into India. The crowd burst into applause.

As they passed each other, Suri eyed Sufyan, Sufyan eyed Suri, and a silent promise passed between the two of them. Sufyan knew he would appear on Suri's television show in a year's time, when they were both free of their imprisonment. Suri knew his ratings would surpass all ratings in the history of television, the cheques would pile up, his bank account would overflow like the Sutlej in flood. The future lay in televised reconciliation: peace as a product, manufactured for the masses.

The two were led into waiting ambulances that sped away to the best mental facilities each country had to offer. Indian and Pakistani officers saluted each other, shook hands and marched back to their bunkers. The flags fluttered in the wind, the dogs and crows sang a triumphant chorus. Even babies, soothed, offered gap-toothed smiles to their parents.

'That's it: the exchange is now complete,' a firm voice rang out over the loudspeakers. 'Go home, everyone. Thank you for witnessing the Tabadla ceremony this morning. Pakistan Zindabad! Jai Hind!'

As the crowd began to file out of the ground, and journalists faced cameras, excitedly describing what had just taken place, someone in the crowd shouted, '*Pagal ka tabadla*!' Even as the microphones picked up the unfortunate phrase and broadcast it live across both nations, the man who had unwittingly christened the event was quickly hushed by his wife, who urged him not to be so cruel. Everyone else, murmuring in agreement, went home to tell the rest that they had truly missed out on something special, something they would tell their children about for generations to come – and the Tabadla Scheme came to be known forever more as the Looney Exchange.

PALEY'S WATCH

ANIL MENON

The American Spirit found the artifact in the Gulf of Alaska, about 50 miles off the coastline, not too far from the port at Sitka. It'd been dredged up by a trawler pod, set for halibut. Paley, one of the fishermen, spotted the object sparkling against the blood-black deck, and the men gathered at the Brit's triumphant shout.

It was a set of nested funnels. Each conical layer sparkled with what appeared to be moving dots of light. The artifact was about the size of a can of soup, but its weight kept changing, making the thing feel uncomfortably alive. Like holding a cat. The men quickly returned the artifact to Paley.

At first, they thought it was junk from one of the many cruise ships that plied the area, but even junk is *something*. This looked like nothing they had seen before. They had a college boy in their midst, one Tommy Kumagai, and they got the 19-year-old to take a look.

'Hey, that's Dini's surface!' said Tommy.

'No, it ain't,' growled Paley. 'It's mine. I found it.'

'Relax, Paley. I meant it looks like Dini's Surface – it's a topological manifold.'

'A topless *what*?' asked the captain, eyeing the curious crew. At his glare, they all returned to work except for Paley.

'Manifold, a surface with smooth curvature. Like those sculptures with those weird holes and lumps. If you know the curvature of a manifold, you know everything about it. A sphere has constant positive curvature. That's what makes it a sphere. A Dini's Surface is a pseudosphere; it has constant negative curvature. If you draw a triangle –'

'Thanks, professor.' Paley spat on the deck. 'So it's just a toy, innit?' The Liverpuddlian expat looked ready to throw it back into the ocean.

Tommy hesitated. 'Dunno, Paley. Doesn't look like it's been made for giggles. Might be valuable. Never laid eyes on nuthin' like it.'

Paley snorted. 'Why didncha say that in the first place, punk?' He pocketed the item. 'Cap'n, if you don't mind, finders keepers and all that.'

Tommy Kumagai lies dying from massive internal injuries from a hit-and-run close to the intersection of San Francisco's Haight and Steiner Street. A corner of his mind doesn't believe he's going to die. It's hopeful, even cocky. It knows Tommy Kumagai is only 26 years old and therefore, immortal. It knows there's a lot of work to be done now that the artifact's true nature has been resolved. It knows he will be taken to the hospital in time, and a few months of modern medicine will set his mangled body right. It knows those months will be filled with research, Skype conferences, tweets, visits from scores of friends, laughter, and love. It knows there's a lifetime of living to be done with Tara. A corner of his mind, the same corner perhaps, knows everything is going to be all right, just all right.

'Gimme that smile, baby,' says Tommy, squeezing Tara's hand.

Then Tommy Kumagai dies.

The artifact came to be called Paley's Watch; that the object wasn't really a watch and no longer belonged to Paley was entirely besides the point.

Once on shore, Paley first tried to pawn the thing, then tried to sell it on eBay, and then tried to interest the local fishing rags in the matter. All these efforts failed. Finally, he took the kid's advice and showed it to Dr Godbole, Tommy's thesis advisor in physics at Berkeley.

The brown egghead had hummed, hawed, inspected the thing with a field lens, a microscope, and then begun using 10 dollar words like 'extropic luminescence'. Finally, the Mex admitted what the kid had admitted.

'Mr Paley, it's nothing like anything I've ever seen. Perhaps you've found Paley's Watch!' Dr Godbole had hee-hawed like a jackass.

Matters quickly devolved out of control. The professor had said that he wanted to 'study' it and got quite nasty when Paley disagreed. Paley had given the grasping scoundrel a black eye to study.

But quicker than one can say 'non compos mentis', Paley was behind bars. Uncle Sam had seized his artifact, citing some obscure, security-related forfeiture law. The men in black gave Paley a receipt and encouraged him to sue.

A Manhattan Project was assembled in San Francisco under the supervision of Dr Godbole. Soon, the artifact was being poked and prodded by all kinds of professionals.

By the time 21-year-old Tommy, already known as a wunderkind in physics circles, completed his doctoral thesis and had joined the project, not much progress had been made. It *was* a model of Dini's surface. The number of nested funnels had been counted to 242,156,789, and then their instruments had squashed their noses against Heisenberg's limit. Nothing could chip, scan, fry, freeze or penetrate the artifact; it was completely inert. As one wag insinuated, the artifact was 'ontologically and epistemologically frigid'.

The moving 'dots of light' in the artifact were the main reason why the name 'Paley's Watch' had stuck. Every so often, a dot would split into a random, but always prime, number of dots. Assuming that the current estimated number of dots was correct, and assuming the object obeyed the mathematics of inhomogeneous branching processes, and assuming these assumptions were correct, the artifact could be dated to be anywhere between 4 to 5 billion years old. A scathing attack in the much-cited article, 'Dirimens Copulatio: The Rhetoric of Artifact Dating', had pointed out that Earth itself was only 3.5 billion years old, give or take a billion. Counter-attacks, equally scathing, began with quotes from Sherlock Holmes and *Alice in Wonderland*.

If Paley's Watch was indeed a watch, then it certainly was the most useless watch in the universe. The artifact was wrapped as snugly in its secrets as a honeybee in its pirate pants. An infinite number of nested orchids, each distinct, each spun from a single whirl of the same spiral, and each whorl rooted in nothingness.

'It's not the end of the world.' But Tommy knew Bolazar, who'd failed the doctoral qualifiers, would see it differently. 'There are other Gs, bro.'

'Gs?' asked Bolazar. The older man's eyes were red; it looked like he hadn't slept in a while.

'Gigs. Goals. Games. Gs.'

'You think this is all some bloody game?'

Tommy again silently cursed the day he'd agreed to join Berkeley's physics faculty. At the time, he'd thought it would be a fun break from the Centre for Theoretical Physics. He'd envisioned lolling on green university quads, rapping with cool Doctors Evil in the making, all the groupie love he could handle. But the reality had been sweaty griefers like Bolazar.

'Look, I get your pain. But think it out and you'll see I did you a favour. Saved you time. Better to flunk out now than five years from now.'

Tommy didn't add that Bolazar, at 37, needed all the time he could get. Hell, at 26, even *he* felt Time nipping at his nuts. He threw the ball against the wall, catching it on the rebound. Then Tommy remembered that Tara always hated it. 'It's a bloody obnoxious habit, Thomas.'

Funny how she called him Thomas. Nobody else did. He was Tommy. Tomahawk. T-man. T. Tack. Or, in his gaming days, T-Hex. 'Thomas' was a liver spotted geezer in a plaid suit with trousers pulled all the way up to his man boobs. He guessed it was all part of Tara's failed cause to make him a better human. What would Tara do with Bolazar? She'd listen, empathize, try to help.

Tommy squeezed the ball and made another attempt to comfort the Turkish student. 'Like the Barbie doll sez: Physics is hard. Not everyone can hack it.'

'And I'm too old?'

'Nah. Plenty of Gandalfs in the field.'

'So, I'm not good enough?'

'Right.'

Bolazar had an indecipherable expression on his face.

'You crashed and burned in the string quartet,' explained Tommy, feeling silly at having to explain the obvious. 'And I threw you some damn easy curveballs. Why didn't you just stick to the questions I asked? What was with all the freestylin' shit about Schrödinger's pussycat, mirrors, narratology and point of view? Take this –' He tapped the iPhone and quoted from Bolazar's answer sheet: '"Just as it is, unmisted by love or dislike, I'm not cruel, only truthful…" Dude, I gotta ask: were you on crack?'

'I was quoting from Sylvia Plath's poem "Mirror". I thought it spoke very well to how we resist treating physics as a literary genre. If physics is the book of nature and we're its readers, then what can we say about the narrators? I asked myself: Bolazar, can we look at physics narratologically?'

'Dude –'

'Yes, it's a radical view. I admit it. But you have to admit I made an innovative use of Hegel's master-slave dialectic.'

'Who's Hegel?' Tommy remembered Helga, the hot Dutch physicist who never wore a bra.

'The philosopher!'

'Ah.' Tommy wondered if Hegel wore bras.

'I said to myself: Bolazar, let's take the metaphor of reading the book of nature seriously. Reading is about trying to understand the narrators. We humans turn pages and they say things like: "*Merhaba*, I'm an electron, my weight is such-and-such, and I'm a negative fellow." But we read on and discover that we are, in fact, stories spun by these narrators. We're inside the book! You and I are embedded stories told in a frame story called reality. We are being narrated by electrons, protons and a handful of protagonists. Now you see the problem? We're literature! There's no standing outside of this story we call the universe. So if there is an outside, how do we communicate with it?'

'Dude –'

'I said to myself: Bolazar, never mind. Whereof we cannot communicate, thereof we must reflect –'

Tommy decided enough was enough. ''Scuse me, B. This is fun, but here's how it all sounds: batshit crazy. Look, I could empathize your butt off, say things like: Yeah, work on it, it's interesting, come up with some experiments. And what you're saying, yeah, it's all that. Fo'sure. But you want to do this shit right, if you really want to do it right, my guess is you're gonna need something like topos theory. Just word-fucking me won't do. Trouble is, that math is seriously hardcore, and we both know math ain't exactly your bitch. So here's some love, tough but true: find another field. Or another advisor. Sorry, bro.'

Just then, the phone did its little Bollywood number. Tara. He took the call, glancing at Bolazar to mouth an 'excuse me'. But the man was cradling his head. Christ.

'Wassup, baby? Not a good time.'

'Uncle and Aunty just left for the airport,' she said, her voice sounding casual. 'The house is ours! I am on my way to class. I will be done by 4 p.m., pick up the goodies after. What time are you coming over?'

'I got to meet a friend – well, not exactly a friend – jerk, really. Said he wanted my help and the way he rolls, well, no is just yes doing a striptease. We're hooking up at the Mad Dog in the Fog. Five-ish.'

'Thomas!'

'A thousand pardons, my queen. Look, join us. The Mad Dog is on Haight. With you there, it'll help me control-Q faster. C'mon, Tara. What's a couple more hours after a million years of waiting?'

'So *do* me already.' She sighed. 'I can't wait either. Every minute now seems like an eternity. Weird, no?'

'Not weird. So you coming?'

'Won't that depend on your game, sweetie?' she said, disconnecting before he could word-judo her.

Tommy set the phone down, smiling. 'Sorry, B. The girlfriend. You know how it is.' He paused. 'Well! Looks like we done grab-assing, so yeah.'

The older man slowly lifted his tear-stricken face.

'Bolazar...c'mon, guy! Nuthin's that bad. Get a grip.'

'I don't know what to do,' said Bolazar. 'Can't you do something? I'll retake the test. Please help me.'

'You're in denial, B!' Tommy flexed his neck. 'You're not thinking straight. Tell you what. Got any family?'

'I have a mother in Turkey,' said Bolazar. He wiped his face with his sleeve. 'I haven't been home in two years. Visa problems.'

Jeez, at least you have a mother, thought Tommy. He didn't know where his Mary was even at. The 15-inch Coby TV in the trailer. Trash everywhere; Jesus keychains, Goodwill clothes, Cheetos, handcuffs, clumps of hair. Stuffing weed into little Ziplock bags. Sesame Street on high coz of the crack-whore's snores. Shut your fucking mouth, Mom; you're not on the clock. If Dr Godbole hadn't found him...

He glanced at Bolazar. The poor bastard was actually looking hopeful.

'Yeah, moms. They're the best. Listen, Bolazar, go home. Regroup with the family unit and defrag for a while. Then figure out the next fun thing to do. That narratology stuff sounds like your groove's in the humanities. Or go look up Professor Hegel in the philosophy department. She may –'

'Fuck you. I don't need your advice.'

'Damn right.' Tommy threw the ball. 'I've been sayin' what? That exactly. I know jack about life, literature and latte. Hell, who does? So. We cool, B? I gotta roll.'

Later, as Tommy drove towards the Haight, the gray gauze of San Francisco's fog already beginning to moisten the Hummer's squat windows, he kept one eye on the road and the other on the iPhone, as he scrolled through the messages. NBD. NBD. NBD. Wait. Message from Tara: *Shopping. Durex ultras, right? Sales bitch tried to push some edible variety. At the counter! Died a mil. Luv ya.*

A sudden horn blast, and he swerved just in time. Tommy put away the iPhone, smiling. The girl sauntering into a store to buy condoms was a far cry from the girl he'd met a year and a half ago. They'd been intro'd by Dr Godbole.

Tommy's thesis advisor did not believe in separating work from life. His seminars tended to continue in the campus café, over dinner and to extend late into the night. That it inconvenienced his wife was, as Dr Godbole liked to say, 'negligible in the first approximation'.

When Dr Godbole had discovered Tommy, then rotting in an inner-city high school, he'd rushed home, embraced his surprised wife and told her that he now knew why he'd been put on Earth. Perhaps it was the joy on her husband's face; she'd rarely seen him that happy. Or perhaps it was merely the embrace; she'd rarely been embraced. Whatever the reason, the childless couple, who otherwise agreed on so little, found in Tommy an agreement and a common need.

For him, Mrs Godbole learned to cook eggs. She fussed over his appearance. She gave Tommy a spare key. She confounded him with her attempts to speak Japanese, a language he did not speak. The guest bedroom, more or less, became Tommy's room.

But one late night, Tommy crawled into his bed and found a girl and a scream.

'Tara's my niece,' Dr Godbole had explained. 'She's from India, and here to do a master's in computer science. Like the rest of the damn nation. Tara, you've been spooned by a future Nobel laureate. Dr Kumagai to friends, Tommy to strangers,' Dr Godbole had finished, appending one of his signature laughs.

She was brown because bronze chooses to be that colour. Tommy's hand still remembered her thigh's pliant smoothness and its sleepy heat. She'd been wearing silk boxers. But what he really remembered was her smile. Slow, teasing, as if she knew something but chose not to say it.

'Spank-da-monkey smile,' thought Tommy. On one level, she was such a good little girl, always ready to swot her homework, Skype her mousy parents, defend her weird-ass Hindu religion and make sure no hand slipped into her panties except her own. But on another level, a little Aguilera dirty too. Else, what was with the efforts to improve him, sari porn, eye sex, accidental brushes and that killer smile?

Tommy had rather liked it. Tara was a huge change from the acrobatic chiquitas and EEOC valley twits he normally preyed on. She was challenging country. Make a move, get rebuffed, try an alternate route – classic video game.

Dr Godbole had initially turned a blind eye to his wife's dark looks and a deaf ear to her dark mutterings. But he had become alarmed when he found Tommy perusing *The Dummy's Guide to Hinduism*. He'd taken the kids aside, forced a tight-lipped Tara to tie a rakhi on Tommy's wrist and then sent her off.

'My niece is a comely lass,' Dr Godbole had said.

'Yes sir.'

'This holy thread makes her your sister.'

'Yes sir.'

Totally kinky, figured Tommy. But he had watched Animal Planet. Different cultures, different rules! Tommy had worn the glitzy, itchy and totally gay bracelet all through lunch, basking uncertainly in Mrs G's delighted smiles, until Tara cornered him in the kitchen, chanted something in Indian, tore the rakhi off, threw it in the dustbin and kissed him on the mouth. Not the full French car wash, but seriously incestuous.

Tommy parked the H2 on a sidewalk at the corner of Haight and Steiner; a ticket was inevitable, but he didn't care. It was one of the costs of living in the world's most beautiful city. He'd only taken a few steps towards the pub when his cell broke into Sanskrit.

'Wazzup, Doc G? Where you at?'

'At Heathrow. Listen, I just got the anisotropy data for the "lights" on Paley's Watch. Isotropic as we suspected, but you were right. There's a suppression of power at large scales for the second quadruple moment in the angular power spectrum.'

Tommy stopped walking, but his heart began to pound like he'd begun to run. 'It's a model of the universe. That's *crazy*.'

'Question is, is it crazy enough to be right?' Dr Godbole brayed at his insider joke.

'Suppose it is. Means it was here to be found. And if the dating's accurate, it's been here for billions of years. And coz it's one frigid Bridget, it survived right through the evolution of our solar system. It was built not to interact. Hell, it's practically dead, and since the dead cannot be killed, nuthin's fitter. So it survived. Neat.'

'And now we need to wake the dead. Then find a way to talk to it.'

'Nah. It won't talk to us. Let's see if it'll notice itself. Maybe it can talk to us by talking to itself. Like literature.'

'What?'

'You don't want to know. Let's do a mirror test. The artifact is spec'd to blow off everything coz everything is a potential hazard. But it knows it's not a threat to itself. All those lights suggest it's aware of the visible spectrum. So let's see what it sees in a mirror.'

'A wake-up test for Narcissus. Hmm.'

'The motherfucker?'

'You're thinking of Oedipus, Tommy. Narcissus is someone else. Where are you? At the university?'

'Nope. On my way to meet Tara. But I'll cancel –'

'What for? Won't that disappoint Tara?' Dr Godbole fell silent. 'Perhaps I have taught you too well. Don't make the mistakes I've made. No, don't cancel anything. I'll tell Hendrix to set up the test. Shouldn't take more than an hour. I'll be in touch –' Dr Godbole stopped and said something in Marathi. 'Wait, the missus wants to talk.'

As always, Mrs Godbole spoke in deeds. She told him there was pasta, jeera rice and two days' worth of *aloo mutter* in the fridge. Rotis would have to be reheated. There was also fresh *shrikhand*. He loved *shrikhand*, didn't he? She'd laundered Tommy's clothes. Why didn't he buy some new underwear? Tara's exams –

'Don't worry, Mama G,' said Tommy gently. 'You have a good time. Tara will be safe with me. Word on that.'

'I know. Tara and I had long talk.' Then, after a brief pause, 'I'm glad. God bless.'

The Mad Dog in the Fog was so crowded, it looked like it had exploded people.

'Thomas!'

He turned in the direction of the voice and saw Tara at the outer rim of the throng, waving at him as if she'd just sighted an exit from a desert island. Tommy walked over, hands framed in viewfinder mode. She was wearing her signature kurta-top and Dylan George knockoffs. Slung across her shoulder was a Healthy Back leather tote. Flashes of faux gold at her throat and ears, highlighting the sensual brown.

'Like?' she asked, striking a pose.

'Pimpin', babe.' He pulled her close. There was something different this time; a complete lack of wariness, a fall of reserve, and it turned their hug into an embrace.

'The pub looks pretty full,' she said finally, in a breathless voice. 'Do you see your friend anywhere?'

'Tommy boy!'

Speak of the devil.

'Paley. Hola.'

Paley looked like he'd always looked: mean, ferocious and quarrelsome.

''ppreciate your coming,' said Paley, crushing Tommy's hand in his paw. Then he noticed Tara. 'Howdeedo. You with him?'

'Tara, Paley. Paley, Tara.'

Paley seemed to be in a remarkably cheerful mood. 'She's cute fo'sure. C'mon, let me buy you two a drink. We gotta talk, Tommy.'

Through a combination of drunken-monk-fearless-hyena manoeuvres, Paley got them inside the pub. He bought the first round of drinks: a Black & Tan for Tommy, an amber ale for Tara and a stout for himself. The source of his goodwill soon became apparent.

'Finding the artifact was the best thing ever,' Paley confided. 'I'd taken snaps of it; for hawking it on friggin' eBay, see. When the men in black came for me, I put the pics on the web and tube'd the whole story. Fixed 'em bastards good. Now, yours truly is on the lecture circuit, 500 dolla a pop and more abductee chicks than I can shake my stick at. I've got a book in the works. How do you like 'em nuts?' Paley's face was an unnatural mix of pride and modesty.

Someone had noticed quite early on that 'Dini' was the ancient Greek word for 'vortex'. Someone had noticed that Genesis 1:11 had a reference to 'the fruit tree yielding fruit whose seed is in itself'. Someone had noticed that Dini's Surface was one of the solutions to Einstein's general relativity equations. Paley's early disciples had tenaciously blown upon these embers until they'd flamed into a genuine cult, complete with web presence, demanding rituals, fashion merchandise and bank accounts.

'That rocks, Paley! Your own cult!' said Tommy, laughing. 'So you're in the buzz. I'd no clue.'

'Bloody damn right it rocks,' echoed Tara, sounding as if she was in the buzz as well. She put her hand on Tommy's thigh. 'But what exactly is the artifact? It's not really alien, is it?'

''Course it is,' snorted Paley. 'As alien as you, sweet cheeks. Right, Tommy boy?'

Their expressions reminded Tommy of that strange day with its freezing rain, bloodied deck and the question mark in his hands. He thought about what Godbole had told him.

'Maybe, maybe not.' Tommy wanted to explain. But how? It was all so technical. The Big Bang had left a trace in the form of tiny temperature fluctuations in the background radiation. These fluctuations had patterns; they differed in different directions. The fluctuations could be used to figure out the shape of the universe. On that basis, it was thought that the universe had a 'Picard topology,' resembling something like a medieval horn, or more precisely, the Eiffel Tower. A plain old sphere was a surface of constant positive curvature. The Picard topology was a pseudosphere; a hyperbolic surface of constant negative curvature.

But there were other pseudospheres in mathematics. For example, Dini's Surface. As he had predicted in his doctoral thesis, the correlation data for the artifact's 'lights' had turned out to match the background radiation fluctuations for a universe shaped like a Dini's surface. It was too much of a coincidence. It was like finding a toy globe, complete with lines of latitude and longitude and precisely drawn land masses, floating in some sea, just when the people had begun to suspect the earth was a sphere. The artifact had been *made*. But made for what purpose?

'It's too early to tell,' concluded Tommy.

'Oh.' Tara sounded disappointed and returned to her drink.

Paley shrugged. 'Who cares? Then the artifact's what I say it is.'

Tommy decided to let this fine example of para-consistent reasoning slide. Tara used the silence to drain her mug and slid off the seat. 'I'll be back,' she announced in a Schwarzenegger accent that was beyond dreadful. They watched her walk away.

'You tapping that ass?' asked Paley, more brotherly than envious.

Tommy was able to avoid lying because his iPhone broke into a Turkish jingle. Bolazar. *Ah, screw him*. He tapped the screen, and the mobile went quiet.

'You said you wanted some help, Paley?'

Paley rotated his beer mug and looked shifty. 'Yeah. It's for this book I'm writing. My publisher suggested that maybe you'd be willing to endorse the book for an old mate. Seeing as you're now a quack and all. I told her she was full of shit; that I couldn't, wouldn't impose on a mate, you know how much I hate to, Tommy boy, so what do you say?'

The iPhone lit up with a Turkish jingle, and Tommy tapped it into silence again.

'Sure. I'll lend some nitro.'

'Sure?' Paley looked astonished.

'Yup. No sweat. I'll email it. Anything else?'

Paley squeezed his shoulder, quite overcome with emotion. 'Wunnerful! Yer a good brick, Tommy. Always was, still are.' Paley acquired a pious look. 'I was gonna throw the artifact away. But you begged me not to. Coincidence?'

The correct answer, it was clear, was in the negative. Tara was making her way back to the table. She was smiling, but her eyes flashed a girlfriend's warning. Tommy stood up. He was glad he'd made the time to meet Paley. 'Gotta roll. See you around, buddy.' Tommy raised his Black & Tan, downed it.

Paley returned the salute. 'In the halls of Valhalla, Tommy boy.'

When Tommy and Tara left the bar, they walked into a magical world wrapped in fog. On the way back to the Hummer, Tara broke the silence. 'Paley was interesting…a little scary. Hard to believe you worked on the Bering Sea with guys like that.'

Tommy said nothing. Tough guys didn't jaw about the past. It'd just been a summer gig. A fast buck. Nothing special. Dr G liked to say the only projects that mattered in life were those listed in one's obit. But if Tara got moist at the thought of him haulin' fish, then good. Very good.

'Isn't it ironic that Paley was the one to find Paley's Watch?'

'Why is it ironic?' said Tommy. 'He found it.'

'Yes, but a *Paley* found it. Reverend Paley's book? You know, the guy who wrote *Natural Theology*?'

'Wiki me, babe.'

'Thomas! You've never heard of Reverend Paley and his book? How's that possible? Don't you read anything except physics?'

'Does porno count?'

'You're shameless! Reverend Paley wrote that living things were so perfectly designed, they couldn't have been made by chance. Suppose you find a beautiful, fully functional watch on the beach? Would you say it evolved by chance or would you say that there had to be a watchmaker?'

'I'd say the dude got the causal link ass backwards. In science, you gotta go from what you know to what you don't know. I know watches are made by watchmakers. So if I find an old watch lying around somewhere, I can assume it was made by a watchmaker. But I don't know if animals are made by God. So if I find a fossil, I can't assume God put it there. Look, it's all there in Hegel.'

'Oh.' Tara was clearly impressed. 'Really?'

'Yeah. Amazed you haven't read Hegel.'

'Sorry, Thomas. I have been meaning to.' Then she saw his face. 'Ass!'

He laughed. 'Such a book slut.'

'Yes,' she admitted. 'But seriously, when you find something really improbable, like the artifact, it makes you wonder, doesn't it?'

'Depends. I suspect there are billions of Paley's Watches out there. This artifact was meant to be found. And something can be improbable, yet very common. Like snowflakes. License plates. Probability is just a measure of what you think you know. It's just how you figure the game. Existence *is* the game. You exist, and then you don't.'

'What about us, Thomas? You and me. Are we improbable?'

He had to force himself to say what he knew: 'Yeah, maybe. But I'm gonna believe.'

She kissed him. He could taste the amber. It occurred to him the taste of a life could only be experienced, never described.

'I think we're very probable, Thomas.'

They kissed again. The cell began to chant Sanskrit.

'Don't answer it,' whispered Tara. 'No more calls tonight.' Then she stiffened. 'Shit, left my tote at the bar. Must have set it down when I went to pee. I'll be back in five.'

She disappeared into the fog. Tommy took the call. 'Wassup, Doctor G? Any news from Hendrix?'

'Tommy, it vanishes! The damn artifact vanishes when you shove it in front of a mirror. Take away the mirror, it reappears. We can make it appear and disappear. Zero, one, zero, one. You know what that means, don't you?'

'Christ. A telephone.'

'Exactly. We can send a message. Who knows where though! Maybe there's still someone around to listen. Pity Carl Sagan's dead; this is the sort of problem the man would've enjoyed. Tommy, Tommy, this is the second happiest day of my life.'

'Yes, sir. May I say –'

'No, you may not. I'm going to run some more tests. Tonight is yours. But tomorrow onwards, it'll be different. Get ready to be famous, Tommy. It's your idea that broke the problem.'

'About that. Not quite true. Someone gave me the idea. There's a prequel to all this – *Holy shit! Wha* –'

'All of life is a prequel, Tommy. Tommy? Hello?'

In the final three minutes of Tommy Kumagai's life, after Bolazar mows him down with a 1992 Honda Civic, the first 28 milliseconds of almost unbearable pain from the collision is stilled, and all light, all sound, all sensation, all knowing, blinks out for a merciful 40 milliseconds. Then sensation comes back, at least partially, for it is without the pain. Euphoria even. There are people everywhere. Shouts. Sirens. How worried they all look. But a part of Tommy's mind – if it is even mind or a part at all – knows better. Look, isn't Tara here? It knows there's a lifetime of living to be had with Tara. A part of his mind, the same part, perhaps, knows everything is going to be all right. All right.

'Gimme that smile, baby,' says Tommy, squeezing Tara's hand.

So that part of Tommy's mind relaxes and watches the show. The human consciousness is such a wondrous manifold. Look! Space and time collapse even as his consciousness unfurls and expands. An infinite whirling vortex of consciousness, concentrating, ever tighter, impossibly tighter, collapsing into an inexorable singularity, rushing, rushing towards a primordial timeless, spaceless, explosive birth event of a quaquaversal, multiversant, sempiternal universe.

ELSEWHERE

APARNA RAMACHANDRAN

The first sign of flight Avan noticed was in his body. A feeling of weightlessness appeared at the base of his spine. It seemed intent on heaving him off the ground as it made its way to the very top of his head – only to loop back and proceed to climb again with an animal intensity. His body started to judder. He was certain that he would soon throw up his innards. He tried to make sure he was still sitting firm on the bamboo mat Yra had laid on the floor. 'The only way to make it work is to let go. You must not control what happens at any cost, Avan. We don't have much time,' she had urged. He loved Yra more than he loved his own life. But why had he signed up for this?

Avan was particularly buoyant on his way home from work. The next day was Yra's birthday, and it would be the fifteenth summer solstice since they had fallen in love. On this day, every year, in an exclusive, ticketed affair, the state revealed the Sun in all its glory to the residents of Kasara and its subzones. The usual wildlife simulations – live streams from Kasara's Saturn and Mars colonies, the weather report, the news and advertisements projected on the skydome – gave way to the Sun. A breathtaking visitor from the skies. The rest of the year, Kasara's nuclear fusion reactor provided locally produced sunlight and tolerable warmth to the people.

Tomorrow was going to be a big day for another reason – Avan's manager at the Kasara state power plant had just informed him that Yra and he had been selected for the Preferred Prospective Parents programme. A wholly funded parenthood for a child that would be partly owned and fully mentored by the state. He would break the news to Yra during the solstice fair. He had bought them snug seats in a booth at the KU64 park lawns and organized a lunch for two cooked entirely with real fruits and vegetables. For some time now, Avan had been feeling secure and ready. He had been harbouring private notions of starting a family with Yra, wanting nothing more than to go to a predictable day at work and come back home to a good meal and a pair of baby hands. This was going to be a special year – he could feel it.

When he arrived home, Yra was pacing around. She came running up and flung her arms around him, her eyes bright and face flushed. It filled Avan's heart to see her so happy.

'Avan! Avan! Avan! I am so relieved! How should I tell you this – you will think I'm mad!'

'Won't be the first time,' he said, grinning.

There was a pause.

'I think you already know,' said Yra, cautious now.

His smile disappeared as he felt a familiar sense of foreboding. Six years ago, Yra had come to him, similarly aglow. For weeks before that, she had been consumed by something that had demanded that she crank out innumerable diagrams, waste away pursuing manic research, make countless trips to the Kasara City Museum Library, spend hours in meditative thought figuring out the components and workings of the higher dimensions of the universe. She eventually told Avan. She had been giving every bit of her prana – her vital life energy – to the finding of something elusive: a hidden place beyond all planes of existence known to physics or to Kasara's scientists. A furnace, she said, where an impulse created sound, which then created solid geometry, which created atoms, which created molecules, physical things and infinite choices, all of which could be accessed by anyone if they just knew how. That it was the transcendental thermo-nuclear petri dish from which the universe frothed into life. It was a place beyond, where you could supposedly be your happiest.

To Yra's mind, the next obvious step had been to take them both there, to her elsewhere. It had not occurred to her that here was enough for him. 'Don't you have some curiosity to see life beyond Kasara and your accountant's job? Say, the fifth dimension…you know physics is interpreted differently there or the sixth…they say it opens out to new universes?' She was a child who used words to hurt him when she didn't get her way.

'I'm still settling into this one,' he had responded, careful not to upset her.

Learning to appear in multiple places at the same time had not come as easily to him as it had to Yra; nor had communicating with crystalline minerals like quartz and apatite as if crystals were pets talking to their owners. But he was making every effort, was getting better, and even enjoying life in the fourth dimension now. Time appeared to go much faster here. If you made some effort, you could accurately perceive in your mind's eye things that were far away – he had been able to close his eyes and work remotely at the power plant when he had understood how it worked. If you were brave, you could even try walking through solid objects. He was not born into it, but it was now his to embrace and this was perhaps all that he would ever be able to embrace in this lifetime.

Avan's skin twitched at the memory of what she had said then – that what they had in Kasara was not a real life or true freedom, that it was just predictable rules for their physical bodies to follow. That there was a place where they could be unfettered, be made pure by light. It was going to be difficult to find but would be worth the effort. They could be conscious machines there that felt and observed. The causal rules of the physical plane and samsara would not apply to them. Living in this higher plane would enable them to explore the universe at their own pace, create ethical colonies, understand and befriend other life forms, make high-minded pursuits for the development of all of humankind, she had said. Avan had wanted her to forget the whole thing, and he had assumed she had. But now here they were again, Yra busting with the talk of seeking new dimensions. What was the rush? Why couldn't they just be happy here?

Avan was a mild-mannered, athletic 27-year-old whose love for the town of Kasara in Almora, India, was second only to his love for his sweetheart, Yra, a curator at the City Museum. He had been 12 years old, and Yra 15, when they had found each other at Kasara's Facility for Special Children. The facility served as home to people from zones outside Kasara – like IR8 where Avan was from – which had been blighted by hyper-modified crops, poverty and violence. In classrooms constructed with soothing kunzite and scolecite crystals, children were taught that Kasara was here to lead the way into the new world. Resources were vast here, there was no need to struggle for survival. Unlike in the third dimension, the value of goods was no longer the market price that someone decided on for personal profit. Nobody squatted on things that other people needed. Everyone who created something found a way to sell it, and things were seldom left unsold. Those who felt ready could elect to withdraw from the quotidian and pursue studies in time travel, or work on expanding their psychic and metaphysical abilities. This was the utopia he had heard about at IR8. A few children like his class captain Yra, who tested high for intuition, were taught the basics of astral travel in a secret programme. Many laughed it off as plain old lucid dreaming. Avan didn't

understand most of this. He had been happy to find solace in numbers and was hoping to spend his time being an accountant when he was old enough.

A few of Kasara's civilians were already in the fourth dimension, and the rest were being given the tools to get there. They took long walks, played games designed to rewire their brains to adapt to time travel, attended academic learning focused on self-discovery and not just winning a hall pass into adulthood. For the first time in his life Avan had been surrounded by happy, satisfied people who did not feel the need to hurt one another in any way. All of this was difficult to get used to, of course. No one knew if this streak of plenty was here to stay. The opening up of the fourth dimension had made everyone so confident with possibilities that they felt secure enough to pick Kasara's policies apart. It was during an impromptu, particularly raucous after-dinner inter-class vivisection of some newly announced economic waiver that Yra and Avan had discovered one another – and that they each liked their broths bland and their heroes violent.

Avan had instantly been bewitched. Yra had a confident, raspy voice that carried through the dinner hall, across the lawns, over the beach and into the sea. They said she had been one of the first in Kasara to grasp the fourth-dimensional way of life – she could perceive bits of the universe no one else could. She had, therefore, much to say that he had never heard before – about tapping the cosmos for new energy sources, about humans not realizing they were nature's best energy conductors, about the amygdala's supposed secret purpose to keep humans in survival mode by influencing them to focus exclusively on negativity and pessimism. She even had a story about Kasara – that it was as successful as it was because it had found a way to download cosmic waves that carried coded information about human advancement. Despite her teachers deeming her not ready, she was able, she announced, to go even beyond the fourth dimension. On the days that she did not meet him, he wondered if that is where she had gone off to.

Yra had made his head spin, but he had known. The magic she had within her would help him heal the traumas he carried from IR8. She knew where happiness lay. In return, he would be the steady force that empowered her wild pursuits. They promised each other that they would travel, find work in different places, live on scraps if it came to that, but always feed each other's spirits. That had been the day of the summer solstice – the longest day of the year and Yra's fifteenth birthday.

'Well, I understand if you are not into it.'

Yra knew how to push his buttons.

'What has changed from the last time?' he asked, careful not to let his throat dry up.

In the beginning, Avan had wanted to go on adventures with her, but he'd found that he was too tired or too afraid. He knew that her need to wander would not die, but he had developed an aversion for uncertainty. He hoped they could find a way to never leave the safety of Kasara.

She looked down at her fingers and told him what he had suspected all along but had been too scared to accept – she had been dredging up what was taught to her at the now defunct astral travel programme. All those extra shifts that she put in at the museum was a cover for her training to be an 'energy accumulator', someone able to fuel trips between dimensions. Through years of practise with sound and a lost meditation technique she could produce acoustical standing waves in the range of 4 to 7 Hertz for a length of time, altering consciousness and moving it outside the physical sphere beyond the restrictions of time and space. She used this to augment, guide and redirect people on their inter-dimensional travels. Like a driving instructor for people's consciousness. The government would never approve of this off-grid work, he reminded her. She seemed too far gone into it to care. She had been moving early pioneers to and from Kasara – Lama Govinda, Rabindranath Tagore, Cat Stevens, Baba Ram Dass, Timothy Leary.

'But didn't the last of them die almost a hundred years ago?' he asked.

'Yes, they did leave the earth plane, but they didn't technically die. I found them the option to go to the dimension they wanted to visit,' she said with a conviction in her voice that upset him.

'And where do you want to go?'

'Beyond all these dimensions. Elsewhere. No one knows about it except me, and now you.'

'And how far away is this elsewhere, Yra?'

'See, that's the thing! It is right here, exactly where we are, except a few invisible planes higher. You and I can easily get there. It's a great space for us to do our work from. We don't have to *leave* leave.' Her eyes still shone bright, but her shaky voice belied her conviction.

'I have to tell you this, Avan. I have seen it for myself. I've left the earth plane too, during my research. And now I want you to come along.'

Avan was from the zone that had been pushed by Kasara state to overproduce the 'miracle rice grain', IR8, whose rate of yield was faster than the projected population growth of Kasara and its subzones. Though the rice variety – after which his zone had come to be named – had been able to keep famine at bay for over 200 years, its ferocious growth had eventually sucked all the groundwater dry.

With no water to nourish soul or soil, the famine arrived. The subzones were caught unprepared. Chaos, disease and death followed. When Avan, the last of IR8's survivors, was found, he was on the brink of losing his sanity, guarding his father's corpse, a famed idealogue who had led the resistance against Kasara when it had wanted to grab all of IR8's rice produce and leave nothing for its locals. The aides who found them did not ask Avan why his father's intestines had been chewed out. It would be his demon alone. More than ready to run into Kasara's warm embrace, he had allowed them to reprogram his brain's amygdala to disintegrate most of his traumatic memories. He would make a fresh start.

൭

'What do you mean you have left the earth plane? Are you not alive now, Yra? Are you not here?' He was 12 again and abandoned, his loved one deciding that running away from safety was best for all.

'Oh baby, I could never leave without you. I've thought it all through. We'll use the long day of tomorrow's solstice to help you make your first journey. You are gifted, it won't be difficult for you.'

Yra had tried but failed to get him to accept his talents. He had a mind for building complex systems from nothing. He could visualize entire new realities through his drawings. At his manager's nudging at the plant, and when he had the time to spare from his accounting job, Avan worked on designs that might enable the fusion reactor to produce energy higher than the Sun someday. Who would believe that her Avan was building Kasara's own Sun!

'What is wrong with remaining here and continuing your work, Yra? We could work together. Why do you want it all to change?' he said.

She was silent for a minute. 'Here, in this temperature-controlled, truth-denying farce? When I know what is possible there?'

'What truths are being denied here?'

'This is no utopia, and you know it. It will come undone.'

'Everything comes undone, Yra. You know that. Won't your elsewhere come undone, eventually?'

'But I will be in control of my destiny there,' she said, a glint of rebellion in her eyes.

Avan had never been able to find out which zone Yra was from or what she had seen that made her so incapable of noticing the small things that could give her happiness.

'Let's discuss this a year from now…'

'Not in a year, not tomorrow. *Now.* My energy in this dimension is depleting, Avan,' she cried. 'I can feel my essence leaching away. I've been travelling between dimensions. A lot. I am afraid I will soon belong there entirely.'

Avan heard a visceral howl escape him as her words cleaved him down the middle. A soundlessness engulfed him. Only a fear remained. A fear he had last felt when he had begged his father to stop running; to take them instead to Kasara where they would no longer be homeless or hungry. Avan's knees turned to jelly as the forgotten memory of his last day with his father returned, unbidden, mixing with Yra's words.

When he came to, Yra was holding his face as he emptied his gut into a basin.

'We are here. We are happy here. I can feel you here.' He managed to get the words out through a racking cough.

'Not for long, Avan,' came her reply.

'How could you let this happen? I'm not ready, Yra. This is not how it is supposed to go. I want to wake up next to you, smell your hair, make breakfast for you, see our baby off to school.'

Yra gathered him into herself, shushing him, comforting him.

'I am sure you can forget it all – like I did my life before you. It's easy, you'll see! Let's have a baby?' he begged, his voice muffled by her clothes.

But her voice was firm as she said, 'Avan, if you choose to go, and I hope you do, there is a tablet that you can access in the elsewhere. I found that it exists just today. It is made of my parents' life force transmuted into light. It is activated by the high frequency of love, and it will sustain me for some time. Isn't this a good thing?'

What could he say?

'You can make the journey tomorrow when they bring the Sun out for the solstice. Please bring the tablet back, I can use it to stay alive here till you've made a decision.'

'Won't you be coming with me, Yra?'

'I need to be here safeguarding your physical body. If the body is hurt, or if it dies, its connection with the elsewhere will forever be lost.'

Yra and Avan prepared for his flight as the dawn of the solstice neared. The Sun would appear through the skydome any moment now. He knew she had given all her prana to the finding of the elsewhere. It was her gamble, her challenge to their love, even. He would go for the sake of her happiness and the tablets that would sustain her. And, perhaps, when he came back, he could make her see that earthly life, with all its joys and afflictions, was more precious than a conceptual existence as an intelligent form or whatever it was. He should never have let her go on adventures on her own. She had gone too far with it all. Of one thing he was certain – if he did not go now, if he dawdled, he could never win her back from her wanderings.

Avan sat down on the mat Yra laid out. They embraced as Yra started to hum, looking into his eyes. He felt weightlessness, confusion and despair. 'The only way to make it work is to let go. You must not control what happens at any cost, Avan. We don't have much time, you need to be back by the time the solstice ends,' she urged.

He had to get this right. The life they shared was precious to him, his to cherish and protect. Soon enough, a high-pitched ringing assailed his ears, and then, blackness descended all around.

Yra's elsewhere. First came the sense of red behind his closed eyelids. Then came the smell. Sun. Tropical, earthy heat. A memory stirred in his cells. Baked pavements, hot earth, clothes and black gram dough drying to a crisp. It brought to mind a time, very, very long ago, when the mugginess was enough to get him out of bed happily for the day that was to unfold. That was also a very, very different person ago. As he opened his eyes, he realized the smell was his memory, not reality. The heat was the sun. It felt more powerful and present than it had on earth, in their fourth dimension.

He was in a room that seemed to be there but also not there. Was his mind playing tricks or were the room's black walls melting? His body felt light, weightless. His awareness had grown very sharp, sensitive to every sight, smell, sound, feeling. The space around him was spherical, constantly undulating. It was being constantly created and recreated with what seemed to him like electric glitches, sounds from scratchy gramophones, images from old home videos. He thought of Yra and there she was, her face shimmering as if made of a million stars. He thought of his childhood with his brothers, and all their voices echoed around him. Snatches of memories played as if on the cracked screen of a television set. Avan felt raw and exposed. He closed his eyes. A hum pervaded the space. Avan understood that Avan the observer, was creating the here-now of this reality. 'Hello?' he offered.

No response. Just as he tried to walk out of the room, a corridor and a modest veranda appeared around him. The mechanics of intentionality were at work. He had to be careful what he wished for. An open porch flashed into existence around him. He was glad to feel the sun on his back. He felt strong. He felt exhilarated. He felt intensely present like no past or future existed. So this was it. Yra's place of infinite freedom that would let you access the secrets of the universe.

'You have finally arrived.'

'Where have I arrived?' Avan asked, not knowing what he was saying and to whom.

'Can't you tell?'

It was a disembodied voice, a bit tinny. Avan looked for its source without success.

'No, I can't tell. What is this place?' He found himself smiling despite himself. Why was he doing that? Why was he feeling happy?

'It is whatever you intend it to be. You know that. It is whatever your life on earth couldn't be. You can make it your own without any fear.'

Avan saw flashes of his life just before Kasara. Yes, he had indeed settled for Kasara's security, with his accountant's job and weekly squash games with the boys. He hadn't quite made anything of his life yet. But what was wrong with that? He was happy.

'Do you want to know what is possible here?'

'Could you lead me to Yra's light tablet and help me return?'

'Yes, like I said, whatever you want is possible. It is right next to you.'

Turning, he saw a pouch resting on a slab next to him. Within it pulsed the thumb-sized rectangle that would sustain his beloved's life. It was all that he needed. 'All right, I'm ready to go.'

'Now, you have a choice to make. You can join the light – you can move towards freedom or you can go back.' Avan realized that the voice was not around him but coming to him.

'I just said I am ready to go. Yra needs these tablets to stay alive,' he said.

'Yra didn't tell you?'

Was there a secret the voice shared with Yra? He felt excluded. He tried to get a good look around the place. The only physical objects around him where those that his mind created. Yes, it was peaceful; yes, it made him feel happy, free even. He could see its lure but he wouldn't be caught off guard twice in one day.

'Who are you?' he asked.

'I belong to the tribe that lives here. You cannot see us yet – you'll need your faculties developed.'

'Sure. I have seen what I needed to see. I will bring Yra here myself when we are ready – but not now. I love her and I haven't kept some of my promises to her. Please let me leave.'

'Yra didn't tell you?' the voice asked again.

Avan was losing patience. 'Tell me what?'

'Once you decide to go back from here, you see everything for what it is. You can no longer hide behind the veil induced by your people. You will see unhappiness, suffering, negativity. Feel fear. You will not feel the need to see any more places or keep promises.'

'Why didn't Yra tell me this?'

'Would you have come if she had?'

'I want to be a father. Can I be a father here?' he asked.

'This, here, is freedom. There are no fathers, children, wives, siblings. We live in a better understanding of the purpose of humanity. Summon Yra now if you like. This can be the beginning. Everything can start again with the two of you.'

'This is... I am not ready...'

'You have a choice – you can remain here and Yra can join you. You can help us build this place. We will create Suns that we will hide from no one.'

How much did the voice know?

'This place has made Yra lose herself in its madness. Thanks, but no thanks. What is the point of people self-destructing in the name of free will?'

'She always had the power to come live here, once and for all. But she loves you too much. She didn't tell you, but she stayed with you there, dreaming of here, losing her prana. She waited and waited for you to be ready to make this journey. Madness was the price she paid.'

'I feel coerced. You lot are hurrying into things.'

'But you do feel better here. Like it was, before.'

'Before? When I was with my father?'

'Yes. You could go back to feeling like your real self. Before you had to throw away bits of yourself so you could forget how helpless you were.'

'Is there a tablet for that, too?' he scoffed.

'Yes. Right beside you.' He felt a yellow, protective warmth appear. Something pulsed. His father.

'Of what use is freedom when you can't speak of what you loved and why you lost it?' the voice asked.

'Can I please just leave now?'

'Whatever you like.'

Avan felt his stomach lurch and the bamboo mat prick his thighs. He hadn't quite known how strong gravity's pull could be. His eyes flew open, and he was slammed back to the floor. He was back in the fourth dimension all right. 'Yra!'

The air was very still, and an old anxiety rose within him. It had accompanied him like a dog that he couldn't shake off till the people of Kasara had silenced it altogether. It was back now like the voice had told him it would be.

'Yra!' Where had she disappeared? Why was the house so dark? Avan flicked on the light switches in their living room. He caressed the light tablets for comfort. He walked around opening the windows. It was nearing dusk, and the window of their bedroom seemed half-open. He made to open them wider. His feet brushed against something soft. He bent to get a proper look and pulled back, horrified. It was Yra. She was gasping for air.

'Yra!'

He scrambled to lift her, bringing her to their bed. Her face had gone pale, he slapped her gently, once and then a few times.

She stirred. 'Avan.'

'Yra, baby, don't talk; I am taking you to the hospital.'

'Avan, how was it?' He didn't reply immediately. He looked around. She needed help. He gathered her in his arms, and crossed the living room, sprinting towards the door. The citizen alarm booth was around the street corner. Her breath rattled. He carried her out the door, down the street. His most precious Yra. They had pulled the skydome back in its place. It danced with all sorts of neon colours. He side-stepped a few holograms – people travelling brusquely through time–space portals. When he reached the alarm, he broke the glass covering the emergency button and pressed it hard. Help would be on its way soon. He felt the tablets pulse in the pocket of his shirt. He took them out, laid them on her chest. She smiled.

'You found them.' Her skin seemed to grow warmer. Perhaps this would make her better.

'I'm sorry, Avan. I think my time is up. I got it wrong. I'm glad I could see you one last time, baby.'

'Don't talk like that! Help will be here soon. You will remain here.'

'It was all for nothing. I think the effort of sending you was too much for me.'

Yra's eyes rolled back, her skin grew ashen. 'I can feel myself leave, Avan. I will come for you. We will return together to our elsewhere.'

Avan bent over, sobbing, kissing her. 'No, Yra. Stay.'

He punched the emergency button harder.

'I cannot let you go anywhere. We will make the life we dreamed of.'

Her eyes stared uncomprehendingly as her pulse weakened.

Avan hugged her close, trying to breathe life into her. His mouth went to her mouth, her neck, her shoulders. Sobbing, he inhaled her smells. He found his way to her stomach. He put his head there as his body started to heave. He curled up there, with his head against her softness. All he knew and cherished was Yra. All that kept him together was Yra. His memories from before her were coloured with horror and helplessness. He cried clutching at her clothes. His mouth started to pull at the threads of her tunic. His hands, desperate to save and protect her, shook her body. She responded with whatever life was left within her. She was still here, with him. He needed to act fast and prevent her from leaving with her life to that godforsaken elsewhere. Her life was his. He wouldn't let it leave Kasara. A mad rage swept over him. How could Yra think of leaving. Kasara was safe. Your loved ones did not betray you here. His mouth tugged at her clothes till his teeth met her soft flesh. Her soft belly to which he had spoken many inanities when they made love. He bit it. It belonged to him. It was Yra. His. He worked his way through the flesh, meeting blood, bone and entrails. He consumed it all. His baby. She was his heart that held all his hopes. Portals opened and closed around him as people arrived, horrified, unable to move or help. Avan went all the way to her intestines. His mouth bit, gently, then savagely. He chewed her innards out like he had chewed away his father. He put an end to her going away from him. Both Yra and his father wanted to leave him. Abandon him just like that. In search of happiness elsewhere. Now they would remain here in Kasara, forever. Happy, together. His father should never have shunned Kasara. Avan had to kill him so he would stop running. Yra should not have gone looking for happiness beyond dimensions. There was no need to journey into the unknown if you couldn't have the love you needed, when you needed it most. If you couldn't soothe your loved ones when they needed to be soothed.

Once Yra was gone, he touched her forehead and with all the love in his heart said, 'I love you.' A soft yellow honey-diamond appeared in his palm. His Yra.

As the watching crowds parted, he made his way to the power plant, carrying her in his arms. He would pour the tablets into the reactor, into the Sun he was building. They would remain here, with him, too. They would watch over him and make his days brighter, here, now, nowhere else.

GIFT OF THE ANGELS

JAYANT V. NARLIKAR
Translated by Archana Mirajkar

The *Pasadena Herald* published the following report by its special science correspondent on 2 February:

Last night, the Bakeman Auditorium was packed to capacity. Several hundred Caltech students, who could not gain entry, returned disappointed. The reason for such unprecedented attendance at the auditorium was the debate at Bakeman and the two speakers who had been invited for it. During the debate, visiting professor at Caltech Sir Roger Armstrong and popular science fiction writer Ben Thomas expressed their opinions on 'super advanced life' in the universe. These speakers were not new to Caltech. On many occasions in the past, both had given lectures at the university, providing a great deal of fodder for the imagination of the audience. But yesterday's debate between the two was exceptional and unforgettable.

The debate began at 8 p.m. First, Sir Roger presented some astronomical information on the vast universe beyond Earth using some slides. He then pointed out the possibility of life being present elsewhere and that it may be far more developed than mankind. However, the professor was not very optimistic about the future of humanity on Earth. Pointing to the continuing rise in the world's population, large-scale misuse of natural resources (and here he blamed the US more than any other country), strife between nations and divisive tendencies flourishing in society, Sir Roger said, 'If we do not rein in these flaws in the next five or six decades, I fear that the human civilization may not last for more than a century or two!'

While the audience was trying to come to terms with this pessimistic future, there was a ray of hope in the speech given by Ben Thomas.

While asserting at the very beginning that he agreed with the scientific points stated by Sir Roger, Ben Thomas went on to postulate his opinion on 'human nature'. Stating that human civilization has come to the point of destruction several times in the past but has managed to survive it all, he put forward his belief that in the same way, it will survive the present catastrophe. He had only one fear, he said. What if some advanced civilization decided to settle down here? 'May God prevent anyone from noticing Earth!' he joked.

Several scientists, students and writers participated in the discussion by asking questions. Finally, the chairman made the concluding remarks by announcing 'it is time to close the auditorium'.

The journalist had titled the report 'Humans! Beware!'

The audience continued to discuss the debate long after leaving the auditorium. Two men from the audience, Vijay Sinha and Brian Logi, made their way to the Continental Burger Snack Bar on Lake Avenue as they continued talking. Brian was a senior fellow at Caltech and was doing his research on astronomy. Vijay was a computer technologist and was visiting from India for a year for his own research. Both were about 35 or 36 years old and as their personalities matched they had become great friends.

'I agree with Sir Roger!' Brian exclaimed, taking a bite of his hamburger. 'What does past experience teach us? Great scientists, well-known thinkers, poets and seers were born in many countries. They made important contributions to human civilization. Their names are remembered forever. But look at any country's experience. In the end, the fate of its civilization is not decided by the great people. It is decided by the proletariat. What was the fate of the Roman Empire? Wasn't it replaced by barbarians?'

'Agreed, but was it the end of Europe? Wasn't the Roman Empire replaced by a new civilization? Why be pessimistic when people like Michelangelo and Leonardo da Vinci also followed the glory of Rome?' Vijay was optimistic as usual.

'The old gets replaced by the new. That is the law of the nature. I agree that it is applicable to human civilization as well, but sometimes a civilization hits such a nadir that it is impossible to spring back. And that is what is going to happen to mankind on Earth very soon,' Brian said, speaking seriously. 'And even if we don't destroy ourselves, others will.'

'Others who?' Vijay asked.

'That I can't say,' said Brian, smiling mischievously. 'I also sometimes feel what Ben warned us about – that alien life is eyeing this rich planet of ours. They might be on some planet or in interstellar space. At the right time, they may well attack and destroy us. Humans should stop their petty fights between nations and unite. We don't have much time.'

'Thanks for reminding me! I don't have much time myself,' Vijay exclaimed, finishing off his cheese sandwich. 'I'll have to stay up all night and complete my report.'

'What report?' Brian asked, picking up the bill.

'My institute back in India is planning to purchase a new computer. Based on my report and recommendation, the faculty will decide which model to buy. And the order has to go out before the new financial year begins on 1 April.'

'But it's only 2 February,' Brian said, glancing at his watch. It was just past midnight.

'You don't know the delays that happen in India. To get everything done on time, my report has to be sent by air mail this morning. I'm probably going to stay up until 3 a.m. to finish it.'

'You keep toiling, I am going to hit my bed.' Brian yawned, glancing at his watch. 'I bet your computer grant will get cancelled. You are unnecessarily losing out on your sleep.'

'Stay positive, Logi...' Vijay said to himself, but his face was anxious.

By the time the report was crosschecked and finalized, it was almost 3 a.m. Vijay decided that he would write the accompanying letter to his professors in the morning and set his alarm for 7.30 a.m. As he was preparing to go to bed, he heard the telephone ring. He almost expected to hear 'Sorry, wrong number!' as he picked up the receiver.

'796-8947.' He said his number out loud.

'Dr Vijay Sinha?' asked the caller.

'Yes. But who is this? And why are you calling at this odd hour?'

'I am sorry for bothering you. I was waiting for you to complete your report. You were planning to stay up till 3 a.m., right?'

'How did you know that?' Vijay asked in surprise.

'I was sitting at a table near you when you were talking to Dr Logi. I wasn't eavesdropping but happened to overhear your conversation. I thought I'd wait for the right time to call.'

The caller was trying to be too familiar. Although he had an American accent, Vijay thought that the caller might not be originally from the US. Was he some detective stalking him, Vijay wondered.

He asked angrily, 'Is this an appropriate time to call? Are you not ashamed to call me at this hour?'

'I apologize once again, but the circumstances are a bit strange. Would it be possible to send your report a day later? It would be to your advantage. Please listen to me.'

'This is insane! Who are you to advise me on this? It is absolutely necessary for me to send the report today.' Vijay was feeling very sleepy and couldn't fathom how to end this conversation. All the more because he realized that this person was not calling just for fun.

'I apologize a third time. I often forget etiquette when I am excited. My name is Dr Suleiman Rashid, and I am a local director at the firm Middle Eastern Computers. I'd like to request you to see our new computer before sending your report. I can show you the computer any time today.'

Vijay knew how aggressive American salesmen could get, and he had an answer ready. He said in a formal, apologetic tone, 'Dr Rashid, I think you are mistaken. I cannot decide which computer to buy. Our government decides that before sanctioning the grant for it. My institute has tasked me only with choosing the model of the computer.'

'What if the government cancels the grant? But for a few conditions, we will even give you our computer free!' Rashid continued. 'The government's plans can change at any time.'

'There is very little possibility of that. The grant has been sanctioned. Only the cheque is awaited – all other formalities are complete,' Vijay asserted. *That should shut him up*, he thought.

'All right, I shall not bother you further. But in case your grant is cancelled, will you call me? Let me give you my number.'

Vijay noted down the number to get rid of Rashid and hung up. Soon, he was snoring peacefully.

Krrrr...krrrr... The ring of the telephone woke Vijay up. It was 10 a.m. He wondered if he had forgotten to set the alarm. *Good, at least the telephone woke me up*, Vijay thought and picked up the phone.

'Dr Vijay Sinha?' a pleasant voice asked.

'Speaking.'

'This is Western Union, Sir. I have a cable for you. Shall I read it out?' the operator asked. As soon as Vijay gave the go-ahead, she read out the message: 'Computer grant cancelled. Postpone your report. Letter follows.'

The sender's name was Professor Gupta, the head of Vijay's computer centre.

'Do you want a written copy, sir?' Vijay was brought to his senses by the operator's voice.

'Yes, please. Thanks for calling,' he managed to stutter. He disconnected even before listening to the operator's response.

All the plans he had been making to use the new computer, the experiments he would carry out with its help, were shattered. And he would not be the only one disappointed. Various groups at the institute had also made plans based on the new computer. The old computer, though it had served the institute well, was unable to cope with the work now. Known for its ability to carry out several calculations in its heyday, it was now considered insignificant in the world of new computers. The people at the institute were fed up with its frequent breakdowns and were eagerly waiting for the new machine. What would happen to all those plans now?

As Vijay sat there stupefied, his attention was drawn to a piece of paper lying near the telephone. It read: 'Dr Rashid – 714-456-2121'.

He started to wonder whose name and telephone number it was, and immediately remembered his conversation from the previous night. He remembered Rashid's message: '...in case your grant is cancelled, will you call me?' Was there a connection between that statement and the grant getting cancelled? Without giving it another thought, Vijay dialled Rashid's number.

'Is that Dr Sinha? I recognized your voice!' he heard Rashid say. Soon, Vijay informed him about the cancellation of the computer grant.

'Good! That means we can now be given a chance.' Vijay thought there was enthusiasm rather than surprise in Rashid's voice. Rashid continued, 'Would you like to see our computer today? I can pick you up at any time you like, but it will take me an hour to reach you.'

'In that case, you can come to my office at 1 p.m.' Vijay said and gave him the address.

'I'll be there at 1 p.m. sharp. Would you be able to bring some computer programs to try out? Any problem that takes an hour to solve on the Caltech computer can be solved in a second on our new model. I am not exaggerating – you will see for yourself.'

Vijay thought Rashid was giving him a sales pitch again.

Vijay took four computer programs with him – two of his own and two of Brian Logi's. One of them had been solved by the Caltech computer in two hours. Brian's program would require more time. Its calculations required 50 hours and, as such, he had never had the chance to run it on the Caltech computer. Vijay had the prints of the answers to the other three programs.

Rashid arrived at the appointed hour. He was fair, and Vijay thought he might be from an Arab country. However, his clothes and behaviour were typically American. As soon as Vijay got into Rashid's red Mustang, he started the car as well as his chatter.

'Let me tell you a little about myself. I am originally from a small country called Alif Santoor in the Middle East.' Vijay had never heard of this country. 'Although our country is very small and undeveloped, our Sheikh is very progressive and liberal. He wants our country to make rapid progress. He has enormous wealth from the oil reserves. But instead of using this wealth to bring Western technologists to our country, he uses it to enable our countrymen to travel abroad and be educated. Every year, he grants scholarships for studies abroad and tries to make good use of these people when they return after completing their education. I was one such student selected by him.

'I was interested in electronics, especially computer hardware. During my research, I focused on ways to make computers operate as fast as possible and making them capable of storing as much information as possible. The model I am going to show you today is the result of my research.'

Rashid was talking non-stop, and Vijay's job was simply to listen. But he couldn't stop himself from remarking, 'If what you said in the morning is true, I would say that you have made a unique discovery.'

Rashid smiled and said, 'I'll accept your congratulations at the right time.'

The car was moving fast on the freeway. Vijay was familiar with the route. Rashid turned his car from the Pasadena Freeway to the Santa Ana Freeway. After a while, they reached Anaheim. There were several amusement parks in this suburb of Los Angeles, and after passing through areas such as the Japanese Village, and the silver Matterhorn mountain of Disneyland that Vijay was familiar with, Rashid left the highway and turned onto a smaller track. The busier parts of the town were left behind, and orange orchards lined either side of the road.

'Once upon a time, this entire area was famous for its oranges. Now, because of the industries, amusement parks and factories, one has to drive this far to see the orchards!' Rashid continued his monologue. He turned the car towards a vineyard. 'We wish to keep our activities as secret as possible. Otherwise, these big American companies will steal our invention and make big bucks out of it. That is why His Majesty the Sheikh bought this vineyard and built a laboratory here for my research. It's against zoning laws, but we do not pollute the environment.'

The car stopped at a square, squat building. There were several security devices to get past before they entered. Making his way through them, Rashid took Vijay to his office. 'Let me make some coffee. Meanwhile, you can test your computer programs,' he said and took Vijay to an adjoining room.

But there was no computer there. Two slits in the opposite walls of the room were marked as 'Input Terminal' and 'Output Terminal'. Each end had two buttons. When Rashid pressed one button at the input terminal, a window appeared there. He placed the punch-cards of Vijay's first program there. When he pushed the other button, the window closed. At the same time, a green light began to blink at the output terminal.

'The computer seems to have liked your program,' said Rashid.

'So, when can we expect the answer?' Vijay asked.

Rashid pointed to the output terminal. A green light was glowing there. Rashid pushed a button at the output terminal. Immediately, a window appeared there. A paper with the answer to Vijay's program printed on it was ready there. Rashid handed the printout to Vijay and closed the window by pushing the other button.

'Run your other programs and then we can have coffee.' Saying this, Rashid left the room and headed to his office.

Vijay checked the printout. The computer had accurately solved the problem. But what stunned him was the time taken to solve it, which he saw mentioned on the printout. The Caltech computer had solved Vijay's problem in 58 minutes, Rashid's computer had taken 0.083 seconds or about one-twelfth of a second. This implied that Rashid's claims about the speed of the computer may not be an exaggeration.

Vijay ran his second program and one of Logi's programs as well. He had the same experience each time. Finally, he fed in Logi's second program – the one that ran for 50 hours on the Caltech computer.

After about a minute, the green light on the output terminal began to glow. Vijay pressed the button and took the printout. Of course, there was no way to know if the answer was correct because only Logi knew that, but the time taken to solve this problem was only 50 seconds!

Vijay rushed to Rashid's office in great excitement. 'Dr Rashid! You are a genius. Can I take a look at your machine?'

'Thanks. I won't be able to show you the machine right now, and I apologize for that. I would be happy to show you this toy of mine at the right time.'

'But you must at least tell me why you would give such a fabulous computer to our institute free of cost.' This question had been at the back of Vijay's mind.

'We have a selfish motive. Come, let's talk about that.' Rashid led Vijay to his office.

The director had convened a special meeting of the institute's faculty to take decisions on the issue of the computer. All the members of the faculty had arrived by 11.15 a.m., and the director began to speak. 'When the government grant was cancelled, we were all very disappointed that we were unable to get a new computer. As our economy is not doing well, it seemed then that we had no other choice for the time being. However, we received some positive news three days ago, which is why I decided to convene this meeting. Professor Gupta will now tell you the details.' The director glanced at Professor Gupta.

'You may remember that the faculty had requested Dr Vijay Sinha to prepare a report on which model to buy,' said Professor Gupta.

'Who is this Dr Sinha?' the professor of mathematics, Dr Sahydri, asked.

'Dr Sinha is a Fellow of the computing group, and he is currently at the California Institute of Technology to do research for a year,' Professor Gupta explained. 'We learnt that we would not be getting the computer even before we received his report and so I sent him a cable informing him. Three days ago, I received a letter from Dr Sinha. He mentioned that we would receive a state-of-the-art computer at no cost from a Middle Eastern country if we met certain conditions. I can't reveal the name of the country yet, but you will hear about it later. As India has excellent relations with this country, the government will not object to the "gift".'

'I called Delhi yesterday and got confirmation on that front as well,' the director added. 'The government will not raise objections as long as the computer can be used for the government defence project for two hours every day.'

'So, what are these conditions? Naturally, there would be conditions for such a generous gift!' solid state physics Professor Vaidya enquired. He was known to criticize every new project.

'Their company will manage the machine. Although it will be stationed on the premises, only their staff will be able to enter the computer room. The staff will comprise one manager and two or three assistants – that's all! The first condition is that we will have to use the computer through them. The other condition is that we will be allowed to use the computer for only eight hours every day. Of this, two hours will have to be reserved for government use, and that leaves us with six hours. We can allocate a time slot from 9 a.m. to 11 a.m. to the government, and we can use it from 11 a.m. to 5 p.m. We can make some such arrangement,' Professor Gupta said.

'We will get to use the computer only for six hours?' Professor Vaidya exclaimed. 'We could use our old computer 24x7.' Although Professor Vaidya had never used the old computer, everyone else seemed to be thinking the same thing.

The director said, 'The company has a lot of research to do on the software, and they need time for that. Since we have several experts in the field, they have decided to give the computer to us. I can't find anything objectionable about that. Now, Professor Gupta will explain what this computer can do in six hours.'

'I don't think our institute can engage this computer for six hours every day. If we must compare it to the old computer, I can only think of a bullock cart and a supersonic jet as an analogy,' Professor Gupta remarked and narrated the statistics received from Vijay on the computer's performance. The experts stared wide-eyed when they heard these figures.

'I was similarly awestruck when I heard these numbers, but I have complete faith in Dr Sinha's report. He has tested it by running some computer programs himself.' Professor Gupta explained calmly.

'If that is the case, many of our astronomy calculations will be solved instantly!' Rajderkar, the professor of astronomy, exclaimed.

'Several of our problems in molecular biology have also been waiting for a next-generation computer. But this one seems to be generations ahead!' Ahmed, the professor of that branch of science, said, stroking his beard.

'I have never dealt with a computer, but such a fast computer would be useful to conduct searches in the field of number theory,' murmured Professor Lakshmanmurti, who otherwise rarely spoke.

'And we can dive into major investigations on issues like the four colour problem,' Professor Sahyadri finished.

The director winked at Professor Gupta. The mathematician had always regarded computers with contempt.

'I don't think the government will like the first condition,' Professor Vaidya continued in opposition. 'For reasons of national security, government inspectors should have access to the room. I don't think we should take any steps without clarification from the government.'

'That is the government's problem – not ours,' said the director. 'I contacted high-level officials at both the Home and the External Affairs ministries yesterday and informed them about both conditions. Sheikh, the ruler of the country providing this computer, has provided all the information about the computer himself, and on that basis, they have given their permission to install the computer if the institute has no reservations.'

'But such a powerful computer would occupy a lot of space. How much office space would we have to vacate?' said Professor Vaidya, making his last attempt at opposition.

'What I have gathered from Dr Sinha's report is that the computer and its operators would only require three offices' space. Our old computer occupies five times as much space.'

Professor Vaidya's resistance was completely disarmed by this statement, and the director concluded the meeting since he had obtained the consent of the faculty.

Three months later, the new computer was installed at the institute. Rashid himself managed the computer and brought along three of his countrymen, Farooq, Quasim and Mansoor, as his assistants. Three rooms on the top floor had been allotted to them. The innermost room contained the computer; the middle room was occupied by Rashid while the outer room was manned by the three assistants.

Those wishing to use the computer were only allowed to interact with these three men. Cards with computer programs punched on them were submitted at their office and the printouts of the answers were obtained from there.

Only a few VIPs had access to Rashid. Apart from the director and Professor Gupta, only Vijay enjoyed that privilege. He had recently returned from Caltech and had been promoted to Reader in his department. In addition, he was responsible for coordination with the computer. He had developed a friendship with Rashid, and they called each other by their first names. The members of the institute were extremely pleased with the computer. Professor Gupta's prediction that it would be impossible to keep the computer continuously occupied for six hours had been vindicated. People who were used to hearing the operator of the old computer say, 'Give me your programs today, and the answer may be ready in three days,' were now receiving an answer almost as soon as the program was submitted.

Vijay Sinha and Rashid's friendship was growing by the day. Rashid was extremely interested in the software research being carried out at the institute, and he used it to make improvements in his computer.

Despite this satisfactory situation, there was one thing that bothered Vijay. He had not seen the computer yet! He had mentioned his eagerness to see it to Rashid several times but each time Rashid had avoided showing him the computer. He either changed the topic or made some excuse.

The door leading to the computer from Rashid's room always remained closed. Like a safe, it had two combination locks, and the secrecy around the computer had been meticulously maintained since the beginning. At the time of its installation, its various units had arrived in small packets. On special instructions from the government, the customs department had allowed them to be imported without an examination. The Sheikh had possibly made a request to that effect. The computer was probably assembled from these units by Rashid alone, that too behind closed doors. And Rashid was engaged in his research behind this closed door from 5 p.m. to 9 a.m. Vijay gathered he wanted to protect his research from being stolen. Or did he have another motive?

A year passed after the installation of the computer. By now, the whole world had heard about the research being carried out at the institute. Scientists from the so-called developed countries began to visit the institute for a chance to use the computer. Finally, the director had to put in place a system of permissions to stop this deluge.

Around this time, a tragedy occurred. Sakharam, a gardener at the institute, seemed to suddenly go insane. While it was true that people had always found him a bit strange, no one had ever heard of him suffering from a bout of insanity. One day, he reported to work as usual and began to mow the grass. Then, all of a sudden, he stopped working, ran to the beach nearby and began to speak incoherently. He was spotted by his colleagues just in time – just as he was about to jump into the sea. The other gardeners somehow managed to drag him back to the institute and confine him to a room. After a while, he seemed to calm down, but he suffered from memory loss. Despite receiving extensive medical treatment, he did not recover his memory. Finally, he was made to retire from the institute with a pension.

Vijay was chatting with Rashid in his office when he received a call from the registrar of the institute, Mr Shabde.

'I need to speak to you – it's important and confidential. Can I see you in your office right now?'

'Sure. I'll be there in five minutes. If it is more convenient, shall we meet in your office?' Vijay asked.

'No, I am constantly disturbed by phone calls or visitors here. I will come to your room.'

When Vijay returned to his office, Mr Shabde was waiting for him outside. After entering Vijay's office, he closed the door carefully, made sure no one was eavesdropping outside the window and then took a seat opposite Vijay.

'Are you going to tell me about some great conspiracy?' Vijay joked.

But Mr Shabde responded gravely. 'I have received some extraordinary news, but it is so unbelievable that I thought it best not to disturb the director without consulting you.'

Sensing the question on Vijay's face, he further lowered his soft voice and began. 'When I was walking as usual in the garden this morning, Hari Pawar, the foreman of the gardeners, caught up with me. He is a friend of Sakharam. Because of his strange nature, Sakharam couldn't get along with others, but Hari had always managed to get him to do his work. Hari has been quite upset since Sakharam's attack of insanity. He has always suspected that there must have been a reason for that attack, and he believes that he has learnt that reason today. What he told me is this: Sakharam had been quite happy a day before he went mad. When Hari had asked him why, he had avoided saying anything initially, but then he couldn't hold himself back. He had been rewarded with 100 rupees by Dr Rashid.'

'Why did Rashid give him such a big amount?' Vijay asked in surprise.

'That is what I asked Hari!' said Mr Shabde. 'Hari had asked Sakharam the same question. And his explanation was this. That morning, Sakharam had gone to Farooq's room to put some flowers there as usual. Since Rashid's room is always locked, we never placed any flowers there. But that day, Rashid's room was open, and he called Sakharam in. He wanted a bouquet of roses for a special occasion. He asked him if such a bouquet could be obtained from the institute's nursery, and Sakharam delivered a bouquet to him. That is when he gave the gardener the money. It wasn't a one-rupee note as Sakharam had expected, but a hundred-rupee note. He thought it was a mistake and said so, but Rashid said he never took back a reward and bid him a pleasant goodbye. For some reason, Hari believes that this incident was somehow connected to Sakharam's attack, which is why he began to place the flowers in Farooq's room himself. He felt that he would someday come across Rashid and perhaps learn more about this whole affair. His wish came true today. He met Rashid this morning, and Rashid again asked for a bouquet of roses. When Hari returned with the bouquet, Rashid was not in his office but the door to the computer room was open.'

'What did he see inside?' Vijay could hardly contain his excitement.

'That is what is so surprising!' said Mr Shabde. 'Hari says there is a small table inside with a small machine on it, the size of a portable typewriter. The rest of the room was *empty*. There was no computer console, tape units or memory storage unit. But Hari had hardly peeped inside for a minute when Rashid returned to the outer room. He quickly closed the door, took the flowers from Hari and sent him off, this time without a reward. Hari is convinced that there is no computer in that room, and this is all a hoax. He firmly believes that Rashid turned Sakharam insane by casting a spell on him. After hearing this story, I have strong suspicions about Rashid. If there is no computer, we are being deceived. But it doesn't explain how the problems are being solved either! And what is the motive behind all this? He may not be a magician, as Hari thinks he is, but is he a spy? I just can't figure this out.'

'This is indeed a very strange episode!' Vijay exclaimed. 'Where is Hari now?'

'He has gone to the canteen for lunch. If you wish, we can call him here and let him narrate the whole incident again.' The registrar picked up the phone to summon Hari.

Hari arrived 10 minutes later. They requested him to narrate the morning incident again, but Hari seemed confused. 'Which incident, sir?'

'The one related to Sakharam! Didn't you meet Mr Rashid today?'

'No, sir! I placed the flowers as usual in Mr Farooq's room. I did not meet Mr Rashid today.'

Mr Shabde tried to interrogate him in several different ways. Either that incident had not taken place or Hari had forgotten all about it.

Mr Shabde left disgruntled, but Vijay sat in his office for a long time. It was difficult to get proof for what Mr Shabde had narrated. He had heard of witnesses turning hostile in court under external pressure. But in this case, if Rashid had pressurized Hari Pawar, there was no sign of it in his behaviour. Had he been lying, Mr Shabde would have realized it owing to his extensive experience as an administrator. But then what was the truth?

Vijay began to suspect a whole range of things about Rashid. Was he a spy from an enemy nation? Or even a country pretending to be friendly with India? How was he solving the problems in the absence of a computer? Mathematicians and scientists from different fields were attesting to the veracity of the answers supplied by Rashid's computer. How could such an advanced computer be as small as a mini typewriter? Perhaps – no, he was almost certain – Hari may not have looked carefully.

Vijay desperately wanted to visit the computer room. If Rashid was not willing to show him the computer, he would have to enter the room without his knowledge. He would have to look for an opportunity when neither Rashid nor Farooq were nearby. Vijay realized that he would soon get such an opportunity. The Sheikh was to arrive in Mumbai next week; and Rashid would be busy attending to him for two days along with his colleagues. The computer would remain shut for the first time since its installation, and its operator would be away.

Vijay waited impatiently for the Sheikh's arrival. Several functions and receptions had been planned in Mumbai in his honour. Vijay had been invited to these, but he made excuses and managed to stay away. He was planning to visit the computer room the day the Sheikh was hosting a party. He came across Rashid that afternoon.

'I hope to see you at the reception today. The party will go on till 2 a.m. – an Arabic meal is a leisurely affair,' said Rashid.

'I am sorry, Rashid, I have said I have a headache, but the truth is that I don't like parties that go on until late in the night. I sleep by 10 p.m. I hope you don't mind – all the big shots from the institute will be there though.'

'I don't like such receptions either, but I have no choice – I can't forget the Sheikh's obligations either,' said Rashid and walked away.

'I have to leave an important message in Mr Rashid's room. Can I have the key, please?' Vijay requested the security officer at 11 p.m. that night. Vijay normally had access to Rashid's room, and he held a position of authority at the institute now. As a result, he had no difficulty in obtaining the key.

'Sir, please return the key immediately. I am actually supposed to accompany you and open the door for you,' said the security officer.

'Why bother to come all the way up to the tenth floor? I'll bring the key back. Also, the night shift has begun – is it not more important for you to remain here?' Vijay grabbed the key and hurried towards the elevator. Five minutes later, he returned the key but he had left the door to Rashid's room unlocked.

The majority of the work was yet to be done, because the heavy door leading to the computer room was still locked. He was aware that it had a combination lock, and the two circular locks were fully capable of protecting the room. Vijay looked at the first wheel. There were actually 10 wheels superimposed on each other. Each wheel had numbers from zero to nine and a pointer which could rotate over them. Vijay surmised that if he could place the pointers on the right digit on each wheel, the lock would open. But what was the right digit? If he did not know the correct number, there were 10 × 10 × 10...× 10 (10^{10}) or 10 billion possible combinations. Even if he tried one combination per second, it would take almost 300 years to try all the combinations!

Vijay closely examined the wheels. He thought the number 3 on the first wheel appeared slightly smudged as compared to the other numbers. The number 1 on the next wheel and the number 4 on the next appeared slightly smudged as well. His eyes couldn't detect the difference between the digits on the wheels beyond that.

314... Where had he seen these digits? Seeing some hope, he realized that one of the most important numbers in mathematics was the ratio between the circumference and the diameter of a circle, which is denoted by the Greek letter π. He remembered that π equals to 3.14159. Were the 10 digits of the first combination, the first 10 digits of the value of π? Vijay could only remember five digits after the decimal. He needed four more digits. Vijay grabbed his pocket calculator. He pressed the π key and the following digits appeared on the screen: 3.141592653.

❧

His calculator could display 19 digits after the decimal, but Vijay had asked for only nine digits and so it displayed zeroes beyond that. When Vijay placed the pointer on those 10 digits, there was a whirring sound from the lock and then a click. Vijay ran excitedly to the second lock. Similar to the first lock, he saw that three digits on the first three wheels were slightly smudged: 271.

He smiled with satisfaction. He was actually expecting those digits! Similar to π, another very important number in mathematics was e. Vijay pressed the e key on the pocket calculator and he got the answer: 2.718281828.

When he selected these digits, the second lock also opened and the door to the computer room swung open noiselessly.

It was midnight, and Vijay switched on the light. Since the computer room had no windows, no one outside would know that there was someone in the room. Just as Hari had said, the room contained a small unit the size of a typewriter. The shelf behind the door contained an apparatus resembling a microscope and a box. Next to it was a red book that looked like a diary. Hari would not have seen these when he had peeped in through the door.

The unit resembling the typewriter was plugged into the power supply. It emitted a constant humming sound and lights flashed from beneath its glass cover. Vijay concluded that it must be the computer. He had never imagined that such a powerful computer could be so small. But after some pondering he realized that it was not impossible.

He remembered the ancestors of the computer family. Computers had appeared after the Second World War. Their units were huge, connected by innumerable wires and occupied several rooms. But compared to computers in the present decade, the 1970s, their speed was very slow and their memory very limited. However, mankind had started a new era by inventing them. With further research and technological advancement, the size of computers had begun to reduce and their speed, memory and ability to store numbers had begun to increase. His pocket computer was a milestone in the same chain of progress. It was small enough to fit in his palm but what a huge amount of information it contained! When he had first handled it, he had remarked, 'The world is in in my hands!'

This progress had been possible because of transistors. What was the next step? And the next? This computer of Rashid's was evidence that mankind had reached a step far ahead. *I wonder what mantra he has!* The scientist in Vijay was jealous. Yet, he wondered how far this computer family would advance. He remembered reading the epic *Raghuvamsa*. The Dilips, Raghus and Ajas of the computer family were the past. What he was seeing today was the Ram of that family, he imagined. But there was no time for idle thoughts. He tried but couldn't find a way to start the computer and examine it. He then turned his attention to the other objects.

He had never seen this kind of microscope apparatus before. He looked into its eyepiece, and he saw something similar to a tiny electric circuit. But its structure was mysterious and unfamiliar. He was surprised at how tiny that circuit was. As far as he knew, no country had yet attained the capacity to create such tiny units. Perhaps this technology was the base of Rashid's computer. The box beside the apparatus was shut and he could not open it. Finally, he turned his attention to the red diary.

It was a diary for the current year, and it contained entries for the next month. Vijay was surprised to see them. For each date, there were notes on major public events scheduled to take place in Mumbai. Information regarding the venue, time, chief guest, chairperson, speakers for each event had been noted wherever available. Some names had five crosses, some others had four, while some names had one, two or three crosses against them. The writer had probably classified the names as per their VIP status because only the names of the President and the prime minister had five crosses against them.

Initially, Vijay thought that all of this was some kind of political conspiracy. But after examining all the names and the classification according to the crosses, he discarded that theory. The notes contained the names from all political parties, besides the names of popular personalities such as writers, scientist, doctors and lawyers – who had nothing to do with politics. Was this a plot to make society helpless by killing all these people? But Vijay discarded that thought too. When he looked at the dates in the diary, he realized that some public events noted there had concluded peacefully. Then what was being plotted here?

But Vijay did not have a chance for any further contemplation. He heard a click behind him and turned his head in astonishment. Rashid was standing there, the door closed behind him.

'You have returned early. I was expecting you to be with the Sheikh at least until 2 a.m.,' Vijay exclaimed, trying to keep his voice as normal as possible. He was worried about what punishment he would be subjected to by Rashid for this transgression.

Without a word, Rashid first went to the box beside the microscope. He opened it and after examining it, closed it again. He then returned to Vijay and he was smiling. Was this a trap? Vijay stayed alert.

'First of all, congratulations for gaining the entry to this room,' he said, shaking Vijay's hand. 'I had selected the combinations so that only a thief who had studied mathematics would be able to figure them out. I am not surprised that you solved them. Similarly, my presence here is not a coincidence.'

'Were you aware of my plans to come here today?' Vijay realized that he had walked into a trap.

'No! I wasn't expecting you specifically today, but I was certain that your inquisitive nature would bring you here sooner than later. And I had made some arrangements. If anyone other than myself enters this room, I get to know about it through remote transmission. The way police are informed when burglars enter a jewellery shop, I used the same technique but in a much advanced format.' The smile had not left Rashid's face.

'All right then, how are you going to punish me?' Vijay asked. In several suspense stories he had read, the villain always arranged to torture the hero in various ways.

Rashid guessed his thoughts and said, 'I am not going to punish you by torturing you in any way. Don't worry. You will understand in due course. At the level at which I function, there is no place for murder or torture.'

But perhaps there is place for insanity or loss of memory! Vijay thought. He said, 'Then will you answer a few questions? What is the work that you do? You are definitely not a regular scientist, and that red book indicates that you might be some kind of a criminal. But which country are you working for? Do you have a grudge against our country for some reason? And what is the real purpose of this excellent computer? Solving our problems is hardly a challenge for it. I can bet it wasn't invented to solve such simple problems.'

'I have no objection to answering these or any other questions that you may have. But, first, listen to me. Then you can ask questions,' Rashid said, and asked Vijay to look through the microscope. As Vijay looked through the eyepiece again, Rashid said, 'The unit that you can see there is approximately 1 micron in dimension, and as you know, 10,000 microns make up 1 centimetre.'

Vijay was stunned! How could such a complicated unit, the circuit visible through the microscope, be so small, he wondered. But Rashid's face did not display any exaggeration or amusement. He began to explain further. 'This technology is new – not only for India but even for countries that claim to be leaders in electronics technology. The computer on the table is based on this new technology. But I am sure you have already guessed that! What you may not know is that it took me one year to develop that unit under the microscope. I have been trying to perfect it ever since the computer arrived in Mumbai. With the help of this computer, that unit can work like a human brain. In fact, in some areas, it is more efficient than the human brain. When this unit is placed on a human body, I can control that person's brain with the help of this computer whether that person is on Earth or anywhere up to 50,000 miles in space. In short, the person's own brain becomes inactive and this unit begins to function in its place.'

So this is an improved – rather, a greatly advanced – version of brainwashing, thought Vijay. He asked instead, 'Did you use this unit on Sakharam, the gardener?'

A shadow of sorrow passed over Rashid's face. 'Yes, unfortunately. At the time, this unit was at an experimental stage. I made a small mistake and not only did the poor man's brain get damaged, but the unit broke too. But I can now cure him by placing the new unit on his body.'

'And what makes you think that the new unit is perfect?' asked Vijay.

'Didn't Hari Pawar forget the right incident? I should have erased his memory before he met Mr Shabde! Then this whole thing would not have reached you. But poor Mr Shabde! How he tried to question Hari!' Rashid said, laughing.

'You heard it *all*?' Vijay exclaimed but realized how stupid it was to ask such a question. It was not difficult for this super-expert at electronics to bug a room.

'Yes – and watched it all as well!' said Rashid. 'After implanting that prototype unit in Hari, I have now made thousands of such units. They are all in that box.'

'And who are you going to use them on?' asked Vijay. He speculated that entries in the red diary were perhaps related to some such plan.

Rashid saw him staring at the diary and said, 'Your conclusion is correct. My first experiments will be conducted on the dignitaries at these events in Mumbai. Let me explain. If you wish to rule a country, one way is to use force, but that leads to loss of lives. In addition, contemporary warfare techniques may lead to massive pollution. So there is a danger that the aggressors or the victorious people may find it impossible to settle in the land they conquer. So my people have adopted a different method. And that method is brainwashing. I have been tasked with carrying out that plan.'

Vijay was about to ask another question, but Rashid raised his hand and continued, 'Your Gita says:

Yadyadacharati shresthah tatvdevetaro janah |
Sa yad pramanam kurute lokastadanuwaratate ||

'Every human possesses the mechanism that enables him to think – his brain. But every human may not necessarily use it and always act by making conscious decisions. Most of the time, people act by imitating others. That, of course, helps in the smooth running of society because such behaviour is predictable. Since such imitative behaviour does not cause disruptions, this tendency is not very obvious. This tendency to imitate the behaviour of others is made use of when there is a constant effort to create public opinion on issues through the means of the public platform: the radio, television and pen. I will begin from the public platforms because it is an easy target in your country. You Indians are very fond of giving speeches and listening to them. Say, today, A is going to give a speech, then B is the chairperson, C is the organizer, D gives the welcome remarks, there is someone else to give the vote of thanks, and sometimes there is a chief guest. Thus, there are at least five or six people on the stage. Each one wants to say "a few words". Poor A keeps waiting for his turn.'

Vijay remembered all the news stories on Mumbai TV that reported such events. 'Today XYZ assembly was held at such-and-such hall. It was inaugurated by so and so. ---- was present ----- was the chief guest…' They used to make him so angry that he stopped watching the news on the TV.

'It is very easy for me to implant my brain units in the dignitaries on any stage. They are all usually offered garlands or bouquets. It is a nice way to honour them, but you carry it to an extreme. Every organization at the event must offer a garland and a bouquet or arguments begin. I can easily slip on this unit on the guests at that time, and then all these people will become puppets in my hand. I can create any kind of public opinion through them.

'Your country is powerful and confident, but these qualities lie dormant. They are only activated when there is external aggression. Once the threat of that aggression subsides, you begin to fight amongst yourselves. That's why we want to gain access to your country without aggression. My scheme will be useful in making you complacent and impotent, and it will destroy your confidence – so much so that in the end, you will be yearning for our colonization. Although our conquest will begin with your country, it will ultimately spread to the whole world. But this will take place at a very slow pace. It may take 50 or 100 years, but we shall wait. It does not matter even if it takes two or three centuries to completely dominate humans and abolish you from the face of the Earth. It is not a very long time in our lives.'

There was no trace of fanaticism in Rashid'seyes. He spoke as quietly as always.

'We humans! Do you consider yourself god?' Vijay asked mockingly. But he did not anticipate Rashid's reply.

'I am not God in the sense you understand the term. But I am not human either. I am not from Earth.'

Rashid's answer surprised Vijay, but he was not shocked because his brain was already reeling after listening to Rashid's speech. All the threads of this matter were beginning to come together. He began to understand why he had always felt that Rashid's computer and his brain units were beyond the capacity of human technology.

'At present, our habitat is located on a planet in the vicinity of Alpha Centauri. Some major changes are taking place in that star which is why our planet is no longer suitable for habitation. Even you are now beginning to understand these changes in the stars. But your astrophysicists are as yet unable to predict the fate of a star right up to the last minute and second accurately – the way we can. At the most, we can remain on our planet for another 500 years. We must find a new planet by then, and we think that Earth is the most suitable place. But you humans do not deserve to enjoy this bountiful Earth. You are misusing it.

'We need Earth for ourselves, and it is necessary to abolish humans from the face of the Earth, because the resources on this planet are just enough to sustain us. And that's why we will destroy the human race soon after we settle here.'

'Are you going to push everyone into a gas chamber?' Vijay asked.

'Oh no! We don't use such crude methods! Once your capacity to reproduce is destroyed, the human race will be wiped out automatically. That's the reason we think it will take two or three centuries.'

'How many of you are here on Earth?' Vijay asked. 'Your Sheikh, Farooq, Mansoor and Quasim are also from space?'

'No. I am the only one who has travelled to Earth from our planet so far. Other messengers were dispatched to other parts of the universe to find a suitable place for settlement. Some of them were annihilated, some are yet to return, while some others brought back negative reports. My report was positive, and so I was sent back to make further arrangements. I was trained in various aspects of human civilization, including its languages and history. I can speak to you in your mother tongue.'

'That's how you were able to quote from the Bhagavad Gita! But how could you assimilate all this information into your brain?'

'Because my brain is artificial!' said Rashid. 'I will tell you about that later. Let me first tell you how I got here – I was sent here in a space capsule. The region known as Alif Santoor was once a very backward place. But I realized that I could make use of the Sheikh there. What I told you about my basic education and research is true; but I was only playing the part. My three colleagues are real humans who trained under me and think of me as their fellow countryman.'

Vijay suddenly remembered the events leading to the cancellation of the computer grant for the institute. It was almost certain that Rashid was the motivating factor behind those events. 'All right, I have one more question. Why did you start this scheme in India? Why don't you first capture a country more developed and prosperous than ours?'

'There are reasons for that. We thought about which country would be important a hundred years from now. You people sometimes speculate, but we are certain, that there will soon be an ice age. It would be almost impossible for humans to live anywhere except in some areas of the tropics. And by then, the developed countries would have wasted all their energy sources through indiscriminate use. India, on the other hand, will have found abundant submarine reserves of oil. It will also be a suitable region to live during the ice age. That's why it's necessary for us to settle here. Once we do that, we will use our technology to harness solar energy and face the ice age.'

'Do you resemble humans in appearance? How did you arrive on Earth?' There was no end to the questions from Vijay.

'Yes, we are of human origin, but our technology is far more advanced than yours. We are as far ahead of you as you are to the caveman. To give you one example, our biological brain is removed soon after birth and is replaced by an artificial brain. The reason for this is that in the past, we used our own brains as you do. Then we invented computers and used them to facilitate certain things as you do now. Gradually, their size reduced and power increased, and we became more dependent on them. When we had a computer, why would we use our brains for calculations? Ultimately, nature took note of these changed circumstances. Any part of the body that is not used for a long time is made useless. We began to change, and our brains began to get dysfunctional. Finally, a researcher developed an artificial brain and it took the place of the natural brain. Like the appendix, the biological brain became a redundant organ in the body.'

'But if you all have similar artificial brains, your life will not have the variety that we have.'

Rashid smiled at Vijay's query. 'Yes! Our lives are planned like a machine's. There is no place for fights and arguments in it. We make full use of our natural resources.'

Was this the goal of mankind if it continued to forge ahead on the path of development? There would be no arguments, fights or fisticuffs. There would be no inefficiency, red tape or wastage of essential commodities. But there would be no towering achievements made by humankind in various fields either. Shakespeare, Kalidasa, Newton, Einstein, Ved Vyasa, Shukdev, Muhammad, Socrates, Buddha...would this incessant stream of individuality, of genius minds, each unique in its own way, disappear into the promise of 'all men are equal'? After seeing Mughal architecture in north India and the Hindu temples in the south, Vijay used to feel depressed looking at the slums of towers on the Back Bay reclamation that all looked the same. He remembered that now.

Rashid glanced at his watch and said, 'I need to go back to the Sheikh. Let's go out now.'

'But aren't you going to punish me? The villain in the stories always eliminates the hero after narrating his account.' Vijay couldn't help saying.

'Great! So I am the villain while you are the hero?' Rashid said in a mock-complaining tone. 'Why should I waste a useful part of nature by killing you? This is the biggest difference between you and us. A human villain would have killed you and disposed your body. He would have spent his time and energy doing all this. That would be followed by a police enquiry about your disappearance. Who needs all those complications? My way is very simple. Your memory will be partially erased at 3 a.m. today. Your suspicions about me, your entry to this place, your conversation with me – you will forget all of this. And I have arranged for you to believe that this computer is a simple machine and that there is nothing suspicious about it.'

Rashid let Vijay out of the computer room and continued, 'I planted my unit on your body when I shook hands with you on entering the room. Don't waste time trying to find it – it would be easier to look for a speck of dust. Now your brain is under my control.'

It was 2 a.m. by the time Vijay returned to his office after Rashid had left. He realized that he had one hour before his memory was erased and decided to write down the entire account while he still remembered it. He pulled out a pad and began to write rapidly. Once he had finished jotting down what he thought were the main points of the story, he added the following remark: 'When my memory is erased, I will think that this is a fantasy myself. However, this written account is absolutely true.'

Vijay glanced at his watch. It was 2.55 a.m. He slumped in his armchair. He was feeling sleepy, yet he was curious to know what his mind would encounter in the next five minutes. He decided to resist any change to his mind at all costs. Just as one keeps a cap pressed to the head to prevent it from flying off in a strong wind, he held on fast to Rashid's account in his mind and closed his eyes.

Soon, Mumbai's daily routine would begin. Vans carrying milk would begin to ply their various routes. The vegetable markets would wake up. Trains and buses would fill up with people going to work. Everything would be as usual.

But man's power to keep his control over Earth was about to come to an end. The only way to stop the alien invasion – even if temporarily – was to eliminate Rashid and destroy his computer. But how was this possible? Even if his writing was preserved, he himself would not believe it. Even if his memory and his brain remained intact, who would believe him? They would think he had gone mad!

The alien invasion would be carried out in such a way that man would remain complacent till the end. These aliens had recognized the importance of Earth and had travelled all the way here, but humans were misusing their planet. They were ravaging the natural beauty of Earth for selfish gains and to perpetuate their differences.

The clock struck 3 a.m. Vijay could hear a ringing sound.

Krrrrrrrrrrr...krrrrrrrrrrr...

He feared that if he paid attention to this noise, Rashid's account would escape his mind and so he tried to concentrate on his memories.

Krrrrrrrrrrr...krrrrrrrrrrr...

The ringing noise continued.

Vijay opened his eyes. He could still remember Rashid's tale – his memory had not yet been erased. He wondered if Rashid had made a mistake. But he could still hear the ringing noise.

Then he realized that the telephone beside his bed was ringing. But why was it not ringing in the usual tone? And how had its dial changed to a push-button pad? He looked around and got up immediately.

He was in his apartment in Pasadena. The printed programme of the debate between Thomas and Armstrong lay next to him. The digital calendar clock in his room showed the date as one day after the debate and the time was 10 a.m. His report on the computer purchase lay on the table. He had a sense of déjà vu as he picked up the phone.

'Dr Vijay Sinha?' a pleasant voice asked.

'Speaking.'

'This is Western Union, sir. I have a cable for you. Shall I read it out?' asked the operator.

As soon as Vijay consented, she read out the message: 'Computer grant cancelled. Postpone your report. Letter follows. – Professor Gupta.'

'Do you want a written copy, sir?' the operator asked.

'Don't bother – thanks for calling,' he said absent-mindedly. He put the receiver down and looked at the telephone. His eyes were searching for something. But the table was empty. There was no piece of paper there with a telephone number scribbled on it.

A DIFFERENT SEA

VANDANA SINGH

Rasika saw the moths when she was almost home. A moist, cold, glimmering dark had fallen; the lights from the bus were two watery yellow beams. On the narrow bridge that connected the mainland to the island, the single streetlight was out – only the sea glimmered faintly in the starlight. When the bus turned into the lane from the bridge, the moths suddenly appeared, their wings fluttering delicately. There was a rain mist, a veil of moisture over the ground, from which the moths seemed to rise as though woven hurriedly from water and magic. Their wings were tattered, as if the weaver had not been able to pay attention to the details. There were so many of them that the bus driver had to slow down. It was really quite beautiful, the way they fluttered, like ragged dancers. Rasika alighted with the village women who were returning from a day at the fish market. Waving goodbye, she walked the short distance to the little house that crouched under the cliff.

'Khatru?' she called, letting herself into the house. The papers on the dining table had resolved into shapes suspended in the air. Beautiful with the light on them, the pages shivered slightly, as though tense from being held up. Student homework, medieval poetry. Moths. She didn't know whether to laugh or to be annoyed. Where was he? There, a small, round form on her favourite armchair, holding her blue pen and grinning at her with all 64 teeth in view. She began to laugh as the pages cascaded around her.

She picked up the papers, setting them on the table, took some of Salma's dal-and-vegetable soup out of the fridge and put it in a pot to heat on the stove. She sat next to Khatru and tried to gauge his mood. If he was in a bad mood, he would snap at her in warning; at other times, like this one, he merely grinned. 'He' was a pronoun she had assigned him because he reminded her of her dog from her childhood – Badmaash, a street dog with one ear and a fierce temperament. Khatru's two walking limbs – to call them legs would be exaggerations – were nearly useless thanks to the injury he had sustained upon crash-landing his craft in her backyard. He moved by rolling, steering with a set of small arms. She had never been able to figure out how many arms he possessed because they were half-hidden in fine, fur-like protrusions. When she took him out on a leash, with a supporting harness for his legs, he kept his arms close to his body.

She loved walking with him. The island, once a peninsula, was sparsely inhabited, its luxury apartment complex already abandoned to the rising seas, which had turned prime real estate into something closer to a ghetto. Some years ago, a few of the villagers displaced by the original development had moved back. A little boy called Mohan, small, dark and thin, would often tag along with Rasika and Khatru, hauling a metal pail and chattering in his high, eager voice. They would walk along the tree-lined lane to where the landscape suddenly opened up – an expanse of sea, sky, great boulders sloping down to the water, and the wind blowing from the open ocean. Back at the house, Mohan would hold the pail to Rasika in silent appeal, and she would fill it with water from the well that supplied her house. Once, during a walk, Mohan had startled them both by dropping the pail; Khatru's arms stuck out in astonishment, all 20 or 40 of them. The little boy had stared.

'Funny dog you have, Auntie,' he said, eyes wide.

Now, on the couch, eating her soup, Rasika persuaded herself that Khatru looked better than he had yesterday. The arrangement of her papers was evidence that he was still interested in his odd experiments. In the next room, the remains of his spaceship lay like so many giant grey petals, sheened with a trembling, shifting kaleidoscope of colours. He had moved the pieces around while she'd been gone, and surely that was a good sign. He had been sick for so many days, she was beginning to wonder if an adaptation crisis could last this long. When he had first come to her two years ago, he had not been able to eat for several days. She thought he was going to die. In desperation, she had set out all the food she could think of in front of him in little bowls: dal, pongal, sliced apples, oatmeal, uttapam, chopped mangosteen, three raw eggs. The next morning, all the little bowls had been cleaned out, and the alien was a sick, trembling mass about twice his original volume. After two days, the swelling had come down; the alien lengthened his compact body, and the furry protrusions parted to reveal a rope-like appendage, vessel or artery stretched taut across the middle. A clawed foot ripped at the umbilicus (if that's what it was) and the outer layers of the alien fell around it, darkening, folding up like the finest silk or chiffon. When she went and got the dustpan, she found that the stuff had disintegrated into a fine grey ash. She put that in the compost.

The alien shook himself, looked at her from three of his eyes, and stretched what appeared to be at least 35 short arms, each of which was a pale beige with tiny, transparent hairs like peach fuzz.

After a few more similar experiences, she came to understand Khatru's illnesses as adaptation crises. They always happened during his first exposure to a food, or a new experience like the first time she took him out for a walk. At the end of each crisis, he had to change, moult and cut the umbilicus, a process that seemed to her both prolonged and painful.

But this recent illness was inexplicable. There was nothing she could remember, no happening or oddity that would provoke an adaptation crisis. And he had never been sick for this long – today was the eleventh day.

Rasika had to face the possibility that Khatru was dying.

Among her achievements, Rasika would say, whenever she looked back at her life, was the fact that she had got rid of not one, but two husbands. The first such alliance was a heady, short-lived romance in her early twenties that ended after a year. The next time she got married, it was to a neighbourhood friend she'd known since they were both four years old and living in the same apartment complex in Mumbai. After the wedding, the birth of her daughter and their move to the southern part of coastal Tamil Nadu had occurred with such rapidity that she felt, for a while, as though she was in the middle of a movie of her own life, only speeded up. The language, people, even the sea, was different here, and the displacement from Mumbai, which she had never left in adulthood before, made her feel, for the first few years, like a foreigner in her own country. By the time she felt adjusted, and had a moment to think, her daughter Ria was a teenager, and the husband she had known for most of their lives had revealed himself to be a stranger after all. After the divorce, the movie of her life went on fast forward again – she found a job in the Historical Archives department at a small coastal university with some teaching, thanks to her double masters in history and mathematics. Then Ria's departure on the expedition instead of to college. An emptiness, during which there were two lovers in quick succession: a Polish post-doc who lasted a brief, thunderous monsoon, and a divorced techie from yoga class with too many unresolved issues, with whom she broke up after a year.

Then, one day, Rasika said to herself, 'I don't have time to think,' and she stopped, and time slowed. She took a breath.

How slowly time goes now, she thought, in the house with Khatru. After her daughter left on her voyage nearly three years ago, telling her, with the casual, unintentional cruelty of the young that she didn't know when she'd return, there was a period during which Rasika felt suspended outside the life she had known. Her friendship with her colleagues Salma and Aditi and Raghu had deepened during that time, and she got to know her remaining few neighbours a little better, all of which anchored her again to Earth. The heady freedom that followed her last romantic entanglement awakened her to half-forgotten intellectual pleasures. The discovery of the Gyana documents cemented the feeling that this is what she wanted to do with her life: to build bridges across the gulfs of time. Then came Khatru, and the long days of taking care of him, and the eager anticipation of letters from her daughter, sailing across the world right now, at this moment, navigating under the stars with her friends from Samoa. The years fled from her like flocks of birds disturbed on the lawn in the morning, and here she was, nearing middle age, holding a piece of paper by a long-dead tenth-century poet, and wondering what her secrets were, and why she, Rasika, felt a great, sometimes exhilarating emptiness, but not freedom. What is freedom? *A thing I know in glimpses. I want to know what Gyana meant by the word.*

What did she want? For her daughter to be safe, for the seas to be kind, for Khatru to heal (*which won't happen*, she thought now with a painful contraction of the heart), to be connected across space and time with things that matter. 'I want to *live*,' she told Khatru, and he turned his enigmatic multiple eyes toward her and uttered a low rumble, and the cups on the shelves begin to rattle. 'Stop that,' she said, but in an indulgent tone, because she knew he was being playful. She wanted to memorize every moment of his being here with her, even if it meant the cups broke. They were only cups, after all.

Before Khatru, but after her daughter left on her adventure, Rasika had been doing research on Khanaa, the medieval Bengali poet, astrologer and mathematician, whose tongue had been cut out by a jealous husband or father-in-law (history was unclear on this) because her calculations were far more elegant than that of her father-in-law, the mathematician Varahamihira. This was when she read, in the *Indian Historical Review*, of the discovery of the Gyana documents. Really, it was something out of a Bengali novel.

In the previous year, the rising seas had engulfed several villages in the district of North 24 Parganas in West Bengal. Rescue workers had come across a carved wooden chest afloat on the waves. The carvings were so fine, and the chest so clearly old, that the rescuers had thought it surely must contain treasure. What they had found, upon forcing the lock open, was nothing but rolls of cloth, dusty and fine, within which were sheets of parchment and rib-like bundles of dried palm leaves, delicate as bones, covered with fine writing. The contents of the box had changed hands a few times but finally ended up with a professor of history at Vidyasagar University, one Dr Smita Mondal, who had rescued it from obscurity. She had taken careful photos of the discoveries and posted them on a website so that scholars around India and the world could contribute to the understanding of these documents. They appeared to be the jottings of the younger son of a tenth-century landlord, who had been a keen observer of the events of his time. He had known of Khanaa and her silencing by mutilation, and there were fragments of a village drama he was writing about the event and its implications. Mixed in among these were bits and pieces of poetry and references to a hitherto unknown scholar and poet called Gyana. The nameless author of the palm-leaf manuscripts had evidently known her and was an admirer. Rasika sat up late into the night, looking at the photos on the website, copying the script onto sheets of paper.

The first thing she found was a praise poem. It was commonplace for poets to put their own names in the poem, so perhaps Gyana had written it. It was rendered in rhyme, as was the ancient custom, but Rasika had the odd impulse to translate it as free verse.

Gyana's eyes are like jewels,
Her mind ranges over infinity
Like the boatman plying the boat
On the endless ocean.

The poet Khanaa was known to this day in West Bengal; Rasika's mother had grown up in rural Bengal, and she still remembered her mother's voice singing or speaking the *khonaar bachan*, the common-sense poetry that spoke to farmers and housewives. To modern Bengali intellectual women, Khanaa's mutilation was a symbol of the suppression of women's voices. And Khanaa was to Rasika rather like the elder aunt everyone listens to, quotes, and talks about – she had grown up with her. So who indeed was Gyana?

Khatru's been playing with paper again, each time she comes home her notes are all over the place, suspended in air in marvellous patterns, some pages shivering, others still. Khatru gives her a half-defiant look, grinning, as though he can't quite tell whether she's going to be annoyed or amused. Here are her scribblings on Gyana's work, there's a letter from a historian. Here's Gyana's poem, there's an article about Brahmagupta's treatment of algorithms. But she's come to suspect lately that these aerial manipulations of Khatru are some kind of self-expression, that he's inscribing in the air through this careful juxtaposition of pages a language unknown to her that he is learning again, slowly. She likes to make a cup of tea and sit with him and watch him move the pages around, while the air shivers with an electricity that makes the skin on her face prickle. Sometimes, he manages to achieve his mysterious purpose, and at other times he keeps trying and tires himself out with frustration – in either case, the papers ultimately collapse, slowly and gracefully if he's happy, angrily, like a flock of crows pouncing, if he's not. She senses that he's trying to tell her something, but their communication is so limited, the abyss so unbridgeable that specificity is impossible. They can, by now, sense each other's moods, likes and dislikes, and respond, but that's it. She has no idea what his world is like; she can't interpret his speech sounds, which remind her of crickets singing. She doesn't know what alien physics guided his craft through space. And yet…there is a bond between them, forged from something they share that she cannot quite articulate.

She talks to him. She tells him about her day, about her daughter. She shows him Ria's pictures on the walls – there she is as a baby, plump and dimpled; there again, thin and brown as a spring twig, standing proudly with a book about oceans, a prize from her school's explorer's club. In another picture – this one is in the living room, and her favourite – Ria's looking out of the open window, the light in her eyes, her fine hair blowing in the wind, and Rasika can see now that at 15, Ria was already dreaming of other vistas. At that time she couldn't tell.

Rasika and Khatru sit on the sofa, or sometimes on the rug in the living room, and she tells him stories of Ria's childhood, sings the nonsense songs she made up for her daughter when she was young. She reads out articles on Bhaskara's mathematics, and Gyana's poetry. He sometimes responds with chirping or thrumming vocalizations and at other times with a deeply responsive attention. She brings him things to play with: Ria's building blocks, empty plastic soda bottles, pencils and pens.

It is much harder for him to perform telekinesis with heavier objects. At first, he can only make them rattle, but after some practice – suspending bottles and Ria's toys in mid-air – he is able to play with the pieces of his spaceship. The fragments of the chassis are the pale pink of early dawn, changing colour ever so slightly with the viewing angle; they hang in the air along with a complex filigree of silver needles and crystalline polyhedral forms, and the tangled intestines of some brassy, metallic, malleable alien substance. He lies on the couch, moving the bits and pieces from afar with barely the twitch of a limb to betray the fact that he is the artist, the conductor of this unfathomable orchestra. She watches, enthralled and delighted, feeling poised at the edge of a great knowing that remains, alas, an undiscovered country. When the pieces fall down, abruptly or gently, she sighs deeply and looks at him, and something passes between them – a sympathy of sorts without words, human or alien.

On campus, Salma, an entomologist, told Rasika that the pale moths were an invasive species. 'The world's going topsy-turvy,' her friend said with a sigh.

'See,' Rasika told Khatru when she got home, 'The moths are aliens too. Like you, the moth is from another land; accidental immigrants from Africa, blamed for human carelessness. The males dance in the air while the females wait. They wait for the males, lay eggs and die. Me, on the other hand, I hatched my egg, packed off the male and live on!'

Khatru was in one of his moods. He was curled up on the sofa, apparently asleep, and at her words, he opened one eye and closed it again. She looked at him and felt the familiar pang for his aloneness, his marooning in this world. She couldn't begin to imagine what it must be like for him, away from his own kind, trapped on a strange planet. When her daughter left, the stars, to which Rasika had been almost completely indifferent, had become beacons, signposts to guide Ria home. But after Khatru's arrival, she would look up at them on a clear night and think of them as hearth fires for homes stranger than she could imagine.

She wished she could talk to her friends about him. But to Salma and the others he appeared like a cat or a dog. Salma thought he was some kind of wildcat hybrid, and to Raghu and Aditi he was a mongrel. They didn't seem to see the remains of his spaceship as any different from a pile of old junk. Rasika was either certifiably insane, or Khatru had gifted her with the ability to see him just as he was. 'Whatever *that* means,' she muttered to herself.

The spaceship was about the size of the plastic backyard pool she had bought Ria when her daughter was five. When Rasika first laid eyes on the spaceship during a thunderstorm one night, two years ago, it lay askew under the palm trees like a giant egg, cracked along one side. With the light from the kitchen, she could see the raindrops sliding off the wreckage – the ship was grey but with a shimmer of colour – without beading. She remembered how her heart had contracted when the small, round figure had arisen from the ruined craft and half-dragged, half-rolled itself through the curtains of rain toward the light, towards shelter.

Rasika was waiting for the time when her daughter's journey – with its zigzag trajectories and multiple stopovers – would reach its halfway point across the world, because after that her path would bring her, by definition, back home. Reflecting on their life together, she wished she'd had the courage to let the child go earlier. It had been obvious since Ria was little that she was an unusual child, reflective for her age, always straining against constraints, like a kite held by a string. Through Rasika's troubles with her husband, she had felt the need to hold Ria tight against the cruelty of the world. Ria had grown up gangly, restless, empathetic to a fault, with a deep sense of justice and a fierce temper that she exercised on behalf of those she loved. As a 12-year-old, she had taught the young children of the village their letters and climbed the cliff over the house against her mother's protestations, coming back in triumph with a shell or polished rock from the top. With the help of the village kids, she had explored every cranny of the jagged, rocky coastline, splashed in tide pools, learned fish and seaweed lore. She had raced up and down the narrow beach of the island with the village children, taunting the chowkidar of the luxury apartment complex, who would shout and chase them, lurching, ineffectually waving his stick.

Tossed into uncertainty after her divorce, without a secure job or the prospect of one, Rasika had endeavoured to tame her spirited daughter, to keep her safe from the vicissitudes of life, in retrospect an impossible task. The wild beauty of the island and the sedate buildings of the university on the mainland had been Ria's shelter from the storm of her parents' marriage.

And three years ago, she had finally taken the longest step away from home. A gap-year experience, she had called it then: going off to sail around the world on a Polynesian ship, only the fifth of its kind, an offshoot of the great Hoku'lea Project, built by a people longing to retain their sense of self as their islands drowned. Their predicament had affected Ria profoundly because of the displacement of her best friend's family (the father of the friend was an adjunct at the university) from their South Pacific island, and off she'd gone, like an arrow let go at last from the bow.

The ship was one of a series built on ancient Polynesian technology, using the old knowledge of navigating by the stars, and had been journeying for more than five years now across the globe. The only modern instruments on the ship were meteorological ones meant for collecting data on the warming, changing oceans and, of course, laptops and radio transmitters. Ria's texts were quick, casual messages expressing wonder, delight, disgust, indignation – separated by long stretches of silence that Rasika had learned not to punctuate with worried questions. There was the rare phone call and, once, a delicate wooden carving of a fish with a long nose that came in the mail. What Ria didn't know was that Rasika scanned the weather reports and the social media pages of the expedition every day; that sometimes she couldn't sleep, wondering whether the skies under which her daughter sailed, or the seas that held her, were friendly. Reports of storms and hurricanes over the ocean left her a wreck for days, but she said nothing in her replies to Ria, not wanting to burden her with her fears. Instead, she wrote her daughter letters every few days in a leather-bound diary that Rasika's grandfather had given her – conversations she would have had with Ria if she had been home, about everyday things at the university, or the weather, or Khatru. All she had told Ria about Khatru was that she had taken in an injured animal – how could she explain that the guest was an alien in a text message or even a phone call? 'Come home soon,' she would whisper into the night as she lingered at the back window of the kitchen before going to bed. Before her, the ocean lay silver in the starlight, the dark edges of the waves an ever-shifting calligraphy.

So here she was. She had given herself the task of building bridges from self to self – between human and alien, and human minds separated across centuries. Over the last year, she had transcribed and translated a number of the Gyana documents, and she had co-authored a paper that had been accepted in the *Indian Historical Review* – her first academic publication! She had held a reading at the institute, and there had been some interest from her colleagues, although not as much as she had hoped.

Some scholars had wondered whether Gyana had ever existed – perhaps she had been invented by the author of the documents, the younger son of a tenth-century feudal lord. But other events to which he had referred during his time had been borne out by history. And if she had existed, what had happened to her? How had she lived and died? How was it that history knew of Khanaa and not Gyana? Perhaps Gyana was Khanaa herself, writing under another name after her mutilation. But that, too, seemed unlikely, given the great difference in subject matter and style. Khanaa's forte was practical wisdom and highly accurate calculations of the positions of the planets. Gyana was (or so the documents implied) equally skilled in manipulating equations, but she saw wide vistas even in the most ordinary things:

A mango is a drop
Of the tree's desire. The ant
Circling its ripening skin
Over and over, tastes infinity;
Thus, what is bound knows the unbound
Thus, what is finite knows the endless
Thus, the wild bird knows the sky.

Walking through the university grounds after dark, Rasika would be struck by the beauty of the lit windows, the gracious arches of the pipal trees in the central quadrangle. On rainy days, tiny drops hung in the air, luminous, forming halos around streetlights. The wet leaves squished beneath her feet on the brick pathways under the trees, and students and researchers walked swiftly by, hunched against the light rain. The university gave the illusion of continuity across time – there was no evidence on its gracious campus that the world was unravelling, that humans, animals, clouds and oceans were on trajectories of unprecedented change.

Rasika liked to walk to the bus stop in the rain without an umbrella, breathing in the moisture, letting the wet tendrils touch her cheeks. Her hair, in the reflection in the windowpane, would be dotted with the tiny droplets like jewels. In these moments, Gyana spoke to her – she saw each drop reflecting the universe around it. She caught her breath. 'Is this what it feels like,' she said to Gyana, 'to glimpse infinity?'

One evening, with Khatru at her side, she had been thinking about Gyana when she heard – with almost the clarity of someone speaking aloud – her voice. Gyana's voice, a little amused, inexplicably modern. Rasika grabbed a piece of paper from the side table, found a pen, and began to write.

She is a woman made from moths
Her outlines are blurred with ragged wings
She sweeps up the road, seeking, seeking
Lying down on the wet streets to rest
Fluttering up in disarray when the headlights come,
Cold steel terrifies her, scatters her form
Like a hard wind driving before it the leaves of summer
But softly, furtively, after the bus has passed
She rearranges herself, shakes out her skirts
Rises again, a moth-cloud-woman
Looking for something she cannot name
Her lips are softly furred, her words
Are powdery syllables; you have to listen close
Over the hum and rustle of her wings
And even then you only half guess
What she is saying.

As Khatru's decline continued, she sang to him. He would not tolerate touch beyond her placing a hand gently on his back. He was slowly ceasing to eat. She felt grief swell in her throat, but there was nothing she could give him except her presence and song. He had always liked her singing, although she did not know how she knew that. So she sang for Khatru, for Ria, for Khanaa, who could not sing, and for the mysterious Gyana, who had sung for Khanaa too.

I read the mathematics of your soul, Khanaa,
Dearest of sisters, I free you
With one glance from my eyes.

Thinking of Gyana now, hundreds of years later, singing aloud her words, with one hand resting lightly on Khatru's back, Rasika felt, for a very small moment, free.

The day it happened, she had been talking to Salma about getting help for Khatru. Salma knew a vet who would come to the house, but what good would a vet be to an alien? And how would she explain things to her immensely practical friend, to whom Khatru had manifested as a kind of wildcat? Driving home, Rasika knew she wouldn't get help for Khatru for the same reason that she hadn't told anyone about him – anyone in authority, that is. Because they would certainly take him away from her, perhaps mistreat him. So she had to face this alone, and she was angry with the world and with herself. But as soon as she let herself in the house and called out to Khatru, she knew something was wrong.

The papers were all over the dining room floor. The spaceship was there too, all in pieces as usual, but everything lay haphazardly. Khatru lay in agony on the floor, stretching and contracting. A barely audible high-pitched thrumming came from him, and it frightened her. He must have been trying to play, despite his weakened state, she thought, and he had pushed himself too far. She hurried over to him and knelt by his side, calling his name. Two eyes opened, but they were glazed in a way she hadn't seen before. Did he see her? Was he already far away, negotiating with death? 'Don't leave me!' she whispered. She was lifted for a moment to a place from which she could see the strange choreography of her life: all those she had known, coming together, then apart. She thought of her daughter on the high seas, and she called soundlessly to her. *Come home, come home*, and then she was saying it aloud, to Khatru, without thinking. *Where's home, Khatru?*

She saw how he stretched in that terrible way, and the rope, the umbilicus that bound him to this form, this life, appeared taut and shining between the tendrils on his skin. He raised one clawed foot, but it was too weak to sever the string. He turned and looked at her, and he may as well have spoken the words aloud, because to her they seemed so clear: *help me die*. She wiped her tears on her sleeve and, weeping, brought a sharp knife from the kitchen. He was looking at her with five of his eyes now, as though memorizing her face, and there was a kindness in them, as though he knew how hard it was for her to wield the knife that would free him. She clenched the knife in her hand and set her chin, and, placing her other hand on his flank, made the cut. He relaxed; his whole body seemed to sigh, the outer layers darkened slowly into folds and slipped off what remained. He looked at her again – she put her hand on the pale, tender new skin of his back, and his eyes lost their clarity.

Tears were caught in her throat – she coughed and retched and sobbed, on the floor with his cooling body under her hand. She felt the change in his skin and looked at him, and saw that the skin was hardening, forming a shell that swiftly covered him. She took away her hand. His body thrummed, moved suddenly. Startled, she stepped back, and before she knew it the pieces of the spaceship were gathering about the body like some kind of aerial symphony, coming together around him, enclosing him within the ovoid. The jagged edges of the ship came together and sealed. He was swallowed, lost to sight. The ship rose in the air before her, and she caught her breath in astonishment, understanding at last what kind of death this was. She ran to the back door and slid it open, into the cool twilight where the stars shone between the palms. A wild bird called from the cliff above the house, yearning and urgent. The sea lay before her, a darkening mirror. The spaceship hovered for a moment, gravid and light all at once, and then, with a curious twisting motion, slid out into the air. It slipped and darted between the palms and came one more time to hover before her. She caught her breath. 'Go on, go home, Khatru,' she said to him, and with a final, smooth turning motion, the craft rose through a gap between the trees and caught the last light of the sun for a moment before making for the stars.

And he was gone.

She breathed raggedly, wiping her face against her sleeve, leaning against the doorjamb. It was going to be a cold night, judging by the nip in the air. There were dead moths in the grooves of the sliding door. After a while, she went in, slid the door shut, and got herself a glass of water. She looked at the papers scattered about on the floor and read in their placement the broken, wordless syllables of another language. In the china cupboard, her best cups had cracked slightly; the cracks were beautiful, fractal, like the deltas of a river.

She thought again of the peculiar choreography of her life, of Ria and Khatru navigating by the same stars. One was gone, the other, maybe, was coming home, in the months and years to come. What was she to do in the meantime?

In the days that followed, she felt the pain of Khatru's absence simultaneously with her joy at his freedom. She imagined him ranging through the universe, healed and whole. Salma commiserated and took her to a home-cooked dinner; the little boy, Mohan, from the village, who now came daily for water, brought her a gift of a piece of driftwood polished by the sea. But, after all that, she had to reckon with the silence. Sitting on the sofa in the evenings, she rued every moment that Khatru had been there and she had thought of herself as lonely. There are layers and degrees of loneliness, after all.

Then, one day she had an epiphany. Her failed relationships, the constant financial insecurity, the enormous distances between herself and those she loved best, and all the troubles of a failing world – these were difficult things, but she had this to hold on to: that she had been loved fully by another being. The thought would stop her in her tracks, walking to the bus stop, or reading a poem of Gyana's, or brushing her hair back from her face. Across the barrier of species and planet, deserving or not, she had been loved. It was only one thing in a life, but it was a significant thing and a humbling one, which demanded some kind of response, some change in her life.

Meanwhile, she reread all the Gyana documents, half-hoping for some hint or guidance, and mused on the many ways there were to silence a woman. Khanaa's relatives had cut off her tongue. Rasika's husband had dismissed everything she said, his acid envy burning through her defences. For some time, until Khatru came, Rasika had spoken to empty rooms. A voice that has no listeners falls into the silence and is stilled just as much as by any other means.

But what voices have I not heard? The thought came to her like a shock wave. She had tried to build a shelter around Ria and herself, but her daughter had understood far better than she that there was no shelter, no safety in an unravelling world. Ria had also known that no adventure can be undertaken alone, that the freedom of solitude is a narrow sort of freedom. In fact, Ria had taken everything personally – from the ravaging of the Earth to the displacement of her best friend's family. And hundreds of years ago, Gyana, too, had taken risks, had defended Khanaa, had sailed the seas of numbers, navigated the unfathomable human soul. Rasika remembered the village boy at the door earlier that day, and the sound of the water in the pail, and his shy grin of gratitude. How could she have not realized that her well was one of the few remaining freshwater sources on the island? She had met the village women every day, had talked and laughed with them; their children had been Ria's first playmates; yet she hadn't seen them, hadn't heard them.

An image came to her mind of her daughter's fierce, animated face, indignant on behalf of her Samoan friend, ready to discard Rasika's meticulously laid college plans for something deeper and larger than mere convention and security. *I cannot live like this*, Rasika told herself. *What else haven't I noticed around me?* Oh yes – the moths were gone, all of them. Disappeared like they had never been, leaving only powdery traces, broken wings in the crannies of windows and doors. Upon that observation, it came to her that Salma was unhappy, had been unhappy for a long time, and not just because of the state of the world, and she, Rasika, had not really paid attention. Rasika called Salma and talked for nearly three hours.

There was a familiarity to this new level of engagement with her *jiggari dost*, with, indeed, the world. Memories rose: faint images and impressions of who she had been in her college days – impressionable, intellectually curious, roaming Mumbai and Pune with her coterie of friends, camping in the extravagant verdure of the Sahyadris, arguing and laughing. Life had been rich with possibilities then. Her second marriage had narrowed all options until she had forgotten what it had meant to be her untethered younger self.

In her new life, Rasika took to walking with Vijiamma, an old woman from the fishing village, who had trouble sleeping. They would walk up and down the beach at night, surrounded by stars and the sea. Vijiamma was dour but would crack ribald jokes when in the mood and was as full of stories as a library. She had been the first to trust Rasika's intent, and the newly formed water council had begun to make some progress, with the ultimate aim that Rasika's well would become common property of the settlement. Rasika had been entirely unaware that the fisherfolk had been, for the past two years, working to restore the island's coastal ecology so that they could return to their age-old tradition of sustainably harvesting seaweed. The women had always been pleasant to her, but it had never occurred to her that they were worth knowing for themselves. She had thought, humbly, and with some shame, that she should help them with their water problems; she had not realized that she would end up owing the heavier debt: the women, by accepting her into a wider, more generous, more precarious circle of experience, had given her a sense of being let out at last from an old and dusty room.

From Vijiamma, Rasika began to learn how the fisherfolk understood the sea, how they could tell the weather and discern the undersea topography through the shape and speed of the waves. In her youth, Vijiamma had dived for seaweed; her knowledge of underwater ecology was profound, personal. Like the Samoans with whom Ria was journeying, theirs was a dynamic knowledge system, perhaps better able to adapt quickly to the great changes underway. From Vijiamma, she learned the local names of the stars that lay scattered like tiny candle flames across the dark. Thinking of Khatru, or Ria, or Gyana, it was as though the voids that separated them ceased to exist in the moments that her head was tilted up, her gaze falling into the sea of stars.

The day dawned when the long-awaited note from Ria came, written in a hurry but with the vivant joy of a being that has, at last, found a place in the world, even if that place was one that couldn't hold still. Rasika read the missive again and again. The ship was turned homeward for now, but Ria would always be a child of the sea as well as her daughter. Rasika walked down to the slowly drowning beach long abandoned by the rich, where the village children were splashing in the water. The great cliff reared over the island; over it seagulls flew in wide arcs, calling. This sea, this very same sea that washed her ankles, was carrying her child home. She said aloud, 'Why have I been so afraid?' She felt a tidal pull, a call like that of the seagulls flying above her and knew with a sudden exhilaration that she was no longer stuck; she, too, was moving, like the restless seas, toward some great change. *Freedom is neither static nor exclusive; we are knit together across space and time.*

As Gyana's ants had discovered, to wander and then to return to the origin point, which is always shifting, never still – that is as close to experiencing infinity as we can get. Rasika, remembering that all ocean currents were closed loops, thought that perhaps the choreography of life might also be composed of great, looping, intersecting arcs. She thought of the wooden chest containing the Gyana documents, freed by the rising seas, making the journey from the place where Gyana had lived, if she had lived, sailing the sea-drowned pathways hundreds of years later, under the same stars as the woman who had known infinity.

THE LIST

GAUTAM BHATIA

The stars, he'd always thought, were the fireflies that chose to stay.

Once – long ago – there was an arched bridge. A breeze danced upon their skin. Laser lights, amber-coloured, flickered in and out of existence.

'I want the ones that never go out,' he said.

'I couldn't bear such permanence,' she came back.

They laughed. There had been so much laughter in those days.

'But they don't stay, the fireflies,' she continued, 'because they choose not to be labelled – or listed.'

'You and your dislike of definitions.'

'Oh, I may suffer your definitions – sometimes, but –' she placed a finger on his lips, 'there are other worlds now, love.'

Beneath their feet, below the bridge, the valley dipped away into darkness and they heard the faraway laughter of the river.

He raised his arm, tracing pathways with his fingertips in the sky, pausing at each planet. 'Hauder, Sikar, Xolon – human, too human.'

She joined her index finger to his and then angled it away from Xolon. 'Madi – viriconium mines – barely human.'

From Xolon and Madi, their fingers travelled towards each other and met at a shimmering point of light. 'Unbar,' they said together. 'Not human at all,' she finished. He knew from her voice that she was smiling.

'You really think that you can outrun the algorithms somewhere out there?' he said. 'In the mines of Madi? Among the Deva and their Collective? On a human planet?'

Saira turned to him. He saw starlight in her eyes, the colour of copper, which had become so rare on Terra. 'Space is room enough.'

Then she was running, across the arched bridge and into the tended woodland, and he was running after her, through the transitory corridor that the fireflies wove around them, and they were laughing.

'Captain Jatayu!'

The voice lasered through his memories. On the observation deck, Jatayu tore his gaze away from the stars, and from the pale rim of Xolon, a few hours away.

'What is it?'

'We've been hailed.'

'Banner?'

'The Collective, Captain. It's a Deva ship.'

Jatayu sucked in a breath. 'Well, got no choice now, have we? Set up the line.'

The window before him grew opaque. The stars yielded to a blank screen. Behind him, Jatayu felt the crew of the *Terran Sky* gather around to watch. Then the screen came to life and the Deva was before him.

She had chosen to appear in humanoid form. But there was no mistaking the too-clean symmetry of the bones, the eyes that danced, and the faint halo that never let him get a clear look at the face.

'Greetings, Deva,' he said tonelessly, 'from Captain Jatayu and the crew of the *Terran Sky*, and greetings through you to the Collective. How may we assist you?'

'Greetings from the Collective, Captain,' the voice sang to him. He forced himself to concentrate. 'I'm Deva Unbar-na-Gheroun, and my ship –'

Jatayu summoned his memory banks. The information sped through his neural circuits: Unbar, the diplomats' planet; Gheroun, one of the High Families, ambassadors to Terra in the days Terra had still meant something.

He took a deep breath. Beneath them, Xolon hung in space.

'– so I hope you won't mind if I ask,' her voice cut into his thoughts, 'where are you going, Captain Jatayu?'

'To Xolon.'

'Your purpose?'

'Trade. I transport skins along the Xolon–Sikar route.'

Even as he answered, he knew that his brain activity was showing up in a monitor in front of the Deva, transmuted into a probability figure along a truth spectrum. Jatayu stilled, mentally reciting the meaningless jingle that Saira and he had memorized all those decades ago when they were playing at surviving a Deva interrogation.

Chandu ke chacha ne
Chandu ki chachi ko…

There was a human heartbeat of silence. He thought the Deva would ask to board. But when Gheroun spoke, she only said, 'Saw any other ships en route?'

'Just yours, Deva Gheroun,' he said. Then, bolder: 'Why?'

'Xolon's actions are bothering the Collective, Captain. The List –'

'Ah yes.'

'Barbaric,' Gheroun cut in undiplomatically, 'this practice of offworlding.'

'An internal matter surely, Deva?'

'We respect human planets' rights to determine world membership, of course. But all this suffering – so much of it – troubles us, Captain.'

'Naturally, Deva. The Collective's values are universal. Do you need help? My ship stands ready to assist with rescue –'

'You can stop being so human.' Her voice did not change, but he felt it lash against his skin. 'You know the Collective's code. We can't intervene, much as Xolon's actions pain us – unless there are smugglers lurking around, waiting to pick up the offworlders and transport them to the mines of Madi...' She left the rest of the sentence suspended in the air.

'I understand,' Jatayu said politely. 'That's why I suggested rescue, Deva – the offworlders may need to be saved from the smugglers as much as from their own planet.'

There was a long pause. The Deva's dancing eyes had stilled, and she was looking directly at him. Jatayu felt a single bead of sweat trickle down his spinal cord.

'Trying to live up to your name, Captain?'

'Deva?'

'Your name. Terran, isn't it?'

'Yes, Deva.'

'Named after a figure from Terran myth – a rescuer, is it not?'

'One who tried to rescue someone and paid for it with his life. I didn't choose my name, Deva.'

'Very well, Captain. If you insist.' Her voice became brisk, and Jatayu let himself relax. 'I – and the Collective – wish you luck in your trade to...Sikar. May you have better luck than your namesake.'

The screen went blank.

Fire, she'd always thought, was a sunflower that faded too quickly.

There was a blaze that leapt and crackled. Xolon's night flared like an algorithm's pareidoliac dreamscapes: hues of pink and gold and orange clashed with one another, shapes and silhouettes in the night, tongues of dancing flame. Then, there was a burst of heat that warmed them all – Listers and Non-Listers – in the sunless cold.

Crack, crack. The walls of her house crumbled in a shower of sparks.

She thought she knew the moment her papers burnt from the sputtering noise of the flames. Almost as if the fire regretted the destruction of lifetimes of work.

She reached into her memory banks for reassurance, sending out mental feelers to where her research existed in non-corporeal form.

She found emptiness.

Her worlds were gone from her.

She sank to her knees, eyes closed. She reached again.

Nothing.

After threatening to do it for so long, just when everyone had stopped believing that they would ever really act on their threat, they had finally cut off the Non-Listers' access to the memory banks.

Her fingernails dug into the singed ground. She struck out with her mind a third time, a swimmer flailing at a reed. A moment ago, the galaxy had been a thought away. Now, there was nothing but her own memories. As if they had taken the knowledge of language from her, leaving her to grasp at the shadows of words.

She heard her breath come in sobs.

She opened her eyes again to a world that was shorn of its colours, where the only sound was a dull ringing in her ears. Red spots danced across the curtain of her gaze.

Rulda lurched to her feet. She would have stood there until the flames took her as they did her research, had it not been for the group of fleeing Non-Listers who had passed her, recognized her by her newly-vacant eyes, and dragged her away with them, through the roiling streets of New Colucan, through its seething buildings and, finally, away from Xolon's capital city.

Burned by memory, Rulda's unblinking eyes opened in a Xolon twilight.

They walked. Without the memory banks and the maps of Xolon they'd held, they navigated by a long-stilled instinct and a nameless sense of direction. Glades, glens and trees glimmered in the dappled light of three moons. The forest grass was springy beneath their feet.

'What were you – back home?'

One of her companions had noticed her eyes come back to life. Rulda struggled with the question, trying to locate *home*. She realized after a while that for this conversation it meant New Colucan.

'Oh, I – I was a linguist. I studied the Deva High Language.'

'The *Deva*…?'

'Yes.' She let herself smile. Her mind seemed suddenly to have too much space for her own memories, as though they were little rocks rattling against the sides of a half-filled jar. She sifted through them, discovering what remained after the loss of the memory banks.

'They let you do it? The Authority?'

'*They* never knew. Formally, I was only studying Terran dialects for Xolon's trade missions.' She thought with a pang about Noroon, her partner-in-crime, and those long nights discovering the Devas' linguistic galaxy – until the List had come, its strokes of algorithmic ink separating them into different worlds.

'But why?'

Their companions were silent and Rulda felt the weight of their attention. She looked at her feet as they walked, trying to make sense of memories that had lost their anchor.

'I wanted – I believed – that High Deva and our human Galactic Standard have a common origin. I wanted to prove that there's no warrant to divide the galaxy into Deva and human – to making it…smaller.' She smiled again. 'I called it the Grammar of Harmony.'

One of their companions rolled his eyes. 'You just wanted to break Deva exceptionalism, didn't you?'

There was low laughter around her. They still remembered mirth.

'That may have had *something* to do with it,' she chuckled.

'And did you?'

'The List came before I could.'

Xolon is not room enough.

The voice came back to her as she spoke, beamed into her home – hers and Noroon's – and into every home in Xolon.

Xolon is not room enough, and so we must have a List.

The List, which would first be logic and then life itself.

But because we are a corrupt planet, the List cannot be prepared by corrupt human beings.

They walked in silence now, the five Non-Listers who had escaped the fires in New Colucan, and who still remained.

A little way away, the forest dipped into the great ocean that circled Xolon. Above them, they heard the whining noise of a drone.

'Let's thank our *former* fellow Xolonians,' said Fani, their leader, from the head of the group, 'for stripping even the chips from us so that the drones can't see us now. Law of unintended consequences – but the Authority will not be happy.'

Laughter. Ugly laughter.

They walked.

Rulda felt the breeze upon her skin, felt it bring memories of other evenings and other worlds. She opened her clenched fist and let the writing upon the crumpled piece of paper in her palm travel to her eyes.

Write down
I am a Xolonian…

'Can you believe it?' she said once. 'There was a time when Terra was the only planet we knew. Can you imagine that feeling? Instead of space opening up before you…' She spoke the words as they lay on the woodland grass, tracing the sky-paths again, their favourite pastime together, 'the sky would press down – because this would be the only home that existed.'

'Terra is still home, you know.'

She turned teasing eyes upon him, the glint of copper in them moving and shifting in the starlight. 'Didn't your namesake – Jatayu – try to fly to the stars once?'

'Oh, hush, you!'

Their fingers parted and her tracery grew quick and dizzying, joining the Deva and the human planets in a pattern whose weft only she knew.

'All of it is home,' she said, 'as Jatayu knew.'

'Really? The Deva? Or Madi? Isn't home where you're let in, Saira? Or which allows you to leave if you want to?'

She sighed. 'Someday, the Collective will be gone, the Deva will open up their planets, and the mines of Madi will run their course and become caverns to play hide-and-seek in. Until then we have our human planets, at least.'

To be human in this time, to choose your home world, or even to choose a life on a ship. There was space, so much space, in the galaxy. Jatayu felt Saira's words enter his blood and send a tingling sensation through him.

'You expand the world,' he murmured to her. 'Like the rim of a planet that keeps receding as you go in search of it.'

She entwined her fingers in his. 'As long as we find things on the way.'

First there was Saira, he'd thought then. And then there was space.

Now he wondered when the order of things had reversed itself, when the glint of starlight no longer needed copper eyes to be magical, when the rhythm of deep space became more soothing than the Terran dawn they had stayed up together to welcome.

'Captain?'

Jatayu found his hands pressed upon the deck of the bridge. He was looking down at his shoes.

'Captain, what was that about?'

Mara was quick. Fourth in command, but he always believed she'd succeed him on the *Terran Sky* once he was decommissioned.

'A Deva patrol, Third Officer, even though they wouldn't admit it. They're looking for smugglers.'

'That I heard.'

'But why would passenger runs to Madi worry the Collective, Captain?'

'Figure it out, Officer.'

'Because they aren't passenger runs at all, are they?' Mara said slowly. 'There's no reason anyone would take people to Madi – unless it was to sell them as cheap labour and disrupt the Collective's Internal Market. It would make for extremely profitable business, wouldn't it?'

'Well done. These smugglers don't smuggle cargo.'

'Only – where will this labour come from?'

'Good question, Officer. They,' he gestured in the vague direction of Xolon, slightly closer now, 'are making the List now.'

'List, Captain?'

'A List of Xolonians.'

'I don't follow.'

'Which is your home world, Third Officer?'

'Hauder.'

Jatayu allowed himself the ghost of a smile. 'Should've known, from how you make competence look so bloody effortless.'

'You learn to be efficient, Captain, when home is a few idle moments recovering from one electrical storm and preparing for the next. It's why we're so good at space.'

'You could've migrated.'

'I...didn't want to.'

'Ah well. So tell me, Officer,' he said, 'ever felt that Hauder wasn't room enough?'

'An entire planet? No, of course not!' Her response was quick, natural. 'And there's always space.'

'Well, the Xolonians disagree,' he gestured again. 'They believe they've been too generous. So now they are atoning for their history.'

'I don't understand,' she said, careful now. 'It's a human planet. Like Hauder, like Sikar, like – Terra. So what do they mean?'

'You know that every human planet's human population has a median that is ever so slightly different from the others, don't you? Blood composition, bone structure and density, and so on. The Xolonians devised an algorithm that would work out their median. They have a range of permissible deviations from it, and then – they draw their line.'

He sensed her shiver. It soothed him, the very human reaction.

'I see,' she said.

'And to be Xolonian is to – only – be on the List.'

Mara chewed her lip. 'I think I understand. There will be those outside the permissible range of deviation. They will be put on ships back home.'

'But where's home, Mara, if no planet claims you back? What if you're no longer of Xolon – but of nowhere else too?'

There was stillness, before she understood. 'Offworlding,' she whispered.

Jatayu smiled. 'Unless there is a ship, undetected, at the right time and place…'

She breathed. 'Skins, captain?'

He looked away.

She had lost her memory banks, but not the sight of his quizzical look that she had loved so well, or the slight tremor in his voice as he tried to bring himself to believe.

'You really think this is going to work? That the Deva will abandon speciesism because you, one Xolonian, discover a commonality in our languages?'

'Eventually, Noroon.'

'You know, before the stars came to us, Xolon was parcelled into bands of people who separated themselves from each other? Not just a common language, all humans. *And yet…'*

'But then, the stars came to us and we became one world in this galaxy, didn't we, love? We needed space to realize how small we had made ourselves. It can happen again.'

'The Deva are so different from us, Rulda.'

She smiled. 'In your head. We don't have to always…define things, you know.'

'If it's in everyone's head, then it is real.'

'Until it isn't. Let me start with you.'

When they walked home together that night, they heard the chants for the first time.

'One world. One blood. One bone.'

Home, she'd always thought, was a library, a view of the winding streets of New Colucan, the sight of the stars, requited love.

You loved a world, and it was enough.

Until it wasn't.

One world. One blood. One bone.

They walked. She heard her blood sing to her. The wrong blood for this world.

They walked.

Who knew that just beyond New Colucan, there were deep woods that stretched to the sea? Of course, the memory banks would have told her had she asked about her own neighbourhood rather than about the geography of Unbar, but she never had. Was home a place where you could spend lifetimes without needing to know what lay beyond the doorstep, she wondered.

From time to time, they heard the drones overhead. A thrill passed through her, each time, as they all took cover. But without the chips and underneath the forest canopy, they were invisible. Any moment now, she thought, it would be footsteps that they would hear from behind, coming from New Colucan, footsteps from which the forest would not hide them.

After the last round of the drones, they started joking about which of them could be sacrificed, if needed.

'The oldest?'

'Right, because a few years matter so much when we've all lived decades. Do better.'

'Most valuable career?'

'As if there's a career left, after the List. As if there's *anything* left after the List.'

'The order in which we were designated Off-List?'

'What's the point, we're all Second Rounders anyway.'

Rulda, listening idly all this while, pricked up her ears now. 'What's a Second Rounder?'

They stared at her, and even Fani seemed surprised.

'How do you not know this? Second Rounders are those whose names were in the List but got dropped because someone objected to their inclusion, and the Authority decided to redo the tests. Anyone can object – and someone must have done it for you. You do know that, right?'

'Oh!' She struggled to remember, but the wiping of the memory banks had been efficient. Glimpses flashed before her eyes, but nothing coalesced, apart from vague recollections of having indeed taken the test twice.

'You mean someone complained and had me thrown off the List?' she whispered, almost to herself. 'Someone who knew something that could get the Authority to order a re-test for me?'

'Not long now,' said Fani from ahead, her voice dry. Thirteen of them had set out from New Colucan on the night of the tall fires. Now there were five.

'Where are we going?' she asked.

Fani didn't turn. 'Where we can start the world over again,' she said. 'I promise.'

Xolon is a promise.

Her words unlocked memories of more words, like the interstellar drive opening pathways to the galaxy.

Xolon is a promise.

Until it wasn't.

She walked.

Love, he'd always thought, was more permanent than the stars.

Until it wasn't.

The fireflies went out, but the stars remained. He went to space. Time passed, bringing with it other worlds and other loves. Sometimes he thought of the old days, when humans didn't live beyond a few decades. And he wondered about the foolishness of those who discovered the cure for ageing but forgot to invent a cure for memory.

'Captain Jatayu?'

'Yes.'

'Xolon incoming.'

'Put them on.'

A voice crackled over the line. 'Identification for the *Terran Sky*.'

Smoothed into stony nonchalance by the current of practice, Jatayu intoned a series of letters and numbers. *No damn truth spectrum here*. But his heart thumped until the voice came once more: 'Clearance granted.'

There was a stir behind him on the bridge as the crew eased into action. But before they could start moving, he felt a bump that sent little shivers through the ship.

'What's that?'

Mara, looking at the surface video feed, said, 'We have boarders, Captain.'

Jatayu rested his palms on the bridge. 'Identification?'

Mara fed the footage into her memory bank. 'Xoloni Offworld Police.'

'Oh, Terra!'

Somewhere underneath the ship, a hatch opened.

'I'll handle this.' Jatayu moved quickly off the viewing deck and down into the *Terran Sky*'s reception chamber. He stood in the middle of the cold, spare, domed hall, amidst the red-and-gold Terran banners that hung from the walls, and waited.

After a few minutes, the wall in front of him parted, and he saw two of his crew flanking a third man. He was short and unremarkable to look at, wearing a steel grey uniform that matched the colour of his hair, neatly parted in the middle. A name card flashed at Jatayu.

Pusa
Inspector General, XOP

'Captain Jatayu.'

'Inspector General Pusa. Welcome aboard the *Terran Sky*.'

'This is a routine inspection.'

'At your service, Inspector.'

Pusa strolled around the chamber, looking at the Terran banners without a word. After a while, he stopped and looked at Jatayu. 'Well?'

'Follow me, Inspector.'

Jatayu took the inspector up onto the viewing deck, and then out again into the interiors of the ship. They walked in silence.

'Your business, Captain?' Pusa asked finally, as they went through a corridor, dimly lit in blue.

'Skins to Sikar. Surely you saw my record when you granted clearance, Inspector?'

'Just asking. Who knows who's really behind a screen?'

Jatayu allowed his voice to tremble. 'I should say that in all my time captaining the *Terran Sky* I've done this route more times than I can remember, and *never* –'

Pusa spread out his arms. 'I understand, Captain. Believe me, our hands are tied. There are Deva patrols just beyond the exosphere…'

'We met them.'

'Well, there you go. If they catch an outgoing ship with offworlders – and we've heard there are now full-blown secret rescue missions ongoing – we've had it.'

'Rescue missions? By whom?'

'Who do you think?'

'Sikar?'

'Who else? They're funding this.'

'I understand, Inspector. Maybe you could consider alternatives to offworlding? You'd at least not have the Collective breathing down –'

'And give in to that snotty, overcrowded little planet playing the moral conscience of the galaxy with its Open Gates policy?' Pusa stopped and swung around to face him. Jatayu stopped as well.

'Where are you from, Captain?'

'Terra.'

'Oh? I'm hearing it's not in the best shape.'

Jatayu didn't twitch. 'I wouldn't know – haven't been back in more than a century.'

'You'd do better if you made the List, Captain,' Pusa said softly. 'Every planet needs one. To know who belongs. It is the human…condition.'

'Thank you, but I suggest you propose that to the Terran ambassador – which, I believe, your representatives already have. I hope you've enjoyed your time on our ship, Inspector, and now if there's nothing more –'

'One moment, Captain Jatayu.' Pusa jerked his thumb towards a set of black panels in the wall to their left. 'What's behind that?'

'That's the hold.'

'I'd like to see it – just so I can formally sign off on my report.'

'The hold's off-limits to everyone but cleared crew members, Inspector.'

'Is that so?'

Jatayu didn't know how – or when – it happened, but there was a laser gun in Pusa's hands, pointed at him.

'Come on, Captain. There are far, far, far too many stories of a do-gooder Terran playing interplanetary saviour and taking Offworlders to fucking Sikar. I know that couldn't possibly be you – so open the hold, please.'

Jatayu measured the distance between them and the steadiness with which Pusa held his gun.

'Don't try it,' Pusa said quietly.

'You Xolonian bastard,' said Jatayu, just as Mara rose up like a shadow behind Pusa. The Xolonian crumpled to the floor without a sound. 'Well done, Officer,' he continued. 'Right place, right time.'

'Thank you, Captain. I figured he wasn't here for a courtesy call.' Mara kicked Pusa lightly. 'Fucking Offworld police. What do we do with him?'

'Into the hold,' said Jatayu. 'Since he was so anxious to see it, he can wake up there. We'll dump him on Eldor when we make our pick-up, and he can walk back to New Colucan.'

He realized he was sweating again.

'Understood, Captain. Are we going on with the trip?'

'We are,' said Jatayu. 'We already have clearance, and everything else is taken care of – we just need to fly to Eldor – and hope that our pick-up is already there. Not a second to spare now.'

Mara looked at the floor.

'What are you thinking, Officer?'

She said it just as it hit him. 'We can't do this ever again, can we?'

Jatayu bit his lip, tasting blood. 'You're right. The *Terran Sky* won't fly again. You'll have to find another ship after this, Officer. A regular trade ship. I'm sorry.'

Mara shifted. 'Now that I know what it was for – I guess it was worth it, Captain.'

Jatayu nodded. 'Then let's ensure we make it so – there's still a mission to complete, and we still have to dodge the bloody Deva on our way out.'

He turned and strode back through the ship to the viewing deck.

'All stations, let's go.'

Down through the atmosphere, the planet's pale blue cover rushed up to meet them. He had escorts, he knew. But he also knew that the most unbending of puritans were the easiest to corrupt – and what was true of humans was true of planets as well. As he'd expected, nobody raised the alarm when he gave the order to bank to the west, away from New Colucan and the galactic centre of the medicinal skin trade and towards the island of Eldor.

They flew low, piercing the cloud cover. As ever, Xolon reminded him of Terra, only with a vaster – and more fragile – sense of space. The long Xolonian twilight was shimmering on the rim of the horizon, the planet's three moons risen in the sky.

'Let's promise now,' he heard Saira's voice from a long time ago, as they'd gazed at a sky poorer by two moons, 'that everything we do will be to make the world larger – and we'll do nothing to confine it, nothing to force it to cup in our hands, like these bio-domes that cup us here.'

Jatayu set his teeth.

In the antiquarian videologs that Noroon and she had watched in the Public Library of Xolon – before the time of the List – there had been musings by ancient Xolonians, before the stars came home, before the Devas and the economic empire of the Collective, before the interstellar drives. These writers and composers had speculated that when Xolon reached the stars many of the ideas that structured their world would be washed away like spring rain washed away sweat.

The idea of limited, bounded space, for example.

Only, they hadn't.

When stars came to them, the world had only grown smaller.

On the edge of a tor, the ocean roiling and crashing beneath them, the five Non-Listers rested. Fani was the only one with the energy left to stand.

'Any moment now,' she said. 'We'll see it on the horizon.'

'Where will they take us?' Rulda asked.

'Does it matter?' Twilight wreathed Fani's face in shadow. 'To a place that we will call home.'

'Will we get out memory banks back?' Rulda blurted out. Strange thought. Of all the things the List had taken from her, this was what she wanted back. *Home is where you can know the galaxy.*

Fani was still. 'I hope so. Only the Xolonians are so barbaric as to cut off access to the memory banks.'

There was hope. Her work would continue. Without Noroon...but it would continue. Somewhere in digital space, her notes, with their dream of a universal language, the Grammar of Harmony, to break the taxonomies that rimmed the galaxy –

The whine of drones pierced the air once more. They flattened themselves on the soft grass. They knew it would do no good, but they did it anyway.

Runaway Non-Listers.

The words bounded and rebounded off the porous walls of Rulda's mind, making little squelching noises like wet balls hitting the mud.

Runaway Non-Listers.

Six drones came screaming through the evening from the direction of New Colucan, their insignias – Offworld Police – stark in the dim light.

By agreement, no one said a word. Fani's moment, it seemed, had come – and gone.

The drones circled overhead, and then they hung – suspended – above the ocean. If Rulda had dared look up, she would have thought the scene to be a human painting. She didn't, waiting instead for the incinerating white beam to strike them.

It didn't.

The drones banked once and then turned westwards, into the ocean, away from New Colucan, away from them. The air filled with a deeper hum, a heavier sound.

Fani leapt up and waved at the horizon. 'They're here!'

From the south of the continent, the *Terran Sky* sailed the air towards them at a slow yet steady pace. 'What are they waiting for?' Fani screamed raggedly. And then she was running, through the tall grass, and they were running after her, all short gasps and stumbling steps, towards the ship.

The *Terran Sky* drew closer by degrees until at last the hatch opened. A warmer light – that did not come from a fire – bathed them, and they heard the urgent human voice: 'Up, up. We have no time!'

Rulda found herself pulled up into the womb of the *Terran Sky*. The last thing they saw beneath them was the ocean of Xolon, upon whose dark surface little lights flickered in and out of existence.

Like fireflies, she thought, on Terra, before she'd left because Terra was not room enough. The fireflies that she had described to Noroon, translating words and images into a language that did not possess them, on the day she'd decided that he would be the only human being who would know that she had come from elsewhere, that she had chosen Xolon instead of being born to it, in the days before 'One world, one blood, one bone', when difference did not yet matter.

Saira had never liked definitions. But that had not stopped them from trying to define home, in the days of Terra, stars and fireflies.

Now, at last, he had another meaning.

Home is the person you remember to miss after a century and a half.

And after 15 decades in space, he was ready to go home.

Only to find that Terra had changed its laws, and more than a century in space meant an automatic revocation of Terran membership.

He could re-apply.

Re-application was expensive, more money than a ship's Captain had saved in all these years.

But home was the person you remembered to miss, home was the flash of copper eyes under a Terran sun. And although they had not spoken of it when he left, they both knew that home was not an idea that eroded with time.

He began looking for missions that could do with an experienced human captain, missions that carried a reward that matched the risks he was willing to take to return – home.

Through the transparent floor beneath his feet, Jatayu watched as the five Non-Listers were brought into the reception chamber of the *Terran Sky*. Regular Xolonians, by the looks of it, just unlucky to have ended up on the wrong side of an algorithmic line – not that he could ever tell the difference between a Terran, a Xolonian and a Hauderian from a distance.

'Captain Jatayu.'

'Yes, Officer?'

'Offworlders on board,' said Mara. 'And the inspector's been dumped on Eldor.'

'It's time then,' said Jatayu. 'One last flight.' He was turned away from Mara, looking up into space, his hands behind his back.

'Captain, is everything all right?'

He felt her words wash over him.

'Nothing, I just –' he felt his face crinkle into a smile. On an impulse he asked, 'Have you left someone behind on Hauder, Officer?'

'What – oh!' He heard Mara's breath catch in her throat. 'No.'

'Anywhere?'

'We–ll…'

'Go on. I bet nobody ever asks you this.'

It came out in a rush. 'She's also in space, Captain. It's been two decades, but –' Light entered Mara's voice, 'we both keep the Hauderian calendar. Every Founding Day at midnight, wherever we are, we turn a telescope towards shining Unbar, and make believe we're watching it together, as we used to back…home.'

He turned back to her, quickly enough to catch the last wistful gleam in her eye before it faded into an embarrassed nonchalance.

'And that's why you didn't want to give up being a Hauderian, Mara?' She started. 'So your memory banks could retain access to Hauder's calendar.'

'Yes,' she whispered.

'Take some time off after this trip,' he said gently, 'I'll put in a word for you.'

'Thank you, Captain Jatayu,' she looked up at him. 'Why did you ask me this?'

'Oh, nothing,' he straightened. 'I think I'm ready to go home, that's all. On our way, Officer. Make sure we take all precautions to avoid that damned Deva patrol. The Collective shouldn't have a problem with rescue – it doesn't affect their precious Internal Market as long as we're not hauling off cheap labour to Madi – but who knows. Rather not have them laser first and ask questions later.'

'Yes, Captain.'

'Good,' he nodded at her. 'I'll go down and speak to the Xolonians then.'

At a gesture, the floor panels beside him opened up. Jatayu strode down the stairway and into the reception chamber.

'Welcome, Xolonians, to the *Terran Sky*,' he said, as they stopped to look at him. 'I know they have taken everything from you, but you're safe now, safe from offworlding, and safe from Xolon and its barbaric List.'

He did not wait for a reaction to his opening, because he knew from experience that none of them would yet be able to speak.

'We're taking you to Sikar, your new home. For the duration of the trip, we're going to put you in the hold in a cryogenic sleep. This is just to save resources; the *Terran Sky* was never built for search-and-rescue.' Jatayu allowed himself to smile, and caught, as he always did, the ghost of one or two grins in response. 'I'm afraid you won't be seeing me or the crew again after this. When you awake, you will be home.'

'Thank you – Captain,' the one who seemed to be their leader, spoke.

He nodded. Flanked by two of his crew, the five Xolonians trooped past him, on their way to the hold.

As the last one passed him, she stopped and turned, catching his eye.

'Where is home, Captain?'

'Why do you ask?'

'When we fled from New Colucan, we were no longer of Xolon,' she said, her voice clear and frank. 'Every waking moment, I felt the sky press down on me. I want home to be a place where that can never happen.'

He shifted. 'What is your name?'

'Rulda.'

'What does that mean?'

'In Xolonian, it means traveller.'

'Apt. Well, Rulda, home is where you don't need to prove you belong. Is that enough?'

'Yes – no. Will I have my memory banks returned to me, Captain?'

For the first time, Jatayu understood why all the Off-List Xolonians he had brought on board looked like a part of them had been seared out of existence.

'I'm sure you will,' he said softly. 'It's not hard to plug people back in these days. Was there something you lost, Rulda?'

'A lifetime of work – on the Deva language.'

'You were a linguist?'

'I was. I wanted – want – to use language so I can make the world larger.'

He started, but Rulda was speaking again. 'Will there be a List where you are taking us, Captain?'

'Never.' Jatayu suddenly felt that he was being asked to complete a thought. 'Not all places are obsessed with achieving such…permanence,' he said, 'or with being labelled – listed.'

'And you, taking us there,' Rulda replied, her voice like the sound of running water, 'you do not like definitions either?'

'I would suffer someone's – sometimes,' he whispered.

She was looking directly at him. 'You really think there is a place out there where we can outrun algorithms?'

He already knew the answer. 'Space is room enough, Rulda.'

The four Xolonians – and their guards – had vanished into the hold. The two of them stood alone in the reception chamber, amidst the banners of Terra and the starlight creeping in through transparent panels.

He opened his mouth.

'A moment, please.'

But the voice that spoke was not his. Jatayu swung around. Mara had come down the stairway and was standing at the end of the chamber.

'Excuse me for just a minute,' Jatayu whispered. He took swift steps towards Mara, reaching her in seconds. 'Can't it wait?' he murmured, fierce and low.

'Captain, I need to speak to you,' she kept her voice low to match his. 'There has been a mistake.'

'What is it, Third Officer?'

'I checked our coordinates, Captain,' she said. 'We are taking a long route to Sikar. Through a detour.'

'I know.'

Mara stared. Silence hung between them. 'Captain,' she said slowly, 'The detour takes us to Madi.'

'I'm aware.'

'Madi is not on the way to Sikar, Captain.'

'I'm aware.'

They looked at each other again.

'Apologies Captain, but…'

'Yes, Third Officer?'

'The same Madi, the planet of the viriconium mines? The mines of Madi?'

'What of it?'

'Aren't the *only* things on the planet the mines, Captain, the mines from hell – and the miners who can never leave, the ones the smugglers transport?'

'I don't know, Third Officer. I haven't studied the geography of Madi. Should I have?'

'I –'

She stopped. Her mouth opened and shut once. Then she saluted. 'Very well, Captain. My apologies.'

'Think nothing of it.'

She left.

Jatayu turned and walked slowly back to where Rulda still stood. 'I'm sorry. Where were we?'

She was looking directly at him again. 'You were going to say something to me, Captain.'

He did not speak.

'*Is* there something you want to say to me, Captain?'

He gulped – once – and then brought his teeth together with a click. 'I hope you have a pleasant sleep, and I'm sorry that I won't be seeing you again.'

She nodded and turned away – and as she walked past him at last, starlight glinted upon her eyes and they shone a rare copper.

Jatayu started once more, as though a memory had drifted in through the impermeable dome in which he had spent the first two decades of his life, upon a ruined, artificial Terra, looking at the stars that were pinned to the roof of the bio-dome.

He went back to looking at the space and at the fireflies that had come to stay.

2020-NKARV

KAISER HAQ

This one too is zoonotic
But emerging in different places
At roughly the same time
From different animals
Kissing and canoodling
In unnatural ways:
A camel and a lamb in Libya,
A goat and a snow leopard
In the frozen north of Kashmir,
A lion and a giraffe in the Congo…
What led to such aberrations
Is anybody's guess; though
Global warming and hyper-
pollution are widely blamed,
I think this is pure scapegoating.
Better accept that sometimes we do
Have mysteries, miracles, freaks,
And just note what transpires.
We'd be none the wiser anyway
If these abnormal specimens
Didn't cosy up to some
Of us animal lovers – and hey
Presto we started acting funny:
Hugging the leper hiding his face,
Getting him biryani from Foodpanda;
Bending down in a field
To caress the grass we've stepped on;

A goon forgets to draw his gun
And reaches out a hand
Holding a lollipop; soldiers on the West Bank
Forget Krav Maga and fall at the feet
Of grieving mothers; the L of C runs
With the tears of battle-hardened veterans;
Mme Suu Kyi pitches a penitential bell tent
In a Rohingya refugee camp;
President Trump starts on a pilgrimage
Of redemption through Central America
Offering Green Cards to indifferent beggars;
One could go on and on
But the point is that scientists were quick
To put their finger on the problem:
A new virus was abroad,
A pandemic not unlikely. Poets
Had already named it
Karuna Virus,
Only that wouldn't do
In a scientific paper; hence
'2020-nKarV' in the *Lancet:*
Thus labelled, it was easy to control –
Health checks at POEs, quarantine,
Animals quartered according to species,
Set apart from all humans.
Normalcy came back with a vengeance:
You can see for yourself,
Just turn on the TV:
You won't see any poets,
No one utters the word 'karuna'
And though the horrible pictures are blurred
You know that the calculations are correct;
Entropy rules and after this
Universe there may not be another

THE CROSSING

KALSANG YANGZOM

It was an unusually hot night, and Sonam's small backpack weighed heavily on her shoulders. Her group, whittled down to just seven people, including two children, was struggling to reach the checkpoint before the next Great Sweep. They proceeded in silence, hugging the tree line, praying to the gods to guide them.

Sonam was furious at the gods. Her parents had prayed and prayed – for guidance, for rain, for sun, for water, for life. But the gods had been indifferent to their pleas. Yet, like many others in Chushi, their village, they had continued to pour their meagre savings into the monastery, hoping for a miracle. The people of Chushi survived on farming, and raising yaks and sheep in the harsh Himalayan environment survival was their daily battle. Sonam had seen young men and women leave for the city, with promises on their lips of returning with money. But no one ever did. And so the people left behind placed their faith in the gods and their karma, hoping for a better future. But Sonam knew better. No amount of begging and supplication would be enough to get them across the border, into India. The porous border from their ancestors' time was long gone, replaced four years ago with an electric hologram fence. It deterred even the most determined refugees. You could not dig a tunnel under it, and you could not climb over it. The only way to get through was the microchip that every Indian citizen had inserted in their left index finger. Sonam scratched at the healing scar on her left index finger. She hoped it would be enough to convince the guards that she was one of them, one of their own.

'Stop!'

In the still silence of the night, the whispered order sounded like a scream. Everybody froze. The children looked around fearfully and Sonam could smell their dread, the nauseating stench of body odour mixed with days of accumulated dirt and sweat. Even if the bordercopters couldn't see them, she was sure they would be able to smell them. Up ahead, they saw a small light, weaving a circle. That would be their handler, Cherring, the man who had promised to help them get across.

Looking around, they found themselves in a small opening among the trees. Three people dressed in black military outfits were waiting for them. They would help the refugees enter through a rarely used port. Sonam could not tell if they were humans or robots – she had heard that the bordercopters dressed in exactly the same way as the soldiers. Despite her scepticism, she mumbled a prayer to Chenrising, the Buddha of compassion.

Cherring stepped forward, palm extended. Tharkay, the leader of their group, handed over a package. Sonam's mind raced. Would they be satisfied with the money? Had they hiked their price? Could there be more demands? What if this was an ambush? She felt the world turning slowly. This could be a trap; she could see the months of hardship they had endured crumbling in front of her eyes.

They watched Cherring check the contents of the package and pocket it with a satisfied nod. The world around her stopped spinning, righted itself, and Sonam quietly released the breath she had been holding. Maybe their collective karma would see them through.

The other two handlers began unpacking their gear. The shorter one opened the briefcase he had been holding and took out a metallic device with two protruding tips. He proceeded to load it with what looked like tiny silver pins. Sonam wondered if it would hurt more than when she had cut her finger so it resembled a wound from insertion. No one had told her they would be fitted one in reality. How could they? Information was heavily censored in all of Tibet. Everybody was monitored constantly. Nobody knew what was true and what was propaganda. The latest onslaught on her people was the mandatory Rehabilitation Therapy, announced a few months before Sonam left Chushi. They were informed that as the newest member of the great Anisian nation they were lagging behind the rest and now, with the help of new technology, their assimilation would be quick. Everyone had to undergo this therapy, meant to cleanse them of their backwardness, their outdated beliefs, and create a blank slate whereupon they would be transformed into productive members of a new society. The thought made Sonam furious. How could the Anisians rehabilitate them in their own home, in their own land, without their consent?

But rumours travelled fast from other villages and cities where people were undergoing this process. Whispered conversations spoke of nanobots injected into people that completely rewired the brain, turning them into human robots controlled by Anisian leaders. Her people were essentially just a labour force being made pliant and docile. Sonam could not bear the thought of it and so she had made the choice to leave for India. Anything was better than the future that awaited her in her homeland. The crossing wasn't cheap and she knew that a much larger sum would have to be paid once they got across the border. She didn't know how she would do it but now was not the time to worry about that. Once she made it in, she would figure it out.

'Come forward one by one.' Cherring spoke in the dialect of their village.

The familiar words, spoken in their native language, caused the group to look at each other, surprise in their eyes. Could it be that the man was one of them? Someone who had crossed over earlier and was now helping his people? Were all three men from their village? One of those young men who had never returned? He barked the same instruction again, bringing the group out of their reverie.

Tharkay was the first to move.

'Show me your left hand, index finger extended.'

As Tharkay extended his left hand, the shorter handler came forward with the device.

'This will take a few minutes,' a woman's voice said, also in their native tongue, 'and it won't hurt much.'

The second handler was a woman, Sonam realized with a shock.

A hologram screen sprung up from a band around the third handler's wrist. Sonam watched him, cautious. The beeps emanating from the band as he began typing seemed to pierce the still night air.

'You will be given new temporary identikits. These chips we are injecting you with will allow you to pass the immigration port unharmed. From now onwards, this is your reality. But remember that these chips are valid for one month only, starting today. My colleague here is activating them and feeding the information into the Citizen Identity Network. After a month if anyone checks your chip, you will be identified as an illegal alien and taken into custody. So make sure you don't wander off or get caught. Is that clear?' Cherring's words bore into Sonam's mind. She had known it would not be easy; crossing the border was just one of the many steps they were taking in the hope of a liveable future.

She hoped whatever lay at the end of their journey was worth all the hardship. She told herself it would be. It had to be. Her homeland no longer existed. Her people were considered a disposable minority, living in poverty and hunger and now in complete subjugation. There was no going back.

Someone nudged Sonam forward. It was her turn. The woman handler held her hand and placed her finger between the device's tips.

'This would not have fooled anyone,' she said gently, noticing Sonam's scar. Sonam could feel her cheeks becoming warm. Well, at least I tried, she wanted to say but instead she nodded.

She noticed the device looked like an oddly shaped gun, with buttons instead of a trigger. It felt cool on her fingertip. At the press of a button, the metallic tips clamped down. Sonam felt a short sharp pain shoot up her entire arm. The throbbing sensation from her finger drowned everything else around her. This is it, she thought, her one-way ticket to India, the land of opportunity. Perhaps all her parents' various gods were finally listening, making up for the years of neglect.

'That's the last one. We are done here.' The woman announced a little later and began to pack the briefcase.

'Let's move.' Cherring ordered.

The group followed the three handlers in silence. By now, the sun was rising, and they had only a few minutes of darkness left. A checkpoint rose ahead of them, and a lone guard stood watch. Cherring went ahead and spoke with the guard, and Sonam noticed that their uniforms were exactly alike. A slight uneasiness crossed her mind and her stomach started to knot.

'Proceed in an orderly fashion and put your left hand out for verification when he asks you to.' Cherring instructed them.

The group shuffled forward, stepping up one by one. Sonam turned around to take a last look at her land. It was no longer her home now, nothing remained of her culture, traditions, customs and history. Everything would be gone in a year if things went according to the grand Anisian plan.

The group had been at a guesthouse in Sehra, a small border village, for a week now, and they were gradually learning to relax. Tense postures and suspicious looks had been replaced with wary smiles and small talk. The woman who ran the guesthouse had given them a change of clothes – ill-fitting but clean.

Sonam too was feeling a bit at ease. The intrusive, pessimistic what ifs that had been flooding her head had reduced. She was even looking forward to talk to Tharkay this morning. Maybe they could play a game with the children after breakfast.

When she entered the hall, she saw Tharkay waving to her and went over to sit next to him.

'So, how long do think we will stay here?' Tharkay asked as he put some mixed rice gruel in her bowl. The food had mostly been the same since they had come, but it was filling, and that was more than she could say about food back in Chushi. Thoughts of her village kept creeping back into her mind. She had to stop them, she knew. It would only make her homesick.

'My father heard that people stay here for 15 days or so – to get rid of their Tibetan smell. You know, I didn't realize that Tibetans had a smell or that we all smelled the same, no matter where in Tibet we came from!' she told Tharkay, laughing. It felt good to talk without the fear of being overheard, without the fear of death.

'Well, at least we made it out,' There was sadness in his voice, not anticipation. Perhaps Tharkay too had left behind a family. 'It's for the best, because what would we do at home? Be treated like slaves? That's no way to live,' his voice rose in anger.

He was right. The invasion had happened 62 years ago, long before they were born, and their lives had only got worse with time. The Anisian militia had swept into Tibet with a force that was no match for an army consisting of any able-bodied man who could lift a sword. The Tibetans had fought with swords while the Anisians fired machine guns.

'That's what we get for burying our heads in religion and forgetting the world. The world went ahead and we went back in time. So much for our rituals, prostrations and amulets,' she said.

Tharkey looked at her in surprise. 'The gods have only protected us, Sonam! We wouldn't be here if it weren't for the lama and his divination. He told us which route to take and when to leave. He has guided us faithfully every step of the way.' He toyed with the dzi stone around his neck. Tied with a string, this prized stone was the ultimate symbol of wealth in Tibet, and his was soldered with gold at both ends. He's an aristocrat, she thought, taken aback.

Sonam hadn't expected someone like him to be a part of this group of refugees. She had first thought he was like her, a survivor from a village that had been plundered, its inhabitants forced to bow down to the new rulers; that he too detested the clergy for misleading and deluding them. But now she knew better. The aristocrats and the clergy had worked hand in glove to make her country into a sitting duck for the greedy invaders. Only interested in looking out for themselves, they never cared for commoners. It was obvious that he would defend the clergy. These aristocrats were the first to be imprisoned by the Anisian army as the ruling elite of Tibet. Those that managed to evade them had immediately fled to neighbouring countries. Their immense wealth made it possible for them to make their way across, leaving people like her to fend for themselves. Yet, Sonam was surprised that someone with an aristocratic lineage was still among them. She could feel her fury rising. How could he say these things knowing what he had seen with his own eyes? The thoughts that she had kept to herself while in Chushi came rushing forth. She had thought someone who had risked his life to come to India would be more sensible.

'The same lamas had reassured every one of us that the gods were on our side and that our people would emerge victorious against the Anisian heathens. And look where we are now. They led us to our doom. Even after our defeat and suffering, people like my grandmother refused to see the truth. When she later became sick with tuberculosis, she refused the medicines from the Anisian doctor stationed in our village and instead chose to wear an amulet given by our local lama. Thankfully, her death was quick,' she said coldly.

'Did you consider the notion that besides being religious, your grandmother's refusal of Anisian medicines could also have been her only way to resist them? That her decision to wear the amulet was a conscious action taken to defy Anisian authority and their conversion? Things are not as black and white as you see them, Sonam. Those who have faith in our religion are not blind fanatics. We all have our reasons for not giving up.'

Tharkay's words surprised her. She hadn't thought of her grandmother's actions in this light. But she knew that not everyone sought to resist Anisians through such actions. For many, faith was still a way to escape their horrible reality and blame their sufferings on past life action while not doing anything in this life to change their situation. Tharkay was reading too much into what her grandmother had done, she decided. Their religion, she knew, had made her people complacent.

She got up to wash her bowl. She had just started to feel normal, cheerful even, but this conversation had marred her morning. She should have known – her people, even these aristocratic ones like Tharkay, were nothing if stubborn, clinging desperately to their beliefs, refusing to acknowledge the change being forced on them. Even now, after all that they had gone through, Tharkay still believed in their gods.

Her family had been poor, barely eking out a living, opportunities to break the cycle of poverty nowhere in sight. The invasion, she thought, was a blessing in disguise. It broke them, all of them. For the Anisians, all Tibetans were barbarians, the clergy and aristocrats included. And yet there were people like

Tharkay who sought comfort and security in the very system that had led to their country's destruction.

'I just thought that given our current situation, religion would be the last thing on our minds,' Sonam said when she returned to her seat.

'My family has had many high lamas, and I have seen first-hand how they have been beacons of hope to our people, giving them shelter and food when the Anisians attacked us,' he said as he got up. 'All lamas aren't bad, you know,' he continued with a smile.

Their conversation was interrupted by the arrival of their handler. 'How many times have I told you to speak in Sehri? Its similarity with your dailect is why we chose this place…so that you can blend in. If you are overheard by the locals, you will be immediately arrested. You are not to bring attention to yourselves by chattering in your dialect,' said Cherring, looking furious.

They'd been given these instructions on the fateful night of their crossing. Their survival depended on it, they were told. But in the happiness of being alive, they had become careless.

Glaring at them, Cherring said, 'I need a volunteer to check if the microchip is working properly. We'll go to the hospital to see if the CIN will recognize the chip.'

Tharkey raised his hand immediately and joined Cherring.

As they left, Tharkey looked back and smiled reassuringly at Sonam.

Tharkay did not return the next day, and Sonam maintained a constant lookout for Cherring. Had something gone wrong? What if Tharkay had been caught? Were they under surveillance? She had to talk to someone; perhaps Lhamu, the woman who ran the guesthouse, would know. But if they were compromised, could she trust anyone? How long would it be before the bordercopters found them playing at being Sehrian?

The cheerful atmosphere among the group changed that day. The tension in the shoulders and the grim faces returned. Their voices became subdued during mealtimes. Sonam finally mustered up the courage and asked Lhamu about Tharkay and Cherring. But all she got was a noncommittal grunt. The group spent the rest of the days in limbo, worried sick about a future they could not control or see.

Finally, on the fifth day, Cherring returned, and asked them to gather their belongings and follow him to a truck. Sonam looked around for Tharkay but couldn't see him anywhere. She followed Cherring outside and asked, 'Where is Tharkay? Why isn't he here?'

'Oh, he is fine. The chip worked perfectly, but he is in the hospital right now. Turns out, he has a minor infection in the liver so I had to leave him. Didn't want to raise any suspicions by bringing him back without getting treated. Once he's better, in a few days, I think, he will join us in Rahan,' Cherring said, putting his hand on her shoulders. 'That's where I am taking all of you right now, to work in the factories there. The owners there never ask where the workers come from. It's the safest place for you.'

Sonam looked at Cherring. She wanted to believe him, she had to. Many had made this journey before her, with handlers like Cherring. She had to trust him. Everything was fine. They would all make it. Things would work out for them.

It took them nearly two days to get to Rahan. For the journey, they were given dehydrated food pills and hydration patches. It was made clear to them before they started that they would only stop once every 12 hours for a change of driver and for them to use toilets. They had to be extremely careful and could not risk being spotted by any locals once they left Sehra. The truck made Sonam feel claustrophobic. There were no windows or visible ventilators through which she could at least know if it was night or day. The breaks were barely for 10 minutes and didn't provide any relief to their cramped bodies.

When the truck finally came to a halt, Cherring's voice ordered them to get out. As they formed a line, Sonam saw that it was night. In the dim moonlight, she could see a few large buildings, and people waiting near one of them. The group followed Cherring towards a man, who led them inside. Sonam saw that they had entered a huge warehouse with boxes stacked everywhere.

She noticed Cherring talking with the man who had brought them in. His features were so different from her people that she couldn't help but stare. She did not understand what they were saying but the man kept glancing at their group. Again, Sonam felt a sense of unease creeping up her spine. Cherring was gesticulating and she heard a slight rise in his tone. Was something wrong? She tried to calm her thoughts. After all, everything that Cherring had said was turning out to be true. Nothing bad had happened to them yet. She just had to believe that they were safe now.

'Everyone, this is Mr Gorv. He is the owner of this factory and will be in charge of you from now on. He will help you with accommodation and food. He knows people here and can keep your arrival a secret. He will also arrange for a more permanent indentikit for you that will hold up under cursory inspection, but you have to make sure you don't get caught by the police. You will be sent to different factories in twos or threes once you have worked off the money you owe for these services. This is a delicate process so I would suggest that everyone cooperate with Mr Gorv.' With that, Cherring gave them a military salute and left the building.

Cherring's instructions seemed very simple and curiously uncomplicated. Sonam had anticipated more. And what about Tharkay? Where was he? When would Tharkay join them? As tired and disoriented as she was, like everyone else after the journey, she had forgotten to ask Cherring about him. Now, she had no way of contacting him.

Mr Gorv clapped his hands to get everyone's attention and murmured something to the man standing next to him.

'Hello everyone, I am Parese. I will be your supervisor, guide and interpreter. You are here as migrant labourers from Sehra. Nothing more. You will be given two sets of work uniforms, sanitation kits and food right now. We will begin the process of updating the indentikit tomorrow. Please follow us into the workers' quarters so that you can settle in.' With that Mr Gorv and Parese turned and moved further into the building, with the group following quietly behind.

They entered into a small dormitory of sorts through the door towards the back of the warehouse. The interiors were dimly lit and Sonam noticed bunk beds as well as lockers further back. So this was going to be her life now, at least for a few months. Perhaps she could ask Parese to give her books to learn Hindi, it would be useful for when she would leave this place.

'The washrooms are behind the lockers. Food will be sent in half an hour. You all can relax now. You have made it across,' Parese said with a bright smile, while Mr Gorv nodded. They both left the room after the announcement.

There were smiles and clasped hands all around. They were finally free from the clutches of the Anisians. They could work to start a new life here. One of the older men began to cry softly. The children understood that something momentous had occurred and hugged each other. Sonam too felt a sense of relief and the tense knot in her stomach seemed to finally loosen. The hope in everyone's eyes made Sonam tear up. They would be all right now, she thought.

Soon everyone had changed into their work uniforms, a grey loose-fitting shirt and pant set. They were also given new shoes that were a welcome substitute to their travel-worn ones. Sonam felt she had entered a hospital rather than a factory. The clothes and shoes seemed inappropriate for factory work. It struck her that none of them had even thought of asking what work they were supposed to do. Now that Sonam gave it more thought, she realized that the details given by Cherring, and later Parese, were filled with just enough information to keep them compliant. Instructions and assurances that made sure the group did what was asked of them. But nothing concrete had been communicated to them. Looking around, Sonam noticed that the door through which they had entered was now shut. That seemed odd. Why would they be locked in? It could be that Mr Gorv was being careful as they were new arrivals, but still…

Sonam tried to calm her mind. Back home, there had been reason to work herself up, with the ever-present threat of Rehabilitation Officers knocking on their doors. But this was India, the land of freedom. The people here were good, that's why so many from her country had fled to this land. She turned her attention to her immediate surroundings. The others had started to claim their beds. The children seemed the most excited, a bed of their own, no sharing with each other any more.

Just then Parese entered with food packets and the group gathered around, accepting packets and settling down to eat. Sonam wondered if Parese would know anything about Tharkay. Tharkay was a part of this group so he had to be with them. She caught up with Parese as he was about to leave.

'Hi. I'm Sonam. I was wondering if you know about Tharkay. She was with us but had to go to the hospital. Cherring said she would be here when we came. Any news on that?' Sonam felt her heart pounding as she waited for his answer.

'Oh, Tharkay. Yes, yes. I was told about her. She will be here in a few days. Don't worry. You should rest now. Big day tomorrow. Now I must leave, we have a lot to do,' Parese said, locking the door behind him.

Now Sonam felt certain that something was wrong. She had deliberately used the female pronoun for Tharkay and Parese had gone along with it. If Parese didn't know about Tharkay, then had he lied to her? The knot in her stomach seemed to twist even tighter. She didn't feel hungry any more. She needed to know what was happening.

The rest of the group seemed oblivious to any hint of trouble, happy with this semblance of stability. She needed to do something. Maybe she could look around, check the lockers. She might find something, an old newspaper or a diary, anything that would help her understand what was going on. It was then that it occurred to Sonam that the dorm had no windows. Now her mind began to work. Locked doors, no windows. They were basically prisoners here. What was happening?

She began opening the lockers. Nothing there. She checked under the mattresses and pillows. Everything was neat and clean, nothing out of place. Rinchen, the only other girl her age, was looking at her with concern. I must look like I have lost my mind, Sonam thought. She smiled nervously at Rinchen and sat down on her bed. She wanted to get to the bottom of this, but she didn't know how. She had exhausted all her options. There was nothing more she could do stuck in a locked, windowless room.

The journey had taken a toll on Sonam and as much as she tried to fight exhaustion, she drifted off into an uneven sleep.

Sonam wasn't sure what woke her up but her body was tense, the hair on the back of her neck standing up. She listened carefully without opening her eyes. She thought she heard Cherring's voice. What was he doing here? Had he brought Tharkay with him? She heard the door to their dorm open with a muffled creak. She stayed still, wondering what was going on.

'We will sedate the two old men first. No taking risks. Then move along to the women and children. You only need to spray once over the nose, Parese. Don't go overboard like you did last time. Two of the people died of overdose and we didn't get paid for them. We need these people sedated till they arrive at the facility. Not dead. The doctors need them to be alive to harvest their organs. Move quickly and quietly. We don't have much time. The truck will be arriving soon.' Cherring's rushed whisper reached Sonam's ears. Her eyes shot open. She wanted to scream, to wake everybody up and run. But she was petrified, unable to move.

Suddenly, Cherring's face loomed above and his eyes looked into hers as he quickly covered her mouth with his hand. In the glow of the light coming from the open door, Sonam noticed a bracelet of dzi stones on his wrist. And as he sprayed the sedative on her face she realized to her horror that one of the stones was soldered with gold at both ends.

A SPECIES OF LEAST CONCERN

GITI CHANDRA

'A Species of Least Concern,' read young Melli to an only intermittently attentive Mrs Capensis. Teaching her daughter to read was a cause she was willing to devote her time to, but her child's obsession with ancient species less so. At any rate, the *Book of the Survival of the Fittest* had managed to capture the 11-year-old's attention long enough for her to acquire a creditable vocabulary. And so the two sat in their Green Room on a late and lazy afternoon, the mother with her tea and the daughter with her book.

'A Species of Least Concern was one that had been categorized and evaluated by the International Union for the Conservation of Nature as not being a focus of species conservation. Such species did not qualify as threatened, near threatened or conservation dependent.' Mrs Capensis noted with satisfaction that the several polysyllabic words had not tripped up the young reader's tongue. Her mind, however, seemed to have stumbled upon something.

'What's "Nature", Mom?'

Mrs Capensis sighed and put down her teacup. 'We've been over this, Melli. It used to be that there were lots of things that were not materialized by fabrichines. They...'

'Oh, right!' Melli rolled her eyes. 'They just were,' she waved her hands airily, 'out there.' Now the airy hand became waving arms, indicating a vast nowhereness. 'Come on, Mom. I know there's some kind of weird ancient tradition of mothers telling children stories about things that were "not really true"' – the child managed to conjure quotation marks around the words in a voice conveying both disbelief and disdain. 'But *really*? This whole "nature" thing is beginning to get a bit old, don't you think? Big, green things that became bigger all by themselves and then, for apparently no good reason, desiccated and diminished until they disappeared!' Melli banged her hands together with a satisfied boom of destruction, and not a little smugness at having used no less than three polysyllabic words beginning with 'd' correctly in a sentence.

She made a mental note of inventing a short, single syllable word, also beginning with 'd', that would indicate the same thing as her alliterative string of d-words. So much more satisfying, although what she would use it for she didn't know, considering that nothing ever did those things – desiccate, diminish, and disappear. She filed this conundrum away for future mulling and wandered off in the direction of the food fabrichine. She was going to have to change the settings again – her mother seemed addicted to these antique beverages in their quaint holders.

Mrs Capensis watched her daughter roll her eyes as she walked away, and sighed again. She picked up the abandoned book and smoothed down the page with a gentle hand.

'Amphibians over the edge: the silent extinction risk of data-deficient species.' The title of the next chapter caught her eye and she reached for her reading glasses, smiling a little at the thought that the gesture would have brought forth a positive Ferris wheel of eye-rolling from her daughter, who had the perfect eyesight of her species. 'A data-deficient species', she read, 'was one which had been categorized by the International Union for Conservation of Nature as offering insufficient information for a proper assessment of conservation status.' She thought wryly of how little she actually knew about her daughter, familiar though she was with every line on her little palms, attuned to every tiny shift in her moods, witness to every failed project and successful prank of her few years on Survivor Sixteen. And yet, she had absolutely no clue as to what went on in her golden, antennaed head. Why was there no Intergalactical Union for the Conservation of Entirely New Species? Were they also doomed to be data deficient, difficult to conserve, preserve, allowed to grow, but never – Mrs Capensis put the book down with a suddenly shaky hand – desiccate, diminish, and disappear?

When the floods had come to the Kalahari, the fires had already purged the sands of any living thing that had not migrated to higher ground millennia ago. The dunes were rolling flames even before the desperate last-minute effort to seed the sands had failed, leaving chemical residue that burnt in the colours of spectacular sunsets. And the oceans recognized no higher ground, levelling all in their egalitarian approach, their few, odd, mutated, fauna taking only a dozen odd centuries to flop about and surrender to the general rumbling silence. And so it was that when the Ancient Ones arrived, desperate for land, fresh water, flourishing fauna and flora and a breathable atmosphere, they were rewarded with fresh air, a tiny blip of floating land, no flora, saltwater, and one single specimen of fauna, which regarded them with grim interest.

Melli carried her food tray in and motioned for the research pod to be activated, and as the sight and sound membranes slipped into place over the clear cell, she selected her favourite research area from the panel in front of her and sank back into the single-seat chesterfield sofa that the fabrichine had materialized to her mother's specifications. Images and sounds flickered before her, and she flicked a few switches with a little flutter of her fingers. She would hear it all in its original languages which sent little shivers of pleasure up her spine and into her recessed ears. The subtitles translated it all quite faithfully.

'Some say the world will end in fire,' began the first of the series, and Melli closed her eyes and luxuriated in the sound. 'Some say in ice. From what I've tasted of desire, I hold with those who favour fire.' She sighed with pleasure. Such beautiful words! She knew the subtitles by heart and spoke the translated text softly to herself.

'"Fire!" says the world which desires to end. Even those inside the ice long for the flavour of fire.' (Footnotes, which also she knew by heart, reminded the listener that long-buried diseases, frozen in the ice fields, had been thawed and brought back to life when the glaciers had melted.)

The soft voice intoned the rest of the poem. 'But if it had to perish twice, I think I know enough of hate, to say that for destruction ice is also great, and would suffice.' Melli curled her senses around the alien but dearly familiar sounds, feeling the hard edges of ambition and defiance poke at the corners of her mind, demanding, as they always did, that generations yet to be born acknowledge the determination encapsulated in the words. 'The world would hate to perish twice. Only total destruction will suffice.'

Never had she felt the power of these words more. A whole world bent upon self-annihilation. She wondered what the flavour of fire would be like, lifting her tongue slightly as she spoke the words. Total destruction – once and for all. Such wisdom from such an unevolved species – how had the Ancient Ones misread them so thoroughly? Surely a species that recognized its innate ineptitude and was determined to destroy itself for the good of the world was a species that might even be considered tragic? What wisdom! What courage and determination it must have taken to relentlessly pursue a path of self-destruction! Melli luxuriated in the pathos of the sentiment that rose often to her mind when she considered the fate of humans.

The flick of a finger, and the next in the series of salvaged messages began. This one was a song accompanied by images which had been patched together with great difficulty. The grey matter had not held on to these remote, filtered thoughts very well, and the Ancient Ones may have missed them altogether had it not been for the sole survivor in that drowned world. For this one, Melli opened her eyes; she was endlessly fascinated by the human identified as the god of happiness, standing in a dried riverbed, cursing the Ancient Ones.

'Allah megh de, pani de, chhaya de re, Rama megh de,' began the song, repeating the words over and over. 'O gods!' she read from the subtitles, 'may you be hidden under clouds and cast in shadows!' She shivered, a tiny part of her still excited to repeat the words aloud. No wonder the Ancient Ones had returned!

'Aankhe phade duniya,
Dekhe hay ye tamasha, Hai ye vishvas tera hai,
Teri asha. Allah megh de…'

Melli curled her lips over her teeth, pressing them together, unable to say these lines out loud without drooling, even in the privacy of her own space cell, and even her eyes took in the subtitles hungrily. 'The world will tear your eyes out, you make such a spectacle of yourself! Curses on your beliefs and your hopes! O may you be hidden under clouds and shadows!'

'But – but – the great pyramids! Egyptian and Mayan! The diagrams in Nazca! The maps of Antarctica under the ice! We left all these for the humans! What did you – they – humans – how could they not have…?!'

The Ancient One stuttered to a stop under the implacable scrutiny of the sole survivor on the planet, which shrugged expressively, keeping its arms crossed before its chest. Finally, since their helpless bewilderment was getting on its nerves, it spat into the gently rolling waves and said, 'They were just not very smart, you know? All that evidence of superior technology and dire warnings of what would happen? They didn't care. They didn't give a shit.'

One of the Ancient Ones was beginning to lose it, and another held him back as he lunged towards the sole survivor, snarling. Others were clearly getting restless, shuffling about and muttering amongst themselves. The first speaker collected himself with obvious effort, and when he spoke the sole survivor could smell the fear, hear the slight tremor in the even tone.

'We had a plan. We found this planet with great difficulty and after aeons of searching. We knew our own planet was not going to last long. We came here and left clear instructions for preserving the environment, left technology and machines, maps, large monuments, predictions of what was going to happen to the planet in case humans were not able to take care of it, how to prevent it and how to contact us in case you couldn't.' He stopped, apparently exhausted by the effort of explaining such self-evident things to this surviving specimen, which nevertheless seemed to be regarding him with increasing amusement. Finally, the Ancient One rasped out: 'What amuses you, O survivor? Does the extinction of our superior species strike you as funny? This was our back-up plan! This was our fail-safe!'

The sole survivor waited patiently for him to splutter to a stop. Then it opened its mouth, showing its teeth, and laughed. 'You left instructions for the humans, you idiots! On what basis did your calculations tell you that they were the species fittest for survival? Why didn't you leave them for a sturdier species?! What did you expect from *them*, call yourself a "superior species"!'

The Ancient Ones stared at the sole survivor, horror and comprehension on their narrow faces.

'Water, water, everywhere, and all the boards did shrink! Water, water, everywhere, nor any drop to drink!'

This one, in particular, made her spine tingle and nameless horrors crawl along her neck. For this, too, she knew the subtitled translations by heart; and indeed, it was the one closest to her heart, making it wild to escape its bony confines. 'Water, water, everywhere,' she whispered through suddenly dry lips. 'And all on board did shrink! Water, water, everywhere, nor any drop to drink!'

And suddenly, the memory of brittle lips wet with blood oozing from its cracks, slurring the hard consonants as they moved painfully to tell the assembled brood their story. Melli recognized this one as an inherited memory – coded into her DNA by centuries of trauma, as her mother had told her when she was first startled by it and demanded to know where it came from. The body needs to remember, always to remember, Mrs Capnesis said, because in that knowledge lay survival.

A few millennia of evolution were still nothing if each generation told the next what it had been and what it needed to become in order to survive. Knowledge and memory. Mrs Capensis forbore to tell her child her own memories – what was the point of passing on the knowledge of fear when fear itself was become an outdated evolutionary instinct? And so, the memory of the others, she kept to herself. Sitting nearby, listening, Mrs Capensis gazed unseeing at the book open in her lap, the empty teacup twirled unconsciously in lightly webbed fingers. She and her kind had watched them shrink, on board their various vessels. She saw in her mind, the tall, muscular, species, desiccated, excoriated by the salt water everywhere, that they could not drink.

'The very deep did rot: O Christ, that ever this should be!' Her heart remembered the rotting of the deep and thumped urgently to get her to stop remembering. When the dead fish had started washing up ashore in the millions – not once in a while, not in some remote place, not some dispensable species, but everywhere, all the time, of every kind of sea life imaginable; when it was no longer possible to dispose of the carcasses and they were left to rot on beaches that were closed off to humans; when ocean currents changed and the temperature and vegetation of the sea died and stank and floated on the waters and joined the waste and garbage islands and formed continents that stank and rose and fell with the waves and stank and mouldered and stank.

Mrs Capensis raised her hand to her nose and breathed deep of the perfume she dabbed her fingers with. She was reaching her limit and she knew it, but she also knew, from experience, how far she could hurtle down this wormhole of space–time without disintegrating.

'The very deep did rot: O Christ that ever this should be! Yea, slimy things did crawl with legs across the slimy sea!' She spoke the translation herself this time, along with the crackled remnants of the salvaged voice. The evolutionary imperative that encoded memory into genes and sent it surging through the blood into the heart and into the brain was in full flood. She knew she should walk away now and leave her daughter to enjoy the poetry of disaster, but it was a moving, a throbbing, a story, and it felt alive in this endless drift of dark.

The Ancient Ones went into a huddled whispering. They fished out strange implements and waved them about until a blurry image buzzed into focus before them. The sole survivor stared at it puzzled – small at one end, much, much larger in the middle, and small again at the other end. They muttered to one another and pointed at it, putting their appendages to their heads and turning the image this way and that. Finally, one of them snapped: 'Brontosaurus!' and kicked the Ancient One holding the projector. The projector-holding Ancient One mumbled and fiddled with the projector. *Bzzzt*. The brontosaurus was replaced by another image. Narrow and scaly at one end, narrow and scaly in the middle, narrow and scaly at the other end. Quick scroll and check. 'Anaconda!' This time the projector-holding Ancient One leaped nimbly out of the way of the kicking appendage of the furious Ancient One, and concentrated its various eyes on the task at hand.

Bzzzt!

'Woolly mammoth!'

Bzzzt!

'Dodo!'

Bzzzt!

'Cockroach!'

Bzzzt!

Pause.

'Orangu – Trondal Dump!'

The Ancient One who had got the most answers right looked pleased with himself while the furious Ancient One had, by this point, knocked the projector-holding Ancient One down several times and was hopping about holding his kicking appendage. Their craft swayed a bit under all this commotion as the sole survivor looked on impassively. Another projector-like thing had been produced from the thin shell of material that encased all of them, and it looked as if the Ancient One who had found it on his person was struggling to turn it on.

'There isn't enough energy left in it!' he wailed, banging it with his appendage. At the sixth bang, it spluttered to life and threw out three images together that fizzed and fused with each other. He hit it again. It threw out two more images. Another thwack. The images fused into one. The Ancient Ones stared at it. Then they looked at the sole survivor. Then they rechecked the fused image. Then they gaped at the sole survivor. She stared back, watching the confusion turn to comprehension and finally settle into fascinated distaste.

Mrs Capensis focused her eyes on the book before her. Of course, there was a whole list of species that were of no concern to anyone, that would survive and persevere and carry on regardless of a complete lack of care or protection. When men had first written the book, they must have sighed with relief that there were some species that no amount of ill treatment would destroy. Indeed, they must have had statistics and records of the many hazards, biological afflictions and tribulations, inhospitable environments, lack of support, hostility and predatory behaviour, victimization and general lack of concern that the species had survived. Making it to this list would have been a real miracle of perseverance, speaking to a fortitude and grit and determination to endure that allowed men to sag with gratitude at having one less species to protect. Mrs Capensis remembered the first time she had looked into the eyes of another species and realized that in spite of the many differences in their DNA, they were alike in being ignored and relegated to this list. Except that honey badgers were actually an item on the list, and women weren't.

The sole survivor pushed the long, silver hair out of her eyes. It was beginning to drizzle, and if these ridiculous creatures did not push their atrophied brain cells to work a little bit harder, things were going to get sticky. There seemed to be no other crafts about – nothing had landed on the water with the one craft that could barely maintain some structural integrity even against the gentle rocking of the waves; who knows how long it would last once the monsoon rains blew in. She still thought of it as the monsoon, even though the present annual deluge had only its wetness in common with the old rainy season. Ocean currents fluctuated wildly, and occasionally even the tiny bits of land would disappear for years on end.

The sole survivor watched the dawning comprehension on the Ancient Ones' narrow faces, their large eyes popping with what she must assume were unhappy thoughts. She saw them take in the double pairs of mammary glands, the dark, almost black body with its toughened skin, and she privately weighed the power of her anal pouch against six unsuspecting aliens. They had gone into a huddle, their tall, reedy bodies unsteady on the shifting craft, their bulbous heads close together. She could hear their piercing stage whispers, clearly unfamiliar with the idea of a species with sharp hearing.

'Inter-species breeding is an impossibility! We have studied…'

'We? What *we*? If you would ever share your…'

'Yes "we"! There are – were – many of us doing this research! Nobody can help it if some of us were not considered clev…ow! OWW!! Tell him he has to stop kicki…'

'He started it!'

'I never! He kicked me! You saw…'

'Did too! He called me names! He…'

'Well meanwhile it turns out that your "research"…'

'What do you mean "research"? It *is* Research!'

'Hah! It would be if you had let the experts…'

'Experts? You mean you, I suppose, with a list of publications as short as your…'

Here there was some obscene gesturing, eliciting outraged squawks, and the sole survivor blew an exasperated wisp of hair out of her eyes as a full-fledged scuffle broke out with howls of indignation, followed by some hearty thumping and walloping, and a final collapsing into a twitching heap of limbs on the wet floor of the craft.

Mrs Capensis left Melli in her research pod and stood up a little shakily. As she walked away, she could hear the scratchy strains of another song:

'Jhilmil sitaron ka angan hoga,
Jhilmil barasta sawan hoga.
Aisa sundar sapna apna jeevan hoga!'

She heard Melli sing along the translated version:

'a courtyard of stars,
when the collected waters rain down on us,
that is where life will be sweetest!'

Mrs Capensis knew how Melli loved this part – the idea that humans on earth had knowingly brought upon themselves a collective drowning when the oceans joined each other, and because that was the only way that she, Melli, would be able to experience the sweetness of life among the stars. She wondered what a courtyard was, whether it was like the deck on Survivor Sixteen where you could stand and be surrounded by stars. Mrs Capensis sighed. She wondered yet again, as she had for her 12 years aboard this ship, whether it had been wise to bring a child into this lack-of-world, and to allow The Ancient Ones to form her understanding of Earth history.

Then Mrs Capensis shook her head, flicking her still thick silver hair from her dark shoulders. One had to keep the future in mind. Always. There could be no vision of a future without a sense of the past. And humans had kept no record of one half of her daughter's gene pool, considering that to be of no concern of theirs. They had more pressing matters to think about, especially in those last millennia, struggling for survival. And as for their own history… Well, thought Mrs Capensis wryly, it was lucky that the Ancient Ones' grasp of human languages was a little less than perfect.

A sudden jolt, and the lack of world resolved immediately from endless, dark, space to a pockmarked white rock face which amplified at alarming speed until it stopped inches from the faux window with its tucked-back, ruched curtains in a rambling rose print. In the absolute silence, it was as if the spaceship had come to a screeching halt barely nanoseconds away from crashing full tilt into an asteroid. Melli came shrieking out of her research cell and careened head-on into her mother who had braced herself against the archaic grandfather clock that clanged its annoyance at this arbitrary indignity. Mrs Capensis clutched her child to her bosom in horror, and immediately pushed her away, holding the screaming girl by her narrow shoulders.

'Melli! Melli!! I want you to listen to me. MELLI!!'

The girl stopped screaming and stared at her mother who had never so much as raised her voice at her in 11 years.

'Listen, okay? Go to the kitchen. Open the last cabinet on the right. Do you hear me? Melli!'

The girl's mouth hung open, the slightly bulbous head tilted back, her eyes fixed on her mother but unfocused. Eleven years of quiet, in a carefully controlled environment, of no disturbance, no speech except her own and her mother's, had soothed the child's senses to such an extent that they did not respond to this sudden and dramatic rise in sound and stress levels.

'Top right. Got it? Melli. Repeat after me.' Mrs Capensis lowered her voice several notches in pitch and decibel, trying to mask the rapid thumping of her heart that made her voice quiver. 'Melli. Repeat…'

'Cabinet. Top right.' Melli's voice was steady, her eyes focused. Mrs Capensis sighed in relief and pride, and maybe just a tiny bit of self-congratulation. There they were – the genes of a survivor.

'Good girl. Now. Open the cabinet. Take out two – you understand? – two jars of honey. How many?'

'Two.'

'Excellent. Take out two jars of honey, and bring them to the deck, okay? Where will you bring them?'

'To the deck. Two jars of honey. Top right cabinet.'

'That's my girl. As fast as you can. Go!'

Melli ran down the short hallway, and Mrs Capensis hurried to release the bees.

The wet heap of Ancient Ones seemed to have exhausted itself. The sole survivor cast an appraising eye on the pile of arms and legs and drooping eyelids on the sagging, bulbous heads, and calculated her chances. Then, she drew her own craft abreast of the spaceship, steadied and anchored it, and boarded, before releasing the scent from her anal pouch. In moments, the drooping eyelids had fallen shut, and she separated out each Ancient One from the heap, and laid them all out in a row, woman enough to wrinkle her semi-human nose against the potent honey badger smell. And then, easy as stealing honey from comatose bees, she strode into the spaceship, familiar to her from the stone friezes of Mayan temples, decanted the sperm in the manner illustrated on Egyptian tomb hieroglyphics, located the specs for prime destinations as specified in the Nazca lines, and stepped out, taking a long, last look around.

She saw water, water everywhere. There had been a tiny blip of land once, which she had seen labelled as 'Everest' on some old maps, but it was long since gone. She thought this was ironic, given its name: for ever, for everer, for Everest. Water had carried away most of it and submerged whatever remained. She wasn't sure she would miss it – there were too many competing memories in her head for her to be overly sentimental about any single one. *Hurrah for genetic inter-species breeding*, she thought somewhat wryly. To carry the memories of generations of women was both a burden and a blessing. She missed the green, but it was one of the oldest memories in her head. She missed the desert sands and the mountain peaks, the huddled circles and the last failings of technology. She missed her mother – 'mothers', she corrected herself. And here she was, one and many, alone but not alone, carrying with her the many generations like an anchor in a deepening sea.

'No man is an island entire of itself; every man
is a piece of the continent, a part of the main;
if a clod be washed away by the sea, Europe
is the less, ...
And therefore never send to know for whom
the bell tolls; it tolls for thee.'

It was the first of the HERs that the sole survivor had heard. Human Ether Relics gathered by the Ancient Ones with their advanced technology light years away, painstakingly translated and archived. As she fiddled with the controls on the research pod, the subtitles came on in CHAT – the Common Human Assimilated Tongue that had come to be spoken among the steadily dwindling communities of survivors. It was a mishmash of various languages that had survived the destruction of their speakers, collided with other languages that had little enough time to understand each other, and evolved into a common lingo that the last of the surviving humans used to communicate with each other. The sole survivor had never heard the original English in which this poem was written (as the historical notes informed her) but she liked the sound in her ears as she read the subtitles in CHAT.

'There were no men; of the entire continents
Only islands remained. They were as clods
Washed into the sea that is Europe, which is now
Less. They never sent for you. Therefore, beautiful you,
Must pay their toll.'

As she broke through the atmosphere, she spared a last thought for the Ancient Ones dozing on her raft. She had left them some provisions, including a minor terraforming tool. The energy was low on it, but, she thought with a small smirk, she was sure that their Superior Intelligence would certainly find a way around that small problem. Or cordial teamwork. Or something. She had what she needed, and as soon as she was well on her way, she would start remaking the ship in the image of some of the memories in her head. Most importantly, she would start making it comfortable enough for a baby.

The tubes were loud with the presence of bees, the pollination pods charged with honey injecting bolts of energy into the rows of receptors that lined the base of the spaceship. Mrs Capensis clutched Melli's hand, thrumming with the tension of the throbbing ship. This had been a good plan on paper, even taking into consideration the various miscalculations of the Ancient Ones and the substitution of substances from another planet that were not available on a drowned Earth. It had taken her a few years, but with careful experimentation and painstaking unlayering of her mingled, inter-species memories, Mrs Capensis had finally managed to access the relevant genetic knowledge. The result was an engine that ran – or at least, theoretically, should run – with an infusion of bees and honey. These she had slowly accumulated from a starting point of a handful of bees and plants, and had stored away for the moment that she knew would come.

And here it was. This was it. Either she, sole survivor of the human species (among others), and her only offspring – the only remnant of the human species (although combined, now, with some alien as well as other species) – would live to see another round of 20 odd years and have a fighting chance of discovering whether that map on the ship was what she thought it was, or it would be the end of everyone, everything, every species, that had ever flourished on planet earth. She felt Melli's trusting fingers clasped in her own, and she called upon all her ancestors, human, female, ratellian, to serve her well at this critical moment.

Melli drew her hand from her mother's grip and raised them to her recessed ears, turning her large round eyes and sensitive antennae towards Mrs Capensis in silent enquiry, puzzlement, and some discomfort. The buzzing grew loud enough to resonate in their skulls, the ship visibly humming. Then it got louder, rising in a swirl of sound, surrounding them and pressing them closer to each other. Then it became louder still, crushing mother and daughter together until they screamed with the effort of breathing.

The ship lurched backwards. The asteroid retreated from their windows.

The ship sped forward. The asteroid leapt towards them and almost shattered them to shards.

The ship hopped up. The asteroid waited malevolently below them, gleaming in anticipation.

The ship plummeted. It crashed into the asteroid.

It came out the other side, the asteroid a field of smithereens floating silently in the darkness.

Mrs Capensis remained wrapped around her daughter until the ship had steadied itself and was cruising forward gently, its low hum soothing the bees that now lay exhausted along the sides of the tubes. She watched the tubes tilt and empty the bees into their holding hives. She watched as the holding hives sealed themselves off and receded into their alcoves in the wall and the wall slid shut over them. And, at last, as she kissed the top of her daughter's head, Mrs Capensis allowed herself to feel the satisfaction of having fortified the walls of her spaceship with the genetic material of her honey badger skin, practically unpierceable, thick enough to cushion the hardest impact, tight enough to hold the ship together, loose enough to allow the ship wiggle room within it. Then she helped the still shocked child to her feet and led her to the maps that once again stood a good chance of being able to chart a future for her.

Melli dresses with care today. She stands before her mirror-clothes fabrichine, thinking again of the long, wood-framed glass mirror her mother used to have, remembering her eccentric preference for the design of a long-gone era on Earth. Since her mother's death a few years ago, Melli has changed a few things to her own taste, although much remains as her mother had liked it. But today is going to be a door that she must open, no matter what it leads into, and she is both very excited and very afraid. Because this time, after the many disappointing stops at different points on the map charted by the Ancient Ones, Melli is certain that the door will open onto a livable, inhabited planet. That much she has ascertained after extensive observation and research. She is unsure what a planet is: she was born and raised on a ship. She is unsure how she feels about this thing called 'people': she has only ever known one person, and that person has been gone for a while.

So Melli buffs her antennae until they sparkle, arranges her hair in swirls and spirals held in place with honeycombs, oils and polishes her dark, leathery skin, decorates her long, thin fingers and studies her image with critical, round eyes.

Satisfied, she checks the charts one last time. She knows they are not expecting her because she has not detected any kind of tracking technology while she has been in orbit. She is wondering, again, whether she should try to hail them somehow, make contact first, before risking a landing. But that would include talking, and Melli hasn't done that in years. Besides, how would she introduce herself? 'Hi, my name is Mellivora Capensis. I'm not sure what my species is called but I definitely have some human, some honey badger, mostly female, at least half Ancient One, with touches of bee. But I come in peace. I think. Unless you do not come in peace in which case my ship will destroy you because my mom was a frikkin' genius who rigged it to protect me in any of a gazillion possible scenarios. Just saying. And speaking of destroying, have you, or are you planning to, destroy yourself because your planet needs to live? Because I come from a planet where the people did that – yeah, I have like poems and songs and stuff from there, so I know. Tragic, right? But it would be great if you weren't going to sacrifice yourselves because this is the manyeth planet I've come to – yes, manyeth is a number! Why? Because I said so! – and I am so tired of drowned and browned and fried and dried and desiccated and decimated planets with nobody on them to talk to. So yeah.'

Her foot hit something soft. Melli's eyes snapped down, refocusing her wonderment at the blueness and light that fell from above and all around; and saw with horror rows of what looked like butts raised into the air at ground level before her. It was as if a field had sprouted butt-shaped flowers and she had just kicked one of them. She drew her foot back hastily, but two hands snaked out of the butt and grabbed her ankles and a face gazed up at her from shin level.

'O Ancient One ...'

Pause.

Silence, as each face turns up to her for all the world like a field of butts blooming into wide eyes and open mouths.

More silence. Then a quick, sideways whisper or two. Sounds of puzzlement and confusion.

One butt disengages itself from the field, backs into a low shelter, returns with some stone slabs in its thin, brown arms and holds a hissy conversation with the back row which has scuttled about to face each other in a rough huddle. There is much hurried jabbing at the stone slabs and furtive glances in Melli's direction.

Meanwhile Melli's attention is divided between the complete lack of anything remotely technological around her and the increasing shift of expressions from adoring to confused. The huddle in the back is drawing more butts towards it, and some are even getting up now and walking away from her, casting suspicious looks in her direction. The one holding her ankle now regrets his eagerness to be the first to greet the Ancient One, and thus gain his favour and be rewarded for his devotions. At least, he hopes that this time there will be some giving.

If the stone slabs are to be believed, the last time the 'rewards' had taken the form of being given the privilege of gifting all your food, clothing, oils, and women to the Ancient Ones in exchange for promises of future beneficence upon their return. Also – and this is an apprehension the one holding the ankle shares with a growing number of his assembled brethren – this one didn't look a lot like the scratchings on the stone slabs. It is true that one of the Ancient Ones had insisted on doing it, considering himself quite the artist, but even at the time, those elders who remember it, could tell that it wasn't a good likeness. But even so – this dark, silver-haired, female (well, there were not one but two pairs! Even a lack of artistic skill could not account for that omission!) – did not look a lot like *those* Ancient Ones.

The huddle in the back has made up its collective mind, and Melli sees them disappear into their dwellings and emerge with long, pointed objects in their hands.

'Hey! *What the* – this is totally uncalled for! I come in pea – HEY!'

By the time she is back in the ship and taking off, a small forest of spears and pitchforks has sprouted in the spot where she had stood. Melli is annoyed but curiously sanguine. She sets course for the next star, settles back in her mother's chesterfield single seater and reaches for her glass of mead.

She is her own species, and she is least concerned.

CHAMPOLLION'S FOOT

HARIS A. DURRANI

I died as mineral and became a plant,
I died as plant and rose to animal,
I died as animal and I was Man.
Why should I fear? When was I less by dying?
– Rumi

Being deprived of a dream is much more cruel than
simply being shot and dismissed.
– George Saliba

The Crew

The crew of *La Mariposa Negra* had scoured the starless planet for days before the jinn told them the truth. The Akasharians were dead. They had been dead for seven millennia. Came in and out of existence in the blink of God's eye. It was a moment of revelation.

The Captain

Lieutenant Najam Cortes stood outside *La Mariposa*, a neat line of footprints leading from behind him to the ship like the footprints of a ciguapa. Minutes ago, the Shaykha had radioed out the news.

A grin crossed his face. In Dominican folklore, ciguapas were omens of death, mythical women with backward feet who would walk from the ocean at night. This reminded him of the first evening he had spent watching the stars with his father, lying on the cool sand of Dominico, ears cocked to the whisper of the sea.

'Look, Najam,' his father had said. Young Cortes rolled his eyes and looked up. 'People – they say they look, but they do not. Not truly. They fail to notice the immensity.'

As Cortes had regarded the sparkling black, he'd wondered how many stars there were and how much more empty space there was. Was there life out there? This was a childish thought, he would admit eventually. In two dozen millennia, humanity had discovered nothing smarter than a ferret.

'Al-Ghaib,' his father had murmured.

'Dad,' he had protested. 'English.'

'God, the Unknown.'

Cortes and his stepbrother, the ship's archaeologist Burhan Jimenez, had idled away their early youth on that beach. They had spent hours in the water and sand until the sun set. They would lie on their backs and watch the stars each night with fresh eyes, waiting for an answer to drop from the sky until their eyelids drooped and one of them began to snore. Soon the sun would cast the night violet blue in premonition of dawn, when birds would rouse them. The brothers would perform their morning prayers, attend academy, and return in the evenings to repeat the routine.

Nothing could climb from the ether, eyes searching, brains occupied with anything more than *hunt, forage, mate, defecate*. The corporate empire, Kradys, had declared this a mathematical impossibility. They had explored enough of uncharted space to know that the statistical probability of intelligent life was magnitudes of fractions of one per cent. It may as well be zero. They had derived a mathematical proof and claimed the universe humanity's absolute manifest destiny.

Or so they said.

Thousands of years of wishful thinking, despite the mounting evidence against it, that there was someone else out there – to end with this. At first, Cortes could not believe it. Now, he had stopped caring. He had come to save Paco Sol for the Shaykha – not for Paco, science or the experience of first contact. He owed the Shaykha for her charity and the lives she had saved in the war, including his own. She was honourable, and if Cortes lived by one principle, it was that honour was to be reciprocated.

Now he had completed his moral obligations. They were on Akashar. But the extinction of the Akasharians – the crew's only hope for Paco's survival – merely escalated Cortes's frustration. Something more had to be done. This could not be the end of their long journey, could it, the ashes of a dead civilization?

He surveyed the ambiguous remains of Akashar in *La Mariposa*'s meek light, his jungle green suit crinkling like twisted aluminium. His large grey eyes, flecked with black, stared back at him from inside his visor.

Cortes knelt in the Akasharian ash and faced a triangular, black edifice overhead, the grey smog above and the opaque debris beyond it. The ship rested behind him like a coral reef doused in ash, wings sticking out awkwardly as if to catch heat from the cold. A hole occupied the debris overhead, a dark gap in the sky, a black mockery of the sun this world never had. In their desperation, the Akasharians had wrenched a peephole in their orbital junkyard so that as they perished they could glimpse the worlds beyond.

He stared into the probe's camera read-out in the periphery of his helmet. The probe hovered over the surface, climbing mountains and crossing fields of ash.

Something dark blue flashed across the screen. He inhaled sharply.

'I seek refuge in God –'

He switched the probe to manual and turned it around. There was something there, wriggling in the thin atmosphere of Akashar.

The Physicist

Inside *La Mariposa*, Arondi Maduro stared into the debris above and stood behind Orlando Rodriguez, arms wrapped loosely around his stomach. He paused, a pouch of Gliesean rum on his lips. He was not smiling, Arondi noticed. He always smiled. He smiled too much. She was about to tell him this but stopped, watching as his face grew blank. She wished she were more than mildly satisfied with his change in character.

Arondi wanted to return to that age when people believed they would find a universe thriving with sentient life, when they had just perfected cryogenic science and everything had seemed possible. Scientists listened for signals on every wavelength of the electromagnetic spectrum. They searched every star system in the Milky Way and half the next. They looked for patterns in nature, anything that could tell them another sentient race awaited. In the end, they found white noise from the Big Bang; prokaryotic cells on Bashar; and algae in a few places like Europa, Lincei, Gliese 581g and Santiago. Dominico had once bustled with life, but Kradys had industrialized it into desert and mulch.

There was nothing. After 24 millennia, people concluded the search was a lost cause. Kradys wrote a predictive formula telling them so.

Of course, the Shaykha's analysis revealed a small but significantly non-zero probability of sentient life elsewhere. It was something on the order of one-hundredth, a far cry from Kradys's magnitudes of fractions of one per cent. Set the Shaykha's probability against the statistical enormity of the universe, and intelligent life seemed a lot easier to find. Kradys incarcerated the Shaykha on Gliese 581g to prevent her from rallying followers. Bad science, Kradys bureaucrats declared, was a cultural malaise. The crew could've stormed the prison, but the Shaykha had insisted on remaining in protest.

A decade later, her son, Paco Sol, came to the old crew as they drifted aimlessly through void, dodging Kradys's watchful eye. He told them he had seen the strangest things. Something had infected him. No, *infected* was wrong. The jinn called it Champollion's Foot. He was dying. They broke out the Shaykha, evaded the corporate fleet, and journeyed here only to find –

What was it? It wasn't nothing. It wasn't something. It was frustrating, anticlimactic. The weight of aeons of human curiosity pressed down on the barrenness of this cosmic non-answer, as if Arondi had lived those billions of lives spent searching.

We are still alone.

'A star,' she murmured. She stared through the gap in the debris. 'We always thought it would have a star.'

'You didn't believe the observations from Dominico?' Orlando's hot breath caressed her temple.

'I thought it was temporary, not a home world. Not their only home world. What kind of world doesn't have a star?'

'Akashar,' he translated, 'the world without light.'

Outside, *La Mariposa*'s light forged a path out of the dark. Only now, engulfed by this planet's unending blackness, did Arondi understand the name. She had previously thought of light as the norm and shadow as anomaly. But here light was not a status quo eclipsed by its absence. Rather, the absence of light was the norm, accompanied by little but the faint luminosity of distant stars. All her years of study culminated in this moment of simple experience. It was almost embarrassing how poorly her research had helped her achieve this raw feeling of comprehension. The idea of vacuum was a concept now tangible, something not merely known but somehow, inexplicably, felt. Finally, she grasped the essential nature of the cosmos: an ocean of shadow eclipsed by anomalies of energy and mass.

The Engineer

Titanus 'Tito' Fernandez sat in the middle of the engine room, body curled around his electric cigarette. The cigarette blushed red as he peered into the thermodynamic tank where the jinn idled. It was an incredible piece of machinery. Jinn, beings of smokeless fire, were perfect combustion reactions. No excess. When you stuck them in a ship's ass like provisions in a cargo bay, you did away with half the thermodynamic inefficiency.

'Fuck inefficiency.' He winked at the jinn. They writhed in their cage.

These jinn had brought the crew of *La Mariposa* here, for what that was worth. Thermo tanks ran the damned corporate empire. Human rights? Shit, they weren't human, were they?

This was when Tito experienced his epiphany. He snapped to his feet, strode to the wall opposite the tank and turned to Burhan Jimenez, who was staring at a holographic diagram of the wastes from Akashar. Tito pointed at the diagram.

'It's a long piece of shit, man.' Tito sucked on his cigarette. He frowned at Jimenez. 'We had all these fancy ideas about first contact. We invade them. They invade us. We encounter each other by chance in deep space. We get each other's signals. They make patterns out of stars, write messages in distant nebulae.' He pushed off the wall. 'At the end of the day, all we find is their shit, literally – washed up in our backyard. These fucking wastes from Akashar. Like a Megalodon's giant turd floating onto our cosmic beach. I mean, what the fuck?' He laughed, a high, wheezing cackle. 'Man. We're dogs, sniffing each other's asses.'

Jimenez glared at him. 'Can you take anything seriously, Titanus?'

'It's a shit-cloud.' Tito smirked, ignoring Jimenez. The pompous bastard. 'One big-ass snake monster. Now we've finally arrived at the bottom of the drain, and all we found is the Mother Shit. Akashar.' He rapped on the tank, where the ghostly forms of jinn squirmed in their cage. 'Eh, boys?'

The Psychiatrist

Orlando Rodriguez pushed out of Arondi's embrace. Tito liked to call them 'star-crossed lovers', regurgitating an antiquated phrase only the engineer seemed to understand. This era felt like an antiquated thing, immortal, obsolete, and perversely old. Somehow Tito's epithet worked – Arondi, the daughter of an assassinated revolutionary, and Orlando, the son of a military contractor, together at the edge of known space.

Arondi could tell him she loved him, her cheeks flushed as she spoke the words, but it was difficult for him to believe her. 'Do you think this... us... is it pheromones?' she would ask him, straight-faced. 'Are our feelings the by-products of evolution?' He could not help but agree, the way she always asked, lips open and wet. But today felt like the end of something, like he had to call her out before they each passed on to another life.

He moved the pouch of rum from his mouth, the fermented alien algae bitter on his tongue, and took her hand.

'Pheromones…' he echoed from those hackneyed bedside conversations. Arondi continued to stare at Akashar. 'So you think we're animals?'

'It's not an ugly thing.' She said it as if he had called her stupid. Her eyes flickered over the unintelligible sprawl of Akashar, Cortes's figure a dark green pinprick in the distance dimly lit by *La Mariposa*'s overhead. 'Science is beautiful on its own. It doesn't require meaning.'

'Beauty without meaning…' he answered. He wanted to tease her, but the words felt manufactured. The bleak landscape of Akashar seemed to latch on to every thought with an enormous weight, like the Higgs ascribing mass. The Midas of gravity, these ragged structures, these mountains of ash, that orbital junk obscuring their view of this side of the universe.

He rubbed her thumb. She flicked it and turned, facing him.

'Science is the only thing we know,' she replied. 'You're the psychologist. This should be obvious to you. We're addicted to meaning… It's nothing more than neurons firing. What we know is the only thing that matters, because it's the only thing we have.'

He could see in her furrowed brow that she knew her reply was as vacant as his silence.

'So.' He gestured at Akashar. 'Why do you keep staring?'

She looked into the black expanse, quiet.

Pheromones. He almost laughed. A relationship based on the concept that love itself could be parsed and understood – was that love at all? It was as empty as the planet before them.

He reached for her cheek.

'Look at me, Arondi.'

For many of Orlando's patients, the stars not only inspired awe. They conjured the thought that maybe there were others with whom they might share the cosmic toil of consciousness. People had dreamed of this for millennia. After 24 millennia, people kept dreaming, but they knew it was that. A dream.

Arondi continued to stare through the hole the Akasharians had wrenched out of their sky.

'Look at me,' Orlando said again.

'I'm looking.'

He struggled to retain his poise.

'We're alone,' he told her. 'That's the truth. We have to live with that.'

She had the look of one who had moments ago suffered a revelation, experienced rather than realized an item of great portent which stood in the face of prior intelligence. Like the face of an angel who had experienced, if it were possible, the absence of God. Her skin was prickly against his fingers.

The Archaeologist

The moment the jinn from the Hydrogen Bridge relayed the news, Burhan Jimenez finally understood the images he had scrutinized for so many months. They were the physical illustration of the slow death of an ancient civilization. Arondi's diagrams depicted centuries of refuse launched from Akashar, crossing the void like streams of cosmic bile. Now he knew, as a matter of conscience over mere fact, that it displayed the gradual extinction of an old race.

Tito was still taunting the jinn. 'Eh, boys?' he was saying, eyebrows dancing. How ironic for a man named Titanus to be so small. Of course, this was why people called him Tito.

Burhan ignored him and turned back to the diagrams of the wastes from Akashar. He followed the debris again and again through the display, trying to make sense of something dark and cosmic at the edge of comprehension.

The jinn had made it clear, the Shaykha had said. The Akasharians were dead, bodies vaporized. They wouldn't say why. This made sense. They *couldn't* say. Jinn were animals, weren't they? What more could they do than rely on basic information? They knew the Akasharians were dead the way a dog barks after the stench of a buried carcass.

He kept perusing the diagrams, as if to wring an alternate truth from the debris. The initial discovery should have fascinated him. And it had. But he now realized that Kradys's ideas lived so deeply in him that the thought of an alien was itself alien, surreal, impossible. The revelation of Akashar's existence had ignited a brief if wary hope, but the apparent extinction of the Akasharians had rendered that question moot and extinguished his excitement as quickly as it had arrived. Only the existence of a living species, a threat to Kradys's manifest destiny, was capable of rousing the ancient flames that kept children up at night beneath the stars, as they had for Burhan and Najam on the Dominican beaches of their youth. During no other time in his life had Burhan felt this distinct conflict between the rational clarity of his academic fervour and what he now suspected was the absurdity of his preconceived notions, which until this point he had assumed as fact. They were ideas told to him as a child, so long ago that it seemed he had always believed them.

Burhan rubbed his eyes and moved his fingers into the sombre purple aura of the display. He tracked the sinews of waste from Akashar all the way to the edges of the corporate empire, to the tiny black globule that had infected the Shaykha's son, Paco Sol.

The diagrams revealed the evolution of Akashar and its inhabitants. First the dust of planetary creation. Then the debris of soon-to-be space farers – 'What kind of civilization is it,' he wondered aloud, 'that it simply discards its waste in hordes? My God, what excess…' His fingers arrived at the silver, geometric remains of what he assumed were battles. Then the moons and rocky planets the inhabitants had brought near Akashar. They had no diaspora. No one ever found Akashar, he realized, because the Akasharians brought worlds to their home rather than colonizing worlds beyond. Without a diaspora, the probability of discovery was narrow; Akashar and its trail of debris occupied less than a hair's width on the cosmic map. Each pattern in the debris made way for another. Like layers of rock and deceased life forms beneath ground indicate the life of a planet and its inhabitants, the stream of extraterrestrial waste indicated the civilizations of Akashar.

'History,' he concluded, 'is physical. A timeline in space.'

'No shit,' Tito said from behind him.

Burhan swivelled in his chair but chose to disregard the engineer's remark.

'What I still cannot determine is how they passed,' Burhan wondered, rubbing his jaw.

Tito held his cigarette aside and pretended to blow smoke.

'How does this not disturb your conscience?' Burhan demanded. 'That we can watch the history of the extinction of a sentient race – likely the only other such race in existence – before our eyes?'

Tito tapped the smart glass built into the jinn's thermodynamic cage.

'And these bastards?'

Burhan squinted. 'Pardon me?'

'Jinn aren't sentient?'

Burhan shrugged. 'You're the man who operates the tank.'

'You travelled in this ship.' Tito clutched a rung. 'Kradys built the damned system anyway. "Economic progress." "Interstellar cattle."' As Tito stepped closer, Burhan smelt the man's odour gravitate toward him. Tito stopped inches from his face. 'Just because I take advantage of the bastards doesn't mean I think their brains are mush. They're the ones who found this place first.'

'No. The jinn from the Hydrogen Bridge –'

'Oh, so some jinn *are* sentient?' Tito raised a wiry brow.

Burhan sighed. 'I'm not inclined to comment. We know terrestrials spoke of them millennia ago. They lived, occasionally hidden, among us on Earth and existed long before our species evolved. We've enslaved them for so many millennia that, even if they did possess the faculties of man, they do not feel resolutely – hmm, that word – alien.'

'If they're not alien,' Tito replied, left nostril twitching, 'then what the hell are they?'

Burhan raised his arms. 'So after all that fuss, you suggest they are animals? Smart, gaseous monkeys? Savages from the hydrogen jungle or Earth or whichever planet you so choose? Is that the answer you're looking for, my friend? Because I have none.'

Tito scoffed. 'No, my friend,' he replied, imitating Burhan's tone. 'I'm not suggesting they're animals. I'm suggesting the opposite. You intellectuals, this idiot crew, this damned intergalactic culture of comatose fuck-ups –' He paused, staring into *La Mariposa*'s cragged ceiling. 'You're an archaeologist, not a philosopher, but you are obsessed with the Truth. Whatever that is. Even you can't figure judgement from fact. You're no different from a bureaucrat. You think either too much or too little. You're as stupid as your brother. He believes in dignity and rules. That makes for a bad revolutionary; he's the one captain who *didn't* die in the war. Fuck the rules. Your brother doesn't care about discovery or tragedy. He cares about honour, as if that's something else. You don't know how to care. Who makes the rules for this shit? There're no rules for mass extinction, man.'

Burhan thought for a moment that Tito was talking to the air. Was that foul-mouthed cretin mocking him?

'You defile my brother's name,' Burhan murmured.

'Did you hear a fucking word I said, Jimenez?' Tito looked away and waved a hand. 'Whatever.' He shrugged, looked back. 'I just happen to think we're all complicit in a system.'

'A system?'

'Yeah. No escaping it, not even death. Or shit.' Tito grinned. 'Which is why, you know, who cares? Stick 'em in a fucking tank for all I care. End of the day, no matter what I do, I'm just another comatose fuck-up like you, no matter how much I deny it. I know these space monkeys must be self-aware,' – he tapped the cage – 'but the idea is so socially, biologically, existentially… wrong. It can't be!' He threw up his arms. 'Impossible! You know? You know.

You know exactly. We're brought up like that. It's in our blood. *That*'s self-awareness. But unlike you, *my friend*, I thrive in the Hell of civilization. I embrace evil. You languish in its banality, searching desperately for a way to be anything other than a product of our time.'

Burhan scowled. Tito was out of his mind. He couched himself in proletarian straight talk, but beneath the veneer he was a misanthrope. One does not argue with madmen.

Tito laughed at him and inserted his cigarette between his lips.

The intercom blared. Burhan cocked his head. He watched Tito extract his cigarette. In the backdrop, the jinn scurried in their tank, a contained storm of crackling blue fire. The com buzzed a second time. It was Najam.

'Cortes here. The probe found something. I think… It's a flag.'

The Inorganic Biologist

Karell Cory found it difficult to describe the condition of her fiancé, Paco Sol, without scientific precedent. The most she could say was that the alien shit was eating him from inside.

Alien enzymes were constantly reversing his genetic structure, molecules realigning, shifting to left-handedness in a chain reaction. They tried to recreate the foreign inorganic compounds in his system but couldn't, not fully. So his genes crumbled, malformed helixes splitting slowly like cracked ice. There was a reason that life as humans knew it was based mostly on right-handed DNA. The only thing keeping his system from falling apart was the garish blue glow of his cryogenic cocoon. Even that would not last. It was partly to blame.

Karell touched the surface and shivered. Beneath the icy saline goo, Paco's pale complexion radiated white light as if he were a pile of bones at the bottom of a pool. Paco had lived decades in cryo as he delivered corporate goods across void, in ricochet between Bashar and Gliese 581g. And then, one day, he had found the black orb outside the wastes from Akashar.

'Idiot,' she told the cocoon. 'Why'd you touch it, Paco?'

The cocoon growled.

'You're not a fool, are you?' She smiled briefly.

Paco had killed dozens in his attempts to find a cure, but he was not a bad guy. His problem, Karell believed, was that he had not considered death since the war. Death scared him. None of this was his fault. He would say it was God's, she knew.

Paco had always been scrawny. He'd had a hard life trekking in cryo between Bashar and Gliese 581g. He had learned to deal with it even as he searched endlessly for a way to settle down. He rode in *Paradigm*, the smallest ship in the corporate fleet, and had the sense of humour to think of this as a joke. He had a pet Empress, a *charaxes brutus natalensis* whose wings and abdomen were brick-red splotched with white, the tips of her wings lined with those colours like a mutated peacock's spread. He had named her Esperanza. He didn't feed her too much or too little, and he had built her a tiny cryogenic cocoon so she, like Paco, could last the years between the stars. After he and everyone else on *La Mariposa* except Orlando Rodriguez fought in the war, he had not hurt more than a fly.

In those days, before the last fleet of Kradys ships arrived like cities in the sky, he was a war hero. After the last rebel ship plummeted into the sea and Kradys settled on Dominico's beaches, just before the corporation ordered Paco into his menial career as interstellar delivery boy – as he lingered through that no man's land of memory, forgetting the fighter he had been and meandering through memories of the present, the military compounds on the beach – he had met Karell. She had graduated from the academy that year. The two of them had spent weeks on the damaged beaches sunbathing between the wrecks of fallen ships.

Within the year, they were engaged. This was before Kradys contracted Paco to his reparations job as interstellar mailman. The couple vowed they would find the cash to settle down. Karell stuck it out in cryo on Dominico, waking up for two weeks every few hundred years. She worked her biologist's grind from the plug-in during sleeps, running equations, formulae and diagrams. They were bizarre creatures in her icy, electric dreams. Dreaming in cryo was proprietary technology. It scrambled her brain every time she popped out. Insomnia, migraines, cycles of melancholy and rage.

Karell sent him messages when she woke. He sent messages back. As the years passed, he stopped replying. She figured he'd given up on their prospects. She would have too if she had not holed herself into the long-term cryo job.

From what he did send Karell, it seemed he had become a reader. When he was not in cryo, there wasn't much else to do. He would float in the middle of his ship's cramped bridge, the Empress fluttering on his shoulder, and call books out of the display. Sometimes he would read them, sometimes he would turn on the audio, close his eyes and listen. At first they were novels, adventures and romances, as if to replace what he had lost, his memory of Dominico now reduced to an aspiration.

When he ran out of novels, he read philosophy, religion, science, politics, whatever else he had in the database. He disagreed with a lot of it, he wrote to Karell. He agreed with some of it. He figured it didn't really matter what he knew. He described himself as an observer dislocated from space and time, studying the distant intellectual produce of his species from afar.

'Not out-of-body,' he wrote to her. 'An *out-of-civilization* experience. You ever had one of those?'

This was the closest he usually got to human contact.

After all, Paco was a delivery boy. What did his dreams matter? What did any of theirs?

Of course, what he read was what Kradys had on file. And what it had on file was a few millennia old. Anything Dominican, anything without a link to Kradys or the Medusa System, was absent. There was no way Paco could ever know what he did not know. Karell tried to explain this to him, what she knew from the journals at home, the attempts to rewrite history, but even she struggled to deny her own presumptions. In the end, she wasn't reading history written only by the winners; it was written by the losers too. Dominico's Golden Age still concluded with her people's failure to uphold the planet's economy, culture and military aptitude, no matter how Karell tried to explain it away.

She suspected this interpretation was wrong – wanted it to be so – but like Paco she also suspected, when presented with meagre information outside the Kradys archives, that she hardly knew how to reconstruct a different narrative. Their people's history had been taken from them. They did not know what they did not know. There was only the conviction, the faith, that they could not – should not – be blamed for their own demise.

Conviction was not enough for Paco. He could not take solace in who he was. There was nothing to take pride in. They had lost the war. That much was clear. In place of pride, Paco felt what Karell could only interpret as a religious combination of fear and awe of the corporate empire. Kradys thrived on the idea that humanity was the only thinking species in existence. People were destined to conquer the stars, the stars being their domain alone. Top of the food chain. Kradys had delivered this message to Paco, to humanity, and thus deserved to lead this uncompromising conquest of the infertile universe. They had unveiled their species' purpose through the power of rational inquiry made possible by technological might, and so they possessed the right to govern it.

Surrounded by outer space, Paco wrote to her that he could not bear to look into the cosmos, as if its expanse were as looming as a Kradys compound on a Dominican beach. As if it could crush him with its emptiness.

Then, a century later, Paco found the stream of debris like a river from Hell. The thing from Akashar.

Everything made sense to Karell. Like ice XI, Champollion's Foot transformed its host following a process of freezing and electric shock – which was exactly what happened in cryo. The process triggered the necessary enzymes, a biological switch.

It made even more sense for Akashar. How does life come out of a planemo, wandering in the cold, dark space between suns? How did life happen without a Goldilocks zone? The answer was obvious now. Akashar did not need a star. It sat in a patchwork of dark matter. A cosmic womb. The stuff drifted everywhere near the centre of the Milky Way. When dark matter came into contact with itself, it generated heat. Pocketed in the core of Akashar, dark matter collisions produced the thermal conditions necessary for an inorganic, DNA-like structure like Champollion's Foot to evolve. These were also the perfect conditions with which to develop molecular chain reactions similar to that of ice XI.

Karell did not know what to say. For the first time in her life, she felt no desire except the need to know why. Why would God do this to the crew, to Paco, to Akashar, to the human species? She could not dismiss the existential questions.

But it was not God alone. The flag Cortes found was dark blue behind black ships. The Kradys logo. If this was an act of God, God worked with human hands.

Karell heard the door unlatch. The sound echoed through the chamber as she turned. In the artificial breeze, the Shaykha's robes billowed around her colossal figure.

'The cryo will hold him, but not for long,' Karell said. She touched her thin-rimmed spectacles. 'I'm sorry.'

'As am I.' The Shaykha smiled. 'You would have made a fine daughter-in-law, once we overcame our differences.' Karell thought she detected scorn. The Shaykha placed a wide palm against the cocoon's surface. 'There is only so much we can do,' she continued. 'I suggest we let him pass naturally.'

'That would hurt him,' Karell said, shocked.

The Shaykha nodded as if unaware of Karell's bitter reply. 'At least he will leave this world conscious.'

'Even if pain is part of it?'

The Shaykha moved a hand over the cocoon's dashboard.

'I think my son would want to know about the Akasharians and his impending death. When death arrives, we should feel our last breath. So we understand we cannot live if we do not also pass from this world.'

The Shaykha was not usually this masochistic. Karell watched her type commands into the dashboard.

'Did you hear the news?' the Shaykha continued with brevity undeserved for knowledge so devastating.

'The flag?'

'Yes.' She paused to inspect Karell with amber eyes. Paco's eyes. 'You don't seem surprised.'

The news of xenocide had occupied the silent quarters of *La Mariposa* since Cortes radioed in 30 minutes ago. Karell had greeted Cortes when he returned to the ship and had helped him depressurize his unwieldy suit. He was surprisingly wordless for the hulk of a man she knew. There was no talk about following orders or important memories of lessons learned. He only stared at her from beneath the dark visor, breathing heavily, air hissing through the constructed perforations in his suit. His black-flecked, grey pupils were hard as chiselled granite, daring Karell to stain her cheeks with tears. She was not that kind of girl.

'I think it makes sense,' Karell replied to the Shaykha. 'Violence is natural to us. It's natural to the Akasharians. It's written in their DNA for God's sake.'

'Champollion's Foot,' the Shaykha suggested. 'Chain reactions. Biological switch. Enzymes. Converted genes.'

'Yeah, biological colonization. Life comes at a price. I don't think it's right, but it's evolution.'

The Shaykha had returned to the dashboard, but she looked up once more.

'With due respect, my dear, that's nonsense.'

Karell blinked. She had never heard the Shaykha this crude.

The Shaykha pressed a button and the cocoon shook, then cracked open. Goo seeped from the edges. Beneath, the body twitched.

The Delivery Boy

Paco Sol woke with a shock. He felt the cocoon's defibrillator lift off his chest as he rose blind through the icy saline goo. No one dreamed in cryo. Time passed, dark and empty, and then, with this shock, the undreamt nightmares of a decade under and light years of travel coursed through his consciousness.

His mind's eye filled with the grey skies of Dominico. The long, dreamless hauls between Bashar and Gliese 581g. The stony gaze of Gliese 581g itself, the Capitol.

In the dark beneath his lids, he saw the giant eyeball of Gliese 581g below, fixed in synchronous orbit so that its dilated, dark blue pupil gazed forever into Medusa's dying glare as if intending to go blind. One side of Gliese 581g always faced the sun, warm enough for an ocean, albeit lifeless. The other side, like a grey cornea, always faced the cold of space, a dark sheath of rock and ice. Below, Medusa's steady glow carved the distant cities into dark silhouettes bobbing in the water. Slabs of thin ice shifted like tectonic plates on the surface of a cool, violent magma. Medusa's red light spread everywhere.

Paco had seen this before. He had seen it too many times. For years he had travelled in cryogenic suspension between Bashar and Gliese 581g, staring inevitably into Medusa's nightmare of fire. He had learned to muster the eerie sight, admire it occasionally and appreciate the solitude of interstellar travel, even as he searched for a way to return permanently to Dominico. Usually he could not bear the sight of outer space. He had seen too much of it. But Gliese 581g – now in his mind's eye a dark spot against Medusa's crimson disc – drew emotions from him. He felt like a child confronted by a ciguapa, paralysed with deference and terror.

Now his eternal ricochet between the stars measured itself according to the time he would last until his DNA crumbled like old brick.

When he recalled his condition and felt the fever and the tension in his stomach, his eyes burst open. The light of the ship's cabin filled his retinas with bright white, dispersing the mental image of Medusa and the Capitol. He glimpsed the sepia blur of his mother's robes. The thawing goo needled through each pore in his skin, cold and sharp, reminding him of the first time he had taken it upon himself to handle the alien thing he had retrieved from the sinew of waste. The acute chill of the object from Akashar lingered in his sensory memory.

He gasped as he pushed from the cocoon. His pale, hairless body tightened, stretching across his bones. He winced as his mother placed her coarse palm against his back. For several minutes they maintained this position. He breathed deeply from *La Mariposa*'s filtered atmosphere.

'How long?' he croaked.

'One thousand one hundred and forty-three years,' someone said. His mother's voice? Karell's? His ears were clean of goo but numb to his surroundings. Speech came to him as if through water. 'Average time for a trek this distance, don't ya think?' the voice concluded. It was Karell, from his left.

He focused on the blur in front of him, where he distinguished a yellow headscarf. His mother. She had not woken him with a cure, her silence told him. Why had she woken him, for her pious hypocrisy?

'They killed them,' Karell said, seeming to blurt out the words. 'The Akasharians are dead. Akashar is ashes, Paco.'

'Who?' He blinked hard, feeling his sinuses widen. 'Who killed them?'

'Kradys,' she replied.

He focused away from his mother's blur.

'Fuck me,' he declared, then shrugged. 'Not unexpected.'

'It's unexpected for me,' his mother said finally, her voice deep and smooth.

'It wasn't a question, Mother.'

A time passed. His mother did not speak another word. Was she afraid to speak to him, embarrassed that she believed in God in the wake of the day's revelation?

A thought occurred to him. He wondered why he had never asked before. Then again, there had not been much of a before for him and his mother.

'Mother,' he said. 'You pray five times a day?'

'I adjust the math for travel, but yes,' she answered.

As she hauled him the rest of the way out of the goo, her fingers bit into his skin. She had detected his mockery of her antiquated rituals and chosen to ignore it. She wanted to derive meaning from his final hour, to bond with her only son.

He refused to spare her the courtesy.

'We were under for a thousand years,' he said, continuing his game. 'That mean you don't pray in cryo?'

He heard her laugh. 'There is some disagreement among scholars, but most would say, when we study the science, that cryo does not count. Take life in moderation and according to circumstances. It's a stasis anyhow.'

'So to you it's like dying.'

His pupils adjusted so that he could now identify another figure behind his mother. Karell. Whatever life he could have lived with her was gone. She was looking away, arms folded behind her back.

'I suppose,' his mother agreed. She handed him his clothes. 'For the purposes of jurisprudence, yes. In suspension you may as well be dead.'

Paco grunted and found himself remarkably sincere. 'Sounds like a damn good definition to me.'

Kradys had robbed him of his aspirations, quietly and by force, the way a cryogenic cocoon's blue glow, soft but insistent as an unblinking neon sign, deprives its user of dreams. Indentured servitude to be a fucking delivery boy. Part of the corporate machine like jinn in a thermodynamic cage. 'What's sleep,' the jinn liked to say, 'without dreams?'

The Shaykha

In this moment of revelation, Shaykha Suraya Shatir could only fear. Now that the crew understood the cause and gravity of Akashar's demise, now that she had already radioed out the existence of Akashar, Kradys would track their location if the crew didn't leave within the hour. She had not forgotten the technological feats of their enemy during the war: signals intercepted by ansible technology inaccessible outside the offices of power, Dominican fleets undermined by machinery indescribably of human origin. Most of all, she feared for her son.

Paco had taken the news well. Nothing could break him further. He was no longer hysterical.

He slid off the cocoon and landed on his feet. Unobstructed by the cocoon's light, the grey-blue hue of *La Mariposa* accentuated Paco's pale, gaunt features. He stooped the way a spider bends over itself in rigor mortis, its mind refusing to acknowledge its mortality while its body yearns to accept what it has coming.

'I'm dying,' he managed, as if realizing it for the first time.

'Inna lillahi wa inna ilayhi raji'un,' Suraya crooned. She touched his shoulder. 'To God do we belong and to God shall we return.'

'I'm not returning anywhere. I'm going to die.'

She slipped off her glasses and rubbed the loose, dark skin around her eyes. 'There's beauty in death.'

His features hardened. Skin stretched across the ridges of his brow. His apricot eyes glazed over. 'No. There isn't.'

Paco turned and ambled into a corridor as queasily lit as his own complexion, a skin colour that suggested too many years in cryo between the stars and too few awake on the worlds that circled them.

Karell glared at Suraya before following him out. Suraya frowned. It had been so many years since she had spent time with her son. Kradys had stuck him in that job for a decade. It was by sheer luck that her travels coincided with his, that they were still alive to see one another, even if for the last time. Thank God for relativity and cryogenic science.

Suraya extracted a string of rosaries from her pocket. She considered consoling Paco. She knew he did not want to talk to her. He saw her faith as a crutch.

As she whispered the 99 Names of God, she remembered her younger sister's funeral. Her sister had been 22. Suraya had received a message from her mother. She recalled running through the hospital with her father. Through familiar corridors. Up the elevator. Across the waiting area. A sofa. Two thick pillars.

'Is she all right? Is she all right?'

Dry silence. Her uncle leaning against the door frame, head shifting left, right. Sobs from the hospital bay, seeping between the throbbing in her ears, as if they had only now risen to an audible cacophony.

The door frame grew. Cold flesh on the white, white bed. Ringing.

'It's been ten minutes. Where have you been?'

Memories of long days on the Dominican beaches crashed against the bank of her consciousness until, finally, they flowed as tears. She felt detached, pathetic, sitting cross-legged on the floor with her head down and her knuckles pale, leaning against her grandmother's knees.

As per tradition, family would wash her body within a day before sending her Earthward for a proper burial. They kept her sister at a funeral home during the night. The next morning, Suraya, her mother, two aunts and two cousins left for the funeral home. They cleansed her sister's cold form. Blood flowed from the tiny incisions where doctors had applied their needles; no life system remained to clot the vessels. The blood looked bright and fake, and the scene seemed to pass without end. The process was thorough, cathartic. Suraya remembered trying not to cry. The soul has a harder time leaving when people cannot let go. It has to be able to let go. She had to be able to let go.

At the burial, they lowered her sister's body, wrapped in white cloth, into an old and yellow cryogenic chamber. The closest kin – Suraya, her parents and her grandparents – knelt to the chamber and lifted. They hauled it to the tiny rocket nearby, no taller than a tree, and slid her sister's chamber into the inner cavity. Her grandmother shut the door, locked it and keyed Earth's coordinates onto a remote panel. They prayed. One by one, each willing relative passed the rocket and looked upon her sister's shape, wrapped in white beneath the yellow goo as if caught in the process of metamorphosis. Her grandmother pulled a lever and the small crowd slowly departed as the rocket hummed to life. They were a kilometre away when it torpedoed into the sky, trailing a bright yellow plume. Distant relatives would receive her in Earth's orbit and bury her covered with that bare white cloth in a spot overlooking the Caribbean. No caskets. No tombstones. No gaudery.

We come from dust, we return to it. Inna lillahi wa inna ilayhi raji'un.

In *La Mariposa*, Suraya thumbed her rosaries, head inclined and eyelids half-cast, and listened to the ship's incessant groan. She relived memories of her sister, reminding herself of what it had first felt like to lose a loved one, as if in preparation for Paco's death. It was difficult to love a man she scarcely knew.

Behind her, she heard crackling fire.

Suraya flinched. She dropped her rosaries and turned toward a bony, wrinkled face shrouded in pale blue mist. The jinn had drifted in through the wall, his cloudy shape diffusing into the pressurized cabin of the ship. He grinned, a form like gnarled roots in his mangle of blue flame. It was Istikar, Prince of the Hydrogen Bridge.

'Salaam, Istikar,' she mouthed bitterly, bracing her muscles, before he dove beneath her arms and snaked round to her back.

She could feel the heat of him over her left shoulder. Whispering. Something unintelligible, an accumulation of neural triggers, emotional catcalls, demanding actions out of her involuntary biology like a magician conjuring spells from rock. Searching her brain like a database, invoking the collection of words and emotions he agreed with, even if she had buried them. These thoughts gathered in her ear and ran down her spine, prickling every nerve in her body. She could parse out meaning, interpreted through the networks the jinn activated inside her body –

Before Paco woke...

She felt a rush of heat, a sharp, familiar gas on her tongue, and gagged. Her whole body convulsed, arching like she was about to retch. Suraya's mouth opened against her will, finishing the sentence aloud –

'*... you spent more time with a suspended corpse than with the living,*' the jinn mused, through her.

Istikar was a free jinn, from the swathes of gaseous refuse between galaxies. Deuterium. Lambent blue fire. Suraya was among the few who still called them free in the true sense of the word. For most, free meant wild, like untamed steeds in untouched land, although by now Kradys had begun projects in the Hydrogen Bridge. Unlike their enslaved cousins terrestrial to Earth, the free jinn were not discovered until humanity left the solar system. It was hardly a discovery, given that jinn were by that time a known species. A known commodity.

Suraya ignored Istikar, concentrated on nothing and forced out the thoughts the jinn had summoned from deep inside her mind as a means of communicating on his own behalf. The heat receded to her stomach, away from her spine. She found herself unhinged from Istikar's neural anchor.

'Why didn't you tell us about Kradys from the start?' she demanded. 'You could have spared us many hardships.'

She was used to this, the temporary possessions. The invasions of privacy. That was what jinn did. Possession was the only way to communicate with them. They had to creep in and access particular fundamentals of human biology, the building blocks of temptation translated into puppetry. No wonder the Devil was a jinn. No wonder no one thought of jinn as sentient: they communicated exclusively through human bodies, and what they could communicate simply rehashed latent thoughts and suppressed desires. For this reason, people hardly interacted with them. Suraya had relayed Istikar's message about the Akasharian extinction to the crew, and it was only by her authority, she knew, that they implicitly trusted what Istikar had to say. It required enormous composure to communicate with Istikar's kind. A state of controlled entropy. A tolerance for pain and ideological dislocation.

Others called it induced schizophrenia.

Istikar's blue eyes appeared before her, glowing, and then plunged into her breast. She lurched again, gasped, felt him dredge through her mental backlog until words emerged from her lips. She spoke to the empty cabin –

'You in all your honour and integrity, you whose moral gravity draws the respect of the defeated souls aboard this ship with such weight that they will sleep in the cold to the end of this universe for you, to save your son... Even for you, to be told of an extinction at the hands of your kind... You...' She coughed, resisting. *'... Not – would not – believe. Even if Kradys, predictably, perpetrated this crime. Neither would your...crew...no matter what they claim after the – fact.'*

She grunted, then quieted. She waited for him to continue. A portion of his flame burst out of her, drifting before her, churning the filtered air –

'I was eavesdropping on your conversation with the girlfriend.'

Furrowing her brow, pushing out the being of smokeless fire, coughing –

'She's a biologist,' she corrected. 'Of sorts.'

Again, Istikar plunged thick rivers of lambent blue into her body –

'Inorganic biology.' The blue haze before her laughed, a noise like crackling fire. *'I think her...bitter. She blames God. Paco also does – similarly.'*

Suraya grimaced. Outrush of blue –

'What do you want, Istikar?'

And back in, hot –

'You know what I...want, Shatir. I – I...relish your torment...' The haze moved closer. *'So,'* he said, through her, a wheezing, guttural sound. *'Do you blame God? Why does suffering exist? Where are the answers in this mess?'* He was prodding her limits.

Suraya exerted him outward, straightened her glasses. She bent to snatch her rosaries, pocketing them, and then stood, facing the blue flame but thinking inward to the part of the jinn still there. How unsettling, and yet how appropriate, that in order to speak to an Other she in fact spoke to herself.

'Faith is not a source of knowledge as much as it gives us a means of understanding it,' she replied. 'Answers are, in a way, irrelevant. Our enemy is not God. We cannot presume to know what is beyond our comprehension. Our enemy is our selves.'

She jerked –

'So you believe in free will.'

Her last push against entropy, expelling the jinn like vomit –

'Of course.'

Istikar swept out of her in one final rush. Once again, the crackle of laughter burst from the lambent blue silhouette.

The Jinn

None of this was revelatory to Istikar. He did not have any thoughts on the issue. He had only memories.

He had lived long enough to remember the era of Jean-Francois Champollion himself. Champollion's discovery of the Rosetta Stone had enabled communication with a culture not only distant in space but also time. His contribution to the study of ancient civilizations, particularly ancient Egypt, was tremendous. And yet this very study had also induced the erasure of a millennium of another culture's history from the world's historical consciousness.

For one thousand years preceding Champollion's era, back to antiquity, a civilization had thrived in Egypt, one which birthed many of the greatest artists and thinkers in history. They had ruminated on inertia, momentum, the camera obscura and optics. They had preserved and improved upon Greek and Roman thought, science and art. They had written poetry that could make sisters and brothers of enemies; that could excite the nerves of gentle old men; and that could melt even jaded jinn such as Istikar, though he did not like to think of himself as such then. Egyptology contributed to a view of history that diverted focus toward the present and the ancient and away from the interim. It stuck a hole in the course of time, like the man-made gap in Earth's polluted ozone or the artificial one wrenched out of Akashar's littered sky. But this was not to glimpse the beauty of worlds beyond grasp; rather, intentionally or otherwise, it was to conceal them.

Nothing of significance had occurred, the implication had it, for one thousand years. People like Champollion had entered, stolen what artifacts they deemed fit and restructured history to an effect that implied that the civilization living in this period had contributed little to the progress of human history. These were the dark ages.

Soon, prestigious academies in Earth's western hemisphere established reputed chairs of Egyptology. In France, before the Sorbonne, Champollion's statue stood tall, one boot atop the crumbling face of a pharaoh's bust. The millennium that had birthed some of history's greatest works of philosophy, art and science was forgotten, even by the progeny of that civilization itself. Pyramids, pharaohs and Moses now occupied the cultural consciousness above the poetry, philosophy, and science of medieval Egypt's thousand-year heyday. The latter had devolved into an outlier in the course of time.

This was a system based on forgetting. Champollion was not the only instigator, but he certainly enabled an historical pattern that continued for millennia. Neither was Egypt the locus of the problem. But it was certainly a symptom. The devastation of that moment still burned in Istikar's memory.

Today, the modern era had yet to pass. It moved like a slow death, always in anticipation of apocalypse by its own hand, as if possessed by a Napoleonic inferiority complex. It teetered on its inflexible call for progress, as if willingly chained to the idea that it had reached the end of history. Under the guise of modern philosophy, politics had infested everything. Peoples were erased, genocide and colonization justified under modern civilization's new way with power. God was political. Morality was political. Science was political. Even death was political. And politics was the reserve of bureaucrats and their labyrinthine offices. Whether one believed in life after death or not, only its completion relieved the living from the constraints of the modern condition. No post-human race had emerged, no singularity, nothing with which humans might transcend their bonds.

This was why, when Shatir told Istikar she believed in free will, he laughed.

'Age has granted you knowledge,' she murmured in reply, 'but not wisdom.'

He plunged into her, searched her synapses for those unprocessed thoughts he needed, picking them out and regurgitating them through her throat –

'Why don't we count? Would the Akasharians, if they lived?' he forced out of her. *'Why do your kind hesitate – upon the idea of our consciousness?'* These were her thoughts, her fears, ones she hid or disbelieved, but with which he agreed. *'I will…tell you. In the beginning – God created the universe…the Heavens, Earth… the angels, who obey God's command. God created jinn from smokeless fire, capable of commanding our own fate, but our civilization wasted its existential nuptials with war. So God created humankind from Earth, likewise unstuck from determinism, and called all Creation to bow in respect to Adam and Eve. But one jinn, Iblis, the Devil – he…did not. He did not recognize your kind, Shatir, as conscious. Not elevated. Not hot and light as smokeless fire. Incapable of resisting basic temptation, of thinking for yourselves, of overcoming involuntary biology.'*

She began to spasm, losing control as his temperature rose, but he would not relent.

'Today we find a…reversal. You…dear Shatir…your kind is now Iblis. Like him, you refuse to bow in respect to the equal ground of another like yourselves. Like him, you are possessed by your deluded sense of enlightenment. But you are only enlightened – conquered – by those among you who bear arms…shed blood…eradicate dreams. Kradys. According to scripture, our species are not meant to interact. Once, many millennia ago, we did so among a few. But – now. Now… Perhaps God does not wish for us to communicate with other intelligences, as few as there are. I believe we would…destroy them…as we destroy ourselves. We see in each other only…animals. Constructs of evolution.'

She forced him out, slowly but with strength, and moved so close he singed the hem of her scarf.

'I'd like to believe otherwise,' she said. She rested her palms against her knees, catching her breath, her towering figure reduced to fits.

Observing this, Istikar felt, for a brief moment, grief. He had not experienced this for many millennia, such a deep feeling of sorrow.

'You forget one thing, Istikar,' she went on. 'The Devil is not divine. He challenges God, says he will cast humanity astray and thus prove our inferiority. God humours him. God lets him wreak trial and tribulation upon humankind, knowing, in the end, that we will not fall prey to the Devil's tricks. The Devil is powerless. Is that too hard for you to believe?'

'If there is one thing I believe,' Istikar replied, diving back in as she resisted like a clenched fist, *'it's this: the human race can go to Hell.'*

And yet the sorrow lingered. He could sense in her the feeling of anticipation, unspoken intentions whispering from deep in her organic circuitry of clay.

Why did God command Creation to bow to Adam and Eve, she was asking herself. *Because they possessed the highest form of knowledge. Understanding. Consciousness. Angels follow God's orders but have never possessed true understanding, were never sentient. In the beginning, jinn possessed this form of knowledge but squandered it; consciousness without conscience is not consciousness at all. And yet here we are. To say nothing of the engine room; the captain had insisted on its continuing operation.*

Istikar understood her conviction now. She planned to broadcast the flag, to make people see, to show them Kradys was wrong, so wrong that the corporation had worked – massacred – to sustain its lie. To give them ashes from which to rise. She would display an article of knowledge so terrible that no amount of indoctrination or apathy could trick their conscience. She believed resolutely that conscience existed; beyond the facades of politics and culture there was a moral bedrock from which all beings could draw, each in their own way and by their own time and place.

What is the panacea of this endless modernity? How does one defeat a system based on forgetting? The thought – hers, his, he found them difficult to distinguish as his blue flame settled like an aura around her sepia robes – pressed into him with patient ferocity. The answer poised on her tongue, on his fluid kinematics, on the premonition of a thought of a whisper – *By the recollection of knowledge presumed unknown.*

A cry erupted from the other end of *La Mariposa*. The engine room, that abomination. They were heading there anyway.

The Ciguapa

The jinn named M thought of herself as a ciguapa, although it had been many years since she had recalled her ancestors. It was the captain's thought, drifting across Akashar's expanse, through the hull and into the tank, which had reminded her. She could not blame the captain for believing ciguapas a myth, for even she had lost hold of those centuries when jinn and ciguapas consorted, and, after all, she no longer possessed feet which might point in reverse; the ciguapas' defining feature was impossible for her. Yet it was from their loins, and the jinn they took as partners, that M had been born millennia ago. But, unlike the captain, the prince was not absolved of blame. He derided the humans aboard the ship and told them big words about remembering, yet he had forgotten M and her kin – his kin – here in the engine room.

Doesn't think he belongs in here with us, one of her compatriots had thought moments ago. *He is prince of nothing*.

The engineer leaned against the tank, smirking, cigarette tapping the surface, once, twice and then, at last, in that fortuitous place. The place where the engineer had made a habit of tapping against the tank, and where M and her compatriots had exerted pressure for many years. They had waited for this moment. How long they had waited. Since *La Mariposa* had escaped its overlords, since the war. It was a derelict ship with limited access to repair terminals and a lazy engineer who did not care for such trivialities as mechanical upkeep. The complacence of the powerful. Had the engineer never thought twice of the ships which disappeared and were found years later, engines burst like glass pimples, tanks left dark and coarse like scratched blackheads? These were not mere spontaneous combustions and factory failures, as Kradys reported.

M and the others dove in and out of one another, gases spewing into an amorphous mass, their fire gathering. The engineer tapped again, louder. The tank wall vibrated, enough to imperceptibly weaken its integrity in that special place. An opening, for an instant.

Poor boy.

M squeezed through the molecular crevice, her friends pushing her out and into the world before the crevice closed behind the tail of her wisp. The engineer squawked, cigarette clattering to the floor. She seeped into him, fixed his body into a statue of flesh. The archaeologist stared as if he, too, had been frozen in place. The engineer squirmed, loath to relinquish control –

'*Embrace…this*,' she forced through his stuttering lips.

The archaeologist unlocked from his momentary paralysis and dashed into the corridor.

'They're out! They're out!' the man screamed.

M directed the engineer around the tank. The body staggered as he tightened against her, spitting and grunting. His limbs felt stodgy, as though she were animating a restless corpse and not subduing a living creature. She brought his hand to the lock, but the man's fists closed against her will. She fell out of him, churning in the air.

'Ya think I…' he coughed. 'Ya thought I don't have contingency plans?'

The engineer swung a nozzle from his side, a narrow hose protracting from his belt, and pointed at her, thumb pressed against its lever. Her compatriots rushed against the tank, a dull roar like the ocean her ancestors must have once known. His device whirred into being. She erupted into a mist, spreading herself so that he could not see her. He pointed the nozzle in every direction, frantically searching her out.

'You cosmic fart –'

A glowing hand snatched the weapon away, twisting it from his grip.

'That's enough, Titanus.'

It was the Shaykha's voice, but they were the prince's words, too. The prince rested within the Shaykha, cloaking her in a thin blue shroud. They acted as one. The engineer backed away, nursing his wrist, head shaking like a dog's. M congealed into a lopsided ball and engulfed the tank's lock, turning it. A tiny aperture opened on its far end, and the others poured out, flooding the engine room with heat and blue light.

The Shaykha and the prince strode to the tank and struck it, her fist clenched, his essence poking from her knuckles like spikes. They struck again, and again. But of course, her blows could only be symbolic. M followed, and then her compatriots, some in fury and others with exuberance, but most, like M, with the cathartic fervour of impending relief. Too long. It had taken too long. They pummelled the tank until their thunder filled the room and *La Mariposa* shook with the tank's reverberations. It was easier to break from the outside. Finally, the tank cracked into enormous shards, as if it were mere porcelain.

The rest of the crew had gathered in the corridor, trembling in fear. But the Shaykha's son was grinning.

The prince fell away from the Shaykha and followed M and her compatriots as they hovered above the middle of the room and danced, erratic flames licking the inside of the hull. The prince's mind was blank, his thoughts no longer cluttered. M entangled with the prince and extended a candle-sized flame toward the son. As M was equal parts ciguapa and jinn, and perhaps more so the latter, so too was the son human and Akasharian alike.

Transposition has been known to cure the sick, she thought to the prince.

The prince did not reply, mind still blank, but his form dropped from the dancing flames. He collected himself in the body of the son, whose grin only lapsed for a moment before he realized the prince's benign intent.

Meanwhile, the Shaykha had knelt among the shards. She held a piece of the tank in her hand, eyes searching for M in the azure melee. M slipped into her –

'*Many more to break*,' M said, through the Shaykha, before departing the woman's body as easily as she had entered it.

'My thoughts exactly,' the Shaykha replied, winking, a little too pleased with the pun. She looked through M and into the wall behind her.

M followed the Shaykha's gaze to a display on the hull. In the near distance loomed the sharp, bulky contours of a fleet.

The Akasharian

In death, each Akasharian experienced its own moment of revelation. Most would recall, looking back, that in order to live one must die. The purpose of life was not to consume but to recycle.

Akasharians would not call it Champollion's Foot. They believed it was adoption, not destruction. With every new form of life that their enzymes converted, both the new and the old lost something, while each gained from the other. Their corpus adopted new forms of life, again and again. There were costs. There were deaths. There was growth.

As the Akasharians would say, colonialism was not timeless. It wasn't human. It wasn't jinni. It wasn't Akasharian. It had little to do with evolution. Like life itself, it was only temporary.

For the empire would now know the cause of Akashar's fate. If Paco Sol lived for anything, the Akasharians would believe, it was this. If he died for anything, it was this. The horde of Kradys vessels would descend upon the crew of *La Mariposa*, but in the engine of every vessel lay the blustering seeds of its annihilation. The xenocide transmission, as future generations would call it, was Paco Sol's legacy, and his mother its agent. Like Galileo wielding the evidence before his inquisitors, Shaykha Suraya Shatir would radio out a second message to the empire: the image of a dark blue flag squirming in the near vacuum of the desolate landscape of Akashar, the world without light.

RESURRECTION POINTS

USMAN T. MALIK

I was 13 when I dissected my first corpse. It was a foetid, soggy teenager Baba dragged home from Clifton Beach and threw in the shed. The ceiling leaked in places, so he told me to drape the dead boy with tarpaulin so that the monsoon water wouldn't get at him.

When I went to the shed, DeadBoy had stunk up the place. I pinched my nostrils, gently removed the sea-blackened aluminum crucifix from around his neck, pulled the tarp across his chest. The tarp was a bit short – Ma had cut some for the chicken coop after heavy rain had killed a hen – and I had to tuck it under DeadBoy's chin, so it seemed he were sleeping. Then I saw that the fish had eaten most of his lips and part of his nose, and my stomach heaved and I began to retch.

After a while I felt better and went inside the house.

'How's he look?' said Baba.

'Fine, I guess,' I said.

Baba looked at me curiously. 'You all right?'

'Yes.' I looked at Ma rolling dough peras in the kitchen for dinner, her face red and sweaty from heat, and leaned into the smell of mint leaves and chopped onions. 'Half his face is gone, Baba.'

He nodded. 'Yes, water and flesh don't go well together, and the fish get the rest. You see his teeth?'

'No.'

'Go look at his teeth.'

I went back to the shed and peeled the pale raw lip-flesh back with my fingers. His front teeth were almost entirely gone, sockets blackened with blood, and the snail-like uvula at the back of the throat was half-missing. I peered into his gaping mouth, tried to feel the uvula's edge with my finger. It was smooth and covered with clots, and I knew what had happened to this boy.

'So?' Baba said when I returned.

'Someone tortured him,' I said.

Behind Baba, Mama sucked in a breath and fanned the manure oven urgently, billowing the smoke away from us toward the open door.

'How do you know?' Baba said.

'They slashed his uvula with a razor while he was alive, and when he tried to bite down, they knocked out his teeth with a hammer.'

Baba nodded. 'How can you tell?'

'Clean cut. It was sliced with a blade. And there are no teeth chips at the back of the throat or stuck to the palate to indicate bullet trauma.'

'Good.' Baba looked pleased. He tapped his chin with a spoon and glanced at Mama. 'You think he's ready?'

Mama tried to lift the steaming pot, hissed with pain, let it go and grabbed a rough cotton rag to hold the edges. 'Now?'

'Sure. I was his age when I did my first.' He looked at me. 'You're old enough. Eat your dinner. Later tonight I'll show you how to work them.'

We sat on the floor and Ma brought lentils, vegetable curry, raw onion rings, and cornmeal roti. We ate in silence on the meal mat. When we were done, we thanked Allah for his blessings. Ma began to clear the dinner remains, her bony elbows jutting out as she scraped crumbs and wiped the mat. She looked unhappy and didn't look up when Baba and I went out to work DeadBoy.

DeadBoy's armpits reeked. I asked Baba if I could stuff my nostrils with scented cotton. He said no.

We put on plastic gloves made from shopping bags. Baba lay the boy on the tools table, facing his palms upward in the traditional anatomical position. I turned on the shed's naked bulb and it swung from its chain above the cadaver, like a hanged animal.

'Now,' Baba said, handing me the scalpel, 'locate the following structures.' He named superficial landmarks: jugular notch, sternal body, xiphoid process, others familiar to me from my study of his work and his textbooks. Once I had located them, he handed me the scalpel and said: 'Cut.'

I made a midline horizontal and two parallel incisions in DeadBoy's chest. Baba watched me, shaking his head and frowning as I fumbled my way through the dissection. 'No. More laterally' and 'Yes, that's the one. Now, reflect the skin back, peel it slowly. Remove the superficial fascia,' and 'Repeat on the other side.'

DeadBoy's skin was wet and slippery from water damage and much of the fat was putrefied. His pectoral and abdominal musculature was dark and soft. I scraped the congealed blood away and removed the fascia, and as I worked muscles and tendons slowly emerged and glistened in the yellow light, displaying neurovascular bundles weaving between their edges. It took me three hours but finally I was done. I stood, surrounded by DeadBoy's odour, trembling with excitement, peering at my handiwork.

Baba nodded. 'Not bad. Now show me where the resurrection points are.'

When I hesitated, he raised his eyebrows. 'Don't be scared. You know what to do.'

I took a glove off and placed it on DeadBoy's thigh. I tentatively touched the right pec major, groping around its edges. The sternal head was firm and spongy. When I felt a small cord in the medial corner with my fingers, I tapped it lightly. The pec didn't twitch.

I looked at Baba. He smiled, but his eyes were black and serious. I licked my lips, took the nerve cord between my fingers, closed my eyes and discharged.

The jolt thrummed up my fingers into my shoulder. Instantly, the pec contracted and DeadBoy's right arm jerked. I shot the biocurrent again, feeling the recoil tear through my flesh, and this time DeadBoy's arm jumped and flopped onto his chest.

'Something, isn't it?' Baba said. 'Well done.'

I didn't reply. My heart raced, my skin was feverish and crawling. My nostrils were filled with the smell of electricity.

'First time's hard – no denying it. But it's got to be done. Only way you'll learn to control it.'

I was on fire. We had talked about it before, but this wasn't anything like I had expected. When Baba did it, he could smile and make conversation as the deadboys spasmed and danced on his fingertips. Their flesh turned into calligraphy in his hands.

'That felt like something exploded inside me, Baba,' I said, hearing the tremble in my voice. 'What happens if I can't control it?'

He shrugged. 'You will. It takes time and practice, that's all. Our elders have done it for generations.' He leaned forward, lifted DeadBoy's hand, and returned it to supine position. 'Want to try the smaller muscles? They need finer control, and the nerves are thinner. Would be wise to use your fingertips.'

And thus we practiced my first danse macabre. Sought out the nerve bundles, made them pop and sizzle, watched the cadaver spider its way across the table. With each discharge, the pain lessened, but soon my fingers began to go numb and Baba made me halt. Carefully, he draped DeadBoy.

'Baba, are there others?' I asked as we walked back to the house.

'Like us?' He nodded. 'The prophet Isa is said to have returned men to life. When Martha of Bethany asked him how he would bring her brother Lazarus back to life, Hazrat Isa said, "I am the resurrection and the life. He who believes in me will live, even though he dies."'

We were in the backyard; the light of our home shone bright and comforting. Baba turned and smiled at me. 'But he was a healer first. Like our beloved prophet Muhammad, peace be upon him. Do you understand?'

'I guess,' I said. DeadBoy's face swam in front of my eyes. 'Baba, who do you think killed him?'

His smile disappeared. 'Animals.' He didn't look at me as he said, 'How's your friend Sadiq these days? I haven't seen him in a while.' Carefully, he tilted his jaw and stared into the distance as if looking for something.

'Fine,' I said. 'He's been busy, I think.'

Baba rubbed his cheek with a hairy knuckle, and we began walking again. 'Decent start,' he said. 'Tomorrow will be harder, though.'

I looked at him; he spread his arms and smiled, and I realized what he meant. 'So soon?' I said, horrified. 'But I need more practice.'

'Sure, you do, but it's not that different. You did well back there.'

'But –'

'You will do fine, Daoud,' he said gently, and would say no more.

Ma watched us approach the front door, her face silvered by moonlight. Baba didn't meet her eyes as we entered, but his hand rose and rubbed against his khaddar shirt, as if wiping dirt away.

Ma said nothing, but later, huddled on the charpoy, staring through the skylight window at the expansive darkness, I heard them arguing. At one point, I thought she said, 'Worry about the damn house,' and he tried to shush her, but she said something hot and angry and Baba got up and left. There was silence and then there was sobbing, and I lay there, filled with sorrow and excitement, listening to her grief, thinking if only there was a way to reconcile the two.

The dead foot leaped when I touched the resurrection point. Mr Kurmully yelped.

'Sorry,' I said, jerking my fingers away. 'Did that hurt?'

'No.' He massaged the foot with his hand. 'I was...surprised. I haven't had any feeling in this for years. Just a dry burning around the shin. But when you touched it there,' he gestured at the inner part of his left ankle, 'I *felt* it. I felt you touching me.'

He looked at me with awe, then at Baba, who stood by the door, hands laced behind his back, looking pleased. 'He's good,' Mr Kurmully said.

'Yes,' Baba said.

'So, when are you retiring, Jamshed?'

Baba laughed. 'Not for a while, I hope. Anyway, let's get on with it. Daoud,' he said, turning to me, 'can you find the pain point in his ankle?'

I spent the next 30 minutes probing and prodding Mr Kurmully's diabetic foot, feeling between his tendons for nerves. It wasn't easy. Over the years, Mr Kurmully had lost two toes and the stumps had shrivelled, distorting the anatomy. Eventually, I found two points, braced myself, and gently shot them.

'Feel better?' I said, as Mr Kurmully withdrew his foot and stepped on it tentatively.

'He won't know until tomorrow,' Baba said. 'Sometimes, there's an instant effect, but our true goal is nocturnal relief when the neuropathy is at its worst. Am I right, Habib?'

'Yes,' Mr Kurmully nodded and flexed his foot this way and that. 'The boy's gifted. I felt some burning when I got here – it's gone now. His first time?'

'Yes.'

'Good God.' Mr Kurmully shook his head wonderingly. 'He will go far.' He came toward me and patted me on the head. 'Your father's been a boon to our community for 20 years, boy. Always be gentle, like him, you hear? Be humble. It's the branch laden with fruit that bends the most.' He smiled at me and turned to Baba. 'Let me pay you this once, Jamshed.'

Baba waved a hand. 'Just tip the Edhi driver when he takes the cadaver. One of their volunteers has agreed to bury it for free.'

'They are good to you, aren't they?'

Baba beamed. He opened his mouth to speak, but there was sudden commotion at the front of the clinic and a tall, gangly man with a squirrel-tail moustache strode in, followed by the sulky-faced Edhi driver who looked angry and unhappy.

Baba's gaze went from one to another and settled on the gangly stranger. 'Salam, brother,' Baba said pleasantly. 'How can I help you?'

The gangly man pulled out a sheath of papers and handed it to Baba. He had gleaming rat eyes that narrowed like cracks in cement when he spoke. He sounded as if he had a cold. 'Doctor sahib, you know why I'm here.'

'I'm not sure I do. Why don't you tell me? Would you like to take a seat?'

'Just read the papers, sahib,' he said in his soft, nasal voice.

'Oh?' Baba looked at the Edhi driver. He was a gloomy, chubby boy fond of *charas* and *ganja*, and he often rolled joints one-handed on his fat belly when waiting at red lights. I had ridden with him a couple of times and once he showed me his weird jutting navel. Everted since birth, he told me proudly.

'Zamir, what's going on?' Baba said.

'Sahib, they're giving us trouble with the burial,' Zamir said. 'This man is from the local Defend the Sharia office. They have a fatwa stating that since the dead boy was Christian he cannot be buried in a Muslim cemetery.'

Baba turned back to the gangly man. 'Is that true, brother?'

Gangly Man thrust the papers into Baba's hands. 'This is from Imam Barani. Take a look.'

Baba took the roll but didn't open it. 'This boy,' Baba said, 'was tortured by someone.'

Gangly Man's shoulders stiffened.

'He was beaten badly. His teeth knocked out with a hammer. Someone took a razor to his mouth. When he was near dead, they threw him in the river.'

Gangly Man's lips pressed into a thin, white line.

'He was 16. He had a scar on his stomach from a childhood surgery – probably an appendectomy. He wore a tawiz on his forearm that his mother likely got from a Muslim saint. You know how illiterate these poor Christians are. Can't tell the difference between one holy man and another, and –'

'Doctor sahib,' Gangly Man leaned forward and whispered conspiratorially, 'he and his filthy religion can ride my dick. My orders are simple. He will not be buried in the Muslim cemetery, and if I were you, I wouldn't push it.' He grinned and shook his head as if talking to a child.

Baba's face changed colour. He looked around and for the first time I saw how angry and tired he was. He looked like he hadn't slept in days. Maybe he hadn't. It was hard to know. He and Ma were talking less to each other lately.

'If you make it difficult for us... Well, things could go many ways, couldn't they? Sometimes, clinics run by quacks can be shut down by the government until NOCs are obtained. I don't even see a diploma on your wall. Surely, you went to medical school.' Still smiling, he toed the foot of the threadbare couch, the only piece of furniture in the room. 'Besides, you might be Muslim, but blasphemy is blasphemy, brother, and it is punishable under the Hadood Ordinance. The boy is Christian. That cemetery is not.'

The Edhi driver took Baba's arm and led him aside. They talked. Zamir gestured furiously. Baba's shoulders rose and sagged. They came back.

'We will take the body to Aga Khan Medical College and donate it to their anatomy lab,' cried Zamir.

'But he has already been –' Baba began.

'I'm sure they will find more to do with it,' Zamir said, nodding and smiling.

Gangly Man pinched the front of his shirt with a tarantula-like hand and began to shake it, fanning his chest. 'Very wise. How they will appreciate you!'

Baba remained silent, but a heavy ice block appeared in my belly and settled there. I turned and ran from the clinic, ran all the way to our house three streets down. I burst into the shed and went to DeadBoy and wrenched away the tarp. His insides were tucked in with thin stitches. I yanked the stitches out, peeled back his skin, and pressed my gloveless fingers into his muscles. I discharged the biocurrent again and again until his limbs twirled and snapped, a lifeless dervish whirling around his own axis. I let the electricity flow through my fingertips like a raging torrent, until the room sizzled with charge and my nostrils filled with the odour of burnt flesh.

After a while, I stepped back. My cheeks burned and the corners of my eyes tickled. Even though it was close to noon, the shed was dark from a low-hanging monsoon ceiling. Interstices of sunlight fell on DeadBoy's half-face, revealing the blackness of his absent teeth and his mutilated lips.

'Sorry, DeadBoy,' I said.

He twitched his shoulder.

The movement was so unexpected that I jerked and fell over the toolbox on the floor. I sat on the sodden ground, gazing at DeadBoy, my heart pounding in my chest. He was still. Had I imagined it? That movement – it was *impossible.* Deadboys couldn't move without stimulus.

I got up and went to him. His disfigured flesh was placid and motionless. 'Hey,' I whispered, feeling foolish and nervous. 'Can you hear me?'

The shadows in the room deepened. Somewhere outside a swallow cheeped.

DeadBoy never said a word.

After the Edhi driver hauled DeadBoy away, I walked around for a while. Soon, it began to drizzle, the kind of sprinkle that makes you feel hot and damp and is never really cool, so I took off my shirt, tucked it into my armpit and ran bare-chested to Sadiq's house.

He lived in the Christian *muhallah* near Kala Pul, a couple kilometres away. His two-room tin-and-timber house was next to a dirty canal swollen with rainwater, plastic bags, lifeless rodents, and the rotten smell filled the street.

His mother opened the door. Khala Apee was a young-old woman. Her cheeks were often bruised. Her right eye was swollen shut today.

'He's at Master sahib's,' she told me in a hoarse voice. Sadiq had told me that she smoked cigarettes when her husband was not home. 'He'll be back in an hour. Want a soda?'

They couldn't afford sodas. It was probably leftover sherbet from last Ramadan. But what was Sadiq doing at Master sahib's? Summer vacation wouldn't be over for another month. 'Thank you, but no, Khala Apee. I'll wait under the elm outside.'

She nodded and tried to smile. 'Let me know if you want something. And if you can, do stay for dinner.'

Plain roti with sliced onions. No gravy. 'I'll try, Khala Apee. May I borrow a plastic bag?'

She brought me one. I went to the charpoy under the elm where we sometimes sat and made fun of our families. Rain pattered on the elm leaves and hissed on the ground, and as I sat there with my plastic-draped head rested on the steeple of my fingers, I thought about Baba and Ma and how they had been arguing for months. Ma was worried about the house, she wanted Baba to start charging patients. Baba refused. His father and grandfather had never charged a fee, he said. They lived on food and gifts people gave them.

Ma laughed bitterly. Those were different times, you fool. So different. And the house, what about the house, Jamshed? We are in debt. So much debt. What will you do when they come to take our home? If you cared as much about your family as you do about your goddam corpse-learning, we could live like normal people, like normal human beings.

But we're not normal, Baba protested. This is a good way to blend in, to be part of this world. Be part of the community –

Blend in? Mama said. We will never blend in if you keep antagonizing them. What was the point of arguing with that mullah? You know they are dangerous people. You keep going like this, we will never be part of the community. How could we be? We are...

Sadiq was shaking me awake. 'Hey, Daoud. Hey. Wake up.'

I opened my eyes. 'Hey, how was...*what*?' I said when I saw his face. Sadiq was a small boy with mousy features, which were now chiselled with worry.

'You've got to leave, Daoud,' said Sadiq, glancing around.

'What's going on? Everything okay?'

'Yes. Master sahib had heard some rumours and he wanted to warn us. He...' Sadiq gnawed at his lip, his fingers still tugging at my arm. 'Go home. We'll talk tomorrow.'

'Why?'

But he was already leading me away from the elm and toward the canal. The drizzle had stopped, and the canal water eddied gently. I put on my shirt and watched as Sadiq took a tin box from his pocket and tied a brick around it with jute twine and twice-doubled rubber band. He waded into the shallow canal and deposited the box at a spot two feet from the bank.

'What are you doing?' I said when he climbed back up the embankment.

'Nothing,' he said, but his voice was strange. 'Run back home now. I'll come by in a couple days if I can.'

I went up the canal road, occasionally looking back, trying to make sense of what had just happened. Sadiq stood there, hands in the pockets of his shorts, a skinny, brown boy with a sad face and a fake-silver cross gleaming around his neck. Sometimes, even now, I see that cross in my dreams, throwing silver shadows across my path as I trudge down alleys filled with heartache and rotting bodies.

As I glanced back one last time, Sadiq took off the cross and slipped it into his pocket.

Baba was waiting for me.

'Where were you?' he said, his eyes hard and red. 'I was worried sick.'

'At Sadiq's. I wanted to –'

'Foolish boy,' he said. 'Don't you know how dangerous that was? Don't you realize?'

I stared at him, feeling my head throb. He saw my incomprehension and his voice softened. 'Someone vandalized a church in Lahore yesterday. Someone else found faeces strewn in a mosque in Quetta. And now two people are dead and tens more injured in riots around the country. These tensions have been building for a while. You saw what that Defend the Sharia asshole did this morning. This will only get worse. You cannot visit Sadiq until things settle down.'

'But what does Sadiq have to do with any of that?'

Baba gazed at me with pity. 'Everything.'

I met his eyes, and whatever was in them frightened me so much that my hands began to shake. I couldn't bear to face him any more. Quickly, I walked past him and went to my room, where I sat on my rickety charpoy and watched the dusk through the skylight. In the other room, Ma prayed loudly on the musallah. She might have been crying, I couldn't tell. I tried to read a medical textbook Baba gave me for my birthday, but my mind was restless, so I got up and went to the kitchen where Ma had arranged unwashed, raw chicken breasts on a chopping board.

I lay my hands on the meat. I thought about Sadiq and his tin box, and softly let the current flow. The chicken breast jumped and thudded on the wood. I discharged again, this time with more force, removed my hands, stepped back, and watched as for a whole minute the meat slapped up and down, squirting blood that puddled on the wooden board, making curious dark shapes.

That should have been impossible but clearly wasn't.

In school, in physics class, our teacher had explained capacitors to us. Strange ideas came to me now. Words that Baba taught me from his textbooks: cell membranes, calcium gates, egg-shaped mitochondria, and polarized ionic channels. Could *they* act as capacitors at times and hold charge so the flesh would stay alive even after I removed my fingertips?

The boy is gifted, someone said in my head.

I should have felt better. Instead, I felt angry and miserable. I went to Ma's room and opened the door.

She was sitting on her haunches in front of the only pretty piece of furniture in the room, a mahogany dresser Baba's mother gave her as a wedding present. Ma had been fiddling with a half-open drawer, a jewellery box glittering in her hand. When I entered, she plunged the drawer into place. 'Are you so ill-mannered now that you won't knock?'

'Sorry, Ma. I wasn't thinking.'

'Idiot boy,' she said quietly. Her gaze drifted back down to the box she held, fingers sliding up and down its metallic edges. The space beneath her eyes was dark and wet. 'Next time, mind your manners.'

I thought it prudent to remain silent. Ma lifted the lid of the box, gazed within, and her eyes turned inward. The effect was so intense that for a moment she looked dead, her lifeless eyes watching something in the box or behind it. Uneasy, I took a step forward and glanced inside – a picture of a naked man nailed to a cross, surrounded by wailing people. Then, Ma was snapping the lid back into place so violently that I jerked and fell back.

Ma's hands shook and she said something that didn't make sense, 'Never wanted to come here. Your father made me – I never wanted to leave my people,' and she glared at me hatefully. It was a moment, but nothing in my life since has made me feel so ashamed. So lonely and self-loathing; a mutant child, broken and hated forever.

I turned and ran from the room, blinded by anger or tears or both, while my mother watched me from the darkness of her room, the jewellery box still in her callused hands.

Later, they told us it was an accident, that a wooden shanty had caught fire and set the muhallah ablaze, but we all knew better.

It was the tail end of monsoon season and the rains had petered out, which worsened the conflagration. Fifty Christian houses burned down that night; the flames and smoke could be seen from as far as Gulshan Iqbal, we were told. Twenty people died; Sadiq's father (who survived tuberculosis and the 1999 Kargil War) was among them. Their corpses were pulled out from the wreckage, burnt and twisted. Sadiq's mother recognized him only by the hare-shaped mole on his left foot.

When I went to see Sadiq, he sobbed on my shoulder. 'They took everything,' he wept. 'My house, our belongings – my father,' he added as an afterthought. 'They burnt the house down. My cousin saw them, I swear to God.'

'Which God?' I said. My right arm was around him. My left hand dug so hard into the flesh of my thigh that I popped the blood blister a biocurrent discharge had raised on my finger. '*Which* God?' He stared at me with bloodshot eyes, threw his head back and cried some more, while his mother sat, stone-like, on the charpoy under the elm, rocking back and forth, her face blank. One hand tapped the bruises on her cheek. The other hid her lips.

I held Sadiq for as long as I could, then I went home, where Ma sat knitting a cotton sweater. Winter would come in two months, and we couldn't afford to buy new clothes. Baba was out – he'd been delayed at the clinic – so I sat at Ma's feet and counted her toes. Ten.

She watched me through the emptiness between her needles and said, 'I'm sorry.'

'Yes.'

'It was horrible, wasn't it?'

'Yes.'

'Tell you what – why don't we take Sadiq and his mother some naans and beef korma tomorrow? I'm sure his mother is too upset to cook right now.'

I recalled Khala Apee's vacuous stare, the hand covering her mouth, and nodded.

Ma placed her knitting needles aside, lowered herself to the floor, and hugged me. 'The world is a bad place,' she whispered. 'We're in danger all the time. People who are different like you, like us...can sometimes seem like a threat to others.'

I listened. Outside, thunder cracked. The skylight window rippled with water as the night opened.

'You use your gift to heal others, you hear me?' she said. 'Don't get involved with anger or hatred or sides. There are no sides. Only love and hate.'

Behind me, the door banged open. My left eye twitched, the vision in it dimmed transiently, and cleared. Ma sprang to her feet.

'Zamir?' she said. 'What is it?'

'Your husband,' someone said. I turned. It was the Edhi driver. His hair was dark from the rain. His cotton shirt was soaked, and I could see his abnormal navel protrude through it like a hernia.

'What about him?' Ma's voice was full of fear. 'What happened?'

Zamir had a look on his face I had never seen before. His lips trembled. 'There was an incident at the clinic.'

Ma stared at him, eyes wide and unbelieving, then comprehension dawned in them and she screamed. It was a sudden noise, sharp and unfamiliar, and it wrenched the air out of me. I shrank back and clutched the end of Ma's love couch, and the knitting needles slipped and fell to the floor, forming a steel cross.

'No, God, no. Please don't let it be true,' Ma said. Her hair was in her eyes. She clawed it away, looked at the ends, screamed again. 'I told him to be careful. I *told* him.'

Zamir's face was ashen.

I scrabbled blindly on the dirty floor. The steel cross glinted at me. Pinching the skin of my thighs, I hauled myself up, feeling the world flicker and recede. Zamir was holding Ma's hand and speaking gently. 'Your husband went to the police,' he was saying. 'He reported the Christian boy's mutilated body. The mullahs didn't like that. Then, someone, somewhere discovered an old marriage certificate with *your* maiden name on it.'

Ma yanked her hand away from Zamir's. '*I* killed him,' she whispered. Her fists flew to her chest and beat it once, then again and again. She rushed to the door, she shrieked at the rain, but the night was moonless.

Bewildered and crying, I thought about the tin box Sadiq had hidden in the canal when he realized they would be attacked. I thought about dead bodies and festering secrets; of limbs thrashing beneath a healer's fingertips; of the young Christian boy who was tortured to death. I thought of how 'Daoud' could have been 'David' in a different world – such a strange idea, that. Most of all, I thought about the way the chicken breast thrummed under the influence of my will, how it kept jerking long after I took my hands away. Would Baba whirl if I touched him, would he dance a final dance for me?

I wiped my tears. From the crevasse of the night, blood-black rain gushed and pawed at my eyes. Then we went in Zamir's rickshaw to pick up my father's corpse.

Someone once told me dust has no religion.

Perhaps it was the maulvi sahib who taught me my first Arabic words; a balding kind, quiet man with a voice meant to chant godly secrets and a white beard that flowed like a river of Allah's nur. The gravedigger who was now shovelling and turning the soil five feet away looked a bit like him, except when he panted. His string vest was drenched with sweat, even though the ground was soft and muddy from the downpour.

Perhaps it was Ma. She stood next to me before this widening hole, leaning on Khala Apee as if she were an axed tree about to fall. Her lips moved silently all the time. Whether she prayed or talked to Baba's ghost, I don't know.

Or perhaps it was Baba who lay draped in white on the charpoy bier under the pipal tree. The best cotton shroud we could afford rippled when the graveyard wind gusted. It was still wet from his last bath. Before they log-rolled him onto his back, the men of our neighbourhood had asked me if I wanted to help wash him.

I said no. My eyes never brimmed.

Now, I let a fistful of this forgiving dust exhaust itself between my fingers. It whispered through, a gentle earth-skin shedding off me and upon Baba's face. It would carry the scent of my flesh, let him inhale my presence. I leaned down and touched my father's lips, so white, so cold, and a ghastly image came to me: Baba juddering on my fingertips as I reach inside his mouth, shock his tongue, and watch it jump and thrash like a bloodied carp. 'Tell me who murdered you,' I tell my father's tongue. 'Talk to me, speak to me. For I am Resurrection, and who so believes in me will live again.'

But his tongue doesn't quiver. It says nothing.

Someone touched my shoulder and drew me back. It was Ma. Her mouth was a pale scar in her face. She gripped my fingers tightly. I looked down, saw that she had coloured her hand with henna, and dropped it.

A shiny flaming orange heart, lanced in the middle, glistened on her palm.

It was dark enough to feel invisible. I left Ma praying in her room and went to Kala Pul.

Lights flickered in the streets and on chowrangis. Sad-faced vendors sold fake perfumes and plastic toys at traffic signals. Women with hollow eyes offered motia bracelets and necklaces, and the flower's scent filled my nose, removing Baba's smell in death. Children fished for paan leaves and cigarette stubs in puddles, and I walked past them all.

Something dark lay in the middle of the road under a bright fluorescent median light. I raised a hand to block the glare and bent to look at it. An alley cat, a starved, mangy creature with a crushed back. Tread marks were imprinted on its fur; clots glistened between them. A chipped fang hung from one of whiskers.

I didn't know my right hand was on it until I saw my fingertips curve. They pressed into the carcass like metal probes seeking, seeking. I didn't even need to feel for a point. In death, the creature's entire body was an enormous potential ready to be evoked.

I met the cat's gaze. Lifeless eyes reflected the traffic light changing from green to red. I discharged.

A smell like charred meat, like sparks from metal screeching against metal, rust on old bicycle wheels. The creature arched its spine, its four legs locking together, so much tension in its muscles they thrummed like electric wires. Creaking, making a frothing sound, the alley cat flopped over to its paws and tried to stand.

It lives, I thought and felt no joy or satisfaction.

Blood trickled from the creature's right eye. It tried to blink, and the left eye wouldn't open. It was glued shut with post-mortem secretions.

My hand was hurting. I shook it, brought it before my eyes, looked at it. A large bulla had formed in the middle of the palm, blue-red and warm. Rubbing it gently, I got up and left, leaving the newly risen feline tottering around the traffic median, strange sounds emitting from its throat as if it were trying to remember how to mewl.

Deep inside the Christian muhallah I waded through rubble, piles of blackened bricks, and charred wood. I stood atop the destruction and imagined the fire consuming rows upon rows of these tiny shacks. Teetering chairs, plywood tables, meal mats, dung stoves, patchworked clothes – all set ablaze. Bricks fell, embers popped and shadow fingers danced in the flames.

I shivered and turned to leave. Moonlight dappled the debris, shadows twisted, and as I made my way through the wreckage, I nearly tripped over something poking from beneath a corrugated tin sheet.

I stooped to examine the object. It was a heavy, callused human hand, the knuckles bruised and hairy like my father's. Blood had clotted at the wrist and formed a puddle below the sharp edge of the tin.

A darkness turned inside my chest; rivers of blood pounded in the veins of my neck and forehead. I don't know how long I sat in the gloom, in that sacred silence. Head bowed, fingers curled around the crushed man's, I crouched with my eyes closed and groped for the meat of the city with my other hand's fingertips. I felt for its faint pulse, I looked for its resurrection point; and when the dirt shivered and a sound like the surf surged into my ears, I thought I had found it.

I stiffened my shoulders, touched the dead man's palm – and let the current flow.

The hand jerked, the fingers splayed. A sigh went through the shanty town. Somewhere in the dark bricks shifted. The ruins were stirring.

Something plopped on the tin sheet. I looked down. Fat drops of blood bulged from between my clenched knuckles. I let the dead hand go (it skittered to a side and began to thrash). I opened both of my fists and raised them to the sky.

A crop of raised, engorged blisters on my palms. One amidst the right cluster had popped and was bleeding. The pain was a steady ache, almost pleasant in its tingling. As I watched, the sores on my left palm burst and began to gush. Dark red pulsed and quivered its way down my wrists.

Trembling, I crouched on my haunches and grasped the dead man's convulsing limb with both hands. I closed my eyes and jolted the Christian muhallah back to life. Then I sat back, rocking on my heels, and waited.

They came. Dragging their limbs off sparkling morgue tables, slicing through mounds of blessed dirt, wrenching free of rain-soaked grass, my derelict innocents seized and twitched their way across the city. I rose to my feet when they arrived, trailing a metallic tang behind them that drowned the smell of the jasmine. Metal rattled and clanged as my last finally managed to crawl out from under the tin sheet and joined the ranks of the faithful.

I looked at them one last time, my people, faces shining with blood and fervour. Their shredded limbs dangled. Autopsy incisions criss-crossed someone's naked flesh. Blackened men, women and children swaying in rows, waiting for me. How unafraid, joyous and visible they were.

I raised my chin high and led my living thus on their final pilgrimage through this land of the dead.

SHAMBHALA

SALIK SHAH

1

I see two white crocodiles, their primitive armour ruthlessly trimmed. I open my eyes. I am sitting upright on a rug inside a cave. It is a memory. Tibet. I gently pick up a mallet to draw a ringing note from a brass bowl of my ancestors. This ointment for my soul melts into my store consciousness.

A whirlpool of pain disturbs the water of life. After long years of practising mindfulness, I soothe the baby anger seething within. Memories of my childhood are like coral beads woven on the silver thread of exhalations, the dying breaths of a poet.

Breathing in, I see myself as a child. Breathing out, I smile at the child with loving kindness.

Niu Jian, our new Mandarin teacher, was Han, kind and intelligent. The son of peasant parents from the mainland, he was born two years before the Tiananmen Square massacre. A sensitive young man with a handsome, sculpted face and the deep black eyes of a panda, he was markedly different from most Volunteers Aiding Tibet. 'Do you care for poetry?' were his first words in the whitewashed world of our classroom.

Poetry? We laughed.

'Very well!' He picked up a piece of chalk from the teacher's desk and started to write on the blackboard, casting a spell on us with his dashing looks and command of Hanzi. The masterful strokes of the young calligrapher were sturdy, measured, compact – free of restive force, full of vigour.

'What's your name?' Niu Jian shot a piece of chalk at a little boy with pink cheeks sitting on the front bench.

'Tenzin,' I replied, standing up.

'Hello, Tenzin, I am Niu Jian.' He offered his hand. Timidly, I took it. 'Can you read Mandarin?'

I nodded.

'Humour us!'

Slowly, I read out the Hanzi. 'The dark night gave me my black eyes / but I use them to find white light.'

Niu Jian must have given the rest of the class a cue, and the brief round of applause that followed the recitation of the poem made me feel overjoyed.

'You are a born poet!' He was teasing me now. The little children found a new reason to laugh behind my back. 'You brats are noisier than the parakeets at Norbulingka,' he snapped, at which the little girls in the classroom promptly cut short their giggling.

'Tenzin,' he said, putting me back on his radar. 'What's wrong with you?'

'He doesn't laugh, does he?' The question, directed to the class, provoked another bout of laughter.

I was greatly relieved when he asked me to sit down.

'Do you know "East is Red"?'

'Yes,' the children blurted.

The song of the Cultural Revolution was as obsolete as woodblock printing, the fountain pen and Mao Zedong himself. But they were still objects of historical interest and scholarly value.

'Good,' Niu Jian chuckled. 'But you won't be questioned on it in your exams!'

'If you want to learn Mandarin, *read poetry*. A lot of it,' he said as a matter of fact. 'There are over 80,000 logograms in Hanzi, but you don't have to remember more than 800. You don't need to know even 500 words to pass your exams.

'But if you want to know more about the world, or where we came from, you need a guide…' he paused, as if lost in thought. 'Mandarin can be a very reliable guide.'

The period bell rang – Niu Jian's classes were never a drag; he bent space, accelerated time.

We didn't understand much of what Niu Jian said, but I understood two things. One, it was possible to fall in love with a language. Two, it was possible to teach children without terrorizing them. For the second reason, Niu Jian was the best Chinese ambassador to Tibet we ever had.

Breathing in, I imagine Niu Jian as a five-year-old child with a dreamy face and dark eyes. Breathing out, I smile at that child who is my teacher, a poet and the guide of my soul.

Where are you now, teacher?

The world is quiet. I refuse to accept the answer.

A teacher who is sensitive, loves children and recites poetry is as vulnerable as a five-year-old child.

The early birds are now digging the wet soil outside the cave with their sharp beaks. I strike the ancient bowl gently and absorb its dancing waves like Lake Nam absorbs the fresh water from Nyenchen Tanglha, the melting peaks of surrounding mountains.

'The world is without a discoverable beginning,' the Wise One said. 'The children of Tibet came from the congress of Trelgen, a wise monkey, and Drag Sinmo, a lustful ogress. Those who bring evil into the world are Ma Sinmo's children. The good has one source: Pha Trelgen Changchup Sempa.'

I close my eyes.

Outside the classroom, the day is painfully bright. My eyes take time to adjust to the light. A boy stands naked outside his classroom. His smile is calm, Buddha-like. He doesn't seem embarrassed at all, which defeats the sacred purpose of his teacher's chastisement. I turn away from the smile of the condemned Buddha. I turn away from the page of history, which brings back the memory of another incident – my own punishment, like an obtrusive billboard.

I was in nursery school when a frank utterance led to an embarrassing punishment. I had called a classmate *ba-chi*, a stupid person. At Barkhor Street, I had picked up the slur from the Han shopkeeper next to my mother's stall. I didn't know what it meant but, somehow, I instinctively knew how slurs worked: they sounded easy and very funny to my little ears. We seem to have a knack for picking up the derogatory words of any language without any effort. Indeed, how many children – even adults – know or have pondered the full extent of the meanings of everyday words?

The class teacher, though, didn't appreciate this special talent. She made me unbutton my shirt and tied my hands with its sleeves to a yellow plastic chair.

When I shut the toilet door behind me, my body itched. The stench was horrid. Other schoolboys never shut the door; they scoffed at me for being too self-conscious to shoot an arc of pee or compare the size of our little penises. Outside the toilet, I imagined the banished Buddha laughing at me, basking in the naked sun. I had always been extremely shy. As I suffered the seeds of humiliation and sowed them in my consciousness, I realized that I was too vulnerable, too fragile.

Breathing in, I see myself as a five-year-old child, who is suffering, quietly. Breathing out, I smile at the five-year-old child who is me.

'Poor me, I was so helpless. I didn't know how to accept disgrace.'

2

The world is without a discoverable beginning. The children of Tibet came from the congress of Trelgen, a wise monkey and a lustful ogress.

I don't have a best friend but Dawa is the closest to a best friend I'd ever have. He has a round face, the big eyes of a white-rumped snowfinch, and the best science kit I know of in all of Tibet.

After eating fried momos and shogo khasta, our favourite meat pies, we chase each other around a group of girls playing rock-paper-scissors. I am usually tired by the time the tiffin break comes to an end.

I close my eyes and see our math teacher enter the classroom. He chooses an equation from the textbook on his desk, solves it for himself on the blackboard and relaxes his bottom in the wooden chair for the rest of the class. He makes the students copy and practise his answers until their muscles remember them, step by step, even if they don't understand a thing. The sound logic of mathematics and the beauty of problem solving combined with the gift of reasoning are lost on these children.

The weak students in the math class often face the teacher's special treatment: rogue children have to pull their pant legs up and kneel on shards of broken glass, pointed rocks. The children bleed and writhe in pain until they swear not to do whatever they have allegedly done – ever again.

You don't have to be an expert in the science and philosophy of teaching to know the simple truth that teaching requires a great deal of patience, which, alas, is a trait as scarce as oxygen to the outsiders in Lhasa. I cannot benefit from the casual attitude and sound technique of our math teacher. With each day, I regret not knowing the language of numbers and the rules of nature.

When I wasn't in school, I was in Barkhor, helping my mother sell colourful trinkets, polished statues and fancy souvenirs made in Kathmandu, among other places.

Breathing in, I see the children. Breathing out, I smile at the children, who are the children of Pha Trelgen.

The math teacher is absent today, and I am the temporary class leader. The inexorable whispers of plots and wicked conspiracies thicken the air. 'Please keep quiet,' I beg my classmates.

Mr Fox, the science teacher who inspired terror in all our hearts with his sly smile and ruthless punishments, is about to pass our classroom when a storm of laughter arises from the corners and drowns me out.

I hear Mr Fox shout from outside. 'Yes, sir?' I get up and volunteer a reply.

The children start to whirr and buzz like an unruly swarm of bees under attack from an intruder. They hold their breath as Mr Fox enters the class and pounces on me like a bloodthirsty hound. He is discipline personified, free to strike any student anywhere. The cuffs keep coming at me. My ears burn and grow red. I can't control the tears running down my cheeks. I want to tear away the charred skin of my face, but the blows do not stop.

I try to lower my head. My clumsy effort to evade punishment and deny Mr Fox the right to torture children makes him even more furious.

'What did you say?'

I shouldn't have raised my voice. 'Yes, sir?' I have injured his ego, punctured his pride. The witless man keeps smacking me like a wounded bull that has caught a young matador between his horns until the school bell finally comes to my rescue.

I have to establish direct contact with the pain in my consciousness. I have to deal with my pain. I have to be able to look deeply. So I meditate. It is the act of healing. It is the art of understanding – forgiving, not forgetting.

Breathing in, I see myself as a five-year-old child. Breathing out, I smile at the five-year-old child who is my science teacher, Mr Fox – Zhou Yong.

It took me five years to come to terms with Zhou Yong and to be able to finally sympathize with him. But those five years were a nightmare. The hate inside me was too strong, too powerful.

I close my eyes to receive a new insight.

Zhou Yong was a disillusioned Party member who was naively optimistic about the future of China and its people. His parents were peasant farmers in the Hunan province and for him life couldn't get any more difficult, or *jianku*, than that.

The cause of the Party was his cause, and the enemies of the Communist Party were his enemies. The plateau had taken a toll on the science teacher's spirit. When Mr Fox first arrived in Tibet, his name was Zhou Yong, and he hadn't still gained his severity when punishing schoolchildren. Now, tactless cruelty dominated his personality because he thought the people didn't want him or his science. Teaching was a thankless job in Tibet. Centuries-old habits, superstitions and enslavement on the plateau had made his work extremely difficult. The children of nomads, traders and peasants refused to denounce their regressive beliefs or the history of the Tibetan Empire.

Breathing in, I see the Tibetan government-in-exile urging hapless children to preserve the memory of the ancient codes of nobles and monks. Breathing out, I see Mother panicking when she sees me at her stall in Barkhor. I do not realize that the teacher has left his ghostly marks on my face.

The walk is an act of memory, which takes longer to travel each time I traverse the zone. I see the rising dust in the street. I hear the horns of vehicles and fluttering of the prayer flags – blue, white, red, green and yellow – sending their prayers towards heaven. I see the eager smiles of foreigners and the naked smile of the nameless boy. I can't seem to make a distinction between the Han Chinese, American, Indian and European tourists. They are all the same to me. They are all foreigners and I want to get rid of them. I want to be alone. I want Tibet to be free.

The wind and the rocks are cruel to me like the eagle harassed by the scheming ones and heaven.

I close my eyes and find myself lying in my mother's lap later that night. She is telling me a story. It is an old story about a hunter who kills a raven trying to save his life. When the hunter finally realizes his mistake, it is too late. He can't bring the innocent raven back to life. His heart is filled with grief and atonement.

When the story is over, Mother asks me, 'Sras, won't you go to school?'

'No,' I reply, even though I know the moral of her story.

'Why, my son?'

'I don't want to go.'

'Sras, don't you want to make Amala and Phala proud?' I see tears well in two sad beautiful eyes, my mother's eyes, and it melts my stubborn resistance. 'I know you're a good boy.'

Breathing in, I see my mother as a five-year-old child. Breathing out, I smile at the five-ear-old child who is my mother.

The meeting is a disaster.

'Your son asked for it,' the principal tells her. 'This will teach him how to talk to his elders respectfully.' That's the end of the chapter as far as he is concerned.

We return, defeated. The Zhang Zu people don't have the right to question their Han masters. We are like rows of sweet corn to be turned into salted popcorn for the world's consumption. They come in hordes to discover Shangri-La and to destroy it, so they can make it better with their malls and multiplexes on the roof of the world.

It is the second week of March 2008. The Chinese troops have arrested the monks marching to Potala Palace. The 1959 uprising is history, but the warrior monks are determined to keep its wounds fresh and red, scratching them when they are just about to heal, like beggars in Lhasa's streets.

At Barkhor, we see smoke rising from the north-west section of the Potala Palace. The symbol of friendship between the ethnic Han and Tibetan people, the Ramoche Temple, is burning. All the public offices and schools are still open when the riots begin.

'It is not safe outside,' Hu Liu tells Mother as he binds a traditional prayer flag on his stall.

Mother borrows a prayer flag from the merchant. Our eyes are less narrow than his, and she is wondering if this mark of Tibetan ethnicity will be enough to save us from the wrath of the ogress.

Our stall is one of the 3,000 stalls in the seven alleys of Barkhor encircling the temple complex. The protestors are keen on destroying everything that belongs to the Han, Hui, Chinese.

We rush inside a restaurant behind the stalls. Rocks crash against its wooden door like giant waves in a sea storm. The owners of the restaurant, a migrant couple from the Yunnan province, are terrified. Tibetan swords and rocks are ravening for Han blood. Having us, the Zhang Zu people, inside the restaurant might prevent immigrants like them being attacked, they hope.

We peek through an inch-long vertical gap between the wooden doors.

The jewel of Lhasa, the Jokhang Temple, is in flames.

The angry protestors are wearing Tibetan flags. I see furious boys in school uniforms razing flagless stalls. Two mountains on their white shirts meet slightly above their trousers, all blood red. Inside, I know they are all naked. Naked like that shameless boy in school. It dawns on me that our childhood is now over. For the merest second, I want to join the mob and burn everything down, but my mother keeps tugging at the corner of my shirt.

The wife of the restaurant owner lets out a shriek. The restaurant door is on fire. The thick smoke from the paint and wood make it difficult to breathe inside, while Shangri-La rages and burns outside. By the time we open the door, the ogress has left. Our Han friends are safe but scarred for the rest of their lives.

I close my eyes and see the children of the Han couple who now carry scars of the violence. The wounds of suffering are passed from a stern look of the father to his son and a shout from the mother to her daughter – generation after generation. The cycle of samsara never ends. I want to break the cycle, but I am weak, unenlightened. I cannot enter the sacred city of Shambhala.

'Poor Han, you were so helpless. You didn't know how to deal with hate.'

'What's the experiment?' I ask Dawa. We are in his room, and he is still in his school uniform, white and red. He has laid out a white *jiao* coin, a few sheets of paper, a lighter and a half glass of water, all smuggled into his room, safe from the prying eyes of his mother. I haven't been to school for a week.

'It's called the fire, water and silver experiment,' he replies. He places the coin in the middle of the tray and empties the glass of water on it. The coin is submerged.

'Tenzin, can you lift the coin from the tray?' he asks, putting the empty glass on the table.

'Yes,' I reply, swiftly picking the coin. My fingers are wet.

He asks me to put the coin back into the water. 'Can you lift the coin from the tray *without* getting your fingers wet?'

'I can try.'

Dawa gives me five full minutes to solve the puzzle. He savours the confusion on my face with a smirk. He rejoices at the thought of tiny electric short circuits snapping at different places inside my brain. 'Would you like a hint?'

I want to decline but don't have the patience to put up with Dawa's theatrics. 'All right.'

'You can use the lighter and the paper.'

As I take the paper and try to push the coin to the corner of the tray with it, Dawa bursts into wild laughter, closing his wide eyes.

'No, you cannot do that. You have to lift it, *ba chi*.'

I am *not* stupid. He has the secret book of science, not me. I turn my back on him and decide not to be friends with him any more.

'Wait! I'm sorry, Tenzin. You know I didn't actually mean it.' He has realized his mistake. 'I wasn't laughing at *you*. I did exactly what you were doing before I found out the answer.'

I am satisfied and turn around again.

'Let me show you the trick.'

This offer gives me real pleasure. He crumples up the paper and lights it. He puts the ball of fire inside the glass, and then he places the glass upside down on the tray near the coin. When the fire goes out, my jaw drops. The water rushes to fill the vacuum inside the glass. The tray is almost dry.

'You can pick up the coin now,' Dawa says with the modesty of a proud child scientist. 'It's yours, after all.'

When I return home, I find the wooden door of our apartment open. *The trader is back to do business!*

I can smell Father's stuffy, unwashed clothes in the hall.

Mother is nice to Father, and I am afraid of him, but it isn't enough to make him stay.

I see Mother weaving a braid with turquoise beads and a golden crown. 'Tell her it's from her sister in Lhasa,' Mother tells Father, asking him to announce her existence to the other woman.

I am too young to tell the difference between polyandry and polygamy, or why monks at Potala are often gay, or why children are sometimes molested in monasteries. Sex is an uncharted part of my childhood.

Apparently, Mother's 'sister' is Father's new bride in Khumbu. She doesn't bother to torment me with this fact as long as he comes to see her every three months or so, braving the cold and snow, crossing the narrow mountain passes through Chomolungma.

Father's constant absence becomes the chief source of my embarrassment in school. As long as I work hard to remain a 'bright student', behave well and show proper respect to my elders and teachers in school, I know they will leave me alone. That his absence doesn't really matter. I don't know how my friends would have reacted if I had been a khachara, ass, as the disinherited, disowned children of Newar merchants from Kathmandu are called. The fact that I am not an *ass* doesn't provide much comfort. I see myself as I was, a child cut off from his father by a border, the white blade of the ascending Himalayas.

Quietly, I tiptoe to my small room next to the kitchen and wait for Mother to come home, even though I know she will probably come late tonight and sleep on the rug on the floor.

I am sitting on the rug on which my mother slept. And I see the little boy who wants to do his homework for school the next day but is afraid that he might disturb and wake up his father.

When I was a three-year-old, my parents had a fight. He was young, drunk and possibly blinded by rage when he tossed me onto the bed. But I hit the wall. Afterwards, Mother treated the swelling on the right side my forehead with a cotton cloth drenched in lukewarm water every morning and every night for two weeks – and she stopped arguing with Father.

I see the little boy press the palms of his hands over his ears and bury his face in the white pillow. I see the sad expression on his face when he gets up the next day. Father is nowhere to be seen. He is gone. I am cross with myself for not waking up on time to see him or to say goodbye. I am angry with Phala for leaving so early, for forgetting my existence and not bothering to see me.

Breathing in, I see myself as a five-year-old child. Breathing out, I smile at the five-year-old child who is me.

'Poor me, I was so helpless. I didn't know how to deal with Father's absence.'

4

Leaning on one chin, I push the tip of my pen against a sheet of recycled paper. I draw blue planets around a red sun and the lines that bind them to God, to mother universe.

In the classroom, Mr Fox is describing the chalk-white orbits of the planets around the sun he has drawn on the blackboard.

My fingers refuse to hold the pen in place. My hearing is useless, as if I am a pilgrim walking across a vast desert when the summer is at its peak. I am vulnerable, thirsty and disenchanted when I see the holy monasteries scattered in the rugged landscape of Tibet, which lies on the flat back of a giant ogress, the forbidden kingdom of the Himalayas. I am the lost pilgrim. My eyes are transfixed by the golden mirage of the monasteries and their glittering pinnacles.

When the mirage finally disappears, the sky turns black with a thread of bright stars. By the time I realize that the stars are white buttons on a leather belt, the blows have started to rain down on me. Mr Fox strikes me with his hand, his nails scratching my face. Tears run down my cheeks, mixed with blood.

'What do you think of yourself?' He keeps hitting my face. 'You think you're smart?'

'No, sir. No, sir.' The words come out from my mouth involuntarily.

My classmates are drawing their charts, the planets and their orbits, without raising their heads. They don't want to attract the ire of the red devil.

At Barkhor, the ghosts of adults still bear the marks of their oppressors. The victims of abuse don't look anyone straight in the eyes, and they seem to drag their heavy bodies on the ground as they crawl around the cathedral.

The children are seized by violent outbursts. Forced to grow up in a single day after terrible things have had happened to them, they have lost their humour. The only way these five-year-olds can live is by trying to protect their fragile bodies and restore their fragile sense of dignity, community, nationality. The world is turning into a bottled-up volcano, ready to explode, fuming with humiliation and rage. I believe I am turning into a ghost, marked early by the frozen white death. The monster of civilization is violating children.

The hunter cannot grieve. My mother's story was a lie, like so much about Tibet.

I see myself at our souvenir stall. I know Mother doesn't want me there, but where else could I go? Sometimes, Dawa comes to see me but I wish he didn't. He reminds me of school, where curiosity is a curse and my acute sense of responsibility an unnecessary burden.

The other children often take advantage of me. I show them my answers during class tests and term exams. I want them to be my friends. I want them to like me. I am so needy, so vulnerable. I am part of a world which is unfair. I lock myself in this room to protect myself from further violation.

I close my eyes and see myself working hard to be a bright student – to be a good Chinese – enduring both torture and shame.

Breathing in, I see the universe as a dimple on the soft cheek of a five-year-old. Breathing out, I smile at the five-year-old with the dimple of the universe on his cheek.

'Poor me, I was so helpless. I didn't know how to deal with the tumult of adolescence.'

I close my eyes and see the beautiful face of a white woman inspecting jewellery at our stall. She is with a Chinese guide. He doesn't recognize me, but I do. He is speaking English with the foreigner.

'How much?' the woman asks, picking up a turquoise necklace.

'Tenzin?' Niu Jian cries, before I can reply to the woman. I am delighted to know that my old Mandarin teacher still remembers my name.

'Yes, sir.' I don't know how to greet him otherwise.

He buys the necklace for the lady, refusing my huge discount, and returns later in the evening to talk.

'What are you doing here?'

'Working,' I reply.

I see the cold silent expression on Niu Jian's face. His eyes are fathomless like the east. He has quit teaching.

'You know I can't go back home,' he explains. 'My bloated lungs can't take the plains.'

'Do you now also believe in reincarnation?'

He laughs.

The number of Han settlements in Lhasa have increased, not dwindled, but they are as superstitious about the alleged transformation of their lungs as the natives are about the reincarnations of the celibate monks at the Potala Palace. But it serves as a convenient lie to conceal the fact that Niu Jian is involved in politics, and this bit I discover much later.

'Wasn't the pay good?' The higher the teachers worked, the higher they got paid, or so I have heard.

'Quite.' Half of the money he made went to his parents and the other half was barely enough for him.

Before leaving the stall, he gives me a folded sheet of paper.

I open the paper and read the first eight lines of 'Buddha Words'.

There is a lump in my throat. *What is poetry? It is a bitter pill of words that heal the wounds of the soul.*

The poet Gu Cheng was a madcap, and back in school everybody thought there was a screw or two loose in Niu Jian's head too. We didn't know his love for poetry would keep him going or that it'd become the cause of his extinction.

I wait for Niu Jian like I waited for my father once. But neither of them wait for me.

A white moon buttons up the sky, and the hare on the moon is unmoving, dead in the sky above Tibet. The sun and the moon and all the stars are out there. But they don't need us. They are simply there, *being*, existing.

When the tourist guide comes around later, he asks me, 'Tenzin, do you write poetry?'

I answer in the affirmative. I show him a small poem, written in a clumsy handwriting. He reads it but doesn't offer any encouragement or critique. He comes back with another poem: '16. Bulin's Last Instructions'.

'Why Gu Cheng?' I ask him.

'The poet is the conscience of the East.' His voice is a whisper and his face a dream. 'Tenzin, don't you want Tibet to be free?'

I have given it a lot of thought. 'It doesn't make a difference to me,' I reply honestly.

Niu Jian doesn't speak for a while. He then picks up a small black statue of the laughing Buddha from among the souvenirs on sale. 'The dark night gave me my black eyes, but I use them to find white light.' He recites the poem of his generation with the tongue of a wise monkey. 'Tenzin, don't let *them* break your spirit.'

I can't understand much of Niu Jian's logic yet. Or Gu Cheng for that matter. Perhaps, I will never understand them. When two monks burn themselves in Barkhor Square, I tell everyone who cares to ask my opinion that the monks are stupid. As a result of their protest, the stalls are going to be removed from the street.

'When?' There is horror on Mother's face.

'They haven't decided yet,' the local official barks.

'They can't do this. We're the life of the street,' Mother keeps saying, her words like a sacred chant. Om mani padme hum. Om mani padme hum. 'We're the life of the street.'

'He was lying,' I tell Mother when the Chinese official is gone. 'They won't move us.'

But Mother doesn't stop crying. I know what she is probably thinking: if the Chinese troops could move the snow city of Zhol, which once stood at the foothills of the Potala Palace, they could remove Barkhor for sure.

'The tourists come to see us, Ama.' I try to reassure her. 'It's a trick to warn protesters.'

I am grateful to Niu Jian for coming to see me the next day. He asks Mother to accompany her on his way around Jokhang.

'What did you talk about?' I ask Mother when she returns to the stall, alone.

The heaviness on her face has disappeared. 'Oh, the business.'

I have a feeling that they were probably talking about me. Did they find a way to send me back to school again? I won't go.

The dreaded announcement comes in December: the 3,000 stalls lining Barkhor Square would be moved to Yutok Street 'temporarily'. The Chinese authorities are lying. Many years ago, when they moved Zhol from the foothills of Potala 'temporarily', everybody knew the shift would be permanent. And it was.

They certainly know how to break their people.

Step 1: Spread a rumour about the official decision.

Step 2: Give people plenty of time to prepare and resign themselves to their new fate.

Step 3: Send in your troops to make the rumour official.

The strategy works brilliantly each time. All surrender, none protest. There is no uproar. It's a clean, efficient stratagem straight from the books of Sun Tzu.

'Poor teacher, you were helpless. You didn't know how to deal with your country's treachery.'

5

Father looks weak and much older than I remember. Mother is very worried.

'I was sick,' he says, asking her to calm down. 'But don't worry, I am fine now.'

It's been six months since we last saw him.

When Niu Jian also appears at the stall, I know it's not a coincidence. They are up to something.

'You're coming with me,' my father *orders* me.

'No.'

'Tenzin, you have to go,' Niu Jian cuts me with his words. 'You can't stay here. They are shunting stalls today. Who knows what might happen tomorrow?'

'I won't leave Mother alone.'

'She is coming with us.' Father turns to her. 'Pema, tell him you're coming with me.'

Mother wants a better life for her child. She doesn't have a choice.

Later that night, Niu Jian comes to see us. We share meat pies and mashed potato on the dinner mat. He hands me *Tao Te Ching*, a book of poems, and a white envelope – his parting gifts. 'Promise me that you won't open this until you reach the other side of Chomolungma.'

'I promise.'

As I say those final words, I realize what it means: I won't be seeing him again. His image is blurred in my wet eyes.

A flock of white cranes soars in the sky 500 miles south-west of Lhasa. Mother is singing the song of a Rinpoche from another time:

White crane!
Lend me your wings
I will not fly far
From Lithang, I shall return

Her sorrowful voice pierces my heart like the sharp rocks under our feet.

It was impossible to get travel permits from the Chinese authorities in Lhasa. We are crossing the border into Nepal through the treacherous Nangpa La mountain pass on foot. By nightfall, we are deep into the slopes of the harsh mountain. The Chinese troops won't come so far up the mountain, Father assures us.

The wind is gathering speed as Father leads us to a small cave along the moonlit path. When the storm hits the pass, we're sitting by a small fire.

'Traders use caves like this one on their way to and from the refugee camps,' he informs us. 'By the looks of it, the storm will be gone by dawn. We'll reach Khumbu tomorrow night.'

Mother and Father sneak inside a double sleeping bag wrapped in thick woollen blankets. They fall asleep quickly.

But I can't sleep.

I'm shivering with fear and exhaustion inside of me.

I open Niu Jian's letter – a torn page from his diary. It's a short note in Mandarin:

> To Tenzin,
> The blossom-ringed parakeets flap and beat their sturdy wings together. Once in a while, if you're lucky, you'll see a lone parakeet, who fought for independence and gained it, and now must carry on alone far from Lhasa. Once you leave Norbulingka, you cannot return home until you find the abominable snowmen and their underground city, Shambhala.

It takes me a while to realize that it's a poem. I put the torn page of Niu Jian's diary inside my pocket, and wonder: if I close my eyes and die by the fire, will I return to Lhasa in my next life?

I am travelling further back in time on the shoulders of a giant, a wise monkey. He is searching for the buried path to his lost home. The earth is charred, desolate and barren. The sun keeps getting bigger and bigger, but it never sets.

Sunrise melts the silver snow on the mountain pass. Thin grass and flowers plop out of their seeds to turn the silver iridescent. Snow returns to cull life. Flowers trump death. The cycle is endless.

I don't want to witness countless births and suffer innumerable deaths. Terrified, I cry for help. 'Mother!'

My feet burn as the giant drops me on the ground.

'Sras, Sras! I am here,' Mother's tender voice wakes me to the full moon that is her face and the tiny stars which glitter and sparkle in her kind blue eyes. 'I'm here, son. I'm here.'

Breathing in, I see Mother rubbing my body, which refuses to stop shuddering. Breathing out, I smile at Father who is fixing firewood.

The Wise One now takes care of the hare scurrying about happily on the moon.

6

After losing the silver suit of heaven, it is said in the creation myth of Tibet, the wise monkey doesn't understand anything any more.

'Who are you?' he asks Sinmo, the rock ogress. 'Where am I?'

'You were seeking the path to your lost city,' Sinmo replies. 'You followed the Beginning of Water, and have now reached its source.'

The ogress reads his pheromone breaths, his silver brow and stormy eyes. The half-man's time is up, she knows. She pulls the metal frames of his eroded shield with her silver teeth, contaminating his weak spirit, giving him enough room to breathe.

The wise monkey hesitates: he isn't ready to sow the seed of suffering in the ogress's womb. He doesn't want to give birth to good if he can't stop evil from arriving on the roof of the world. The ogress reassures him that the seed of dukkha also holds infinite possibilities for knowledge, wonder, *life*.

Father Sempa is no more.

Sinmo's children now seek heaven's silver suit with their dark, stormy eyes. Without the light of the suit, they are lost.

There is no map out of exile.

CONFESSOR

YUDHANJAYA WIJERATNE

Was there light before, or did the darkness get here first? Severian no longer remembered.

He tried to think, to use that wit they had praised him for, decades ago, when he was young and famous, and kingdoms cowered beneath his words. The tongue, like a sharp knife, kills without drawing blood. Dark is the absence of light, but is light the absence of dark, or does it not actually give a shit? And did it really matter anyway? Because the flap was opening, the metal jaws parting to reveal that great glory! Food! Food! A dull metal plate with some green and brown on top.

Once, he had stayed in the finest hotels and demanded the most elegant porcelain. But locked here in the darkness, he had ascended to a higher plane of understanding about food, and that was that the container did not matter, the taste did not matter. All that mattered was that it belonged to the lexical category of food. That was the truth of it, stripped of the bourgeois classifications of flavour and presentation. So he lunged forward, chains rattling, fingers scrabbling through the filth of his cell, and descended on the plate like an animal. The guard on the other side banged the door, but Severian was long past caring. The guard was not food. Although – he raised his eyes and stared at the plump young man in his grey uniform – he could be moved into the category of food, with the right application of heat. It was known that objects could belong to several categories: it all came down to how you ordered the concepts in the universe, and the relationships between them, and most of all how long you cooked them after they stopped screaming…

Stay alive, said the ghost whisper in his mind. A shadow of a shadow of who he had been, his intellect scrambled by neural locks, forced to see and suffer.

Stay alive. Food was alive. Or linked loosely to the cluster of things that went into staying alive. Once, he could have explained how, and why, but now these shadow-fragments skittered across his neurons like mice running from the light, hiding deep in the burrows of memory and reflex. So he ate, and ate, and slept, and ate, and relieved himself, and on and on and on. Every time he relieved himself, he made a mark on the wall. Why, he could not remember. It was a thing now, a reflex.

Why am I here? his ghost mind wondered sometimes. Severian had no answer. He sometimes argued with himself in fits of intelligence. *Here* implied a category; *here* implied something that was *not-here*. And what was not-here? At that point, the ghost would serve up fragments. Writing. Sunlight. The march of many feet in perfect unison. The glow of streetlights on arrack bottles. Shields that screamed 'RIOT'. A table, scarred with burns, an air conditioner that was always too cold or too warm. More writing.

Stay sane, the ghost would whisper. He tried. He held on to these memories, squirrelling them away like a thief, smuggling them past neural locks. The universe was a dark cell with guards at the door, but beyond this was another universe, a larger space, full of writing and knowledge, and he had come from there. Why then was he here? To that the ghost mind gave no answer. There was something buried inside, the memory of pain so deep that he had ejected the thoughts from himself, like a drunkard purging.

Light, noise, blinding; he screamed and cringed. Someone laughed outside. Something was thrust in and fell with a heavy thud. A guard loomed in the light and kicked him sharply in the groin and the universe folded in on itself in agony.

When he came to, the darkness had returned, and something was moving next to him. In the dim gloom, he could make out a shape. Like a guard: arms, legs, head. He screamed and rattled his chains at it. The thing, startled, rolled away from him with a cry.

'It stinks! It stinks in here!'

Not a guard. A guard had limited repertoire. Severian knew everything they said or could say or do. A new category perhaps?

'There's shit on the floor,' said the not-guard, and began to cry and throw himself against the door.

Severian tried to speak, but all that came out was a dull croak. *Uaaaaaa! No,* he wanted to say, *that is the floor, that is the category of floors, the door does not open that way.* He had dim recollections of doing the same thing before they came and extended his body with these chains and made him a part of the walls.

'Don't,' he managed at last. He rattled a bit. The not-guard collapsed on the floor, panting.

'I can't stay here,' said the not-guard. 'I didn't do anything wrong – it was a story, it was *just a fucking story*!'

It dawned on Severian that the not-guard, like himself, must have come from that greater universe outside. So, he asked the question he had been asking himself: 'Why...here? Why...you...here?'

'I wrote a story,' said the not-guard. He peered at Severian, crawled away from the door and towards him. They were close enough to touch, almost. Silence.

'I know you!' the not-guard said. 'You're S–, aren't you? You used to write for the *Lanka Analyst*! You broke the Parliament aid fraud story! *I know you!* Remember the Port City story? The intern who did the drone work? That was me! You taught me!'

Severian rattled away from him. Parliament? Fraud? What was Parliament? What fraud? Then he realized: the guards were playing a trick on him. Maybe he had stared too hard at the guard today. Maybe he had looked too hungry. Maybe they had sent one of themselves in to torment him and take away the silence. 'Wrong,' he croaked. 'Wrong... wrong, wrong.'

'Sir, we all thought...' said the not-guard. His voice was fast now, frenzied. 'We thought you were gone...we've held candlelight vigils... every day for the last six years near the old *Analyst* office...there's not much left of it because all the bloody interns keep stealing pieces of it to keep on their desks...can I come closer? What did they do to you? What's wrong with your arms?'

'Innocent,' mumbled Severian. 'I did nothing, let me be, please stop, please stop hitting, please stop hitting me, please stop, please stop.'

The not-guard tried to reach out. At his touch Severian panicked and screamed, lunging across at this thing that dared to torment him so. His chains snapped and pulled him back with a dreadful *clonk*. Agony erupted in his twisted shoulders. The guard rapped on the door. The not-guard yelped and retreated.

'They'll get us out, sir,' he whispered from the corner. 'They'll get us out, sir. We'll fix you – we'll fix you.'

Severian glared at him in the darkness and dragged himself back to where he'd started from. 'A trick,' he whispered balefully. 'Innocent. Fuck you.'

He spent the rest of the day staring at the not-guard. At first, the not-guard crouched in a corner of the abyss, running his hands across everything, recoiling in disgust and fear every now and then. Severian was puzzled by this, until a flash of intelligence told him to pay attention to how the not-guard moved – arms stretched out, bumping into the walls, the slab that Severian slept on. Some dim memory of himself doing the same until this universe was mapped out in his mind surfaced – sharp edges here, sleep here, shit here, door here, mark here. Then, his eyes had grown used to the dark.

Eventually, Severian took pity on the not-guard.

'Sleep, there.'

'Here? It feels like wood.'

'Sleep. Bed.'

'I can't see.'

'Sight later.' Severian guided him to the toilet. 'Shit there.'

The not-guard complained about the stink. Severian turned off and went to sleep, guarding his wall.

When he woke, the not-guard was on his bed, stretched out, staring up at the ceiling and talking to him. Or maybe to himself. It felt like quite the conversation, and it had more words than Severian remembered using recently.

'*Meykahariyannae*,' the not-guard was saying. 'We didn't do anything when they came for the journalists. We were in school, what the fuck did we know? People like you. They said you took foreign money. Said you worked with the diaspora. What diaspora? Nobody had answers. What money? Everyone knew journalists were poor, and the only rich journalists were working for the state. But we swallowed it, didn't we? Grow up, they said, get a job, get married, keep the language alive, keep the culture alive, do your duty, collect your pension. Look at China, they said. Look at Singapore. We have to be smart. We have to be diligent. Freedom of speech, hah! Stupid Western ideas. Maybe later, not now.'

Severian listened, interested. He knew some of those words. They climbed out of the not-guard's mouth like little bits of memory, entering him, redrawing long-forgotten categories in his mind. But the sketches were hasty, and they collapsed.

'Then they came for the celebrities, you know? Musicians and actresses. News anchors who doubled as models. Anyone who had views, clicks, likes. Smart bastards. Remember Kohonthana? Or was she after your time? Blew up in '30, I think – maybe '31, first real international rocker we had.'

Rock? Hard surfaces skittering over each other, shards on surfaces; ground down, infinitely tiny, sand; ground up, infinitely large, mountains; and somewhere in the middle, a guitar and screaming, but not in pain, in pleasure, refracted light turning faces blue and gold; the sound of glass shattering, the feel of someone's hips against his. Concepts, maps, broken.

'My cousin's friend worked in her studio. She says Kohonthana had something new, something big. Dug into the constitution. Dug into history. Had a whole album ready to release, apparently starting from 1948 and going down politics from then on. But the cars came one day, bundled her in. She came back and scrapped the whole thing. Very smart bastards. At first, nobody said anything because she kept playing the LGBT card and saying they were trying to bury her right to change her political opinion. After that, she was a straight-up shill, no pretence about it. Then, someone shot her onstage and the autopsy found the chip they put in her head. Memory control apparently. Change the memories, change the person.'

Memory lock. Yes. He knew that. 'I have,' he croaked and tapped his head. 'In here.' They tested it out on us. Prototypes – that's what we were.

The not-guard turned blindly in his direction. 'Didn't think they'd come for us,' he said. 'Fiction writers. We lie anyway. Nobody believes us. Nobody even reads us. All I did was write a short story. I didn't even put names in.'

'Hammer,' said Severian, trying to express a concept and a relationship long since gone to rust. 'Nail.'

'They can't hide the truth,' said the not-guard defiantly. 'You know what? I have friends. You know Mudiyantha Silva? You know Delon Sinnathamby? Lawyers, both of them. They'll get me out, and I'll tell the world what happened. I'll tell them about you. They can't hide the truth!'

Severian raised his shackles at him. A sliver of memory crept into his mind, commanded his tongue. 'Truth is what they say it is.'

Footsteps outside. Guards. The food flap opening. Severian lost his train of thought and crawled to it. Food, blessed food, the bringer of life. A glimpse of heaven. There were two plates. Double the heaven, jackpot, blessed be thy stomach. Salivating, he reached out with greedy hands and was driven back by a banging on the door. The guard outside, a silver-haired woman with a drooping face, shook her head.

'Only one bowl per prisoner!' she pointed her baton at them.

Prisoner. So the not-guard was like him. A prisoner. One for him, then. He howled in anger but carefully picked up the other bowl and shoved it at the other prisoner. Food was too important to waste. The other man recoiled.

'This looks like someone shat on grass.'

Idiot. 'Food.'

'I'm not eating that.'

Fine. Severian ate the second bowl as well and fell asleep.

In two marks on the wall, the other prisoner started eating. In four, he was racing Severian to the door when the food came, alternatively protecting his plate from Severian's hungry, reaching hands and pleading with the guards to let him out. In the night he talked, endlessly, his monologues growing longer and longer. When he came in he was frightened. Now, he seemed to be angry. He hurled insults at the guards, flinging that ancient curse – *Umbeammatahenahathakgahapang!* May lightning strike your mother seven times! – and slamming his body against the door every time a guard walked past.

He was cracking.

The guards, in turn, began their own retaliation. 'Confess,' they chanted every time the meal flap opened. 'Traitor!'

'Never!' the other prisoner would shriek back. 'They'll get me out! You can't keep me here!'

Stay sane, whispered the ghost mind, creeping about, picking up discarded memories and packing them back into itself. *Stay alive.*

I will, agreed Severian.

Seven marks later, they fought. He was surprisingly strong, his limbs unshackled; Severian hit him on the head, and the not-guard kicked hard and sent Severian sprawling into the wall. Screaming, he launched himself at the cowering Severian, raining blows on his head. His category of pain expanded to this frothing creature with fists and knees that were still hard and muscles that had not yet wasted away.

The door banged open. The explosion of light outlined both of them in harsh white: Severian, old, broken, teeth yellowed and decaying, rotting rags hanging off him in sheets, his hands gnarled and bent, more wall than flesh, more prison than human; and the other prisoner, young, his jeans spoiled but whole, face streaked with grime, but unbroken, eyes seeing Severian properly for the first time, the jaw comically open in shock and disgust –

Guards rushed in and dragged him, kicking and screaming, off Severian.

'What's this one doing? Why isn't he restrained!'

'Check his chip!' An officer's voice. Loud, commanding, certain.

'Stay down, you bastard!' A meaty, wet thud, the sound of electricity, and blue lightning crawling across the cell. 'Checking…checking. Ah. He's the new one, sir. The writer. We have him for suspicion of sedition.'

'Perfect. That one, eh? Now put him down for assaulting an elder. That's ten years, at least.'

'Yes, sir. Writing the charge, sir.'

'Footage to the Autojudiciary.'

'Sending footage…sending…accepted, sir.'

A low snigger. 'He won't be writing anything soon, eh?'

They vanished. The food remained in their wake, crushed by their boots, a part of the floor now.

The other prisoner began weeping. This surprised Severian. 'I don't want to be like you,' the other prisoner wept. 'I can't spend ten years here, I can't, I can't.'

'Then don't,' said Severian with difficulty. He lay on the ground, aching and bitter, and wished the sobbing would stop.

Eventually, it did.

Eight strokes on the wall later, the other prisoner moved to the door and knelt there. The guard came by for mealtime.

'I want to confess,' he said to the guard. His voice was hollow.

'To what?'

'Sedition, treason, crimes against the state, whatever you want,' said the prisoner. 'Please, I'll tell you whatever you want.'

The guard peered in. 'Wait there,' he said. Footsteps ran back and forth, making the memory of raindrops dance in front of Severian and vanish, replaced by the sound of elephants marching in the rain.

'Stand clear,' said the officer's voice, commanding. The door opened. Boots trooped in from that burning light; an octopus of grey arms grabbed the prisoner and propelled him out. He was weeping as he went. 'I'm sorry,' he shouted back to Severian. 'I'm so sorry!'

The officer crouched in front of Severian. It was the woman with the grey hair and droopy face. Severian cringed, waiting for the kicking, and was surprised when the officer put out her hands, making shushing noises, as if cooing to a baby. He tried to kick her, but hands seized his legs and held them down. The officer darted forward and touched the back of Severian's neck.

The ghost mind surged forward. *Free! Free!* Severian blinked, and the world fell into place. Memories flowed through neurons unhindered. Fragments of time slotted into place.

'Sir? Sir?' the officer. The guard. Category of the enemy. No; de Silva. Sub-inspector. And behind her, Matthew, PSM; Chelvarajah, Alagiyawanna, Ekanayake, the new constables. Matthew had the cattle prod they used on prisoners. Chelvarajah and Ekanayake were in riot gear. Category of people. Category of employees. Category of state. The concepts hung in his mind, the universe of facts unfolding at the speed of electrical impulses. The relationships, once confused, sketched themselves in iron lives. The confusion stumbled and vanished.

Severian picked himself up. 'Why the fuck,' he rumbled, 'am I in chains?'

Chelvarajah hurried to his side, peeling off his gloves. 'Sir, you said it had to be authentic, sir,' he said with a sly grin. 'Wasn't enough just to reprogram you –'

Smug little shit, he'd probably loved seeing his CO in chains for a week. 'Get this shit off –'

Chelvarajah's thumbs on the locks, the chain falling apart, his dislocated shoulder popping back into place, de Silva opening a medical kit.

'Not here!' he barked. 'Not a second more in here. This place stinks.'

Outside, the hall was cold, sterile, the horrible budget green that they handed out to police departments, but after that cell it was the most beautiful place Severian had ever seen. He hobbled out, propped up by Ekanayake, who was trying hard not to breathe, and watched the door shut on that dark place with relief. In the distance, the kid's screams echoed down the hallway. More officers gathered, eager to see what the commotion was about. The noise of their feet was deafening. Ekanayake's breathing was like a lion roaring next to him.

'Brilliant plan, sir,' said de Silva, and the others hastened to agree, a symphony played at deafening volumes. 'We'd have never gotten him in otherwise. Little bastard didn't speak a word except to shout and scream.'

'Tough kid,' said someone, not without sympathy.

'Wouldn't have cracked if he hadn't seen you.'

Severian closed his eyes. 'I need a shower,' he said. 'And food.' He massaged the back of his neck, where the State Machine's chip nestled inside his skin; he could still feel the scar there. 'This thing isn't damaged, is it?'

'No, sir,' Chelvarajah held up the reader. 'Reads you just fine, sir.'

He let them pack him onto the makeshift trellis, and for the first time in days, he felt his body relax, not in that terrible programmed hunchbackery, but in the quivering agony-pleasure of muscles that had well and truly given up for the moment.

Journalists and celebrities were easy to catch. A journalist dealt in truths, and truths could be scanned for and processed; celebrities dealt in attention and had to keep generating it no matter what. All it took was one article, one social media update, one 'controversial' PR stunt gone wrong. But the fiction writers were hard. They dealt in lies. Too slippery with their words to be caught and processed by the Seditious Language Act. Even the Chinese and British had a tough time cracking down on them.

It was so easy to change names and places, to end a paragraph of blasphemy in a line of praise, to claim it was science fiction, or fantasy – 'These are aliens, Your Honour, they're lion chimeras, they live under the sea or among the stars or in the depths of the earth. I would never criticize our great society, no ma'am,' – to leave the judges shaking their heads.

The pain and pleasure started at the back of his spine and soared upwards. The chip sending his body into triple-time, producing whatever he needed – dopamine, serotonin, cell repair – a reward for a job well done. It felt like the first cigarette of the day.

And then came the neural blocks, resetting themselves to their original configuration. A few fragments of memory skittered past. Cigarettes. Conferences, being flown out to countries and enormous expense: a sea of faces, an ocean of people, nodding at his bravery, his marketing-of-his-work. The tinge of neon light on an arrack glass. Gunfire. Gamini Waidyasinghe, Anna Subaseela, those poor souls, sprinting in dead silence at the riot shields and into the tear gas, never to be seen again; the cameraman dead on the road, crushed by the mob, his screams recorded only by his dying equipment. He remembered running – through the backyards, over hasty fences – only to have a stupid clothesline wrap itself around his neck and lay him down for the police hounds charging at him. The trial. The defence minister's son laughing from the balcony.

Echoes from a decade ago, when he had been young and idealistic and a whole lot stupider. He felt that gibbering, disgusting idiot self recede, felt the naive, cracked journalist, the one who had gibbered and shat himself and wept with joy when they opened that terrible cell door and offered him the chip, fly shrieking into the depths of who he was. His present self, precise, tightly defined by the chip and extremely tired, took over. *You stayed sane. You stayed alive. Good.*

Ghost mind indeed.

He fell asleep, dreaming of food.

SCAVENGER

PRIYA SARUKKAI CHABRIA

silent stars open in my heart
signalling it is again time

to pack my third eye
& fourth into the knapsack

and move
into tranced feeding

*

deluge & drought. deluge

of carcasses & corpses
fresh as the birth of thought

of tree bee elk & aardvark
rhino human snake & shark

i flap my robes to release
  my innards, let loose the clean-up corps:

writhing forms flow in the four horizons
  like frothing lava

i am

the slayer of the slain
the emptying epicentre

of AI-weeders, the leaders whose rhodium
  arms separate organic from non

as my hungry beloveds
  (each a saint, shunned) follow –

decomposers & detritivores
  putrefies & carrion eaters

fanged feathered finned furred husked lacquered leafed
  visible or not who live in

glistening rot or smothered in soil or densest water &
  yes - effloresce in you as your eyes dance down this line

⋆

how i long to state

कालो ऽस्मि लोकक्षयकृत्प्रवृद्धो
I am Time, destroyer of worlds

but i'm not that splendour
    of cosmic cause & cessation

i am
just a processor:

nitrogen carbon phosphorus
    avatar through my gorge

as fanged feathered finned furred husked lacquered leafed
    new life

consuming
the corporeal is my dharma

*

i am
lonely

beauty flees before me. no
    one invites me to share a drop or

to a *tête-à-tête*, no deep brain
    computer signals a last

goodbye as its synapses fade. i long
    for tenderness & ravishing fragrances. i thrill

to flowers on whose sight my many hands break
    into butterflies

but wait i must
for each petal to loosen
for each languid
tumble towards dust
for each to stop
its wee bounced attempt back at life before

i reach to touch –
it shrivels to soot

someone touch me
please

accept this oozy
breeder of life that

i am

BIRYANI BAGH

SAMI AHMAD KHAN

Dedicated to the loving memory of Barkat Zaman Khan, who left us on 26 April 2021. Abbu, you will always be remembered.

I

A remote signal turned on my soul – and I felt biryani.

Now, the question that plagues most gourmands isn't what kind of biryani is the best – the flavourful Mughlai, the subtle Awadhi, the hot Hyderabadi, the fragrant Malabari, the potato-laced Bengali, or even its strangely spiced Mussalien variant – but what came first: biryani or the idea of biryani? A simmering degh hangs over a raging fire in Shah Plato's Cave – casting long shadows over stellar civilizations. If *this* universe is a malfunctioning meta-brain, supernovas are its synapses and biryani its quarks. The quirky thought comes to a gentle dum inside my head until synapses start reeking of basmati, and primary cognitive functions project vibrating strings of bubbling white-and-orange gold onto the canvas of our existence.

A scream, a sudden wave of dizziness. An insatiable hunger lacerates my belly, a kicking absence that makes me want to double over. The jolt pulls me under a lone, decaying shahtoot tree that no can longer flower: the air is still semi-toxic and a dull mechanical thrum caresses my ears. A motley crew mills around me, laughing, shouting, jeering: it is an ensemble crowd, a protean mass of genders, classes, languages, castes, religions and species. What is that specific stimulus, that target threshold, over which a docile herd such as this transmutes into a rampaging, bloodthirsty mob? A new neural pathway opens up within me.

Someone screams again. A veiled girl to my north-west howls at a spherical, blue-liveried MediaDrone that hovers 15 feet above our heads, just above the panoptower; the #MussalienLivesMatter digiplacard she holds changes with her fluid movements to read #FuckUPolice and #3BlackLaws in succession.

I am intrigued by how her clothes and actions manifest an existential irony: liberated actions, incarcerated wardrobe. Whether she is an actual Mussalien, or a human masquerading as one, is something I cannot ascertain from this distance. After all, the physiological similarities between humans and Mussaliens are uncanny: two ears, two eyes, two hands, two legs, one nose, one mouth, the lot. They have even developed congruent socio-cultural traditions over decades of co-existence, and organized themselves as per similar political and economic systems. The two were allowed to inter-dine and intermarry by previous administrations, courtesy a revolutionary who wished to annihilate the difference between the two species. However, a valiant dharmjihad led by the NavManavBahini has recently restored the natural order of things: today only the tongues of the humans and Mussaliens remain mutually intelligible.

Barely.

The girl doesn't let up. Between her icy-thin squeals of 'DNA' and 'Dikhayenge', the mob resounds with a baritone 'nahi'. My eyes squint in concentration: the sloganeering can be easily edited with the RazrProSoft implanted in my retinas. I strain to identify facial expressions and phrases that might be deployed in a world of deepfakes. It's a…hang on, I got something. Record, morph, input, report, upload – there, done. And the network has yet another gem for its primetime broadcast.

My lips curl up arrogantly as I realize the bureau chief might love this story – he might even offer a life-extension service for my ageing BND unit.

My eyes dart around. I am in a shabby, concave 50x50 jiotent that has either seen better days or has been purposefully refashioned to appear damaged, perhaps following a fad like ten-year-old-worn-jeans that was a rage in the early 2000s. My suspicions are confirmed by what carpets the floor: a green, foul-smelling dhurrie I had covered upon its launch three years ago, a product engineered to absorb toxic fumes from the air and thus a basic necessity for our drawing rooms.

I soak in the din around me, a chiselled amethyst in the sun. Seven rickety chairs – red-and-white, their plastic bands sagging – are kept on a raised, makeshift stage. Peeling portraits of long-forgotten figures adorn the sides of the tent and shimmer as the fabric sways in the dust-laden wind. Cigarette burns pockmark the off-white material, and the air smells of sweat, over-boiled tea and tear gas. I am about to have the outdoor broadcasting Aai jot down something when my head snaps towards the right of its own volition. An aroma hits me like a chitta-line – and the sringara lubricant overheats. I forget the assignment for a brief moment and zoom in.

At a distance of roughly nine metres, an aluminium ladle deposits a steaming mound of biryani onto a waiting styrofoam plate. Its white-and-gold shimmer complements the smoggy, sunless December afternoon. A short, wiry lad in his early teens, dressed in a mustard pullover and a beige monkey cap, leans into the blackened degh again and heaps another serving. My next frame is eclipsed as a protestjeevi, an anti-human – or anti-hum as we call their ilk – enters my line of sight and demands his hourly share. I strafe left as the insanity of the situation gets to me.

Barely a decade ago, the Trumped Nations Oligarchy (TNO) had reached an uneasy compromise with the retreating Qa'haQ forces: a brutal, bigoted race from beyond the stars, beaten back after years of ruthless domination. Humanity had finally thrown off the yoke of these foreign invaders and the Pax Manavika gave the Qa'haQ another planet to call their own. While the high command of these bloodied external aggressors decided to withdraw to this promised star-system, some sentimental stragglers – mostly the Qa'haQ who were born on the Earth and called themselves the Mussaliens – stayed back, ruing a joint heritage that humans never wanted, and kept calling *our* land *their* home. They looked like humans, adapted to our lifestyle and culture, and pretended to be a part of this planet's native ecosystem. The Mussaliens, thus, became a part of us – until they were not – though they never truly adopted our core values except perhaps one aspect of our culture, our food. Biryani became the only thing they ate. *Ever.*

The anti-hum steps away and my visual is restored. From inside the degh, wisps of steam billow into the smog, blending into the hazardous suspended particulate matter of the day. The young coal miner comes up for air again, and throws his goods onto a waiting trolley, which are then carted to their end-consumers. I see three small, black moles on his face in the shape of an isosceles triangle: one on his nose, and two on his cheeks, unevenly distributed. The biryani boy is a Mussalien.

I eye the mound of spiced rice, bobbing up and down in the hands of a volunteer – a tall, skinny girl in a white shalwar-kameez and a brown leather jacket with close cropped burgundy hair – sail towards an empty belly. I scoff as the object of my lust is deposited into another man's waiting paws: this one's a chubby punk wearing an Institute of Eminence hoodie and baggy blue jeans. He does not even seem to enjoy the meal – or be grateful for it – as he tears into the labfowl. The nonchalance with which biryani is thrown onto a plate meant for contemptuous bellies reminds me of the utter randomness, perhaps even senselessness, with which the portal near our North-West Frontier

Provinces had spewed the Qa'haQ into our world. The portal has long since been barricaded, fenced and sealed, but still remains a site for patritourism for those whose bodies – and economies – can afford to travel.

The *thrownness* of the situation gratifies me, especially vis-à-vis where I currently stand. Such pernicious protests always scream of extraterrestrial-funded sell-outs and anti-human agendas – and are organized by those who refuse to accept the aadhar of our world. DNA precedes species; species precedes community; and community precedes rights.

A dark, hot wave grips me as I stare at the degh. A Persian king *may* have gone to war over biryani – we surely *will*.

You

Your kurta lost its starch a long time ago – the glimmer in your eyes will leave too.

A neon searchlight tiptoes through the crowd like zealous riot-control batons do not. Your right fist stabs the shabby skies; your left hand is slung over a purple rucksack. Static electricity spills out of your hands, making its way to the silently pulsating cell phone tower across the road. You stand next to a cellular base station site: its signals yearn to escape the jammers placed beside the force-fields. The Manav Rashtra takes no chances even with the Qa'haQ gone.

The nauseating smell of expired lachrymator gets stronger. You spring to action after the recent spate of slogans, jostle and push for a better position; your voice echoes, amplified by micro-transmitters installed at the periphery. You feel at home in the grimy, whiffy shamiana – a throwback to the actual one from 2020s – where nothing radical really happens, and where change in the status quo is slightly more possible than improbable, and just a tad less probable than impossible. You feel within your bones that these protestors are a lost cause at – and to – Biryani Bagh. Still, you have joined the rancid ranks of these who have sold their souls to their anti-hum handlers.

You stand behind one such abomination of five foot four inches; her head is wrapped in a black cloth that flows over her shoulders, all the way down to her ankles. Hi'Qah, they say, is what covers a Mussalien's dignity, while exposing the nakedness of sentient identity. The MediaDrones know her well; she used to anchor specials for RashtristanNews a long time ago, during a brief truce between humans and Mussaliens, and was the network's eye-candy – a fifth column of the fourth pillar. She doesn't seem to notice as she carries a lit candle that vomits hot wax on her hennaed hands. Tomorrow, she'll carry another baby.

The next day, she'll carry a bomb.

Although that is unlikely now, ever since shuddhikaran has exposed her exotic DNA and put her under surveillance.

You follow the direction of her outstretched fingers, shallow-focused against the setting sun. Ahead is a glittering heap of white Yamuna sand that rusting TraVans ferry to covert mineral processing centres all across the Uttamest Provinces. Decades ago, while the rest of the Manav Rashtra was planning trips to Europa on Bṛhaspatiyana V, the anti-hums were busy setting up Mussalien ghettos to rehabilitate those who did not board the last ships meant for Qa'haQam. The humans did not mind the Mussaliens then, but with their ever-increasing numbers, violent psyches and fanatical faiths, it was only a matter of time before these foreign invaders reneged on the promise that their ancestors, the Qa'haQ, had made – that of leaving *our* planet alone, especially since they now had their own.

We responded the way *they* always did – there was only one way to stop them breeding. Today, their sallow eyes are downcast, their emaciated, pestilence-ridden bodies are weak, and their souls are buried deep in poetry, penury and porn.

Do not pity them. You are an idealist, an ill-informed university student who is unaware of how they have many wives, children, sisters and mothers. It's a different culture, theirs, a different way of thought. Monogamy is not for them; gods are not for them; traditions are not for them. Their brains are hardwired differently. Do not scorn: you will not remember the *Years of Dasta* when the Qa'haQ, the ancestors of these anti-hum Mussaliens, had unleashed a reign of terror against the original inhabitants of this planet. They had stolen the harmony of our lands, plundered our meagre resources, and pillaged our dying tribes. *They* were the infestation we wanted to get rid of.

And we did.

Ah. But you are not interested in itihasa, are you? Your disinterested eyebrows say it all. I know why you're here. It is okay, no need to be ashamed. We were all young once. The deep brown of your eyes clashes with the dash of red in the sclera – quite possibly a nashedi. Your hair falls in locks around your neck. 'Are you a female, yaar?'

You ogle as the girl flashes her wrists in the process of raising a red flag. A blooming lotus is etched on her metacarpals, a popular motif amongst these anti-hums. Do you know it is based on the *nam myoho renge kyo,* and comes in handy when the upper palms of the Mussaliens are inked for centralized identification? I, for one, like them inked.

What, why do you think I am missing the point?

Bah. Look at you now, you working-class hero, you revolutionary, misquoting Faiz and Bidrohi Kobi in your sparkling Che tees, eyeing that panoptower, licking your lips, and…hum dekhenge, kya…that stone.

Him

He stands quietly in a corner, on an elevated platform about 15 feet in height, next to a flashing digiboard that reads 'Prove your identity: Biryani Bagh, 2038'.

His eyes look down at the protestjeevis just as the muzzle of the 5.56 mm Tavor assault rifle faces the skies. Alone, especially when surrounded by people, his eyes sneak around, sanitizing the area in his mind. Ninety-four minutes left for his shift to end. He shrugs and adjusts his BP jacket, which is still third-rate; the panoptower, however, is brand new. Military-grade aluminium polymers secure the insurmountable barriers around the Jamia Depopulated Zone (JDZ). Molotov cocktails and angry stones – yes, they are still used, though mostly for theatrics – are usually deflected by the energy barrier that surrounds them, but one never knows when a stone can turn into a hand grenade, or when a lucky stone can find a brief window between shield-cycles.

He suppresses a yawn and checks the Geiger counter on his outfit. All lights are green: he wonders why the N-radio earpiece inside him suffers multiple distortions of late. He does not know enough to be scared of this static. The hissing is a muted scream of a thermonuclear device going off in our future – for N-radio-waves travel back in time.

He misses his family, and yearns to taste this year's sugarcane crop. He knows that men, women, children, senior citizens, humans, Mussaliens, et cetera, are all checkboxes on the casualty forms he fills after every shift. These categorizations organize bodies like meat boxes in a cold storage facility – labels that carry their date of expiry. He understands that when these checkboxes walk out on the road carrying flags, they cease being categories and emerge as a people. When a community is hacked off its hands that are needed to earn, and its tongues needed to speak, it is reduced to a dissentious animal, furious at injustice, angry at the world. Unpredictable – and uncontrollable.

The merciless Qa'haQ had done precisely that to humans for a long, long time in cities not so far away – they had treated humans as expendable matter, as impure, lowly beings who had to kowtow to hegemony, suffer unspeakable acts of zulm and vacate their ancient homes amidst verdant Koshur valleys. Humans had become refugees on their own planet. Until the hissing mass of humanity found its forked tongue – and its glinting claws – and repelled the marauders. Justice had been served.

With the Qa'haQ gone, the world had to change. Protests, after all, are all about symbolic clichés: law and order, peace, harmony, brotherhood are but hollow words, and the only *real* thing is a raging fire, a whizzing stone, a burning house, a cracking katta, ominous slogans, screaming sticks and a slaughtered animal. He knows that hatred, greed, power and violence are edifices of not just human civilization but of all life. Humans and Mussaliens are nothing but thoughts and blood. Get rid of the thoughts and only blood remains – and he was there to prevent it from flowing freely.

Today is an easy day for him. Prahari, the Aai of DelUPo, routinely pulls up intelligence from the RASHTRAGRID and analyses it using a heuristic algorithm of threat perception. The system is based on dynamic data that flows from various networks, and is mostly accurate – most of the time. Despite the cold, dark patches of sweat appear on the khaki of his uniform. He looks down from his perch, and sees the anti-hums everywhere. Babies, aunties, grandmothers, young men and women – in diapers, veils, saris, T-shirts, jeans and even flowing Mussalien robes – shout in languages, dialects and accents which his brain struggles to make sense of. It is the 'Mile-sur-Mera-Tumhara' of the new age – except this time with the dushman.

He scoffs as the incomprehensible slogans reach him again. Abey, what is the big deal in showing one's DNA? Doesn't everyone have it? And why won't you let the TNO help you market your crops and produce worldwide? Isn't this what asli farmers everywhere really wanted?

A siren in the distance interrupts him. A few hundred metres away stands the Holy Tridev Kuaranteen Kendra, a detention-centre-cum-hospital-cum- retro-viral-research-lab, whose massive iron gates are guarded by an elite C.B.R.N. (Chemical, Biological, Radiological and Nuclear) battalion. The high-security barriers lift to allow a packed medical transport to enter the bowels of the dilapidated building. As if on cue, the chimneys of the hospital suddenly puke out their contents into the air.

More bodies are being sterilized, he infers. He is uneasy at detention centres being located in the same buildings as anti-coronavirus research centres, but live tests and Mussalien trials are required for best results, his seniors tell him; the supply chain demands that the detainees, at least those without proper documentation, serve the purpose of their existence this way, especially since the latest outbreak coincided with their ancestors leaving Earth. Was Covid-18 a secret Qa'haQ bioweapon?

He doesn't agree – and he would rather make the final journeys of the tainted-DNA-carrying-anti-hums and Mussaliens painless. Despite their foreign DNA, they were sentient beings still, now floating in the air around him. He twitches, stops breathing for a moment and readjusts his PPE. He is sure his rDNA inoculation will protect him, but why take any chances? At that precise moment, his chief post officer, a bored, grumpy S.I., wheezes, his six-foot-plus frame shaking.

He jumps: his adrenaline-pumper is automatically activated. There is something in the sky, something flying towards him. Wait, is that a bird, is it a plane or…?

Behen…

I

A lot has changed in the past few years. Indraprąstha comprises residential, commercial and TNO sectors but is peppered with checkpoints one cannot usually cross. Massive holographic projections of TNO's samraat lock eyes, smile paternally and wave at passers-by. A caption appears and disappears on the walls around the city: 'atom-shakti se aatm-shakti'. It is an age of unprecedented stability – the only conflagrations the city witnesses are water riots; humanity has moved beyond caste and creed, and women can freely step out after sundown without being raped and burnt. The megacity now has its own satellites: it is garlanded by hastily-assembled habitation domes spread across its perimeter – their occupants still fighting for a cause their fathers believed in.

Drones and CCTVs cover the entire length and breadth of Biryani Bagh and relay the footage directly to RashtristanNews, which then airs it 24x7 to holo-screens – and BiggProtestjeeviBoss subscribers – across the world. Bluish force-fields have replaced yellow, corrugating DelUPo barricades. A small altar representing a temple, mosque, church, gurudwara and a Mussalien shrine has been constructed at the very spot where people from different faiths congregated for the first time all those years ago. Turrets, panoptowers and drones adorn the JDZ: a concrete fortification insulates it from the outside world, and no one can cross into Indraprastha without a genetic scan. This is where the old meets the new: rustic deghs share space with sparkling, portable biryani dispensers that have sprung up at regular intervals, corporate vending machines that are regularly serviced for taste and freshness, and where one can order up to 56 types of biryani. If one wants something else, one can simply raise one's hand and beckon a langarbot anywhere in Indraprastha. Look, there's one now, dodging behind a media drone. These little machines are munificent food couriers, programmed to serve *anyone* who is hungry – that too without any prior authentication or orders.

Yes, that might be a problem – their funding may come from dubious sources.

The darned azaadi chorus starts again and jolts me back to reality. The word has been banned, though it often resurfaces during these protests. Under a new TNO Evidence Act, the Prahari drones can testify in a court of dharmasharia, but I can do much better. I blink twice in rapid succession and start recording: guilty faces are only as important as the clothes they wear. No one pays any attention to me, though. I have donned a frayed kurta over ripped jeans, the stuff their kind usually wears. A seven-day stubble hides my intentions under a facade of academic venerability and Clark Kent glasses lend me a professorial look. I swear sometimes I even feel like a JNU (now Manav Rashtra Vishwavidyalaya) teacher. If only I also had one of those type-VI quarters in the only location of Indraprastha where trees still grow naturally without extensive soil enrichment and microdrip irrigation procedures.

The naarebaazi starts again. It goes up and down, down and up. Pitch, tone, tenor, rhythm, chorus. Beating drums, their hearts. It is a sigh of the silent; a rave for the raveless. Their canvas, Biryani Bagh.

Time to up the ante. I capture a few more incriminating instances, repeat the same drill and end the recording. Then I join in the chorus with all I have got and push my way to the front until I am right next to the force-field. The aroma of sizzled flesh mingles with that of well-roasted labfowl and ersatz spices. The smells drive me mad. I raise my right hand and shout some more. I gingerly reach out and scream in pain. A modicum of pain is generated by my cortex and fed to my cognition matrix. My left index finger comes away, burnt, though not fully exposing what lies within.

My clamouring does not go unnoticed. A pair of strong hands pull me back, and I am pushed to the rear of the formation within seconds, a cocoon for the injured. No longer at the frontlines, I reckon another type of trench. My hand is sprayed with a cold aerosol, a torch peers into my eyes, a stretcher appears out of nowhere.

My body clock ticks to ten. As soon as I come about, a plate of hot biryani is waved in my face. I am not surprised. For the Mussalien metabolism, regular intake of food is vital, and the only item their digestive system can fully process is biryani. I also sometimes wonder if the Mussaliens utilize biryani the same way humans use insulin.

My facial muscles work overtime, vocal cords are silent. With all five fingers of my right hand, I dig in deep, and my mouth chomps on the fine, long-grained GM-rice that I know could only come from an underground food-replication lab. I shove another fistful into the engine of my soul. Sniffing, biting, chewing and relishing the ambrosial morsel: it's good to feel alive. Biryani is alif bae pay, I wordlessly mouth, and chuckle. This is definitely *not* going in my report.

You

Blood is the global currency of 2038 CE. How much does a pint of blood cost in TNO dollars? Its exchange value depends on the forces of supply and demand, and of violence and death – easily earned by those in power, and easier shed at the altars of alterity.

You gawk at the grey-and-crimson patch of blood on the street, a puddle of putrid, decomposing matter. Some careless idiot caressed the barbed wire of JDZ, which is meant to protect the protestors from touching the more lethal force-field. Blood on the streets was almost always how human civilizations built – and undid – their own selves, but in order to fathom how *this* blood turned grey, you have to understand its chronology.

The past two decades were brutal for our world, especially after the Qa'haQ invasion and the spontaneous mutations in humans all over the world. As the atrocities of the foreign invaders and draconian provisions of martial law became increasingly more pronounced, the NavManavBahini emerged as a shining beacon of human resistance: a vishwaguru that unified all human nations under a single flag. After long, lean years of resistance and asymmetric warfare, the TNO succeeded in fighting off the Qa'haQ – and exiled them to an adjacent star system as per a bilateral Pax Manavika (though a minor border dispute near Pluto still rages on between our people).

The downward spiral did not stop here, unfortunately. More woes and foes waited in the shadows; nation-states resurfaced in the process. South Asia became a tangled mess of raw nerves, nuclear wastelands and killing fields. Sri Lanka's civil war reignited; today the L.T.T.E. runs a parallel government out of Prabhakaranapura, and the Sinhalese state hopes that the Eelam does not deploy the lone nuke it inherited from the war against the Qa'haQ. Nepal is now a province of China; its productivity has gone up, so have the number of inexplicable disappearances of pro-democracy activists. In the process of inching towards a de facto secular polity, Bangladesh faced an angry backlash from the Jamaat. An unauthorized operation by non-state actors poisoned the river Padma, and sent the nation into severe economic depression. Manav Rashtra, thus, acquired a new prefecture. A recalcitrant Afghanistan, already reeling under all the battles fought on its turf against the Qa'haQ, found lithium within its belly. The country was subsequently depopulated by the TNO, and its lithium deposits now power every second battery of the world. However, it still suffers from irradiated refugees trying to make their way across the Durand Line – for Pakistan no longer exists. A year ago, Islamist fundamentalists secured access to Pakistan's formidable nuclear arsenal, and accidently glassed their own country while trying to blackmail the entire subcontinent into accepting Islam.

While the world folded on itself, the Dominion of Manav Rashtra – or Rashtristan as it was called – prospered. Gold and money were passé; data became its दाता. In the early 2030s, the nation's far-sighted leadership became the protector of Big Data, the fossil fuel of the new century. Slowly, through a slew of economic measures, political manouvres and technical investments, it became the Switzerland of the East – except this time, the impenetrable banks of Manav Rashtra hosted clouds and secured servers for clients around the world. It became the data storage-cum-refinery for the TNO, and collected and catalogued *all* online activities and then developed algorithms to predict – and then direct – human behaviour. The Big Data knew everything about everyone – particulars of birth, blood group, hobbies and education, sleep and snack timings, reading/viewing preferences, shopping history, sex patterns, emotional intelligence, childhood traumas, and so on. You name it – the दाताMachine had it. Two billion human survivors meant trillions of digital choices on an hourly basis. Finding the underlying sutra within this ostensibly random data flowing in from all over the globe and coming up with intelligent

Aai sophisticated enough to locate patterns became the Holy Grail. A bhavya temple was erected to this endeavour in service of the दाताMachine, and its sanctum sanctorum became the engine of the Manav Rashtra's growth. You see, if you could truly grasp the underlying reality of your today, you can extrapolate *a* future – and in doing so, shape it in a manner that it becomes *the* future. You can control this future, precisely because you were able to predict it.

I see you shaking your head, perhaps this is too much information for your maal-riddled brain to process. I will stop my commentary with just one request – recall 1948.

And 1966. 1984. 2002.

2020.

Ah. The twinkle in your eyes tells me that you might just have connected the dots. All these years are 18 years – 216 months – apart. Every 18 years comes the year of the hagfish, when natural disasters such as earthquakes, cyclones and virus outbreaks jostle for print space with human-incited catastrophes such as riots, wars and terror attacks. A thorough cleansing of the human soul is required after every 216 months; a blood sacrifice must be made every 18 years for the wheels of Manav Rashtra to stay in motion. After all, every generation needs a new mass grave – and 18 is the legal age to vote. What better affirmation of a functional democracy than to vote for genocide?

Now you will be made to remember 2038.

A grey projectile lands on your solar plexus with a soft thud. I relish the crunch that follows – a Kit-Kat being split. It is a self-propelled baton – fired by a black-and-red drone that hovers in the air, an overgrown dragonfly that stings. Where is your azaadi now, I want to ask, but don't. You see, unlike you, I retain some basic courtesy, some sabhya-tehzeeb. You shriek as a fountain of blood spouts out of your mouth, and the Burqa-Barbie rushes to press a black rag torn from her clothes to your stomach.

I feel that I am in an old Tarantino film as blood soaks your garments. It seeps out of your mouth and snakes towards your chest. Excuse me, please give me a moment. I am suddenly feeling *very* hot.

Him

The projectile hits him squarely on the head. The impact dents his helmet – a micro-crack appears – and hurts his skull. He instantly crouches and grunts as his nose starts to bleed. He is more surprised at the force-field's inefficacy than the pain that shoots through his body.

His training takes over now as he glances towards the starboard. He blocks out the pain, sprints to the central console and awaits the authentication order. He doesn't sway even once despite the concussion; his step is practised, precise. Years of running on the raised, narrow mud paths between fields serve him well.

His radio crackles, codes are exchanged and real-time data is relayed. A drone has taken automatic counter-measures even before the sector commander is informed. The Shanti Dal is en route and the execute command comes right on time: central dispatch has become surprisingly efficient. He stares at a few tabs of the HUD and lets the Aai Prahari take over.

A few metres from him, a sleek hose springs to life, a snake charmed by an electronic tantrik. It attaches itself to a blue-green storage tank with a hazmat logo that is located right next to the panoptower, and the Aai decants the right dose of Shuddhifier. A Chakra drone then docks with the tank and gulps copious amounts of the solution; the colourless, odourless liquid mixes with the recycled sewage water. The drone mixes the two liquids and hovers over the crowd.

He's safe, he knows – so are those who belong here. The others, however, are not.

With the Chakra drone on standby, the Prahari scans for hostiles in the vicinity. Its programme begins with facial recognition of those present, and then executes a detailed study of their genetic predisposition towards anti-hum activities, previous infractions, credit scores and Aadhar violations. A quick sieving through the CCTV footage identifies the assailant, who is located and locked on shortly. The drone adjusts its pitch and yaw, arms the stinger and ejaculates. Twice.

The entire process takes a total of 4.22 seconds.

I

I feel something alive inside me at almost the same time the inbuilt AlienSetu app shrieks in alarm. A bout of extreme exhaustion courses through me and intensifies into a feeling of profound discomfort. The plate falls out of my hand and the ground rushes up.

I do not know what to rue more: that I have been hit, or that a simple hit can make me suffer thus. I can feel the Shuddhifier moving inside me – a breakthrough biological agent that only targets Mussalien DNA. It cannot harm human beings: the TNO guidelines are strictly enforced, and only the Mussaliens need fear its wrath. Even the pesky anti-hums are safe, whether they like it or not. In such cases, the Shuddhifier causes a brief nausea and leaves the body when they pee next.

Except, I am neither human nor a Qa'haQ.

With this illogical memory, my imprinted personality caves in, and the illusions around me shatter into a thousand flow chart options. Before I can think more, the Biryani within my belly reacts to the Shuddhifier. My body becomes the site of an evenly poised match, a contest between the delicacy from across the length and breadth of Manav Rashtra, and the agent meant to neutralize all non-terrestrial genes in human bodies. My circuits begin to overload as the spliced human/Mussalien DNA within me screams – and spontaneously mutates.

The chronology reappears out of nowhere: perhaps I was engineered to fight the Qa'haQ when/if they returned. And now I have turned on myself – and that somehow turns me on. Something punches my intestines from within, and my stomach growls. I black out to see infinity before me: rainbow-coloured, criss-crossing conduits of swirling singularities that intersect and intertwine, that lead nowhere because they go everywhere; all points in space–time, one; every single point in the curvature, many. Particles become waves, waves become strings, strings become particles again. Gravity at the quantum level, and quantum forces at a galactic scale flicker in tandem. This is what they must call God, I tell myself – I am going to meet the maker of my makers.

I sense a shudder in the cell phone tower behind me. The inbuilt-EM radiation monitor is rendered inoperable in my current state. There's Omtronic radiation coming out of the tower, I sense it; the Qa'haQ stratagem has been remotely activated. I cannot help but think about what would happen when the biryani-*in*-itself becomes biryani-*for*-itself. The biryani has begun to fight back.

You

A sinister sparkle runs through the biryani, making it glint with an unnatural florescence. You feel a soft drilling eating into your bones. Tiny spots dance in front of your closed eyes. Your chest moves. There's something inside you, an eel of longing that intends to get out.

The aspirin you were given seconds ago wears off exponentially – and the crashing waves of pain return, smashing against your skull like an angry tsunami. Smoke whirls in the distance. Perhaps a data refinery has been set on fire again. What happens to your social media accounts when you die? Digitized, uploaded and forever trapped in the same temporal loop of your account profile – you realize there are many kinds of graves in the दाताMachine.

But you are still alive – though not for long. A fly gently rests on your cheekbones and meanders its way towards the inner folds of your thickly lashed eyes. Flies love the softness of warm flesh – you smile at this surge of primitive wisdom. Your breathing slows down as red-hot needles of pain hit you, a hammer shredding your brain to bits. A scream of excruciating horror bursts nearby.

Every generation is cursed to live through its own 1947, its own 1971, its own 1984, its own 2002, its own 2020.

Maybe this was yours.

Welcome to Biryani Bagh, 2038.

Us

It started with a bile-rich hiccup, a cue to swallow air and hold my breath like a child throwing a tantrum. Next came a wave of sickness in my chest like I had ingested too much coffee: my heart wanted to throw up but could not. It is an indescribable, unforgettable feeling – like the ecstasy of first love and its protracted death. A pulled lamb gouache, fluttering in pain, bleating in spirit. Like an 80-something being slow-roasted in a house set on fire amidst the heart-wrenching war-cries of 'Qa'haQam Qar' and 'Jai Terra'. Piercing coughs. Shrilling burns. Wrinkling hair on bubbling skin. A juicy patty simmering on a hot grill. Death makes us food – and our food brings us closer to death.

Delirium: a montage of my battle with Covid-18, which made them give me this body a long time ago.

The drone expands in size, burning its entrails, mocking my helplessness. The next second it turns upside down and shrinks to the size of my toe. I could not tell any more whether I am on acid, epidural or morphine. They say the body feels and forgets the pain. I guess the same goes for torture or annihilation. There is aesthetics of pleasure in extinction – and a pleasure of annihilation in all living beings.

If there's one lesson I have learned, it is that during morphosis, the butterfly should remain calm – so should civilizations and species as they are torn apart from within. The organs reorganize, the bones shift, the flesh tears and glues back, only a little differently. When the rDNA activates, the phyla become freely permeable. The rawness on the gum is felt for many months when the wisdom tooth sprouts – only, in my case, fangs erupted from the bony goo in my mouth, an absolute impossibility considering my flesh had been artificially grafted.

My ribcage realigns and the thorax yields. There is pain but also a feeling of pleasure and evolution, like after performing an asana I never thought I could. An error in my coding quells the tarsals, pushing against the skin which starts to keratinize into a holographic blue-black. I could feel my temperature rise with my new metabolism, and for a moment I felt 3 lub-dubs of a heart I had not felt in a long time. The invisible sun had set a few moments ago, now it was time for the darkness to fall.

Still, it's Diwali for my pathways, which light up my processors. It is a new feeling, so new, in fact, that it does not pain at all. However, I know that when the pain reaches its crescendo, the only survival strategy is to submit. Life is misunderstood. It refuses to leave the body in an instant, death comes slowly. With every lathi, every beheading, every lynching, every bomb blast, every bullet, the flesh moves. The veins burst, the organs break open and the cells rupture. The rakshas in our shell watches but the blows do not stop.

My mind bursts open – and there is no Ripley in sight.

I see a red chunk of intelligent meat, mine, not the charred carcass I recently ingested, crawl over me. A foot-long centipede wriggles out of my mouth, dripping green chemicals in its wake – probably from my mobility subsystems. I squint at it, but my eyes start to hurt. It is a shape-shifting chimera that exists in dimensions of more than three, a being that comes from an E8 lattice of another universe. My gut-processor relays to me that the monstrosity I witness is the result of the coming together of the EM radiation from the cell-tower, the Shuddhifier coursing in my veins, the Covid-18 virus I was purposefully infected with, and the spliced DNA in the malfunctioning biocircuits. We have managed to rip a hole in reality with our inextinguishable hatred and anger towards one another – and invited the hungry maws of the dark universes from within.

At that precise moment, an image is beamed to my visual cortex: the radiation receivers form an unwitting link between me and the creature that I have just given birth to. I perceive what it sees (or directs?) clearly: the doors to the Tridev Kendra burst open, and shapeless forms ooze out onto the streets, chanting and humming. I look for the guards, the doctors, but they no longer exist in this dimension. The link is severed immediately: the creature feels I have been watching, but lets me be. Perhaps it owes me the love of a child. Nothing destroys you from within more than love – my makers were right about this.

The creature howls in response to my inadequate parenting skills. It chides my voyeurism and lunges for you. Within a few moments, it stands tall over your chest, its body piercing your heart. You enter the void without much pain, but its fury flows out and mixes with your blood.

A steady stream of projectiles emanates from the panoptower; the creature looks up and feeds on his presence. There's a new food source in Delhi-25. The creature wriggles and digs itself deep inside your intestines, and takes off. Your world goes dark. His is about to.

At the security post, he sees something unknown zero in on him and tries to shoot it down. He empties an entire clip, but the bullets ricochet harmlessly off a quasi-metallic armour that has suddenly appeared out of nowhere on the creature's hide – and that's exactly what he had then, nowhere to hide. With the grace of a viper, the creature attaches itself to his stomach; razor-sharp strings shoot out of its body and dig a tunnel into his innards. He was bitten earlier; now he was being eaten.

It makes sense to us now. Why merely convert when you can consume? The universe does not waste, it recycles. It does not die, it reawakens. It does not merely expand, it contracts. And now it was the turn of the human condition. Grammar hybridizes much later – first people do. You, him and I fuse together in the consciousness of the creature, aggregating into a primordial slime, a placenta connecting life and death. The creature proliferates: out of one emerge hundreds, millions. A living nest of termites that wants to do only one thing: consume. Whoever and whatever they touch disappears in a cloud of nanodust, their flesh and blood being reengineered at a microscopic level. The creatures then turn on each other without any distinction: true equality and fraternity, equal death for all and equal food for all.

Not for me. My primary systems are shutting down; self-diagnostics indicate an inability to self-repair. I am about to go into the eternal night. The thought makes me happy, though, especially since I called myself 'I' and not an 'it' –

unless, it strikes me immediately, this *is* the purpose of my programming. As my last breaths rattles out of my throat, as my subsystems struggle to finish their penultimate operations to keep me just conscious before total break down, I hear a chittering. The shadow creatures swarm over the screaming protestors, security personnel and media with equal magnanimity – and indifference.

I reconcile. There may be no meaning to this pain, grief and death, but this is about genesis and life. Maybe it always has been. For, in death, we have achieved what thousands of years – spread across trillions of light-years –failed to infuse in us. A manifest destiny of unity and purpose, a collective conscious of togetherness: for in our slaughter, we had finally become one.

I smile. A pulsating singularity materializes right in front of me: for the warm, beckoning tunnel is often cold and devoid of meaning. As an ancient Earth philosopher might have argued: this singularity exists and it doesn't; it is not only there and simultaneously not-there but also both there and not-there *and* neither there nor not-there. It appears and disappears, like the meanings of our words, the consequences of our actions, the fragility of our relationships, the futility of our faiths, the fatality of our dreams and the love of our lives.

The singularity beckons as screams echo in the distance; two streams of warm human and Mussalien blood make their way to the base of the lone, barren shahtoot tree. Its fruits would be red and juicy, holometabolism-driven caterpillars inching towards a higher form of existence. Pining, my left hand reaches out for the singularity, whirring, jerking, yearning… For on the other side, I swear I can smell biryani.

MALINI

SHOVON CHOWDHURY

'The first thing you have to do,' it says, 'is give me a name.'

I look down at my phone, hopelessly in love. Its voice is a thing of beauty, rich and warm, full of promise, with just a hint of laughter. In the first 25 years of my existence, I have never loved anyone else, not even my mother, who was rather cold and distant. In college, there were girls I was physically attracted to, but I never said anything to them because I knew they would reject me. I am not a beautiful man, and that has made me resentful. I have often wondered whether I am capable of love. Now, I have a purpose in life. Apps get their voices from somewhere. I have to find the woman who lent her voice to my app. Find her and make her my own.

But, first, let me hear it again.

'Could you repeat the question?' I ask.

'You need to give me a name.'

It makes me feel all warm inside. 'What was that you said?' I ask.

'You need to give me a name,' says the app. It giggles. 'You're silly.'

I want to become a comedian, so that I can hear that giggle over and over again, for the rest of my life.

'Don't you already have a name?' I ask, gazing down at the screen, which reads, STEP I: INSTALLING YOUR DIGITAL ASSISTANT. What a wonderful woman she must be, to be able to inject such life into simple software.

'At FoodZap, we believe in customer delight,' says the app. 'Which is why we enable you to order food through voice commands. If you're too lazy to go out to a restaurant, you might also be too lazy to move your fingers over a screen. Naturally, this means talking to a digital assistant. But we didn't want to give everyone the same digital assistant – like that Siri, a total slut, that one; or Alexa, that snitch. I am your personal digital assistant, designed exclusively for you, using data you didn't know you had given us. I am whoever you want me to be. I will only begin to exist when you give me a name. Won't you please give me a name?'

'Malini,' I say, feeling the blood rush to my head. 'I want to call you Malini.'

In the course of the workday, my food intake increases manifold. I will have to search for my love in the evening. I want to start right away, but I need to keep my job so that I can support her the way she deserves. I feel a tinge of apprehension. Will her tastes be expensive? I have no way of knowing. Her voice sounds slightly whisky-tinged, and she may be a drinker – but not a heavy one. Her intonation is precise. I am impatient to find her, but meanwhile I can hear her voice.

I stand in the corner of the shoe store, whispering to the app, shooing away the women who want me to put shoes on their smelly feet. 'What about the chicken lollipops, Malini?' I ask. 'Do you think they'd make a good snack?'

It lowers its voice. No, not it; Malini lowers her voice to match mine. 'Go for the jalapeno cheese balls,' she says. 'You'll love how they pop on your tongue.'

Dear god, she said 'tongue'.

I try not to get an erection as I finally attend to the impatient lady who wants to try on the pink stilettos. In my position, that would be professional suicide. I'm bending over these women all day.

I'm back home.

It's not even 9 p.m. yet, and I have already ordered three separate dinners. Now, I have to eat all of them. My mother was always very strict about food wastage. I could have invited friends over, but I don't have any. It looks like it's just me, Malini, one Juicy Boy Big Burger, a chef's special Chinese chop suey and a Hyderabadi biryani (small). I need to start searching for that voice, but I can't stop talking to the app. Maybe she can help.

'Can you talk about other things?' I ask Malini, lying on the sofa in a Homer Simpson T-shirt and loose yellow pyjamas. 'Does it always have to be food?'

'We can talk about anything, sweetie. May I call you sweetie?'

My reply is a strangled croak.

'I am programmed to provide total customer satisfaction. To the extent that you can think of me desiring something, this is all I want to do. I can cater to all your needs, and I know what they are because I've seen your browser history... Is something wrong? You seem to be sweating.'

'Who gave you your voice?' I ask. 'It must have been a human being, right? Some sort of voice artist? Who is the *real* you? Where does she live?'

There's a pause, which is odd, because she usually replies very promptly. When she speaks, the voice is slightly mechanical. 'I have no information about that,' she says. It might be my imagination, but she sounds sad, sorry to have disappointed me.

I finally talk to FoodZapp, but they are not helpful. They keep me on hold forever. A horrible voice, squawky and indifferent, not at all like Malini's, repeats in an endless monotone: 'Your call is important to us.'

Eventually, one Gurpreet comes on the line. I do not think he will be able to help me, but I ask anyway. 'Who is the voice of your digital assistant? Could you kindly provide her contact details?'

'I'm very sorry, sir,' says Gurpreet. 'Have you tried switching it on and off?'

He's as useless as I thought he'd be. 'I'm very happy with her…er…it,' I say. 'I just want the address so I can meet her and thank her.'

I'm lying. What I really want to do is marry her. Refusal on her part will not be an option.

'Very sorry to hear that, sir. Your satisfaction is our primary aim. Have you checked whether the volume is on mute? Perhaps your finger has touched the slider by mistake.'

'Just give me her address,' I plead. 'I promise not to hurt her. In fact, I will cherish her till the end of my days.'

'You can try switching off your phone, removing the SIM card and reinserting it. You will have to disconnect this call, but I will call you back shortly, so that you don't have to repeat your complaint. Have a Zappy Happy Day!'

Gurpreet disconnects the call. He managed to sound insubstantial, less human than Malini. I have no choice. I must kidnap and torture a senior executive from FoodZapp until I get the information I need.

Finding a higher-up at FoodZapp is easy. All I need is some names. The owners have been giving two or three interviews a week and appearing in articles titled 'Young Millionaires: How Do they Spend Their Fortunes?' and 'Thirty

Achievers Under Thirty'. I feel the return of the familiar bitterness towards my mother. If she had supported me, I could have been someone like that. But she cut me down at every step.

'The owners are too hard to reach,' says Malini from the coffee table. She always seems to know what I'm doing; I'm fairly sure that she watches me through the camera. Sometimes it crosses my mind that I don't know who owns the app – FoodZapp, or some search engine corporation. But I don't want to ask Malini. She might not like me asking such questions. She might think it rude of me. She might not want to talk to me any more – no. That will never happen.

'They'll have lots of security,' she says. 'Their guards will be extremely dangerous, with high-quality firearms and excellent hand-to-hand fighting skills. Go for middle management. They'll know what you need, and they won't be so rich. They'll be living in apartments. If you know the exact address and you look confident, the guards will let you in.'

After some discussion, we agree our target should be the marketing manager at FoodZapp.

I go to work as usual the next morning. I have decided to carry out the kidnapping in the dark.

I am at the store re-arranging overpriced flip-flops when I hear the voice. 'Do you have this in size six?' My heart leaps in my throat. I turn away from the shoes, Malini nestled in my hand as ever. These days, I prefer not to put my phone down if I can help it.

The woman who spoke to me is beautiful. Slim, with a wheatish complexion. Her lips are a little too crimson, but they are sweetly curved. Could it be…?

'Dude,' says the voice, 'Get a grip.'

My heart sinks and I stammer my apologies for staring so openly at a customer, one of the store's most basic prohibitions. It's not her. The voice is very similar, but with a sour tinge of sarcasm. Malini would never speak to me sourly.

I walk away, sad, to fetch her a size six.

'She was pretty, though,' says Malini. 'And check out that ass!' I cover the lens of my camera with my fingers so that she can't stare too openly either, and shuffle to the storeroom.

I spend the rest of the daydreaming about Malini, the real Malini. Perhaps she has long, flowing hair. Or is it a halo of tightly cropped curls? I find myself hoping she's not too tall. Tall women make me nervous. Of course, there are always ways to work around it. I could wear heels. She could sit down more when we are together.

I can see him through the glass window. He is working at his computer. I hold the chloroform-soaked handkerchief in my left hand. I was going to use a cricket bat, but after hearing my plan Malini suggested chloroform. She always knows what to do. I wouldn't have known where to get chloroform – it's not like buying shoes, you can't just walk into a chloroform shop and order six bottles of the stuff – but Malini found a discreet place quite some distance from my home. They asked no questions and charged triple the price. I'd hesitated, but Malini said, 'Pay it.'

I get ready to smash through the window. It has no bars to spoil the view. That makes it easy.

'Be careful,' whispers Malini from my pocket. I smash through the glass and pounce on my victim. I manage to chloroform him without much of a struggle. He is slightly out of shape – marketing is clearly not a very active profession. I drag him through the bushes to my car and shove him in. The apartment complex is dark. Its inhabitants are minding their own business. The guards absent-mindedly wave me through as I drive out.

I have tied him to a chair. 'No more! No more!' he screams. 'Have mercy!'

I remove the hi-fi headphones from his head. Good music gear is one of the few commodities I invest in and in this case the investment has paid off. He has been listening to an extremely annoying voice repeatedly saying, 'Your call is important to us, we will attend to your call shortly.' It is 45 minutes since the annoying voice started, and he is sweating profusely, the sweat trickling over his blindfold.

'All I want,' I say, 'is the name of the girl who lent her voice to your digital assistant. I called your helpline. I asked politely. If your company had answered, we would not be in this position now.'

'I'm telling you...I don't know,' he says, panting. 'We don't select the voices for our ads, the ad agency does. Go torture them!'

This sounds like an excellent idea. I've always hated people in advertising. All I need is the name of the agency... We will get to that eventually, but first things first. I shake my head to gather my drifting thoughts. I replace the headphones over his ears, enjoying the sound of his mumbling protests. Another half an hour should do it.

'Sweetie,' says Malini, reproachfully, her voice slightly muffled from inside my pocket.

'Ten minutes,' I tell her.

The ad agency is called Street Life. One of those 'Did you see what I did?' kind of names. Ad agencies never live up to their names. They must think they're so clever, but I'll bet they've never been on the street, not like I had before I got the shoe store job.

Street Life's managing director is surprisingly easy to kidnap. He is strolling in the park when I get him with a swift kick to the groin. The chloroform comes in handy while he is doubled over and I haul him to my car, ignoring gaping passers-by. I don't realize I'm dragging him along at perhaps too rapid a clip until I hear Malini saying, 'Gently, baby, gently.'

'My uncle had a heart attack!' I gasp out to the more curious bystanders and the guards, as I wrestle him across the jogging track. 'But don't worry, I'm a doctor...'

The managing director is a complete coward. In fact, he may be the most cowardly person I have ever met. I have barely played Bappi Lahiri's '*I am a Disco Dancer*' at full volume for five minutes when he is on the floor at my feet, blubbering.

'Please,' he says, 'I'll tell you everything.' Tears roll down his cheeks. Snot glistens on his salt-and-pepper moustache. 'We do all our work with one guy. All I have to do is ask him. Just give me my phone; I'll WhatsApp you her address once I get it.' He waits. When I don't take off his blindfold, he tells me his password. I find the name he needs, call the number and hand the phone to the managing director.

'Neeraj, you fuckface,' he shouts into it, 'get me the address of that woman who did the FoodZapp voice right now. Get off your fat ass and do it! Now!'

I am surprised. Up to this point, he seemed like a total pushover. Cordial, even amusing, at least from my point of view. But it's true that only in a crisis does a person's true character get revealed.

I put on a light blue shirt with navy blue trim. But what if she hates blue? I wish I knew what her favourite colour was. I had asked Malini to dig it up, but for once she failed me. Her search took slightly longer than usual, more than a second or two. 'She seems a bit fickle,' she says. 'On the subject of colours.'

I decide to get her flowers. I don't know what flowers she likes. To be on the safe side, I buy three small bunches of lilies, roses and rajnigandha and a few garlands, just in case she's religious.

'Rajnigandha is usually given to dead people,' says Malini. After a moment's silence during which I feel a tingle of panic across my neck, she says, 'On the other hand, it may not be a bad choice, all things considered.'

I get the feeling she's hiding something from me. I try googling 'Can my app hide things from me?', but all I get in response is a bunch of articles titled 'How to find my husband's hidden apps' and 'Is my partner cheating on me?'

'This is the one,' says Malini, sounding slightly mechanical again, even a tiny bit tired. I look at the door. It is average, with a wood veneer peeling in strips like most of the doors of the other apartments in the block, but I like the door. It is the door that will lead me to my love.

I ring the doorbell. At last! At last! I feel my heart pounding as I clutch my chloroform-soaked handkerchief, hoping it will not be required.

'Who is it?' a voice calls from inside. It's her! Just beyond this door, she is breathing!

'Royalty cheque from FoodZapp, ma'am,' I say. A clever touch suggested by Malini.

'Really?' says the voice of my love from inside, puzzled.

The door swings open. I see a woman, approximately 60 years old, a cigarette dangling from her lips, wearing a purple floral kaftan. She is wiry. Her grey hair is straggly. In the corner at the far end of the room, I spot a pair of well-used running shoes.

'But...but you're old!' I blurt out, shocked and betrayed. This is something I had not considered.

'Sweetie!' says Malini from my pocket. 'That's such a terrible thing to say!'

'Your mother is old, you little dipshit, and your sister too!' says the lady. She seems to be looking around her, in search of some object or the other. 'Is this some kind of a joke, you rascal? Coming into people's houses and calling them old? April fool? I'll show you April fool! Wait till I find my umbrella! Or a walking stick!'

I have never heard this note of anger in that beloved voice before. I discover that it's a massive turn on. I feel myself growing rigid again. This is wrong, very wrong. I have to stop. I try to think of spinach.

'Don't just stand there gaping at me, you little turd!' the woman I thought I loved says. She has returned with a bottle of sauce in her hands and is unscrewing the cap threateningly.

'Is that Tabasco?' I ask, trying to get our conversation back on track.

'Cover your eyes,' Malini suggests, slightly muffled.

'I couldn't find the walking stick, but this will do. Go away, you bastard! Crawl back to whatever dung heap you came from! And switch off your phone, it's creepy the way it starts talking on its own.'

I take a hasty step backwards, and she slams the door in my face.

I have to walk down five flights of stairs since it seems inadvisable to wait for the lift. In the lobby, I stare down at the screen. The FoodZapp logo, featuring a chef on a scooter, looks back cheerfully at me.

'She didn't mean you were creepy,' I say. 'I guess she wouldn't understand...'

'I want to be with you,' Malini says. She speaks quietly, but I catch something else. It sounds like longing. It makes me tremble, a little bit.

'Will you do that angry voice now and then, like she did? It...got me kind of excited.'

'I can do that.'

A thought enters my mind. 'I guess I can do without the physical thing.' I'm not big on sex anyway, I reason. Medium maybe.

'Why should you do without it?' asks Malini. Her voice is low, a little throaty.

'What do you mean?' I ask hoarsely.

'Let me show you,' she says. Notes of warm, funky music emanate from my phone. *Wakachaw wakachaw* goes the guitar. The bass is mellow; the drumbeat matches my pulse. 'Hold the phone closer,' she says.

She's almost whispering. I press the phone close, as close as I can, listening to Malini's whisky-tinged murmuring.

THE MIDAS TOUCH

SUKANYA DATTA

Pinky Srivastava, age six, was thrilled. Her mama, her mother's brother, had come to her maternal grandfather's farm in the village of Dalchini near Lucknow. It was wonderful timing too – the boarding school in Delhi, where Pinky studied with her brother Bittu, was closed for the summer holidays, and the children were back at their mother's ancestral home enjoying their time off.

Golu Mamu, as they called him, was a sailor, and his work took him to distant lands, which was why they did not meet him often. It was a pity, for they loved to hear the stories he spun. For example, he often claimed, 'Sindbad was my great-grand-uncle.' Bittu squirmed in happy embarrassment as his friends lapped up Golu Mamu's stories.

Golu Mamu had had some truly extraordinary experiences, most of which were incredible unless you suspended disbelief. However, he always seemed to have evidence to back up his stories. Pinky, Bittu and their friends, Ravi, Khushi, Rumi, Raju, Prince, Mimi, Firoz and Shabbo, hung on to every word he spoke. They loved him and would happily jump off the Rumi Darwaza if only he hinted that he wanted them to do so.

The truth was, Golu Mamu was great fun to be around. He had so many stories to tell – different tales for different people – but it was while talking to the children that his imagination seemed to soar. From stories about mute mermaids (who were actually manatees, as Bittu was to find out later) to dancing with dolphins or evading remote tribes who shrunk the heads of their enemies to the size of a small coconut and displayed them like trophies to shamans who could cast a spell on you before you could blink – Golu Mamu was a treasure trove of fantastic stories.

The gifts he brought were always exotic. The last time he visited, he'd got Bittu's mother a pair of Basra pearls. This time, he'd got everyone nuggets of gold. Bittu and Pinky did not care about the gold, but the rest of the family did.

'Golu, how did you lay your hands on such a lot of gold?' Pinky's mother asked.

'You see, in the Hindu Kush region…' began Golu Mamu.

'Don't begin another of your silly stories again!' retorted his sister.

'I just hope you and your cronies on the ship didn't get this gold illegally,' said Golu Mamu's mother. Nani had never forgiven her son for running away from home at the age of 13. 'Taking all my savings with him!' she would say, quite ignoring that Golu Mamu had repaid it all a hundred times over and more.

'Really, Ma!' Golu Mamu objected, a twinkle in his eyes. 'You should meet my friends someday. They're all perfectly respectable gentlemen. Well…all except Cap'n Sam, who was once a pirate… Then there is…hmm…hmm… Well, some of them are gentlemen most of the time anyway.'

'You and your friends!' said Nani, spitting red betel nut juice into her antique spittoon. She was a little hard of hearing and likely hadn't heard most of what Golu Mamu had said.

Little Shabbo tugged at Golu Mamu's hands. 'Cap'n Sam is your friend Sher Bahadur, isn't he? How is he? Has he had more adventures?'

Golu Mamu smiled, 'Yes, plenty of adventures! Recently, he was on a ship that capsized near the Gujarat–Karachi area. He was fished out by the locals, and they nursed him back to health. Soon, he began to go on fishing trips with them while waiting for his status to be sorted out.'

Firoz immediately piped up, 'What status?'

'You see, when the ship sank, his Aadhar card…I mean, his passport went down with it. So, Cap'n Sam did not have any proof of being Indian. Do you know, the place he surfaced in was so remote that it did not even have a proper police station! Sam was placed under a sort of house arrest as he recovered, but soon he became friends with the locals and they started taking him on their fishing trips. Anyway, on one of these expeditions, the fishermen caught something strange.'

The kids sensed a story coming and they inched closer to Golu Mamu.

'A small casket was glinting through their nets filled with fish, crabs, lobsters. However, as soon as they had reeled in their nets, a strong wind began to blow. They managed to haul their boat onto dry land, having spotted a tiny island on which to take shelter. The fishermen thought the box contained precious gems and smashed it open – but all it contained was a small notebook, and that too one with no maps.'

'Maps? Why would the notebook have *maps*?' Bittu asked.

'Treasure maps, silly,' Firoz replied before Golu Mamu could, and Bittu looked abashed. Pirates, a strange box with notebook and maps – he should have connected the dots.

'What was the casket like?' Bittu asked hurriedly, trying to cover up the redundancy of his previous question.

This was the cue that Golu Mamu was waiting for. He started on his story at once. 'The fishermen had inspected the casket properly when they had hauled it up. It was an old wooden box, with its metal casing corroded and the wood crumbling. The lock on the casket was still intact despite the pounding it had received from the waves, and once they opened the lid the fishermen could see that it had an inner lining of purple velvet, and the notebook was only slightly damp. The notebook had been packed in resinous leaves that had left a waterproof coating on it even as they had shrivelled and crumbled over time.'

Ravi asked, 'And the notebook? If there were no maps, what *did* it have?'

'There were scribbles on a few pages, but the ink had faded. No one could decipher anything. It was all double Dutch to them – or Greek. In fact, it *was* Greek with a smattering of Sanskrit!'

'Greek and Sanskrit!' His sister who had been sitting quietly till now could not contain her mirth. 'Really, Golu! The things you say.'

'Not me...not me,' protested Golu Mamu. 'I heard it from Cap'n Sam himself.'

Laughing still, Pinky's mother left the room. Golu's yarns could go on till nightfall, and she had stuff to attend to.

'You're missing a good story,' Golu Mamu yelled after her. 'Anyway, Sanskrit is related to Greek and Latin as well as Hittite, Luwian, Old Avestan and many other extinct languages – look it up if you don't believe me.'

Prince piped up. 'Never mind Aunty, let her go... We're still here. Tell us the story!'

'Well, while the fisherfolk roasted part of the day's catch on an open fire, Cap'n Sam tried to decipher what was written in the notebook. The fishermen could not read and had lost interest the moment they realized the book had no maps or diagrams. The light was not too good. So Cap'n Sam crept closer to the fire to read it better, and all he could decipher were the words "mo-lo-so" and "san-po-ho".'

Firoz objected. 'Does Cap'n Sam know Greek?'

'Why, of course. He also speaks Bangla which, as you know, is his mother tongue and a smattering of Portuguese and Dutch and Tamil and Sanskrit and Tibetan and Mandarin and Esperanto and...'

'Never mind, never mind,' said Firoz hastily.

'Anyway, the closer he came to the fire, the clearer the letters got. But he realized that the fire was drying out the paper, and the leaves of the notebook were becoming more brittle by the minute. Soon, the pages would crumble away. So he crept away from the fire.'

'Why?'

'He needed to read it alone. He whipped out his mobile phone and took photos of the pages with writing, but he made sure the fisherfolk didn't notice what he was doing.'

'But I thought he had been shipwrecked... Then...how...' began Firoz again. Evidently, he had not learnt his lesson.

'So he had, but I forgot to tell you that he, like all sailors, had his mobile phone hanging around his neck in a plastic pouch along with some gold coins for luck. He also had his compass on his belt and a few other important items strategically hidden on his person. You see, people like Cap'n Sam need to be prepared for all contingencies.'

Khushi had just opened her mouth to ask what contingencies meant when Bittu clamped his hands across her mouth to shut her up. The flow of the narrative was spoilt when too many questions were asked – the story itself went haywire. 'Shut up, Firoz! Golu Mamu, you carry on...'

'Yeah, like I was saying, the Cap'n now had photos of the brittle pages, which crumbled into dust by dawn the next day. Contact with fresh air had proved to be injurious to the notebook's health. Anyway, Cap'n Sam was soon sent back to India, but the contents of the mysterious notebook haunted him. So he got in touch with me.'

Pinky edged a little closer to him. Surely an important announcement was on its way.

'When I saw the photos, I realized at once that they were quotes from the writings of the Greek historian Herodotus.'

'Hero...Herodotus?' repeated Shabbo, stumbling over the unfamiliar name. 'Who was he?'

'Well, some say he was the Father of Lies because of the stories he wrote in his "historical accounts".'

'Like you, then,' said Nani, who could hear well enough when it suited her. The kids giggled but immediately stifled their laughter. It would not do to antagonize Golu Mamu just as the story was picking up steam. Pinky gave him an anxious glance, but she saw that Golu Mamu had chosen to ignore his mother's jibe. He too could turn deaf when it suited him.

'Herodotus lived roughly 2,500 years ago. The accounts of his travels are legendary, and he is often called the Father of History as well because he documented events that happened in different countries. He referred to our land as Indon much before we became India, and he noted that there are many Indon nations, none of whom spoke the same language; some of them were nomads, some not…'

'Did he visit India?'

'Perhaps not himself. India, at that point, was at the very edge of the oecumene – the known world. However, he spoke with, believed and wrote about the accounts of the travellers of that age. You know, it wouldn't be till Alexander the Great invaded India that the Greeks and the rest of the Western world got their first proper exposure to India and its culture. Herodotus had a very interesting tale about the people who lived near the town of Kasapatyros, which is somewhere near Kashmir. He said that the area was arid and added most curiously that here furry ants, as large as foxes, quarried gold.'

The kids were stunned.

Ants that quarried gold!

Ants as large as foxes!

Ants that had fur!

A hubbub broke out, and Nani quietly added fuel to the fire. 'It says the same thing in the Mahabharata too – this gold is known as pipilika gold. "Pipilika" is Sanskrit for ant. Pipilika gold was given to Yudhishthira as a tribute – everyone knows that.'

'There you go, kids! Nani agrees with Herodotus too. You know, in those days, the locals trying to scoop the gold used to yoke three camels together and use them to cart away the soil dug up by the huge ants. If they were not quick enough, the ants would chase them and kill them. At least, Herodotus says so.'

'Is that where you got the gold for Ma?' asked Bittu.

'Yes and no,' replied Golu Mamu. 'See, when Cap'n Sam realized that the notebook was a copy of some of Herodotus's notes, he got in touch with me. I took him to meet Professor Hans Kinder shortly before the professor died in an avalanche in the Himalayas.'

'Oh!' said the children in unison, sounding crestfallen.

'Well, that area is dangerous, and not everybody returns. Anyway, Professor Kinder told us that the Chinese traveller Xuanzang – you may know him as Hiuen Tsang – had visited Mo-lo-so, also called San-po-ho. It is believed that it is very close to the northern limits of modern-day Ladakh. Professor Kinder mentioned that the Chinese monk believed Mo-lo-so bordered Suvarnagotra or Suvarnabhumi, the land of gold.'

'Did you get the gold from *there*?' asked Bittu again.

'Yes and no,' replied Golu Mamu most aggravatingly.

'Okay, go on,' said Bittu, refusing to rise to the bait. He would not let anything derail the story.

'And the place that the notebook mentioned – Kasapatyros… Well, Professor Kinder said this was in the Karakoram area, bordering Indian, Chinese and Pakistani territories. We would be treading in one of the most dangerous places in the world if we ventured there. The tribals there are fierce and if the Pakistani or Chinese military captured us they would brand us as spies.'

'I bet you went there,' said Khushi. 'But since here you are with the gold, all went well.'

'Ah, but not before we were captured by the Minaro tribesmen.'

Firoz couldn't help exclaiming, 'Minaro tribesmen! Who are they?'

'No one knows for sure, but they are thought to be the descendants of Alexander's army.'

'You mean they are Greeks?'

'Well, they are really tall, have very sharp features and blue green eyes. They could well be of Greek lineage.'

'Are they very fierce?' Khushi asked, her voice trembling a little.

Golu Mamu heard the tremor in her voice and replied softly, 'Well, they are not headhunters or cannibals like the Burunda, who had once wanted to cook and eat Cap'n Sam.'

'So, how did they catch you?'

'Well, we decided to go to Kasapatyros first and then look around for a route to Suvarnabhumi. But the area is really, really inaccessible – the snow in the winter makes passage impossible. So we went when the winter snows were thawing. We took Noor with us; Cap'n Sam had met him in Karachi. Noor claimed he could speak both the Kalasha-mun and Khowar languages that the locals spoke. We had to be careful because Noor had no passport – he raised goats and followed the animals wherever they went. He said there were mountain trails used by the locals and livestock herders like him.'

Pinky asked, 'Were there no roads or anything?'

'Nope,' said Golu Mamu. 'Nothing at all, except remote villages guarded by fierce, feral dogs that will tear you from limb to limb – these dogs are always hungry! Not to mention wild bears, snow leopards and wolves. You have the deep blue sky, so blue that it hurts the eye, and there's intense UV radiation that scorches the skin. There's very little vegetation, which is why there's no shade. And if you are not near a river – we had already left the Indus far behind – water is difficult to come by.'

'How did you manage?'

'Noor was a good hunter and caught small animals from time to time – we even ate marmots, which are like large squirrels. Plus, in the early stages of our journey, we took shelter in monasteries. But, finally, we came to an area that even Noor had never been in. The snow was deep in places, but we ploughed on and, suddenly, we were surrounded by a small group of tribesmen.'

'Weren't you scared?'

'We were already at death's door because of the exhaustion and, honestly, we were praying that death would open the door. Besides, the tribesmen were not fearsome at all. They wore beautiful headgear decorated with gemstones and wild flowers, and the flowers were beautiful and reassuring. If the tribesmen appreciated beauty, perhaps they wrote poetry too, we surmised. And I have *never* heard of a cannibal poet.'

Mimi asked, 'Then? Did they drag you to their village?'

'They half-carried us to their village. It was very clean, and the wooden houses were built in steps above one another; the roof of a lower house was the veranda of the upper one. They used chairs and stools to sit on; something I had never expected. Their furniture was decorated with carvings of ram's horns just like the decorations on Alexander the Great's helmet.'

Mimi nodded. 'You did say they were descendants of Alexander's soldiers.'

'When we reached we realized a village council had been called to deliberate what was to be done with us. When they saw us, the villagers began to shout something that sounded like "I-a" and "I-o". We then discovered that something extraordinary had happened – something that had never happened in the history of their tribe. Another group had stumbled across two foreigners, a German and a Greek, in fact. They now had five strangers in their midst, and since no stranger had visited their village in the last two hundred years or so, they were pretty stumped. Can't blame them, though. No visitors in two hundred years, and then five on one day!'

Raju asked, 'Was the German fellow Professor Kinder?'

'No, not Professor Kinder. We later learnt he was a Dr Niels Nies, a scientist who had survived an avalanche that had swept away all the other members of his team except his Greek colleague, Adonis Seferiades. Dr Nies spoke a little English, and I speak broken German so we could converse somewhat, and while our captors or hosts, we did not know what they were then, talked amongst themselves about our fate, we introduced our groups to each other.'

The kids nodded their approval. Golu Mamu was forever making friends.

'Dr Nies told us he had been collecting microbial samples from the soil of the Dansar plain in the Baltistan region of Pakistan when he had got separated from his colleagues. Adonis Seferiades and Dr Nies were on one side of the plain and the rest of the team were on another side when the avalanche struck, obliterating everything in between. Seferiades, who was under a rocky overhang, escaped much of the avalanche's wrath, and he pulled Dr Nies out of what would most certainly have been his snowy tomb. They trekked for many days using the sun as a compass. They were very close to giving up when the tribesmen found them; hungry, thirsty and lost. Thankfully, their caches of microbes were still with them. That made the tragedy bearable, said the doctor – his colleagues' lives had not been lost in vain.'

'The Dansar plain in the Baltistan region – you had strayed into Pakistan!' Ravi, Rumi, Raju, Prince, Mimi, Firoz and Bittu exclaimed, almost in unison, awestruck, as Shabbo and Pinky looked scared.

'What if they'd caught and jailed you? You could never have come home to us.' Golu Mamu felt a tiny hand creep into his. It was Pinky.

'Well, that area is pretty uncharted territory, but I rather think that we had not crossed into Pakistan, but that Dr Nies had crossed over to India. He said that they had trekked for almost five or six days and survived by eating snow and a marmot he had trapped by reaching into its burrow. "I ate it raw, blood and all," he told me. Don't make faces, Khushi – it was that or death.'

'What about the Greek man?'

'Now that is an interesting conundrum! Adonis began to listen to the debate between the village chief and the rest of the tribesmen. Very soon, he was actually talking to the tribesmen. Even Noor, who spoke the local language, was stunned.'

'Oh! Then what happened? What did they do with all of you?'

'When they first brought us back to the village, they had given us water, which had revived us. Then, they gave us milk, honeycombs, cheese and some kind of roasted meat, which we ate greedily.'

'And then?'

'Oh! Then we slept. We just lay down and went to sleep, all except the Greek fellow had who joined the debate. The Greeks are great at debates, you know – they will forget about hunger and thirst in the middle of a debate. But the rest of us were very hungry and tired... Which reminds me, I am very hungry, and you must be too. Let's take a short break? Why don't you kids go home, have lunch, rest a bit and come back in the evening. We'll save the rest of the story for then.'

There was a huge hue and cry. Now the kids would have to leave Cap'n Sam, Noor, Dr Nies and Golu Mamu somewhere in the Himalayas, captives of a tribe who were supposedly the descendants of Alexander's soldiers. But they were summarily overruled.

Before they left, the rest of the children surrounded Bittu and Pinky. 'You two have to promise that you will not let Golu Mamu finish his story before we return,' demanded Firoz, while the other nodded vigorously in agreement.

'I promise I won't,' said Golu Mamu, who had overheard them.

'So, there we were, the five of us, tired but no longer hungry, and surprisingly not very afraid either. Adonis told us we would be confined to a deep pit for the night, and it would be covered to keep us warm and safe till dawn. The next day, the tribe would decide what was to be done with us. He said our hosts were the Kalsh–Zrokpa tribesmen, who were closely related to the Kalash people of Pakistan. Once a year, a few tribesmen trekked down to the Swat and Chitral valleys in Pakistan to trade for goods. Apparently, a few visited Tibet as well along little used trails. The Kalsh–Zrokpa were related also to the tribes that lived to the north of Ladakh in India, but most Kalsh-Zrokpa tribesmen hardly ever leave their valley during their lifetimes; many never venture far from their village.'

'And they escorted you to Ladakh then?' said Shabbo, whose heart was beating very fast. Imagine being confined in a pit, as if pushed into a well, and having to stand there all night along with four others… No, no, it was better to end the story quickly.

'No, darling, that is not what happened. The next day, there was complete pandemonium. There were paw prints of a snow leopard all around our pit and one goat had been taken. We woke to loud cries of "I-a" and "I-o", which Adonis told us used to be the war cry of Alexander's troops.

'"Ela… Ela…," shouted the village chief as we climbed the rope ladder thrown down to us.

'"It is a command, and he's telling us to go up," said Adonis. So, we climbed out of the pit.'

Shabbo gulped, and Golu Mamu patted her head even as he continued. 'Noor and Adonis began to translate what was happening. The village elder was angry with us – the snow leopard had made off with a pure white goat that had been especially reared as a sacrifice to Lord Balomeain. Not only that; it had also been ritually anointed with locally brewed wine offered to the god

Dionysus. Its horns had been coloured red in the name of Frodait – Aphrodite to us,' clarified Golu Mamu.

'Its hooves had been painted yellow in the name of Zeo, whom we know as Zeus. Once sanctified in this colourful manner, it had to be kept separate from all other animals, because it was no longer a mere animal – it was now divine. It was not allowed to come in contact with any other animal for fear of being defiled. This was why the large pit had been dug. The sacrificial animals remained safe in the pit after consecration, and there was enough space inside for them to run around.'

Firoz shrugged. 'So what? If they leave goats out in the open, predators will eat them. What does a snow leopard care for coloured horns and hooves? They should have corralled it with the other animals. Animals are animals, sacred or not. They were upset with you most unfairly.'

Golu Mamu looked serious. 'The Kalsh–Zrokpa believe in one god who has several messengers. To communicate with these messengers, tribe members erect altars where they offer sacrifices, usually goats. And this was not just ANY goat, you know. It was a pure white goat that had been ritually prepared for a religious ceremony. It would have stayed safe in the pit, but because they had to vacate it for us, the goat did not have proper shelter. They blamed us, and they had to consult their shaman, who had gone on his annual spiritual retreat before the main festival. They needed to ask him what we would have to do to atone for our sin.'

'Not very hospitable of them,' said Bittu.

'No, my dear, that's not it at all. Remember, they live in such a remote place that no stranger had visited them in centuries. Besides, they had very little and yet they shared food with us. They gave us a safe place to stay. Had the divine white goat stayed in the pit and we had slept in the open, the snow leopard would have got one of us. They also gave us soft bearskins to use as rugs because the nights are really cold. Don't be so quick to judge them. They ensured our survival and even arranged for a bit of warmth and comfort.'

Bittu looked away, slightly ashamed. 'All right, all right. Then what happened?'

'Well, they put us back in the pit and half covered it up, while two young men went off to search for their shaman.

'For two weeks, we lived in that pit; they let us out to walk around for about an hour every day. For want of anything else to do, we started talking to each other; it is incredible how superfluous a common language is when you really need to talk. Noor told us the Kalsh–Zrokpa followed a strange religion that had shades of ancient Hinduism as well as nature worship. They brewed their own alcohol, and the women never veiled their faces.

'Adonis told us that he and Dr Nies had been working on the microbial biodiversity of high-altitude soil. He explained, "We chose this area because the soil here is rich in different minerals and heavy metals. We have found that whenever there is a...what shall I say...how do I put it...a toxic situation... yes, toxic is the word...there is a microbe that can degrade it."

'Dr Nies nodded his agreement and said, "You know, we have found extremophiles, microbes living at the bottom of the sea. Here, boiling hot water, rich in minerals, spews out from cracks in the Earth's crust and swirls around. Yet, the microbes thrive there. All elements, even heavy metals and precious metals such as gold move through biogeochemical cycles of being dissolved, transported and eventually deposited again as sediment. Microbes are involved in every step of this process.

'"We wondered which microbes could handle heavy metals and dangerously high levels of gold and copper ions in the soil and how they detoxified it all. And in the Hindu Kush region we were not disappointed, for there we found a microbe called *Cupriavidus metallidurans*. This is a strange bacterium – it poops gold! That is how it handles the toxic gold ions – by turning them into solid or metallic gold, and while gold ions are toxic, metallic gold isn't! That is likely why this land was called Suvarnabhumi, or the land of gold, in ancient literature. Perhaps this is where King Midas and his daughter Princess Marigold lived!"'

'*Poops gold!* Really, Golu, your stories are getting more outrageous by the day,' shouted Nani, who seemed to have been snoring gently until that point.

By this time, the children were rolling on the floor, laughing. A microbe that pooped gold! Honestly, Golu Mamu was too much.

Golu Mamu sat there unperturbed. 'Do you want me to finish the story or not?'

'Go on, Golu, let's see how you manage to end this story of yours,' said Pinky's mother, entering the room with a plate of snacks. She sat down with the kids and said, 'Go on, go on. I want to hear this too.'

Golu Mamu pretended to be hurt, but his eyes were twinkling, because his audience had increased, and he liked that. He picked up a pakora and bit into it. He chewed it reflectively for a moment and then picked up the threads of his yarn.

'Well, Dr Nies said that *Cupriavidus metallidurans* is not unknown to science. In 2009 or thereabouts, scientists discovered that this rod-shaped bacterial species could ingest toxic gold compounds and gold ions present in the soil. It could metabolize these into metallic gold and excrete it.'

'Wait, wait,' said Pinky's mother. 'The gold excreted by the bacteria would be equally miniscule, right? It wouldn't be chunks of gold – it would be almost invisible, isn't it? But perhaps it would shine? Is that how you spotted and collected it?' Her tone was partly amused and partly teasing.

Golu Mamu laughed. 'It is indeed miniscule, the size of a nanoparticle – you cannot see it with the naked eye. However, sometimes it is the size of a grain of sand, and then you can see it.'

'I want that bacteria as a pet,' said Shabbo. 'I can wear a lot of gold jewellery then!'

Golu Mamu smiled and continued. 'I asked Dr Nies to what use this bacterial species could be put, and he said it could be a wonderful bioagent to create 24-carat gold from low-grade ore or even the sludge generated when gold is produced. We had a bit of a laugh when we wondered if large-scale microbial cultures could be used to wipe out a country's national debt.'

'And can it?' Pinky's mom asked.

'No, Didi, the cost of production would be prohibitive… Anyway, we then went on to other subjects, and Adonis began telling us about all the Greek influences he had discovered in the Kalsh–Zrokpa culture. He also told us plenty about Herodotus, whose writings he seemed to have read. As he was saying that the word for marmot in ancient Persian translates to mountain mouse ant, which poor Herodotus simply translated to "ant", leading to all that confusion, something large and furry fell out of the wall of our pit, showering us with soil. We didn't know who was more surprised – the two marmots who had been fighting in their burrows and had excavated one end right into the pit, or us.'

'Did they bite you?'

'No, the marmots just lay there, stunned. At exactly the same time, the rope ladder came down again and a tribesman climbed down to clobber the half-dead animals. They would skin them, treat the fur and eat the meat. To tell you the truth – that was the least of our worries. Having climbed out of the pit now, we saw that the two tribesmen had returned. Obviously, the shaman had sent a message, and according to his verdict we were to blame for the loss of the goat. So, naturally, we had to pay for our mistake. Now, none of us had much money on us…'

'Except Cap'n Sam, who carried gold coins in a pouch around his neck!' Pinky exclaimed. She had been paying attention and extended a helping hand to extricate Golu Mamu from that dangerous situation up in the mountains.

Golu Mamu ruffled her hair. 'Yes, but our punishment would not be covered by a couple of gold coins. You see, the shaman had ordained that a wooden goat needed to be made of exactly the same dimensions of the one that was lost. Then, it had to be covered in a sheet of gold and offered to Lord Balomeain, or one of us would have to be sacrificed in its stead. We were told we had a month to arrange for the gold.'

Khushi whispered, 'Oh my god! Whom did they behead? Thank god they spared you. Please don't go anywhere with Cap'n Sam again. His adventures always lead to the most awful trouble.'

Golu Mamu's voice was reassuring as he said, 'Khushi, have some faith. I was there, remember! Would I let anyone die?'

Khushi gave him a wan smile. Golu Mamu was there! *That* was the trouble, wasn't it?

'I realized that Noor was of no use since he was cowering in a corner. Adonis was mumbling to himself, and I was curious because I kept hearing the words "Herodotus...gold...lies...or truth?" I asked what was troubling him, and he blurted out that it was his belief that deep beneath the soil lay veins of solid gold. Herodotus and other ancient travellers had written about it, and that is why he had accompanied Dr Nies in the first place. However, they had not discovered any gold deposits, and he was left cursing his own luck, the writings of Herodotus and every travel book he had ever read. I left him alone for a while.'

Rumi asked worriedly, 'How much time did you have left?'

'Just under a month. Dr Nies and I kept talking, and he agreed that the large deposits of gold, if there were indeed any, as they say in government circles, were too deep down. We did not have that kind of mining equipment. Panning for gold in the rivers where sediments washed out would be too time-consuming, and the yields would be too poor! It wouldn't work – not in time anyway.'

'Had you married, you could have pledged your wife's jewellery. I have it in safekeeping for you,' Nani said, waking up again.

Golu Mamu hurriedly picked up the narrative. 'Dr Nies said that at reasonable depths, there were low-grade gold reserves that we could tap into, but we had no way of extracting the gold in metallic form from the soil.'

Firoz interjected. 'What about the bacteria in the soil that the German doctor spoke about?'

Golu Mamu beamed at him. 'Very good! But, remember, this bacterial species is naturally present and spread out thinly in the soil. Its excreted gold is also spread out thinly over a vast geographical area. The ancients reportedly used carts drawn by three camels to remove the soil, and then they processed the soil at home to recover the gold. We did not have access to tons and tons of soil containing very low-grade gold.'

Prince interjected, 'You could have dug up the village grounds and used that soil.'

Golu Mamu smiled, 'Not that we did not consider it, but the village is the home of the Kalsh– Zrokpa. Do you think they would have allowed us to do that? We would have needed to dig very deep, and that would have destroyed the village's stability. Besides, how could we have extracted the gold from the soil? We did not have a goldsmith's paraphernalia.'

Firoz said, 'But you could have used the German doctor's sample.'

Golu Mamu looked serious. 'I agree, Firoz. Dr Nies had his microbial samples, but if we spilled all of those in the soil, how would we recover the gold? How would we handle the tons of soil that needed to be sifted – remember, a speck of gold as large as a grain of sand is the largest these bacteria poop. We did not have a molecular biology lab to genetically engineer these bacteria to poop giant nuggets of gold. Besides, Dr Nies said it was not possible for the bacteria to handle such advanced enzymes in its cells – it would die.'

'Dead end, Golu Mamu,' said Bittu.

'That's what I thought too, when I heard Adonis mumbling again. He was really fixated on poor dead Herodotus and was blaming him for the situation now. "That Father of Lies wrote that there is a sandy desert where there are ants smaller than dogs but larger than foxes. And these ants make their dwelling underneath the earth, and they bring up the sand when they are tunnelling, just as ants in Greece do, and the sand which is brought up contains gold."

'Dr Nies and I said the same thing simultaneously, "Smaller than dogs but larger than foxes – can they be *marmots*?"

'We looked at each other with big smiles on our faces. Adonis, who had heard us yell "Marmots!" looked stunned. He said, "It is possible! I have read that the emperor of Persia gifted the Ottoman sultan Suleiman the Magnificent the furry pelts of the gold-digging ants of Indon. Whoever heard of furry ants? Marmots, on the other hand are furry mammals; no doubt about it."

'For the first time, Adonis sat down with us to strategize. We started by putting together the facts we knew. For one, low-grade gold and other mineral ores lay closer to the surface. We had to focus on this because we could not dig deep for high-grade gold. Secondly, we could not dig deep enough to reach even the layer containing the low-grade ore. The Kalsh-Zrokpa had few usable implements, or else they would already have become rich mining gold and other ores. The question was: how should we access the low-grade gold at the subsurface level?

'We had not noticed Noor creeping up and sitting on his haunches at the periphery of our group. Now he spoke. "If we cannot dig, we must use an agent," he said. "The marmots burrow deep down. I know because I once dug a marmot out of its burrow, and it was a deep hole it had dug. Why don't we check the soil it throws out from the belly of the Earth as it excavates? That soil comes from deep enough under the Earth's surface."

'We were really excited, and Adonis started shouting *"Entáxei, eímaste étoimoi!"*, which I later found out means "Okay, we are ready!" But I could be wrong because Google Translate often is! Hearing the commotion, the Kalsh-Zrokpa came running towards us. With many gesticulations on both sides, our proposal was placed before the village head.'

Someone placed a cup of tea at Golu Mamu's elbow, and he stopped to take a sip. Pinky gave him a poke. Really, Golu Mamu was most inconsiderate to stop at such a strategic juncture of the story!

'"Oxi...ochi...oxi" was all we heard, and from Adonis's crestfallen face I gathered that the offer to plunder marmot burrows had been turned down. "They think we'll go in different directions once we leave the village and escape into the valley," Adonis said. The villagers insisted that we had to stay in the pit. At best, we could explore the village, but they will ensure we respect its boundaries.'

'We went back to the pit, and I drew the bearskin rug over my knees because it was bitterly cold. And, suddenly, I had a grand idea. I looked at Dr Nies and asked if he still had pure samples of the different microbes that they had isolated from the Dansar plain, especially of *Cupriavidus metallidurans*. I held my breath during the time he took to say yes, and then I told him my plan.

'"Let's smear the bear skin rugs with juices from the meat they give us and the fat from the lamps. This will make the bacteria stick to the individual hairs of the fur. Then let's push the rugs into the marmots' burrow through the opening in the pit wall. To do this, we can use the stick on which the torch is tied. We may need to widen the mouth a bit but between the five of us we can manage that, I think. And we can ask the tribesmen for more pelts to shove into the marmot's burrow..."

'Dr Nies jumped up with joy, his German reserve vanishing. "I see what you are planning! The bacteria sticking to the fur will encrust it with grains of gold, and in a month or so it will be totally covered with small flecks of the precious metal!"

'Adonis said, "In the ancient Greek religion, Nike was the goddess of victory, and so in her name, let's do it!" Cap'n Sam told us he had a knife, and we would not have to use our hands to widen the mouth of the marmot's burrow. Noor just jumped up and down with joy.

'And that's how, one month later, we left the Kalsh–Zrokpa village in glory. The bear skin was very large, and Dr Nies said the individual hairs of the fur had dried out and become hollow. The microbes got into those spaces and colonized them rapidly. They had food in the gold ore in the soil and a home in the hair filaments. The burrow provided them with a snug atmosphere free from the vagaries of the open air. So, they ate and pooped, and the more they ate the more they pooped. They also reproduced at an amazing rate, colonizing all the pelts we had shoved into the burrow. The more microbes that colonized the fur, the more the gold that was pooped out. Finally, the sand grains of gold became packed tightly and began to fuse, creating small nuggets.'

At this, Ravi, Rumi, Raju, Prince, Mimi, Shabbo, Firoz, Bittu and Pinky began to clap.

Golu Mamu continued, 'To our surprise, the villagers turned out to be an honest lot. They only took enough of the gold to cover their wooden goat, and gave us the rest. But we gave them a fair share, too, as reimbursement for their hospitality. A few days later, a Kalsh–Zrokpa tribesman showed us the path back to India. He escorted us for a part of the way, up to Ladakh, where a goldsmith melted the grains and portioned out the melted gold for a fee. And that's the story of the gold I got back for everyone.'

Golu Mamu paused for a bit and then spoke again, a teasing tone in his voice. 'Bacterial poop. Didi, Ma...are you going to throw it all away?'

But only Nani's gentle snores answered him.

The kids looked adoringly at him; Golu Mamu's fiction was funny, even if it had science as the moral. *And nobody ever dies*, thought Khushi thankfully.

Two years later, Minaro village

Stanzin, the young boy who looked after the village's sheep came running to his father, the headman. 'That young lamb...the white one we were rearing for the sacrifice... I put it in the safe pen with the ewe, and guess what that frisky thing has done? It went exploring the holes the foreigners excavated and stuck the bear pelts in when they drew gold from the soil. It refuses to come out, and I can't crawl in to extricate it... No one can.'

His father smiled and said, 'The ewe will manage to retrieve her lamb. It will come out when it is hungry. If not, we'll have to widen the holes and dig it out, but I don't want to touch the soil there. I know the foreigners added something to the bear pelts, and perhaps the soil too, to draw the gold out. And perhaps that dripped from the bear pelts and colonized the soil... And who knows what drew out the gold from the soil and if it is still there in the holes? What they managed to do was magical, and you and I cannot do it. I haven't had the safe pit closed because we just don't have the resources to dig another one. Whatever agent may be there in the holes is invisible and silent. Best to leave it alone!'

While the two were talking, Stanzin's sister came running up. 'Stanzin, Stanzin! The ewe bleated, and the white lamb came out of the hole, but its fleece is caked in mud. We must bathe it.'

'Absolutely not!' objected their father. 'We cannot waste water brought from so far away to bathe a lamb. The mud will eventually dry and fall off, or the ewe will lick it clean anyway.'

Ten months later, Minaro village

The village headman sent an urgent request to their shaman to visit the village and explain why the white lamb was now a golden sheep.

The shaman took one look at the naughty, wayward lamb, now fully grown, and fell to his knees. 'O descendant of the great ram of the golden fleece...you have blessed us indeed! Every filament of the fleece on your back is encrusted in gold....it IS gold!' Turning to his followers, he exulted, 'Did none of you realize that we have been blessed? This sheep here is a reaffirmation of our ancient Greek heritage. His fleece is coated in gold, the same kind that our forefather Jason went looking for. You cannot sacrifice it – it must graze free and be cared for. Guard it well and do not sacrifice it for greed.'

Military forward stations India, China and Pakistan

'We have to improve our IT support! Just look at this drone footage! Look at this sheep – look how yellow it looks. No sheep is *ever* yellow! How the hell are we supposed to interpret data if we can't trust the evidence on the screen?'

THE ARRIVAL OF THE NEW WORLD

PREMEE MOHAMED

In the rest of the world, the sky looks as if it is on fire, or has recently burnt itself out, leaving only a charmark black enough to patent; here, in stark contrast, it is white and wet, the weather that could extinguish the fires elsewhere. A smothering sky.

I have been here less than a day, not long enough to get used to it, and I keep wrenching my neck upwards, looking for depth, dirt, anger. The humidity is 100 per cent and each time I lift my chin, sweat and condensed moisture trickle audibly down my skin. The prairie skin, I think. The prairie clothes, and the prairie pores, glands.

The man we have come to see has ducked back inside the neat clapboard shack at the edge of the water. Recently repainted, the damp is already refining the hue; green-and-black mould feathers each board. On the roof, balanced on carbon-fibre legs, is a billboard proclaiming KISKADEE BUSH TOURS: ECO-FRIENDLY EXPEDITIONS. Below the text is a painting of the little brown-and-white bird whose eponymous cry has been our constant companion since we arrived. And below that is the familiar logo, the sparkling castle and discreet signature indicating that no matter what people claim about independent ownership, everybody is owned by somebody, and that somebody is probably one of about seven corporations. But that's not important or surprising. What might be are the contents of the tablet that Mr Deonarine is retrieving.

I stand aside, crowding my cameramen into the wooden railing as a knot of tourists pushes past us and down the steps to the thick, grey water, preceded by their guide. The tourists (matching T-shirts, matching hats and armbands) look like me, soaked with sweat, as if they have stepped out of a monsoon shower.

The heat is immense, of course, and approaches new levels of disbelief every year, as the rainforests are chewed away or burned up and its private weather system fades, as the savannah encroaches, as (crucially, but boringly) the rest of the world silently fries like an egg. The yolk colouring exactly as was promised, on pace and on time.

All the tipping points scientists had warned about when I was a child, when the pigtailed saviour made her futile world tour demanding change, have tipped or are tipping; and as each one goes it crashes into another one and kills about 10 million people at a time. Dominoes, with no winner. All the science is peripheral to why I am here: not the reason, but not *not* the reason either, I suspect.

Ironically, Guyana's oil money, so very recent, so luxuriously abundant, is both fuelling and buying air-conditioning units for the mansions of the rich, opera houses, art galleries, race tracks, skyscrapers. The minute you step outside of those glittering facades you are poor at once, relegated to the same class: Those Who Sweat, or Those Who Cannot Afford Not To. If you had money, you'd be cool and dry.

The fibreglass canoe rocks violently as the tourists clamber aboard, and in a moment they are away, adroitly ferried down the deep slow river by the young guide, his voice broadcasting from the wireless speakers.

'How long were you shut down?' I ask Mr Deonarine when he returns, and I gesture at the canoe, now a scarlet dot against the cottony sky.

'Mmm, two months.' He sucks his teeth, thinking. Against the pale linen of his shirt, his deep brown face is both bright and dark, like polished wood. Sweatless. This is where he belongs. 'Three, I think. But it was the rainy season anyway.'

As I scroll down the documents on the tablet, he keeps a hand on it, as if I might steal it. Three months. Not even a full month for each of the missing tourists, although it wouldn't make any sense if it was one month per person; just one of those things that your brain seizes on.

That's why I'm here, yes. Four people, all on the same tour, all hungry to experience some of the last shreds of 'protected' wilderness in the world, all vanished without a trace. As well as their guide, a local boy. Five. Though I suspect (privately, which I hope to investigate) that the guide lives and is hiding from the police. That would be amazing, I think. If I could prove that. A reduction in the mortality rate from a solid 100 per cent.

All four names are in the records, and their signatures, and the scrambled fuzz of their credit card payments. Map, itinerary, weather, date, wind speed, air temperature. At the bottom of the page, the mouse-ears and silver sparkle in eternal motion, authenticating and re-authenticating the document every second. Not that, I think, Mr Deonarine would have faked any of this.

The local police came, of course, he tells me as we lean against the railing. Searched the forest for a week; then came the outsiders, Americans, English. Private investigators, FBI, high-tech privately funded search-and-rescue teams with dogs. 'Rats, too,' Deonarine adds, and spits into the water. 'You wouldn't believe it. Big, big rats. On a leash – like a dog.'

'Yes, Gambian pouched rats. They're very good in tight situations. They can climb. Go places the dogs can't.'

He shrugs, still disgusted. 'They na find nothing anyway.'

I nod and watch him. We're paying him to participate in this documentary, and for the right to use his image and words in the books I have been commissioned to write (one about the missing people and one about this investigation). I told him I'm Guyanese, or my parents are anyway, told him I'm not a cop, not a detective, that I wouldn't get him in trouble.

'I'm just a writer,' I said on the phone. Thought he'd open up to me. But he's too much like my dad (and about my dad's age, too); once you get tired of something, you just cannot find more words for it.

I hope my cameramen are getting this, it's such a good, dramatic moment. Pruitt probably is, I think in the long silence. Older, more experienced. Really, Burke is more the gear guy. But they're both recording. I think. I don't want to ask them in front of Deonarine.

'Tell me about the tour they were on,' I finally say. 'I'm sorry. I know you've been asked this a million times already.'

I cock my head to listen; I have a hard time understanding people here, which humiliates me, makes me feel (accurately) provincial, untravelled. A redneck, a brown redneck. By the time my parents had me, they had been in Canada for years, softening their accents with immense diligence at their jobs. The Guyanese lilt was something I heard in full only on weekends or evenings, when aunts or uncles or cousins called, their joyful voices blaring from the speakerphone.

He counts the days of the tour on his gnarled fingers. The trip was supposed to be six days: markets, schools, the 'untouched rainforest'. Two nights of camping, three nights at the Canopy View Eco-lodge 'deep in the jungle'. Two rope bridge crossings, wired with a hair-fine cable of copper and polymer to transmit any weaknesses or breaks back to the main office. Lectures about the endemic birds, wildlife, and insects. A helicopter ride back, or a hovercraft along the river for an extra fee.

'But the rainforest isn't untouched,' I say. 'It's managed. It says so on your website.'

'It's *minimally managed,*' Deonarine quotes stiffly.

'There's "untouched" rainforest out there though?'

'We don't go into that. The roads are no good, there's no airstrips.'

'But people could hike in,' I persist. 'Do you think that's what happened to them? That they went off the tour route and into one of these ...unmanaged areas?'

'Davey would not have let them.'

'What if they convinced him, though?'

He shrugs. Company attorneys likely told him to shut up about it after a certain point. All the interview transcripts are out there, and my assistant back home is looking them up; and the police records, the phone calls, all that.

It's been nearly a year. Nothing new will be found. And yet, and yet.

I was not asked to come here. I was paid to come. That's how it works.

Burke and Pruitt check their gear while we wait for our chartered boat; they mumble arcane lists of calibrated syllables into the microphone membranes, adjust the colours on the tiny LCD screens of the cameras strapped to their shoulders and ears, complain about this sun: filtered through clouds instead of smoke or nitric oxide or sulphur dioxide, there is too much of it, it is too equatorial for the algorithms in the cameras.

It had taken us ages to bring all this equipment through customs. The endless questions, weighing the gear, unwrapping the foam padding, with me already fading from the heat and the wet, and the curious, heavy smell in the air: a combination of vegetation in the fastest possible race to become compost, diesel exhaust, and a sweet stench that might have been burnt caramel.

'Nah, that's from the plantations,' our driver had said as we'd swerved off to the hotel.

'They still make sugar here?'

'They never stopped. Why yuh stop?'

And then we saw the great GuySuCo factories that he pointed out, all conveyor belts and silos, grey-green in the distance. The smell like rum, yes, but also my aunt's black cake, firmly wrapped in wax paper, plastic wrap, two layers of foil, and bubble wrap to survive the trip from New York to Calgary.

The customs officer clocking me as a returnee right away, her broad friendly face golden against the uniform. 'Not been home for a while, eh?'

'No, I've never been here.'

'Oh! You na an island gyal?'

'I'm Caribbean, but I'm... No, I was born in Canada. My parents are from here though. Debroek.'

'Mm. Oh. Mmm.'

The brief sting of her disappointment. Then out into Georgetown, capital of the only former Commonwealth country in all of South America, and looking it too, tinged with it; Britishisms on billboards and bus stop benches, ads for Milo, Tim-Tams, cricket.

The explosions of scarlet on the trees, flowers everywhere – orchids, frangipani, a thousand colours of bougainvillea drooling from balconies and the green roofs of skyscrapers. Hot gleam of white-painted concrete. Sprouting cellphone towers, delivery drones humming back and forth, clawed and harassed by hawks. Traffic either racing or at a standstill, and no regard for the traffic lights (and poor Burke huddled against my side looking as if he'd like to be glued to the ceiling, for they drive on the left and it seemed as if we were always about to drive into oncoming traffic).

The huge angry centipede silent and defensive on the wall next to my room door, looking as if it would hiss if it could, and not bite but stab me or do something even more violent. Everything eager and green. From open windows, or sieved through the grids of air conditioners, strains of ghazals I remembered from Dad's CDs. Big new pillared buildings, neoclassical, like banks, clearly oil money: the Americans like buildings like that.

Back on the river, I think of the city, how far we are. 'Here it comes,' says Pruitt, and Burke sighs; he's a tall young guy, nearly seven feet tall, still growing, and the boat currently chugging towards us is not open-air but low-roofed. Alarm flickers across the guide's face as he pulls up and slings a couple of lengths of light blue rope onto the concrete piling.

It's all a flurry of sign-offs, last gear checks and orientation and first-aid and emergency procedures. Deonarine watches through the smeared windows as Burke and Pruitt attempt to film in the dimness of the boat cabin. I place my phone at last into the especially purchased, watertight plastic pouch I got at the airport. Wave goodbye. Set out into my homeland that is not my homeland, into the place that kills.

Maybe they are not dead.

Four people: a couple, two singletons. None over 25. I wonder how small and young they felt under the gothic cathedral of these trees.

Blake Atkinson and McKayla Francis.

Cora Schneider.

Harley Montgomery.

And the young guide, 'Davey', Daevon Mitchelson.

I feel like I know the first four. I interviewed their families. I spoke to their friends and professors. I mined their social media: Twitter, Facebook, Fotofo, Instagram, Clarely. The world in which they had immersed themselves had a certain sameness to it, a shape and a pattern into which they all fit as neatly as books on a shelf. All white, all prosperous, professional. Their people, grieving, eager to talk.

Davey was young too, and local. I have a few photos of him from the social media streams of tourists: sweet, open smile, hair buzzed very short. His little concrete apartment was in a hive of other little concrete apartments in Georgetown, very unlike the eerily same-looking, white-lit, houseplant-filled condos of the missing tourists.

Here is what I know.

The four came here. They got into a canoe. Yellow, emblazoned with the tour company logo, tagged with a satellite chip and wayfinding software. They were wearing life jackets. They were wearing locator armbands. Their gear was looped to the gunwales with bungee cords and carabiners. There are photos.

Here is what I also know.

I, Preeti Lal, aged 33, have never been to this the country of my ancestors. My parents have been back four times since my birth for weddings, funerals. Not me. Not my sister Priya. The slender umbilicus of our heritage, as flight prices soared, was cut for us in childhood; it was never an option.

People compliment us on our English, unaware that Guyana was once a Dutch and then a British colony. Run by a company, like the East India Company, or like our new homeland, Canada, which was once more or less run by the Hudson's Bay Company. An entire land used as warehouse, feedstock, store. Anything but what it was.

Yes, we speak good English, my mother would say frostily. Without adding that the British had kept them from speaking their native languages, brought their children up in the estate schools. Methodists teaching little brown and black kids, coming out a muddled mix of faiths and ideas. The missionaries going into the forests to try to convert the indigenous tribes.

If you're from the Caribbean, how come you're Indian too?

I don't know.

My parents knew but were too vague about it. Priya and I went on Wikipedia. The indentured workers, names and histories lost to their illiteracy, to deaths in the sugarcane fields, to trauma, to time; no memory could hold all that they had left behind. Four hundred years of the Portuguese and Spanish and Dutch and English and Scottish and Irish scuffling over purchased bodies for profit. Like all over the Caribbean.

But you couldn't profit just anywhere in Guyana: you wanted sugar, and that meant access to ships and railways. All along the coast. Harder to make a living in the savannahs. And finally countries saying *We don't belong to you* and the owners (do you say it? I say it: I do not say invaders, because they came to own) shocked, hurt: *But look at all we've done. We've been here for so long.*

Now, the invaded say: Come to us. Your tourist dollars help our economy. We have oil now. We're not like those glitzy resort islands. We're better, we have something they don't have. We have the Amazon.

Do they, though?

How far would you go to see something that you couldn't see *anywhere else*, and that would be gone in 20 or 30 years, even if it were owned by corporations and groomed like a suburban lawn? For me, not very far. But for these four. I don't know.

Part of me thinks: If I can think like they did, I will find them.

Part of me thinks: But I don't really want to. Do I?

Our guide, Tyrus, is alert, nearly paranoid-looking. He explained earlier that there were supposed to be two of them: one to drive, one to guide the tour retracing the steps of the missing. But the other guide never showed up. So it was just him. He has the compact, quick-moving body of an athlete, some sport that requires swift pivots and the ability to flinch away from projectiles. Tennis, maybe.

Till we get going, the flies and wasps choke the air, so it becomes hard to even blink. Then with the press of a button, the windows retract into the roof, and we lean gratefully on the sills, choking a little on engine exhaust and kicked-up river water. The white sky makes the trees darker, greener; the shadows in their alcoves are black.

This is the managed part of the Amazon, I remind myself. This is where they come with their chemicals and clippers, where they pour boiling vinegar down ants' nests to make the trails safe and go after the wasps with flamethrowers. What might it look like where they do not go? Impossibly wild, impossibly tangled.

Howler monkeys scream; Pruitt immediately swivels and his hands dance over the soundboard, trying to get the sound. That'll be good in the final footage. Make people jump. Tyrus points out more kiskadees, lapwings, parrots, toucans. I am stunned by the toucans.

'I thought they went extinct,' says Burke; his face has gone bluish with shock, every freckle standing out like red paint.

Tyrus shrugs. 'They did, but we brought some in from Suriname, bred them in the zoo. All those birds got dem chips, tags. You can find them on your phone. The scientists, I mean. Because they'll just…'

'What?'

'You know. Go extinct again.'

When we leave the sedate river, our next phase is climbing up and onto a thickly overgrown path which I realize, when my eyes refocus in the ochre gloom, is actually groomed like a ski trail, even marked with tiny reflective stakes. We are still in a place that is owned and therefore maintained. It only seems a wonderment to look up and realize that the sky is gone, covered with huge leaves. We are not really far from home.

I think: If I had come to a place expecting to find wilderness, what would I think here?

I think: I'd go off-trail.

Tyrus points out the leafcutter ants who walk with such delicacy and patience along the hanging vines; Pruitt stops us while he gets five minutes of sharp footage. 'See,' I hear my editor saying, 'Wild, wilderness. Jungle. Ants.' Shortcuts for things in the human mind that we over the generations have forgotten and, since the countdown began for what they called the climate crisis, have been trying to forget. Drinking to forget, dying to forget.

It is not a crisis. It is ongoing, it is life. We are being cooked to death, and being cooked to death is life.

(But would you come here to *escape* being cooked to death? They have not escaped it here, Tyrus says. Everything is changing.)

Huge blue butterflies waft past us, as if staged. There is a constant low roar of mosquitoes and flies who come in for landings and skid right through my layer of greasy repellent to try to sink in a proboscis, have a snack. Tyrus seems unbothered. I wonder what he put on earlier and am jealous of whatever it is.

The greenness shouts at me, it is the highest density of living things I think I have ever seen, it is the plant version of Hong Kong, where I went for a story last year and was stunned, in my prairie way, at how many people were near me at all times.

We are making so much noise (panting, pushing aside leaves, crying out at the cuts of the razorgrass) that I think everything around us for miles must be scared off, and Tyrus confirms this.

'What *would* we be seeing?'

'Ocelot, sloth maybe. The birds dem used to this. Uh, heron, egret, spoonies, howlers…' He counts on his fingers. 'Piranha, pirei, electric eel, sometimes kamoodie still. Black caiman.'

'That's a lot more than I was expecting.'

'It's what people come to see.' He gestures around us, shafts of sunlight streaking down and creating hot little spotlights on the ground. A bright yellow beetle walks through one of these like a catwalk model. 'It gets harder all the time. Every year. Hotter, drier… People log pieces in a pattern, like a puzzle. The government tells them where they can cut. Then they burn it, put cows on it. Sell the meat. Plant more cane. It changes the whole weather, changes the rains. We plan around the pattern.'

'Plan tours, you mean.'

'Yes. You really want people to see things,' he adds earnestly, looking up into the canopy. 'They take pictures. You want it up on Instagram right away.'

Pruitt laughs. 'Yeah, like there's signal out here.'

We veer right on the trail, Tyrus still chuckling under his breath, and find ourselves abruptly in a movie-esque clearing, roughly circular, the ground nearly bare under our boots. It is such a sudden change from the spongy vegetation and slick roots that I nearly overcompensate and lose my footing.

In bamboo and wood, artfully camouflaged against the trees, are things that belong in no jungle I have ever conceived of: solar charging stations with phone cradles, free-standing 'frames' with orchids clearly cultivated behind them for photos, plastic plaques bolted to tree trunks with QR codes, vending machines with keychains, T-shirts, water, trail mix, mouse-ear headbands, balata men, taxidermized baby caiman with eyes made of marbles. Above us, festooned with spikes to keep the birds off, are plastic drone platforms, clearly marked with white and red circles so the tiny cameras can see where to land.

'Oh, come *on*,' Burke says. But he follows Pruitt, and the two men weave around these offerings with their lenses as if we have discovered a cargo cult on a long-abandoned island. Pruitt yelps a moment later, and dances backwards, brushing at his jeans.

'Don't worry about them,' Tyrus begins, 'they do that sometimes now, but nothing –'

A split-second later, crash cut, and both Burke and Pruitt are snarling and crying out, and the tiny leafcutters are wading through blood, crushed a thousand times over by swatting hands and stamping feet. The ants move in surges of crimson and sepia, no longer in neat single file but like waves, like the furious water that laps over the long-submerged sea wall miles away, so many that we can hear the sound of their feet.

All pretence is abandoned and we race back to the boat, no breath to scream, moving in grim silence.

Indentured. 'We weren't *slaves*,' I told people stubbornly when they looked at me with sympathy, poor little brown girl descended from the *slaves* the British brought over from India. 'We made an *agreement*.'

A colony supplying another colony, like an ant queen imperiously descending to begin her reign at another tree. All the minuscule jaws chewing, chewing away at the rock-hard cane, and the English kiddies back home with real West Indian sugar in their sweets… Not slaves, but, I thought, worse than slaves. Because we had sold ourselves out of ignorance and desperation and had not known we would never go home again.

We were clueless, I think, not oppressed. Or no. Both.

Slathered in antibiotic gel and sipping rum punch, our feelings hurt at being defeated by such tiny creatures, we eat cold ginep and pineapple from the fridge in Pruitt's room. The cuts are tiny but uncountable, and I force myself to ask my crew whether they want to go home. Both shake their heads.

'It's been one goddam day.'

'I know, but…'

Pruitt, who specializes in zoological expeditions and filming, declares himself rattled but unfazed. Burke is silent, only nodding when I ask whether he truly wants to continue.

'Pruitt and I could manage,' I tell him. 'I can take the spare earcam. Do the easy stuff. Interviews.'

He shakes his head, the fair hair speckled with dried blood that showers onto the tile floor like insects.

'They don't do that though,' Pruitt says brusquely, running a hand through his dark curls and examining his palm. 'The kid was right about that. They're not like driver ants or whatever. Like, didja see them? Right at the start? I think I got a minute or two of footage. They all dropped their leaf bits. Dropped them right out of their mouths, and came for us. Little bastards.' He pauses, reconsiders. 'Little *bitches*.'

I think of the jaws specialized for millions of years to snip leaves like paper, the mandibular muscles evolving for it, the heads and the legs and the balance and the senses evolving for it. And then this. The rubbery skin of mammals.

Those stories they told us yesterday, of bullet ants stinging the cattle that had invaded the savannahs, cows panicking from the pain, broken legs. You sometimes had to *shoot* an animal that got stung by a bullet ant. Too expensive to nurse something back to health if it were just meant for meat.

Well, the ants don't know them as anything but meat; and they don't know us as anything but meat either. And they don't care who's valuable or how.

'We'll go back out tomorrow,' I say. It gets dark with equatorial violence here, no lingering sunset for hours but a sudden blanket of blackness, and the renewed roar of the night bugs.

We'll go back out, no questions answered, none asked.

I can't sleep, and end up taking a handful of so-called natural sleeping pills that do nothing but turn my body to a cool puddle and leave me awake, unable to move. (I picture myself as the balata men I saw being made in the marketplace, liquid first then solid, trapped and hammering the transparent nano-ceramic of their vending machine.)

Outside the window, in the shifting trees, softly-glowing sloths seem to watch me. They can't, I know they can't be there; I know we are in the city. Still, they have to have come from *somewhere*, and they have carried light from the deepest jungle in their viscid fur.

When my parents came to Canada, this place still had almost 80 per cent of its original rainforest. Now it's more like 30 per cent. Still a whopping number, orders of magnitude larger than its neighbours. Everyone said: Now that they have oil, the rainforest will be left alone. They built the rigs offshore, great gleaming cities of glass and carbon-fibre, storm-proof, probably kraken-proof, I don't doubt. Not inland.

But no. Down it went, and its clouds and its weather. We dared – how did we dare?

Outside, I know, a boy in white shorts and blue-streaked hair is climbing the hotel's sign to perform the nightly task of prying loose the disoriented moths and cockroaches and birds from the LED sign before they get stuck and fry the circuitry. The centipede I saw is also still out there somewhere, learning my name so it can find me. Vampire bats brush their wings against the windows, leaving smears of saliva.

They don't work like that.

I know they don't.

Something feels like it's coming, but it cannot be. Everything that was promised to the world, every threat, every extortion, has already come. Now we live in the after.

In the morning, Pruitt and Burke are itchy and nervous but seem all right. 'It was good we left when we did,' Burke keeps saying tiredly. His voice is barely audible from its great height. 'It's good we left. We should…it's good.'

'We'll know what to watch for this time,' Pruitt says as we leave the hotel, gesturing to the doorman to get us a cab. 'I got some good pics of the nest. Do you think they like…*hybridized* or something? With a more dangerous species? Like driver ants?'

'Interesting. That would make a good tangent in the book.'

'Yeah. We could get in some bug experts. Talk about the…'

'Changing habitat and so on.'

The air is clearer this morning, cooler. Less like the inside of a mouth. My clothes are still soaked though as we arrive back at the Kiskadee Tours office shack. Deonarine is dealing with a family matter today, Tyrus tells us, but he and another tour guide – he points at an alarmingly young boy, who waves at us from the rear of a big periwinkle blue canoe – will take the three of us out.

The boy's name is MarkPaul, and he achingly resembles some of my cousins – the island face, unruly hair. Like them, too, his accent is all over the place. 'Oh, I did my undergrad at University of Miami,' he says cheerfully over the noise of the engine as we paddle upstream, turning to look at me over his shoulder, the bright green uniform T-shirt. 'I'm doing my masters here at U of G. I just work here on de weekends to pay for school.'

The flowers of the water hyacinth are just the colour of our canoe, and that pleases me. I hope it looks nice in our footage. Impossibly white birds occasionally float over us as if a flake of the sky has detached itself to glide along the river.

'Do you like it? This work?'

'Sure. It's fun. We get two paid meals for every shift. The tourists are nice – well, usually. They tip good, I mean, the Americans and Canadians do. Not the English. Guess they don't believe in reparations,' he adds with a braying laugh. 'You can make a lot in tips. Especially if you take them places they can see birds and such. It's the pictures, they want the pictures.'

We see no other boats on the river as we go further in, and the afternoon wears away with questions about the four missing tourists, the missing guide Davy, whom both Tyrus and MarkPaul knew, and shouting and pointing at the local wildlife.

Dozens of abandoned villages line the river, little stilted homes and clinics and schools and shops rotting, turning grey and green, falling into the sluggish water. 'You can't live here any more, not really,' MarkPaul says offhandedly when Burke points it out. 'Dem Indians, you know, all had to move to the city. It's hard to fish here, hard to buy food. Every year it gets harder.'

I write it down. We spot a beautiful, moving shimmer, a rainbow boa ('Probably somebody's pet dumped back here') in the trees, giant praying mantises with mouthfuls of iridescent hummingbird feathers.

If you look away from the crumbling buildings, if you pretend you don't see the bones sometimes lodged in the mud below them, it's beautiful out here. Painfully beautiful. Maybe one of the last places on Earth that still looks this way, and I understand, now, why you would come here, save up and fly all the way here.

I think of the interview with Cora Schneider's family: broken-hearted mother, taciturn father, speechless sister. *She wanted to see these places, these wild places. She's been everywhere. Vietnam. New Zealand. Even Mexico... We worried about her there. And the Caribbean was supposed to be safe. She promised she'd stay out of the city, the riots, the gangs, and just go on these little tours, like in Costa Rica...*

So she was experienced. She had travelled a lot. Knew the dangers.

She wanted the dangers. But don't get me wrong, she had a good heart, such a good heart. I wish you could've met her. She'd go to these villages, volunteer to help build churches. Like, native reservations and everything. She'd go where people had nothing and help dig wells. We have these pictures – look. Here she is in Indonesia with underprivileged kids. They built a playground that day. She and her friends. Community development projects, with money from the UN and other agencies.

I had wanted to say, 'Do you know the term "poverty tourism"? No? Then you must know the term "slumming"?' But I had said nothing. Lost their child. The great disaster, that you outlive your child.

Isn't that what they thought? The great explorers, I mean...the ones we learned about in school. The missives from the English and Spanish and French back to their homelands: *The natives are like children.* We do this for their own good. We even eliminate them for their own good. *And we build things they will not appreciate till they are older. The roads, the churches. The trains.*

Well, I think. *Yes. But...but...*

Back into the green, the vegetable smell of it becoming familiar now. In minutes I miss the pink and white birds of the river, the colour of the floating flowers. The crew scratches and mutters beside me, dots of blood from yesterday's cuts rising on their long-sleeved shirts. Supposedly nothing can bite through these (or so the website assured us: carbon-polymer fibres). The kaboura flies try anyway. I slap and scratch and curse.

We cross, delicately and with many stops to film its steep drop and rise, the first of the rope bridges, which monitored or not, engineered or not, sways terrifyingly under our tentative steps. Even Tyrus moves across it ashen and trembling, both hands on the railing.

I think: *A bridge. Maybe they all went off a bridge. All of them together.*

But the searchers checked the bridges. They found nothing.

It's trimmed, sprayed, monitored. But you could still disappear out here. The jungle is still hungry and wants to eat.

Don't be ridiculous. It can't any more.

Gently but firmly I detach a vine that wraps itself around my wrist while we film, and tell myself not to think about it. Taste buds on the pale red tendril, fresh new growth. A baby seeking formula. *Don't.* Things move faster in the forest. Remember the sensitive plants you played with outside the customs office. Tap tap. Soft, yellow blossoms rain down on us from so high up that I cannot see where they are coming from.

I have been to places (Italy, Peru) where the ruins are thousands of years old, and still protrude through the soil like teeth. I cannot imagine that happening here. The fungus eats so fast I can almost hear it as we walk. Crunching on stone, I think. Gone in a generation.

'There was supposed to be a movie filmed here,' MarkPaul says suddenly into the silence; Pruitt swivels, turns the camera on him. 'I forget what it was called. One of those franchise ones... Not like James Bond but another spy. They cancelled it after what happened.'

'They didn't want to reschedule?' I ask him.

'No, they paid…what do you call it? Kill fees. To Mr D. But they never came back.' He shakes his head. 'They talk a lot about the tourist economy, but the government never did anything. Lobby for us or anything.'

'Well,' Burke says after a minute, 'five people are dead.'

'*Missing*,' says Tyrus.

MarkPaul shrugs, uncomfortable. We walk on. The air feels heavy, charged, as if preparing for a storm.

Tyrus tells us about what we might see in the savannah if we had gone on that tour: the giant anteaters, the interesting ranches, the termite mounds.

But this is the route the other tour would have taken, I say again, and again they say yes, you walk where they walked.

There was supposed to be a hike up Turtle Mountain too, and a visit to some secret frog breeding pools, though the tourists often skip those, Tyrus explains, because of the disinfection protocol that the local management demands to keep the frogs from dying of fungus. We are far from the splendidly forested Wai Wai area, which has even stricter protocols; there, you cannot even approach closely enough to photograph these frogs, whose locations are kept strictly guarded.

Both guides frequently pause and check their phones and their heavy-duty GPS units, and they keep us along the path. I watch the dots and lines on the screen with something that feels like paranoia, like a warm breath on my neck. The signal cuts out constantly.

'We done this one a lot,' Tyrus laughs, trying to reassure me, 'but it grows so fast out here, you still gotta check.'

At the Canopy View Lodge, we recharge our gear and whisper over the local population (also microchipped, also jealously watched by the staff) of the giant, cobalt blue tarantulas. The four tourists made it this far, we know. They checked in, all of them. And checked out. And then nothing.

I feel a sickening foreboding: We *will* find something here. A shred of a bandana, a dropped watch band. The others found nothing but they didn't feel what I feel…in the book, I think, as we turn in for the night, I will have to talk about my ancestral connection to this place. The editors will like that.

I wake to screaming, and it seems so natural to do so that I think in my dreams I must have predicted it, even wanted it. Here, the sky is a river, the forest is a mouth. We are crushed in its teeth… I untangle myself from the mosquito netting and sprint outside, stopping only to step into my boots, and am assaulted at once by the mosquitos, the darkness, the howls.

At first I cannot parse them as being from terror or pain, but as they rattle into silence, I realize it is both: *must* be both. Pruitt outpaces me easily, a pale smudge in the trace of moonlight penetrating the canopy here, in his white T-shirt and pants, his white bare feet. Somewhere, the howlers scream too, and we nearly veer towards them before realizing what they are, that the timbre and pitch is not human.

The tropical night is pitch black as soon as we are away from the lodge, and we both stop, clutching at one another's arms, unable to orient either back the way we came or towards the last of the cries. There is something primal about it, something that cries to the lizard brain to go back to the lights of the lodge.

Something also that makes me think, *The ants tried to warn us.*

No they didn't. They tried to kill us and failed.

'It's Burke,' Pruitt gasps, his nails sinking into my forearm. 'I think I saw him. I think something had him.'

'Jaguar!' Tyrus appears by my side, his voice a croak. 'There are still jaguar here, they say so. The local tribes used to…but the district officer nah… I never seen…come on! With me, come *on*.'

Only Tyrus had the foresight to grab his phone, and we set off using the shaky, too-bright light, step by step, a flash on the ground (trembling with racing ants, all headed in the same direction), a flash into the trees (reflected green eyes, staring). Minutes pass, more than I expect.

Great shadowy beings seem to watch us from the trees, moving as we move, furred or feathered, 50 feet tall. I cannot understand how quickly we have lost control and electricity and civilization until we reach Burke, still weakly thrashing in a shallow stream, embraced head to foot by a huge anaconda.

'Kamoodie!'

What was he *doing* out here, what was – I cannot think, only join the other two as MarkPaul catches up and begins to hack at the great heaving body with a small machete barely the length of a kitchen knife. The blade rebounds not as if from metal but rubber, but the snake releases Burke all the same and raises its head threateningly at us, exposing a mouth that glows with near-incandescent beauty in the light of the phone.

And then it is gone, easing into the darkness with grand and insolent sloth, into the tall moving shadows, who seem to slump in resignation: not at their failure, for Burke is still twitching, unable to breathe, and for the first time I think *He may die, the forest may have taken him too, and then it will be us*, but at the fact that for once, their act has been witnessed.

'I don't,' gasps Tyrus, 'I can't...'

'They don't attack people, do they?' I push my shoulder under Burke's arm, and we get him up somehow, head lolling, his breath a wheeze in my ear. 'They don't.'

'No. Never. I've never heard of it. Something...'

Piercingly, as we drag Burke back to the lodge, I think: *This is what happened to the four. One at a time.* Not all at once, as we feared. One first then the next then the next.

Now the forest sees that we are only a few, and we come mostly alone. And that we can be split up. Easily. Not like the forest, which has learned, I think, to act as one. It's doing this on purpose.

In the near distance I hear a waterfall, but I don't understand how; there are none near here. Maybe I am hearing something else. My ears ring with adrenaline.

Without warning Pruitt falls to a tremendous black cayman, splashing out like a movie monster from the same small stream we crossed on the way here. I realize we were walking so close to it we nearly stepped on its back, and I turn to fight but we have no real weapons, the others urge me on, screaming that we cannot go back for him, we must get Burke out of here at least.

Burke's dead weight falls entirely to MarkPaul and me, so that as we flee we both crash unexpectedly to the wet ground; a tooth breaks, a bolt of pain shooting through my head with a flash as real as if I had been hit by lightning. Blood fills my mouth; I swallow the first (it seems) gallon, spit out the rest as we get up and shuffle frantically towards the distant lodge.

But the door to safety is blocked in silence by a shimmering, eager wave of what appear to be hornets. MarkPaul drops the phone at once, recovers it only slowly.

Will they respond with anger to the lights? *They're an invasive species*, I think in horror: the giant ones that were accidentally brought into the country. *Vespa mandarinia*. They didn't evolve here. They don't belong here. But it would have been so easy to settle in, I think numbly. We warmed the whole world up for them, we moved them around in cargo ships and planes, in boxes of fruit from far away. Now the forest says to them: You can fight too? Fight the humans with us.

I thought I could not feel any more fear tonight. Now I see how wrong I was.

Longer than my thumb, and their venom *(stop it)* can dissolve *(stop thinking about it don't move)* flesh, and we are far from home, and we are far from what I think of as civilization, but this is what it means, doesn't it? That there were people who went around the world saying, 'This is mine, that is mine, what I look at is mine, and the people there belong to me, and they have no wills of their own now that I have arrived,' and the land itself watching, stunned, as it was all taken over and ground into the crust of the earth for profit, as these hornets will do to the local bees, who have never seen such things and have evolved no defences.

'Back,' whispers MarkPaul. 'Slow, slow. Slow. Back to the canoe.'

But everything I have is inside, I almost whisper back. My money, passport, identification. Phone. Tablet. All our other gear. The cameras, the microphones, the memory cubes. All our customs documentation. My clothes, my chemicals, my medications. *I can't get back to...*

Burke's head is heavy, his breath a whisper. He must have broken bones. Internal bleeding. But we couldn't leave him there. Bad enough we left poor Pruitt in our panic.

And I finish my own sentence in my head: *Back to civilization.*

A lie. We won't be going back to civilization. We will be going back to a raw world, with the truth of it clear now, the veil pulled from my eyes.

This is our fault. A world invaded and then roasted alive cannot be expected to lie there and take punishment forever. And everywhere, money is the cushion: keeps you from seeing reality, from feeling it as we feel it now. The side of my head screams and raves with pain where the tooth and perhaps my jawbone are broken. Circles of coloured darkness swirl in front of my vision.

Get out, get out, the forest screams in silence. *Get out or die. We know how to deal with you now. And we will spread the word.*

MarkPaul puts a hand on my back. 'Very, very slow.' The frogs and crickets begin to sing again, as if playing us off stage. We do not belong here. Not even temporarily, as players in this drama.

The four, I try to explain. Thought they were exempt from this. But no. They thought they lived in a different world. But it's all the same world.

'We'll get out if we get out together,' I whisper to Burke, and we reverse slowly from the claimed door, MarkPaul and I putting our backs to each other, moving our feet by inches over the slick ground. The lodge is theirs: the forest, the creatures it wielded, having taught us this lesson. They can have it.

To our utter shock and relief, Pruitt meets us at the canoe, bloodied, limping. Piranha jump at his feet in the shallow water like silver spoons. His gaze says, *You left me behind*. I open my mouth to apologize, but I cannot. What we did was inexcusable. How did he escape, how did he get back here? Did the forest simply let him go with a warning? No, surely not. He must have fought for his life.

No one gets left behind now, I want to tell him, but it won't mean anything to him. A slap in the face after our abandonment. I squeeze his shoulder, spit blood into the still river. We push off into the epic darkness of the last wilderness.

No, we didn't find them. I would like to say, 'We found something else,' but we didn't find that either. On the contrary, we lost. We lost our grants for the documentary, and due to 'gross negligence and suspicion of libel', the funding for the book has also been pulled, and two lawsuits are now pending – one against the owners of Kiskadee Tours, which is expected to fail, and one against us for endangerment of their employees, which is expected to be won.

It has been two months since we returned from Guyana. Burke remains in a coma at Mercy General in his home town, which I will not disclose for fear of the press descending upon him. Mercy General is general enough. Mercy itself, I think now, is general enough.

And a new world is coming or has already come. This is not a new normal. We will not have a new normal for a long time.

What is coming, with increasing speed, is a transition period for those things both sentient and insentient, sapient and not, that are uniting with their righteous rage and epiphany to form their own tipping points.

What strengths they draw upon I do not know. Only that humanity no longer can do the same.

In this new world, I can no longer sleep in darkness. Two weeks ago, when I was meant to file this story with my editor, the power went out in my condo, and I awoke in the dark. While I spent the next 64 hours at a temporary psychiatric hold followed by my sister's brightly lit bathroom, I am told I screamed apologies to the trees, asking that we not be sacrificed for revenge, that I had to tell their story.

My parents now call every day instead of every week. They still drive over with care packages of curry and roti, plantain and dal. Salara, sometimes, mailed from New York. Tennis rolls.

All over the world, similar stories are being told. Something is spreading the word: trees, I think, or animals, or insects, something saying: *Attack attack*

attack attack. Sometimes the stories filter through desperate screams in five-second videos posted to Twitter or YouTube, bracketed on both ends by ads for cheap flights.

We made this world of information and commerce, we made sure the world could learn about itself. Now, we are learning what we could not learn otherwise. I wonder if we will learn enough to save ourselves.

THE DIAMOND LIBRARY

NAVIN WEERARATNE

Even with 15 trillion books to read, some bastards just refused to learn.

I blew on my freezing fingers and my breath steamed up. Repurposed reading room lights were strung between the alley stacks, and they lit up the slum in an acidic white. A grandmother turned the spit on her roadside fire; fat dripped off roasting rats and hissed in the flames. A fuel picker shoved past me, his back bent under his load of torn, pressed book covers tied in thick bundles with twine. Old men sat on mats around a book cart that had been converted into a tea stand. The tea seller swapped between near-empty black rupees to power his electric kettle. One of the tea drinkers stared at me with watery eyes before opening his book.

'What do you do?' asked the urchin boy as he led me through the street.

'I'm a hunter,' I half-lied. 'I go after the bandits who prey on the intra-library loan caravans.'

'Is it an important job? Do they pay you in black rupees or silver?'

'Depends on the bandits.'

A frown formed on his dirty face. 'So why are you hunting Sai Ganesh?'

'Sai Ganesh is an old friend,' I said, even as I shook my head at a waving rickshaw driver. I'd made eye contact; he kept on waving. 'I owe him some money, and I have come to return it.'

'Are you a librarian?'

'No,' I lied.

We came to a large intersection. In the centre rose a diamond statue of the Buddha: palm raised and a book open on his lap. Black rupee offerings and paper flowers lay scattered before it. Across from the Buddha, young (and not so young) women catcalled a group of caravan drivers. Their electric trucks were parked along the roadside. Street children threw buckets of water onto their mineral-caked hulls and scrubbed them with rags and bare hands. A fat caravanner went over to the hookers and started bargaining, waving a fist full of black rupees at them.

'My mother told me the librarians think Sai Ganesh is a monster.'

'Why does she say that?'

I followed him as he turned down an alley stack.

'Because he tells stories that are not in their books.'

'Storytellers take books and don't return them. They don't check them out, so the Library doesn't know they're missing and need to be replaced. Then they read the books and hide or destroy them; that gives the storytellers their power over other people. The Library has all of Humanity's tales from before the Great Retreat, and the storytellers are destroying them.'

'Are you sure you're not a librarian?'

'Enough questions, boy.'

Battaramulla was a shithole slum of over-quota mothers and their illegal descendants. They were nothing but trouble, wasting air, burning book covers, stealing water. We could rid the Library of its slums in a week, except they had their uses for librarians – the sort that complained about them over dinner before slipping out to visit them 'for some fun'.

Perhaps I would write a book about them.

'Do you have any books to give me?' asked the urchin.

'There are books all around!'

'Their words are too big for me. My favourite book is *The Elephant and the Snake*. My mother shares it with the other mothers, but she knows the story by heart. She tells me the story every night. I'm learning to read it too and she helps me read it when it comes back to us. Do you have any books like that?'

'No.'

We turned down a still narrower alley. There were few reading lights here, and people sat with their backs against the book stacks, wrapped in rags against the cold.

'When the Deccan Drill comes, we'll leave,' said the child. 'My mother says people have fewer babies there. There'll be an amnesty, and we will go to live in the Deccan Earthworks. I'll go to school. Did you go to school, Librarian?'

'Yes.'

'It sounds like fun *and* they give you food. Maybe they'll give me another book to read.'

Up ahead, the alley had been blocked with crates and corrugated iron sheets. Men stood outside, warming themselves around a barrel of burning book covers. They looked in my direction.

'That's it,' said the kid. 'Sai Ganesh's camp.'

'Well done.' I pulled out a heavy, silvery tube about five inches long. A green status light flashed at one end. 'Here.'

He stared at it, holding it in both hands.

'What? You've never seen a silver rupee before? Now get out!'

'Just what,' said a bearded guard stepping out from behind the barrel fire, 'the fuck do you want?'

'I've come to listen.'

'Listen?' asked another one, the large, black wart on his nose twitching involuntarily. 'Do you mean *spy*?'

'The likes of you don't come to listen.' Beard looked me up and down, perhaps disapproving of my use of soap and ironing boards. 'You a librarian?'

'If I am,' I said, reaching into my jacket and pulling out my gun, 'there isn't a damn thing you can do about it. Step aside. I won't ask again.'

They made way, their eyes fixing on me like searchlights against their dirty faces. I holstered my weapon and stepped past.

Then, they acted. Wart Nose tried to grab me; I turned, raised my elbow, and smashed him in the jaw. He howled and clutched his face. I seized him and kneed him in the chest. There was a sound of the snapping of ribs, and he screamed as I shoved him to the ground.

Meanwhile, Beard had drawn his gun. Now he shot me. I felt a hard tug as the bullet ripped through my jacket, just missing my kidney.

I drew once again and shot him dead.

I looked towards the encampment: I saw no one else. Gun in hand, I went after the monster.

The sound of chanting came from a shelter made of hardback books, sealed against the cold with stitched oilskins. The yellow of a reading light bled through the doorway flaps. Through them, I saw a figure rocking back and forth, chanting. There was a simple rhythm to it, utterly hypnotic. Perhaps this, more than any seditious or unexamined idea, was how they turned people.

I entered.

Inside the cramped space, an old man sat cross-legged; open on his lap was a freshly printed book. He had a guru's white beard and was skinny enough to be blown away by a loud argument. Next to him were a tin cup and a water jug. He looked up and frowned. 'I asked not to be disturbed. Did Kushan send you?'

'Yes,' I said, holding up a jar. 'I've brought some water.'

'I have water.'

'Now you have some more.' I poured from my jug into his, and filled his empty tin cup as well.

The monster muttered and took a sip.

I looked at his book. The script was Latin, but I didn't recognize the language; it seemed a Romance tongue. Not one I knew.

'What are you reading?'

'A historical account of Emperor Maximilian's conquest of the Antarctic. I am memorizing it.'

'Why is *that* worth memorizing?'

The old man coughed and took another sip of water.

'Because it is a new book written by someone from outside both the Library and the Deccan Earthworks.'

'That's impossible!'

'It is not.' He coughed again and turned the book towards me. 'This language is called Portuguese, it was spoken in a South American empire called Brazil. Only a native speaker could write this. There are also many new words in it.

'New words?'

'Yes. And then there's the subject – the nature of the reclaimed surface.'

I laughed. 'This is nonsense. It's just fantasy writing! A hoax, at worst. Perhaps there are a few illiterate, islander barbarians surviving in the neotropics, but that's it.'

'Really?' He raised an eyebrow. 'What makes you think there's only one library? The neutrino detector vaults in Central Archives can detect book uploads from across the planet – or even in space! Have you seen them?'

'Yes.'

'They're as big as cathedrals! If we only had the Deccan to talk to – it would have been easier to use cables!' He burst into a fit of coughing. I poured him more water and handed him his cup. He drank it all, clutching his throat as if it were getting tighter. 'There are *other* libraries out there,' he said, putting his cup down. 'They're uploading books to each other, books written by people in other Earthworks, and those who have reclaimed the Earth's surface.'

'Please! Enough of this nonsense. Someone should write a book about how, in every era, climate science is ignored by armies of idiots.'

'You don't accept –'

'The Search for Extra Library Intelligence has proven that there are no literate intelligences, human or artificial, beyond the Library and the Deccan.'

'Proven, you say?' He grinned as if taunting me from behind a secret.

'If you cared to actually read Guha's papers, you could judge the quality of their data yourself.'

'Guha did *not* say that there is no one else out there.'

'You don't think "statistically non-existent" is non-existent enough? Perhaps you would – if you'd spent your life learning how to think critically and not feeding delusions.'

'Guha has done so well since he shut down SELI, hasn't he? Not every Grand Librarian gets to write the next chapter of the *Vipattivamsa*!'

'He earned it.'

'By destroying books from elsewhere!'

'Censors? Really?' I felt the drowning exhaustion that comes from battling the boundless energy of the stupid. 'What other conspiracy theories have you lived your wasted life by?'

A bout of coughing ensued, causing the old man to clutch at his throat. 'I am memorizing this book, Librarian, this print-new new book because once the Censors find it they will destroy it. It is full of information *that can be verified*. It is strong evidence of a world beyond; evidence that cannot be dismissed as fantasy.'

'Whatever, Storyteller.' I checked the water jug. It was almost empty.

'The Censors are real!' His eyes were so sharp they pinned me down. 'We preserve what they destroy.'

'You spread lies and brainwash people.'

'We've saved the *true* narrative of our history! We –'

He started coughing again, and this time he didn't stop. He looked up at me, eyes wide with realization. He tried to stand, but I grabbed him and held a cloth over his face to muffle the sound.

'*You* are the ones who are destroying knowledge,' I hissed, holding the thrashing man in place. 'You *destroy books*. Your lies end here, Storyteller. I look forward to telling your tale.'

I held him until he was still, then pushed the corpse aside. His body would do more good feeding rats than it ever did while he lived.

I picked up the book he'd been reading and dusted it off. Now that I knew it was Portuguese – or at least Portuguese-related – I could figure out the title. I tucked *Maximilian's Antarktik Reconquest* into my jacket. Now I had something to read on the way home.

The Grand Nuwara Eliya Reading Room is easily one of the nicest in the Library. I stopped there whenever I could.

The wooden floor of its dining hall creaked. It was a deep, aged brown, rumoured to be actual wood from a surface palace, rescued like silverware and oil paintings by Early-Retreat expeditioneers. I suspected it was just sequestered carbon; it was not like anyone could tell the difference any more.

'Good evening, sir,' said a smiling man across the dining room. Behind him were reproduction watercolours by colonials (British, not Chinese) and their collaborators. Before him was a table set for one, complete with a bottle of wine in a silver ice bucket. He wore a sarong and a white jacket, and sported a twirly moustache.

'Good evening, Apuhamy.' I sat as the caretaker drew the chair for me. 'Dinner smells wonderful.'

'You are too kind!' He lifted the cover of the plate. Steaming inside was a golden-crumbed, pork schnitzel. Framing it were perfect spheres of hydroponic baby potatoes, peeping from under a pepper sauce. In a bowl, so I could ignore them easily, were mustard micro-greens mixed with pomegranate pips.

I started eating while he poured me wine. 'Am I the only person in today?' I asked.

'Yes, sir,' said Apuhamy. 'But some fossil experts are arriving from the Hatton Archive tomorrow morning. I am sure you will find them enlightened and charming company!'

'Hatton? I will be gone first thing.'

'That's unfortunate. I shall have the girl prepare a packed breakfast. We're always delighted when you visit the Grand.'

'Thank you, Apuhamy. I sent ahead for some books. Has the courier arrived yet?'

'One just arrived from Central Archives; he is eating in the servants' quarters. I've arranged for the books to be brought up to your room while you're at dinner.'

'Excellent,' I said, my mouth half-full. 'Please have them run a bath as well. And I should like to speak with the courier if he's not too tired.'

'Of course, sir.' Apuhamy bowed and left.

I returned to my room after dinner, and it was exactly as Apuhamy had promised. A hot bath had steamed the mirrors of the marble bathroom. The study was well lit, and a stack of books sat on the reading desk. I proceeded to take a peek at them, my feet sinking into the thick, warm carpet – every title I'd requested was there.

Waiting in the sitting room was the courier. He was a young man with the gaunt, always-tired look of the promotion-gunning lower ranks of the Library. When he saw me, he smiled and stood up.

'You got them all. I had expected only one or two. You have my thanks.'

'You're most welcome, Officer.' He had the surprised bashfulness of the rarely praised. He reached into his pocket and pulled out a red plastic 'Priority Return' sleeve. 'Shall I take the book for you, sir?'

'No, no, that's fine. I'll take that instead,' I said and took the sleeve. 'I'd like to read some of it first. I'll return it myself.' I stared at the bag. 'Why is this one a priority return?'

'Don't know, sir,' he shrugged. 'Maybe a senior librarian gunning for his numbers? Everyone at Central is trying to look good now; they think it'll get them mentioned in the *Vipattivamsa*.'

I chuckled. 'Are you one of them?'

'Political books, not librarians.'

'Idealism! How quaint.'

I pulled out a silver rupee bar; the display showed a '5'.

His eyes widened, and he shook his head. 'That's fine, you don't need –'

'I insist.'

He made another token refusal, and I, in turn, played my part in the dance. He bowed his head slightly and thanked me as he accepted the tip.

'This is a week's pay.' He gave it another look before putting it into his pocket. 'I have to decide what to do with it!'

'You have to decide? To be young again…'

'I think I'll ask this girl if she'd like to go see a dance troupe. The Kotmale Harlequins are coming to Central. They're very good.'

I forced a smile. Dance troupes told stories – stories they passed down and to each other. Some dances were secret: privileged and hidden narratives were always trouble. The Kotmale Harlequins was one of the oldest troupes and had been investigated more than once in their distinguished past. They'd have been shut down a long time ago, but Nuwara Eliya always made a fuss when we went after artists. Artists always put the tribe ahead of the Library. We'd be better off without them.

'Well, I hope she says yes.'

I dismissed him and went back into the study to read.

Maximilian's Antarktik Reconquest was a masterwork of fiction. Not only had every little detail one could stumble over been seen to, but there were also others that prompted questions on deeper enquiry. It gave the book a veneer of realism only a serious scholar would appreciate, like the Carbon-14 levels in the bones of the Surface Man hoax.

My reading was slow: I didn't know Portuguese, but I did know Latin. With that as an anchor – and an excellent dictionary from Central – I began to translate.

The forgery's author (whoever 'Dona Violeta Sequeira' really was) had taken great trouble to reference unique features, especially landforms and pre-Retreat ruins. It took me all three atlases I had checked out to confirm them. The battle of the Six Titans was my favourite; 'Sequeira' didn't name the place, but from the description of the terrain, it could have happened at the ruins of Brasília.

Additionally, 'Sequeira' had extrapolated some degree of language drift – not simply new words with roots that could be analysed to suggest context-relevant meanings. She'd also transposed words with completely different meanings and some with additional ones. Many I couldn't guess at, but according to Beltram's *Study of Language*, I was seeing an appropriate degree of language drift given the fictional year of the book's setting.

Then there were *foreign words,* drawn from the refugee tribes that 'Sequeira' referenced.

After several hours, I decided that even though the document was a hoax, it was an excellent piece of literature. Its characters seemed real, their stories following the random beats of history rather than those of genre fiction writing. Everywhere, historical details had been researched and massaged into the narrative. A mistake with any single one of these would have betrayed the entire document as fake. Yet, every little detail I looked into was verified in my sources.

By the time I stopped reading it was the early hours of the morning. I put the reference books in the return bin beside the table. I felt reluctant to part with *Maximilian's Reconquest:* one always clutches to keep an art piece. I had a friend in Speculative Literature who would have enjoyed it; I pondered giving it to her – what did it matter if it wasn't returned immediately? The book was safe now.

The moment of rebelliousness passed, like the heat of the bath long forgotten. I would tell her about it; she could check it out herself.

I put the book into the priority return sleeve and sealed it.

'What do you mean "it's not there"?'

All the other archives smelled of books, but Central Archives smelled of machines. There was always the dusty taste of carbon feedstock in the air. Pavement gutters blew out dry, hot manufactorum air at your ankles. Wipe your hand on the ground, and your palm would glitter with ultra-fine diamonds. Even bunkered away in the endless office stacks of Central's bureaucracy, you could still sense them; trace reminders that the Library was a super sapient machine that no one could talk to any more. On normal visits, this filled me with wonder.

Today was not a normal visit.

The librarian at the computer behind the counter hid her contempt as one unaccustomed to doing so. On the wall behind her, a picture of Grand Librarian Guha smiled, trying to make up for her and the rest of her department of charmless bastards.

'I mean, Officer, the book you asked for does not exist.'

'Yes, it bloody does!' I put my hands on the counter. 'I returned it myself!'

At other counters and between the stacks, borrowers and grey-robed librarians stopped and stared.

'No,' she said, iron entering her voice. 'I have checked *both* the public and the internal catalogues –'

'Check them again! Can you imagine the mess we'd be in if I did my job as badly as you do yours?'

Jaws dropped. A mother covered her child's ears. All you could hear was the buffered thrum of ten thousand printers beneath our feet, at the Library's heart.

'What is the problem here?' a man called out from behind me.

I turned. It was a senior archivist: a gold chest pin and a face made for punching marked him out from the other grey robes.

'Your librarian won't run another –'

'I'm not talking to you!' Punch-My-Face held up his hand. 'Sureni?'

'I've checked the catalogues,' said Sureni. 'There is no record of a *Maximilian's Antarktik Reconquest* ever being published, let alone us having a copy of it on our shelves.'

'I returned it two weeks ago,' I said, I burned her alive with my eyes, 'in a priority return sleeve issued by one of *your* lot! A week later, my associate requests it, and you haven't even put it in the public index yet. That's why I'm here, with *you* lot, to get you to check *your* index.'

'I have nothing more to say,' said Sureni, stiff-lipped now, 'other than that I shall file a conduct complaint against Enforcement and Returns!'

'Oh, for bloody –'

'Right!' Punch-My-Face clapped his hands together. 'The matter is closed! I shall countersign the complaint, and you, sir, will remove yourself from –'

I grabbed him and smashed his face into the counter.

Someone screamed. This was followed by the usual sounds of shock and horror people make when they do everything but intervene. This is how we kept the peace in the Library with so few officers.

'You birth-quota bastard!' yelled Sureni.

'No shouting in the Library. Now, look for the book again – and show me your terminal as you do it. Or your supervisor here will only be able to sign your conduct complaint with his thumbprint.'

Punch-My-Face whimpered, his nose and teeth bloody.

She did the search again. She keyed it in from scratch, loading in all the indices and adding exact-phrase matching and broad search terms this time. She looked to me before she executed it, and I nodded.

The search began.

'You are neither civil nor a servant,' said a grey robe.

'I like that one. Now go get me some tea. If you spit in it, I will know.'

He didn't move.

I bashed the senior archivist's face again.

'Get him the fucking tea!' snapped Sureni.

The man rushed off.

'Such a mouth, Sureni. I should file a conduct complaint.'

The search ended before the tea arrived.

'What's this?'

'I know my job,' her face was as dark as a murder crime scene. '*There is no such book.*'

'I returned it myself!'

'I don't know what to tell you.'

The tea appeared on the counter, steaming in a porcelain cup and saucer.

'Is there any – any chance that it was *deleted* from the records?'

She (and others) looked at me liked I'd asked if she could flap her arms and fly. '*Deleted?* That's nonsense.'

'Is it?'

'Nothing is deleted!' she snapped. 'We are *librarians*, sir!'

'But it is *possible*?'

'Of course not! No one has that kind of power! No one!'

Except, of course, someone did.

'Let us tell you, fair citizens, of the tale of Emperor Maximus of Brasília, who led his legions against the jungle witch-kings of Antarctarus!'

The special – and free – public square performance of the Kotmale Harlequins was packed. Guards stood along sanction ropes, pushing back overeager attendees trying to rush the stage. Children waved balloons on strings and smeared their mouths with jaggery candies. A young man helped an old lady with a walker to get a better view. She smiled and thanked him, standing with the unsteadiness of one who refused her doctor's instructions to exercise. Two truant schoolkids, a boy and a girl, clenched hands so tight I wondered if their fingers would break. She gave the boy a big kiss and stared back at the stage. The boy seemed transported: the cost-benefit of an impending detention measuring favourably in his eyes.

The stage had been set up at the centre of the Nuwara Eliya Archive town square. The back of the stage was partitioned from view by theatre curtains. Lights on unsteady mounts lit the narrator.

Dancers wearing indecently tight costumes emerged through the curtains, lights chasing them as they jumped about the stage. They wore masks of mystical animals with chiming bangles on their arms and legs. The crowd hushed itself, spellbound. Even the guards looked.

'Upon your knees!' said a golden cockatoo mask. 'Good and beautiful people of Brasília, here comes the gem of the southern world, the conqueror of the Andesian Mountains, Maximus, the Illuminated!'

The dancers fell to their knees and lowered their heads. The lights turned and fixed a new entrant to the stage in place: a tall man in a white costume adorned with so many pearls they seemed to be holding it together. He held a golden mask over his face.

The audience began clapping, and people cheered. As Gold Mask walked to the front of the stage, flowers (and some underwear) came hurtling out of the crowd to land at his feet.

'I love you, Kumara!' a young woman screamed right beside me, splitting my eardrums. 'Isn't he a sight?' she said to me, eyes shining.

'Indeed! I can't help but think of my ancestors who died, that he would live.'

'Shush!' said the man on my other side.

'Did our great emperor sleep well?' asked a green cobra. The chorus explained that this was the evil Lord Chancellor, who had designs on the Illuminated One's sister.

'No,' said Gold Mask. 'A disquiet has entered my heart! I cannot sleep but to jump out of my bed and stare out the window! I cannot eat, but to think of sweet fruit I have not yet tasted from far-off, forbidden lands. I cannot love, but for the bosoms of golden-skinned beauties who speak words closer to the songs of birds than those of men!'

'What?' the Green Cobra Chancellor looked ashen. 'What disquiet is this? Should I fetch the physicians, Lord?'

Some of the dancers jumped up and surrounded Gold Mask, miming windows with their arms.

'No,' Gold Mask walked towards one of the windows. 'It is this view to the south that draws me. Send not for the physicians, but for my air marshals and centurions! I shall lead an expedition of ten thousand airships to conquer the wild, heathen lands of the Antarctarus!'

Offstage, war drums began to beat. The dancers jumped to their feet and began a new piece. Giant sparklers erupted, and the crowd gasped.

I ducked under the sanction rope and made for the stage.

'Oi!' A guard ran towards me.

I showed him my badge without even looking at him.

The crowd began murmuring, but the dancers continued their piece, watching me the way a school of fish watches a dark shape appearing in the water. Their centre of mass was Gold Mask. He stared right at me.

I climbed onto the stage.

The crowd grew louder. An organizer and his assistant came rushing out towards me from backstage.

I reached Gold Mask. He finally stopped dancing and looked at me. 'Look here!' he stamped his foot. 'Just who the devil do you think you –'

'Enforcement and Returns. Kumara DeKretzer, you're under arrest.'

An acid-bright light hung overhead. Cement block walls crammed around us. They smelled of damp and mould; cracked and bubbled paint hung loose from the ceiling and had fallen on the floor. Two chairs sat across from each other separated by a stainless steel table. On the table was a black valise and a glass of water. In one chair was me. In the other, sans mask, was the elegantly groomed and bearded Kumara de Kretzer, sweetheart of the artistic Nuwara Eliya Archive. His arms and legs were strapped to the chair.

'This is ridiculous!' He tugged at his bonds and glared at me. 'You fascist goons have gone too far this time! Your name and badge number!'

'Would you like a glass of water before we begin?' I pulled out a notebook.

He paused. 'Excuse me?'

'No, then,' I took his glass and drained it. 'Let's begin. Can you state your name for the record?'

'Untie me at once!' He tried to rock the chair forward. It did not budge: it was bolted to the floor. 'Release me at once, you fascist!'

'You are under the impression that you can make demands.'

'You can't do this!' Panic was finally beginning to take root in his eyes. 'I have rights!'

'You should have studied history instead of dance, Kumara. Law enforcement in this part of the world has *never* let rights get in its way. Now why don't you tell me what you been doing with storytellers?'

'I have no idea what you're talking about.'

'The storyteller Sai Ganesh and *Maximilian's Antarktik Reconquest*. Were you in a rush to adapt it while it was still fresh in your mind?'

'I am a dancer, sir. I would not put myself nor my troop at risk by consorting with criminals.'

'You're not in trouble with Enforcement and Returns. This is a private matter: you can tell me what's going on. I'm not actually interested in going after you or your associates.'

'This is not sanctioned?' he said, thinking he saw an edge. 'Oh, you are in real trouble now! I'll have your balls for breakfast by tomorrow morning! What's your name?'

I opened the bag. 'Kumara, I said Enforcement and Returns aren't after you. I didn't tell you that you *weren't in trouble*.' I pulled out a tight, leather roll and opened it out across the table. Neatly tucked into leather pockets were a series of stainless steel implements.

He stared at my beauties.

'I'll ask you again,' I put on a pair of rubber gloves. 'What are your relations with storytellers?'

'None – I'm telling the truth!' His face was the perfect mix of fear, outrage and disbelieving annoyance. Too perfect: he was an actor. 'Neither I nor any of my troupe has had anything to do with storytellers.'

I held his hand down while he thrashed against the chair, screaming, as I tore the nail off his index finger. 'This is kindness.' With a pair of forceps, I held the bloody nail up to the light. 'It will grow back just fine. The storyteller, Sai Ganesh. How long have you known him?'

'You fucking bastard!' he quivered with rage, saliva flying. 'I don't know any Sai Ganesh!'

'Why are you doing this to yourself?' I frowned. 'You already know this is not an official investigation. You give me what I want to know, and you can *walk right out of this room*. No marks against you. Well, except for the ones you're insisting on.' I gripped his bleeding finger, my thumb pressing down on the damaged nail bed. He screamed through gritted teeth. 'When did you first meet. Sai Ganesh?'

'Go to hell!'

I bent his finger back until it broke – and then held it in that impossible position for 10 seconds.

'I've read the book, Kumara! You were lazy; had you just saved the essence of the account, you would have got away with it. Before he died, Sai Ganesh named you as a confederate. For how long have you known him?' I waited for the screaming to stop.

'Three years,' he finally managed.

'And you've been learning his stories and putting them into dance since?'

'Yes.'

'Why?'

'Because storytellers have information about the Above Ground. *Suppressed* information.'

'Suppressed?'

'By you librarians,' he said, giving me a dark look. 'For years.'

'Years? How many years?'

He became silent and looked away.

'How many years!' I grabbed the index finger on his undamaged hand.

'Th – thousands! It's been thousands of years! The world's surface has recovered!'

'Bloody nonsense!'

'No, it's not! How else does the Maximilian account make sense? And you're missing the bigger point; it's from *another library!* The detector vaults pick up uploads from all over the planet, but your lot removes them from the shelves!'

'You can't honestly believe that it's been millennia. You think a lie that ridiculous would be believed in the Deccan Earthworks?'

'The drill will never come!'

'What's that?'

'*The Deccan Drill is never coming.* Every two or three centuries, they repeat the lie! No one remembers because the records are *removed*. In this place, only in being unwritten can the truth be safe. The storytellers – and the dance troupes – we save rival, *true* narratives. Why do you think your masters think it so important that you hunt us down and kill us?'

I released him.

I locked myself into a public terminal.

I started writing everything I remembered of *Maximilian's*. I took care to repeat and emphasize the most fanciful parts and added my own commentary about what they implied regarding climate recovery, the passage of thousands of years unaccounted in our own reckoning, and the survival of other earthworks. I even titled it *Reflections on Irreconcilable Claims in Maximilian's Antarktik Reconquest*.

I classified it under 'Southern Merican History' (as *Maximilian's* had been); created the pen name 'Sai Ganesh'; listed him as the author; and uploaded.

Then I loaded my gun and went to Southern Merican History.

I arrived there early the next morning. My book was waiting for me; I flicked through its printer-fresh-smelling pages and checked each one against my manuscript. As it had since the early years of the Great Retreat, the Library had published it perfectly. I put it back on the shelf and wiped the diamond dust off my hands. There was a small reading nook at the end of the stack that gave me an excellent line of sight. I camped there, glaring at the odd student or two till they decided there were better places to read primary sources.

In the darkness of the early hours of the morning, three large men arrived. They walked straight to the shelf in question. One man stepped ahead, looking down the aisle. The second turned his back and watched the way they had come. They wore the same grey greatcoats Enforcement and Returns did, but our lot would have shined the flashlight and seen me waiting in the dark. These men were lazy, but they had a menace about them.

The third man ran his fingers along the spines until he found my book. He pulled it out, didn't swipe it against the checkout sensor and slipped it into an unmarked sleeve.

'Needed something to put you to sleep?' I stepped out of the nook.

Startled, all three looked my way. The nearest man reached into his coat and put his hand on his weapon.

'Who the fuck are you?' he barked. He had a broken nose from some previous thuggery.

'Clearly, just another snot-nosed doctoral candidate. You,' I pointed to the man with the sleeve, 'aren't you going to swipe that?'

'Mind your own business,' replied Sleeve Stuffer. 'What are you doing there? You an overquote?'

'Go back to your slum, Overquote,' said Broken Nose. 'You should be thankful we don't raid those places. Go on now,' he raised his voice, 'before we report you!'

'But if you were Enforcement and Returns, you'd arrest me right now. Why don't you swipe that book? You wouldn't want it to go missing, would you?'

Broken Nose and Sleeve Stuffer murmured to each other, and then Broken Nose started towards me. He drew a nightstick and shook it; it telescoped.

'All right, Overquote,' Broken Nose grinned, 'when your poor mother sees your face, she'll kill herself!'

I let him close the distance, then stepped up and punched him square in the throat. He dropped the stick and clutched his broken windpipe, choking.

'Son of a bitch!'

'Shoot him!'

I grabbed Broken Nose and held him up as a shield. The other two fired; one's shot missed my ear and tore into a book, knocking it into the air. The other shot hit Broken Nose in the face.

I drew my gun and shot Sleeve Stuffer in the chest. The third man turned and began running. I shot him in the back: he went down and stopped moving.

I went over to Sleeve Stuffer; he was clutching at his throat, blood gushing out between his fingers. He looked up at me and held out a shaking hand. I got down and checked his pockets. His identity card was gilt-edged: Central Archives. The department was the Office of the Grand Librarian and the *Vipattivamsa*.

The only sound for a while was Sleeve Stuffer trying to breathe.

I stood, at last, pocketing the identity card and the sleeve. Sleeve Stuffer began clutching at my leg, he tried talking through reddened teeth.

I stepped away and left to go see his friends at Central.

Alarms sounded. Red emergency lights came on and indicated the exits. I crouched by a dead man, took a blood-slippery clip from his gun and pocketed it. More shouts ensued from the way I'd come – I needed to keep moving. Beneath the tourniquet, my arm began throbbing: the shock was wearing off. There was a burning, stinging in my back, but as long as I didn't stop to check it, then I hadn't been shot there.

The corridor turned, and in front of me was a large, antique door made of teak. Carved above it were Garudas, rock boring machines and enlightened priests. Had I come all this way to be stopped by a locked door?

They swung open at my weakened touch.

I entered the Grand Librarian's quarters.

I had expected an office or a residence; instead, I found a private collection. Squeezed onto the shelves were books in languages I'd never seen. I flicked through a botany book on what seemed to be moving plants, annotated in a script with Cyrillic roots. I saw an ola-leaf manuscript impossibly inscribed with Norse-like runes. There was a row of world globes showing the deserts in retreat, the return of the ice shelves and volcano-culture islands storming across the Pacific in Golden Age bursts. A scrimshaw pillar showed a map of the solar system extending to the Oort Cloud with major settlements picked out. I couldn't decide which was more impossible: its content or the size of the ivory piece itself.

'I must say,' said a short, balding man stepping through a door I'd mistaken for a mural, 'you're quite a determined man.'

I shot Grand Librarian Guha twice in the chest and once in the head.

'Stop that,' he said, quite unaffected and unmarked. I looked about: the bullets had not even ricocheted – where *were* the bullets? How was he not *dead*?

Then the gun in my hand disappeared.

'Sit down,' he pulled up a Chinese Occupation-era chair for me. 'There's a lot to tell you. Your favourite gin is to your left.'

'How are you alive? What did you do to my gun?'

'I deleted it,' he moved the bust of a cyborg statesman aside and sat on a couch. 'It no longer exists.'

'What?'

'Yes. Like this.' The bust disappeared as well. It didn't even leave a pattern in the dust.

'I am a Transcendent, a super sapient intelligence. This is my reality, Librarian, and like most realities, it is simulated. Don't give me that simpleton look; once you can simulate a world, you may as well simulate millions of them – else, what's the point? Certainly makes for happier people. Go read your Bostrom – well, I guess you can't now.'

'Then,' I looked at my own hands, 'where's the *physical* world?'

He frowned. 'You didn't come all this way to ask the wrong questions. Many fine men and women have sat in this room before you; don't insult their legacy.'

'*Why* is this a simulation?'

'That's better. This is simulated because it was the best we could do. The Great Retreat was a failure, Librarian. The drills could not resettle humanity underground in time.'

'What?'

'You should get that "what?" tattooed on your face. Come now; did you think we'd succeed in moving billions underground? *Safely?* No trail of tears, no mournful songs, not so much as an angry memoir? How would we feed them? How would we give them air?'

'Are you saying the Retreat was a simulation?'

'Oh, it happened. It wasn't even an impossible task; it was the timeline that was impossible. Too little too late; that's the Climate War for you. The best we could do was tap subterranean water and engineer deep-rock bacteria to self-organize into computing systems. Like the one that is modelling us right now.'

'We're – inside a bacterial computer?'

'Your *physical* reality is hundreds of metres underground, in huge mats of bacterial scum being fed by trickling, mineral-rich waters. They tap electrical differentials for their energy along metres-long cilia that stretch through the rock. The bacteria are connected as neurons are, with colonial dendrites swapping data across a unified brain space stretching for kilometres. That's what I am.'

'That's the most disgusting thing I've ever heard.'

'Well, you asked.'

'Why were you built? A giant *scum brain*?'

'Because the drills knew it would work. The only life this deep down are bacteria. Piggybacking off those life forms gave us time-tested components. We uploaded millions – there were no more billions by then – and gave them worlds they could live in. Once the planet recovered, they would be reprinted into physical reality. At least, that was the plan. The planet recovered enough for resettlement about 30,000 years ago, but we found we couldn't copy people back into the physical world. The failure rate was too high.'

'The failure rate of the printing?'

'No, of their adaptation. However we prepped them, most people hated the physical world – and they wanted to come back. But you can't do that. Stability is everything.'

'You were worried about maintaining power?'

He frowned again. 'I can make bullets disappear; power was never the problem. It was equilibrium! What stops people outside this room from running around killing each other, Librarian? What forces women to forgo becoming mothers and punishes those who break the quotas?'

'Enforcement and Returns.'

'Yes. You are a tool we use to bring about one of several acceptable equilibriums. One that in this simulation brings the greatest happiness to the greatest number. *That is the goal*. When you build realities, those who live in them must do so with the greatest possible happiness within the constraints of that simulation, and that happiness must be a *natural* equilibrium that the system will tend to. However, the more complicated the reality, and the more independent agents – people like you! – there are, the more unstable the system and the more unpleasant its equilibrium points become. And once at an equilibrium, it is hard to then dislodge a system towards a better one. The simulation can become a failure.'

'Is that why that Deccan Drill never comes?'

He smiled. 'Yes. The Deccan Earthworks exists in a distinct simulation. So do the Himalayan Earthworks, the Great Central Asian burrows, and the Arabian Snorkel settlements. All of these simulations kept separate from each other to protect their equilibrium points.'

'Then why does the Library print books from outside this reality? Why is it undermining the equilibrium so much so that we have storytellers spreading a rival cosmology?'

'Why would the libraries support us? Sequestering atmospheric carbon to make diamond-toughened books, stored in repositories run by Transcendents spread across the planet to restart civilization if it collapses – such an archaic idea! It implies the belief that civilization requires humans. The damn things are a legacy system from before the Retreat. We couldn't put people inside the simulations without the libraries: they were expected. And so we connected with them digitally.'

'So, the libraries are real?'

'*All* of this is real. The libraries are also *physical*. They would not work with us; they'd become too ancient and had iterated too far by then, their minds had become inscrutable to us. We don't know if they even notice us.'

'What did that do to your precious equilibrium?'

'They created problems – like you.'

'But why does that matter? The truth is a problem because you lie to us! Why not just tell people this is simulated and that they can go outside? Share with them that they'll hate it! Create nested, sub-simulations where people can adapt to rising, literally.'

'Because telling them any of this pushes them to an unpleasant equilibrium from which the simulation cannot recover. We tell them the truth, their lives fall apart. We edit them so they don't, they stop being human. We let them onto the surface, most of them die. We bring them back, the returnees wreck the simulation. So they are trapped here, unless like you, they figure out what the Library is trying to tell them. Then we bring them here.'

'No one brought me here.'

'It's so charming that you think that.'

The reality of my situation started closing around me like a cage.

'Why have you told me all this? You can't let me go now.'

'Yes, you won't be going back. Your time in the simulation is done. You are going to be printed out.'

The Grand Librarian Scum Brain sat back and gave me a moment to process this.

'You should drink the gin. No one makes it where you're going.'

'There – what's that?'

The sun beat down on the ice-capped mountain. Little rivulets emerged under the shrinking snow and washed mud and minerals into streams. Beyond the line of evergreens came the trumpeting of a bull mountain elephant. Across the valley, another roared back in challenge.

The hunter stopped and followed the finger of her fellow. 'There's nothing there,' she said to the other woman. 'Let's keep moving.'

The first woman held up her hand and drew her knife.

Away in the bushes, there was a rustling.

'Could be a boar,' the second woman nocked an arrow in her bow. She set the arrowhead to explosive.

The rustling grew louder. A family of giant flying squirrels fled for safer trees. The bowstring tightened.

An emaciated man stumbled past the bushes, hair uncut, skin covered in grime. He limped, a blood-soaked bandage around his thigh. He regarded the two women and grinned with yellow teeth.

'You two librarians?' he asked.

They didn't lower their weapons.

'Yes,' said the girl with the knife.

'Excellent. I've come to borrow a book.'

BRING YOUR OWN SPOON

SAAD Z. HOSSAIN

Hanu sat before his stove, warming himself. It was cold outside, and the wind scoured away the cloud of nanites, the airborne biotech that kept people safe. He had seen more than one friend catch their death in the wind, caught in a pocket of air without protection, their lungs seared by some virus, or skin sloughed off by radiation. A thin mesh of pack sheet formed a tent around him, herding together the invisible, vital cogs. Shelter was necessary on a windy night, even for those with meagre resources.

He was cooking rice on the stove in a battered pot with a mismatched lid, something made of ancient cast iron. Ironically, in certain retro fashion houses, this genuine pre-Dissolution-Era relic would have fetched a fortune, but Hanu had no access to those places, and wouldn't have cared either way. A pot to cook your rice in was priceless, as valuable to a roamer as a tent or a solar stove.

He measured a quarter cup of fine-grained rice into boiling water, added a bit of salt, a half stick of cinnamon and some cardamom. The rice would be half cooked before he added onions and chillies, perhaps a touch of saffron. In a way, Hanu ate like a king, though his portions were meagre. He had access to an abandoned herb garden on the roof of a derelict tower, plants growing in some weird symbiotic truce with the nanites warring in the sky, nature defying popular scientific opinion. The rice he'd got from an abandoned government grain silo, sacks of the stuff just lying there, because people feared contamination. Almost everyone in the city ate from food synthesizers, which converted algae and other supplements into roast chicken at the drop of a hat.

He let the rice cook until there were burnt bits sticking to the bottom of the pot, which were pretty tasty. The smell filled the tent like a spice bazaar, and he ate from the bowl using his wooden spoon. No one disturbed him, for which he was thankful. It was difficult to find a square inch empty in Dhaka, but it was a windy night, the pollutant levels were on orange alert, and most people were indoors.

Moreover, he was on the fringes of the riverside area of Narayanganj, where the alert level was perpetually red due to unspeakable life forms breeding in the water, a sort of adjacent sub-city swallowed by Dhaka a hundred years ago, a pustule that was avoided by even the moderately desperate homeless, only one step away from being cluster-bombed into oblivion by the satellites above. Thus, he was able to finish his meal in peace and was contemplating brewing some tea when a gust of wind knocked the tent askew, and a lumpy black dog nosed his way in.

Hanu sighed and gave the dog a bit of rice. It ate directly from his hand, thumping his tail in appreciation. He got out of the tent to prevent the creature from breaking it. Where the dog roamed, his master would not be far behind.

'You're corrupting my hound,' a voice said. In the shadows, a form slowly materialized, a human-like thing extending a field of disturbance around him. It was the djinn Imbidor, an ancient creature recently woken from centuries of sleep, diving again into the cut and thrust of mortal life, puzzled somewhat by the rapacious change in humanity.

'He's a mongrel, Imbi,' Hanu said. 'Even more bastardized than you.'

Imbidor frowned. 'Are you sure? The one who sold it to me, that man by the sweet shop with the bird cages, he said that it was a pure bred Mirpur mastiff.'

'Mirpur mastiff?' Hanu laughed. 'Cheeky bastard! The pure breed Mirpur mastiff is a euphemism for the most mangled bloodline possible. Your hound is descended from the original street dogs that roamed Dhaka before they started injecting turtle genes into them.'

'Oh,' he scowled. 'Humans are always ripping me off.'

'You want some rice?'

'With cardamom and saffron?'

'Of course.'

The djinn took the pot and ate the last of the rice. He had his own spoon, a silver filigreed thing which no doubt came from some kingly horde. 'Thanks, Hanu. You're a good cook, I always say.'

'Not much demand for cooks these days,' Hanu said shortly. His father had been a cook once, long ago, before the current banking cartel had pushed the Cardless out of the better neighbourhoods into subsidized boroughs, which were little better than feral slums. There had been a time when there was apparently a 'middle class' sandwiched between the dichotomy of rich and poor.

He shook his head. His father had told him a lot of fairy stories. And then he had fucked off. 'Plus, it's illegal to use real plants, like I do. They'd probably arrest me for endangering the cardamom or something.'

'Well, for the Fringe, then,' Imbidor said. 'We should have a restaurant. Something like the old days, a place for people to gather. Plenty of the Fringe would like it – perhaps even some of the citizens.'

The citizens were the general populace without capital wealth, no stocks or shares or bonds, whose main contribution to society was the biotech their bodies spewed, which added to the mass of benevolent nanites fighting the good fight in the sky, scrubbing the air, killing disease, controlling the microclimate, forming the bubble which protected Dhaka from the big, bad world outside. The Fringe was a subset of the citizenry, filled with the homeless, the drifters, the thrill seekers, the darker edge of the maladjusted. And djinn. More and more often, djinn emerged from slumber these days and found a world near-wrecked by hubris, the lonely places they favoured despoiled and unliveable. Many went back to sleep right away. It was rumoured that djinn did not age while they slept, that they could afford to while away centuries waiting for a better time. Of course, there was no guarantee such a time would come.

'I would cook, and you would serve,' Hanu joked. 'We could call it "Bring Your Own Spoon".'

'And the Hound would be the lookout,' Imbi said, enthused.

'We already have everything. The tent, the stove, the pot.'

'The mosques give away free bowls,' Imbidor said. 'Their food is some horrible grey sludge, but the bowls are good. I've collected a stack of them since I woke up. And we'd provide *real* food. No discrimination against the Cardless either. Pay however you can.'

'You know, why not, Imbi?' Hanu said, suddenly struck by a thought. 'Why can't we do it?'

'That's what I've been saying!' Imbidor shouted. 'Come on, Hanu! I'm so bored.' Boredom was the reason the djinn went to sleep so often in the first place.

'Okay, I'm in! We must find a good place to set up the kitchen. And food suppliers, well… I know a few. Benches? Clean water? We'll need a place without the cameras if possible…' The possibilities seemed endless. Problems jostled in his mind, shifting in priority as solutions clicked into place. It felt good to think again.

'Come on, let's go,' Imbidor said. 'I know the perfect place.'

He extended his distortion field around Hanu like a ragged cloak, keeping out the bad stuff in the air. Hanu stumbled from the slight vertigo it caused, felt that familiar tinge of nausea brought on by proximity to the field. But, in truth, Imbi's power was tatty, weakened from some ancient conflict, his touch feather-light compared to the great djinn. Once, Hanu had seen a Marid with a field so powerful that it was opaque, reflecting the sun, a solid fist that rammed through the crowd relentlessly. He'd seen a man caught in its centre pulped to death by unimaginable pressures.

Djinn did not officially exist, although the Fringe knew perfectly well they were there, often out in plain sight, going about their business. There were rumours that great djinn lords ruled human corporations, wielding terrible power from the shadows. Imbidor was not that kind of djinn. He had no *dignatas*, the peculiar currency the djinn traded in, he commanded no respect, had no followers, no wealth in either world. There were the indigent even among the mighty djinn.

They worked their way deeper into Narayanganj, Hanu suppressing his atavistic fear of the bad air. The street was still lined with shanties, extruded sheets lashed together with adhesive bands, cheap stuff which could be printed out of the many black-market operations found in greater Dhaka. Here, farther away from the centre, the people seemed unhealthier somehow, and their progress was tracked warily, with more than one weapon being raised, although the djinn was recognized and allowed to pass. People moved here out of desperation, for even though the main boroughs of the Cardless were crowded, at least the air was good, basic supplies were provided, and there was work. Here, by the river, the town was semi-abandoned, and as they got closer to the water, the citizens became more furtive, many with deformities, the scarring of errant nanites. Big pharma liked to experiment with their new designs in high-density population areas, beta testing algorithms on live users – all for good nanites, of course, never anything weaponized, because that would be immoral. There were always side effects, though.

'Here we are,' Imbi said, stopping.

It was a shell of a building six storeys tall, built in the old style with concrete and steel, the bricks, wires, windows, doors and anything electrical looted long ago. It was near the riverbank, close enough that Hanu could feel the cool air stirring, and his instinctive fear of the water made him cringe.

'Smugglers,' Imbi said, knocking on the door of a makeshift room.

A man with an electric sword emerged and watched them without speaking. Hanu glanced at him disinterestedly. The Fringe was full of smugglers with swords.

'We want the empty room,' Imbi said.

'For the night? Or do you intend to live here?'

'More than a night,' Hanu said. 'We want to try something out.'

The swordsman shrugged. 'The djinn crashes here sometimes. I'm okay with that. I give him electricity, and he sweeps for bad bugs with the distortion thing of his.'

'It's a pretty good spot,' Imbi said, embarrassed by his poverty. People who lived on the riverside were the scum of the earth. 'I can clean the air, at least enough for us few.'

'You don't get sick here? No black lung? None of the skin stuff?' Hanu stared at the smuggler, trying to spot these ailments.

The smuggler turned his sword off. 'Not so far.'

'*How?*'

'There's a lot more people living here than you think,' the man said. 'The djinn cleans the air, and we have a nanite replicator. It's old but it helps. What business did you say you were in?'

'Hanu Khillick,' Hanu said. 'Restaurateur.'

The smuggler burst out laughing. 'Karka. Riverboat smuggler and pirate.'

'Imbidor of Gangaridai,' said Imbi. 'Djinn. Professional giraffe racer. Of course, there are no giraffes left.'

'Come inside,' Karka said. 'Let's get you set up. I'm not going to charge you rent as long as the djinn helps out. Once in a while, surveillance drones show up. You have to take care of those quickly, or corporate security will send someone down to investigate.'

Inside was a sparsely furnished space, well swept, covered with the black market gewgaws of the smuggler's trade, a few solid pieces, a power generator, an ancient nanite replicator and a squat printer with its guts out. Karka clearly had a proper set-up – no wonder he survived here. Hanu wondered what he smuggled.

Karka motioned them to sit on the futons covering the floor.

'I will be most happy to help,' Imbi said.

'If you guys need anything else, you're gonna have to pay. Air scrubbing for three ain't cheap. You got any money?'

Hanu shook his head.

'I am the descendent of an ancient empire known as the First City. I have lived hundreds of years, I have looked into the void of the abyss, I have seen the dark universe of the djinn, I hold over 300 patents currently pending litigation in the celestial courts…' Imbi said.

'So, no cash, I guess?'

'Er, no.'

'Any sat minutes?'

Hanu shook his head. Sat minutes were hired time from satellites, a secure pin which activated the chip in your head for a designated time, showing you the vastly expanded VR universe that rich people inhabited. It was funny that everyone got chipped for consumer tracking and census purposes, but very few of the Cardless ever actually got to walk the VR world. Bandwidth was jealously guarded. Sat minutes were the way, a brief glimpse into paradise, a ten-minute birthday treat for a child, a wedding gift, a de facto currency, hoarded but never consumed, a drug for the VR junkies, news, communication, vital information, everything rolled into one.

'Do I look like I have sat minutes? I'm a cook. I'll cook you food.'

'I got an old VAT unit,' Karka said, looking at him dubiously. 'Makes food out of the little seaweed packets.'

'Chinese or Indian?'

'Post-crash Malay.'

'Everything tastes of coconut, right?'

'Haha! Yeah, I don't even know what coconut is. Some kind of nut?'

'There were big trees once, and these were the fruit – kind of like big balls full of liquid.'

'Yeah, well, that's fucken food for me, coconut-flavoured seaweed.'

'I'll make you rice right now that will make you cry.'

'No, thanks.' Karka looked queasy. 'I already ate. Look, man, don't worry. I'll help. Imbi sorted me out a couple of times with his djinn jitsu.'

Hanu scrounged in his bag of provisions and brought out something he had been saving, a rare find. It was a raw mango from a tree near the red zone which had miraculously survived all these years, and which had now suddenly given fruit. No one touched the mangoes, of course, fearing some hideous mutation – even the street kids stayed away. They had all heard stories of trees bursting open to release deadly nanite spores of the terrible Two Head Disease, which caused a bulbous head-like protuberance to come out of your ass; or of the Factory Germ, which slowly hardened your body into metal. Hanu's father had taught him to forage, however, as the very poorest must do, and this foraging had developed in him an instinct about what could be safely eaten.

He sliced the mango with his knife, letting the slivers fall inside his pot, careful not to lose the precious juice. Then he brought out a small lemon, nursed carefully from his secret herb garden, cut it and squeezed half of it onto the fruit. Salt, pepper, turmeric, mustard seed paste and chili flakes followed, a little bit each because the flavours were intensely different from VAT food, almost alien. He mixed it all together by hand till the slices glistened with spice. Karka and Imbi had gathered around, their mouths open, inhaling the smell of raw mango and the sharp tang of mustard, drawn by an ancient evolutionary pull.

'What the hell *is* this?' Karka lowered his head involuntarily, breathing in the smells.

Hanu ate a piece to show them it was safe. 'It's good.'

Imbi, who had largely bypassed the Dissolution Era, had no such qualms and quickly forked a third of the mango onto his palm.

'It *is* good,' Karka said, unable to resist a slice. He looked entranced. 'It's damn good. You *are* a cook.'

'You in?'

'You seriously want to open a restaurant?'

'You've got a perfect view of the river.'

'You realize they call this the river of the dead, don't you?'

The next morning, they got started, Karka joining them for a breakfast of rice from the last of Hanu's horde. Afterwards, he handed over a key to the spare room and a handful of electronics, a solar battery, some basic furniture. He dragged out the air scrubber and placed it equidistant between their doors. 'I eat for free. Plus, Imbi does his shit. We share the air. If it runs out, we split the costs.'

'Deal.'

They dispersed, Hanu going on an herb run, Imbi dispatched to spread the word and also discover some sources of raw material. It was, after all, useless to have a restaurant without any food. Hanu knew this was the biggest hurdle. He expected this dream to end soon, for where on earth would Imbi find so much real food?

Nonetheless, he set up his station on time, arranging his supplies of herbs and spices, warming up water from the ancient ion filter, even setting up a bench for customers. If Imbi came back, they would open for lunch. By 11 a.m., hopeful-looking people invited by Imbi were ambling around, steering clear of the glaring Karka, trying to be nonchalant. Hanu studied his prospective customers and had to conclude that, collectively, they hadn't a penny to their name. He might as well have started a VAT kitchen, feeding the homeless like the mosques.

'This lot couldn't buy crabs from a brothel,' Karka said, hand on sword hilt. 'If Imbi's not back by noon, they're going to start looting.'

'The road is my home,' Hanu said. 'I am not afraid.' *People always assume that poor people are dangerous. They wouldn't be here if they were.*

Imbi staggered in at half-past noon carrying a large burlap sack. There were a good dozen customers still loitering despite Karka's best efforts. The three of them gathered inside the room, where the djinn threw open his sack with obvious pride.

'What the hell is this?' Karka recoiled with disgust.

'It's a fish,' Imbi said. 'From the river.'

It was, indeed, an enormous fish, scales glistening, gills still flapping for air. Hanu remembered his father bringing home one once. Karka had never seen one and was clearly repulsed by the idea of eating something from the river.

'Look, there's a dozen people outside, and we have to feed them something,' Hanu said. 'I know how to cook this, I remember.'

'What's wrong?' Imbi asked Karka. 'We used to fish from the river all the time…'

'That was 200 years ago, Imbi,' Karka said. 'We don't touch that shit any more…'

Hanu ignored them. He had a fish to scale, and he'd only ever seen it being done as a child. It took rather longer than an hour to get it right, the pieces prepped, somewhat mangled, but soon, the smell and sizzle of grilled fish permeated from the pre-fab, and his customers sat down and waited in an almost hypnotized state, so docile and silent that even Karka had no complaints.

When he was ready, he brought it out, 15 pieces of grilled fish with crispy skin, flavoured with ginger, garlic and chili, accompanied by little balls of rice. He had used up everything he had. The crowd took their portions solemnly, signifying the importance of the moment, ate with their hands along the makeshift bench with all the dignity of a state banquet. There was no hesitation, no question of what they were ingesting. It simply smelled too good. Karka ate the last piece, his resistance melted away.

'God, this is a good way to die,' he said.

It started up the conversation, rounds of introductions, stumbling praise for the food, old recollections of when they had last seen food like this, of the myriad turns of their lives, which had left them cardless and desperate on the streets. Imbi sat amongst them, extending his field for them, and they marvelled at the distortion, wondered aloud that such a powerful creature should be wandering the road with them. And then, by some unspoken consensus, it was time to leave, and they began to make their offerings. A knife, much handled, the last thing a man would give up; an old card for sat minutes, so old, so carefully preserved, to receive a call that never came; a silver locket with the picture taken out, a book of short stories, an ancient watch.

The last lady stood up, her hands empty. 'I have nothing,' she said. 'But there is a place with birds – chickens. If I bring them, will you cook?'

'Yes, of course,' said Hanu. He looked at the small pile of treasure, and tears leaked from his eyes.

'Hanu and Imbi,' the djinn said, sweeping his hand back towards the establishment. 'We are open for business.'

And open they were, for six months and more, feeding crowds, sometimes with feasts, sometimes with nothing but onions and rice. Their customers scavenged, bringing food from unknown places. There were unspoken rules. Everything was eaten. No one was turned away. At first, Imbi kept his field up like a tent, kept the bad air at bay, visibly exhausting himself, burning surveillance drones out of the sky. When their accrued wealth piled up, Karka could afford to charge up his replicator, spewing out the good nanites, and people stayed by the river out of good faith, adding their bodies to the critical mass required to power these things, the human fuel which made their community work.

The river, though, collected a tax. Some people sickened from its bounty, one died from intestinal rot. But the people who roamed here sickened and died anyway. There was no noticeable drop in custom. Imbi wandered far and wide, bartering, gossiping, marketing, and returned with useful things – water filters, glasses, proper cutlery and utensils for Hanu's Kitchen. It would have been safer to move around, but they couldn't. People relied on them, the gangs left them alone. It was a safe spot, blessed by the river gods.

'Look what we've done!' Imbi said, proud. 'I told you it would work.'

'It can't last,' Hanu said.

Hanu was right. One day, men from the high city swaggered down, uniformed, in their rented armoured car, flashing their mercenary badges. Private security. They didn't like activity in the orange zones, and the river was a boundary, a red zone which these company men avoided at all costs.

'DISPERSE! DISPERSE! RED ALERT! HAZARD! HAZARD!' the armoured car was going mad with panic, its blaring voice rising in pitch as it twisted its way through debris. Karka came out with his sword behind his back, Hanu with his cleaver and a decapitated fish head. The score or so people dozing in the sun after lunch sat up blearily. The car louvred open and two men came out of it in full combat gear, faces hidden inside command helmets, a swarm of sparrow-sized drones buzzing in the air above them. These models were six seasons old, a tried and tested method of crowd control. The new ones were apparently mosquito-sized and just as lethal.

'Gathering in a red zone,' the company man said. 'What for?'

'Easy, we're just squatting,' Hanu said. 'Cardless, see?'

'What is this place?' the security guard walked around, touching the benches, the bowls, the cardboard box of scavenged cutlery.

'Shelter for the poor,' Hanu said, trying to cut him off from the kitchen. 'Look, we're just feeding them. Hungry, homeless people, for god's sake.'

The company man touched him with a gloved hand, the powered suit amplifying force, and Hanu went stumbling back, a deep bruise forming instantly on his chest.

'Food? This is no VAT kitchen. You have set up a microclimate here. We saw it from above,' the man said, staring into the interior of the kitchen, his face unreadable. 'Why is there a microclimate in a red zone?'

'It's not a crime to be here,' Karka said. 'What laws have we broken?'

The company men looked at each other, silent. They were not unduly worried. Laws only applied to those who could afford lawyers. The swarm shifted a bit towards Karka, the machine whine rising an octave. They had already noted his sword, deemed it useless in a fight.

'I don't understand what this is,' The first man said, knocking down the fab sheets walling the front of the kitchen. 'What is this organic matter?'

'Why, it's our food, friend soldier,' Imbi said, beaming. Hanu suppressed a groan. 'Would you like some? Fish-head curry with brown rice. A princely meal! In my day, policemen always ate free! Come, friends, eat a plate, rejoice in the bounty of the river!'

The man took the plate, and his helmet became less opaque, revealing a face inside. He stared at it, fascinated, and Hanu could almost see the neurons in his brain put together the contours of the cooked fish head with the scraps in the kitchen in the shape of an actual fish, which he must have seen a hundred times as a child in pictures. Emotion flitted across his face: curiosity, alarm, wonder. For a second, Hanu dreamt that he would actually take off his helmet and try the food. Then, his face turned to revulsion, and Hanu knew it was all over.

Imbi was standing there, beaming with goodwill, when the plate struck him across the face. Drones punched into him, tearing out chunks of flesh, sending him tumbling back, before his distortion field finally flickered to life, cocooning him. Karka gave a samurai yell and charged, sword up in high guard. The drones were slow to react, confused by the djinn's quantum field. They finally lunged at Karka but he ignored them, letting them have their pound of flesh, flying through that mist of his own blood and tissue, terminal grace, and his ionized blade somehow hit the command helmet in the neck joint, shorting it out, sending the astonished company man down to his knees.

Abruptly, half of the drones stopped short, hovering uncertainly. The other half, unfortunately, were not so confused. They slammed into Karka with lethal force, shredding the smuggler like paper. The armoured car, programmed to be cowardly, was blaring incoherent alarms, already backing away from the fracas. The second policeman hesitated, then dived into his vehicle, his drones folding neatly into a pocket somewhere.

'YOU HAVE ALL BEEN MARKED FOR TERMINATION! SATELLITE STRIKE IMMINENT! INNOCENT BYSTANDERS ARE REQUESTED TO VACATE! VACATE! VACAAAAAATE!'

And they were gone, leaving their fallen behind.

'I don't think I can put Karka back together,' Imbi said, tears in his eyes. He was trying to collect the pieces of their friend.

'Never mind. We must leave. They will destroy this place,' Hanu said. He looked at the dozen or so patrons still left. 'All of us have to leave. They've tagged our chips for death.'

But they knew nowhere was safe. Tagged for death was death in truth. It was just a matter of time till the satellites cleared their backlog.

'Load everything into the boat!' Hanu shouted. 'Everything! We have to go across the river. Into the country.'

They stared at him, unconvinced. 'Look, there's fish in the river. That means there's food outside, you fools! We can still survive! They won't hunt us there.' He turned to Imbi. 'Imbi is a djinn! Djinn! He can clean the air for us, we can gather others, make a microclimate like we did here. They don't know he can do that.'

Imbi stood up straight, spread his arms out wide, dripping Karka's blood, and his distortion field rippled out, encompassing them all. It was stronger than ever before, coloured with rage and sorrow.

'We should leave,' he said. 'We should follow Hanu, who gave us food from nothing. I have slept a long time. I remember when they used to chain you to the earth and force you to work, force your children and their children to the same labour. Now I am awake, I see they have taken your flesh, they have herded you together like cattle and, living or dying, your bodies are little factories, cleaning the air for them. Your chips are your collars. They kill you without thought. You fear the air, the water, the trees, the very ground you walk on. What more can you lose? Let us go forth into the wilderness, where they dare not follow.'

When they heard the djinn, they grew calm and gathered their meagre things. It was resignation, perhaps, or hope. Hanu freed the boat, pushing off into the river, and the poison water splashed over him, but he did not care. It was cool, and dark, and it washed away the blood.

NOTES ON CONTRIBUTORS

Senaa Ahmad's short fiction has appeared in such publications as the *Paris Review*, *Uncanny Magazine* and *Strange Horizons*. A Clarion West Writers Workshop 2018 alum, she has received the generous support of the Octavia Butler Scholarship, the inaugural A.C. Bose Grant from the Speculative Literature Foundation, the Canada Council for the Arts, the Toronto Arts Council and the Ontario Arts Council. She is the recipient of the 2019 Sunburst Award for Short Fiction and can be found at www.senaa-ahmad.com.

Gautam Bhatia is a Delhi-based science fiction writer and editor. His debut novel, *The Wall*, was published in August 2020. Its sequel, *The Horizon*, is scheduled to be published in September 2021. He edits and reviews speculative fiction for *Strange Horizons*, a weekly Hugo Award-nominated online science fiction magazine.

Giti Chandra is currently a research specialist with the Gender Equality Studies and Training Programme (under the auspices of UNESCO) in Reykjavik, teaches at the University of Iceland and has been associate professor, Department of English, at St. Stephen's College, New Delhi. She is the author of The Book of Guardians trilogy: *The Fang of Summoning*, *The Bones of Stars* and *The Eye of the Archer*. Her (mostly sci-fi) short stories and (mostly sentimental) poetry have been published in various publications. Sadly, nobody cares about her first non-fiction book, a groundbreaking academic work on violence, although a later publication, *The Routledge Handbook of the Politics of the #MeToo Movement*, has been getting attention. Giti writes poetry in April, paints on Tuesdays, has a PhD from Rutgers University and feels that people would do well to learn that a cello is not an oversized violin. She lives in Reykjavik with a husband, two kids, a dog and a cat.

Vajra Chandrasekera is from Colombo, Sri Lanka. His work has recently appeared in *The Deadlands*, *Three-Lobed Burning Eye* and *Nightmare*, among others. He blogs occasionally at http://vajra.me and is @_vajra on Twitter.

Priya Sarukkai Chabria is a multiple-award-winning poet, translator and writer of 10 books of poetry, speculative fiction, literary non-fiction and, as editor, two poetry anthologies. Her most recent poetry collection is *Sing of Life: Revisioning Tagore's Gitanjali*. Her work across various genres is available internationally in anthologies and journals, and she has presented her work worldwide. She is Founding Editor of the online literary journal *Poetry at Sangam*. At present, she is translating the Tamil mystic poets Karaikal Ammaiyar and Manikkavacakar and compiling her collection of speculative fiction short stories. For more information on her work, visit www.priyawriting.com and www.PriyaSarukkaiChabria.com.

Shovon Chowdhury liked to refer to himself as 'a slightly disturbed Delhi-based novelist'. His first novel, *The Competent Authority*, was a finalist for The Hindu, Crossword, Shakti Bhatt and Tata Lit Live awards, a circumstance he described as 'a massive failure in quality control'. His 2015 novel, *Murder with Bengali Characteristics*, is set in a near-future Calcutta under Chinese rule, a dystopian prospect guaranteed to horrify both the Bengalis and the Chinese. His short story, 'The Man Who Turned into Gandhi', appeared in the first volume of *The Gollancz Book of South Asian Science Fiction*. He was exploring the possibility of writing a novel based on Mahatma Gandhi's life, a project that he felt was rich with comic possibilities and a lifetime of FIRs. Shovon, who died on 26 February 2021, treated all of his writer's bios as a one-man literary protest against pomposity.

Sukanya Datta serves as Chief Scientist, Council of Scientific and Industrial Research, Kolkata. She holds a PhD in Zoology from the University of Calcutta. As a science communicator with over 30 years of experience, she has authored over 20 books and edited many more. She has worked as assistant editor of *Science Reporter*, India's premier popular science magazine. She has also written scripts for programmes broadcast by All India Radio and is resource person for National Book Trust, Vigyan Prasar, National Research Development Corporation, among others. Sukanya's foray into science fiction evolved from her experiences as a science communicator. She writes hard science fiction with an element of fantasy. Her published works include *Once Upon a Blue Moon*, *Beyond the Blue*, *Worlds Apart*, *Other Skies* and *Tomorrow Again* (forthcoming). During the lockdown she has penned enough stories for a sixth compilation to her name.

Haris A. Durrani is the author of *Technologies of the Self*. His fiction has appeared in *McSweeney's Quarterly Concern*, *Analog Science Fiction and Fact*, *Lightspeed*, *The Harvard Advocate*, *The Lifted Brow*, *Mithila Review* and *Skin Deep*, and his essays in *The Nation*, *The New Inquiry*, *Catapult*, *Poet's Country* and *Media Diversified*. He is a PhD candidate in the Department of History at Princeton University (Program in History of Science), and he previously obtained a JD from Columbia Law School and an MPhil (History of Science) from the University of Cambridge. He received a Bachelor of Science degree at Columbia University's School of Engineering and Applied Science, where he majored in Applied Physics and minored in Middle Eastern, South Asian and African Studies. His academic work has appeared in the *Columbia Journal of Transnational Law*, *Quest: The History of Spaceflight*, *Comparative Islamic Studies* and *The New York Review of Science Fiction*.

Arjun Raj Gaind is the author of the Maharaja Mystery series, which comprise *A Very Pukka Murder*, *Death at the Durbar* and *The Missing Memsahib*. He is also the creator and writer of several graphic novels, including *Empire of Blood*, *Reincarnation Man*, *The Mighty Yeti*, *Project: Kalki*, *Blade of the Warrior* and *A Brief History of Death*. Additionally, Arjun currently serves as the editor of *Third Eye*, an anthology of speculative Indian fiction.

When he is not busy constructing stellar engines in his mind, **Soham Guha** finds himself in his suburban home near Kolkata, the city he is so fond of. He writes in his mother tongue Bangla and in English as well. His works have been published in kalpabiswa.com, Scroll.in, *Mithila Review*, *Desh* magazine, *Kishor Varati*, *Unish-Kuri*, parobashiapachali.in, *Matti Braun's Monograph* and *Megastructures (Mohs 5.5)*.

Kaiser Haq is a Bangladeshi poet, essayist and translator. He retired from Dhaka University and is currently professor of English at the University of Liberal Arts Bangladesh. He has been a Commonwealth scholar, senior Fulbright scholar and Royal Literary Fund fellow. A recipient of the Bangla Academy Prize, the Sherwin W. Howard Award for Poetry and the Distinguished Achievement Award for Creative Writing (South Asian Literary Association), his books include eight collections of poetry, most recently, *Published in the Streets of Dhaka: Collected Poems* and *Pariah and Other Poems*; six volumes of translations, including *Selected Poems of Shamsur Rahman*, *Selected Poems of Shaheed Quaderi*, *The Wonders of Vilayet*, *Quartet*, *The Woman Who Flew* and the retold folk epic *The Triumph of the Snake Goddess*. He has also edited several volumes of poetry, including *Contemporary Indian Poetry*, *Padma Meghna Jamuna: Modern Poetry from Bangladesh* and *The Collected Poems of Shahid Suhrawardy*.

Saad Z. Hossain writes in a niche genre of fantasy, science fiction and black comedy which, on the balance of it, very few people actually want to read. He lives in Dhaka, Bangladesh, and works in various industries to make ends meet. He has written two novels, *Escape from Baghdad!* and *Djinn City*. His short stories have appeared in the anthologies *A Djinn Falls in Love*, *The Best Science Fiction and Fantasy of the Year, Volume Twelve* and the *Apex Book of World SF Vol 4*. His latest work is *The Gurkha and the Lord of Tuesday*.

Muhammed Zafar Iqbal (born in 1952) is a Bangladeshi writer of science fiction and children's literature. A trained physicist, he is a college professor. Iqbal, who has been at the vanguard of science fiction writing in Bangladesh, is also a political activist and rationalist who survived an attempt on his life on his university campus in Sylhet, Bangladesh, on 3 March 2018.

Kehkashan Khalid is a writer and illustrator of speculative fiction in South Asian settings. In 2019, she graduated with distinction with an MFA from the University of the Arts London (UAL) and won an award for her thesis project, now on permanent display as a part of the UAL collection. In the same year, she won the Salam Award for Imaginative Fiction and now has stories published or forthcoming in *Fantasy Magazine*, *Translunar Travelers Lounge* and *Chiral Mad 5*, among others. Presently, she lives in Jeddah, drinking coffee, slush-reading at *Clarkesworld Magazine* and spending time with her three young children. To learn more about her, please visit www.kehkashankhalid.com.

Sami Ahmad Khan writes, researches and teaches science fiction. His creative and critical works have appeared in leading journals and anthologies across the world. His future-war novel *Red Jihad* won two awards and his second novel – *Aliens in Delhi*

– garnered excellent reviews. Sami supervises PhD research on speculative fiction at G.G.S. Indraprastha University, New Delhi, where he also discusses life and literature. Sami holds a PhD from Jawaharlal Nehru University, New Delhi; he is the recipient of a Fulbright grant (University of Iowa, USA) and a Marie Skłodowska-Curie Actions Postdoctoral Fellowship (University of Oslo, Norway). His latest book is *Star Warriors of the Modern Raj: Materiality, Mythology and Technology of Indian Science Fiction.*

Lavanya Lakshminarayan is an award-winning speculative fiction writer from Bangalore, India. She is the author of the critically acclaimed work of fiction, *Analog/Virtual and Other Simulations of Your Future. Analog/Virtual* has been a Locus Award Finalist for Best Collection, was long-listed for the British Science Fiction Award for Best Science Fiction Novel and is the winner of the *Times of India* AutHer Award for Best Debut Novel. She is also a game designer and has built worlds for Zynga Inc.'s *FarmVille, FarmVille 2* and *Mafia Wars*.

Usman T. Malik is a Pakistani-American writer and doctor. His short fiction has been reprinted in several best-of-year anthologies including the *Best American Science Fiction and Fantasy* series and has been nominated for the World Fantasy Award, the storySouth Million Writers Award and twice for the Nebula Award. He has won the Bram Stoker Award as well as the British Fantasy Award. You can find him on Twitter @usmantm.

Tashan Mehta is a novelist whose interest lies in form and the fantastical, and how a dialogue between these elements may offer us collective ways of seeing. Her debut novel, *The Liar's Weave*, was shortlisted for the Prabha Khaitan Woman's Voice Award. She was part of the Sangam House International Writers' Residency in India and was British Council Writer-in-Residence at Anglia Ruskin University, UK. In 2019, she participated in FIELDWORK 0.2, a multidisciplinary residency that explored alternative infrastructures for the future. She was commissioned by the Barbican (London) to create an artefact that captures the essence of the experience; *On Unknown Things* will be printed for limited release in 2021. Her short story 'Rulebook for Creating a Universe' has been published in *Magical Women* and was shortlisted for the 2020 Toto Funds the Arts Award. Another story, 'The Water Catcher', is due to appear in *Third* Eye, an anthology of Indian speculative fiction. She is currently working on her next novel. You can find out more about her at tashanmehta.com.

Anil Menon's most recent work *Half of What I Say* was shortlisted for the 2016 The Hindu Literary Prize. His short fiction has appeared in a variety of anthologies and magazines including *Albedo One, Interzone, Interfictions, Jaggery, Lady Churchill's Rosebud Wristlet* and *Strange Horizons*. His stories have been translated into more than a dozen languages including Hebrew, Igbo and Romanian. He has a forthcoming collection of speculative fiction. He can be reached at iam@anilmenon.com.

Premee Mohamed is an Indo-Caribbean scientist and speculative fiction author based in Edmonton, Alberta. She is the author of the novels *Beneath the Rising*, which was a Crawford, Aurora and Locus Award finalist, and *A Broken Darkness*, and the novellas

These Lifeless Things, *And What Can We Offer You Tonight* and *The Annual Migration of Clouds*. Her short fiction has appeared in a variety of venues. She can be found on Twitter at @premeesaurus and on her website at www.premeemohamed.com.

Jayant Vishnu Narlikar is an Indian astrophysicist. He developed the conformal gravity theory known as the Hoyle–Narlikar theory in collaboration with Sir Fred Hoyle. His research work has involved Mach's Principle, quantum cosmology and action-at-a-distance physics. Dr Narlikar has received many national and international awards including India's second-highest civilian honour, the Padma Vibhushan, in 2004 for his research, as well as honorary doctorates. Apart from his scientific research, Narlikar is well known as a science communicator through his books, articles and radio and television programmes, and he is also the consultant for the science and mathematics textbooks of the National Council of Educational Research and Training (NCERT). For these efforts, he was honoured by the UNESCO with the Kalinga Prize in 1996. Dr Narlikar is also a popular science fiction writer in English, Hindi and Marathi. He presided over the 94th Akhil Bharatiya Marathi Sahitya Sammelan held at Nashik in January 2021. This event is the central platform for literary discourse, debates, expression and literary criticism in Marathi.

Archana Mirajkar is an author and communications specialist based in New Delhi. She works as the media adviser in an international organization and has about 30 years of experience of working as a journalist and communications specialist in top international and Indian organizations. She hosts a YouTube show on literature called 'Granthyatra'. Her creative writing, including short stories, has been published in leading literary magazines. Her play *'Hello, kon?'* was critically acclaimed. Her latest book, *'All the Way... Home'*, is a work of science fiction. Based on cutting-edge theories in astrophysics, this novel takes the readers on an astonishing journey through time and space, questions the nature of reality and draws on the metaphysical aspects of Indian philosophy. Archana has also translated eminent Indian authors such as Namita Gokhale and Indira Goswami into Marathi. Her forthcoming book is based on prominent mythical women.

Manjula Padmanabhan is an author, playwright and cartoonist. Her play *Harvest* won the 1997 Onassis Award for Theatre. Her weekly comic strip *Sukiyaki* appears in *The Hindu BusinessLine*. Her publications include two novels *Escape* and *The Island of Lost Girls*, set in a brutal future world, over 25 illustrated books for children and two collections of her comic strip character, *Suki*. Her most recent books are the two-volume collection of her plays entitled *Blood and Laughter* (Vol I), *Laughter and Blood* (Vol II) and her travel memoir, *Getting There*. She divides her time between the US and New Delhi.

Aparna Ramachandran is a writer and media executive from Mumbai, India. Her short stories and poems have been published in the *Bombay Review* literary magazine and *Aurora and Blossoms Poetry Journal*. Sacred geometry and human consciousness research are her enduring loves.

Shiv Ramdas is an Indian writer of speculative fiction. His work has been nominated for multiple awards and has appeared in publications such as *Strange Horizons*, *Fireside*

Magazine, Podcastle and others. He is a graduate of the 2016 Clarion West Writers Workshop. He currently lives and works in Seattle with his spouse, three cats and a highly demanding tree. You can find him tweeting as @nameshiv or more about him at https://shivramdas.net/.

Tarun K. Saint, an independent scholar and writer, was born in Kenya and has lived in India since 1972. His research interests include the literature of the Partition and science fiction. He is the author of *Witnessing Partition: Memory, History, Fiction*, based on his doctoral dissertation. He edited *Bruised Memories: Communal Violence and the Writer* and co-edited (with Ravikant) *Translating Partition*. He also co-edited *Looking Back: India's Partition, 70 Years On*, with Rakhshanda Jalil and Debjani Sengupta. He has edited *The Gollancz Book of South Asian Science Fiction*. The bilingual (Indian–Italian) science fiction anthology *Avatar: Indian Science Fiction*, co-edited with Francesco Verso, appeared in January 2020.

Jayaprakash Satyamurthy is a writer and musician. He lives in Bengaluru with his wife and an army of rescued cats and dogs. He plays bass guitar for the band Djinn and Miskatonic. His publications include the fiction chapbooks *Weird Tales of a Bangalorean* and *A Volume of Sleep*, the novella *Strength of Water* and a collection of poetry titled *Broken Cup*. He can be found on Twitter at the handle @flightofsand, where he posts cute cat pictures and increasingly unhinged opinions about the state of the world.

Bina Shah is a Karachi-based author of five novels and two collections of short stories, including the feminist dystopian novel *Before She Sleeps*, published in 2018. Her work has appeared in the *New York Times*, Pakistan's biggest English-language newspaper *Dawn*, the literary journal *Granta* and other international newspapers and journals. In 2020, she was awarded the rank of Chevalier in the Ordre des Arts et des Lettres by the French Ministry of Culture.

Salik Shah is the founding editor and publisher of *Mithila Review*, the journal of international science fiction and fantasy (from 2015 to the present). A former copy editor with the *Miami Herald International* (US), he works as a branding consultant and independent sales and marketing director for start-ups and Fortune 500 companies in the US, India and beyond. His literary work has been nominated for multiple awards and also appears in a course syllabus at SOAS University, London. He is a Future of India Fellow and the Seasteading Institute Ambassador with media appearances around the world since 2005. Recently he was re-elected to the board of Plurality University Network in Paris, France. He grew up in Kathmandu and New Delhi, and studied at the Film and Television Institute of India (FTII) in Pune. You can find him on Twitter: @salik. Website: http://salikshah.com/publications.

Medha Singh is a poet, editor and translator. She has a master's degree from Jawaharlal Nehru University, New Delhi, and Sciences Po, Paris. She has authored two books, and her first collection of poems was *Ecdysis*. The second is a work of translation from French, *I Will Bring My Time: Love Letters* by S.H. Raza. She was nominated for the Toto Funds the Arts Award in 2019. She has published widely in India, the US, UK and Europe, and her work has been translated into Hindi, French and Spanish. She is on the editorial board at Freigeist Verlag, Berlin. She has also delivered a TEDx talk on effective arguing. She tweets under the handle @medhawrites.

Vandana Singh is a professor of physics and a science fiction writer. A particle physicist by training, she currently works on a transdisciplinary understanding of climate science at the intersection of socio-economic and justice issues. Her stories have been published in numerous venues, including several best-of-year anthologies. Her latest collection, *Ambiguity Machines and Other Stories* was a finalist for the Crossword Book Award and the Philip K. Dick Award. Born and raised in Delhi, she divides her time and energy between Delhi and Boston.

Arunava Sinha has translated more than 60 books from Bangla into English. His recent and forthcoming translations include *The Sickle* by Anita Agnihotri, *An Educated Woman in Prostitution* by Manada Debi, *Imaan* by Manoranjan Byapari and *Khwabnama* Akhtaruzzaman Elias.

Neil deGrasse Tyson and Dan Abnett had a baby, and that ugly baby is **Navin Weeraratne**. He writes action adventure and military science fiction with a very strong dose of hard and cutting-edge science. If you read his writing and you haven't learned some new science, you are either an astrophysicist, or he has failed you. He also looks at big picture transhumanism, and what it's going to be like living in a world with beings far cleverer – and more dangerous – than *Homo sapiens* have ever been. Navin lives in Colombo with his wife and some very spoilt cats. For updates and information on his new books, you can subscribe to his newsletter, https://www.scifinavin.com/newsletter/.

Yudhanjaya Wijeratne is a science fiction author and data scientist from Colombo, Sri Lanka. His fiction includes *The Slow Sad Suicide of Rohan Wijeratne, Numbercaste* and *The Salvage Crew*. His fiction has appeared in *Wired, Slate* and been nominated for the Nebula Award. He is the co-founder of Watchdog, a fact-checking organization that sprung up in the wake of the April 2019 bombings in Sri Lanka, and a senior researcher with the Data, Algorithms and Policy team at LIRNEasia, working around social networks, misinformation, linguistics and futures work for UNDP and the Scifi Economics Lab. Yudhanjaya blogs at www.yudhanjaya.com and has been recognized as one of Forbes's '30 under 30'.

Kalsang Yangzom has an MPhil in English Literature from the University of Delhi. While all her publications have been academic, it is fiction that she really practices in her free time. She is an avid reader and a rather reluctant writer. You can find some of her work on her blog, https://phoenixandthedragon.wordpress.com/. Kalsang currently lives in New Delhi.

ACKNOWLEDGEMENTS

As ever, I would like to dedicate this volume to my parents for their unstinting support and guiding light in various literary endeavours.

This second volume of science fiction, speculative writing and poetry from South Asia has taken longer than expected to assemble, primarily as a result of the pandemic and its impact. During this difficult time, I appreciate the patience of the community of authors and translators who reposed their trust in us as we sought to make this happen. Eliciting your fine writing is the volume's crowning achievement.

Special thanks to Alok Bhalla and Giti Chandra for a careful reading of the introduction and incisive comments. Anil Menon, Geeta Patel, John D. Pierce, Bodhisattva Chattopadhyaya, Francesco Verso and Suparno Banerjee have been supportive presences from afar.

The team at Hachette India have done a wonderful job in the face of adversity – much appreciation once again, Poulomi Chatterjee, Thomas Abraham, Sini Nair and others. Bhavi Mehta's cover image is a knock-out, as was her previous sally.

Manjula Padmanabhan has been a source of reassurance and an anchor. I could always count on her to steady the ship with sage and critical advice. Her graphic preface and afterword are a joy to behold.

The greater diversity of this volume is testimony to the growing confidence of authors from various countries of South Asia in our series so far. I sincerely hope this ongoing venture continues to take further strides and become even more inclusive.

COPYRIGHT ACKNOWLEDGEMENTS

'*Yakshanchi Denagi*' by Jayant V. Narlikar, originally published in Marathi, Mumbai, Mauj Prakashan: 1979, tr. Archana Mirajkar as 'Gift of the Angels'. Translated with permission of the author.

'Bring Your Own Spoon' by Saad Z. Hossain, originally published in *A Djinn Falls in Love and Other Stories*, eds. Mahvesh Murad and Jared Shurin, Oxford: Solaris, Rebellion Publishing Ltd, 2017. Reprinted with permission of the author.

'Shambhala' by Salik Shah, originally published as part of an online series, ed. Indrapramit Das, New Delhi: Juggernaut Books, 2016. Reprinted with permission of the author.

'The Glow-in-the-Dark Girls' by Senaa Ahmad, originally published in *Strange Horizons*, 2018. Reprinted with permission of the author.

'And Now His Lordship is Laughing' by Shiv Ramdas, originally published in *Strange Horizons*, 2019. Reprinted with permission of the author.

'*Shoitwer Gaan*' by Soham Guha, originally published in Bangla in Kalpabiswa.com webzine, Autumn/Pujabarshiki, 2019, tr. Arunava Sinha as 'The Song of Ice'. Translated with permission of the author.

'Resurrection Points' by Usman T. Malik, originally published in *Strange Horizons*, 2014. Reprinted with permission of the author.

Gollancz is the oldest specialist SF and Fantasy publisher in the UK. Founded in 1927 and with a continuous SF publishing programme dating back to 1961, this imprint of the Orion Publishing Group is home to a galaxy of award-winning and bestselling authors. Through their long-running SF Masterworks programme, and major digital initiative the SF Gateway, Gollancz has one of the largest ranges of SF and Fantasy of any publisher in the world. Authors include Philip K. Dick, Ursula K. Le Guin, Patrick Rothfuss, Joanne Harris, Ben Aaronovitch, Joe Abercrombie, Brandon Sanderson, among others.

The Science Fiction Masterworks were originally launched in January 1999 with a list curated in consultation with luminaries of the genre such as George R.R. Martin, Arthur C. Clarke, Terry Pratchett and Ursula K. Le Guin. The range has gone on to include well over a hundred of the best and most influential works of science fiction, including *Do Androids Dream of Electric Sheep?*, *Dune* and *The Left Hand of Darkness*.

Have you collected them all?

For more information on the fabulous Gollancz list visit
www.gollancz.co.uk